TRUTH IS THE SOUL OF THE SUN

A Biographical Novel of Hatshepsut-Maatkare

by

Maria Isabel Pita

In memory of my father
Mario Pita
I love you, papi

TABLE OF CONTENTS

BOOK FOUR
Mistress of the Two Lands

BOOK FIVE
The Female Falcon

BOOK SIX
Facing the Horizon

AUTHOR'S NOTE

Shortly before Hatshepsut, translated as Foremost of Noble Women, was crowned Pharaoh she took the throne name Maatkare. The concept of Maat—depicted as a goddess—is one Egyptologists still struggle with but it can essentially be summed up like this: Maat is the Divine force or energy that manifests through the sun and flows through the world. Maat is the spirit of beauty and order. Maat also represents truth and justice when, through human beings, she becomes the conscious exercise of faith in the transcendent creative power embodied in the solar disc. Because Maat breathes life into everything, the more someone opens their heart to Maat the healthier and happier they are as circumstances seem almost magically to favor them. Hence the famous scene from *The Book of the Dead* (actually entitled *The Book of Coming Forth By Day and Opening the Tomb*) where a human heart is shown balancing on a scale with the feather Maat always wore in her hair. Everyone possesses the mysterious ability to enrich the world with joyful flights of the imagination. The ancient Egyptians recognized that "Life, health, strength" was the reward for what they called "Cutting Maat" with their every thought, word and action. Immortality could only be achieved through "the intelligence of the heart." Maatkare means Maat is the Ka of Re, i.e. The True and Beautiful (proper) Manifestation of the Sun's Divine Life-force. A more poetic but still accurate translation of Hatshepsut's throne name is Truth is the Soul of the Sun.

For more than three years I immersed myself in all the available information to date about Hatshepsut-Maatkare (inevitably there are gaps in the physical evidence Egyptologists fill with various theories) then I let the "intelligence of my heart" lead the way along the mysterious currents of a life lived thousands of years ago in a time and place very different from our own. And yet, I will admit, writing this book felt like finally going home.

Cast of Characters

(Fictional characters are indicated by an *, all others are documented historical figures listed in order of appearance)

Ahmose – Sister of Amenhotep I, Chief Wife of Thutmose I, Hatshepsut's mother

Thutmose I – 3rd pharaoh of the 18th Dynasty, Hatshepsut's father

Hatshepsut – King's Daughter, God's Wife, Great Royal Wife, Queen Regent, 5th pharaoh of the 18th dynasty

Inet – Hatshepsut's Royal Nurse

Ahmose-Meritamun – Sister and Chief Wife of Amenhotep I, God's Wife

Amenmose – Son of Thutmose I and Mutnofret

Wadjmose – Son of Thutmose I and Mutnofret

Ramose – Son of Thutmose I and Mutnofret

Ruiu – Deputy of the King's Son of Wawat

Senimen – Hatshepsut's tutor and the third tutor of Neferure

Neferubity – Hatshepsut's little sister

*Meresankh – Hatshepsut's personal attendant

*Seshen – Hatshepsut's personal attendant

***Kanefer** – Hatshepsut's Chief Litter Bearer

Mutnofret – First wife of Thutmose I, mother of Amenmose, Ramose, Wadjmose and Thutmose II

Thutmose II – Son of Thutmose I and Mutnofret, 4th pharaoh of the 18th Dynasty

*Nafre – Hatshepsut's personal attendant

*Sinuhe – Steward of the Royal Household under Thutmose I

Hapuseneb – First Prophet of Amun, Governor of the South

Puyemre – Second Prophet of Amun, Supervisor of the Treasury of Amun

Neferiah – Royal Nurse of Thutmose II, Mother of Puyemre

Amenhotep – Wife of Hapuseneb, Royal Ornament and Concubine of Amun

Ineni – Overseer of the Double Granary of Amun, Headman of Thebes and supervisor of all the works of Pharaoh

Akheperseneb – Northern Vizier under Thutmose I, Thutmose II and Maatkare

Senmut – Neferure's Tutor, Steward of God's Wife, Steward of Amun, etc.

Min-Hotep – Brother of Senmut and Priest of Amun

Djehuti – Chief Treasurer and Overseer of Works

Amenhotep – Steward of Amun, Priest of Anukis, Maatkare's Royal Butler

Duauneheh – Royal Herald, Director of Amun's Granary and Overseer of Works

Useramun – Maatkare's Vizier and Scribe of the Treasury of Amun

Hapu – Father of Hapuseneb, First Lector Priest of Amun

Ahmose-Penekhbet – Steward of the Royal Storehouse, Royal Treasurer, first tutor of Neferure

Neferkhaut – Chief Secretary of the Crown Princess Hatshepsut

Amenemhet – Brother of Senmut, Priest of the Bark of Amun

Pairi - Brother of Senmut, Overseer of the Cattle of Amun

Ah-hotep - Sister of Senmut

Nofret-hor – Sister of Senmut

Harmose – Singer and Harpist to Hatshepsut-Maatkare

*Mentekhenu – Head of Palace Security, husband of Meresankh

*Nebamun – Scribe and Counter of the Grain, husband of Seshen

*Nomti – Great Army Commander under Thutmose II and Maatkare

*Ka-hotep – Royal Artisan

*Ibenre – Priest of Sekhmet, Hatshepsut's personal physician

Neferure – Daughter of Hatshepsut and Thutmose II, God's Wife

Hatnefer – Senmut's mother

Tjuyu – Wife of Useramun

Henut-nefert – Daughter of Hapuseneb and Singer of Amun

Ta-em-resefu – Daughter of Hapuseneb and Singer of Amun

Senseneb – Daughter of Hapuseneb and Wife of Puyemre

Isis – Secondary wife of Thutmose II, mother of Thutmose III

Ahmose-Ruru – Overseer of the Prophets of Min

*Khenti – Nomarch of the Sistrum

*Setau – Nomarch of The Great Land

Satepihu – Headman of Tjeny and Overseer of the Priests of Hut-Sekhem

*Patehuti – High Priest of the Temple of Thoth in Khemnu

*Rasui – Nomarch of the Oryx

Dhout – Maatkare's Royal Steward

Tai – Overseer of the Seal Bearers of God's Wife of Amun

Ptah-Sokar – High Priest of the Temple of Re in Iuno

*Kallikrates –Prince of the Keftiu

*Nekhetmut – Foreman of the Servants of the Place of Truth

*Kamut – Deputy of the Servants of the Place of Truth

Djehutihotep – Oldest Son of Ruiu, Deputy of the King's Son

Amenemhat – Son of Rui, Deputy of the King's Son, True Royal Confidant

Nehesj – Overseer of the Seal Bearers

Inebni – Senior Military Official, Troop-Commander, Overseer of the Weaponry

Tjeni – First Prophet of Horus at Nekhen

*Sobekmose – High Priest of Sobek in Nebet

Thutmose III – Son of Thutmose II and Isis, 6th Pharaoh of the 18th Dynasty

*Sobekmut – Nomarch of the Crocodile

Ipu – Wife of Ahmose-Penekhbet, Royal Nurse of Thutmose III

Tinet-iunet – Wife of Satepihu, Royal Nurse of Thutmose III

Satnem – Royal Painter

Tanefert – Second Wife of Puyemre

Paheri – Headman of Nekheb

*Ptah-Hotep – Son of Rasui and High Priest of Ptah in Mennefer

Hatshepsut – Wife of Amenemhat

Nebiri – Senmut's Skipper

Satioh – Daughter of Ipu and Ahmose-Penekhbet, first wife of Thutmose III

Kheruef – Official in charge of Turquoise Mines in Roshawet

Ty – Overseer of the Seal Bearers after Nehesj

*Thutmose – Chariot Driver, King's Sandal Bearer and Chamberlain

Amenemnekhu – King's Son and Overseer of the Southern Foreign Lands

Tusi – Overseer of the Cultivators of Amun, administrator under Senmut

Goregmennefer - Maatkare's Northern Herald

Chancellor Neshi – Maatkare's Secretary and leader of the expedition to Punt

Meritre-Hatshepsut – Wife of Thutmose III

Antef – Great Herald of the Queen and Director of the Granary

Ahmose – Brother of Antef, Scribe and Overseer of Horns, Hoofs and Feathers

Senenu – High Priest of Amun and Hathor in *Djser-Set* and *Djser-Djseru*

Ahmose – First King's Son of Amun, Pure Priest

Maiherperi – Kushite Fan Bearer

Wadjrenput – Royal Steward after Dhout

Djehuty – Army Commander under Thutmose III

Amenemhat – Oldest son of Thutmose III

BOOK ONE

Daughter of Re

1

Great House

Hatshepsut first experienced fear in her royal nurse's milk. The unfamiliar flavor made her cry in protest. Desire and fulfillment formed the twin peaks of her life until the first words she believes she remembers hearing, "The falcon has flown!" were whispered against her cheek, and then suddenly the generous nipples she loved so much trickled only a frustrating bitterness. Fortunately, her mother came and took her away and in the arms of her new nurse life became unremarkably pleasant again.

She was too young to understand that her mother's brother, Amenhotep, Amun is Content, had gone to his Ka and another man had taken his place as Lord of the Two Lands—her father. She loved the way he swept her up in his arms and spun her around and around, transforming the room into a cloud of bright colors in which the only real thing was the firm warmth of his arms holding her against him. When he set her down she clung to the pillars of his legs, giggling helplessly as the room settled solidly back into place. The world outside entered the house in her father's flesh and she inhaled it curiously as he perched her on his lap. She loved snuggling up against him while he conversed with the queen even though his deep voice vibrated so soothingly through her body she had to struggle not to drift off to sleep. She pressed her ear against his chest, listening in wonder to the drummer living inside him who never needed to rest. Intriguing shapes sometimes hung from a leather cord around his neck, and although they did not taste like much their bright colors never failed to entertain her.

 She hated it when Inet came to take her away; she would much rather have slept in Pharaoh's arms than in her bed. Knowing it might be a long time before she saw him again made it doubly hard to let go. The first sentence she clearly remembers understanding was spoken by her father: "She is a little queen fighting for her throne."

"My throne!" she echoed and clutched the head of the jeweled bird resting with open wings against his chest. Determined to hold onto him, she endured the pain of its beak digging into her skin.

* * * * *

Hatshepsut traced the contours of a gold figure that formed part of a small wooden box but was cooler and smoother to the touch. Its face was missing and it seemed to be wearing a skirt. Only its lovingly open arms looked familiar.

She said, "Who is this odd little person, Mami?"

"That is an *ankh*, my love, the symbol for life."

"It looks like a person," she insisted, not knowing what a *symbol* was.

"Because a human being is the pinnacle of life," the queen replied patiently, "the brilliant star at the summit of the pyramid."

"And what is *life*?"

"Ultimately, life is the mysterious ability to ask that question, Hatshepsut."

Whenever Ahmose spoke her name in that particular way she knew it meant something and she should listen carefully.

"I do not know what a symbol is," she admitted. Words she had never heard both excited and affronted her. It made her feel annoyingly stupid how many objects had the power to hide from her even in the bright light of Re, until a new collection of sounds suddenly made her see them as if for the first time.

"Symbols, my daughter, are all the masks worn by Maat, the goddess who can also take the form of an *ankh*. And before you ask me who Maat is I will tell you even though you will not yet understand. Maat is one of the two daughters of Re."

It soothed Hatshepsut's frustration to sit on her mother's soft lap and forget the sharp edge of questions. It was true she did not understand but with someone lovingly caressing her shaved head it did not matter.

"I am very proud of you, Hatshepsut. The intelligence of your heart is as sharp as Thoth's beak. There will be time for more questions later but now you must go and clean the body your heart brings to life with its voice."

"I have heard father's heart talking, and yours and Inet's as well, but it does not use words as we do."

"Listen carefully, my love. The feelings burning in your heart are *sia* and the thought-words which serve to express them are *ais*. The difference between them is the difference between the sun's life-giving heat and the moon's cold reflection of its light. Lord of Time through the phases of the moon, Thoth is Re's servant. Remember that, Hatshepsut."

"I promise I will remember even though I still do not understand."

"You will."

"When? After I take my bath?"

Ahmose laughed and pushed her gently off her lap. "Perhaps after you take as many baths as there are frogs in the palace ponds! Now off with you, impatient one."

* * * * *

The River had risen five times before experiences began flowing with increasing clarity and depth through Hatshepsut's awareness, shaping the banks of past and present while the future remained a formless brilliance indistinguishable from her first conscious sight of the great pyramids.

Sitting on her favorite goose-head stool beneath a pavilion erected in the center of the vessel, she kept her back straight and attempted to hold herself motionless as a statue. Only her eyes moved, squinting and blinking in the face of the world's brilliant colors. On both sides of the River, stretching all the way to the edges of the desert, golden fields of wheat were divided by shadowy groves of date palms or by herds of peacefully grazing cattle.

The royal barge turned into a canal lined by limestone walkways and her breath caught as the horizon blinded her. For a gloriously unsettling instant she failed to understand it was a pyramid filling her vision. Its dimensions were so vast it was difficult to distinguish its solid edges. The monument soared up from the desert into the boundless sky and ended in a star brilliant enough to shine in Re's company. The pyramid's gleaming point sent long, luminous arms directly into her squinting eyes and she felt it silently telling her something wonderful.

As the ceremonial ship glided along the still waters of the canal, she turned her attention reluctantly back down to earth. Above the rhythmic whisper of the oars, more voices than she had ever heard before surged in powerful waves toward the pavilion where she sat behind her father, The Good God Akheperkare, and her mother, Queen Ahmose, King's Sister[1] and Pharaoh's Great Royal Wife. Also with them that morning was Ahmose-Meritamun, Born of the Moon-Beloved of Amun, King's Daughter, King's Sister and God's Wife.

An intermittent breeze—strengthened by attendants slowly waving great ostrich feather fans—wafted myriad scents beneath Hatshepsut's nose. In contrast her hearing felt oddly numbed by the cries of joy rising from the multitudes lining the banks. The crowds rippled like fields of wheat in a powerful wind as some people regained their feet and others kissed the earth as the royal ship approached. She was happy everyone loved her family so much but she was more interested in the giant lion—its human face framed by a striped cloth like the one her father was wearing that morning—that crouched on the horizon guarding not just one pyramid but three.

She squirmed against the spotted animal skin sticking to her naked buttocks, eager to disembark. It was an overwhelming relief when she was at last able to stand up and walk. The white temples of the pyramid builders reflected the light so intensely she was glad Inet had painted her eyelids with soothing shadows. All she remembers after that is standing between her mother and Meri facing a marvelously life-like statue. They were alone; father had vanished into one of the shining walls with the *hemu* Ka. It had made her nervous when the priest stared down into her eyes as if there was no end to how far he could see inside her. She had been glad when he left and she could grasp her mother's hand and the hand of her mother's sister safely in hers.[2] She felt very grown up in those moments even though her only adornment was a girdle of golden cowrie shells Inet had said would help keep her beautiful and healthy. The insides of her sandals were decorated with scorpions she magically crushed with every step while invoking the protection of Serket.

Mindful of being a visitor in the royal couple's offering chapel, she whispered, "Who are they, Mami?" The nearly life-size statue was carved from a smooth dark stone.

It was Meri who replied, "That is Menkaure the Divine and his Great Royal Wife, Khamrenebty, the goddess Hathor embodied."

"He is almost as handsome as father." She was careful to continue speaking quietly. "But his queen is wearing a funny looking wig."

"That funny looking wig," Ahmose squeezed her hand as if by way of reprimand, "was the height of fashion a long time ago, Hatshepsut."

"Well, she looks *very* nice, and she loved her husband as much as you love father."

Meri asked, "How do you know that?"

"Because she is embracing him and holding him close beside her, as if she does not wish for him to go away all the time the way father does, and she looks happy. How could she be so happy if she did not really love him?"

"An excellent observation," said God's Wife. "And an even more astute question."

"Notice, Hatshepsut," her mother added in the tone of voice that commanded her to listen attentively, "that Khamrenebty is as tall as her husband. In reality her head may only have reached his shoulder but in truth she was his equal and ruled Kemet by his side. So it always was between The Good God and his Great Royal Wife before the darkness of chaos swept over Kemet in the form of invaders from the north. Now there are only a few of us left who remember."

* * * * *

"Hatshepsut!" Inet cried her name urgently. "Come, my lady! It is time to give a road to the feet!"

"But I cannot leave without Bubu!"

As she spoke his name, the cat strolled into her room from the Pleasure House.

"There he is." Inet frowned. The large young feline never listened to her. "Now hurry, my dear. The boat has been furnished and Pharaoh awaits his daughter."

"Come, Bubu, we are going on a journey!" She was not at all nervous about leaving home because everyone who lived in her heart was going with her.

It turned out to be a very *long* journey. Land gave them to land as the River never ended. Thankfully, being onboard the *Falcon* was great fun. She was not limited to the pavilion, except for during the hottest part of the day when Inet made her take a nap after they ate. She spent as much time as her father permitted by his side. She enjoyed listening to him talk with the captain, a tall man named Manu whose especially nice smile inspired her to favor him with her questions and observations.

As the solar bark began its journey through the dark hours of the night, the royal ships turned toward shore and a Mooring Place of Pharaoh. Unless she was too tired to remember their arrival, Hatshepsut always enjoyed studying new faces and smiling up at each one to see how it reacted. She liked the people who grinned warmly back at her, but she was disappointed and bored by those individuals who shifted their eyes away, as if the daughter of Re was too bright to look at.

She knew from listening to her parents talking together alone, as they invariably did in the evenings, that how well equipped the ports were pleased them.

"Soldiers and chariots are all kept properly anointed," her mother said. "And I have it from Akheperseneb that Pharaoh's army occasionally eats as well as the court, enjoying short-horned oxen from the west, fat calves from the south and succulent birds from the reed swamps in addition to the customary wheat loaves, dried meats and honey cakes. My lord is truly generous."

"It is best to keep them happy now for the closer we draw to Wawat the louder their bellies will speak longingly of home."

Even though she was full of duck, Hatshepsut could not resist helping herself to another fig. "Where is Wawat?" she asked.

"Near the end of the world!" Ahmose sighed.

"Then why do we have to go there?"

"Pharaoh is honoring all the gods with a visit to the Nome of their birth. The Ba of each Nome enriches the land in its own unique fashion but they all share a single Ka in the king who wears the Two Ladies on his forehead—the vulture Nekhbet, guardian of the south, and the cobra Wadjet, protector of the North. Wawat is in Down Below, the realm of chaos and despair where Sekhmet feasted wildly on blood until Thoth transformed her into Bast by plunging her into the sacred waters of Osiris at the birth of the River. Pharaoh is once again taking the shining lances of his army Down Below to pierce its darkness with Re's light and enforce the Divine order of Maat. Now off to bed."

"Tomorrow we reach the city of your birth, Hatshepsut." Her father kissed her goodnight on both cheeks. "Waset,[3] home of the King of The Gods, Amun-Re. Together you and I will visit the Hidden One in his temple."

Wide awake with questions, she lingered disobediently. "But how can we visit a god that hides from us?"

Laughing, Ahmose glanced at her husband, her eyes intent on his reply.

"She is exhausting," he groaned, falling back across the couch. "I keep expecting Manu to throw her overboard, the poor man. He has earned a golden collar!"

Hatshepsut watched in fascination as her mother leaned over her father and gently raked his skin with her red fingernails from the base of his neck all the way down to his navel. She nearly forgot her question as her parents suddenly reminded her of two kittens playing in a basket.

"Husband," Ahmose whispered, "she will not leave until you answer her question."

He grasped her slender wrist, inhaling appreciatively as he sat up. "My dear daughter, your Ka asks questions your Ba is still too young to understand the answers to. Go to bed and see if a dream will enlighten you. We learn as much, and often more, when we are asleep, which is what you should be."

"Yes, father. Goodnight. Goodnight mother."

"Goodnight, my love," they said as one.

Re felt more powerful in the Town of Amun, where Inet said everyone was celebrating the festival of Renenutet, giving thanks for the bountiful harvest and the good fortune of health and abundance that augured the birth of many future scribes. However, when Hatshepsut asked where her mother and Meri had gone, her nurse's bright expression dimmed to one of respectful sadness.

"They have gone to offer the first fruits of the harvest to the dead and to remember your little brother who went to his Ka only one moon after he was born, on that ill-fated day when Seth celebrates his birthday."

The jaws of the little wooden hippopotamus sitting in Hatshepsut's lap closed with a loud snap as she tugged on the string connecting them. "Mother had another child besides me?"

"Please do not tell anyone you know, Hatshepsut. Your mother did not wish to upset you with his death."

She tossed the toy away. "I am *not* upset!"

Bubu pounced on it like a lion, intrigued by the string.

The Temple of Amun-Re affected Hatshepsut like her first sight of the pyramids. Rays of light streaming in from openings in the dark ceiling, decorated with golden stars and flying birds, looked almost solid enough to touch. Erected on her father's command, two rows of immense wooden pillars evoked lotus and papyrus stalks. As Re traveled across the sky, the great columns seemed to bloom with paintings and hieroglyphs inscribed on all their sides. The shafts of sunlight spoke in silent statements she felt her heart understanding almost as clearly as her eyes could see them. The hall was dark enough to hide the mysterious Amun-Re even as his luminous arms welcomed them.

While the queen and God's Wife spent the day with the ancient cobra Renenutet, Pharaoh and his daughter visited the *Per Ankh,* and there her favorite half brother, Amenmose, Born of Amun, joined them. She was delighted to see him. He kindly cured her boredom by giving her a ride on his back into the inner garden, where there was no one to hear her scream as he tossed her into a pool, flung off his kilt, and promptly joined her in the cool water.

She splashed him happily. "What is father doing in that stuffy old room?"

"Consulting with some of the wisest men in the Two Lands."

"If they were truly wise they would be out here with us!"

He laughed. "Well said, sister."

* * * * *

After Waset, the royal family stayed for a few days in Nekhen before sailing even further south to Djeba. All Hatshepsut remembers about the Temple of Horus is dazzlingly painted columns and a sky blue as lapis lazuli. Every time she looked up she glimpsed a falcon flying so high its wings appeared as motionless as those of the jeweled hawk resting against her father's chest. Djeba was special to Pharaoh for he was the spirit of Horus made flesh, or so her mother told her and she believed it even though she had no idea what that meant. She was certain of only one thing—the whole world belonged to her father.

She never got bored on the ship, from which there was always something new to see. One afternoon she happened to be looking at some wet rocks rising from the water near the west bank when one of them suddenly opened its mouth and she realized it was a hippopotamus. Its tongue was as big as her bed;

it could easily have crushed her little bones with the square rocks of its teeth and buried her forever in its dark belly. The thought thrilled her with terror.

"The Great One." Ahmose stretched forth her right hand with two fingers extended in the gesture of protection. "Tawaret, she who destroys to protect and to nourish. If you had to give two words to what the heart repeats over and over with its double beat they would be *creation* and *destruction*, the rhythm of life as we experience it."

Even though Re was still high in the sky, she shivered. "But when something is destroyed it dies…"

"Do not be afraid, my daughter. When we die we are born to the Divine power behind all creation that lives inside us."

"But Inet told me the hippopotamus goddess protects women in childbirth."

"That is so, but Tawaret also protects the soul in the magical womb of the burial chamber, through which we are born to our eternal nature as we assume command of the laws of manifestation." She pointed upriver. "See that crocodile?"

Hatshepsut shaded her eyes with both hands. "Yes, I see it!"

"The first *neter* to emerge from the starry womb of Mother Nut, Sobek swims with Tawaret, the goddess who wears him across her back in the northern sky. To our body the crocodile is a dangerous creature, but our Ka understands that the death and destruction it represents lead to the transformation of state which returns us to our celestial source. Even so, the journey through the Dwat can be a perilous one. Ammit, who is half crocodile and half hippopotamus, devours any heart which does not balance with the feather of truth, forcing its owner to begin the journey of life anew."

"The feather worn by the goddess Maat?"

"Yes. Maat is the Divine energy embodied in the sun. If you have faith in life's eternal nature, and are true to what you believe with all your thoughts and actions, then your heart receives, circulates and exhales Maat as you speak in a perfect balance. But doubts and fears, evil words and deeds block the free flow of cosmic energy through your body, which drains you of health and strength and prevents beautiful things from happening to you."

Hatshepsut thought a great deal about that conversation. She resented being afraid of anything and it seemed her mother had given her the words she needed to in the future defend herself from the sensation of powerlessness she disliked so much. When she mentioned the hippopotamus to Inet, her nurse changed the subject by once more telling her the story of a fish that fell in love with a boy. For a while she managed to forget the concepts—as dark and intense as the star-filled sky—her mother had planted in her heart.

* * * * *

Hatshepsut began to feel they would never reach Wawat. She did not want to admit she was increasingly nervous about traveling to the end of the world. It reassured her to stand at the ship's railing and look out at the army traveling with them. The points of spears—all properly polished and anointed—reflected the light of the rising sun so that another glimmering river seemed to be flowing across the earth. At times there was barely enough room in the water for all the boats sailing behind the royal barge. As twilight fell, the gilded *Wedjat* eyes painted on the curving bows saw into the darkness and guided them safely toward the torch-lit shore.

Every morning the world was born anew and the baboons were there to rejoice in the miracle. Their raucous celebration woke Hatshepsut and forced her to face another day of the seemingly endless journey. Time flowed slowly by in a waking dream of golden desert mountains and vast turquoise skies her mother described as the jewels worn by the falcon god whose right eye was the sun and whose left eye was the moon.

When they reached the first wild waters, all the ships turned into the canal she learned her father had recently emptied of the stones blocking it. But when, days later, they came to a second place where the River was not navigable everyone was obliged to travel by land as Pharaoh commanded the boats be dragged behind them. Hatshepsut's heart beat fast with mingled fear and excitement as the nearly deafening power of the rushing River, carried toward her by the wind, coolly stung her skin and lips and enabled her to taste its dangerous beauty.

Several mornings later the Soul of Isis rose on the horizon. The star burned a pure blue-white and announced *Wep-Renpet*, the birth of Re and the Opening of the Year, Pharaoh's birthday. They were far from home in Wawat, which made the excess of lamps lit that night in celebration look even more comfortingly beautiful, and yet the skin of the royal court's local host remained as dark as night. No Kushite had ever smiled at her the way Ruiu did, Deputy of the King's Son and Overseer of the Southern Foreign Lands. She liked Ruiu and his wife very much because they were not afraid to look her straight in the eye. It was disappointing they never touched her; she would have liked to know if their skin was as cool and smooth as the black ivory it resembled.

Inet complained of the plainness of the rooms and garden but wherever there was a pool Hatshepsut was happy, and it especially pleased her when Amenmose joined her in it. She relished distracting him by diving beneath the water and tickling him as he swam. Afterward they embraced the shade beneath a pavilion where he attempted to silence her curious questions by slipping slices of fresh fruit between her lips.

"How much farther do we have to go, brother?"

"A long way, little sister." He wiped away the cool juice trickling down her chin with his warm thumb. "Deep into wretched Kush."

"But if Kush is so wretched, why are we going there?"

He frowned. "So it does not come to us."

This disturbing conversation replayed itself monotonously in her mind until five large monuments, all proclaiming her father's victory over the Kushites, brought the barren landscape to life with the reassuringly clean and colorful lines of hieroglyphs. The royal party spent that night in one of the newly constructed fortresses and several days later an even larger fortification of Pharaoh rose welcomingly on the horizon.

The ships were pulled over land again and then, at last, they united with their final destination. Generals, priests, scribes, the most elite members of the court, the queen, a prince and the princess—everyone had come all that way in order to watch Pharaoh's scribes drawing on a big rock. They had reached the end of the ordered world of Maat and Hatshepsut wanted desperately to turn back and go home. It seemed to take forever to complete the great monument marking Kemet's new southern boundary. Through his bodily son, Thutmose-Akheperkare, the power and compassion of Amun now reached all the way to that desolate place. The mountain became a closed door locked by magic. Those foolish enough to ignore its warning would perish like shadows on the shining lances of Re's army.

2

Divine Words

During the journey home, the queen's belly gradually grew. Every night Hatshepsut prayed to Tawaret to protect Ahmose when the time came for the new person to be born, and destroy the perfect happiness of having her mother's love all to herself.

The gods both punished and rewarded her for her selfishness in the form of Senimen, the young nobleman honored with the position of tutor to the princess. He was not as handsome as Amenmose but at least he was not as old as the Wisdom Texts he made her copy and recopy until her wrist and fingers ached. Despite how hard he inspired her to work, and yet also because of it, she found his company much more interesting than that of her half brothers, Ramose and Wadjmose, who did nothing but tease her the rare times she saw them. Never having met Thutmose—her father's youngest son by her mother's half sister, the Lady Mutnofret—she had no idea yet how she felt about him. It was not long before she had fondly nicknamed her tutor Seni. She loved knowing she could ask him endless questions and that instead of dismissing them like a cloud of annoying flies he would answer each one in detail.

After perfuming her mouth with milk, fruit and bread, she had her lessons in the cool light of morning in her Pleasure House. Sitting on a papyrus mat in front of a pool, she often looked up from the motionless little pictures and soothed her physical restlessness by watching the fish flitting freely back and forth. Yet they too were confined to a square space akin to her tablet, which magically became the whole world through the *medu neters*—Divine Words.

Using black ink she copied each symbol Senimen pronounced for her. The red ink stored in a recess on the other side of her palette he later used to correct her mistakes. He met her in the garden every morning with several freshly cleaned tablets hanging over his shoulder. He also carried a little drawstring bag containing all the ingredients he needed to mix the colors. She watched attentively as he stirred soot and papyrus juice together with the tip of his rush stem brush, and then carefully added a little water to produce black ink. He showed her how to make red ink with burned ochre which first had to be ground into a fine powder so it could be bonded with papyrus juice then thinned with water. She soon learned how to mix her own colors and earned her own little leather bag.

The Wisdom Texts she copied and memorized passages from consisted of two separate books—*The Instruction of King Amenemhet* and the *Adoration of the River*.[4] In the first book, Pharaoh Amenemhet gave his son, Sesostris, advice on how to protect himself from treachery. Some of the old king's courtiers had tried to murder him in the night but he had survived the attack by bravely fighting them off. Hatshepsut found the story disturbing. She could not understand why some people had been so murderously unhappy with Amenemhet, who had tamed lions, captured crocodiles and made certain no one in Kemet hungered or thirsted.

"No one would ever dare attack my father like that!" She waited tensely for Seni to confirm her confidence and banish the invisible but chilling shadow abruptly fallen over the garden.

"By the Ka of Ptah, I pray such evil will never come to pass, and yet we can never know with absolute certainty what will or will not happen, Hatshepsut. The important thing to remember is that Amenemhet, Lord of All, was victorious in the darkness against those who betrayed his justice and trust with ingratitude and violence. Remember also that by then he was an old man prepared to give the care of the Two Lands into the hands of his son. Sesostris was like your father, strong and wise as Horus, his people knowing only happiness when they gave him praise."

Even though she was reassured, Hatshepsut much preferred copying the *Adoration of the River*. She had become familiar with the River's different moods during the trip to and from Wawat, and depending on her own mood she sometimes felt it took almost as long as the journey had lasted to write two short sentences:

"Praise to thee, O River, that issues from the earth and comes to nourish Kemet. Of hidden nature, a darkness in the daytime, the light that comes from darkness, the strong one that creates all that is good."[5]

For the purpose of learning the correct writing of individual words, she copied the list compiled by the scribe of the God's Book in the House of Life, Amenemope, son of Amenemope, entitled *The teaching that makes clever and instructs the ignorant, the knowledge of all that exists, what Ptah has created and Thoth has written, the heaven with its stars, the earth and what is in it, what the mountains give forth and what flows from the ocean, concerning all things that the sun enlightens and all that grows.[6]*

She was immediately intrigued by how different combinations of little pictures formed specific words. The first thing Seni taught her how to write was her own name, of course. He explained to her how the *shenu* ring that enclosed all royal names was linked to the *shen* ring—the word for eternity written as a circle over a line which, amongst other things, represented the solar disc perched on the horizon.

"The *shenu* ring is the closed loop of your personal destiny which flows out of an eternal reality when you are born and returns to it when you die," he told her. "Your body rises and sets like the sun, but the *shenu* ring, which encircles the hieroglyphs spelling your name, symbolizes the power your Ka possesses to contain an infinite Divine force in a temporary physical form."

The long *shenu* ring spelling her name *Hatshepsut* contained a feather, a senet board, the row of little pyramids representing water, a vase with two different sized handles, the head and front legs of a lion drawn in profile, and a man with a royal beard who was wrapped up like a mummy and sat on a lion-paw throne holding a fly whisk scepter against his heart. For some reason those different images spelled out her identity. She studied the signs with puzzled curiosity trying to understand what they might tell her about herself.

One morning when she was frustrated by how slowly her skill and understanding were growing, Seni smiled at her and said, "You are doing very well, Hatshepsut, do not be impatient but rather persevere in asking my counsel and in mastering the Divine art of writing. Set your heart upon words for you will find them infinitely profitable. 'It is good to study many things so that you may learn the wisdom of great men. And while you are on your journey, you need never hide your heart. Step out on the path of learning, where the friends of Man are your company'."[7]

* * * * *

"Come in, Hatshepsut."

She hesitated before stepping tentatively into Meri's bedroom. She had never been invited inside before and this fact, coupled with her mother's confinement, made her nervous. The large space was full of fascinating furniture revealed by dozens of burning oil lamps.

Meri was sitting at her cosmetics table. She had just returned from somewhere important because she was wearing the queen's vulture crown. After her attendant gently separated it from her wig, she took it from the woman's hands and rested it on her lap as she said, "Leave us, Nepthys." The lines on both sides of her small firm mouth seemed more pronounced than normal.

Hatshepsut went and stood obediently before her mother's sister, her eyes irresistibly drawn to the golden vulture. Meri's fingers looked strangely swollen and nearly as stiff as the bird nesting in them.

"Your mother has gone to the birthing arbor, Hatshepsut. I would be there with her now if she had not asked me to stay with you instead."

"Will she be all right?"

"Only the gods know. She is no longer young. She is, however, healthy and strong and attended by midwives from the House of Life, so do not be afraid. You should never be afraid. Death exists only in fear. Fear cripples and can even kill the ability of your Ba to exercise the creative power it shares with Re through your Ka. Fear is worse than a hundred thousand armed Kushites. Fear seduces with reasonable excuses. You must always fight fear and triumph over it. Only then will you be worthy of the vulture crown. Do you understand, Hatshepsut?"

"I understand nothing can truly hurt me for I am the daughter of Re so there is no reason for me to be afraid of anything. Mother told me so. She said destruction and death are only *transformations.*"

"That does not mean they cannot be painful," Meri warned sternly. "While blood still flows through our bodies the fear of pain is one of the strongest of all."

Hatshepsut began to worry. She had recently scraped both knees in a fall and had no desire to repeat the experience, which had been both painful and bloody. She hoped that did not mean she was not brave enough to be queen.

"Never doubt yourself!" Meri said harshly. She glanced down at the imperishable vulture lying in her lap and added more gently, "Would you like me to tell you about Nekhbet?"

"Yes, please," she replied dutifully even while secretly hoping Inet would come and take her back to her room soon.

"The vulture Nekhbet and the cobra Wadjet protect Kemet from their throne on Pharaoh's forehead, but the Two Ladies are a single goddess in the Great Mother Mut, the consort of Amun and Mistress of the Two Lands. The vulture is a loving mother who conceives by opening her wings, glimmering with all the colors of Creation, to the celestial wind. But you are only a child. You will not understand if I tell you more."

"I am *not* a child." Indignation destroyed her anxiety in a flash and blinded her to the fact she was speaking rudely. "I am a princess of Kemet. I can understand anything!"

Amusement lightened the corners of Meri's mouth for an instant but her smile died before coming to life. "And one day you may be a queen. You need-"

"*May* be a queen?"

"Never interrupt me again, *princess.* When a queen wears the vulture headdress she is consciously marrying God who uses her body for His own pleasure and purpose. By way of the vulture crown, the queen becomes the mother of her people's Divine nature as she nourishes their bodies with food and their hearts with wisdom. Every person must awaken the Akh within them. Akh is the process of your Ba becoming fully conscious of the beautiful truth that Amun-Re is feeling through your heart and seeing through your eyes. The vulture lives off dead meat just as your Akh transcends the mortal flesh which gives birth to it."

"Amun-Re is hidden inside *us*?"

"Yes!" Meri stood abruptly and placed the vulture crown on top of a featureless wooden head.

"Is father's other wife, the Lady Mutnofret, so far away because she does not live in father's heart the way mother does?"

"You are much concerned with love, Hatshepsut."

She did not understand the remark for the only thing which concerned her about love was the possibility of its loss.

"Come and sit with me," God's Wife commanded gently.

Hatshepsut followed her across the room to a couch in which the two front legs, carved of gilded wood, were topped with Hippopotamus heads. The open jaws revealed red tongues and large, square white teeth lined up behind evil-looking ivory fangs. The couch's four unnaturally slender legs ended in lion's paws that rested on a rectangular black base and the seat evoked a crocodile's long and slender back.

"That is Ammit," she observed anxiously.

"Do not be concerned. Ammit devours only those hearts which do not prove as light as the feather of truth." Meri seated herself on the frightening creature's spine and stretching her legs before her leaned back against the golden *djed* pillars and *ankh* signs decorating both the head and the baseboards. "Come here, Hatshepsut. It is fear that blocks the flow of solar energy through the heart. If you are not afraid and believe in Maat, Ammit will not devour you. Ammit even becomes your friend by ridding the world of bad people who *would* hurt you. I am not impressed with how well you listen to what I tell you."

She quickly climbed up beside her mother's sister.

"You are fond of Amenmose, Hatshepsut?"

"Yes!"

"And what about Wadjmose and Ramose?"

"I do not know… I suppose I do not like them very much."

"A king's wife must be a good judge of character if she truly wishes to be of service to him. You are right. Wadjmose is the eldest but he is unfinished. He is delightful at a banquet but in the Seal Room he would be disastrous; he is perfectly happy hunting ostriches and collecting women. Ramose is a disciplined soldier but a small man. He is strong and brave as a bull but the wisdom of Thoth and the enlightenment of Horus are beyond him. That is why your father favors Amenmose. It seems your favorite brother is destined to be Pharaoh one day and you will be his Great Royal Wife." She paused before adding, "Unless your mother gives birth to a son tonight."

"Then the baby will become Pharaoh instead?" She hated to think how disappointed Amenmose would be.

"Perhaps. Perhaps not. Offices have no offspring, sometimes not even the king's. Your father is not of royal blood and yet the gods saw fit to make him The Eye Of All Men. However, if my sister gives birth to another girl then *you* will have a rival, for Amenmose's affections."

Hatshepsut abruptly felt her heart talking very quickly, urgently telling her something… If Amenmose grew to love her baby sister more than he loved her, this nameless creature whom she already disliked would become his Great Royal Wife and Queen of the Two Lands. Her chest felt disturbingly hot at the thought, as though Ammit was already chewing on her heart and threatening to swallow her future.

* * * * *

The following morning Inet greeted her with a bright smile that cast a strange shadow in her eyes. "As the earth became light and the next day was come, your mother gave birth to a baby girl," she announced, removing the ivory wand she placed at the foot of Hashepsut's bed every night. Various gods in their animal forms drawn in black ink protected the princess from demons who wore their terrible faces on the backs of their heads and preyed on helpless children.

"Your sister's name is Neferubity, Beautiful Daughter of the King, and I am to take you into her presence as soon as you have perfumed your mouth and had your lessons."

Hatshepsut had no patience that day for silly little pictures which all seemed to spell out her great losses. She did not care that she was disobeying Meri and dishonoring herself by being afraid; she could not help it.

"That is enough copying for today," Seni said abruptly and removing the tablet resting on her lap replaced it with a fresh one. "I would like you to write *mer* for me."

"The word for love?"

"The very one."

"But *mer* is only one little picture of a plow."

"Write it."

She did so slowly, making an effort to remember exactly what it looked like, for he had assured her every detail was important.

"Very good, Hatshepsut. Now tell me why you think a plow is used to write the sound which means love."

"I do not know," she said impatiently, thinking of her mother's love divided in half between two daughters and of Amenmose's affection for her threatened by a sister.

"What does a plow do?"

"It makes a path through the earth."

"And what is that path for?"

She looked at him incredulously. "You know what it is for, to plant seeds that grow into food, of course."

"And what do we do with the crops that spring forth from the seeds sown in the path formed by the plow?"

She rolled her eyes. "We *eat* them."

"And what happens when we eat them?"

"We feel full and happy. If we did not eat we would die. Our flesh would shrivel up and all that would be left was bare bones." She was in such a bad mood she took a perverse pleasure in the gruesome image.

"Then you understand why the hieroglyph which means *mer* is written by a plow."

He sounded so flatteringly certain of her comprehension she thought very hard, not wanting to disappoint him. The answer was so obvious she nearly missed it. "Because we could not live without it!"

He smiled. "As you said, when people are starving they are a terrible sight. Their bones press against their withered flesh like the twigs of an empty nest. A Ba that does not love is one through which the Ka cannot shine, a miserable personality already dead in life. Do you begin to see how in a single hieroglyph many truths can be hidden and expressed?"

"Yes!" Abruptly she realized how stupid she was being. She had not lost anything she had *gained* a sister she could love who could also grow to love her. If love was food for the Ka, the more there was of it in her family the better. "Do all hieroglyphs mean so much, Seni?"

"As much and more. If you add an 'e' to *mer* it spells 'subjects', *mere.*"

"Because my father loves his people and they love him?" she guessed eagerly.

"Yes. And because the only thing which truly has any power, the only thing worthy of ruling our lives and which all our thoughts should serve to protect, nourish and assist in growing, is love."

A deepening respect for her tutor drew the features of his face more distinctly in her vision. Perhaps he *was* as handsome as Amenmose, only in a different way. His skin was not as attractively gilded by the sun's as her half brother's but that was only because he was a scribe and spent almost as much time indoors as ladies of the court. In that moment she decided Senimen might also be worthy of her love.

"Meri told me last night I was much concerned with love," she informed him proudly.

"Yes, I know." He smiled again. "Now write the letter *b* for me."

She obeyed him at once, relieved it was much easier to draw than a plough. "B is a foot."

"No, Hatshepsut, a foot is *b*. The reality of *b* exists before the sound. Everything comes into being when its name is spoken but what is embodied in the foot existed before the foot itself. The hieroglyph *b* represents a foot that walks or runs until you draw a rolled papyrus scroll beside it."

He waited until she had complied with his unspoken request before continuing.

"The rolled papyrus scroll alerts the reader to a hidden meaning behind the obvious and is used to indicate an abstract principle. A scroll written beside it transforms *b* into the concepts of placement, of support and of duality, because you cannot walk on just one foot. When you are older, and continue your education in the Temple, you will better understand why *b* is one of the first sounds uttered by Thoth."

Ladies of the court were often invited to visit the residence and those with young sons and daughters brought them along in the hope the princesses would honor them with their attention. Since Neferubity was still only a baby it was Hatshepsut who entertained herself with the assorted children of the nobility. She looked forward to spending time with the more adventurous boys and girls and it was always fun when one or more of them brought along their favorite pets.

No one owned as many animals as the oldest princess and she never tired of showing them off. Except for Bubu, and two small birds in a cage, Inet would not let any of the creatures into her room so they all lived in their own wing. Several moons after she mentioned a pair of little black-and-white monkeys she had seen in the company of a lady, four of the same species were delivered to her growing menagerie. Their faces were adorably intelligent and, in her opinion, they were smarter than many people. Her mother said she could have a tame gazelle when she was older and Amenmose had secretly promised her one of his lion cubs.

In addition to her living pets, Hatshepsut owned a large collection of cats, most made of wood or alabaster with glass eyes. Her favorite was carved of black ivory and had life-like turquoise eyes. She enjoyed arranging her toy felines around Bubu while he slept and pretending he was Pharaoh attended by beautiful women all coveting the position of his Great Royal Wife. Naturally, he did not desire any of them because they were not really alive. She was confident Amenmose would behave just as wisely when the time came for him to choose the woman he would marry and set above all others as queen.

She was forbidden to bring any of her animals with her when she met with Seni in the Pleasure House for her lessons. The restriction had annoyed her at first but it was not long before she actually enjoyed learning the profound ideas and meanings expressed through the *medu neters*. Sometimes, however, the complexity of hieroglyphs made her head hurt and her tutor seemed to notice because the next morning he always set her an easier, if more tedious, exercise. She was obliged to copy the names of all the Nomes in Kemet and, even worse, to memorize them. She learned to list all the northern and southern cities and the names of foreign peoples, their lands and *their* cities, a task she found perversely interesting. She could not help feeling sorry for anyone who lived far from the River because obviously the gods did not love them as much as they loved her and everyone else born in Kemet.

* * * * *

Neferubity stopped eating. Seven magic wands were placed around her bed but, Inet said sadly, evil spirits had run off with her appetite. Hatshepsut was aware of what happened in her little sister's room because her nurse told her everything. She knew Nefi had been born so weak and sickly that she was put on a diet of ground fragments of her own placenta mixed with milk taken from a woman who had borne many strong male children.

"What is placenta, Iny?"

"It is what comes out of the mother after the baby."

"But what *is* it?"

"The placenta is the remains of the baby's residence in its mother's belly, which still shines with the magic of the Ka that shaped it."

"But that means Nefi's Ka was not great enough of magic to create a healthier body."

"How can you say that, Hatshepsut? Your sister is not yet two years of age. It is not her fault she is sickly."

"But her Ka *must* be to blame for not making her healthy," she insisted. "It was not powerful enough to fight off the evil spirits."

"Are you not sad your sister may soon go to her Ka, powerful or not?"

"I do not really know her. I am only worried because mother will be so unhappy."

"If your sister goes to her Ka you will be the only child born of Ahmose who has lived to walk. You are very special to her, Hatshepsut." She took her in her arms. "To all of us!"

No one was surprised when, on the birthday of Horus the Elder, Neferubity's Ba stopped fighting the desire to fly back up to the sky.

3

Creative Fire

In the month of Epiphi, in Year Eight of the Good God Akheperkare, three days after Princess Neferubity went to her Ka, the evil winds of Seth began blowing. The River was at its lowest point and so were Hatshepsut's spirits. Her mother was ill and her father was away on a military campaign with Ramose and Amenmose. She did not know, or care, where Wadjmose was. She was obliged to remain indoors and boredom made the scorching winds feel even worse. The servants were forever cleaning up and their constant presence only added to the aggravation of being stuck inside all day. It was so hot and stuffy in her apartments, the only emotion she had the energy to muster was one of pure mindless longing for the pool in her garden. She craved the water's cool clean depths, and the occasional slick caress of a fish against her skin, with all the passion left her to desire anything in Seth's embrace.

During this time, Senimen became even more special to Hatshepsut. In the early morning—before Seth woke and marshaled his terrible army of sand—her lessons continued, engrossing her with the unchanging discipline and stimulating her with the profound challenges they presented. Later she entertained herself thinking about what she had learned as she curled up with Bubu on her bed for most of the endless afternoon. Inet insisted on wrapping her up in linen to protect her from the stinging lances of sand. Feeling like her own mummy, she listened to the wind howling through the city sounding like the lost souls of all the people devoured by Ammit desperate to find their way back into living bodies. It was an indescribable relief when Seth at last retreated and the peace of evening descended. The cool of twilight in her Pleasure House had never felt so wonderful and the colors flowing across the Celestial River in the wake of Atum-Re's barge sailing into the darkness had never looked more beautiful.

After assuring her the queen felt better and would soon ask to see her, Inet sighed and said, "The land thirsts for the return of the Goddess!"

"Why does she leave us every year?" Hatshepsut demanded. "Where does she go? Is Kemet not good enough for her? Why does she make us all suffer so? And I thought Hathor was the goddess of music and pleasure, the wife of Horus, not *Seth's* consort."

"When the Goddess smiles at us we see Hathor but when she frowns it is Sekhmet we must deal with. Sekhmet was born wild and deep in her heart she always will be. Her destructive nature can only be tamed by her Father through the gods he sends to transform her."

Hatshepsut spread herself out on a papyrus mat and rested her chin in her hands. "Tell me again about The Mistress of the Year!"

Beyond the roof of the pavilion, the western sky was her favorite color. She felt purely happy gazing up at the heavens when they shone like an amethyst. And even as the lovely hue was slowly consumed by darkness, she was consoled by brilliant stars that all sent fervently friendly arms straight toward her as she struggled to keep her eyes open listening to Inet telling her the story of the Divine lioness.

"At the beginning of time, Re wept because he was lonely, and as his hot golden tears fell to earth, bees and men were born from them. Re was pleased with himself, but soon there were so many people he could not control them. Angered by their disobedience, he commanded his daughter to kill as many of them as she desired. In the end, however, her thirst for blood was so intense that Re found himself threatened with eternal loneliness again. Witnessing the terrible carnage wrought by Sekhmet's selfish hunger, he suffered a change of heart. Commanding vast quantities of beer to be brewed and then dyed red, one night he flooded the world with it. When Sekhmet woke the next morning, she drank deeply of what she believed was blood and was pacified. Yet she can never forget what she was, before Re set her on his forehead as his fiery eye. Every year she travels Down Below to satisfy her boundless appetite for men's bodies. And every year she returns to Kemet as the dry land begins drinking the red waters of the inundation like blood bringing it to life again. And so the wild lioness is transformed into the gentle cat, Bast, lapping the milk of moonlight and purring contentedly at the feet of men whose hearts are warmed by Re's bountiful compassion.

"Sekhmet protects and preserves from all evil," Inet concluded, "everyone who believes she is the beautiful daughter of Re and the Beloved of Ptah even though death is forever part of her nature."

* * * * *

Neferubity was in the *Wabet*. Hatshepsut was surprised it took such a long time to make such a small mummy.

"Your sister's heart still belonged in great part to your mother so they will not remove her organs," Seni told her. "The princess will rest beside the queen in her tomb."

"Is that why Meri spends so much time in Waset, to make sure their Houses of Eternity are properly built and furnished?"

"Yes. The God's Wife oversees the work in the Necropolis, as well as the health and happiness of all those entrusted with it."

"I think she misses her brother and husband very much. If he had not died, she would still be the Great Royal Wife and Mistress of the Two Lands. Do you know when father will be back?"

"Pharaoh's army has been victorious in The Land of the Two Rivers and the rule of Maat now extends as far as the circuit of the sun. We should soon be blessed by his return. Already I have received instructions from him as to how your education should progress."

"Father wrote you about me?"

"Indeed he did, in response to my letter informing him what a diligent and excellent pupil you are proving to be."

She resisted the urge to reach over and hug him fondly, and not only because she did not wish to spill the ink in her palette. Except for members of her immediate family, no one was allowed to touch her unless expressly given permission to do so. Even her own two best friends, Seshen and Meresankh, denied her the pleasure of wrestling them for air in the pond, or of being captured in a mock hunt, by virtuously refusing to touch her.

"You will be leaving for Waset soon, Hatshepsut," Senimen informed her abruptly. "There you will continue your lessons in the Temple of Amun."

Her heart sped up, passionately protesting the pain of another loss. "Will you be coming with me?" she demanded.

"My place is by your side until there is nothing left for me to teach you."

"There will always be something for you to teach me!"

She regretted her outburst when he looked away. His throat moved as he swallowed and the one eye she could see blinked furiously even though Re, still the young and mild Khepri, had not yet risen above the garden wall.

He cleared his throat and straightened his back while staring fixedly over her head. "In any case, you still have much to learn here in Mennefer[8] before we leave."

"Are you angry with me, Seni?"

"You are still only a child," his eyes were shining as they met hers again, "but I can see, as your father and mother both do, that every god is in you, Hatshepsut. You have entered my heart. I could never be angry with you."

* * * * *

"When Thoth spoke the desire in Atum-Re's heart, it was Ptah who gave it a shape and became the patron of all craftsmen. It was Ptah, Lord of Sekhmet, who fashioned the world from the Divine Word and assigned a form, color and texture to everything. Ptah's blue skull cap represents the celestial dimension in which the body of man took form wrapped in feathers and furs, because the Ka of all creatures lives in the human heart."

Ptah, a handsome man, was himself bound by the laws of nature he commanded using the three objects grasped in his hands—the *ankh*, the *djed* pillar and a strange black scepter with human eyes.

Hatshepsut was familiar with the *ankh* and the *djed* pillar; she saw them everywhere on furniture and worn as jewelry. Inet owned dozens of amulets, including numerous *djeds* made from a variety of colorful materials. Her nurse said the *djed* symbolized the backbone of the resurrected Osiris and helped keep her strong and healthy. She was very glad that, so far, the amulets seemed to be working because she could not imagine life without Inet, who was naturally going with her to Waset. Some days she was so excited she could hardly wait to depart and continue her education in the Temple of the King of the Gods. Other days she had no wish to leave all the familiar comforts and pleasures of home in White Wall, as Mennefer was also called. She did not wish to see her mother's House of Eternity. She hated to think about Ahmose, or anyone else she loved, going away forever. Neferubity did not really count.

"Hatshepsut, are you listening to me?"

"Yes, Seni, but I was also thinking."

They were standing before the statue of Ptah at the heart of his temple, *Kwt-Ka-Ptah*. It was so quiet in the shrine that her thoughts struck her as strangely loud and her ability to collect them, in an effort to put her feelings into words, as more clumsy than normal. The High Priest had left them alone; she was Pharaoh's daughter and was permitted to speak directly with the gods.

"Were you busy thinking about Ptah, Hatshepsut?"

"I was thinking about the *djed* pillar in his hands and how it blends with the *ankh* as well as with the *was* scepter and his beard."

"Go on."

"Well… if the *djed* is supposed to be the backbone of Osiris, why is Ptah holding it? And why is it so short? A real backbone is longer than that." She tore her eyes from the *neter's* enigmatically smiling face to glance up at her teacher. "And why does it have four black bars running through it?"

"That is three questions with one answer. It is a symbol."

"A symbol of health and strength?" She was disappointed he seemed to be giving her the same answer as Inet.

"It is a symbol of a vital quality in the Laws of Becoming."

That was a term she had never heard before and it threatened to make her head hurt. "Becoming *what?*" She was careful to keep her eyes on Seni's face so Ptah would not think she was impatient with him and the complexity of his divinity.

"Becoming *you*."

The straightforward reply surprised and pleased her but then also annoyed her because she still did not understand.

"Have you noticed, Hatshepsut, that the *djed* pillar resembles a tree?"

"Those are tree branches?" She turned her head and studied the symbol again doubtfully. "They do not really *look* like branches."

"They symbolize branches which in turn symbolize the four cardinal elements and directions of the created world—the mysterious backbone of Osiris, the *neter* who embodies the power every individual possesses to conquer death just as seeds bury themselves in the dark earth and are reborn in another form. The *djed* promotes health and strength because believing in our eternal health gives our Ka the joyful strength it needs to protect our bodies from the ravages of fear disguised as disease."

"Is that why our Ba is symbolized by a bird with a human head, because when we are born we fly down from heaven to nest in the *djed* tree of our spine, and when we die we fly back up to the sky again?" Excitement made her forget to keep her voice down and it reverberated through the shrine with a trapped energy that both embarrassed and fascinated her.

He smiled. "You could say that. The *neb-ankh*, the Master of Life in which a mummy lies,⁹ is decorated with a *djed* pillar against which its spine rests, and a *djed* amulet made of gold is often placed against its neck—the column of flesh joining heaven and earth, Ba and Ka."

"And is that why the *djed* Ptah is holding merges with an *ankh*, because they are both symbols of life?"

"Not just of life, Hatshepsut. The *djed* and the *ankh* symbolize life's eternal and transcendent nature, the Divine creative fire housed inside all physical forms. There is a spiritual power latent in consciousness which can be awakened and developed through the intelligence of the heart. Pharaoh, your father, represents the fully developed personality that recognizes itself as the bodily son of Amun-Re. That is why only the gods and the king are permitted to hold the *was* scepter of dominion and power over the sensual world."

"And that is why the *djed* and the *ankh* and the *was* scepter all merge with Ptah's beard, the same beard I have seen father often wear! But why does the scepter have eyes? It reminds me of the jackal god Anubis, Lord of the Dead."

"Look down, Hatshepsut, and you will see it also has legs. The *was* scepter symbolizes mastery over our animal nature, not through the cruelty of suppression but through the profound appreciation made possible by wisdom. Anubis is another subject for another day. We have come here to honor Ptah who, as you can see, is standing on the hieroglyph for One-Half—the divided unity from which all numbers and physical laws emerge."

"And he is speaking with us, Seni," she whispered in awe, staring at the *neter's* smiling golden face. "Now that you have explained the meaning of the amulets he is holding, I can hear what he is telling us even though his lips do not move and my ears do not actually hear his voice."

"God reveals himself in many ways and particularly in the inspired skill responsible for all beautiful creations. Tomorrow we will visit Pharaoh's workshops. There you will witness the mortal limbs of Ptah exercising his Divine skill."

* * * * *

"The greatest craftsmen and painters in Kemet," Seni began his lesson for the day, "those men in whom the creative power of Ptah shines most brightly, are employed by your father. It is a sign of the highest favor when Pharaoh lends one or more of them to someone else. The individual so honored shows he has proven, by way of his words and actions, that he lives intimately with the knowledge of his innate divinity and has earned the sublime pleasures the intelligence of the heart makes possible. The Royal Goldsmith, the Royal Jeweler, the Royal Woodcarver and the Royal Statue Maker occupy special places beside Pharaoh at banquets and festivals. Today's subject is the materials Ptah uses to express Atum-Re's desire."

She had parted the curtains of their litter in the hope of admitting a breeze and had to force herself to listen to her tutor. She was oddly distracted by one of the men carrying her royal chair through the streets of Mennefer. There were other litter bearers walking behind and ahead of him but until that moment she had never really noticed any of them. For some reason it was only today her eyes had decided to actually *see* one of them.

"The material from which an object is made is of the utmost importance," Seni was saying. "Let us consider the properties of stone."

The litter bearer's shoulders were close to her feet and she was impressed by how broad they were, strong enough to support the weight of two people, and his oiled skin glistened beneath Re's intense regard as if God was as interested in him as she was.

"The physical properties of stone translate into spiritual qualities," Seni went on, "for example strength, incorruptibility and permanence. Less obvious are the patience, experience and skill required for the long and difficult task of wresting stone from the earth, not to mention the subtlety essential for shaping and transforming it into something even greater than what it was before."

The litter bearer's shoulders and arms were as smooth as stone and she wondered if they would feel as hard. Suddenly he shifted his grip on the pole and serpents seemed to slither beneath the flesh of his back all the way down into his loincloth. His skin reminded her of polished copper but he was most definitely not a statue; he was alive and carrying her wherever she desired. Because of him she was floating over the ground like a bird and not dirtying her sandals.

"Hatshepsut, I believe you are not listening to me. Tell me what you are thinking."

"I am thinking this man," she pointed down at the litter bearer, "is not a statue. I was also thinking that perhaps I should thank him for carrying us such a long way for it must be a thirsty task."

"He is only one of eight servants." Seni studied her face. "Why do you feel the need to thank this particular litter bearer?"

"Because it seems to me that when Ptah designed all my litter bearers, and Khnum fashioned them on his potter's wheel, that they both took more time with him than with the others."

"Beware of superficial perceptions, Hatshepsut. An attractive vessel is not necessarily as full of good things as others less pleasing to the eyes."

"Father would never pour his best wine into an ugly jar!" she retorted, affronted by his illogic.

"But do not forget that the father of Horus has a brother. Like Osiris, Seth is strong, handsome and virile, qualities to be admired and valued, yet Seth is also to be feared because his heart is empty."

"I will not forget, Seni, but I still wish to thank this particular litter bearer. When we arrive at the workshop, please inform him he will forever attend me when I travel."

The moment the royal chair came to a stop and was set down, she got off and extended her right arm, with the hand cupped and facing up, toward the handsome servant, offering him her praise and thanks. The surprise she glimpsed in his eyes before he quickly grasped his knees and bowed was intensely gratifying.

Senimen informed the attendant the gods had decided to smile upon him through the princess, who was letting it be known to him that she desired his presence beneath her royal chair whenever she journeyed forth from the residence.

Hatshepsut was very pleased with herself for acquiring the servant by making it official that *she* was the only person he was permitted to carry on his strong shoulders. In the future, she decided, she would be attended only by men Ptah had designed when he was truly inspired.

"Tell me your name," she commanded.

"Kanefer, my lady!" came the astonished reply.

"You see, Seni, I knew it. He has a beautiful Ka as well as a nice body."

"Hmm… yes." He covered his mouth with his hand and coughed.

"Meri told me I was a good judge of character."

"So it seems, but it is time now to continue your lesson."

She had hoped they would begin with the Royal Jewelers but Seni insisted it was best to start with something more basic. "The simplest stone vessel," he said, "can be beautiful and sacred by way of the excellence exercised in the craft of its creation."

She failed to suppress a yawn.

"Pharaoh's stone cutters are the most skilled in Kemet, Hatshepsut, deserving of your attention and respect. You admired the statue of the pyramid builder and his queen?"

"Yes! How did you know that?"

"When God's Wife is in Mennefer she honors me with a conference every evening in which you, Hatshepsut, are the principal subject. Would you say the sculptor responsible for that statue succeeded in capturing the unique beauty of Menkaure and his queen?"

"Oh yes, he was a master stone cutter!"

"Indeed, but before he began working on it that statue was nothing but a hard and featureless block of stone he brought to life with his special tools—his eyes, his hands, the strength of his arms, his mind and his heart. The sculptor performed the supreme act of giving form to his desire, which in this case was to create a house for the Ba's of Pharaoh and of his Great Royal Wife which, like their Ka's, would live forever. If it was not for the magic of his talent you would not have been able to look upon the face of a man and a woman who lived over one-thousand years ago."

"It *is* magic," she agreed.

"Let us return to the subject of the spiritual qualities inherent in the physical properties of materials. Stone is the perfect symbol of adversity so great it seems impossible to overcome. It is relatively easy to create featureless fragments of rock by hammering away at stone angrily, impatiently, aggressively, foolishly. You will exhaust yourself and achieve nothing. It is something else entirely to overcome the resistance of stone with the understanding that spiritual qualities are embodied in all earthly substances. Stone obliges us to exercise our intelligence, strength, skills and vision. Stone forces us to sharpen and hone our imagination and to embrace the virtues of patience, subtlety and accuracy. The characteristics of all the materials created by Ptah are reflected in the human heart."

"I think I understand, Seni."

"I believe you do, Hatshepsut."

In the stone cutter's workshop the men were so engrossed in their respective tasks they barely seemed to notice her. She was the Daughter of Re—her mere presence should have commanded attention despite the fact that she still wore the side-lock of youth. How invisible she felt would seriously have annoyed her if the Royal Overseer, Ptah-Hotep, had not been so attentive. He smiled so warmly at her in between explaining things that she soon forgot to resent how insignificant she felt in the midst of so much purposeful activity.

She actually found herself interested in the machine drilling perfect holes through a stone vessel. A man held it in one hand and turned a wheel with the other. When she went home she would look at the furnishings in her room differently, remembering they had not always existed even though they seemed always to have been there. It was a revelation that countless people had taken the time and trouble to create and shape every single vase she owned. Other craftsmen smoothed the insides of the finished vessels with what Ptah-Hotep explained was a hard mineral called quartz they had ground into an abrasive powder.

"But it is only a powder," she protested. "How can a powder affect a material as hard as stone?"

"An excellent question, princess. The grains of the quartz powder are too tiny for our eyes to see but each one is extremely hard, much harder than alabaster, for example. When the inside of this particular vase is rubbed with the mineral powder the rough surface will yield to the quartz's superior strength by dissolving into another fine powder, leaving behind a nice smooth finish."

"Stone can dissolve like water?" The thought was alarming.

"Before there was stone there were the Primordial Waters of Nun," Seni reminded her.

"Yes." Ptah-Hotep glanced at him almost impatiently. "But the *fact* is that the inner surface of this vase is not dissolving like water but rather disintegrating into such infinitely tiny particles that a single breath can blow a handful away as though it never was."

Hatshepsut imagined the statue of the pyramid builder and his wife suffering the same fate and felt sad. She looked up at Seni, hoping he would explain how stone could be a symbol of incorruptibility and eternity even though it was weak enough to vanish completely. He met her eyes but said nothing and his expectant expression encouraged her to think the matter through for herself.

"The stone powder is actually still there," she concluded, reassuring herself. "When you blow a handful away it seems to vanish, but it is really now everywhere!"

In the potter's workshop, it was fun watching the wheel spin so fast the clay almost appeared as motionless as the old man's hands gently caressing it into whatever form he wanted it to possess. Trying to imagine Khnum shaping her father in this fashion filled her with an even greater appreciation for how powerful the gods were.

The carpenter's workshop was the largest and busiest of all. She was surprised and intrigued by all the different phases of construction required to create objects she took completely for granted. Beds, chairs, stools, chests, pavilions, everything she relied on for her pleasure and comfort had not, incredibly enough, always been there. It was so noisy in the large room she could barely hear Ptah-Hotep's explanations as she observed a bed frame being attacked with a curious instrument resembling a spindle somehow controlled by a bow. Perfect little holes appeared in the wood through which two other men threaded cords while two more carpenters polished the frame.

Elsewhere, men were sawing off portions of tree trunks and cutting them into the familiar planks that composed chests and chairs, although how they could ever get the boards soft enough to make comfortably curved seats with them she could not imagine. The freshly hewn wood was smoothed with a dangerous-looking tool which managed to defeat the hard knots and ugly lumps without damaging it.

Watching a man repeatedly striking a chisel with a wooden mallet she remarked, "It seems nothing could ever be finished if we did not know how to make perfect little holes."

"They do often make it possible to join separate elements," Seni confirmed.

Pins were slipped into the holes to join the wooden planks and at last something resembling a chair began taking form.

"Why did Ptah not simply create chairs and beds and chests for us?" she wondered out loud.

"Because to create is a joy, Hatshepsut. Through our efforts we learn to reflect God's power which, ideally, is perpetually growing and developing within us."

Miniature deserts of sawdust and wood shavings were swept away by servants as chairs, beds, door frames and columns—crowned with either papyrus or lotus bud capitals—took shape all around them. They followed a new cedar wood chest into the eerily fascinating domain of the metal workers, where it was oppressively hot and strangely quiet. No one spoke as they went about their respective chores, which had the effect of making every little sound carry significantly—the crackling of the flames, the clink of cooled metal against stone and the deeply dangerous rushing sound of molten ore being poured into various molds. Seni permitted her to linger there only long enough to watch a sheet of gold-leaf being carefully removed from a box by one man and applied to the chest by another.

Hatshepsut learned that many of Pharaoh's jewelers, painters and sculptors also worked in shops linked to the Royal Palace and the Temple of Amun-Re in Waset, where the furnishings for her family's eternal homes were currently being manufactured. The subject of her parents' tombs tended to put her in a bad mood, which was probably why she became annoyed with Seni when he refused to let her see the glass worker's shop.

"It is not safe in there," he explained.

"But the glass vials in which mother and Inet keep their scented oils are small and lovely. How can such delicate little things be so dangerous to make?"

"You have already grasped how materials can behave in ways you would not expect. Glass is still one of Ptah's most fascinating mysteries. The skill to create glass was brought to Kemet by your mother's father, from where it was hidden in the Land of the Two Rivers waiting to be discovered. Because the efficacy of Amun lives in your family, Kemet is now even greater in magic. So far, however, only a handful of Ptah's servants have mastered the art. Suffice it to say that as a material glass is a potent symbol. Dry sand is poured into a pan and placed over a fire until it becomes as hot as the heart of Re and transforms into a burning red liquid. A clay model shaped like the interior of the desired vessel is quickly plunged into the molten solution, and when the model emerges the vessel's core is covered with soft glass, which must be quickly shaped and decorated before it cools. Afterward, the clay is scraped away."

"The inside of the vessel is made *first*?"

"Yes, and then the surface is shaped from this magically malleable material called glass."

"That is very interesting, Seni. It seems all materials can somehow transform themselves." She was remembering what her mother had said about death and destruction being necessary for transformation. "Do such *transformations* occur by themselves or only in the hands of servants of Ptah?"

"If water flows over a rock long enough, it will change its shape. If fire from heaven strikes a tree, it may burn and turn to ash. Metals and precious gems form deep in the earth. But you are right, Hatshepsut. Only man has the power to *consciously* transform the substance of God."

4

Lady of Life

The journey south to Waset was a festive one. Pharaoh, accompanied by his Great Royal Wife and daughter, set sail on the feast of Hathor's birthday. It was a truly joyful occasion for Hatshepsut embarking on a new stage in her life surrounded by those she loved. She would miss the palace in Mennefer but she was even more excited about going to live in the city of Amun-Re, King of the Gods. She tried not to think about the tombs waiting for her family on the other side of the River. The night before they left, the side-lock of youth was ritually shorn from her head. It was a thrilling moment, after which Inet wept.

"I am not leaving you, Iny." Once they were alone together, she climbed onto her nurse's lap and slipped her arms around her neck, fighting the burning behind her own eyes which threatened to ruin the wonderful adventure of growing up. "I will *never* leave you!"

"Oh my dear…" Inet spoke in a choked voice. "When you are queen, you will not even remember me."

"Of course I will remember you! When I am queen of Kemet not only will I remember you, I will order a statue made of us so we can be together forever!"

Inet's dark eyes overflowed like the River.

"Do not cry, Iny!"

"I am *not* crying!"

Hatshepsut giggled, her nurse heaved a sob that transformed into a chuckle, and suddenly they were laughing as happily as if Bes had possessed them. Hathor's mischievous companion could be heard running around outside and announcing in joyous gusts of wind the coming birthday of his beautiful Mistress, the Lady of Dance and Drunkenness. Hatshepsut preferred to forget Hathor was also called the Lady of Life when she welcomed the dead into her winged embrace. It was in the desert long sacred to the Goddess, on the west bank of the River in Waset, that the mummies of Queen Ahmose and of her sister, God's Wife, would rest forever when their Ba's flew off to the Land Beyond the Sunset.

* * * * *

Presents celebrating the princess' tenth birthday were waiting for her at the *pr-nswt*, King's House, in the Town of Amun, where from now on she would be living in her own rooms apart from Inet. However, her nurse was with her the morning they arrived, and sharing in her joy. Because of her lessons with Seni, Hatshepsut could appreciate how long and hard Pharaoh's craftsmen had worked to fashion so many beautiful objects, all created especially for *her*, the princess of Kemet. Her favorite leopard-head girdle and cat claw anklets, the latter fashioned of gold and dark amethyst, seemed almost plain compared to the splendor of all her new jewelry. There were also gilded cedar wood chests filled with white linen sheets, towels and dresses, colorful woolen shawls, beaded leather sandals and eight finely braided wigs.

"Oh Iny, look at *this*!"

"If you want me to see it you can bring it here!" Inet said breathlessly. Dropping into a chair she rested a hand against her chest. "I do not have your energy, my dear."

"Oh but you *must* see this!" Hatshepsut spread the collar reverently across her nurse's lap as she crouched beside her chair. "Is it not splendid!"

"Oh yes!"

"And I recognize all the symbols." Four rows of alternating *ankhs, djed* pillars and *was* scepters, all forged of gold inlaid with turquoise, were connected by strings of golden beads that ended in two falcon-head clasps. The *neters'* golden eyes, beaks and cheeks were high-lighted with lapis lazuli. "Do you think I should wear this one to the banquet tonight?"

"That is for the queen and God's Wife to decide," her nurse replied with odd formality.

"Are you all right, Iny? You cannot be tired yet! We have only just arrived and there is still so much to see!"

"The journey was too short," Inet murmured, but then she smiled and added, "I am fine! Show me the others."

Every single collar was magnificent but Hatshepsut particularly liked the one made of white, red, green, and yellow beads shaped like flower petals. There was such a quantity of jewelry to admire—necklaces, girdles, rings, earrings, bracelets, armlets and anklets—it was impossible to linger over one piece for long. Most spectacular of all were the crowns designed to go with her wigs. She kept reaching up to caress the stimulatingly rough growth on her skull. She could not wait for her hair to grow out; she felt as bald as a baby vulture without her side-lock. She lifted one of the wigs and, for the first time, wondered if it might not be pleasant to wear such a stiff and lifeless thing on her head.

"You will get used to it," Inet said, smiling at her dubious expression. "They are for special occasions. I am sure your natural hair will be as beautiful as your mother's."

Gladly suppressing her doubts, she set the wig back down and turned to a small black ivory box decorated with a golden *ankh*. Shining magically in the dark depths was a single floral circlet. Her gasp was echoed by Inet's. The fillet was designed to resemble a handful of flowering water weeds but the delicate branches twining around each other were forged of solid gold and, her nurse told her, the miniature flowers were made of carnelian, lapis lazuli and turquoise.

"I will wear *this* one to the banquet!"

The morning passed quickly. Inet had to force her to eat something. Her imagination was so full of dreams inspired by all the beautiful things which now belonged to her that her body completely forgot to be hungry.

"You will be drooping like a lotus in the desert tonight if you do not take a nap after your bath," her nurse warned, and Hatshepsut was persuaded. She was exhausted by happiness and betraying the fact with yawns deeper than her excitement. Two adorable female lion's heads rose from either end of the wooden frame at the foot of her bed. It helped her relax in her new room knowing Sekhmet would protect her as she slept. The last thing she remembers is the reassuringly familiar sight of Inet adjusting the mosquito netting around her.

* * * * *

Hatshepsut woke abruptly. The basket-work shutters had been parted and she could see out into her new garden. The lamps and candles in her room had already been lit even though trees and flowers were still gilded by Atum's golden light.

She sat up. The awe she felt gazing around her was tainted by anxiety. Where was Inet? Was everyone already waiting for her in the banquet hall? She opened her mouth to call out for her nurse, but stopped herself remembering what Meri had said about being afraid. Quickly, she determined that being nervous was foolish. Her living quarters were so beautiful it was a sin against Ptah not to fully appreciate them. If she failed to do so he might give his wife permission to hunt her cowardly Ba, and if the blood-thirsty Sekhmet made a mistake and attacked someone else in her family instead, the tragedy would be all *her* fault because she was not brave enough to be a princess of Kemet.

She flung aside the mosquito netting. Tonight a banquet was being held in her honor. All the greatest lords and ladies of the Two Lands had been invited to formally meet Pharaoh's daughter and she still had no idea what she was going to wear.

The sound of her mother's voice wafting gently toward her from the garden was sweeter to her than all the perfumes in existence.

Walking side-by-side the queen and God's Wife stepped through the open doorway.

"We will help dress you this evening, Hatshepsut," Meri said in a tone that informed her she should appreciate the honor. "Beginning tomorrow you will be served by your own personal attendants."

"But what about Inet?"

"She is also being honored at the feast. From this night forward, the Lady Sitre will wear bracelets of gold and green on her wrists, for it was she who nursed to health and strength the Good God's beloved daughter."

"So naturally," her mother added, smiling down at her, "you can no longer expect Inet to help bathe and dress you like a servant."

She was so happy to discover that her beloved nurse was being honored the only shadow she was aware of was her cat's absence. "Have you seen Bubu?"

"He is undoubtedly out exploring his new territory. He will be back soon enough. Now let us get you ready for the banquet."

It was thrilling but difficult to sit perfectly still while the two most powerful women in Kemet painted and adorned her as if she was a statue sacred to Hathor. The goddess' strangely flat features and bovine ears adorned the handle of the polished bronze see-face in which she avidly studied her reflection. Her image pleased her profoundly even though she sensed Ptah had not yet finished working on her. The mirror had come in a linen bag with a strap attached so she could drape it over her shoulder and carry it around with her if she wanted to. She could scarcely believe she was sitting at her very own dressing table. Beside her the queen and the God's wife perched on stools with soft black-and-white seats resembling a cow's hide. Ahmose looked as beautiful as ever, but it distressed Hatshepsut to detect fine wrinkles forming around her mother's eyes. Perhaps the mirror showing her her own smooth young countenance had something to do with the fact that she suddenly noticed the queen was growing older.

In addition to her mirror, she now owned a wooden cosmetics box filled with glass and alabaster vials, their dark-gold and blue surfaces decorated with wavy brown, yellow and white lines indicating they contained liquids. There was also a knife, a razor, little metal blades for trimming her nails, tweezers to pluck her eyebrows, and a miniature box filled with bone splints to keep the skin beneath her fingernails clean. Some of the items she was familiar with, a few were intriguing novelties, and all were special because they belonged entirely to her. At last, she possessed her very own linen bags filled with balls of malachite and galena for making green and gray eye paint, and ivory palettes on which to grind the minerals to a powder and mix them with oil. She could apply the eye makeup right away or pour it into tubes for later use. A delicate glass vial contained a red powder which diluted with oil gave a rosy hue to her cheeks and lips.

"What is this razor for?" She picked it up gingerly; her curiosity tempered by caution, for it looked sinisterly sharp.

The sisters smiled as they glanced at each other.

"When you are a little older you will use it to shave beneath your arms," Meri explained, "and between your legs."

Hatshepsut glanced down at the puckered lips between her thighs that never said anything, and then picked up her mirror again, irresistibly drawn to her reflection in the polished disc.

"Why does Hathor sometimes appear with a woman's face but the ears of a cow?"

"Because she is the Daughter of Re," Meri said. "It was Hathor who heard the words spoken by Thoth and made the desire in her Father's heart flesh and blood."

"But it is Ptah who gives a form to everything."

"Ptah gives form to the Substance generated by the Goddess. Hathor is God's Hand, the Unique One who stimulates into existence the physical forces that serve to manifest the Divine desire, popularly known as the four children of Atum-Re—Shu, Tefnut, Geb and Nut. A person possesses two hands and two eyes, two arms and two legs, because One must first become Two for nothing to transform into everything through the power of Number. Hathor is also called The House of Horus for she-"

Ahmose interrupted her sister, "I think she is still a little too young to fully understand Hathor."

"But how can Hathor be the Daughter of Re?" Hatshepsut was confused. "I thought Maat and Sekhmet were his daughters."

"Sekhmet is an aspect of Hathor," Meri explained. "Hathor-Sekhmet and Maat were both born the instant the burning star of Atum-Re's desire to manifest His pure existence lit up the darkness. Maat sets into motion and forever maintains in harmony the laws of the substance generated by Hathor and given form by Ptah."

"Now that I know this, does it mean my heart will balance with Maat's feather after I die?"

"It is not enough to merely know something," it was her mother who replied, "simply because you are told it, Hatshepsut. You must truly believe it. And, more importantly, you must feel it. Maat is the essence of Re contained in everything, the truth of the eternal present behind every beginning and end.

Maat is both the source and the fulfillment, the beautiful truth of the world's Divine heart."

They had finished painting her eyes and Hatshepsut eagerly raised the see-face before her again.

"Not yet." Meri snatched the mirror out of her hand. "Wait until we are finished fashioning a worthy shrine for the Goddess with your body." She picked up a wooden unguent spoon carved in the form of a naked girl swimming, her arms outstretched and her head held high as in her hands she offered up a covered bowl in the shape of a duck. Meri gently parted the bird's wings and turned toward a large alabaster unguent jar.

"No." Ahmose stopped her. "I wish for her to wear the oil of lilies tonight."

Meri turned toward another container Hatshepsut particularly liked because its handles were shaped like two *ankh* signs to which arms had been attached so they could grasp *was* scepters in both hands. A *shenu* ring protected her name *Hatshepsut* painted in black ink and dominating the center of the vase. The top of the jar, just below the rim, was decorated with Hathor's bovine-eared face. The goddess wore a ceremonial wig and a collar but her body was merely suggested by a lotus flower.

Meri's perfume-slick fingertips lightly touched Hatsheput's temples, both sides of her neck, the flesh over her heart and the bottoms of her wrists.

"Now let us put on your dress," her mother took her hand, "and pick out your wig!"

She loved the tunics with the bright red, blue and yellow patterns, but they were not fine enough for a banquet, to which noblewomen, not to mention princesses, always wore white. The fine material clung to her body, but she quickly accustomed herself to the restricting sensation by admiring the soft glow of her skin through the mist-fine linen.

The short wig her mother chose for her was not as heavy as she had feared it would be. In fact it felt almost pleasantly cozy embracing her head, like a sleeping cat, a sensation that reminded her Bubu was still missing.

* * * * *

The sound of quiet laughter and soft voices flowed along the corridor toward them like an invisible current and made Hatshepsut shiver with excitement. The torches keeping the darkness at bay crackled in the cool breeze wafting in through the windows as she walked directly behind the tall figure of her father. Amenmose was holding her hand and every time she glanced up at him he smiled at her.

Leading the procession, Queen Ahmose held gilded wooden sistrums strung with bronze snakes in both her upraised hands. When she reached the double doors opening into the banquet hall, she paused for an instant before crossing the threshold and vigorously shaking Hathor's sacred instrument.

At once the joyful sounds of life in the banquet hall were extinguished.

Suddenly, Hatshepsut could hear the River lapping softly against the sides of the canal flowing alongside the palace. The rippling of the black waters outside seemed mysteriously reflected in the muscles flowing beneath her father's skin as he straightened his back and clenched his hands into fists.

The queen shook her sistrums eight times before advancing into the banquet hall at the head of the royal line. Hatshepsut could scarcely believe Meri was walking behind *her*. The God's Wife was also holding two sistrums, which she began shaking the moment her sister moved forward. In her wake followed the Lady Inet resplendent in a brand new floral collar, and behind her came Mutnofret, Pharaoh's first but secondary wife who had wed Thutmose when he was still only the Great Army Commander. Mutnofret, who looked shockingly old, was missing several teeth. It was no wonder the king spent most of his time with Ahmose, his chief and beautiful wife. A few minutes ago, Hatshepsut had finally met her six-year-old half brother. The youngest of Pharaoh's five living children, Thutmose had been reluctant to let go of his mother's hand when his nurse came to take him to bed. Pharaoh's two oldest sons were not present that night. Ramose was in Mennefer at the head of the army and Wadjmose was in charge of the forces stationed even farther north in Perunefer. Senimen, tutor to the princess and a special member of the family, brought up the end of the procession.

The moment Pharaoh entered the banquet hall his subjects sank to one knee and extended their right arms with the hand help open. Then they clenched both their hands into fists and beat their chest four times. The gesture of praise and rejoicing was complete when the people rested their clenched left hands over their hearts and raised their right fists over their heads.

Supported by brightly painted wooden papyrus columns, the ceiling of the banquet hall was a radiant blue illuminated by more candles than Hatshepsut had ever seen burning in one place. There were countless candles made from sesame oil blended with salt and scented unguents, and an even greater number of candles shaped like the animals from which the fat had been rendered. In the center of the room, set on a raised wooden dais decorated with golden *ankhs*, *djed* pillars and *was* scepters, the royal family's tables bloomed with mounds of food.

Sitting to the right of her father and mother, Hatshepsut shared a table with Amenmose. God's Wife occupied the royal couple's left and her dinner companion was a corpulent man who wore a transparent short-sleeved robe which flowed all the way down to his ankles. Many of the older nobles seemed to favor this fashion. She was glad Amenmose was dressed like their father in nothing but a pleated knee-length kilt. The Crown Prince wore more jewelry than clothing and he was so beautiful she could not stop looking at him. Only once did she glance behind her to smile at Inet where she sat with Seni near the Lady Mutnofret's solitary table. Throughout the night, her eyes were drawn to the lapis lazuli scarabs adorning the golden bracelets on her brother's wrists. The wings of the sacred beetle shimmered myriad shades of green and blue and its legs held up a gold-rimmed white stone flecked with red that evoked a blood-stained moon. The heavy jewelry made the prince's arms look both elegantly slender and strong, and his chest and shoulders, nearly as broad as the king's, supported a blue, green and gold bead collar with ease. He wore a wig composed of hundreds of fine black braids that were slightly longer in front than in the back, and the way it framed his painted eyes and ready smile was irresistible.

All around the dais, the guests' tables were arranged in groups between the pillars. At first, it seemed to Hatshepsut that every pair of eyes in the great room was on her. Then she began to fear that everyone had already lost interest in her. Both extremes made her uncomfortable—she felt awkward drinking and chewing beneath the intent regard of so many people and yet it was even ruder for everyone *not* to be captivated by the princess of Kemet. She was convinced that once Ptah was finished shaping her no one would be able to take their eyes off her. The more she drank the more her first formal banquet felt like a waking dream. The polished silver cup filled with grape wine shone like the moon magically fallen into her hand as serving girls wearing only gilded leather belts around their hips kept appearing to refill it.

The table was piled high with so much food they could never hope to eat it all, but it was wonderful to try. There was roast duck (her favorite), raw salted quails, juicy beef ribs and kidneys, assorted cheeses, stewed figs, a variety of fresh berries, little pyramid-shaped loaves of wheat bread and meltingly sweet honey cakes. Eating was never so much fun as when Amenmose joined her, and that night was especially enjoyable because everyone saw how the Crown Prince fed her with his own hand. He offered her slices of duck fat, knowing how much she loved it, and did not draw his hand back until she had licked his fingertips clean with her eager tongue. The pleasing scent of his perfume blending with the subtle flavor of his skin added an oddly exciting spice to every bite. His public devotion to her appetite made the feast they shared that night taste better than any other meal of her life.

"Brother, who is the man sitting with Meri?"

"That is Kemet's northern vizier, father's Hands, Ears and Eyes. Akheperseneb sees to it Pharaoh's will is everywhere realized."

"Then I like him!"

Laughing, he gently forced a fig between her lips. "You look beautiful tonight, my sister." A female servant immediately wiped his sticky fingertips clean with a damp linen cloth.

Watching him caress the girl's naked buttocks as she turned away, Hatshepsut wondered if he collected special attendants the way she had begun doing with Kanefer.

"Does father really know all these people?" Her curiosity was growing deeper than her hunger.

"A man who does not know the names and character of all his children is a poor father indeed." Absently, he helped himself to a beef rib while once more looking around the banquet hall.

She observed with pride how people abruptly stopped laughing and talking whenever they felt the touch of the prince's eyes on them. Amenmose was the young Horus; anyone he turned his attention toward naturally felt honored. Young women in particular seemed to smile more broadly beneath his regard although they never dared to look directly at him.

She reached for a sesame cake and said, "Do you collect women like Wadjmose?"

Amenmose's eyebrows disappeared into his wig. "What did you ask me, sister?"

"I asked if you collect women."

"I enjoy them," he admitted soberly, "but I do not *collect* them. They are too much trouble. First I must have a wife who can control them and save me the effort."

Pharaoh spoke mildly, "Amenmose, what are you discussing with my daughter?"

"I am simply answering all her questions, father."

"An exhausting task, my son, I commend you. However, be careful not to let the wise Ka looking out through her eyes seduce you into forgetting her Ba cannot yet understand everything." He leaned forward in his chair and smiled at her. "Are you enjoying yourself, my dear?"

"Oh yes father, very much!"

"Good," he said firmly, and returned his full attention to the queen.

Amenmose leaned over the table toward her and whispered in her ear, "You must hurry and grow up, sister!"

"I will!" she promised softly, but then found it necessary to take a long sip of wine and avoid his eyes.

"The man at the first table on the left," he changed the subject, "is a Prophet of Maat from Nekheb and the Temple of Horus."

She followed the direction of his gaze and made an effort to pay attention. "What do Prophets of Maat do?"

"They decide who is right and who is wrong, who is lying and who is not. Any citizen of Kemet can lodge a formal complaint against someone he believes has wronged him in some way. The Prophets of Maat decide the case. If the offense is serious, a special group of people is organized to help the Prophet make his decision. The most important disputes are judged by Pharaoh and his viziers."

"What sorts of disputes? What bad things do people do to each other?"

"Seth is everywhere, little sister."

"He is not here now, is he?"

"I said *everywhere* and you would do well to believe me."

"Senimen told me Seth is to be feared because his heart is empty. Does that mean Seth needs to steal men's hearts? And how can you tell when a man's heart is possessed by Seth?"

Amenmose took a long drink of wine and waited for a serving girl to refill his cup before replying, "You look into his eyes."

She nodded. That made sense. She had been fascinated by what people's eyes could say without words, and by the character revealed in their smiles, ever since she could remember.

Her brother continued pointing out important men, including the Steward of the Royal Household and the Royal Jeweler. Also present at the banquet held in honor of the princess was the Overseer of the Cultivators of Amun, the Keeper of the Property of His Lord, The Royal Sandal Bearer, the Overseer of the Cloth, the Supervisor of the Dancers of Pharaoh and, most distinguished of all, the Hereditary Prince Ineni, Overseer of the Double Granary of Amun and Supervisor of all the Works of the King.

A group of female musicians had been performing from the moment Pharaoh took his seat. The singer knelt on a small platform strumming a harp, and Hatshepsut kept turning her head to watch her in admiration for it looked like a difficult instrument to master. Supported by a wooden *tiet* knot, the half-moon shaped instrument rested on the musician's left shoulder. The long and slender neck on which the chords were strung was crowned by a vividly painted head of Maat distinguished by the tall feather tucked into her hair band. The singer was elegantly attired in a form-fitting white dress decorated with little red pyramids arranged in the shape of open flowers. Behind her, standing in the shadow of a column, a young woman playing a lute wore a gown that looked almost black. The dark material was decorated with white circles and accented by white sashes flowing beneath her breasts and around her hips. Her garment evoked the starry figure of Mother Nut stretching over Kemet, her toes touching the western horizon and her fingertips poised in the east. Beside the lute player, a woman clad in a simple white shift beat a tambourine and was accompanied by four kneeling clappers, the straps of their white dresses covering only one of their breasts. A seventh musician played a thin double flute.

Enraptured by the wind instrument's haunting melodies, Hatshepsut closed her eyes and imagined birds flying over the River at sunset and soaring up into the pure realm of colors trailing in the wake of Atum-Re's bark as it sailed into the darkness... It was odd how the voice of the flute found its way into her heart with its long drawn out notes which spoke to her feelings more eloquently than words. Then abruptly the clappers snapped her out of her reverie with a brisk new rhythm her pulse immediately responded to as she turned her head to smile happily at Amenmose again.

When a troupe of female dancers ran gracefully into the open space before Pharaoh and his family, the queen shook her sistrums, commanding silence. Each young woman wore only a short red skirt with a yellow solar disc embroidered over her right hip and a white moon over her left. Visible beneath the fine braids of their long hair, round metal earrings caught the light and glimmered with colors. As soon as the silence in the great room was absolute, the harpist ran her fingers lingeringly over the strings, and obeying the rhythm set by the clappers the young dancers proceeded to do amazing things. Amenmose was so captivated by the performance he seemed to forget all about his sister. The girls were as supple as cobras and Hatshepsut was especially impressed when they arched their backs, planted their hands on the floor behind them, and then kicked their legs up into the air to circle gracefully back to a standing position.

As the dancers ran off, the harpist began to sing:

I worship the Golden One, I praise her majesty,

I exalt the Mistress of Heaven,

I make salutations to Hathor,

And glorifications to the Unique One.

I made my entreaties to her, and she listened to my pleas

And the mistress sent my "sister" to me.

She has come to see me of her own free will,

What great wonder has happened to me!

I was joyful, exultant, elated,

When I was told: "Look, here she is!"[10]

When most of the golden unguent cones—worn on top of the head attached to floral fillets—had melted into their owners' wigs, Pharaoh rose. Hatshepsut watched proudly as he presented Inet with two special bracelets of honor, but it was strangely difficult to stand up when he announced, "My daughter, Hatshepsut, Foremost of Noble Women!"

She was very grateful for the supporting arm Amenmose slipped around her waist, and for the fact that he kept it there the whole time people paraded past her murmuring greetings and names. A smile painted effortlessly on her face, she paid little attention to the official introductions. All that mattered was the bracing warmth of her brother's body pressed possessively against hers.

5

Cities of Eternity

When the new day was come, Hatshepsut's head hurt like never before and her mouth tasted offensive. Worst of all, Inet was not present to help soothe her discomfort. Warm cow's milk and freshly baked bread were brought to her room by young women who were all strangers to her. She was not tempted to accept them as a replacement for her beloved nurse when the sight of the food they carried made her feel even worse. She waved them away without a word; she had absolutely no desire to perfume her mouth.

She got out of bed slowly and forced herself to brave the painfully bright sunlight of her garden hoping a brief swim would help her feel better. The cool water was refreshing but Bes still kept pounding his drum between her temples. As she pulled herself out of the pool one of her new attendants appeared on the garden path holding a linen towel. She permitted the girl to wrap it around her shoulders. Her head was unnaturally heavy and hot, and yet her body felt oddly light and chilled.

After she was vigorously rubbed down with her favorite oils, the mischievous Bes finally began to tire of prolonging the previous night's festivities in her head. Lying on her stomach, she reached gingerly for some bread, took a tiny bite and chewed tentatively. Remembering the way Amenmose had whispered in her ear, "You must hurry and grow up, sister!" caused her to suffer an odd sensation deep in her belly, or maybe it was just the food she forced herself to swallow.

Her new attendant offered her a fig.

Clamping a hand over her mouth, she sat up to get away from it.

The girl quickly emptied the bowl of fruit and positioned it beneath her mistress' face.

It surprised Hatshepsut that completely humiliating herself could prove such an intense relief. She allowed her mouth to be wiped clean and then weakly accepted a sip of milk.

"What is your name?" she scarcely recognized her own voice it was so hoarse.

"Nafre, my lady."

"Nafre. *Goodness.* Your parents named you well."

The girl smiled without meeting her eyes.

Hatshepsut glanced over her shoulder, and then winced as the motion threatened to make her nauseas. "What are you staring at?"

"Nothing, my lady."

"You are looking at something out in the garden." A sudden fear struck her. "Is the prince coming to see me?"

"No, my lady."

"Then why do you not look at me while I am speaking to you?" She took another cautious sip of milk. "There should never be anything more interesting to you than what I am saying, Nafre."

"But my lady, that is not why... I was told never to-"

"Forget what someone else told you." It was seriously annoying her that Bubu was not there to comfort her. "From now on you will do only as *I* say."

"Yes, my lady!"

"Now go away."

Nafre dropped to her knees and assumed the crouching position, her arms stretched out before her and her forehead planted against the floor.

Hatshepsut looked down at her in consternation. "I told you to go away."

"Good morning, my dear."

"Father!" She quickly set the cup of milk down and got up. However, she stopped herself from running into his arms because if he spun her around in circles her Ba would fly off.

He rested his hands, heavy with seal rings, lightly on her head. "How are you feeling?"

"Awful!"

He smiled down at her. "I am not surprised. You worshipped Hathor with a passion last night. You will feel better soon, and hopefully you will also have learned something. How the Goddess is making you feel now should serve to teach you that all actions have consequences."

"But why? I felt so wonderful at the banquet. Why must I feel so terrible now?"

"Not so terrible that you do not have the strength to ask questions, as always." He bent and kissed her forehead. "Unfortunately, I do not have the time to stay and answer them. Just remember that Maat is the spirit of balance."

"Are you going away again?"

"No. I will remain here in Waset for a few weeks."

She hugged him happily. The firmness of his body felt very different from her mother's yielding tenderness, but she loved it just as much, and perhaps even more, because it was so rarely within reach.

* * * * *

As soon as the River receded, it would be time to plant the seeds that would grow into wheat and barley and all other good things. And so would Queen Ahmose, and God's Wife Ahmose-Meritamun, plant their mummies in dark tombs from which they would rise transformed. Hatshepsut had no desire to visit the western desert. Her only consolation was that it meant being freed from her lesson with Seni and spending the whole day with her mother. Her education in the Temple would not commence until after the spring sowing. In Waset, where the River divided life from death, everyone worshipped Amun-Re, but Seni assured her Ptah had not been forgotten there.

"God can have different names," he said, "and yet be the same everywhere."

She had to make a serious effort not to miss Inet. Commanding her own attendants was pleasant but not as comforting as her beloved nurse's company. And yet the knowledge that her Ka had chosen for her to be born in Waset helped her feel at home there. Her family's roots were in the Town of Amun, where a series of pharaohs had ruled during the time when the Two Lands were divided by the Setiu. She could scarcely imagine those terrible years when unclean foreigners reigned in the north. It was her mother's father, King Ahmose, and his queen, Ahmose-Nefertari, the first God's Wife, who had finally driven away the invaders.

"Your mother's father's name will live for millions of years," Seni's voice resonated with respect. "The Good God Nebpehtire will be remembered alongside the great Mentuhotep, the king who first made the Two Lands whole again and rekindled the beautiful light of Maat after a long and painful darkness."

Pride in the power and achievements of her family went some way toward alleviating the anxiety roused in her by the knowledge that dirty, demon-worshipping foreigners had twice dared to wield the crook and flail over Re's children. She disliked being obliged to write the names of the Nine Bows, all of Kemet's traditional enemies.

"Father has conquered them all," she told Seni firmly.

"It is true, Hatshepsut. Kemet's borders will soon be as secure as they were in the time of Menkaure the Divine."

The morning the queen, God's Wife, and the princess made their first crossing together their boat rowed right up to the residence. There were many other vessels, large and small, out on the River. Gazing at a transport barge loaded with lovely white cows, in her heart Hatshepsut promised all the papyrus she plucked on Hathor's joyful feast day to her beautiful brother, Amenmose. The thought made her smile as she climbed the landing steps on the west bank behind her mother and Meri. Strict as Ahmose's older sister was with her she loved and respected her. She was not entirely sure, however, if Meri loved *her*, or if the attention she showed her was principally due to the fact that she would inherit the position of God's Wife. She could not imagine what Meri and God did together. She fervently hoped growing shorter was not something that happened to a person who lived intimately with the deity. When she was a little girl her mother's sister had seemed tall to her but now she barely reached Ahmose's shoulder and every day her face looked sterner.

The sight of Kanefer's handsome figure standing at the head of her waiting litter made her smile again. Perhaps she would save the smallest papyrus for him. Amenmose would never miss it.

* * * * *

"The daughters of the goddess!" A female voice cried from somewhere amidst neat rows of little white houses rising into the desert mountain. "Behold the daughters of the goddess!"

People poured onto the streets. The Servants of the Place of Truth were men, women and children of all ages. Except for the babies, which some women wore strapped securely against their hearts, and for toddlers still naturally close to the crouching position, everyone sank to one knee as the procession of royal women made its slow way along the road of packed sand fronting the tomb workers' village. The curtains of their litters had deliberately been pulled aside and to Hatshepsut all the right arms extended with hands held open seemed to joyously offer her love and praise or to desperately beg for something.

With a curiosity that overrode her deepening thirst, she studied any features she could distinguish over the village's enclosure wall. Odd feelings swarmed around her heart, crowding it with questions and prompting her to wish Seni had accompanied her so she could relieve herself of the mysterious pressure. Palm trees planted in painted pots offered her vision refreshing sips of color, as did a handful of brightly decorated shrines, but it was impossible to imagine how anyone could truly enjoy life without a pool and a garden. She looked over the rooftops—littered with shading screens, sleeping mats and stores of grain— at footpaths twisting through the desert mountain which also loomed over the city of the dead spread out to the left of the living village. The modest cemetery consisted of small eternal homes entered by way of miniature pyramids fronted by large doors.

Beyond the storage buildings, a smaller and much poorer looking community housed those who served the professional craftsmen and their families. Listening to the shouts of love and joy rising from a multitude of throats, she did not doubt the Servants of the Place of Truth were making her mother's tomb as beautiful as possible. Unless some of those cries were actually caused by fear and grief? She wondered if these people might be as melancholy as she was that morning thinking about her loved ones forever flying away beyond the reach of her embrace. Were they praying to the daughters of the goddess to help them endure their sorrows? Seni had told her that Ahmose-Meritamun was in charge of everyone who worked in the Necropolis.

When I become God's Wife, she thought, *the workers in the Place of Truth will be so happy, they will be inspired to create for me the most beautiful House of Eternity imaginable!*

As they left the tomb workers' village behind an absolute silence once more reigned in which the whispers of the litter bearers' sandals across the sand began communicating significantly with her heart. Even as she enjoyed the view of Kanefer's shoulders below her, she found herself truly appreciating the power of Thoth—the ibis-headed *neter* who uttered the first sounds in existence and wrote them out as words to express the desire burning in Re's heart. Rising from the lifeless desert, the Temple of Mentuhotep mysteriously helped support her thoughts and all the feelings flowing through her heart as her eyes drank in the vision of tall, confident columns and thriving trees.

Leaving their attendants outside the enclosure wall, the queen, God's Wife and the princess followed a ramp into The Temple of Mentuhotep of the Domain of Amun. The inner forecourt was alive with shade trees and the avenue was lined with colossal statues of Mentuhotep as Osiris. Walking beneath the towering figures, Hatshepsut gazed up at them in awe, and as they ascended a second stone causeway it seemed to her the king's broad shoulders were not only reaching for the sky but also magically supporting it. She was disappointed they ignored the covered portico at the rear of the first courtyard, which Seni had told her was decorated with scenes of mighty river processions and victorious military expeditions. On the middle terrace, three rows of seven sycamore trees and three rows of seven tamarisk trees formed a natural colonnade. The uppermost level of *Akh-Sut-Nebhepetre*, Splendid are the Sacred Places of Mentuhotep, was entered by way of a double row of columns which brought them to an aisle surrounding a forest of eight-sided pillars. Penetrating the gloom, shafts of light illuminated the King in the company of Horus and Seth, the vulture Nekhbet and the cobra Wadjet. Mentuhotep forever received the *neters* in the temple of his incarnation, accepting the palm branches they offered him that symbolized endless years of life.

Meri did not proceed along the aisle but instead headed directly into the imperishable grove of stone pillars, the heart of which was a sloping square monument serving as a sanctuary for the conquering spirit of Horus—the warrior falcon Montu-Re. The featureless limestone thrust up toward heaven through an opening in the roof and Hatshepsut knew it represented the Primordial Mound of Creation, believed to be located in the desert just south of *Akh-Sut-Nebhepetre* in *Djser-Set,* Holy is the Place, the smaller and more ancient temple dedicated to Amun where they had first made offerings.

At the back of the upper terrace—intimately flanked by the tombs and chapels of six royal women beloved by Mentuhotep—a door led into an open court.

Her tutor (who seemed to know everything) had told her that beneath the stone floor of the court lay a room filled with small wooden statues and models of everyday objects surrounding an empty alabaster container large enough to hold a body. The king was not buried in that chamber, which was dedicated to the creative power of his Ka. The world, and everything in it, was as a child's toy to the Ka, stimulating and entertaining but ultimately expendable. The stone cenotaph was deliberately left empty as an expression of Pharaoh's transcendent power, exercised through his imperishable Ka. The endless physical bodies the Royal Ka willingly inhabited and shed was represented by the broken wooden statues.

Because Seni had explained facets of Mentuhotep's temple to her, Hatshepsut was better able to appreciate it. Although the design of the monument was founded on tradition, no other like it existed. The empty court, so full of meaning, led them even farther west into another great hall of eighty-two columns. Two of them stood alone at the north and south ends and eighty more stretched before them in eight rows ten columns deep. The numbers "eight" and "two" expressed the perfect completion of the cycles of corporeal existence set into motion by the division of One into Two from which the eight ensuing numbers arose. That was why, Seni had told her, one-hundred-and-forty pillars, each possessing eight sides, "One", "four" and "eight", surrounded the monument symbolizing the Primordial Mound of Creation that emerged from the cosmic waters of Nun, Lord of Infinity, on the First Occasion. The separation of heaven and earth engendered the four cardinal directions of space and time and the four principal elements popularly referred to as the four children of Atum-Re—Shu and Tefnut, Geb and Nut. She had not really understood but it did not matter because she would soon be continuing her education in *Ipet Sut*, sometimes called the Place of Number, where she knew everything would be made clear to her.

At the west end of the stone grove was the entrance to a long and narrow chamber evocative of a god's phallus, their final destination. The chapel, dug straight into the mountain, incorporated eight of the eighty-two pillars supporting the hall around it. Inside, the air was sweet and cool, and in the flickering light, she discerned the smooth expanse of a vaulted ceiling. Like moths hovering around flames they never allowed to burn out, priests dedicated to the service of Mentuhotep's Ka stood around a limestone altar. Two of the *hemu-kas* silently handed the queen and God's Wife the ritual objects they needed to make their offerings. Hatshepsut, her hands feeling awkwardly empty, followed her mother and her mother's sister up a short ramp onto the altar itself. She suppressed a gasp when she saw Mentuhotep, Horus of the Strong Arm, waiting for them sitting on a throne carved directly into the natural rock. Meri wafted incense, the breath of the gods, toward him with a burner shaped like an arm, its open hand holding the bowl. Meanwhile, Ahmose slowly poured streams of milk and water at the great king's feet from two small circular jars.

If not for the servants of his Ka, Mentuhotep's image would have sat there in darkness forever. The thought chilled Hatshepsut as a deep disappointment threatened to drown her admiration for the pharaoh who had resurrected Kemet's greatness. Mentuhotep's sculptor had *not* been inspired. Even though he wore the red crown on his head, and his skin was painted the black of divinity, the king's wide open eyes made him look more like a startled child than a powerful man capable of reuniting the Two Lands. His arms were crossed over his chest but his hands were empty of the crook and flail, and his legs and feet were disproportionately larger than the rest of him.

"Do you see what happens in times of darkness, Hatshepsut?" her mother whispered without turning her head to look at her. "The spirit of Ptah is diminished and not even the greatest man in Kemet can find a sculptor talented enough to create a beautiful home for his Ka."

If anyone dares to create such an ugly statue of me when I am queen, she thought, *I will have him killed on the spot!* She did not blame Mentohotep, he had done his best, and because he had been such a splendid ruler, Kemet was filled now with highly skilled servants of Ptah, Amun be praised.

* * * * *

The litters bore them back in the direction of the River, but before they reached it they stopped at the temple devoted to Meri's husband where the *hemu-ka* offered them alabaster glasses filled with cool water. Hatshepsut found the Osiris statues of the Good God Djserkare refreshingly different from those of Mentuhotep. Amenhotep's features were as distinctive as Mentuhotep's were crude. Both the queen and God's Wife made offerings to their brother and afterward conversed pleasantly with the *hemu-ka* who was a good friend of theirs.

Feeling free to walk around, Hatshepsut found herself wondering how much of this noble pharaoh, whose cheeks had been boyishly plump, still lived in Meri's heart. His firm and determined-looking mouth resembled the mouth of the woman who had also been his wife. However, when viewed from the side his face struck her as more pleasantly approachable than Meri's. She concluded that Amenhotep, Amun is Content, had been a nice man. She was not surprised the Servants of the Place of Truth worshipped him for while he lived Djserkare had taken such good care of them they did not doubt he was still watching over them. His mother, Ahmose-Nefertari, was also revered as a goddess and it filled her with pride that the blood of the great queen who had been the first God's Wife flowed through her own body. Amenhotep was the first pharaoh ever to separate his mummy's eternal resting place from the temple where his Ka received visitors and offerings. His tomb was located somewhere in the Valley of the Gates of the King, where her father was building his.

Their small army of attendants was embracing the shade behind the temple and because it was not one of Djserkare's many feast days the desert outside the offering court was silent and empty. Returning to her mother's side, she stared out at the horizon, marveling at the faint yet exquisitely lovely colors she discerned shimmering where the earth and the sky met. The longer she fixed her attention on them, the more the infinitely delicate hues spoke directly to her heart through her eyes... *The air is a veil*, they said, *a veil concealing unimaginable beauty*...

Outloud she wondered, "Is that the desert sacred to Hathor?" unintentionally interrupting the queen's conversation with the priest.

"Yes, Hatshepsut, it is."

"I see her veil on the horizon and it is softer than the finest linen. All those beautiful colors *must* be Hathor's veil for they never stop trembling with her heavenly breath."

* * * * *

Work on Pharaoh's eternal home progressed with no one hearing, no one seeing, although it was hard for Hatshepsut to understand how that was possible when so many people were involved in its construction, decoration and furnishing. It was dawning on her that her father, the bodily son of Amun-Re, was in many ways vulnerable. A well-aimed spear, a snake slipping into his tent as he slept when he was on campaign, any number of dangers threatened his mortal flesh. He could even be trampled to death hunting elephants in Roshawet, but she trusted he was much too skilled and intelligent to ever let *that* happen. It was inconceivable that when he went to his Ka (countless years from now) she might still have to worry about him not being entirely free from harm. Surely the gods, led by Horus, would protect the king's tomb more effectively than a million armed guards. Horus always stood behind Pharaoh, his open wings resting on his shoulders, and no matter how many earthly falcons died, their Divine Ka remained forever unharmed. And so too would the Ka of Thutmose-Akheperkare live forever no matter what happened to his physical form. Still, she hoped the illustrious Ineni was doing his best to keep the location of her father's tomb a secret, truly building it with no one hearing and no one seeing.

Hatshepsut distracted herself from these unpleasant thoughts by anticipating the upcoming feast of Hathor and the joy of picking the papyrus with Amenmose from his Pleasure Barge. She was also eagerly awaiting the arrival of her two best friends from Mennefer. She had quickly grown fond of Nafre but had so thoroughly disliked her other personal attendants that they were dismissed and Seshen and Meresankh sent for to take their place.

Her forthcoming lessons in the Temple of Amun-Re were shrouded in mystery. One day she looked forward to them, the next she dreaded them. But in the afternoons, after her lessons with Seni, she invariably forgot all about tombs and temples in her beautiful Pleasure House. After she tired of swimming, she embraced the sweet-scented shade and either sent for Inet to tell her a story or for Nafre to play her one of the new love songs she had learned which always made her think of Amenmose.

But then, abruptly, it was thoughts of another brother that possessed her. Memories of Ramose guiltily filled her heart with their brevity when a messenger arrived in Waset everyone could see had the black jackal of Anubis nipping invisibly at his feet. Pharaoh's oldest son, the mighty soldier Ramose, Born of Re, had been pierced by an enemy arrow and gone, still young and strong, to his Ka.

All of Kemet grieved for the brave prince and for the father who had lost a part of his heart.

6

The Spirit of Isis

Amenmose was bound for Perunefer to take charge of Pharaoh's army while the body of his brother was being prepared by the embalmers. The festival of Plucking the Papyrus for Hathor was honored by the queen and the princess without any real joy for Pharaoh had also left Waset in the company of the Lady Mutnofret. Together they would wait in Mennefer for their son's Master of Life, preparing to accompany him home to the city where he had been born and where he would now live forever on the other side of the River.

Even though Kemet's forces emerged victorious from the border skirmish in which Ramose perished, Hatshepsut was distracted from her lessons by the fear that Amenmose would also be fatally wounded in battle and never return to her.

One afternoon, God's Wife appeared in the princess' Pleasure House unannounced. Surprised, Hatshepsut stepped down from the shade of a pavilion and extended her arms, bending them slightly at the elbows and holding her open hands respectfully up toward her guest. She was shocked to see her mother's sister hunched over a walking stick. Two young male attendants followed closely behind Meri, their concerned expressions revealing they had already prevented her from falling at least once that morning. But she was the daughter and widow of kings and refused to accept their help climbing the steps. Instead, she rested her free hand on Hatshepsut's right shoulder and together they ascended slowly.

Carefully, God's Wife seated herself on a stool. She sighed but not with relief; her expression remained tense.

Kneeling beside her on a papyrus mat, Hatshepsut gazed up into eyes she perceived as shining with stubborn memories of health and beauty. "Are you well, Meri?" she said gently.

"No. When my Master of Life is ready for me, I will be glad to join my brother in the Fields of Hotep." Fixing her eyes on the gnarled roots of her fingers, she steadied her grasp on the gold handle of her wooden staff, forged in the shape of a goose's head. "When I am gone, Hatshepsut, the spirit of my mother, Ahmose-Nefertari, Beautiful Companion Born of the Moon, will continue to live in my sister and in you. It was the queen who ruled in Waset and who cared for Kemet while Pharaoh was away fighting to make the Two Lands one again. Ahmose-Nefertari was in charge of cleaning up the mess left by the foul winds of chaos. Acting as the first God's Wife, she supervised the beautiful work of refurbishing the temples and appointed men rich in the wisdom of Thoth to positions of power, men whose hearts were true to Maat. Many a foolish

Nomarch who had bowed weakly to Seth during the darkness was stripped of his titles and sent into exile."

"She was a great queen," Hatshepsut agreed.

"Do you know, Hatshepsut, how old I was when I married my brother, shortly after he became Pharaoh?"

She shook her head.

"The River had risen only seven times in my life when I became a bride. Amenhotep was five. Ahmose-Nefertari ruled Kemet after her husband's death, until their son was old enough to take the crook and flail into his own hands. Then, much too soon, my brother and my mother both died, almost as if they could not bear to live without each other, and I became God's Wife. My sister was crowned queen when she married your father. Thutmose had been anointed by Pharaoh as his successor because he himself remained childless."

"Did you mind very much?"

Waiting at a discreet distance from the pavilion, Meri's attendants seemed startled when she laughed. "Yes. At the time I *did* mind, very much."

"Are you jealous of mother?" she dared ask.

"No, Hatshepsut, I am not. I came to tell you to be prepared because my Ka is growing weary of this twisted body. No, do not protest. It is a foolish heart that fears death."

＊ ＊ ＊ ＊ ＊

As the embodiment of Isis, Queen Ahmose journeyed north to Abedju in search of her husband. It was said the head of Osiris was was buried there beneath the ancient temple. Other parts of his body, torn to pieces by his jealous brother, were scattered all over Kemet. His phallus, which neither Isis or her sister Nepthys were able to find, had apparently reappeared in Mennefer where it was enshrined.

On the streets of Waset, outside the Temple of Amun-Re, the mystery of the death and resurrection of Osiris was being enacted by noblemen chosen by the queen for the popular spectacle. Hatshepsut was not permitted to attend, and she took her resentment out on Senimen.

"It does not make sense," she snapped. "Isis found all the pieces of her husband's body except for his penis and put them back together. So why, then, are they all over the place again?"

He smiled. "You seem to have forgotten your lesson on symbols."

"I am tired of symbols! I want to go see the Mystery Play!"

"If you want to see the Mystery, look inside yourself. Men wearing masks and playing parts is entertaining and can prove enlightening but you, princess, already know in your heart what others can only be shown."

"There is nothing inside me today except anger!" She deliberately ignored the compliment. "I am *angry* I cannot go watch the play!"

He laughed, but then his expression sobered so abruptly it captured her full attention. "Do not be too eager to understand the mystery of Osiris, Hatshepsut. You are young. Enjoy it. You will look into the face of death soon enough."

Fearing she might catch a glimpse of the terrible countenance between the leaves of her sycamore trees, she glanced around the garden and said softly, "What does the face of death look like?"

"It will look like *your* face, only you will not have eyes with which to see it."

She did not care to pursue the subject by asking him to explain what he meant but he went on without her prompting, in a voice as stern as she had ever heard from him.

"When you become an initiate, Hatshepsut, you will play every part in the Mystery by ridding yourself of masks. Your fear will be dangerously real, but so too will be the joy of your victory over the darkness. It is no longer your place to be a child at a play, *princess*." He stressed her royalty again, something he rarely ever did.

"Do I *have* to become an initiate, Seni?"

"That is for your Ka and your Ba to decide as they battle each other like Osiris and Seth in your heart."

"But why must they fight? They seem to be getting along just fine."

"You are young."

"But why must getting older cause my Ka and my Ba to fight?" She was not looking forward to such inner strife even though she could hardly imagine it. She remembered what Amenmose had said at the banquet, "Seth is everywhere, little sister" and wondered if he had meant inside herself as well.

"Before I answer your question, Hatshepsut, tell me in your own words, as briefly as possible, the story of Osiris and his brother."

She did not see the point of this, but she had learned not to argue with her tutor when he told her to do something.

"Seth was jealous of his brother Osiris, the first king of Kemet, and of how much the people loved him. Desiring supreme power for himself, Seth invited Osiris to a banquet and presented him with a beautiful jeweled Master of Life as a birthday present. He convinced his brother to lie down inside it to make sure it fit him and immediately he and his followers sealed it shut and threw it into the River. The current carried it all the way to a foreign land where it was caught by the roots of a tamarisk tree. Isis, the beautiful sister and wife of Osiris, and their sister, Nepthys, the wife of Seth, found the chest and brought it back to Kemet. But Seth discovered it again and this time he cut his brother up into sixteen pieces and scattered them all over the world. After searching everywhere, Isis at last finished gathering all the parts of her husband's body. She could not find his phallus, which had been swallowed by a fish, but she was still able to conceive their son, Horus, by spreading the wings of her love over him. Afterward, Osiris hid deep in the earth to renew his powers."

"Very good, Hatshepsut. Now I will tell you this. Your flesh belongs to Seth. The smooth golden contours of your limbs are the hills in which his power lives. Osiris resides in your heart as the seed of divinity that must be cared for by all your thoughts and actions and watered by your feelings. Fear and doubt, jealousy and greed, anger and hatred are arid Sethian emotions that weaken the Osiris within you, just as pestilence and drought can kill a growing field of wheat. It is easy for the body to believe only in itself. If we fail to exercise the intelligence of our heart, we run the risk of trapping our Ka in a coffin of reason adorned with earthly riches and nailed shut by fear. Seth tossed Osiris, the Divine half of himself, into the River because he believed when his brother's body was reabsorbed into the womb of the world he would cease to exist forever.

"It is easy to think like Seth. When we turn away from the wisdom which lives in our heart and empowers us, we become Seth's subjects. Followers of Osiris know how to elevate the evidence of their senses to a true nobility so that, like hieroglyphs, they reveal more than they seem to. We are all of us Osiris. If not for Isis and her infinite love, our body would merely be a collection of parts. When we truly feel and believe a Divine force breathes life into our flesh, Horus is born in our hearts.

"Pharaoh sees to it that the story of Seth and Osiris is told to all his children every year by way of a spectacle in which they can participate by playing the subjects of Seth in one scene and the faithful followers of Osiris in another. So do you see, princess, how the most profound concepts can be expressed to everyone? Some people will experience inspiring glimpses of the truth, most will merely be entertained."

* * * * *

As a natural extension of her lesson on the death and resurrection of Osiris, Hatshepsut was taken to witness the spring sowing. The River had receded and, wherever the ground was firm enough, furrows stretching all the way to the edge of the desert were ploughed by the wood and metal versions of the hieroglyph for love. It was hard work. The royal lands adjoined those of the

Temple of Amun but only scribes knew where one began and the other ended for there were no physical markers. Pharaoh, who owned all the land in Kemet, awarded generous portions to the temples, his Nomarchs and courtiers, and what was left belonged to small farmers. Everyone paid a tribute of the tenth part to the crown. The extra grain was stored throughout the land, kept in reserve for those terrible times she knew only from legend when, because Hapi was displeased for some reason, the River did not rise high enough to slake the land's thirst and leave behind the mysterious nourishment that made life possible.

From the comfort of her litter, Hatshepsut watched as men wearing only white loin cloths walked the neat rows ploughed in the earth tossing grain to the left and to the right, every few steps reaching into the leather bags slung across their left shoulders for more seeds.

She yawned. That was the second morning she had spent in the same spot and she was bored. Yet Seni insisted they return again the following day, and every few days after that. He said it was important. When she asked him why, he told her life was a process requiring patience and an intimate knowledge of the way things worked if it was to be properly lived. The deepest suffering, he said, was caused when people strove to avoid making an effort in the mistaken belief only the result was pleasurable.

"But would it not be nice to be able to wish for all our favorite dishes," she used the example because her stomach had just grumbled, "and have them immediately appear in obedience to our will?"

"No, for an image without substance only makes the heart grow hungrier."

Meri had used the word *substance* in relation to Hathor, who was God's Hand, even though it was Ptah who had shaped the *substance* produced by the Goddess as she responded to the desire in Re's heart. She pondered the connection sucking on a little ball of frankincense mixed with cinnamon that made her mouth taste pleasantly sweet.

"Did Re *see* what he desired, Seni, before Hathor made it real and Ptah gave it form?"

"I do not know."

She stared at him in astonishment. "But you know everything!"

He smiled. "You are very sweet."

"You are right." She leaned toward him and blew gently on his face with her perfumed breath. "Do you like it?"

"It is very nice, but you do not need it."

The following morning they returned to the same place to watch flocks of sheep herded across the field, their hooves trampling the newly sown seeds into the ground before birds could eat it. The silly creatures bleated incessantly while eagerly following virile young rams led in the right direction by little boys waving tempting sprigs of hay in their faces.

Throughout the month, the princess and her tutor occasionally returned to observe men carrying water to the seeded land from the nearest canal in buckets hanging from both ends of a long pole balanced on their shoulders. Their muscular backs looked as strong as seasoned leather and the tedious chore they performed made carrying the litter of a princess seem luxurious by comparison. Over and over again all day long, they poured the precious contents of their buckets into what Seni informed her were grids of small dikes dividing the field into sections which held the water as it was slowly absorbed.

"You could easily have explained that to me back in my garden," she said impatiently. "Did we really need to come out here *again?*"

He did not reply.

She had no idea what he thought she was learning. Then one morning, as her litter was set down in the same spot, she noticed tiny green shoots breaking triumphantly through the black earth.

"Osiris has risen!" she cried, and for the rest of the day did not complain about observing what only appeared to be nothing slowly, but significantly, happening.

* * * * *

Hatshepsut was sitting cross legged on a papyrus mat, mixing the ink for her morning lesson, when she was delighted to see the queen accompanying Senimen as he appeared on the garden path.

"In ten days time, my daughter," Ahmose smiled at her, "you will enter the temple. First, however, you must become intimately familiar with the ways of the serpent. Renenutet may seem a humble goddess always close to the earth but without her we would perish from lack of care and nourishment. It is Renenutet who guards the residence and every other home in Kemet from evils both embodied and invisible."

"I know," she said confidently. "My attendant puts a bowl of milk out for her every morning."

"The serpent is the first form assumed by the Goddess," her mother went on, "but she has many others and *Aset*, Isis, is the throne from which they all rule as The Mistress of the House. Before you leave the nest, Hatshepsut, you must become fully aware of the tree in which it rests."

Before she could ask any questions, Seni took over, "Using the symbol of a living tree, the craftsmen you observed in Mennefer were all part of a large and vital limb supporting a variety of different branches. What farmers grow is another crucial limb in the tree of life, as is how animals are kept and made to flourish. It is time for you to study the limbs closest to home. You will meet the Royal Supervisor of the Cloth, the Overseer of the Royal Weavers and the Chief of the Laundry. You will also observe how a banquet is put together, from the peaceful activity of baking bread to the violent act of slaughtering cattle. The way that animals you eat live and die is such an important part of your life that to remain unaware of the process can do you great harm. The food you put in your mouth always speaks to your heart of its source, but if you fail to listen to it you will not be fully nourished and your health will suffer."

"But if all animals are a part of our heart why is it not wrong to kill them for food?"

"No, Hatshepsut, for without the human heart animals would not exist. Put very simply, animals embody our feelings and emotions, our base characteristics and spiritual qualities. When we butcher and consume a creature designed by Ptah to be our food, we are honoring the truth it is already a part of us."

"But that also means that when we mistreat an animal—like the man I saw beating his ass the other day because it was not moving fast enough to please him even though it was really all *his* fault for putting too much weight on its poor back—we are mistreating ourselves."

"Precisely. The man you mention was doing himself as much or even more harm than he did his ass."

"I understand. I imagine he was so impatient because he was not happy about something. Perhaps his wife had left him for being so unpleasant. Perhaps he was hungry as well as unhappy and that made him angry with his ass. Yet the animal could not possibly make his wife love him again or satisfy his hunger, not unless he stopped to kill it, but then he would be worse off than before because he could not carry all his burdens himself. Yet the poor creature was too overloaded to move any faster, which must have made the man even angrier -"

Smiling, her mother interrupted her, "We get the point, my love."

Hatshepsut began the lessons that would occupy her for the next week[11] with an introduction to Sinuhe, the Steward of the Royal Household. She had often seen him entering and leaving the queen's receiving room but she had not realized how important he was. She liked his even little features and plump face, into which no real worries had been carved, even though the way his eyes drooped down at the corners made him look tired all the time.

"Chaos is everywhere," he warned her. "For instance, if just one servant becomes lazy and neglects to clean that one hard to reach place all sorts of foul things are given the opportunity to make their nests there."

"Really?"

He nodded solemnly. "Really."

"Are you in charge of everyone who works in the residence?"

"I am in charge of everyone who works in the palace and *for* it. My Seal travels as far north as Roshawet and as far south as wretched Kush. I make certain Pharaoh and his queen and their beautiful daughter are always pleased and happy."

"Well, we are very grateful to you, Sinuhe, Son of the Sycamore. Never doubt it."

He suddenly seemed to stop thinking about where else he needed to be as he studied her face closely. "I live to serve," he declared, crossing his wrists over his heart and gripping his beefy shoulders.

They were sitting together in his Seal Room. It amused her that the man in charge of maintaining order in the residence was himself so messy. Papyrus scrolls were strewn across a table, stacked in piles in every available corner and crammed into recesses lining the walls.

"What is written on all these papyruses, Sinuhe?"

His response was a dramatic sigh, "Everything!" He shifted on a stool that had obviously been made by a fine craftsman for it sustained his considerable weight without complaining.

"Like what?" she insisted curiously, looking around her. "And how do you ever find anything?"

He gazed down at the rings decorating his thick fingers. She thought he was considering his reply until he held up both hands and said, "Every papyrus is sealed by one of these. They tell me to which beautiful facet of the residence and its furnishing each individual scroll belongs."

She leaned forward and curiously studied the multi-colored scarabs.

He removed one of the rings to show her the tiny hieroglyphs carved on the back.

"*Belonging to Nefertum*," she read, "the son of Ptah and Sekhmet."

"Yes." He sniffed as if catching a whiff of the *neter's* sweet scent and slipped the ring back onto his finger. "With this particular scarab I put my seal on all the scrolls pertaining to the breath of the gods—incense and oils, unguents and perfumes, many more precious even than silver. They number in the hundreds," he concluded in a tone of mingled pride and weariness.

She discovered Sinuhe was not only a comfortable servant of pleasure but also a battle-weary soldier.

"They will never be defeated, my princess." He was referring to mice, the curse of his noble life. "Their numbers are too great and they can chew themselves into anything."

"Bubu brings me one almost every night as a present," she sympathized. "I have trained him not to drop it on my bed."

"I do my best." He straightened his back and gripped his knees. "Cat's grease is regularly applied throughout the residence and the royal cats hunt freely."

From Sinuhe, Hatshepsut learned about all the important little things the servants she never noticed did for her. Snakes were kept at bay by balls of natron left before any suspicious holes. The residence was regularly fumigated with frankincense and myrrh mixed with cinnamon bark and honey. The fat of the golden oriole helped keep away flies as well as other annoying insects. Natron water sprinkled on the floor, and then swept through the room with a broom, discouraged fleas from breeding. Physical life could prove quite unpleasant if chaos was not fought on a daily basis. She realized how fortunate she was to have so many people devoted to her comfort.

The Steward of the Royal Household made certain every department worked together smoothly and efficiently. Therefore it was Sinuhe who introduced her to the various overseers.

The Supervisor of the Royal Weavers was a tall, thin man whose small eyes regarded her as sharply as one of the needles being scratched out under his exacting supervision. She immediately liked Sen-nefer and listened to him with a curiosity sharpened by amazement as he described how the finest mist linen was made from flax, one of the crops she and Seni had watched being planted in the royal fields. First the plant was carefully pulled out of the earth intact, then it was prepared in a complex fashion (at that point her thoughts had drifted to a song Nafre had sung for her the day before and she had forgotten to listen). The flax was then spun into a ball of thread with a spindle, an activity Bubu would have found very frustrating to watch. The thread was then ready to be woven into cloth on tall looms worked by men. She was impressed by the way countless individual threads merged into a single expanse of linen that did not look anything like the plant it had come from. Hatshepsut concluded she would never tire of observing a material's magical ability to transform itself in human hands.

The age of the plant from which the cloth was made determined its intended use. Only the youngest flax threads became dresses fine enough for a princess. The finished material was then marked at one edge by Sen-nefer, after which it was either rolled up or spread out for storage in large rooms designed for the purpose. It could also immediately be sent to the dying room.

"I will show you a material being colored," Sen-nefer said, "which will be woven into dresses very much like the one you are wearing today, princess."

The pure white cloth was spread out on the floor and naked little girls were using tiny brushes to apply special substances that would create different colors when the fabric was dipped into a dying vat—a large stone cauldron boiling with a dark-red liquid.

"But how can it come out looking like my dress?" she protested as the length of cloth was plunged into the hot dye. "It will be all red!"

He did not reply but merely smiled and a few moments later the material emerged white, yellow, dark-green *and* red.

"Oh!" she exclaimed. "There is great magic in those *substances*."

Discarded household cloths and bandages were sent to the *Wabet* where they were used by priests of Anubis. Hatshepsut was very glad embalming was not one profession she was expected to study, at least not yet.

The Royal Kitchen, regulated by numerous officials, extended far beyond the actual area in which the food was cooked. The Overseer of the Cattle of the King worked closely with the Overseer of the Cultivators of the King, the Overseer of the Royal Granaries, the Overseer of the Hunting Nets, the Overseer of the Royal Vineyards and the Overseer of the Bees of the King which provided the honey for her favorite cakes and, she discovered, for many other things, including life-saving medicines. Clad in white knee-length skirts, women prepared the food, obeying the detailed instructions of the Royal Chefs who were all men.

The kitchen was attached to the eastern side of the residence by a long covered walkway ending in an open courtyard. Cooking fires boiling meat in pans, roasting birds on skewers and grilling fish directly over smoldering embers sent a mouth-watering smoke up toward heaven, fulfilling the Divine appetite for all things sensual and delicious. One side of the courtyard was dominated by clay ovens from which wafted the irresistible aroma of baking bread and date-sweetened cakes. Hatshepsut watched hungrily as a woman opened one of the beehive-shaped mounds, removed three loaves, and then scooped out the ashes that had collected on the bottom. As soon as the oven was empty, more balls of dough were placed on the shelves, some of which had holes in the middle for filling with boiled beans and vegetables later. First, however, the dough was kneaded on a flat stone table by the only male servants working in the kitchen. They shaped the moist flour by beating it, slapping it around and thoroughly mistreating it.

"The wheat is struggling against its transformation," she observed. "And yet it must enjoy being handled so roughly, otherwise it would not become something so delicious."

Depending on what kind of bread was desired, salt and other spices were mixed into the batter along with milk, eggs and butter. It took a long time for the dough to swell up but finally it was ready to be baked in balls or in long loaves shaped by conical molds.

The courtyard opened onto rooms filled with pots used to store dried and pickled meat and fish, fruits and vegetables. The stone jars also contained chick-peas, lentils, green peas, onions and garlic. Milk was kept cool in damp earthenware pots and stored well away from the sunlight. Animal fat was preserved in special *adj* vessels. An entire room was occupied by jars of salt and spices, including cumin, coriander, cinnamon, dill, marjoram and thyme. There were numerous cooking oils but the most frequently used were sesame oil, safflower oil and olive oil. *Ben* oil derived from the horseradish tree was the most delectable of all.

The fuel used to ignite the fires and heat the ovens was made of animal dung. Matter-of-factly, Sinuhe informed her that the Royal Kitchens only used sheep dung because it burned the longest, although every variety was equally clean and, as she had certainly noticed, completely odorless. The manure was collected daily—by young women and children not yet assigned a more important and less onerous task—mixed with water and straw, dried in the sun and shaped into bricks.

Hatshepsut especially enjoyed visiting a field alive with beautiful horned cattle. The Goddess lived in the lovely eyes of cows that regarded her with a humbling indifference, their deep, liquid-black gazes shining drops of the Primordial Waters.

The Royal Slaughterhouse was not so pleasant. It seemed to her there was enough blood flowing across the stone floor to satisfy Sekhmet for a month. With their skins carefully stripped away and used elsewhere to make sandals, loin cloths, shields and numerous other items, she scarcely recognized the animals all the raw hides had been only moments ago. She was glad Sinuhe did not linger there even though there was a disturbing splendor to the place. The insides of living things was such a vivid, gleaming red all the hanging carcasses and limbs looked as elegant as freshly painted hieroglyphs spelling one thing—Amun-Re, the creator god.

* * * * *

Seshen and Meresankh arrived at last, their eyes swollen from weeping. They made an effort to hide the sadness they felt at leaving their families behind in Mennefer, but for the first time in her life, Hatshepsut felt guilty. She did not know what to make of the unpleasant emotion, which was neither anger nor impatience or the frustrated desire for something. She felt sorry for herself as well as for her friends; wilting with homesickness, they proved dull company. No one was happy and it was all her fault. She did not like that at all.

"Go home if you cannot appreciate the great honor of attending the princess," she told them. "I give you permission to leave!"

Their eyes widened and their unshed tears seemed to sparkle sharply with fear.

It was Meresankh who said, "But... but we would be completely dishonored!"

"You are dishonoring yourselves already by being so miserable instead of rejoicing in the happiness I have generously granted you. You may visit your families whenever you please. I have Nafre. At least *she* is wise enough to appreciate her good fortune. Your loved ones can also visit you. It is not as though you have gone to your Ka's and can never see them again!"

"And think of all the handsome young nobles," Nafre added mildly, "who will now look upon you with even greater respect and admiration."

Meresankh and Seshen became bearable again. After a week, they even managed to be amusing as they attempted to replace Nafre in the royal affection. They did not succeed but the princess found their efforts enjoyable.

* * * * *

Hatshepsut entered the domain of Amun-Re through a small wooden door concealed by a grove of sycamores. The temple itself was hidden behind a high sandstone wall that had been erected by her father. On feast days, two great wooden doors, strengthened with gold, opened onto a public court where the multitudes were permitted to make offerings.

Her fantasy of entering the temple in a litter as the gates ceremoniously parted before her shattered like a bird's egg falling out of its high nest; the secret little door made a mess of her expectations. Her images of dark chambers misted with the Divine breath of incense, in which the secrets of the gods would be revealed to her in reverent whispers, vanished like a dream as she woke to blue sky, green trees and white houses. Within the enclosure wall thrived another neater, more peaceful city.

She had not been inside the temple since her father had brought her with him when she was too young to remember anything except rays of light streaming into the darkness between tall pillars like Divine arms welcoming them. Kanefer remained outside with her litter as, accompanied by Senimen, she entered the sacred grounds on her own two feet clad very simply in a white linen shift. She wore no jewelry, not even a floral collar. Her sandals were made of unadorned leather and her natural hair framed her face. She could easily have been mistaken for a servant yet the thought did not upset her. She was the beautiful Princess of Kemet no matter how humbly she was dressed.

Palm trees shaded modest dwellings made of mud-brick plastered to resemble polished limestone. Seni told her the houses served as temporary and permanent residences for select priests, students and important visitors. Behind them stretched enclosed gardens and a confusing collection of buildings he said were workshops and storage houses. Then at last, she glimpsed the interior of the gilded wooden doors beyond which lay the public offering court where special posts had been provided to which animals could be tied and left to nourish the Hidden One through the bodies of his priests. Amun's compassion was famous throughout the Two Lands and on feast days there was hardly room to move around all the jars filled with milk and beer and countless baskets containing eggs, bread, flowers and produce.

Hatshepsut stood with Seni between the outer gate and the entrance to the inner temple. To the west lay the world framed by four flag posts and the Monuments of Heh, erected by the Good God Akheperkare—two slender shafts of red granite thrusting straight up into heaven. Whenever she saw them, her breath caught with pride at her father's achievement. To the east rose the great doors which led into the Divine realm. They were supported by two rectangular sandstone towers covered in bright white stucco and inscribed with sacred symbols. The sloping walls of the towers—linked near their summits by a walkway—narrowed as they ascended, and from two high wooden masts, their tips sheathed in gold-leaf, red flags responded to Shu's slightest breath. The towers evoked the *Akhet* hieroglyph and the two lions of the horizon—the substantial mountains of past and present between which the sun rose on the First Occasion. Behind the copper-studded doors lay the pillared hall where she had walked with her father. It would look different now; Pharaoh had recently replaced two of the northernmost wooden columns with ones made of imperishable stone.

Senimen looked into her eyes and said, "You have taken the first steps on the path of Maat. Are you prepared to follow it or do you wish to turn back?"

Her heart skipped between excitement and dread as she said, "I am ready to follow the path of Maat."

BOOK TWO

The Hidden One

7

The Path of Maat

Hatshepsut strove to listen attentively to the First Prophet of Amun. Hapuseneb was also Governor of the South, like his father's father before him, and he was such a handsome man it proved extremely difficult for her to concentrate in his presence.

"Kemet is often called *Ta-Nutri*, Land of the Gods," he told her, "and *Ta-Meri-*"

"Beloved Earth," she said, pleased. But she had not meant to interrupt him and her smile wilted self-consciously.

"Already you recognize the nature of the One, Hatshepsut."

The satisfaction in his voice gave her the courage to look at him. His firm features were as mysteriously slippery to her thoughts as wet stones were to her feet. "Love?"

"Why do you sound doubtful? Is that not what your heart tells you?"

"Yes…"

"Do you question the voice of your heart?"

"No…"

His lack of expression as he waited for her to tell him exactly what she was feeling and thinking was almost as difficult to endure as a disapproving frown. His eyes held hers in a way that made her strangely breathless and she was reluctant to speak for fear she might shame herself by displeasing him.

"My heart tells me that love is the nature of the One," she began tentatively, "but another voice I do not recognize, a voice I fear may be Seth whispering in my ear, tells me that is too simple… too easy."

"It is easy to doubt." Abruptly, he closed the short distance between them and knelt beside her on the papyrus mat. "Does Seth whisper in your ear *like this?*"

She straightened her back and clenched her hands against her thighs as a chill traveled from the base of her neck all the way down to the space between her legs. "No!" she nearly gasped the word. "It does not feel anything like that."

He whispered directly in her ear again, "What does it feel like?"

She closed her eyes wondering what was happening. Was he casting a spell on her? His power was terrible and yet wonderful. Carefully considering her reply she said, "Seth's voice is small and cold and yet also strangely loud, impossible to ignore. It is not a warm and wonderful whisper…"

Embarrassed she had told him how she felt about his nearness, she paused for a moment before continuing. "Seth's voice tells me I cannot be certain of anything except uncertainty, and that my heart only pretends to know everything because it is unable to face nothing."

"It is the voice of a coward ruled by fear who believes only in what his eyes can see. Pay it no heed. Teach yourself to ignore it. The longer you refuse to acknowledge it the weaker it will grow, until one day it will fall silent and trouble you no more."

"But it is my own voice Seth speaks with, which is very confusing." What felt like a long time ago Seni had warned her Osiris and Seth would one day do battle inside her.

"I do not believe you are as confused as you think, Hatshepsut. You have studied the myths. If you truly understand them you have the power to master yourself."

Hereditary Prince, High Priest of Amun and Governor of the South, Hapuseneb crowded Hatshepsut's heart so there was scarcely any room left in it for Amenmose, who she rarely saw anymore for he was always away with the army. Hapuseneb was a young man but he had already fathered one son and two daughters. His wife, the Royal Ornament Amenhotep, was beautiful but, in her fervent opinion, scarcely worthy of him.

"The correct and joyful application of every science," he said on the morning he taught her about the different temple offices, "is a sacred act that makes everyone who engages in it a priest or a priestess. Anyone who excels in his craft, anyone who loves and masters the materials he works with, is a servant of God.

"*Wab*-priests serve part-time in the Temple. In addition to their administrative duties they observe the heavens and calibrate the festival calendars, peform animal sacrifices, receive offerings and carry the *neters* on procession.

"The Lector Priests live in the Temple and are the most revered. They read from God's book and guard from decay the scrolls containing the sacred laws and measures."

"The *hemu-Kas* serve the revered dead.

"*Sem*—priests are always High Priests. They officiate at the Opening of the Mouth and other special ceremonies."

"What about the priests of Anubis?" she said, morbidly curious.

"Embalmers constitute a special caste of the priesthood. Chief amongst them is the Overseer of the Secrets of the Place who is also simply called Anubis. At certain times during the rite, Anubis wears a jackal-head mask. The priest who performs the actual operation of embalming is called the Chancellor of the God and his assistants are The Children of Horus.

"But do not make the mistake, Hatshepsut, of believing all priests of Anubis are confined to the embalming house. There are priests of Anubis who possess the power to travel between this world and the next through the doorway found in dreams. It is their task to heal the body by discovering the spiritual source of its illness. Such winged priests were once as common in the Two Lands as flocks of ibises are on the River's edge."

"Mother said once 'there are only a few of us now who remember'. Is that what she was talking about?"

"In part."

"But what has been forgotten and why?"

"In the beginning, the door between the worlds was wide open but it is slowly closing. Eventually it will be locked by Seth and the key, lost in the River of time, will travel through ages of darkness where it will be grasped by those who recognize it and seek to open the door again. But you need not be concerned, Hatshepsut. The present belongs fully to your heart and to Amun."

From the moment she entered his presence, she had sensed Hapuseneb was as far above all the other priests as Pharaoh was over even his most noble subject. She had no doubt he was a Sage of the House of Life, one of the few who knew the secrets of the Letters of Thoth. She missed him intensely on the days when Senimen took over her instruction. She loved Seni dearly but she was distracted from his lessons by the painful absence of her new, and very special, teacher. Only the possibility that Hapuseneb might ask her to tell him what she had learned enabled her to concentrate on anything except the thought of him.

She familiarized herself with the individual *neters* while at the same time studying nature's elements and how they worked together.

On the First Occasion everything bloomed from nothing as Khepri, Lord of Becoming. The sun rose from the Primordial Waters of Nun as a child's head emerging from a lotus flower. Every night the solar disc—called Khepri in the morning, Re at noon and Atum in the evening—returned to the dark womb of light.

It was Atum who, stimulated by his Hand, gave birth to Shu and Tefnut, Geb and Nut—air and light, heat and moisture, earth and sky, the substance of space and time. Hathor was both the sensual world and the Divine creative power behind it, the Ka of Re and the House of Horus, a truth expressed by the statues of Menkaure where he stood between two identical women—the celestial Goddess and his earthly wife. From the separation of heaven and earth emerged the four children of Nut and Geb—Osiris, Isis, Seth and Nepthys, the *neters* constituting the human soul.

Hatshepsut already knew her Ka had fashioned her body. She recognized her Ka in the smiling face that lived in her mirrors. Nothing could ever hurt her Ka, which Hapuseneb said possessed the power to harness every material element and energetic force in its creative service.

However, there was much to study and learn when it came to the body and everything that could go wrong with it. Medicine was now almost exclusively the domain of the priests of Sekhmet. The prevention of disease relied on cleanliness, but once a person fell ill, or was injured in some way, it was imperative their Ka assist in the healing process.

"The body is fashioned from physical elements and is therefore vulnerable to them," Seni explained. "It is never a question of the Ka being weak or sick. Those personalities who cultivate a clear connection to their Ka's are less prone to illness. Yet often the Ka, for reasons which cannot be fathomed, desires to unravel the body it has woven more quickly than seems desirable.

"Disease is a symptom of an imbalance in *whedew*[12], a substance produced by internal processes affected by the relationship between the individual Ba and its Ka—in other words, by how freely the life energy we call *Maat* enters and leaves the heart. From the heart extend channels called *metu* that link all parts of the body. Good health depends on the free flow of Maat and disease results from blockage, whatever its cause. Physical imbalances often reflect the process of fine-tuning feelings and consciousness in the vital act of growth for *whedew* responds to spiritual impulses.

"When a person suffers a head wound received in battle, for example, the damage may be too great for their body to be saved. That is very different from illnesses caused by an imbalance. The stress bred by fear has stopped many a heart that refused to listen to the calming reassurances of its Ka. Life, health and strength depend on the unobstructed flow of Maat through the heart. The heart receives cosmic energy and returns it in a mysteriously enhanced form to its Divine source through the breath of enlightened speech. People who are true of voice are healthier than those who lie, thereby blocking the circulation of Maat through their hearts and, as a result, through the world."

Hatshepsut thought about her brother, the great soldier Ramose, and of the enemy arrow that had sent him to his Ka when he was still young and strong. Every time the River rose and receded it took a member of her family with it back to their heavenly source. She was beginning to dread the season she had once looked forward to the most. Only the high walls of Amun-Re's house helped keep her deepening fear at bay. If she lost all those she loved, what would be left of herself?

First Ramose had died in battle. Then—almost exactly a year later—the Ka of Wadjmose hunted his body all the way to the Dwat. Chasing an ostrich was a foolish way for a prince to perish. He was flung from the chariot when his driver swerved to avoid the monstrous cobra he swears suddenly reared before them. No one had been inclined to doubt the faithful servant's story. Wadjmose's Mother had called him home sooner than expected. He was, after all born of Wadjet. It was said that those who bore the name of the goddess either lived longer than most or left earth early in life with the swift suddenness of a snake bite. The bloodstained rock against which the prince struck his head had been brought home to Mennefer with his body. The ostrich got away.

The following year, in the same month of Hethara, on the feast day of Maat, God's Wife, Ahmose-Meritamun, rested from life to join her husband, the Osiris Amenhotep, in a world exactly like the one they had ruled over together but a million times more beautiful. Hatshepsut had been shocked by the sight of Meri's Master of Life, which was big enough to hold three of her. The painted wooden coffin was so magnificent she was effectively distracted by it from the sadness of knowing she would never again speak with her mother's sister. Only when she herself entered the perilous realm of the Dwat might she see Meri again in the golden feast hall of Osiris.

Ahmose-Meritamun's wooden wrists were crossed over her chest beneath her heart and her upper body was enfolded in a design evoking great blue and gold wings. She grasped a lotus scepter in both hands and her broad wig, also painted gold and decorated with a scale-like blue pattern, tapered near the ends and fell just below her matching collar. From where her wrists met a straight ribbon of hieroglyphs flowed all the way down to the base of her magnificent coffin.

For several nights after the funeral, Hatshepsut dreamed of Meri's young and seriously smiling face. The royal artisan who had captured her Ka in painted wood must have known God's Wife very well for Meri's personality truly seemed to shine in the lifeless stone irises, outlined in royal blue beneath her intelligently arched eyebrows. She hoped Amenhotep had gone to meet his beloved sister as soon as the tomb doors were sealed behind her and they could be alone together. How he could ever get his arms around the ponderously large bed his wife now slept in was not something she cared to think about...

But she could not *help* thinking about it. She was forced to remind herself that Amenhotep and Meri were both their own beautiful Ba-birds now. Their wooden coffins could no more confine them than a tree imprisoned winged creatures perched on its branches. Meri could fly out of her tomb and return to it at will and no one—not the soldiers who guarded the Necropolis and the workers living in the village nearby—would ever see her for she lived in the Dwat now.

Hatshepsut understood the Dwat to be the place between heaven and earth where all magical transformations took place. The Dwat was the moment between night and day and day and night, a realm of transition. The Dwat was like the River on which boats sailed one way while others traveled in the opposite direction—some Ka's were busy shaping bodies and being born while others were discarding their mortal flesh the way snakes shed their skin. In the Dwat everyone appeared just as they had on earth despite the fact that their mummies were nearly as dry and fragile to the touch as serpents' empty husks.

Meri, young and beautiful again and free of pain, stood tall and straight beside her brother, whose heart would have rejoiced to see her smiling and happy the way he had known her in life, before his death made her sad. In the Dwat people did not age and but there were other dangers because every thought and feeling that lived inside you—freed from the corral of your physical limbs—suddenly surrounded you.

"That is why to live in fear," Hapuseneb told her quietly, "is to be devoured by it in death. If darkness and emptiness are all you expect to see, that is all that will be."

"But that is not all there *truly* is…"

"There is no truth apart from what your heart conceives. The only light in the Dwat is cast by love, from which it emanates eternally. It can be extremely unpleasant not to have the courage to fight Seth and believe you are a powerful Osiris. But even more dangerous, and potentially fatal, is never to love, for then if you become lost in your own emptiness no one will be able to help you."

"But how is it possible people are born who never love? Surely everyone loves at least *one* person?"

"It is difficult for a heart as rich as yours to comprehend spiritual poverty, but do not make the mistake of believing it does not exist. While on earth a loveless person hurts all those he encounters, in one way or another, but in the Dwat he becomes his own miserable victim."

At least she knew that would never happen to *her* or to anyone else in her family. Nevertheless, she did not care to walk past the statues of her father as Osiris that lined one wall of his colonnaded hall in Amun's temple. She did not need to see his confident and magically repeated smile to feel he would always be with her.

Senet no longer seemed a child's game to Hatshepsut. In her hand each leopard-head gaming piece, made of reddish-brown jasper, challenged Sekhmet's blood lust for her family. She had to believe those left to her, the most precious persons of all, would endure. Her favorite human opponent in the game was her new special friend, Puyemre. Every time she beat him life triumphed over death, love over emptiness. Each of the five pieces on the board was a member of her family—her mother and her father, Amenmose, Inet and Seni. Hapuseneb did not need her help; he was powerful enough to protect himself. Every time she rolled the smooth little bones marked with black lines she closed her eyes and prayed very hard. In the end she always achieved her heart's desire—everyone she loved lived forever.

Then one day it occurred to her Puyemre might be letting her win.

When she accused him of manipulating the fate of her pieces, he stared back at her sadly. His large black eyes glimmering with intelligence did not seem to belong in his boyish face. At ten he was two years her junior and he was so small and slender he looked younger.

"Do you not desire to win?" he said in the quiet respectful voice it was frustratingly difficult to argue with.

"Of course I do, but that is not the point! *You* have to try and win too or it does not count!"

"But I want only what you desire, princess, and you desire to win."

It was maddening that he could argue convincingly without ever raising his voice the way she often did. Hapuseneb had told her she enjoyed letting her passionate nature get the better of her, but she seldom found herself exercising the control she supposedly possessed.

"You actually *desire* to lose?" she said more calmly.

He thought about that. His full lips always seemed to be smiling slightly, even when he was at his most serious, as if behind whatever he was thinking at the moment there was one special thought forever pleasing him. "No, I do not wish to lose," he replied at last, speaking even more softly than usual.

She was thrilled. Perhaps she had finally gotten the better of him in an argument.

"I desire to see you happy," he went on. "If you are happy when you win, then I win even if I *seem* to lose."

"But then *I* never really win!" she was exasperated with him again.

"I do not always *let* you win," he admitted, looking away with a sudden shy humility that effortlessly endeared him to her again.

"You do not?"

"No." He shook his head. "If I desired to beat you I would have to try very hard. You are an excellent player, princess."

"But not as good as you, apparently, the great Puyemre who can win or lose at will!"

Yet even when she was annoyed with him, she could not help being secretly pleased with his devotion to her happiness and the subtle skill with which he achieved it.

Puyemre was the youngest son of Lord Puya and the Lady Neferiah, Royal Nurse of Pharaoh's youngest son, Thutmose. Puyemre made the formal visits of her little half brother something to look forward to. Fortunately, Thutmose's mother, Mutnofret, rarely accompanied him when he visited the princess. Hatshepsut would not have known what to say to the illustrious lady with the missing teeth and sons. Of the four boys Mutnofret had borne Pharaoh, only two still lived. She could not imagine why father had married her in the first place. She reminded herself Mutnofret was the daughter of the great pharaoh who reunited the Two Lands, which meant she had inherited a little of his Divine blood even though her mother had been only a minor wife. The royal part of her must have seduced her father through the serpent of her smile, for the Goddess lives in every woman's lips.

Thutmose was only nine-years-old and such a stiffly polite child she might have perished from boredom if ever left alone with him. Fortunately, the pavilion in her Pleasure House was more than large enough to accommodate his pretty nurse along with her son, in addition to Nafre, Seshen and Meresankh. She had assigned her attendants the task of keeping the young prince entertained with stories and music while she played Senet with Puyemre. Thankfully, Thutmose was more interested in pretty girls striving to please him than in board games requiring his concentration and effort and in which he risked being defeated.

* * * * *

Hatshepsut continued spending fifteen days studying in the Temple of Amun-Re every month. "I am afraid of death," she confessed to Hapuseneb. "Yet Ahmose-Meritamun, True of Voice, said it was a foolish heart that feared death."

"You are not foolish, Hatshepsut. An enemy who threatens your peace and well-being must be faced and defeated. Your fear is natural but so too is the courage with which you struggle to conquer it. Your thoughts are soldiers armed with concepts and beliefs and the voice of your heart is the Great Commander. You would be foolish only if you chose to be weak."

Like Seni, he always knew what to say. It was the direct, challenging way he looked at her when he spoke that was so different and so strangely exhilarating. Seni was her friend and she welcomed their lessons together as she embraced the shade on a bright day—Hapuseneb had the uncomfortable power of Re to reveal all the thoughts and feelings hidden inside her. She had discovered that some of her emotions shamefully resembled the foul things the Steward of the Royal Household said lived in dark and neglected corners. A part of her could be likened to a crocodile submerged in the River blending with the water weeds with only its eyes rising above the surface as it waited to devour all her beautiful feelings and thoughts with a perfunctory snap. Gradually she began to understand what it meant that all animals lived in her heart.

"I am ashamed, Hapuseneb." They were sitting before the shining waters of *Isheru* late one afternoon watching the moon rise over the enclosure wall. "I always believed I was beautiful and yet in truth I am full of ugly fears and doubts and other feelings not worthy of a noble heart."

She wanted him to tell her that she *was* beautiful, much more beautiful than his silly Royal Ornament of a wife, but he remained silent. She could never get him to say or do what she wanted him to and that stirred up desperate feelings inside her she was not proud of even as it deepened her respect for him. *His* thoughts and feelings were mysteriously powerful currents that drowned her childish efforts to manipulate him like flimsy reed boats.

When he did not reply she began to worry. She could not let those be the last words she spoke to him before they parted for the night or she would not be able to sleep with his silence still loud in her ears.

"I *am* beautiful," she declared with quiet defiance, looking away from his sternly handsome profile across the half-moon of water fronting a small temple to Mut, Amun's consort. "More beautiful than anyone else! I will show you, Hapuseneb. One day you will see!"

"I already see, Hatshepsut." His quiet voice felt like a natural extension of the silence, intensifying rather than disturbing it. "It is you who do not seem to realize that the clearer you see the more beautiful you become to me."

Infinitely relieved she would be able to sleep peacefully that night she relaxed and opened her heart to him. "Every animal, even the most terrible and fierce and deadly, is beautiful because Ptah shaped it to reflect a part of us. Therefore, I must not be ashamed of my natural tendencies, no matter how base and ugly, for they have something to teach me of my nature, which is both earthly and Sethian, heavenly and Osirian. I should only be ashamed of my inability to separate my true self from my baser instincts, for not to do so would be like willingly living and sleeping with hyenas."

"Everything is Amun-Re-Ptah, Three in One, One in Three," he said, his eyes meeting hers.

"Yes!" she breathed. Every day she seemed to better understand the statement with which he began and ended all her lessons.

"The Hidden One is well pleased by how clearly you are beginning to see, Hatshepsut, Foremost of Noble Women."

Three days after that special evening with Hapuseneb on the shore of *Isheru*, she wiped herself clean between the legs after urinating and saw blood on the cloth.

"Nafre!" she cried. "Send for Inet! Quickly! And for the queen!" She was so excited it was almost frightening.

"My lady, what is it?" Nafre came running, torn between concern and obedience. "Is everything all right?"

"Hathor has pricked me between the legs with her horns, Nafre!"

"Oh my lady!" Joy blinded her to the forbidden and she embraced the princess as happily as she might have done her own little sister, until she abruptly remembered who she was touching and quickly released her.

"That was wonderful, Nafre. Please do that again whenever you feel like it, but now you must go get my mother and Inet!"

While she waited, Hatshepsut studied the stained linen in fascination. Blood was life and its loss could mean death—the child inside her had died today so the woman could be born. She held the preciously stained cloth close to a lamp. Her royal blood was a bright red more beautiful than any she had ever seen. No painter could hope to reproduce the richly gleaming color that flowed out of her Ka's magical depths. Yet even as she gazed at it in awe, her blood began to darken and suddenly she feared she might never *stop* bleeding.

Her elation ebbing, she became aware of a dull ache low in her belly just above the place from which her blood emanated. She felt a growing pressure there, as if for the first time in her life the wordless mouth between her thighs was making an effort to speak.

She was a woman now and Hapuseneb would find out. The next time he saw her he would know she was no longer a child. She had made her first sacrifice to Hathor-Sekhmet.

"My lady," she whispered, "I hope you will be well pleased with your daughter!"

8

House of Horus

Amenmose was back in Waset but Hatshepsut could not see him. For five long days and nights she was confined to her rooms and garden. Being a woman was proving uncomfortable and messy. She felt sorry for the royal laundry.

Her mother came to see her everyday, which was wonderful. And yet, strangely enough, the queen's presence did not have the power to assuage the restlessness she suffered because Hathor-Sekhmet had killed, and was selfishly devouring, three of the precious days she was supposed to have spent with Hapuseneb in the temple.

She did not voice her concern but the deep ache in her belly worried her. The first two nights of her confinement, she woke whimpering with pain and fear. She felt as if the lower half of her body was caught in the jaws of the Divine lioness. The invisible fangs of the goddess were digging relentlessly into her tender skin and causing her blood to gush through the linen bandage. A battle was being fought inside her the nature of which she could not understand. She had never been so acutely aware of her slender thighs, which reminded her of the eastern and western horizons when she spread them open. She could sense the unimaginable force of her Ka working inside her to shape her flesh and felt both awestruck and anxious.

Finally, Hathor assumed her smiling human face again and Hatshepsut was free to leave her rooms, only now she was torn between her longing to return to the Temple and her desire to see her beloved brother. Her heart passionately debated, "Hapuseneb or Amenmose? Hapuseneb or Amenmose?" but in the end the decision was made for her. She discovered the High Priest had left Waset for a time, traveling in his capacity as Pharaoh's southern vizier. The frown that possessed her face when she received this news was soon replaced by a smile of delight inspired by the lion cub Amenmose gave her.

Forgetting to embrace the dignity of her new status as a woman, she cavorted happily with the adorabe creature. The cub's cushioned paws were more suited to the hard floor than her human knees. She had to make an effort to keep up with him as together they crawled across a painted fish pond into reedy swamps where he effortlessly pinned flying birds beneath him and stalked the little walking people she made of her fingers.

"Oh I adore him!" she cried. "He is so beautiful!"

She picked him up, loving the restless way he squirmed in her arms, and followed Amenmose into his garden. She set her new pet down outside and knelt beside him again. She plucked a gold-flower and laughed as he attacked it.

The cub's mother, reclining beside the pool, thumped her tail and closed her eyes in lazy approval.

"I rejoice in the knowledge that my gift pleases you, sister." Amenmose seated himself in one of the gilded wooden chairs servants had quickly placed beneath the largest pavilion.

When the food arrived, the piercingly clear eyes of the lioness opened again as she lifted her head off her paws. The serving girls carrying platters of meat and fowl received her undivided attention as she drew her lips back over her teeth to expose the scent glands in her jaws.

Suddenly, Hatshepsut remembered herself. She stood and smoothed her dress, dismayed by how childishly she had been behaving around her brother. Before she saw the lion cub she had fully intended to show him how grown up she was.

A Keeper appeared at the end of the procession. The lioness glanced sharply up at him as he slipped a leash around her neck, but then she pushed herself to her feet and followed him tamely down one of the garden paths. Another man smilingly caught her cub up in his arms and followed them.

The sophisticated feast Amenmose had arranged for them reminded Hatshepsut that, after her long confinement, she was ravenous for a man's company. She had seriously missed her games of Senet with Puyemre and grown heartily bored of Seshen and Meresankh's company. Even Nafre's lovely singing had frustrated more than it pleased her because the only thing that seemed to matter to the writers of banquet songs was the love of brother and sister. Listening to her attendant's enigmatically soaring voice had made her feel awkward as a bird with one wing confined to the empty nest of her garden. She had become intensely aware of the fact that, apart from her mother and Inet, the most important people in her life were men.

She ignored the buttery leeks and fava beans, concentrating on the plate piled high with duck meat deliciously washed down by pomegranate wine.

"Unless you are planning to sacrifice the evening to Hathor," Amenmose smiled at her approvingly, "I suggest you also eat some cabbage."

"Cabbage is boring!" she retorted.

"Not as *I* instructed it to be prepared for us," he disagreed, his eyes fixed on the naked hips of the serving girl refilling his cup. "The leaves are stuffed with spinach and raisins, garlic and sweet little onions. Try one." His smile deepened indulgently as he watched her take a small bite and chew it tentatively.

"Mm." she moaned appreciatively. "You are right brother. It is delicious." She quickly devoured the tightly wrapped sheathe.

He waved a ringed hand and the serving girls immediately left them. A fan bearer remained standing at the foot of the pavilion slowly waving the great black-and-white ostrich feathers in the mild evening. Two other attendants held whisks that proved almost as annoying as the flies they briskly shooed away from the prince and princess.

Hatshepsut met her brother's eyes across the table. Suddenly, she felt more inexplicably breathless than she was understandably full.

"Every night before I die to dreams," he spoke with quiet intensity, "I pray to Hathor that my beautiful sister will reveal to me the color of her bosom. Do you desire to become the Mistress of my House, Hatshepsut?"

She thought of Hapuseneb and his smoothly shaved skull covered by the dark shadow of the hair he did not let grow. She remembered the expression on his face when he listened to her, and the smile that made him even more handsome whenever her responses pleased him, which was often. But then she recalled how he had worn the wig of a nobleman the night the Royal Ornament he had chosen to be his wife accompanied him to a banquet, and how much she had suffered beneath the intangible flail of the lady's gratified smile.

She said, "Ever since I can remember you have lived in my heart, Amenmose. There can be no other for me. Every beat of my heart speaks your name, my beautiful brother." In that moment, it felt like the truth.

He smiled. "Then come and give me a kiss, sister." He reached over and grasped one of her wrists.

She had not sat on a man's lap since she was a little girl but she clearly remembered the sense of happy security. It felt perfectly natural to relax against him and slip her arms around his neck.

His left hand resting on her waist, with his right hand he gently grasped a fistful of her hair. His smile was replaced by an intent expression she had glimpsed on men's faces before but it had never been directed at her. She was thrilled. The painful and uncomfortable process of becoming a woman was worthwhile if it meant that one day soon the High Priest of Amun might look that way at her. The thought was more exciting than the feel of her brother's mouth pressing against hers. The sensation became even more surprisingly curious when his tongue, tasting of pomegranate wine and other delicious things, insinuated itself between her lips.

After a moment, she pulled her head back. "What are you doing, brother?" she laughed, strangely nervous and happy all in a single breath.

"Kissing you," he said firmly and forced her head down again.

She was amazed by how hungry he was even after eating so much and oddly exhilarated by the fact that he appeared to find the inside of her mouth more succulent even than roast fowl. It made her happy to be pleasing him but she also felt somewhat insulted he was treating her like food. She was the daughter of Re, the future queen of Kemet, not a goose.

She pulled away from him, lithely escaping the exciting but peculiarly demanding throne of his lap. Giggling, she fell back into her own chair and shyly avoided his eyes as she took another long swallow of wine.

He did the same but then stared at her so soberly she began to worry she had offended him.

The queen appeared on the garden path at the head of a procession of attendants. Amenmose frowned and his reaction upset Hatshepsut, deepening her confusion to the point where it became impossible for her to fish any words out of it. All she could manage was the anxious question, "Have I made you unhappy, brother?"

"Not at all, sister." His easy smile returned and he raised his voice slightly as he said, "After we are wed I will be the happiest man in Kemet. Until then I live only for that day."

"Ah, but a prince should not be so selfish," Ahmose remarked with a smile as she stepped up into the pavilion.

While her mother and her half brother exchanged pleasantries, Hatshepsut glanced from one face to the other wishing she had not drunk so much wine. She could not seem to understand what was being said; words were spoken which somehow bore no relationship to what they really meant. In the end, she knew only that she had agreed to become Amenmose's wife and that her mother had approved the union but refused to set a date. The crown prince was forced to yield to the queen's will and wait a little longer for his dreams of happiness to become real.

* * * * *

The following day, Hatshepsut accompanied Ahmose to the Temple of Amun-Re. After the sunlight outside, she could make out only her mother's white dress walking before her. Then a finger-like shaft of illumination touched all the gold embracing the queen and for a magical instant her slender figure shone like a constellation.

Hatshepsut could not stop wondering what it would actually be like to be God's Wife. The shadowy shapes of the powerful predatory birds flying amidst the ceiling's golden stars felt almost threatening as she tried to picture the nature of the sacred duties she would inherit from Meri. It worried her she might not after all be wise enough to serve Amun. Then she remembered how her mother's sister had commanded her not to be afraid and felt comforted if not confident.

A courtyard opened up beyond her father's hall of pillars and there Ahmose-Nefertari awaited them. The great woman who had helped her husband reunite the Two Lands stood tall and beautiful as a goddess where she lived forever on the stone wall. Standing below her, Queen Ahmose seemed only the dim mortal reflection of her vividly painted mother.

The space between the columns swiftly grew darker as beyond the Temple's enclosure wall across the River the solar disc kissed the hills of the western desert. More than ever, the intense silence that reigned in God's house impressed Hatshepsut. She became aware of how much Hapuseneb's voice and company—like a hand held up to protect her eyes from Re's direct light—helped shield her from the full and profoundly demanding effect of the Divine presence. The absolute stillness was a pressure against her heart and the silence felt mysteriously pregnant with meaning as each second passed more slowly than a snake with a rat lying heavy in its belly—the impatience of her body to return to the palace and enjoy another feast with her beloved brother.

"The time has come, my daughter," Ahmose spoke, "for you to understand what the goddess Ahmose-Nefertari is offering to her Lord, Amun-Re."

A refreshing River breeze found its way over the stone wall into the slight crack between Hatshepsut's forehead and wig as she studied what the beautiful woman on the wall held out toward Amun who, true to his nature as The Hidden One, was barely visible. His ghostly figure was in striking contrast to the exquisitely carved and colorfully defined lines of the queen's face and body. In her hands, Ahmose-Nefertari held the thick and heavy bead necklace all queens wore on special occasions.

"The *Menit*," Ahmose said, "is the medium by which the power of the Goddess is transmitted."

Hatshepsut savored the statement and waited eagerly to hear more. She was a woman now and the Goddess was revealing her secrets to her through her mother.

"Hathor is the Great *Menit* and every woman is her priestess." Without taking her eyes off the sacred object, Ahmose reached down and grasped her daughter's hand. "Hathor is the cosmic mother and wet-nurse, the House of Horus. The *Menit's* three rows of beads symbolize the trinity of God, Goddess and Divine child, the One that divided into Two and gave birth to Three."

She nodded. "Three in One, One in Three."

"The Goddess is the House of Horus. Mirrors are sacred to Hathor because she herself is God's mirror."

"Then, if Amun is hidden inside us, does that mean that when we look into a mirror God smiles back at us?"

Her mother squeezed her hand in response, an indication she was so pleased with the understanding revealed by the question it was already effectively answered.

Encouraged, Hatshepsut went on slowly, collecting her thoughts, "Hathor is the Hand of God who holds the mirror of incarnation up for Him. And yet Hathor is also the material substance from which the mirror is made and in which His reflection lives... and *I* become Hathor whenever I hold up a mirror and see Amun-Re smiling back at me. I *think* I understand..."

"You clearly do, Hatshepsut. But be careful not to let the wisdom blooming in your heart become lost in the complicated reeds of your thoughts, behind which debilitating doubts lie waiting to sink their fears into your confidence and happiness.

"Soon, when you become one with your brother, Amenmose, you will fully understand the *Menit* and the shape of the weight which balances it. When a man penetrates a woman's body he reflects Re's Divine force contained in the substance of the Goddess and creating life as we are experiencing it now, here, today, in this special moment that will never come again and yet will exist forever in Amun's heart.

"Everyday the miracle of life is repeated at sunrise and is reflected by the shining disc of a baby's head emerging from the dark womb of its mother's belly between the horizons of her legs. This is the magic of the *Menit*—the power of Hathor to manifest her Divine Father in a physical form as she becomes both His mother and His wife through all the Sons of the Sun.

"Like her sistrum, Hathor's *Menit* can be played as an instrument, for Music is Number and Number is Substance."

Hatshepsut was fascinated but distracted as she wondered how exactly Amenmose's body would penetrate hers. She knew it would involve that special part of him she had often glimpsed hanging between his legs when they swam together, before he concealed it beneath his kilt again. She wondered what it would feel like to be with him when Amun, in his virile form of Min, possessed him.

"Will it hurt, mother, when Amenmose enters me?"

"Yes, it will hurt a little, but only once or twice, and even then you will feel the Goddess coming alive inside you. Every time you embrace your brother you will be filled with joy as you savor a small taste of your Divine nature through each other."

"Then why do you not wish me to marry him yet?"

"Your body has aligned itself with *Sopdet* but the spirit of the Goddess still shines low and dim on the horizon of your girlish limbs. When the star of Isis burns more brightly in your blood, *then* will it be time for you to join with your brother in The Castle of the *Menit* in Tantera."

What Hatshepsut really wanted to know was why she was not expected to marry the High Priest as well. How else could she join with Amun and become God's Wife? Yet that was one question she did not dare ask.

* * * * *

The Hereditary Prince Ineni, Headman of Waset and Overseer of the Double Granary of Amun, was a slight man with a kind smile which seemed to apologize for the directly assessing way he stared into her eyes. Hatshepsut liked him at once despite the fact that the papyrus scrolls spread out on the table before him contained plans and progress reports for her father's tomb.

Akheperseneb, Pharaoh's northern vizier, wore the long wrapped kilt of his office held up by braces that revealed his little pointed nipples but concealed all his dignified rolls of fat. He was as slow in his movements as Ineni was light, each statement he made weighty with importance. Everything tended to sound like a problem in his mouth. His well carved lips turned up in a faint smile only when Pharaoh agreed with him the issue under discussion was indeed serious.

Ineni's speech was quick and precise as a stone cutter's tool and he seemed much less troubled by ponderous problems than the vizier.

Pharaoh had sent for his daughter to attend him in the Seal Room. Bubu slept on her lap as she listened dutifully, with only partially feigned interest, to the inventory of supplies needed to pay the foremen, scribes, painters and laborers working "secretly" on Pharaoh's House of Eternity. She realized that Meri, who had been in charge of the well-being of the Servants of the Place of Truth, must have worked closely with Akheperseneb, which meant that in the future she would too. That realization prompted her to observe the vizier more closely. She was relieved to determine he was really not as gloomy as he seemed. She could see in his eyes—which turned toward the window whenever Pharaoh was engaged in a conversation with Ineni—that he considered the colorful profusion of blooming flowers out in the garden inspiringly beautiful. Perhaps it was only men, and the quality of *their* work, he distrusted. She also thought she glimpsed a flash of envy in his eyes as they followed birds in flight. It made her wonder if he was secretly critical of himself, of his heavy and potentially lazy Ba, and if this made him harder on everyone else than was strictly necessary. She was relieved when she decided she could grow to like him.

There was no doubt, however, she would prefer Ineni's company, and not just because he made it a point to glance at her when he spoke, showing he understood and approved of the fact that she was to be included in the proceedings.

Akheperseneb did not meet her eyes so openly but the stance of his body—slightly turned toward her even as he faced Pharaoh—showed her a respect she found more than adequate for the moment.

She also kept looking at her father where he stood between two of his most important officials studying the scrolls and tablets a pair of silent scribes placed on the table before them. She was trying not to be upset by all the white hairs which had spread from his temples and across his whole head almost overnight. Her father was getting old. It was a distressing thought. And yet, she reminded herself, he was not like other men for the timeless vigor of Amun-Re, whose bodily son he was, lived inside him. His chest and arms were not as firm as she preferred to remember them, and he was not quite as tall as she had thought, but the new lines on his face only carved his features out more handsomely and his strong deep voice never changed.

One of the royal heraldss entered the room and announced, "The Royal Scribe, Senmut, requests entrance into the Divine presence."

Pharaoh said, "It will please me to see him."

The herald stepped aside and a young man immediately crossed the threshold. He sank to one knee and performed the gesture of praise and rejoicing.

Bubu lifted his head, abruptly abandoned his choice spot on Hatshepsut's lap, and striding quickly across the room leapt up into Senmut's arms. Had her feline approved so heartily of Ineni he might have knocked the small man over.

"Your animal is an excellent judge of character, Hatshepsut," her father remarked. "The cat belongs to my daughter, Senmut. Please return it to her and fill your arms with these instead." He indicated the growing pile of documents.

"Senmut will review them all," Pharaoh addressed her again, "and make certain everything is in order. Our Royal Scribe has the eyes of a young falcon. No mistake or omission ever escapes him."

As he sank to one knee struggling to gently return her pet to her, she regarded the young man curiously. Bubu was not cooperating—his eyes were open but his body was utterly relaxed, which had the effect of making him even heavier. She was obliged to reach up and help Senmut drape the seemingly boneless cat across her lap.

He quickly let go of it and took several steps back.

She experienced a strange sensation deep in her belly as she looked up and he met her eyes. No one had ever looked at her quite so boldly before, almost as though he was challenging her. Then abruptly she recalled the sensation of her fingers brushing against his and understood the blend of anxiety and defiance in his expression.

She said lightly, "The Goddess smiles upon you, Senmut, Brother of Mut."

Purring so passionately that his voice broke, Bubu settled himself more comfortably on her lap.

* * * * *

Large clouds swept across the sky and swallowed the sun. Nut's laughter grew increasingly louder, frightening in its power, and the day swiftly darkened to night.

Hatshepsut and Puyemre, watching in awe from the door of her game room, gasped as one when the Celestial River suddenly began pouring down into her garden.

"Water from heaven!" she cried and ran outside with her arms held high, her face tilted up to receive the cool blessing. She saw the Great Mother weep a long silver tear and suddenly one of the Persea trees lining the path burst into flames. She could not hear her own scream as Puyemre pulled her back inside, either forgetting or ignoring that he was not permitted to touch her.

That afternoon Pharaoh sent for his daughter. The queen was attending her husband. Also present in the private receiving room—to Hatshepsut's concealed joy—was the High Priest of Amun returned from his travels. Sitting beside her husband, Ahmose glanced up at Hapuseneb where he stood just behind her right shoulder. Hatshepsut saw her father observe the look that passed between them before he rose to embrace her. His arms were as strong as ever but there was no denying they were not as muscular as she remembered.

"Is everything all right, father?" She managed to make her voice sound light and happy as if she was confident the answer would be "yes" forever.

"Need there be something wrong for me to embrace the daughter of my heart? It is I who was concerned about *you*, Hatshepsut."

"Me? Why?"

He turned away toward the cedar-wood chair he favored as a throne in that private chamber. Heh—the handsome *neter* who symbolized infinity—formed the gently sloping back where he knelt on the hieroglyph for *gold* holding two notched palm branches, the bottom ends of which rested on the symbol for one-hundred thousand years written as a tadpole perched on the *shen* sign for *eternity*. A large *ankh* hung from the god's right arm and the columns of hieroglyphs framing him, topped by falcons wearing the red and white crowns, proclaimed her father's kingly titles. The chair's slender legs ended in lion's paws that rested on square golden pedestals. A winged solar disc forged of gold, and from which arms emerged in the form of cobras, spread protectively open behind Pharaoh's neck when he seated himself. Hatshepsut promptly went to kneel at his feet, turning her body toward the queen and the High Priest as she slipped an affectionately protective arm around one of her father's legs.

Hapuseneb said, "Amun-Re pointed at you today, Hatshepsut."

"Since the night you were born," the queen spoke, "there have been other signs the gods favor you, my daughter."

"There have?"

"Yes," her mother said firmly but did not, to her disappointment, provide any examples she could fatten her vanity with.

"Today's sign, however," her father said mildly, "was too obvious to ignore."

"We have never ignored any of them," his wife pointed out without looking at him so that it was not clear who exactly she meant by "we".

"You will spend three days of the week with me in the Seal Room, Hatshepsut," Thutmose announced, resting a hand on her head as he looked steadily down into her eyes. "The following five days you will spend pursuing your education in the Temple of Amun under the sole guidance of Hapuseneb. On the ninth day, you will do as your mother says. On the tenth day, you will be permitted to rest. And so it shall be until your marriage to my son, the Crown Prince Amenmose, exactly two years from today."

Pharaoh had spoken.

In a rush of emotions, Hatshepsut saw everything his words meant. Senimen would no longer be her teacher. She would also dearly miss playing Senet with Puyemre. But her consolations would be great. She would be spending more time than ever with her father and half a week with Hapuseneb *every* week. The Celestial River had washed away her old life and fire from heaven had pointed her down a more disciplined and demanding path. She was thrilled and honored the gods seemed to be watching her so closely.

9

Re's Garden

The priest poured clean water from a *heset* jar over Hatshepsut's hands four times. In the hot morning, the sensation of cleansing coolness was especially welcome. The water was caught by a *shes* bowl made from layers of alabaster, each one a different and subtly luminous color in the sunlight. Every time she dipped her hands into the bowl—used in the *medu neters* as a determinative for the word *heb* which meant *festival*—she felt she was doing much more than cleansing them. During the ritual purification, she celebrated the beauty of the person she became as she divested herself of all joyless thoughts and feelings before entering the Temple's sacred precincts.

A second priest handed her a linen cloth with which to dry her hands and a third servant of the god knelt before her to remove her sandals. Another *shes* bowl, resting on a stone close to the ground, received the water that flowed over each of her feet four times. This part of the rite was less elevating for as the priest dried her skin she was reminded of the intense pleasure she experienced whenever Nafre massaged her feet. But the effect her attendant's skill had on her limbs was merely a reflection of the profound satisfaction she took in absorbing Hapuseneb's penetrating words and looks. The High Priest of Amun-Re relentlessly massaged her feelings with his demanding wisdom. The discomfort she experienced when he made her aware of her limitations was indistinguishable from the intense fulfillment of self-discovery. When she was with Hapuseneb, her thoughts and perceptions felt more energetic and supple; they seemed to dance with inspired confidence instead of merely to walk or stumble from one fact to another.

The individually unique layers of the *shes* bowl served as a reminder of the wholeness within all multiplicity, also expressed by her two hands and feet animated by a single heart. By the end of her purification, any discontented thoughts or emotional annoyances she might have brought with her had been washed away by the beauty of the sacred objects designed to hold and pour the life-giving water. The true meaning of being unclean and unworthy to enter God's house was failing to realize that *awareness* was the most sacred vessel of all containing as it did its own mystery.

Her favorite days were the ones during which she had Hapuseneb all to herself. However, she also enjoyed sharing the feast of his knowledge with other special students since Puyemre was one of them. She was not surprised her friend had been admitted into the Temple on the recommendation of his tutor for his thoughts were as agile, and often as entertainingly mischievous, as monkeys. He was able to leap directly to conclusions others struggled to reach and to pluck the answers to complex questions as casually as fruit.

Hatshepsut was the only girl in the group of seven students.

Djehuti had come all the way from Khemnu, The One of Thoth, to complete his education in the Temple of Amun.

Min-Hotep was a local boy from Iuny, located on the West Bank of the River just south of Waset. He had learned to read and write at home before furthering his education in the Corp of Pages like his older brother, Senmut, the Royal Scribe Bubu had taken such a liking to.

Amenhotep had been born in Abu near the first wild waters, a child of Anukis, the daughter of Khnum and Satis.

Useramun, the oldest son of Pharaoh's northern vizier, and Duauneheh, were both from Waset. Like Hatshepsut and Puyemre, they did not live in the temple but went home every day after their lessons.

At first Hatshepsut found it hard to concentrate in the company of so many young men who either stared at her as though they had never seen a girl before or did their best to avoid looking at her. Then Hapuseneb addressed her directly by asking her a question and she ceased to care about anything except capturing the truth for him in her answer. After that she relaxed somewhat and began studying her classmates with the avid curiosity a new face always aroused in her.

Puyemre sat on a papyrus mat beside her and his ability to make everyone laugh soon made her feel they had all been friends forever. She was possessed by the distinct impression they had all been together like this before. The sensation was like trying to remember a dream too late in the day for the details to still be fresh in her head.

In all the gardens, large and small, throughout Kemet, Amun ceased to be the Hidden One as He revealed himself in every flower. God was everywhere and nowhere, within her and outside her, in a single breath. The Temple's immense Pleasure House was divided by stone walls with gilded metal gates and every day Hapuseneb chose a different location for their lesson. The fruit trees and flowering shrubs growing where he led them were often symbolically relevant to the subject under discussion. Hundreds of trees were planted in neat rows—sycamores and date palms, Perseas, dom-palms and moringas, pomegranates, tamarisks, willows and other more exotic species. Flowers bloomed in square beds and along straight paths leading to ponds filled with fish. Pretty bridges spanned canals flowing beneath shaded pavilions. The heart of the garden was Amun-Re's vineyard.

The first time Hapuseneb brought his seven students together he asked them to observe how God's Pleasure House was equally beautiful everywhere, its divisions deliberate and effective but ultimately artificial. Then he requested that Amenhotep, Djehuti and Min-Hotep each tell everyone about the city of their birth and the local deities sacred to it.

Hatshepsut immediately understood the day's lesson—the garden was divided into many beautiful areas just as there were many great cities in Kemet, where Divine truths were expressed in a variety of ways, like different types of flowers blooming from the same dark soil. She longed to say so but remained politely silent, and it was not long before she forgot the selfish thrill of triumph as she was captivated by the love each youth revealed for his birthplace.

The name *Anukis* was a strange, exotic blossom she tentatively held for the first time with the fingers of her thoughts. Her feelings became the mysterious scent glands of her Ka as she listened to Amenhotep speak of the goddess worshiped in Abu and as far south as the wild waters leading into Kush. Also called The Embracer, Anukis was an ancient goddess of the hunt, a daughter of Re, like Sekhmet, who could also be as gentle as Bast. Anukis was the daughter of Khnum, the ram-headed Ka of Re who fashioned all living things. As Lord of the Crocodiles, Khnum controlled the life-giving force of the River from his home in the caverns beneath the first wild waters.

Satis, Mistress of Abu, was Khnum's consort. Like Hathor-Sekhmet, Satis was an Eye of Re. A silver amulet statue of Satis—a woman with a cobra rearing from her forehead beneath the horned white crown—always hung from a black leather cord around Amenhotep's neck. Hatshepsut felt less confused when she thought of Khnum, Satis and Anukis as flowers thriving in their own special area of a single Divine garden where also grew Amun, Mut and Khonsu and the even more ancient trinity of Ptah, Sekhmet and Nefertum.

Min-Hotep began by speaking proudly of his older brother who, fresh out of the Corp of Pages, had been offered a position as a minor clerk to an important nobleman. Senmut had risen so quickly in the ranks of his master's staff that he caught Pharaoh's eye and was soon promoted to Royal Scribe. The brothers had grown up in close proximity to Waset in Iuny, where they called Hathor *Iunyt* and Horus *Montu*, Horus of the Strong Arm. The names were different and yet they were the same *neters*, part of a single tree with multiple limbs. The shadows cast by all the trees growing in God's Pleasure House appeared chaotic and confusing but the sap rising through each one shone with the same creative magic. All diversity, Hapuseneb told them, arose from a single and unimaginably powerful seed.

"But a fig tree cannot grow from a pomegranate seed," Min-Hotep protested. He was so reluctant to challenge the High Priest he often remained silent even though the restless way he wriggled against his papyrus mat made it clear he wished to speak.

"That is true," Hapuseneb agreed. "But I refer to the seed of all seeds that is also the soil in which it germinates and the air and light in which it grows—the One that is Three and Three in One."

Hatshepsut felt sorry for Min-Hotep when he looked ashamed at failing to see the obvious. His father, the Honorable Ramose, was not of noble blood and yet no less than two of his sons had found their way from provincial Iuny to Waset, one of them to the great Temple of Amun-Re and the other to Pharaoh's Seal Room.

Duauneheh was the tallest of the boys, a fact that seemed to make him feel awkward rather than superior whenever he stood, and was forced to look down on everyone. Perhaps, she thought, the gods had made him that way in order to force him to be less boringly humble. It was clear he was already good at seeing beyond himself and respecting others. If he stopped being ashamed of his natural pride the Goddess would probably be more inspired to nurture him and fill out his bony limbs. If that ever happened, he would be quite attractive, especially from the neck down. There was nothing at all wrong with his face, it was nicely proportioned, but his perpetual concerned and somewhat uncertain expression failed to hold her interest.

Djehuti's expressions, on the other hand, were fascinating to watch for they passed across his features as obviously as light and shadow. He did not say much but she sensed his thoughts swimming swift and abundant as fish beneath the surface of his dark-brown eyes. He was only a year older than she was and of the same slight build as Puyemre.

Amenhotep's devotion to his local goddess pleased Hatshepsut, although she hoped he would come to realize Satis was only an aspect of Hathor. She found herself glancing his way whenever he reached up to stroke the little silver woman's body resting against his bare chest. The relaxed intensity of his concentration as he listened to Hapuseneb attracted her, and when he spoke, it was always in a quiet but decisive voice. She liked that he did not doubt himself but rather valued the power of understanding which could grow from the hard-to-crack seed of every profound question.

Useramun was the oldest of the group, nearing his fifteenth year, and a credit to Waset in appearance and demeanor. The Goddess had blessed him with long strong legs and broad shoulders. There was always the hint of a smile on his lips (at least whenever she was around) and it was easy to see that when framed by a wig his face would rival even the Crown Prince's in masculine perfection. He was not shy about meeting her eyes, a fact she immediately respected him for. However, his failure to look away after she turned her attention elsewhere came close to annoying her by making her unnaturally aware of all her movements and gestures.

It occurred to Hatshepsut to wonder how all her new friends had come to be there with her in the Temple, and the next time she was alone with the High Priest she asked him.

His reply was to instruct her to take her scribe's materials out of the leather pouch she always carried with her and, when she was ready, to make a small circle with red ink in the center of her palette.

"That is the heart of Kemet," he said, "Pharaoh's residence—Beloved of Maat, the Horizon of Re—joined with the great Temple of Amun, earthly rule reflecting Divine order. I now wish you to draw, with black ink, slightly larger and larger circles around the red one until you have seven in total."

She obeyed him, striving to do so as neatly as possible only to discover that drawing perfect circles was more difficult than she would have thought.

Without touching it and smearing the ink, he indicated the outermost ring with a fingertip. "Here live the poorest citizens of Kemet," he said as she admired the way his nails were all trimmed down to the flesh and perfectly clean, "those who own no land and perhaps not even a single ass to do their bidding. People who must work all their lives for others."

"But no citizen of Kemet ever goes hungry," she quickly pointed out.

"Never," he agreed firmly. "The heart of Pharaoh beats wisdom and compassion, for you cannot have one without the other. Even the poorest man can find employment every year, when the River overflows and everywhere reflects heaven, by building and maintaining the temples of the *neters*.

"But you asked me a question, Hatshepsut, and you can answer it for yourself by drawing a straight line from any point in the six outermost circles that leads directly to the heart at their center. No matter where a Ba is born in the Two Lands its Ka has the power to fulfill its destiny. A common man may become the Eyes and Ears of the King. One of the many evils that plagued us—in those dark times when the Ba of Kemet was cut off from its Ka by unclean foreign blood—was the disruption of a system that has existed since the beginning of our history. Promising children from poor families are educated together with children of the nobility, even of Pharaoh, and groomed for positions in the priesthood, the civil service and the military."

"But how are they determined to be promising if they are all the way out here," she indicated the largest circle, "so far from the residence and the Temple?"

"Amun-Re and his bodily son command many pairs of Eyes and Ears, Hatshepsut. Every city and town in Kemet, no matter how humble, has a temple with a pendant cloth signaling the Divine presence beneath which there resides at least one priest who can see into the hearts of his flock. Restlessness and unhappiness are often signs of potential, especially in persons born to ignorant and superstitious parents. There are many other signs of wisdom and intelligence which can be discerned by those who know how to."

"Do all priests have the power to see into a person's heart?" she said, wondering what he saw in hers.

"No."

His abrupt negative response surprised her and the frown accompanying it seriously distressed her.

"There was a time when the answer to that question would have been 'yes'," he added, "but no longer."

"Why?" she demanded.

"Many temples that contain images of gods and goddesses are no more sacred than rotting barns filled with unhappy animals where priestly privileges are claimed by those who worship only their bodies. False servants of God stink of selfish emotions that contaminate them and all those they are in contact with like excrement. The sweet scent of the Divine is only a dream in their presence."

Hatshepsut was shocked. "But why are such priests allowed to live?"

"They do not live, they merely exist. Their noses inhale only air and not the breath of Shu."

"But they should not be allowed to remain priests!"

"That is why the Good God needs as many Eyes and Ears working in his service as possible. When such foul priests and officials are discovered, they are rooted out like weeds strangling all the flowers which would otherwise bloom in their vicinity."

Although lately she was making an effort not to display too much emotion around the High Priest to show him she was capable of exercising self-control, she could not keep the relief and excitement out of her voice. "Is that what you do when you travel as the Eyes and Ears and Mouth of the King, root out and punish evil doers?"

"To diagnose an infected wound is easy. To awaken and promote the strength of health is a more difficult and lengthy chore. The temples and secular offices in which unworthy persons exercise power in the name of God and Pharaoh are part of a living whole. In every temple, the relationship between heaven and earth is sustained and nourished by the receiving and offering of Maat. When an important office is profaned by an unworthy person, whose selfish heart blocks Maat, a dangerous imbalance is created that disrupts the flow of cosmic energy through the world."

"What do you do with such awful men when you discover them?" The idea of the High Priest being forceful—perhaps even justifiably violent as the spiritual general of Pharaoh—awoke a strangely delicious sensation of warmth between her legs.

"It all depends on the nature and extent of their transgressions," he said. "True justice is complex for if the punishment does not also serve to teach it becomes a crime in itself. The important thing is finding people to replace those who are unworthy to serve in positions of power, which brings us back to your initial question. Are you satisfied with your answer?"

"I am always satisfied with the answers you give me, Hapuseneb, but I am distressed to realize Maat still suffers so throughout the Two Lands. That means many people who were meant to find their way here to the Temple or to the residence may still be living in poverty and ignorance, unable to read and write the Divine Words that would help them understand themselves and what special thing they were born to do."

He smiled. "Exactly."

"When I become God's Wife and the queen," she vowed, "I will dedicate myself to restoring Maat throughout the Two Lands."

He stared into her eyes. "My heart rejoices in your words, Hatshepsut."

She looked away shyly. "You will help me in this task, Hapuseneb?"

"You have only to express your desires," he said quietly, "and I will do everything in my power to fulfill them."

Even though his voice entered her body through her ears she felt it deep in her belly.

* * * * *

Hatshepsut learned that Duauneheh was apprenticed to the masters of various crafts. He was familiarizing himself with the knowledge and skill exercised by men who productively enhanced the transformative power of materials. He had worked with tanners, saddlers and carpenters and was looking forward now to learning from spinners and weavers, smelters, metal-beaters and jewelers.

"Are you trying to decide what you wish to become?" she said curiously.

"I suppose so." He shrugged. "Although I believe I am more interested in all the different processes than in one craft in particular. The skills exercised in each of Ptah's workshops are separate and yet they often come together in one thing, a chariot, for example. A chariot is a marvelous blend of materials and designs that must be precisely followed by all the various crafts involved in its construction. They all work together to-" He stopped speaking abruptly, as did everyone else, when Hapuseneb appeared.

"Today's theme is composition," the High Priest stated without preamble.

Their lesson was to be held in the bark shrine of Senwosret, beside which Meri's brother had erected an alabaster chapel. Amenhotep had died before it was finished but Hatshepsut's father had completed it. The blue sash across his chest proclaiming his status as a Lector Priest of Amun, Hapuseneb's father, Hapu, had escorted them to there, and then left them to talk amongst themselves. He looked more like Hapuseneb's father's father for his wife, Ah-Hotep, had born their two sons late in life. There was always a kind smile on Hapu's thin mouth, which he seemed to open only when he had something important to say in the name of God. He did not need to waste his breath addressing his son's students for they always followed him obediently wherever he led them.

Senwosret's limestone bark shrine was truly magnificent. Exquisitely detailed carvings covered every available surface. On the exterior west wall were depicted the emblems and deities of Kemet's southern Nomes. On the eastern wall, the northern Nomes were all represented. Hatshepsut followed Hapuseneb up the steps cut into the short ramp leading into the sanctuary. Everyone else walked behind them.

The priest's quiet voice sounded even deeper surrounded by stone walls flowering with colorful scenes of Senwosret being crowned with eternal life by the gods Horus, Ptah and Amun, the latter also portrayed in his virile form of Min with an erect penis.

"The nature of life is composition," Hapuseneb began. "Different substances compose our bodies. A single desert mountain is composed of various rocks and minerals. Our eyes see different colors which compose what we perceive as a single image. Yet everything works together. Nothing is independent of anything else.

"Shu—the personification of air—enters your lungs through your nose and makes it possible for your heart to beat and for the blood to flow through your body because of the warmth and moisture personified by his sister, Tefnut. Generated by the division of a primordial wholeness, opposing and yet mysteriously complimentary forces compose incarnate life by way of attraction. Shu and Tefnut are the two lions of the horizon, called the *Ruty*, which symbolize the division of the One into Two—the First Occasion that engendered space and time. The lion facing west is yesterday and the lion facing east is tomorrow. The four cardinal directions are the children of Atum-Re who also embody the four primary elements contained in all that is created—Shu and Tefnut, Geb and Nut. When Shu separated Nut from her twin brother, Geb—heaven from earth—the space necessary for their Father to experience Himself was created. Geb twisted and turned furiously, spitting out the flames that formed mountains and deserts while Nut arched peacefully over him, the Divine womb of all the stars in the universe. Every evening Nut kisses the solar disc and swallows it as night falls. In the heart of winter the brightest star in the sky burns in the space between Nut's thighs, from which were born Osiris, Seth, Isis and Nepthys—the four *neters* which compose the human heart.

"The chapel where we are standing was designed to house the bark in which Amun-Re travels when he is on procession. Not a single figure or hieroglyph is randomly sized, colored or placed. The limestone into which they are carved also once interacted significantly with other materials—including fire, incense and water—all of them a vital symbolic part of the chapel's composition. Art is the language of Mystery. Art affects the heart directly whether or not the mind yet possesses the ability to read and understand it."

He paused and looked at each of their faces in turn, inviting questions or comments before he continued.

Everyone remained silent.

Except, Hatshepsut thought, *the silence itself.* She said in a respectfully hushed voice, "Why does silence have the power to ring in my ears when it is nothing?"

Hapuseneb looked directly into hers eyes and did not reply, which meant he expected her to think the question through and answer it herself.

"Is it because before the First Occasion there was nothing except emptiness and silence? Which means silence is the seed of everything, including sound itself, and I can hear only because of my ears, which are part of my physical *composition?*"

"You are correct, Hatshepsut, to a certain extent. Silence is the space between your heartbeats—the Divine force that always has been and always will be and from which all forms of life bloom and into which they all *decompose.* However, your senses did not themselves create hearing or vision anymore than a delicately woven dress brings to life the woman wearing it. Your Ka is not an insensible ghost, it is eternally beautiful with creative power, which it exercises over the elements constituting corporeal existence to fashion your physical body. Sensuality and the powers of attraction are poured into carnal forms but not limited to them anymore than the water contained in jars confines the River from which it was drawn. Like the elements composing it, only your mortal body is forced to obey the laws of growth and decay."

She inclined her head, smiling with pleasure at his response. Much of what the High Priest told them that day she had already known but he brought everything together in a way that made her feel as she had when she was a little girl and learning the names of all the things that surrounded her, at which point she seemed to see them clearly for the first time.

Size was profoundly significant in a composition. The king was always as tall as the gods because he was their earthly incarnation. Any other persons present in the relief or painting were invariably rendered on a more modest scale. Grown men and women often appeared small as children in Pharaoh's presence, their size in relation to the rest of the elements in the composition determined by their relevance. Prisoners of war and dangerous animals were portrayed much smaller in order to magically diminish their negative power, and to this end they were sometimes cut in half or beheaded.

The material from which an object was made was a vital part of its symbolic composition. The avenues of trees leading to temples represented the many long years of a wisely lived life in which every thought was turned toward its heavenly source like leaves to the sun. The bark of Amun, *Userhat,* Mighty of

Prow is Amun, was made of wood as a symbolic expression of the journey from sunrise to sunset, and from birth to death—the process of growth and decay set into motion by the desire in the Hidden One's heart to experience Himself.

The gold accents adorning the sacred wooden bark resting in a stone shrine spoke of Amun-Re's solar, incorruptible and immortal essence. Silver symbolized the moon and through its waxing and waning was associated with Thoth, Lord of Time and Measure. When mixed with silver gold became *neb-hedj*, white-gold, the most precious substance of all. It seemed to Hatshepsut that electrum embodied a perfect state of being in which it was possible to exercise command over the forces of light and dark, sun and moon, life and death, instead of being helplessly subject to them. She thought of her Ka as shining like *neb-hedj*.

Amun-Re's bark was now located in Djeserkare's alabaster shrine next door. Therefore, incense—the breath of the *neters*—the fire used to light it and water's cleansing coolness were now absent elements of the chapel's original composition. Incense, *senetcher*, was significantly related to the word *senetcheri*, to make Divine. When Senwosret made his burning offerings, he inhaled God, revealing the interaction between human nature and Divine energy whenever a sacred perspective is awakened.

Through colors, Hapuseneb said, their eyes perceived metaphysical forces at work. "The pure light from which specific colors emerge exists beyond the confines of the physical senses and yet, at the same time, is responsible for their highly specific palette which is composed by the infinitely creative force behind all forms of life, Atum-Re." An object's color could not be separated from its substance. *Iwen*, the word for color, could also mean *personality*, *nature* and *being*. Colors were mixed from pure minerals that defied decay, a fact that was, of course, a vitally important symbol.

There were six primary colors:

Black *kem* was sacred as the visual expression of silence, the cosmic seed of all light and life.

Red *desher* was the color of power, both positive and negative, of blood and attraction and the lifeless desert. Red ink was sometimes used to write the word *evil*.

White *hedj* symbolized pure unlimited Being. Priests wore white sandals because, ideally, their hearts were as free of doubts, fears and harmful desires as their bodies were clean.

Blue *irtiu* was water and the sky, the color of health, fertility and perpetual creativity. Blue embodied the transcendent nature of the cosmic energy that circulates through the world and everything in it.

Yellow *khenet* was the soul of the sun and the heart of gold, the only color besides black worthy of a *neter's* flesh as the embodiment of incorruptibility.

Green *wadj* was the spirit of growth, decay and regeneration, the color of Osiris, Lord of death and rebirth.

"All artistic compositions appear motionless," Hapuseneb concluded, "but in truth they are, like the senses composing our awareness, magic in action."

* * * * *

Prince Amenmose had been confined to his bed for several days with a terrible toothache. Hatshepsut felt sorry for him but was too busy to dwell on his indisposition.

Lately it pleased her to have her attendants arrange her hair in the style currently favored by unmarried women, which she would still be for another eight months. Her hair had indeed grown in as lustrous as her mother's hair but not as dark; the sun revealed glimmers of red-gold in the dark-brown strands she was very proud of. On her day of rest she had her hair washed in the morning, and then allowed it to dry in the sun as she was oiled and massaged. Afterward she sat in a low chair—either in her dressing room or beneath a pavilion in her garden—her legs languidly extended as Seshen trimmed her toenails and then painted them red. Every time she glanced down at her slender ankles it pleased her to be reminded her attractive powers were daily growing stronger despite the fact that her breasts were still disappointingly small; barely discernable buds crushed by her tight linen dresses. Meresankh painted her fingernails the same deep red while Nafre smoothed and softened her hair with a special mixture of beeswax and resin before parting it into three sections, bringing most of it forward over her shoulders. She left enough hair hanging in the back to divide into an additional three plates she braided tightly together, exposing the delicate sides of the pricness' neck in a provocative fashion which also helped keep her cool. Finally, the front sections were neatly composed into a mass of delicate braids framing her face.

Every tenth day Hatshepsut was more than happy to let Seshen and Meresankh's superficial chatter disperse the administrative details crowded into her head during her long afternoons in the Seal Room. She was becoming increasingly aware of the relationship between her body and her Ka, which was sometimes like comparing mud with white gold. The only things her flesh allowed her to care about when she was tired was the water refreshing it, the invigoratingly clean scent of the linen towel caressing it and the softness of the bed embracing it. Her magical Ka was only a dream.

As her attendants gossiped amongst themselves, Hatshepsut's awareness drifted off on a flow of memories in which faces and words rose before her eyes as randomly as fish leaping out of a pond shining vividly in the sunlight for moment...

A few days ago in the Seal Room, she had been pleased to see again the Deputy of the King's Son, Ruiu. She had never forgotten the night they stayed with him and his family during that endless journey up the River when she was little. He wore a floral collar and a stiffly pleated linen kilt that looked even whiter against his black skin. The magical power of the monument she had watched being carved so far away and long ago had not yet been breached except, occasionally, by a few raiding parties Ruiu easily crushed beneath his gilded sandal in the name of Pharaoh.

She spent one special afternoon alone with her father in the Seal Room. He showed her an ancient map where beneath the starry womb of Mother Nut the world was drawn as a circle composed of four rings. The outermost ring represented the Great Green—the vast body of water on which floated the island of Kemet's long-time friends, the Keftiu.[13] The second ring marked the location of all other foreign lands. The third and innermost ring was resplendent with the forty-two standards representing the Nomes of Kemet. The center of the map was the Dwat, the magical heart of the world marked by the east-west course of the sun and the south-north flow of the River.

"Kemet is the image of heaven, Hatshepsut," Thutmose caressed the map as lovingly as if it was living flesh, "the place where all the forces that actuate and govern the Divine will are properly sustained and nourished."

She would never forget those hours alone with her father. Whatever the reason for the note of sadness in his voice it rang distressingly through her heart. In that moment she loved him with such force she had to blink back tears that threatened to flood several Nomes. More than ever she appreciated the fact that he was sacrificing some of his valuable time to educate her himself.

"The materials we need to build and to make all those things you cannot imagine living without," he smiled at her, "come from many different places." He unrolled another papyrus on which she immediately recognized most of Kemet's Nomes by their individual emblems set atop a standard. This second map was new and very detailed, identifying each Nome's principal cities and towns, irrigation canals, production areas and residential lands. Miniature hieroglyphs, almost impossible to read, described the type and quality of the Nome's soils along with their locations and, if it varied from the norm, the length of the local cubit. All the temples, and the *neters* to which they were dedicated, were also listed.

"The River looks like a flower with a very long stem," she observed reverently.

"It is the heavenly lotus," he agreed. "And see how rich the lifeless sands surrounding it are in materials precious to gods and men?"

Gold, she was pleased to note, was mined not too far south from Waset in the eastern desert, although much of it came, along with black ivory, from wretched Kush.

Also near Waset, on the western side of the River, stretched rich quarries of limestone also found near Djeba and not far from Mennefer.

Copper was mined in the eastern desert, deep in Seth's territory, as well as farther north in Roshawet, the Land of Turqoise.

Granite lived just north of Abu in the west and north of Abedju. Looking at the map deepened her respect for Menkaure the Divine, who had built his pyramid entirely of red granite. The heavy stones used for its construction had journeyed a formidable distance from their quarries.

That afternoon her father must have sensed she was particularly tired because when a herald announced the Royal Scribe, Senmut, he gave her permission to leave. "It is hot," he said. "You may go for a swim, my dear, and enjoy yourself for the rest of the day."

Her right shoulder brushed against Senmut's arm as she ran eagerly out of the stuffy room...

"We have finished arranging your hair, my lady," Nafre told her.

She blinked, returning lazily to the present.

"You are a vision of loveliness," Seshen declared, as always.

She was glad they had not yet painted her eyes as she relished rubbing them like a cat with the backs of her hands and yawning. "Is my brother feeling better?" she said absently, contemplating a visit to her menagerie. She missed her pet lion, which was no longer an adorable little cub but an impressive young beast she had named Shu. In truth, she was a little frightened of his deadly teeth and claws but she was determined to teach herself to feel absolutely safe and superior in his presence.

Abruptly, she realized no one had answered her question about Amenmose.

"Well?" she snapped, sensing the tension but refusing to acknowledge it for fear of what it might mean.

"He is suffering from a fever, my lady," Nafre admitted.

Seshen declared, "Everything he eats and drinks comes right out again!" her morbid glee only slightly tempered by concern for her mistress' feelings.

Nafre cast Seshen a disapproving glance. "The priests of Sekhmet are with him night and day, my lady, and everyone knows they are great of magic."

"The prince is also young and strong," Meresankh added hopefully.

"They say-" Seshen began, but a stern look from Nafre stopped her short.

"*What* do they say?" Hatshepsut demanded.

"They say demons invaded the prince's body through the black hole left in his mouth when the priests pulled out his tooth," Seshen made an effort to sound concerned as she repeated what she had heard. "They say these demons are consuming all his food and getting drunk on his wine so nothing he eats nourishes his body."

"Even if that is true, my brother is strong enough to defeat them!" She sounded angry because she was desperately trying to convince herself.

Her attendants glanced dubiously at each other but did not dare contradict her.

10

Oracle of Amun

"*F* stands for air and breath," Hapuseneb said, "an essential quality of physical life. *Ner* expresses the concept of Divine energy contained within the substance through which it becomes incarnate. *Nefer*—*ner+f*—refers to the form of the person or thing in which the Divine desire is actualized and fulfilled. As you know, the common meaning of *nefer* is *beauty* but *nefer* also forms part of the words for happiness and good fortune, health and perfection."

"Is that why so many vases are shaped like the *nefer* sign, because the Divine energy responsible for the *neters* of Creation is contained in everything just as jars hold life-giving water?"

"Yes, Hatshepsut. The absolute life poured into and contained within all mortal vessels is eternal."

"And the word *ner+t* is *neter*, meaning *god*."

"Yes," he prompted, his eyes urging her to go on.

"*T* relates to earthly things. *Ner* expresses the absolute power that pours itself into the forms of matter without ever being limited by them. That is why *neter* is the word for god."

"Correct. The universe is the Mother of Atum," he said, "and the gods are the Laws of Becoming—*neter-nefer*."

She stared at him longingly. The shadow of the beard he never allowed to grow was once more mysteriously darkening her thoughts. His mouth was not as sensually full as Amenmose's, it was longer and firmer, and she could feel all its expressions as though it was touching her. Unfortunately, it never came close to actually doing so.

He clenched his right hand and held it out toward her. "Touch it," he commanded.

Her breath caught and she dared to obey him only because she was afraid he might change his mind if she hesitated.

"Tell me what it is," he said.

The longed for sensation of her skin caressing his made it almost impossible for her to think. "Your hand?" she replied foolishly.

He smiled.

For a wild moment she dared to think her touch was pleasing him.

"What *sign* is it?" he clarified.

She felt incredibly stupid but it did not matter because he was actually letting her hold his hand in both of hers. "*Khefa*," she said, surprised and relieved she was able to remember anything.

"Can you tell me just by feeling it what it means, Hatshepsut?"

She was glad they were sitting down because she was increasingly weak with joy. Not only was she touching him, he was giving her permission to continue caressing him!

"What it means?" she echoed, then took a breath and made a supreme effort to concentrate.

His flesh was warm, not as soft as hers but certainly not rough. The most distinct impression she got was one of firmness. Clenched into a fist his hand was hard, full of suppressed strength.

"It feels hard beneath the tenderness of your skin," she began breathlessly, glancing up into his eyes, "closed and contained... like a seed that can burst open at any moment. It feels powerful." She never wanted this particular lesson to end.

"That is correct," he said, but did not pull his hand away. "*Khefa* is both latent creative energy and the Divine will actualized in all the laws of creation represented by the fingers of the open hand."

When he slowly unclenched his fist, she pretended not to be expecting it so she could continue holding on to him. "God's Hand!" she whispered reverently.

"No." Grasping her right hand in his, he gently curled her fingers over her thumb to make a fist as small and cool as his had been large and warm. "*Yours* is God's Hand, my lady, and soon you will be God's Wife."

* * * * *

When the queen and Inet suddenly appeared in her gaming room where she was playing Senet with Puyemre—a pleasure she had not enjoyed for more than three months—the first thing Hatshepsut noticed were all the white strands sinisterly decorating her former nurse's hair.

Puyemre's mother, Neferiah, was watching the game while petting Bubu, who had managed to curl his considerable bulk up on her small lap. Now that he was old and enjoyed napping even more than he did hunting, he was more sociable with the few people he approved of.

Hatshepsut was so surprised by the unannounced visit that she simply stared at the newcomers. She had been about to make the final move which would secure the health and happiness of all those she loved.

She set the lion-head gaming piece down on the appropriate square. "Mother?"

Neferiah whispered something in Bubu's ear.

The cat promptly leapt off her lap and headed toward the door as with her eyes the lady silently commanded her son to follow them.

Hatshepsut watched them go with her voice caught in her throat. "Is… is father all right?" It took all the courage she possessed to ask the question, and then to wait an endless moment for the reply.

"Thutmose, may he live, is as strong as the Buchis bull," her mother assured her. "Unlike his ill-fated sons."

Hatshepsut pushed herself away from the table and got to her feet. She could not face sitting down the battle of sadness and anger being fought on the queen's face. The crocodile about to devour her happiness had blessedly turned away only to lash her agonizingly with its tail. For a moment she was numbed by the impact of the inconceivable news she was about to receive.

Inet said miserably, "Oh my dear!" and clutched an amulet that hung from a leather cord around her neck.

"Amenmose has gone to his Ka!" Ahmose announced loudly, almost impatiently, as if the prince had deliberately done something foolishly inconvenient.

The blow was so great she scarcely felt it. The next thing she was conscious of was Inet embracing her. It seemed to her she was a child again as the years were swept away by a flood of tears more devastating than the wild waters of the River. The only comfort available to her was to become a little girl again crying over a scraped knee, except the pain she experienced now was much *much* worse. The boundless ache burst her heart like a rotten fruit and made a horrible mess of all her feelings every time she thought *Amenmose is dead! Amenmose is dead!* She had never tasted so foul a fact in all her life. She sobbed so hard she could hardly catch her breath.

Inet crooned unintelligible words while gently stroking her hair. Her nurse's caress was all that kept Hatshepsut aware of the vessel of her body struggling against the drowning depths of the sorrow she suffered for her brother, so young and beautiful but now gone forever.

* * * * *

I love you through the daytimes,
  in the dark,
Through all the long divisions of the night,
  those hours
I, spendthrift, waste away alone,

and lie, and turn, awake till whitened dawn.

And with the shape of you I people night,

    and thoughts of hot desire grow live within me.

What magic was it in that voice of yours

    to bring such singing vigor to my flesh,

To limbs which now lie listless on my bed without you?

Thus I beseech the darkness:

    Where gone, O loving man?

Why gone from her whose love

    can pace you, step by step, to your desire?

    No loving voice replies.

And I (too well) perceive

    how much I am alone.[14]

Hatshepsut embraced a bitter-sweet comfort weeping in silent accompaniment to the sad songs Nafre sang for her. The emotion in her attendant's voice made her feel less wretched and alone. It did not help that countless others before her had suffered this same sorrow which was both agonizing and numbing—a fever of the soul that sapped the health of joy from her heart as nothing ever had before. She was plagued by memories, and then tormented by how few there were and how many more there should have been.

Amenmose's smile haunted her. Whether her eyes were open or closed, she could still clearly see his smiling face. His grin still had the power to make her feel the way it always had even though it lived only in her heart now. And yet his smile remained so vivid it felt like mysteriously more than a memory.

As the days passed, Hatshepsut came to believe, with a relief too deep to express, that Amenmose continued to live in the magical body of his smile. It was his Ka she had seen and loved in his carefree grin, the visible expression of the Divine energy shaping his physical form. Only his physical body was resting from life now. His Ka was the cosmic soldier that had armed his Ba with the bow of a joyful smile and it pierced her heart now with faith in its eternal nature.

One evening, half a moon after the Crown Prince's death, as Nafre strummed her lute in the lamp-lit pavilion, Hatshepsut defiantly raised her voice over the melancholy notes and said, "The pain of sorrow gradually decays, like the lotus flower I kept from my brother's grave."

Her attendant lifted her hands off the strings and a sudden quiet fell over the garden; all the frogs and crickets stopped singing their own songs as if to listen.

"Where tears end," she concluded fervently, "smiling memories play!"

Nafre bowed her head.

Once she determined it was vital she never doubt Amenmose was Divine, Hatshepsut stopped crying every day. To continue disconsolately grieving for the absence of his body would have been selfish on her part and insulting to him. Whenever she recalled the contagious joy of his grin she made it a point to smile back at him with her lips even though all she could think was, *I miss you, brother!*

One afternoon—while she was reliving one of the many times Amenmose had caught her by surprise from behind and tossed her in a pool—she felt herself genuinely smiling as she listened with her heart to his triumphant laughter. She did not doubt that Nepthys—inevitably charmed by the young prince's beauty and wit—had immediately taken him under her protective wings. Nepthys understood how much Hatshepsut missed her brother, and how much it hurt he could no longer return the earthly love she still felt for him. The lonely wife of Seth, the sweet and gentle Nepthys would surely heed the prayers of the princess of Kemet and lead Amenmose safely along the dangerous paths of the Dwat straight into the golden hall of Osiris, where every true heart became one with Maat.

She was very glad Hapuseneb had taught her the true meaning of *nefer* because it seriously comforted her. Amenmose's mortal vessel was broken but who he truly was could never be destroyed.

Not even her beloved brother's death had been able to make her forget her last day in the Temple when Hapuseneb commanded her to hold, and even encouraged her to caress, his hand. The memory was like a light in the darkness holding her fears at bay and giving her heart direction. She cherished it in secret while openly grieving. She took it to bed with her at night and woke with it in the morning.

She could no longer marry Amenmose but *nothing*, she vowed, would prevent her from becoming God's Wife. She had betrayed her brother a long time ago in her heart and at first his death had seemed to punish her for it. But the truth was the person she missed the most while she was confined by her sorrow was the High Priest of Amun.

* * * * *

All the people of Kemet—those magically living in the Dwat and those still doing everything they could to enjoy life on this side of the River—were happily preparing to celebrate the festival of *Apet-Aset*.

Since she moved from Mennefer to Waset, the princess had formed part of the procession from *Ipet Sut* to a smaller temple called *Ipet-Reseyet*, God's Favored Place. The festival—which had been conceived of in the time of Ahmose-Nefertari—had invariably proved rather uncomfortable for the princess, who still found it difficult to sit still and smile surrounded by so much excitement.

Hatshepsut almost envied her attendants' freedom. Meresankh, Seshen and Nafre would be out on the streets, just three of the hundreds of people laughing, drinking and dancing, invisible as drops of water in the surging currents of life. Wondering what it would be like to lose herself in the crowd for a while and become an anonymous part of one huge joyful body, she was unable to imagine it because the last thing she desired was to be like everyone else.

She had participated in the festival three times already but she had not truly understood what was happening until yesterday, after she spent the afternoon with her mother and Hapuseneb. It had been difficult for her to concentrate and not only because she was so honored by their combined attention. Whenever she was with the High Priest her blood seemed to purr through her heart and she felt utterly content. She was surprised he seemed unaware of the intense pleasure she took in his company. And yet sometimes—in moments as mysteriously hot and blinding as glancing directly up at the sun—she was sure he knew exactly how she felt about him. When he stared silently into her eyes she suffered a sensation between her thighs that almost hurt even though it was more wonderful than anything she had ever felt before.

Yesterday, however, she had not been alone with Hapuseneb but rather had been forced to share his company with her mother. She was disturbed by her jealous reaction to the quiet conversation the First Prophet of Amun and the queen had been engaged in when she entered the room. Thoroughly ashamed of herself, she had ignored the emotions fighting inside her and passionately concentrated on understanding the true meaning of the popular festival of *Apet-Aset*.

When the new day was come and it was time for her attendants to bathe and oil, dress and adorn her, Hatshepsut was more excited than ever because she now fully grasped the mystery of the First Occasion that would be enacted by the procession of the god and his family. Also oddly exhilarating was recalling the way Ahmose had studied her face yesterday, a pleased smile on her lips, as Hapuseneb raised his arms in respectful praise toward them both before he left the room.

On the other side of the River, Amenmose would also be enjoying the festival, although of course it would have been so much more splendid if they had been able to celebrate the gifts of boundless love and prosperity together. Hundreds of men and women would become one in the eyes of the gods during the eleven days Amun spent in his Favored Place, the popular name for what the priests called The Palace of Maat. Hapuseneb would be walking at the head of the procession, and yesterday before he left the room he had commanded her to be prepared. He had not given her a chance to ask "For what?" so she had directed her question at the queen, who had answered her only with that enigmatic smile.

Apet-Aset was a joyful festival of the inundation. Hatshepsut selected a girdle of miniature golden fish that seemed to swim around her hips held together by three strings strung with red and yellow beads. Her attendants slipped it on over her head because it had no clasp and she wore it provocatively beneath her white mist-linen dress. The thin straps holding the dress up were concealed by a floral collar composed of alternating rows of blue and white lotus petals, green Persea leaves, gold-flowers and red poppies. Seshen and Meresankh adorned her with it wistfully, obviously wishing they owned such a beautiful collar themselves even though the ones they wore, made of willow leaves and white lotus petals, were certainly lovely enough.

Her hair was pulled tightly back and contained beneath a ceremonial wig that fell forward over her shoulders in two long plates of black braids while a single plate fell heavily down her back, exposing her slender shoulders. It was her favorite wig because every braid was encased in evenly spaced golden tubes, hundreds of them designed to catch the sunlight and draw all eyes toward her. The wig was resplendent enough without the crown Nafre set on her brow made of solid gold inlaid with flowers made of lapis lazuli, carnelian and faience. The colorful stones surrounded the jeweled cobra coiling up in front of her forehead and protecting her with its all-seeing red eyes.

Made of gold, carnelian and turquoise, the bead bracelets she chose to wear reflected the colors of her collar. Meresankh and Seshen wrapped one around each of her wrists before locking the slide piece engraved with her name. The thirty-seven rows of gold, red and blue stones reached almost all the way to her elbows.

Onto each of her mistress' fingers Nafre slipped gold wire rings, their ends coiled around each other like linen thread, set with scarabs made of turquoise, carnelian and amethyst. The scarabs could swivel back and forth as if given life whenever she felt like playing with them.

Hatshepsut was gratified by how Kanefer's eyes widened when he saw her. He forgot to look down for a moment she gladly forgave him for. He had long ago been honored with the privilege of touching the princess so he could help her onto her litter where it rested on the ground. All she had to do was sit down but it pleased her to pretend she required his assistance. The thrill she sensed he experienced every time he felt her soft skin beneath his rough fingertips tasted better than the sweetest wine. She never said a word to him—the royal heralds always told him where she wanted to go—and she enjoyed anticipating the day she would address him directly and savor his reaction.

Her litter bore her the short distance from the royal family's living quarters to the ceremonial and administrative residence located just north-west of Amun's Temple. Pharaoh's lesser wife, Mutnofret, and his now only living son, Thutmose, owned their own elegant home but she knew (even though she had never seen it) that there was another palace nearby where dwelled the king's concubines and their children. Hatshepsut preferred to think that whenever they were in the same city her parents spent every night with each other just as they had when she was little. It was hard to picture how many beautiful women her father had collected. It seemed that every other moon a Royal Ornament was given away to a favored official. Even the High Priest of Amun had married one of them. She relished the gossip eagerly related to her by Seshen and Meresankh that Pharaoh's concubines pined away with loneliness, and were reluctantly glad when he offered them to a lesser man who would pay more attention to them.

Even on the private royal road, the sound of rejoicing drifted into Hatshepsut's ears. The citizens of Waset, as well as people from neighboring cities and towns, were already gathered in the marketplace outside the Temple buying and selling and giving thanks for the abundance the gods blessed Kemet with year after year. When the crowds waiting outside the ceremonial palace caught sight of her litter, the overwhelming sound of their rejoicing rushed in through her ears and filled her chest so that her heart almost ached from the wonderful pressure. Her lungs and throat were a living *nefer* vase from which a feeling of happiness—indistinguishable from the knowledge of her true imperishable beauty—flowed out of her freely through a smile she imagined warmed the hearts and stimulated the dreams of all who saw it.

Hatshepsut joined her parents in the antechamber of the palace *The Horizon of Re Beloved of Maat*. On the outside its blindingly white-washed mud-brick walls bloomed with colorful scenes of Pharaoh vanquishing the evil forces of chaos and death, *Isfet*, in the form of Kemet's enemies, all run through by the spear of truth and bound submissively at his feet—fear and despair conquered and controlled by faith and wisdom. Guarded by twelve shining golden cobras crowned with solar discs, the great double doorway was flanked by two rectangular towers which narrowed as they rose toward the sky and supported wooden flag posts flying red, blue and green banners.[15]

Inside the palace, the beautiful ordered universe of Maat thrived in giant columns carved in the shape of a papyrus blossoms and lotus buds rising into the ceiling's star-filled sky. She felt short of breath recalling what Hapuseneb had said about these columns as their upward thrusting force excited her like never before. She was surrounded by the virile power of Amun-Min manifesting in shafts of Divine procreative light that conceived the universe in a sperm-like shower of stars. She gazed up at the ceiling for a moment before looking down at the floor teeming with painted life as it gradually rose in the direction of the throne room—the heart of the palace embodying the Primordial Mound of Creation. All manner of realistically detailed fish swam down the broad isle between an abundance of vividly rendered plant life. The lower sections of the walls were adorned with animals which almost seemed to move and breathe in the flickering lamplight. Symbols of the god's phallus uniting floor and ceiling, heaven and earth, the mighty columns created the space necessary for the adoration of life, corporeal and eternal. The common people of Kemet, the *rekhyt*, were represented on the stone stalks in the form of lapwings with human heads flying in the direction of the throne room, their arms raised before them in the gesture of praise and rejoicing.

Queen Ahmose had donned an unusual collar made of willow leaves, blue lotus flowers and amethyst-colored petals. Hatshepsut had never before seen the armlets her mother was wearing made of solid gold and studded with red, green and blue stones. A raised *shenu* ring lying on its side contained Pharaoh's name, *Thutmose-Akheperkare*, and was protected by two miniature lions with human heads wearing the striped *nemes* headdress. The queen's tight-fitting white tunic exposed the heavy armlets linking her husband's kingship with the fertile curves of her body. Her long black wig was adorned by a freshly plucked lotus blossom that hung over her forehead. The wrinkles decorating the corners of her eyes and mouth were scarcely noticeable, and when she smiled her beauty shone as powerfully as ever.

For the festival of *Apet-Aset*, Pharaoh wore the ritual *shendyt*—a short pleated kilt held up by a belt of colorful beads to which a black bull's tail had been attached. The white head scarf framing his face decorated with blue stripes represented a lion's mane and the union of Divine and physical strength, for there was truly no separating them. The same symbolism applied to the bull's tail which made him look even taller and stronger. Around his neck he wore a magnificent broad collar composed of blue beads made of glass alternating with fresh leaves and flowers arranged in nine rows on a half-moon shaped papyrus base. To his wrists clung matching rigid gold bracelets on which winged lapis-lazuli scarabs held up green solar discs while cradling the *shen* sign for eternity between their bottom legs. On the back of the bracelets, visible when he raised his arms in praise, *shenu* rings contained his two great names crowned by solar discs.

The joy of the people outside the palace was heard to intensify and a few moments later the Lady Mutnofret, accompanying Pharaoh's youngest son, joined them in the ante-chamber. For more than four months Hatshepsut's heart had relentlessly beat grief for Amenmose and desire for Hapuseneb. She had not even thought of her remaining half brother. It struck her now that this boring little boy would one day be Pharaoh. Thutmose, who disliked games because they injured his pride if he lost, had won the ultimate prize without even trying. His three older brothers had been knocked off the board one after the other. She did not believe the gods played with men's fates, it was her opinion life was like Senet—her Ka controlled the circumstances of her destiny like gaming pieces and determined if her desires were fulfilled or thwarted. Ever since the death of her baby sister, Neferubity, she had believed everyone rested from life when they were meant to. She had tried, and failed, to suppress her conviction that Amenmose was in some sense responsible for his own death. Her brother's Ka had pulled him abruptly from life, almost as though his body was only a rotten molar in its magical mouth, which was full of endless forms through which it could dig into its mysterious hunger for sensual experience. If what she believed was true, the Ka of her stiffly handsome little sibling was potentially quite powerful. On the other hand, he was only eleven-years-old; it was entirely possible he would prove no greater of magic than his older brothers.

The festival of *Apet-Aset* officially began after the royal family was carried in their litters from the palace into the Temple of Amun. The polished lances of Pharaoh's personal guard reflected the sunlight and gilded the edges of the crowd's darkly surging mass. The throngs of people made Hatshepsut think of malleable mud in which the fine linen worn by more affluent spectators stood out in refreshingly lovely groups like white lotus flowers. Hapuseneb had told her yesterday that most people did not realize the festival's sacred spirit was actually initiated the very moment Pharaoh and his loved ones emerged from the ceremonial palace heading in the direction of the Temple.

"The deliberate move from the earthly center of power to its Divine heart is an expression of the enlightened individual's grasp of his true eternal nature," he explained to her. "The journey from the palace to the Temple symbolizes God become fully aware of Himself through His own creation, which as you know is the definition of *Akh*—the knowledge that death is only a return to our cosmic origin. The rituals enacted in God's house honor the mysterious processes of incarnation—the unfathomable pumping heart of Creation."

The great double doors set in the wall surrounding *Ipet Sut* were already open and the outer public courtyard within was full of people as even more kept flowing in. A path was effortlessly cleared before Pharaoh more by respect and awe than by his personal guard. The frightened bleating of goats and sheep abandoned as offerings contributed sour notes to the elevating music of a trumpet announcing the arrival of Amun-Re's bodily son.

As always Hatshepsut hated not being able to look freely around her. She longed to study the faces turned up toward her and to gaze up in wonder herself at the rays of light of the First Occasion symbolically captured in her father's two Monuments of Heh. But when the great inner doors began opening for the king and his family she forgot everything except the fact that Hapuseneb was waiting for them.

The queen had said a few things yesterday about the festival but mostly she had deferred to the High Priest of Amun, as if she knew her daughter was more likely to listen attentively to him.

Apet was the word for "joining together" and for "gestation" which related it to *Ipet*, the benign white hippopotamus goddess, mother of Osiris, who personified the city of Waset as an aspect of the Great One, Tawaret.

Aset was the word for "throne" and the name of Isis, wife of Osiris and mother of Horus.

It was all rather confusing until Hapuseneb said, "The festival of *Apet-Aset* celebrates the Divine Mother. As you already know, a female hippopotamus is the personification of the physical substance which gives birth to our sense of self, and then seems to devour it by way of death and decay. But in truth when we die, we enter an even greater womb where we develop and grow into our latent powers.

"When, in the company of Pharaoh, God journeys forth from his home to the House of Mut built beside the sacred waters of *Isheru*, and from there travels to the Palace of Maat where he spends eleven days and nights, what is happening, Hatshepsut?"

"In *Isheru* Amun enters the moonlit waters of the womb of the Goddess, and in The Palace of Maat he assumes flesh and blood through his bodily son, the king."

"And when God returns to *Ipet Sut* accompanied by Pharaoh, what is happening then?"

"Amun-Re is returning to his Divine source—the timeless force that penetrates and shapes the sensual substance of the Goddess just as the male seed enters the female womb and engenders all the beautiful pleasures made possible by our highly specialized senses. Amun, Mut, and their child, Khonsu, are Three in One and One in Three."

When she finished speaking the priest and the queen glanced at each other in a way that inspired her to add, "The festival is called *Apet-Aset* because the womb of the Goddess is the seat of earthly life, the throne from which God issues the Laws of Becoming. *Aset* is Isis, the wife of Osiris, the man in the god, and the mother of Horus, the god in man."

Yesterday evening as she ignored her food and drank more wine than usual, as she lay in bed attempting to sleep, all that morning as she was bathed and adorned, and now as her litter entered Amun's sacred precinct, Hatshepsut kept remembering the way Hapuseneb had looked at her after she finished answering his questions, before he suddenly commanded her to be prepared and left her alone with the queen's satisfied smile.

Waiting for Pharaoh and his family inside *Ipet Sut* were all the greatest men in Kemet accompanied by their wives. Both sexes were resplendent in luminous white linen, their sweetly oiled limbs adorned with colorful gemstones. Directly across from the nobles, on the eastern side of the courtyard, over one-hundred priests formed a three-layered crescent behind Amun-Re. The god's bark was placed in the center of the great open court with its prow facing west, the direction from which the king approached traveling east toward life. Beside *Userhet*, facing north and south, sat the smaller gilded wooden vessels of Amun-Re's consort, Mut, and their child, Khonsu, each one surrounded by eight priestesses, the Songstresses of the God.

Clad in a red-and-blue dress sewn with feathers, a papyrus staff grasped in her right hand, Mut was a beautiful woman wearing the queen's vulture headdress surmounted by the red and white crowns of the Two Lands. Her son, Khonsu, was a tall and lovely boy sporting the side-lock of youth and the short curved beard of a god. Around his neck hung the vividly colored *Menit* necklace—the attractive force of the Goddess which holds creation together. In his hands— emerging from the white garment in which he was swathed almost as tightly as a mummy—he held the crook and flail in addition to a *djed* scepter.

The First and Second Prophets of Amun, both wearing leopard-skin cloaks, stood before the large central bark. God's statue, removed from its permanent stone sanctuary, occupied a temporary wooden shrine visible over their shoulders.

Hatshepsut's litter veered to the left and was set down directly across from Khonsu's bark shrine as the queen's litter turned to the right and headed for its rightful place before Mut. The instant he was set down Pharaoh stood before his Father.

She concentrated on the figure of the High Priest resplendent in white sandals, a short white kilt held up by a golden belt inscribed with sacred symbols, and a leopard-skin cloak draped over one of his shoulders, the anmial's head and two front paws resting against his stomach. The conquered predator drew attention to his sleekly oiled muscles, and the pronounced tendons in his right arm revealed the controlled force with which he planted his magical black staff against the white stone floor.

The sound of the crowd outside, rejoicing in the official commencement of the festival, was muted by the stone walls and columns of the interior offering court which was closed to the public. To Hatshepsut, the voice of the multitudes sounded like the deep rushing sound of wind unfurling the sails of a ship sailing across the waters of heaven as she distinctly sensed currents of magic swirling around her body. Magic caressed her flesh and vibrated in her vision. She was caught in a net of magic woven by her senses. Gazing at Hapuseneb, her heart beat like a wild bird's wings soaring on a rush of longing to feel herself pinned beneath his strong leopard-clad body.

Holding a *shem*-scepter in each hand, one for Horus and one for Seth, Pharaoh stepped forward to make and consecrate the offerings. Hundreds of loaves of bread, dozens of jars of beer and wine, flowed into the bowels of the temple carried by young men and women dressed in plain white linen kilts and tunics. The first offerings were succeeded by baskets brimming with fruits and vegetables, then by casks of milled wheat and barley, followed by alabaster jars heavy with oils and unguents, which preceded precious boxes of incense and spices. Led by naked little girls, fat black-and-white cows entered God's House, their heads bobbing up and down as if silently saying "Yes, yes, yes!" to happiness and life with every step. The placid bovine procession was succeeded by a noisy stream of cages containing ducks, geese and other wild fowl clamoring for the freedom of heaven.

All during the king's adoration of Amun through the celebration of life's diverse beauty and abundance—on which God thrived through the well-nourished bodies of his priests—the Songstresses gave sound and form to the joy in everyone's heart:

A pilot who knows the waters, that is Amun,

> *a steering oar for the helpless,*

One who gives food to the one who has not,

> *who helps the servant of His house to prosper...*

My Lord is my protector,

> *I know his strength;*

He aids with ready arm and caring look,

> *and, all alone, is powerful—*

Amun, who knows what kindness is

> *and hears the one who cries to Him;*

Amun, King of the Gods,

> *strong Bull who glories in His power.*[16]

In reality, the offerings went on forever but during the festival they necessarily came to an end. The singers fell silent and temple musicians—hidden in the shadows of the colonnade—began pounding an urgent rhythm on their drums which made it seem as if God's heart was beating deep inside the body of His House, nourished and vitalized by all the offerings it had swallowed.

Hatshepsut's pulse sped up as the sistrums joined in and her breath caught watching Hapuseneb reappear before the god. His magical wand had been replaced by a crook and a flail made of dark-blue glass and metal cylinders overlaid with gold. She thought about how the hieroglyph for *flail* contained the word *akh*, and seeing it in his hand its significance fully struck her—discipline, control, the courage to punish herself for negative thoughts and foolish fears, were all qualities it was vital she embrace. Truly believing Amun-Re lived in her strengthened her physical health and helped make all her actions wise and effective by promoting the free flow of Maat through her heart.

The High Priest of Amun-Re handed Pharaoh two of the symbols of his office—the ability to lead compassionately while defending ruthlessly. She watched with pride as her father grasped the crook and flail and crossed his wrists over his chest like Osiris, who had been the first king of Kemet and was now Lord of the Dwat. She remembered the map he had shown her in which the Dwat was the heart of the world and understood that Pharaoh ruled over both the living and the dead as the General of Maat. It was impossible to imagine spoiled little Thutmose ever standing in his place. The thought made her want to laugh and cry at the same time. Then abruptly the very real possibility she was now expected to marry him, and everything this implied, hit her like a swarm of locust. Within seconds, nothing remained of her happiness. She had hoped, and almost dared to believe, she would somehow become one with Hapuseneb when she was crowned God's Wife. She had ceased to care about being queen. When Amenmose died she had set that desire aside like an old toy. More than ever all she wanted was to be God's Wife. She would *never* marry Thutmose!

As though he could hear her thoughts, Hapuseneb looked over at her.

Her desperation and anger at once transformed into hope and excitement beneath the breathtakingly discerning touch of the High Priest's eyes.

* * * * *

Like morning and evening, youth and old age walking timelessly side-by-side, the First Prophet of Amun, Hapuseneb, and the second Prophet of Amun, Amenhotep, led the procession out of the temple. Another priest strode ahead of them clearing a path through the crowd that parted in awe before his falcon-head mask fashioned of gold and precious stones. Wearing stiff knee-length kilts tied closed above the waist, twenty-four priests bore the bark of Amun on their bare shoulders while half as many carried the shrines of Mut and Khonsu. Eight more priests wearing black jackal masks over short red kilts and gilded leather sandals walked on either side of the celestial boats, tirelessly wafting incense over them. The doors of all three shrines had been closed because the multitudes could not look directly upon the gods.

From her place near the rear of the procession, Hatshepsut could see, and was fascinated by, the priests of Anubis. Their jackal heads, with their fiercely pointed snouts, turned slowly from side to side as though smelling the crowd. The masses of people seemed animated by a single pulse as the musicians of Amun never for a second stopped beating their drums. Hundreds of people talking and laughing merged into one vast and soothing sound like the goddess Bast purring as hundreds of sistrums were shaken over and over again unceasingly. One of the priests of Anubis was taller than the others, his shoulders broad and his back lean and strong. Hatshepsut focused on him gratefully as the sight of him made it easier to look straight ahead and ignore the lure of the crowd.

Some of the lesser priests walking behind her began clapping in rhythm with the drums and abruptly a dwarf acquired a choice spot beside her litter by darting between a soldier's legs. In the corner of her eye, she glimpsed his full-size head and muscular limbs imprisoned in a child-size body. She longed for the vision of the High Priest in his leopard-skin. From the moment she saw him she had longed to touch the sleek animal flesh warmed by his body and to test the sharpness of the claws resting against his firm stomach. Wondering if the leopard's claws beat against his skin and scratched him as he walked, she gripped the sides of her chair in response to the hot stab of sensation she suffered deep between her legs.

The procession soon reached the Temple of Mut. Once they were safe behind the enclosure wall, the doors of the shrines were opened to admit air and light. She saw Hapuseneb again where he stood on one side of Pharaoh on the western shore of *Isheru* watching the bark of Amun being carefully lifted from its stretcher and placed onboard a ceremonial ship. The priest in the falcon-head mask stood at the prow seeing the way ahead. Two of the priests of Anubis, who had exchanged their incense burners for long-handled oars, flanked God's shrine and propelled the boat forward while Pharaoh steered the course. At both the prow and stern two horned ram's heads faced east. The royal cobra rose from their foreheads as they merged with the ship through *Menit* shaped bodies ending in golden falcon heads regally regarding each other across the elegant vessel.

Hatshepsut gazed at God's body inside its glimmering shrine decorated on all three sides with kneeling figures of Maat surrounded by solar cobras. Directly overhead Re was a burning yolk in the curved shell of the sky through which the full moon was also faintly visible just above Mut's temple. Amun-Re's red face—reflected by the kilts of the Anubis priests dipping their oars into the shining water in a pulse-like rhythm—was both bright and dark, like night and day, life and death existing as one in his flesh fashioned by the magic of the Goddess. Amun's shirt, sewn from blue-and-white feathers, mirrored the heavens as twin golden feathers, each one divided into seven sections, rose tall and erect from his red crown. His short kilt was identical to Pharaoh's as he strode forward on his pedestal, the *was* scepter extended before him and an *ankh* held close to his right leg.

For the first time, Hatshepsut watched the slow progress of the bark without feeling bored. The mystery of the Goddess was being celebrated here in the House of Mut and it meant something to her now that she was finally a woman. Her eyes spent much less time worshipping the motionless figure of Amun than they did feasting on Hapuseneb walking beside the sacred lake—shaped like the half moon it was named after—at the head of the priestly procession which would greet the god's bark on the eastern shore where the queen and the princess stood waiting for them. The heat of the sun was intensifying as uncomfortably as her feelings, her excitement confused with anxiety. She prayed the High Priest would look at her again in the special way that made her feel as if she was about to die of joy. She knew he would not speak to her because it was not part of the rite but he absolutely *had* to look at her.

As he strode by, she inhaled an intoxicating whiff of his richly perfumed skin. Disappointment might have crushed her heart when his eyes failed to meet hers if she had not glimpsed Amun's golden shrine sailing on the dark waters of his vision, which at once worshipped and nourished God.

As the procession made its slow way out of Mut's complex and back into the deafening embrace of the multitudes, male and female acrobats twirled and leapt alongside the bark shrines, their supple bodies a stimulating contrast to the armed soldiers staring stiffly ahead of them as they walked protectively alongside the royal litters.

Hatshepsut was looking forward to the feast awaiting them in God's Favored Place just outside the Birth Chamber where Amun would dwell for eleven days and nights, during which vast quantities of food and beer would be freely distributed by Pharaoh to his children all throughout the Two Lands. But before Amun could enter the Palace of Maat eight bulls had to be ritually slaughtered. The excited voices of the spectators hushed to a reverent rumble as the sacrificial priests intoned inaudible prayers over the animals before swiftly slitting their throats. Spurts of magically virile blood dyed their kilts red, drenched the ground at their feet and flowed into the River through the canal.

The three bark shrines had once again been hoisted up onto strong shoulders when the old blind priest who served as Amun-Re's voice suddenly strode forward. At once the beating of the drums and the shaking of the sistrums ceased and left in their wake a deep sense of expectation. Those who could see what was happening mysteriously communicated their silent anticipation to the crowd's farthest reaches and the sound of hundreds of voices swiftly died away to a hushed murmuring.

From the vantage point of her litter, Hatshepsut stared curiously down at the oracular priest. She was enthroned beside the shrine of Khonsu with Thutmose and his mother occupying seats of honor behind her.

God's voice issued clear and strong from the old man's throat:

"Daughter of the Good God Akheperkare, Hatshepsut, Foremost of Noble Women, may only a princess be but through her body flows the shining blood of divinity!" His blind countenance turned unerringly in her direction and drew everyone's eyes toward her. "In her right hand the flail will smite Kemet's enemies and keep the Two Lands safe and whole. In her left hand, the crook will hold her children close to the heart of Maat in beautiful monuments splendid with the light of eternity. All of this Amun-Re foresees and is well pleased!"

There was a moment of silence, and then joyful exultant cries sprang up as the temple musicians beat their drums even more vigorously and sistrums purred approvingly. All the priests whose hands were free clapped a swift and irresistible rhythm that soon had people jumping up and down with their arms stretched up toward the princess. Her name was chanted until the drums were forced to obey its rhythm. "Hat-shep-sut! Hat-shep-sut! Hat-shep-sut!"

As if in a dream, she saw the High Priest of Amun turn his head in her direction. He met her eyes and she knew that when she died she would take the memory of his smile into the Dwat with her, where it would give her the power to conquer every obstacle on the path to her immortality.

11

Crook and Flail

As if she had dared to look directly at Re when he was at his most powerful, Hatshepsut was strangely blind to all the once enjoyable details of her life. At night she slept fitfully, her dreams black spaces surrounding the memory of a moment that lasted mere heartbeats and yet mysteriously gave life to a whole other person inside her. More than once she woke with her right hand crooked between her thighs as she remembered the secret way Hapuseneb had smiled at her.

One morning she cried out in fear when she seemed to feel her Ba beating its Divine wings in her heart and soaring away on a shaft of sunlight. Breathless with joy she closed her eyes but when she opened them again, she was still lying safe inside her body. Her heart beat so vigorously in her chest she could feel it all the way down between her legs.

The High Priest of Amun was working an irresistible magic on her which made it impossible to concentrate on anything except the thought of him. His magic was so powerful she had no desire whatsoever to break the spell he had cast on her. The only thing that mattered was when she would see him again. With every hour that passed the painful pressure in her chest intensified as if she was drowning on air because it remained empty of his presence.

Four days after the end of the festival of *Apet-Aset* Pharaoh summoned his daughter to the throne room of the ceremonial palace beside the Temple of Amun-Re. She had not seen him since the great feast outside the Birth Chamber in God's Favored Place, where she had found it nearly impossible to swallow food and temptingly easy to drink. Everyone had kept staring at her except for her father, who had only looked at her once, his eyes inscrutably dark. But then he had blessed her with his usual affectionate smile and helped restore her appetite. The priests had not taken part in the public feasting.

Her attendants quickly prepared her for the royal audience. Ever since the Oracle of Amun, Seshen and Meresankh had behaved even more respectfully toward her. They seemed almost afraid to touch her, as though her skin might burn their fingertips. She was more grateful than ever for Nafre's ability to take gentle but firm control of everything. Nafre applied her make-up before helping Seshen and Meresankh adorn her with a fresh floral collar, matching bracelets, a long wig and a golden circlet fronted by the royal cobra. She dearly wished her mother would come to see her and tell her what was happening but the queen did not appear and she found it difficult to think clearly wondering if the High Priest of Amun would be there.

Her half-brother was waiting for her in the antechamber. For once he was unaccompanied by his mother and stood with his shoulders thrown back looking almost as stiff as his own statue. The vulnerability she glimpsed in his eyes when he looked at her struck a compassionate chord in her heart and she smiled at him. For some reason his discomfiture made her feel more confident.

They were announced by the joyful sounding of trumpets. In the throne room, high ranking courtiers formed a living colonnade offering praise to the children of the Good God Akheperkare with their raised hands held before their faces. Smiling, Hatshepsut walked a few steps behind her half brother. She could see Akheperseneb, Ineni and Ahmose-Pennekkheb occupying positions of honor near the dais. Senmut stood much farther down the line. She noticed him because he was considerably taller and younger than the officials around him. Hapuseneb stood behind the queen. Pharaoh and his Great Royal Wife were at their most awe-inspiring seated on thrones made entirely of gold and precious stones. Akheperkare wore the double crown and in his hands—crossed at the wrists against his bare chest—he grasped the crook and the flail. Such a quantity of gold embraced and surrounded the king and queen of Kemet it was hard to look at them directly. Dozens of alabaster lamps—shaped like lotus chalices flanked by figures of the god Heh kneeling on papyrus plants holding up *ankh* signs and *shenu* rings containing the king's name—rested on stone bases carved in the form of low tables. Light washed over the gilded wooden dais, transforming the man Thutmose and the woman Ahmose into a god and a goddess luminous with all the beauty of an abiding power at once earthly and eternal.

Hatshepsut prostrated herself before her beloved parents, glad to give her eyes a moment's rest from trying not to look at Hapuseneb instead. Striving to move as gracefully as possible, she regained her feet and stepped up onto the dais behind her brother. Two smaller thrones had been placed on either side of the royal couple and as she claimed the one next to the queen, she still did not look at the High Priest. Instead, she found herself focusing on Senmut's distant face during the long formal speech Pharaoh delivered to the assembled company. Until the Royal Scribe dared to meet her eyes, then she quickly averted them. She recalled the feel of her skin caressing his and wondered if he was also remembering the oddly stimulating sensation. He was a non-royal, a commoner, the mere possibility that he was thinking such a thought should have affronted her and yet, for some reason, it did not.

Princess Hatshepsut's forthcoming marriage to her half-brother was announced and Thutmose's position as Crown Prince was made official. What surprised everyone—she later learned from her mother—was the order in which the king informed the court of what it already expected to hear.

"Everyone was led to understand, without it actually being said, that his youngest son's claim to the crook and the flail is contingent upon his marriage to you, Hatshepsut."

"The High Priest was also pleased by this?" It distressed her that Hapuseneb did not seem to care if she married someone else. He was already wed himself to a silly Royal Ornament yet everyone knew powerful men were not limited to one wife if they also desired another...

"He was *very* pleased," Ahmose assured her with a smile. "Think about it."

"Think about what?" she said petulantly. "That I am soon to be married to a child?"

"You are being foolish, Hatshepsut. Your young woman's heart is making it difficult for you to think like the queen you will one day be."

"But the voice of my heart is all that matters," she dared to argue. "You told me so yourself, mother. You said my thoughts were as cold and unreal as moonbeams compared to the beautiful power of my feelings which burn as warm and powerful as the sun."

"I am pleased you remember what I tell you, my daughter, but you are deliberately misunderstanding me now. The sun and the moon are the two Eyes of Horus and without one, he would be half blind. Thoth, Lord of the Moon, is the scribe of Re and the master of Divine self-expression. It is Thoth who provides the words that enable you to understand the feelings burning in your heart and to *control* them, empowering you to create a life devoted to Maat."

"But what of Hathor? Why has she suddenly transformed into Sekhmet and devoured my happiness with a painful and yet terribly wonderful feeling?"

"The wonderful feeling you speak of is Hathor's sublime gift. The blinding hunger and frustration you suffer is the domain of Sekhmet and of the flesh. And yet, as you said, there seems no separating them. But remember who it was brought Sekhmet back from Down Below."

"Thoth?"

"Yes. Re sent Thoth disguised as a baboon, and Shu in the form of a lion, to bring his daughter home again. Sekhmet traveled far into Down Below to indulge her voracious carnal appetites but she was never satisfied. The gods found her and brought her back to Kemet where they plunged her into the sacred waters beside the tomb of Osiris, from which she was born again as a beautiful young woman who can also take the form of a cat. Ever since then Sekhmet has been at the service of men and women in love through the tenderness and understanding of Bast.

"You must call upon Thoth who, as a baboon, can help you laugh at yourself when you become so self-involved and foolishly morose that you forget your heart is as strong as a lion. While you still breathe, you possess the ability to conquer everything blocking the path of your desires as long as they remain faithful to Maat. Your heart, like Re, must ask Thoth and Shu to help you master Hathor's power that becomes destructive when blindly indulged. When you burn with lust, Sekhmet has you by the throat. When your heart glows with love Bast licks your hands and purrs at your feet."

"But mother, I feel as though Hathor and Sekhmet are *both* possessing me!"

"They often do," she agreed, and her smile looked sad. "You must learn to master the force of the Goddess, Hatshepsut."

That was a daunting thought. It did not seem possible, especially since Sekhmet always came to her when she was lying helpless in bed dreaming of Hapuseneb both asleep and awake. She wondered if she dared tell her mother about the way her right hand was often possessed and moved to fiercely caress herself, as if the Goddess was greedily digging for the luminous sensation buried deep in the magical space between her legs. But the queen gently dismissed her before she found the courage to ask her about that irresistibly beautiful experience the mere thought of Hapuseneb unerringly led her to. Her love for the High Priest of Amun was a flail that kept transforming her right hand into a crook between her thighs.

* * * * *

Before departing for Mennefer, Pharaoh awarded one of his lesser but more astute and efficient courtiers, the Honorable Neferkhaut, the position of Chief Secretary to the Crown Princess. Hatshepsut had no idea what to do with him. She met Neferkhaut, along with his wife, Ren-Nefer, Mistress of the House, at one of the numerous banquets held by the queen. The provincial couple— unable to keep up with the other guests' sharp-edged wit—appeared a little stunned by their new position. In a word, they were boring. The queen and the princess shared a table in the center of the room and were privy to all the conversations going on around them.

The more grape wine she drank, the more Hatshepsut felt as light and excited as a bird flitting from branch to branch as an amusing comment here, and a serious statement there, captured her attention while drawing her eyes to the speakers' lips and faces. These small gatherings were more entertaining than large formal affairs where she could not hear what everyone was saying from her elevated position on the royal dais. The fact that Ahmose had begun inviting her to her banquets meant she considered her daughter to be a grown woman capable of understanding all that was said, and of contributing her own views and opinions. Unfortunately, the High Priest had yet to attend any of them.

During one such event she said, "Mother, why do you never invite Hapuseneb to your parties?"

"Because I know he does not much enjoy idle gatherings."

"But you are the queen, you can *command* him to attend."

"Of course I can. But why would I?"

"I am the princess. Can *I* command him to attend?"

"No! However," Ahmose seemed to force a smile as she said less sternly, "you will be seeing him again when you resume your lessons in the Temple on the Feast Day of Maat."

"Will I be alone with him or will his other students be present?"

"That is for him to decide. Remember what I told you about mastering Hathor."

"I do not understand how I can because it is impossible!"

The guests fell silent, their wide eyes and broad smiles expressing a skeptical curiosity for surely *everything* was possible for the princess of Kemet.

Hatshepsut had already been looking forward to the Feast Day of Maat but now she could hardly wait for the day to arrive. She would ask Maat to help her find again the emotional balance she had lost. One moment she was overcome with elation as she touched herself remembering the way Hapuseneb sometimes smiled at her. The next moment she felt so frustrated and unhappy she was forced to dismiss her attendants so they would not see her crying, and ask her questions to which she had no coherent reply.

People were supposed to tell the truth all the time but on the Feast Day of Maat no one dared lie. She was in her pool, swimming back and forth from one side to the other, when she realized she had not actually told her mother how she felt about the High Priest of Amun. She suspected Ahmose knew but that was not the point. Was it a lie to conceal a truth, particularly one so all-consuming?

She came up for breath, shook shining drops of water off her lashes, and suddenly knew what she had to do. On the Feast Day of Maat she would tell Hapuseneb the truth. She would tell him she loved him. She *had* to. She risked blocking the flow of Maat through her heart if she kept lying to him by concealing her feelings. Her shyness, her timidity, her fear he would reject her love were all negative Sethian emotions endangering her soul with their selfishness.

She stepped out of the pool and the thrilling dread she suffered was indistinguishable from the chill of the early morning air making her tremble. A coward was not worthy of becoming God's Wife; she *had* to be brave and tell Hapuseneb how she felt even if it meant discovering he did not love her as well. As Nafre wrapped a towel around her, she tried not to think about how she would feel when the High Priest also told her the truth. If he ever lied, the sun would fail to rise; it was impossible. She was sure he would be honest with her, a truly frightening thought.

Perhaps because she knew what she wanted to accomplish on the Feast Day of Maat Hatshepsut was reluctant to prepare for it. Her resolve to tell Hapuseneb how she felt died as many times as there were tadpoles swimming in the ponds but she kept bravely resurrecting it. Fear of rejection, and of a loss too great to conceive, was the flail she lived under for seemingly endless days. The fond hugs of Inet who often came to see her, and her mother's farewell embrace before she left for the Temple of Maat in Nekhen, were loving crooks that failed to comfort her.

Then at last the stars fell from the graying sky into the River and sparkled with joy as the sun rose on the Feast Day of Maat, Daughter of Re and Mistress of Heaven and Earth.

As her attendants dressed and adorned her, Hatsheput's courage felt frail as a baby bird and as small as the way Maat was sometimes depicted in Pharaoh's cupped hands when he offered her back to God. In addition to her simple white linen dress, she would have liked to wear a fresh floral collar and her loveliest bracelets but that was not appropriate attire for her lessons in the Temple. She hoped Hapuseneb would remember how beautiful she had looked during the festival of *Apet-Aset*. She felt much younger and less confident when her face was not fully made up and her body richly attired—she still looked too much like a child, her breasts only modest little buds. On that special morning it was depressingly clear to her she was not yet beautiful and sensual enough for the virile priest of Amun-Min. She could not blame him if he did not want her in the same way she desired him. She would understand and they would simply be friends again. She soothed her nervous insecurity with that comforting conclusion, until she realized the sun had barely risen and she was already lying to herself. It was not an auspicious beginning.

Walking to her litter she whispered a prayer Seni had taught her, "Oh Thoth, help me be brave so I will be loved and praised and protected by you, lord of kindness, of time and of the moon, that shines down upon lovers where they lie together in the houses built by your power of measure!"[17]

When she arrived at the Temple, she was surprised not to see the group of lesser priests who normally waited for her on the other side of the humble door through which she entered. Hapuseneb himself was there to greet her.

She stared at him mutely, unable to find any words to give wings to her feelings. She had not been prepared to see him so soon and all she could do was gaze helplessly up into his eyes. As if Thoth himself was present to grant her wish, time seemed to stop when the High Priest grasped both her hands in his. He placed them over the *shen* bowl and she managed to hold them steady as he poured water over them, and then firmly caressed them with his own two hands. The ritual made her breathless as her ability to think struggled to keep up with her racing heart. When he knelt before her to bathe her feet, she stared down at his smoothly shaved head longing so intensely to touch and caress it that she swayed, and nearly stumbled, as he grasped one of her ankles to slip off her sandal. He purified her feet and she resented the soft linen separating her skin from his as he dried them. She never wanted the cleansing ritual to end yet she could scarcely wait because only then would she be permitted to speak and tell him everything that was in her heart. But the way he looked at her as he stood somehow had the effect of commanding her *not* to talk. Words could not describe the heaven into which she was transported staring up into his eyes, where she felt she saw all she desired in their luminous darkness.

He took her hand, leading her in the direction of Amun-Re's garden, and she followed him as silently as a tame gazelle devoted to her human master, who knew and understood so much more than she could yet hope to. When she saw his six other students waiting for him beside one of the numerous fish ponds, disappointment and relief mysteriously balanced in her heart. More than anything she longed for what his eyes had promised her but how hard his mouth had looked also told her she was not ready to receive what she desired. For now, it was enough that the High Priest of Amun did not let go of her hand even when her classmates could see him holding it.

* * * * *

Mighty one, foremost of the goddesses
Ruler in heaven, Queen on earth…
All the gods are under her command[18]

The sister-wife of Osiris and the mother of Horus, Hathor in her form of Isis dominated Hatshepsut's thoughts. Hapuseneb had revealed the goddess' transcendent nature to her on one of the special afternoon's they spent alone together. Every faithful wife and loving mother in Kemet was Isis made flesh but that was only the personal reflection, he said, of her cosmic role.

"As you know Isis, *Aset,* means *throne* but Isis is also called *Weret-Hekau*, Great of Magic, when she takes the form of a cobra with a woman's head. That is why mothers pray to her to protect their children and to give their husbands life, health and strength. They do not care or understand *why* Isis is great of magic so long as their prayers achieve the desired ends."

"*I* care."

"I know you do." He smiled. "That is why I never feel I am wasting my breath on you, Hatshepsut."

She realized he was speaking the truth even while teasing her but she did not mind. Ever since the morning he purified her with his own hands everything he said to her felt like a caress. Sometimes she wished she could live in the Temple like some of the other students. Even though the High Priest always left in the evenings at least she would still be breathing the same air he had, her memory

143

of the time they had spent together uninterrupted by tedious formal visits from her little brother or by Seshen and Meresank's idle chatter.

In an ancient myth Isis, desiring to know the true name of Re, asked him to tell her. Her Father refused but she was determined to learn it and to that end she fashioned a magical serpent to bite him—if Re said his true name the venom would not affect him. The ruse worked. It was difficult to reconcile this ruthlessly ambitious goddess with the protective mother peacefully nursing a child at her breast. And yet it was precisely the magic she gained from Re's true name which enabled Isis to conceive a son with her dead husband and give birth to Horus.

Hatshepsut pondered the myth while forced to play Twenty Squares with Thutmose, who now insisted on partnering her and taking the place of her favorite opponent, Puyemre. The prince's new and excessively solicitous attitude toward her was both flattering and aggravating. She hoped that once they were married he would stop pretending he cared about how she passed her days. She could not respect the fact that he hated the time he was forced to spend with his tutor every morning. He in turn was obviously disappointed to discover he did not have an ally in his older sister against all those "insufferably conceited scribes" as he described them. The first time he complained about his tedious lessons her displeasure was so obvious he never again brought up the subject. The only thing she enjoyed about her half brother's visits was watching him suppress his dismay and anger whenever she beat him, which was often.

Hatshepsut could not imagine herself a devoted wife like Isis, who had magically created the snake that bit her Father. Or was Isis *already* the serpent?

Once she answered that question, the deep truths contained in the seed of the myth were revealed to her.

"According to the story, Isis created the snake that bit Re but she was *already* the serpent of substance generated by the Goddess who acts as God's Hand," she told Hapuseneb exultantly. "The desire to know Re's true name symbolizes the process of becoming enlightened to our Divine natures so we can learn to share in the deathless power that created us. The serpent's venom is the terrible fear which sometimes sinks its fangs into our heart and causes us to believe death is the end. But when we understand the Divine origin of substance, when we comprehend it issued from the desire in God's heart, we are healed of fear's destructive venom with the knowledge that Amun-Re lives in us all."

"Babies and young children cannot eat and drink as adults do," was Hapuseneb's apparently unrelated reply but the satisfaction in his voice told her he was quite pleased with what she had said. "Infants must be fed directly from their mothers' breasts, and then their food must be softened so they can swallow it without chewing, until more substantial fare is gradually added to their diet as their teeth begin growing in."

"Do you mean some myths are like baby food?" She recalled what Seni had told her about the Mystery Plays. "Priests feed myths to the people so their hearts and souls will be nourished by spiritual truths even though they cannot yet... *chew* the facts for themselves and come to their own understanding?"

"Are you asking me or telling me, Hatshepsut?"

"I am *telling* you, Hapuseneb."

* * * * *

During the journey to Tantera, the princess would wear a girdle beneath her blue, red and yellow dress from which hung sixteen *tiet* knots, also called The Blood of Isis, made of carnelian and red glass. When she was a little girl the *tiet* hieroglyph, which meant *life* and *well-being*, had looked to Hatshepsut like a drooping and oddly lazy *ankh*. As she grew older, she understood it was its own distinct sign and yet it still made her think of a sensually languid *ankh*, especially when it formed the body of Hathor's bovine-eared face on unguent jars. She was not entirely wrong. The queen was tired that afternoon, which perhaps explained her rather perfunctory description of the popular amulet's meaning. Ahmose had been away from Waset a great deal visiting neighboring cities and temples because there was always a festival being celebrated somewhere. Hatshepsut preferred to think her mother looked older than usual because she missed Pharaoh, who was as they spoke sailing south from Mennefer to Tantera for the union of his son and daughter. She and her mother were leaving for the castle of the *menit* in the morning.

"The *tiet* knot symbolizes the female sex organ and the womb of the Goddess," Ahmose said, then sighed and held still as her attendant gently began removing her make-up with a fine swab of linen dipped in a moisturizing cream.

Even though she was wearing a dress, Hatshepsut could not help glancing down at her legs and thinking about the magical space between them she had come to think of as Down Below. When she imagined Hapuseneb putting his hand there she suffered a hot stabbing sensation in her belly.

"In the Isis Knot all three stages of a woman's life are represented," Ahmose added, her eyes closed as her attendant rubbed her shoulders. Her arms had always been slender but now the bone was beginning to show through her skin in a way Hatshepsut tried not to notice. "The central open space is the erotic fertility of a mature woman flanked by the closed loops of childhood and virginity on one side and old age and sterility on the other."

There *was* a sort of opening between her thighs she had dared to tentatively explore with her fingertips, but she feared making herself bleed and always pulled her hand back before discovering anything.

"Do you understand, Hatshepsut?"

"I think so… Is that why the *tiet* knot and the *djed* pillar so often appear together, because Isis is the wife of Osiris whose backbone is symbolized by-"

Ahmose sighed "Yes!" She stood and raised her arms over her head. Immediately, two attendants removed her dress. Naked, she spread herself face-down on a couch.

Hatshepsut had often glimpsed the place between a woman's thighs but that time she studied her mother's cleanly shaved sex with avid interest. "It looks like the mouth of a fish," she thought out loud.

"What looks like the mouth of a fish?" Ahmose murmured, her eyes closing.

"The lips between a woman's legs. It was a fish that swallowed the phallus of Osiris…"

One of the young attendants vigorously massaging the queen laughed.

"And it is the fish between your thighs, my delightful daughter, which will swallow your husband's phallus once it is big enough to get a hold of."

* * * * *

In Tantera, the days dragged by in a nightmare of disappointment from which nothing had the power to wake her to happiness again. If it could not be Hapuseneb then at least it should have been Amenmose walking beside her. The Temple of Hathor was so beautiful it made her want to cry as she entered its sacred precincts in the company of her little half brother. His childish vision limited the profound pleasure she otherwise would have taken in her first visit to the Castle of the *Menit*. She was surrounded by people she loved—her father and her mother, Inet, Seni, Nafre and even Puyemre, whose mother was charged with the task of watching over the princess' beloved cat—and yet the black gaps in the Lady Mutnofret's smile looked more dreadful than ever as they seemed to reflect the emptiness she herself was feeling inside her. Thinking about how difficult it must be for the woman to chew her food made her feel even more despondent about her future and all the responsibilities she would have to make an effort to discharge with dignified efficiency, whether or not they actually succeeded in nourishing her with happiness.

Assembled in Tantera for the great feasts being thrown to celebrate the royal union were courtiers and officials, noblemen and Nomarchs from across the Two Lands, many of them accompanied by their whole families. Beneath the sun all the gold they wore flashed a pure power and even when darkness fell their jewelry shone an incorruptible sensuality in the banquet hall, where the hot tongues of burning wicks floated in richly scented oils and animal fat. It seemed everyone except the High Priest of Amun took part in the festivities, which lasted seven whole days and nights and culminated on the Feast of the Hand of the God.

It was the beautiful time of the harvest, when the granaries were overflowing, like the joy in Pharaoh's heart knowing all his subjects were safe and well fed. The days were growing longer, *too* long in Hatshepsut's morose opinion. Because nothing inspired her, everything began annoying her. More than once, she brought tears to Nafre's eyes by yelling at her. Thutmose presented his bride with exquisite gifts fashioned by Kemet's most talented craftsmen but she took no more pleasure in them than she did in him. Her face began to ache from smiling all the time without her heart's permission. After standing for hours beside her mother in the Temple of Hathor watching the priestesses anoint hundreds of pregnant women—who waited for the blessing as silently as a herd of human cows—her body finally saved her from another interminable day of rites and sacrifices by growing so weak she could not rise from her bed in the morning. With her forehead burning, certain hieroglyphs suddenly struck her as revealingly meaningful. Hathor's High Priestess was sometimes called *Hetra*, House of Re, but *hetra* was also the name for a woman's womb, which seemed to explain why her belly felt so deliciously warm whenever Hapuseneb looked at her in a certain way…

Hapuseneb! She tried to get up with the intention of finding Kanefer and commanding him to take her to the Temple of Amun but for some reason Nafre stopped her. She liked Nafre very much, she loved her like a sister really, but that did not give her the right to wrestle with the future queen of Kemet.

"Release me, Nafre!" she snapped. "I must go! I know he is waiting for me to return to him! I know he is!"

"I will send for him, my lady, but you must not get up. You are ill. You need to rest."

She fell back across the bed wondering if after she died her Ba would feel so awful when it attempted to live again inside one of the stone statues carved to look exactly like her. Her body had never been so heavy and uncooperative. She reached down and anxiously caressed the space between her legs. Her skin was still soft and tender but it felt dry and lifeless. She experienced only a faint memory of the overwhelming joy she knew was buried Down Below.

"I have sent for him, my lady," Nafre assured her gently. "He will be here soon."

It took all her strength but somehow she managed to push herself up into a sitting position as she gasped, "Hapuseneb is coming?"

"The High Priest of Amun?"

All the objects in the room seemed to be swimming around her as if she was sitting at the bottom of a pool instead of on a bed. She closed her eyes in an effort to control a rising nausea. When she opened them she was lying on her back and her attendant had vanished.

"Nafre?" she whispered because it was almost impossible to speak underwater. "Come back, Nafre… you must make me beautiful for him…"

She was losing her battle with Tefnut. The air had transformed from the light breath of Shu into his sister's hot and heavy moisture pinning her against the damp linen sheets…

The next time she opened her eyes Nafre had returned but instead of Hapuseneb, she had summoned the queen. Sitting on the edge of the bed Ahmose said angrily, "You cannot leave me, Hatshepsut! Listen to me! The High Priest has sent you a message. He says the Oracle of Amun promises you will be healthy again soon and even stronger than before!"

"Hapuseneb sent me a message?" The room thankfully belonged to Shu again and it was not such an awful effort to speak.

"Yes! Already you have what you wish for, Hatshepsut, believe me. Now be a good girl and get better so we can sail home to Waset together."

12

Lady of the Sycamore

The Festival of the Conception of Horus was approaching but as a woman Hatshepsut did not yet feel great of magic and she seriously doubted Kemet's future falcon would choose to fly into her womb anytime soon.

Over a year had passed since her marriage. The River had risen, the seeds had been sown and hair had begun sprouting on her husband's face. Other parts of his body now also needed to be shaved and his deepening voice sometimes cracked like the dry earth.

After they returned to Waset from Tantera, Thutmose moved into Amenmose's old rooms where she visited him in the early evening four times a week. She also occasionally saw him in Pharaoh's Seal Room where he was accompanied by his new tutor, her beloved Seni. She felt sorry for her former teacher even though she was happy he had been honored by the position. Perhaps he would be able to inspire the Falcon in the Nest to take a greater interest in the *medu neters* and all they had the power to command.

She was able to enjoy her games of Senet with Puyemre again because the only piece her husband was interested in playing with now was the one beneath his kilt. He never seemed to tire of showing her his penis and of proudly commanding her to touch it. She obeyed him with a rather disappointed curiosity for it did not look anything like Amun-Min's long thick phallus, which rose before him like a weapon. Her little brother's organ was soft and vulnerable, until she cupped it in her hand, then it began stiffening and growing. The effect her caress had on him intrigued her—his eyes closed, his mouth fell open and the rapt expression on his face made her wonder if he was seeing God. She rather resented that he might be having a vision when she was experiencing nothing at all. Two pretty girls removed her dress before stepping back into shadows thickened by dozens of young female bodies—the Crown Prince's personal attendants, many inherited from Amenmose, some long in his service and a few acquired more recently. A handful of them, the daughters of Akheperkare's concubines, were related to the prince and princess but Hatshepsut could not see that they resembled *her* in any way. Of all the people in the room, including her husband, *her* blood was the purest.

"Your beauty blinds me with its radiance, sister," Thutmose said as he fondled the pointed little buds of her breasts.

A lovely young harpist strummed her instrument. Four more girls beat drums and tambourines in an urgent rhythm Hatshepsut's pulse reluctantly responded to as Pharaoh impatiently helped his attendants remove his kilt. She thought he looked rather funny wearing only a floral collar and sandals but did not say so.

She had taken note of the power her touch had over him and it helped her feel confident in the midst of her inexperience. It was thrilling to feel she was indeed God's Hand even though it seemed she was practicing her mysterious future duties with a toy. It merely felt like a game when her brother caught her in his arms and victoriously pinned her body beneath his. And yet, after a brief struggle, he was always the one defeated by her absolute submission. As he lay breathing heavily on top of her his limp organ slipped out of the damp space between her legs like a dead fish. She was so intrigued by his overpowering need that, the first few times he penetrated her, she scarcely noticed the pain, which dissolved almost at once into a mild discomfort. Nevertheless, the desperate way his body beat against hers was oddly enjoyable as she felt Hathor whispering an important secret in her ear she could *almost* hear...

She did not find visiting her husband unpleasant but she did not look forward to it either, especially when he began making her kneel on all fours so he could mount her from behind like a lion. She never let him possess her more than once and the experience was so predictably brief she was able to forget about it almost immediately. Every month she was both relieved and disappointed when she once again began bleeding. Hapuseneb's wife had borne him two more children but she did not like to think about that. She could not for an instant picture the High Priest reduced to imitating a fish flapping desperately on the River's edge, as whole schools of them sometimes did when the waters of the inundation receded. She was sure the experience of worshipping Hathor would be very different with Hapuseneb even though she could not imagine how.

She met Seni's wife and son at one of the queen's parties and was mildly surprised because she had never realized he was married. It had been quite childish of her to consider him her exclusive possession since everyone naturally had families of their own. Abruptly she understood what was wrong with Seshen and Meresankh—their hearts longed for husbands.

Wondering if her favorite attendant also wished to wed, she asked her, dreading the answer.

"No, my lady," Nafre said firmly, her eyes fixed on a date palm in bloom. "I am perfectly happy here with you."

"And I am very happy to hear that, Nafre, but I suppose I should find Seshen and Meresankh promising young men as soon as possible." Remembering she now had a secretary, she sent for Neferkhaut.

"I will be honored to arrange a banquet for you, princess." Focusing on his palette he began writing. He seemed very glad to have something to do. "I will draw up a list of esteemed young nobles and their sisters for you to consider. Is there anyone in particular you wish to invite?"

Smiling in delight, she shook her head, suddenly feeling quite fond of the provincial scribe.

"The princess will require her own group of musicians and dancers?" It sounded like a question but the way he looked at her, brush poised expectantly over his palette, seemed to say that *naturally* she would.

She nodded.

"Then tell me, my lady, when it will be convenient for you to hear various candidates perform so you may select the most talented."

She laughed. "Kemet is flooded with servants of Hathor?"

"Yes, princess." He dared to return her smile before lowering his eyes to his tablet again.

"I have changed my mind, Neferkhaut. There *are* some people I wish to invite to my first banquet." She supplied him with the names of all her fellow students in the temple, beginning with Puyemre. She did not include Hapuseneb because she did not want to risk boring and displeasing him with her inexperience as a hostess. She would need to practice her entertaining skills a great deal more before she dared invite the High Priest of Amun to her gatherings. "Also put Min-Hotep's brother, the Royal Scribe, Senmut, on the list."

Bubu will be pleased to see him again, she thought, and suddenly wondered if Seshen or Meresankh would like him as much as her cat did. Would they also long to fall straight into his arms?

"My lady, have I displeased you? If so, I hope you will find it in your heart to forgive me for I long only to serve you to the best of my ability."

"What?" Apparently, she had been frowning at her secretary without even seeing him. "Of course you have not displeased me," she replied somewhat impatiently, still preoccupied with the strangely annoying image of Senmut sweeping Meresankh up into his arms and holding her close against his chest.

"Do not be silly, Neferkhaut," she added with a smile. "I am *very* pleased with you. And I also intend to make much better use of you in the future."

* * * * *

The queen was delighted her daughter was hosting a small banquet of her own even though she politely refused to attend. "It will be *your* night, my dear. Enjoy yourself. But also remember to listen more than you speak. Grape wine tends to open men's mouths and reveal the quality of their hearts."

Hatshepsut understood what her mother meant. She was accustomed to forming her initial opinion of people by studying their faces and looking into their eyes but what they said and how they expressed themselves was also important. Mouths, throats and chests were Thoth's sacred instruments expressing by way of speech how abundantly Maat flowed through the heart.

It was the hot season of the harvest so she decided to hold her first formal gathering in her garden. A large pavilion was erected for the occasion and together she and Nafre chose the eight musicians who would play beneath two sycamore trees, because Hathor, their patron, was also called the Lady of the Sycamore. A great deal of serious thought went into planning the carefree event, from the lamps chosen to illuminate smiling faces, to where they would be placed as her guests drank wines especially selected to go with certain dishes. It was exciting but tiring because the Steward of the Royal Household, Sinuhe, politely insisted on supervising all the various overseers she met with. He said he wanted her to be perfectly satisfied with their service, but she suspected it was the queen who had asked him to make sure her daughter did not forget anything important.

When she learned that Min-Hotep was blessed with even more siblings than Senmut, she instructed Neferkhaut to add them to the guest list. They arrived all together, the two youngest sons of the honorable Ramose, Amenemhet and Pairi, holding the hands of their sisters, Ah-hotep and Nofret-hor, who appeared to be the same age as the princess. Senmut was not wearing a wig. His black hair was cut close to his skull and the stiff little black beard adorning his chin made Hatshepsut feel as if a great nobleman had stepped into her garden from a thousand years ago. He was the only man present who had chosen to come bareheaded with his hair cut in a style popular in the time of Menkaure the Divine. He looked quite distinguished and perfectly comfortable. She was surprised that neither Seshen nor Meresankh chose him as her table companion. Apparently, they did not think the Royal Scribe fashionable enough. Hatshepsut fondly concluded they were pretty but regrettably silly girls. Bubu was more astute than her attendants. When Senmut stepped into the pavilion, her cat immediately lifted his head off her feet where it had been resting with lazy possessiveness. That time he kindly waited for his human prey to sit down before he leapt onto his lap, where he curled up contentedly.

"You have cast a spell on my animal, Senmut," she accused him with a smile.

"Forgive me, my lady, but I cannot have done so, for I do not believe in spells of that nature."

His brothers and sisters laughed with a rather forced cheer that sparked her interest. The glances they exchanged told her they were worried he had said something so odd it might prove offensive, and seemed to hint at the fact that he often made such remarks.

"My cat would seem to disagree, Senmut, but please quench your thirst with some wine before you explain to me, if a spell of some sort is not responsible, why Bubu is so extraordinarily fond of you."

He accepted the cup an attendant handed him and took a quick sip before replying, "Perhaps he likes the way I smell."

"Does the fragrance of Nefertum permeate your limbs, Senmut?" She thought *certainly not, for you are a commoner.* "Or can you afford oils even more priceless than those Pharaoh enjoys?"

"Forgive me, my lady," he repeated quietly but his features carved themselves out even more sharply, "I was lazy with my words. What I meant to say is that perhaps your cat can smell, as in sense, my respect for him and for all of his kind. Cats do not need words to communicate and therefore never say what they do not mean, an admirable trait indeed. Cats can also see well enough in the darkness to become what is feared. Cats are unlike many men, who live enslaved to superstitious terrors because they lack the wisdom and the courage to root them out and kill them, preferring instead the marshes of their rudderless emotions. Unlike cats few men are fully aware of what surrounds them."

"Indeed!" She regarded him with excited pleasure. His prominent black eyes and hooked nose evoked a falcon's intent, almost indifferently superior, expression. "It *is* very sad so many people remain unaware of the fact that God lives inside them and instead of using their powers of perception to enlighten themselves become the helpless victims of their fears. But it is most interesting what you say about the sense of smell, Senmut. The nose is the seat of life and we use it to capture scents and odors whether or not they delight or disgust us."

She sipped her wine while pursuing her thought for a moment. "Feelings burn in our hearts the way incense does in an offering bowl... so perhaps the quality of our Ka emanates its own distinctive aroma, which other Ka's can smell, in the sense you describe it, and find pleasant or noxious according to their own natures." She smiled at him, thoroughly enjoying the conversation.

"Unfortunately, my lady, there are far too many people who suffer from hopelessly congested perceptions."

Puyemre, who was sharing her table, barked a strangled laugh around the fruit stuffing his mouth. Judging by the manner in which he waved his hands wildly back and forth in front of his face, he had swallowed some without properly chewing it.

Regarding him with fond concern, Hatshepsut decided he could benefit from a slap on the back. Everyone laughed and began conversing freely amongst themselves, pausing only to savor all the delectable dishes their hostess had commanded be served in groups of two and three as the evening progressed. Stars glimmered in the darkest depths of lamp lit eyes as cheerful voices ascended into the sky, until harp strings gently strummed commanded silence. Transcendently lovely musical notes rose over the sistrum-like rustling of leaves and a girl began to sing:

"The wind blowing through my garden

sighs with desire for the sycamore,

but upon entering my garden

you desire only me, my brother!"

The man's voice which answered hers belonged to Harmose, a handsome young harpist Hatshepsut was quite pleased to have acquired:

"It is true, sister!

When I kiss you and your mouth opens beneath mine

I am filled with joy without drinking wine.

Your teeth taste as sweet to me as pomegranate seeds

Your breasts are lotus buds, so lovely,

and our sycamore never a word will breathe!"[19]

Hatshepsut decided the next time she threw a party she would invite Senmut to share her table. His unpretentious yet quietly superior attitude intrigued and attracted her. There was not a drop of royal blood in him and yet he possessed more presence where he sat simply watching and listening than most noblemen did at their most eloquent and charming. She hoped his way of seeing things would pose more irresistible challenges for her in the future. It pleased her he seemed even less interested in her two pretty attendants than they were in him. It was the soldier Mentekhenu who won Meresankh's hand. Seshen's heart was captured like a wild fowl in a net by the expertly woven compliments of a young scribe named Nebamun.

Several young men attempted to impress Nafre with their titles and positions but though she smiled at them politely, she did not look impressed. She seemed more interested in their sisters.

* * * * *

The morning after her first banquet Hatshepsut entered the Seal Room expecting to see her father. Instead, she came upon Ahmose-Penekhbet, Akheperseneb, Ineni and Senimen talking quietly but intently. No scribes were present. After the Royal Herald announced her, all four men turned their heads and stared at her. Senimen was the first to reflect her respectful greeting by raising his arms toward her. His expression warned her she was about to receive the ultimate lesson in faith, courage and strength she had always dreaded.

"Pharaoh," she said.

Seni inclined his head.

Ineni informed her in his usual quick efficient voice, "Messengers have been dispatched and will travel without rest until they reach the queen. Fortunately, she is not far in Nekhen and the current is with her." He seemed relieved to have something positive to report.

"I must go to my father!"

"No." Akheperseneb finally stopped staring out the window. "Pharaoh desires his daughter to take charge of the Seal Room until he feels... until he is ready to receive her."

All she wanted to do was curl up on the floor and weep. Instead, she took a steady breath, bracing her resolve on Seni's sad but encouraging eyes. "What ails Pharaoh?" She was proud of how calm she sounded.

"We do not know," her former teacher admitted gently.

She started when directly behind her a herald announced loudly, "The Royal Scribe, Senmut!"

"Half of Pharaoh's body has..." Akheperseneb's mouth, so accustomed to voicing problems, nevertheless had to struggle to utter the dreadful words. "Half of Pharaoh's body has turned to stone."

She realized Senmut was standing beside her when he quickly explained what the vizier meant, "He means your father can only move his right arm and his right leg."

"The left side of his face has also been carved for eternity," Akheperseneb almost seemed to enjoy correcting the young scribe, who supposedly never missed an important detail.

"But he can still speak with the right side of his mouth," Ineni added confidently, "and he has clearly expressed his wish you serve in his place today."

Not the Crown Prince. The fact did not need to be spoken for it to resound significantly through the room.

Senmut informed her quietly, "The scribes are waiting outside, my lady."

Instead of being offended, she was grateful for how close he was standing as his body emanated a determined strength she desperately needed. She looked up into his eyes feeling she had found a rock to cling to in the torrent of grief she was forced to keep her head above until she was alone, and only Nafre could see she was already drowning in despair even though her father still lived.

"Tell the scribes to enter, Senmut."

* * * * *

Ten priests of Sekhmet clad in long white robes covered with black hieroglyphs surrounded Pharaoh's bed. They formed a breathing *shenu* ring protecting the living god's present name and identity, Thutmose-Akheperkare, while quietly chanting "Horus-Anubis, Horus-Anubis, Horus-Anubis" ceaselessly. Their presence both comforted and confounded Hatshepsut as it prevented her from seeing her father. Her mother, standing at the head of the bed, looked shockingly old. More than half of the King's body was unresponsive as wood or stone. Already his Ba-bird perched on his immobile limbs preparing to build its magical nest in the branching corridors of his tomb.

Hatshepsut strove to remember the things Hapuseneb had told her about the Ka. For thousands of years the Falcon had flown and been reborn, there was nothing to fear, but this time it was very different because Pharaoh was her beloved father. What would happen to his uniquely special personality when he became one with *his* Father? Would *her* father vanish forever? That was the only truly important question and one the High Priest of Amun had answered again and again without actually doing so. Or so it seemed to her as she waited for the king to open his eyes again and speak, or to silently leave the world through the doorway found in dreams. Only a selfish need to hear his voice, and to tell him how much she loved him, made her beg the Goddess—who could be heard impatiently rustling the leaves of the sycamores outside—to wait a little longer before she invisibly entered the room and enfolded the Divine egg of Pharaoh's heart in her infinitely colorful wings.

It is the warmth of the mother vulture's body that brings her eggs to life, she thought, *and so is it love that surrounds and protects the soul in the stone nest of its tomb, where it slowly grows the wings of its power over the forces creating the world and our bodies, until we become as falcons soaring on the wind and diving freely back to earth to feast on our senses!*

Like a sip of water in the desert of her desolation, the thought helped soothe her misery somewhat. The relief it gave her from grief did not last long, but she knew a determined stream of such clearly defined beliefs was essential if she desired to survive the death of her beloved father and, even harder, to go on living afterward without becoming Seth's despairing subject.

The air in the room was made uncomfortably thick by the sweet scent of incense mixed with the musky odor of fear. The prince and the princess were not the only ones about to lose the man who had loved and protected them. Hatshepsut fervently hoped Kemet's fear and sorrow did not carry like smells across the borders and entice her enemies to attack while the General of Maat lay helpless and dying. It struck her as a dangerous fact that there was no Great Army Commander to lead Re's army. She would have to do something about that as soon as possible.

"Hatshepsut?"

She stiffened and listened with all her being as the chanting ceased abruptly. Had the king called her name? She got her answer when the priests standing on

Pharaoh's right side turned toward her, and then moved back so she could approach the bed.

She suppressed a gasp when she saw her father's face. His left eye and the left side of his mouth both sagged like melting clay, as though Khnum had sunk his thumbs into Thutmoses' flesh to deliberately distort and ruin what had once been a noble creation. But then, blessedly, she recognized the man she adored in his gaze, which was even more shiningly alive than normal and free of all limitations through his thoughts. He was looking up at her with such feeling that nothing else mattered as in his eyes she beheld a passionate love and pride indistinguishable from joy.

"Hatshepsut!" He squeezed her name out of the right side of his mouth while slowly raising his right hand.

She grasped it in both of hers, ignoring how frighteningly light it was as she bent close to his stricken face and whispered, "I love you, father! I will always, *always* love you!"

"I know." His voice sounded deeper than usual as he projected it past the dead half of his mouth. "I always knew... you were the child... of Pharaoh's heart." He pulled his hand out of hers and it fell back onto the bed. His eyes now told her to step back and listen, like everyone else, to what he was about to say.

"My daughter!" His voice commanded the same attention it always had. "Hatshepsut, the Female Falcon!"

He caught his breath as if planning to say more but all that emerged from his throat was an awful sound like the hollow echo of rocks clattering down a tomb's steep shaft, and then abruptly she saw nothing in her father's eyes except the reflections of candles burning around the bed on which he rested from life.

* * * * *

In the throne room of Osiris

Thoth says to the assembled deities:

Hear the words I speak:

the heart of the deceased is true to Maat.

No falsehoods corrupted him.

Greed did not diminish his offerings.

He never destroyed what had been created.

He did not use words to deceive

but spoke always from the heart

and of treachery remained free.

Standing in her garden—her body facing north and her face turned up toward the imperishable stars—Hatshepsut whispered, "Thank you, father, for my life!"

An unbearable grief was making it hard for her to breathe.

"Is love the light in the Fields of Re?" she went on between sobs. "It must be. I *know* it is for I feel your love in the sunlight even more strongly now than I did while you lived here with me.

"You have crossed the horizon of fear and freed me from it forever, father, because I cannot, even for a moment, surrender to the intolerable thought that I will never see you again. I *know* we will talk and laugh together again in the endless Field of Offerings. I cannot possibly doubt this for to do so is to let you die forever instead of only to my eyes for a little while.

"True of Voice you rule as an Osiris now embraced by Isis and Nepthys and I promise you that, for as long as I live, not one of your subjects will suffer the hopeless tyranny of fear. Kemet's children will rejoice in the certainty of their Queen Mother that those they love who have gone to their Ka's live on not only in their hearts but in *fact* as luminous *Akhs* in the Dwat, where all our joyful thoughts and dreams are received as gifts nourishing to the heart of Amun."

Akheperkare's body was in the embalming house. It was hardly the first time someone she loved had been in the hands of a man wearing a jackal-head mask. How long she was forced to wait to accompany her father to his House of Eternity was bearable only because her lessons with Hapuseneb continued uninterrupted. She now spent four days in the temple every week and six full days in the Seal Room with her husband and his officials. After Akheperkare's burial his son and daughter would be crowned king and queen of Kemet and, even more importantly, she would officially assume her duties as God's Wife. Tainted now by grief, her desire to marry Amun-Re possessed the feverish desperation of a dream, from which she had no desire to wake as she faced the fact that it could never be in Hapuseneb's embrace.

"Is a mummy in its tomb a mysterious kind of seed?" she asked him late one afternoon when they were alone in God's House. No matter how hard she tried she could not banish the image of her father lying in the *Wabet*.

"A mummy is a map back into realized magic," he replied. "The body's organs are vital functions in the Laws of Becoming. A mummy fixes the form through which the powers of sight and taste, touch, hearing and smell are actualized in a way that makes it possible for the Ka to develop, control and enhance them. Mummies also serve as a way of recording experience so that we can learn from it as our ability to emulate Divine creativity grows and develops, eventually freeing us from slavery to the dangers and limitations inherent in all corporeal manifestations of life.

"The reverent use of our five senses is the practice of magic, Hatshepsut. Our senses do not give birth to our ability to feel, they serve it. That is the message of the mummy and of the ceremony of The Opening of the Mouth.

"The human body is an instrument created and played by God and his Hand. An infinite Composer tunes the specific vibrations of the physical senses like musical strings. The mummified form serves as a map back into a realm of experience where we can continue to learn about the god within us. That is the meaning of true growth, the growth that transcends the self-perpetuating laws of earth. Osiris symbolizes the processes of matter—the cycle of birth, death and decay—as well as the spiritual force that transcends them."

"My father is an Osiris now."

"He is, and the beautiful tomb in which his body will soon rest, securely wrapped in spells and linen bandages, will help protect him from the forces, both creative and destructive, surrounding his soul. If he was not nourished by the enlightened power of faith, if he did not continue to live deep in the hearts of those he loves and who love him, he would be as a seed lying exposed to wind and rain, the hunger of birds and the trampling of beasts. In his tomb he will be as a baby growing safely in the womb of the Goddess."

"But a baby leaves the womb when it is born and father will never leave his tomb. It is his House of Eternity. He will live there forever for its doorway opens magically onto the Fields of Hotep."

"Do you really believe that, Hatshepsut?"

"It is what everyone believes."

"You did not answer me."

"Yes!" She was suddenly so upset it made her angry. "I believe that!"

"When you were a little girl did you play with only one doll?"

"Of course not! I had dozens of dolls made of wood with obsidian eyes and animal hair."

He smiled. "Then why do you imagine your Ka is limited to playing with only one body?"

"Are you saying father's tomb," her voice rose incredulously, "is only a *doll's* house?"

"To his Ka it is. But you should not say 'is *only* a doll's house' for the game of incarnation is a serious one."

"But why do we go to all the trouble of mummifying one body if our Ka can create as many as it wants?" Her sense of self felt threatened as never before. "I will be Hatshepsut forever!"

"Just as craftsmen employ designs and diagrams," he ignored her outburst, "the Ka uses mummies to record the highly specific equations governing the laws necessary for the fashioning and functioning of the physical senses. If you truly wish to become an initiate of the First Occasion you must realize that mummies are as appropriate to our cosmic age as dolls are to childhood."

"But my father was Pharaoh!" He was offending her now in addition to shocking her. "A fully grown and powerful man not a child!"

"You are being deliberately obtuse, Hatshepsut."

The sternness of his voice reminded her the only thing she truly could not endure was his displeasure.

"Forgive me!" She stared earnestly into his eyes. "I do not *mean* to be obtuse."

"I know." He grasped both her hands and held them firmly in his. "And I do not mean to be impatient with you. Words can only lighten the weight of sorrow caused by the knowledge that in this life you will never again see the person you loved more than anyone. But never forget the doorway of dreams is always open and that through it love travels freely between all possible worlds."

"I love my father, I love him more than I can express in a way I will never love anyone else." The sycamore beneath which they were sitting rustled loudly in a sudden breeze. "But I do not love him anymore than I love-"

"Do not say it," he whispered, pressing two fingers against her lips that made her think of the double plumes of Amun. "Not yet."

13

Lord of the Necropolis

Anubis, the Overseer of the Secrets of the Place, his assistants, the Children of Horus, and a Lector Priest of Amun reading from sacred scrolls as they worked, had finished preparing the body of Thutmose-Akheperkare for his battle with the forces of eternity. A spell written on new papyrus invoking the celestial cow *Ihet*, Mother of Re and Mistress of the Hidden One, was placed beneath the dead king's head, which had set like the solar disc in the west, to protect him in his magical efforts to live again.

A flame has been lit beneath the sun's head

the one who is your Ba, see him!

His name is Atum, and he is you![21]

The *djed* pillar of Osiris was set beside the *tiet* knot of Isis on the royal mummy's chest close to its neck. Directly on its throat rested the Heart Scarab through which the Divine energy embodied in the solar disc continued flowing through his supernatural body, for while he had lived on earth Thutmose had been true to Maat with all his thoughts and actions.

Oh dear heart, which my mother gave me,

oh my heart which beat my life on earth,

praise to you my beautiful heart!

May your voice always be loved by Re

so that my Ka may go forth by day forever

never setting but rising in the west eternal![22]

Hatshepsut would have preferred to remain ignorant of the procedure by which her father's lungs, liver, stomach and bowels were removed and then reverently placed in gilded cedar wood chests. His brain was softened with special substances and pulled out through his nostrils. Priests of Anubis were brave men indeed—their souls entered people's dreams and their hands thrust boldly into the body's dark fluid depths in search of the organs vital to the mysterious process of Becoming.

When only the heart remained inside it, Pharaoh's corpse was filled and surrounded by natron wrapped in linen. It stayed that way for an entire month, during which the intolerable grief swelling his daughter's heart, and causing her to weep nearly as much as she breathed, gradually began diminishing as his dead skin dried up. After thirty days the king's body was washed with perfumed wine, purified with incense, then filled with myrrh and other divine-smelling things. His desiccated flesh was painted like a statue's with fragrant oils designed to imbue it with a life-like softness and glow, his skull was stuffed with warm liquid resin and the empty cavity of his torso fattened with resin-soaked cloths. A young priest of Anubis had come to the palace to explain the process to Hatshepsut. She did not ask him if the queen or the High Priest had sent him. It was entirely possible he had come from the *Wabet* of his own accord because she was the princess of Kemet and therefore expected to know the Secrets of the Place.

The final seventeen days of the rites of mummification were occupied in imitating the Ka's creative magic. The body was imbued with a semblance of life using red-brown paint and glass eyes. For a second time the man named Thutmose at birth was brushed with oil and perfumed, after which his back was massaged as though to help him relax after the long ordeal of being dressed for the festival of his death and resurrection. Only then was he wrapped like an infant in a sheet of yellow linen, except for his fingers and thumbs which were individually sheathed in gold. It took seven days to oil and bind his head because of all the prayers that had to be said, then it was oiled a third time and his body was wrapped in red bandages. Finally, a third layer of white linen completely embraced him, leaving only his hands free where they crossed at the wrists against his chest. The *heka* crook of the south rested on his right side and the *nekhekh* flail of the north on his left.

In the end, Hatshepsut was glad she had seen and spoken with an infamous servant of the jackal, for the truth was he had looked and smelled much the same as everyone else. It made her wonder how many other liberties, no matter how innocent and well-intentioned, Inet had taken with her stories. She could not imagine the man who had come to see her being tempted to have sex with the corpses of lovely young girls because no living women would even look at him. He had, in fact, been quite personable *and* a priest, a desirable husband for any woman with a heart more sensible than superstitious. She remembered what Senmut had said about most people suffering from hopelessly congested perceptions. Even though Puyemre had nearly choked on a mouthful of fruit laughing, she sensed the Royal Scribe had not been joking. The mummy's nose was stopped up, and its closed eyes were covered with stone or glass, because it no longer required air to live or light to perceive. But on earth, everyone needed to breathe and desired to see and the more freely and clearly they did both, the stronger, healthier and happier they were. Even though it was possible to breathe without realizing it, and to understand what the eyes beheld without great effort, there was much more to the power of vision. Just as the lungs could deliberately take a deep and expansive breath so too was it possible to make an effort to see more consciously and profoundly.

The body of Queen Ahmose continued to inhabit the east bank of the River but Hatshepsut feared her mother's heart had already moved to the residence in the western desert, where she waited to join her husband in the Land Beyond the Sunset. Made of brightly painted mud-brick, the false palace would not survive the gradual but relentless attack of time the way tombs were designed to do, and yet its beauty would exist forever even when all that was left of it was an insubstantial veil of colors on the horizon. The residence in the west was in some respects even more exquisitely furnished and appointed than its reflections in the east. Hatshepsut looked forward to the day when—an unimaginable span of years in the future—she would join both her parents there. She did not allow some of the things Hapuseneb said to shatter this dream. After all, he had told her himself that simply because one thing was true did not necessarily imply another was false. It was vital for her to believe she would see her father again as he had been in life, and that her heart would once more be warmed by the indescribably special quality of his smile.

A few days before Pharaoh was ready to go forth by day to his House of Eternity, the spacious apartments in the palace belonging to him and to his queen swarmed with servants. The excessive activity struck Hatshepsut as indecent. She had no desire to exchange her current rooms for those of the Great Royal Wife even if they *were* larger and more splendid. She was not happy that the Lady Mutnofret was planning to move into the palace even though she had every right to do so bearing now the highly prestigious title of "King's Mother". She struggled to accept it all until it abruptly occurred to her one intolerably hot afternoon in the Seal Room that she did not have to.

"I intend to build myself a palace," she stated without preamble.

Ineni looked at her, his thoughts unreadable.

Akheperseneb stared out the window the way he always did when he needed to think about something which had been said before voicing his opinion.

She followed the vizier's gaze in the direction her heart was always facing. "I desire to live even closer to my Father, Amun."

"As you wish, my lady," Ineni said mildly. "I will consult with the royal architects and draw up a variety of plans, one of which I trust the young Falcon and his queen will both find pleasing. Building will then commence as soon as the River begins rising."

"No."

He blinked. "My Lady?"

"The new residence will belong exclusively to me, the queen and God's Wife, and will not be a separate structure but rather an addition to the ceremonial palace that already stands beside *Ipet Sut*. The garden of *I Shall Not Be Far From Him*, as the new wing shall be named, will adjoin the garden of Amun so a single gate opens onto both."

Akheperseneb, shifting his eyes back into the room and her face, bestowed upon her the same admiring regard he normally reserved for birds in flight.

When she informed Neferkhaut of her plan he was, in his restrained provincial way, ecstatic. The project would keep him busy for months. She decided to retain him as one of her personal secretaries even though after she became God's Wife of Amun she would be awarded her own retinue of male administrators to help her manage her vast endowment of lands and goods. She almost forgot her father was dead when she met with the royal architects and tasted the novel joy of designing her own residence, albeit within conventional lines established long ago. She knew the High Priest would find out and fervently hoped her initiative would please him.

In the Seal Room, other important matters were attended to, including the appointment of a new Great Army Commander. She relied upon the information and recommendations provided by her advisors, and especially on the brief but incisive comments made by Senmut concerning the character and experience of each candidate. A man Ahmose-Penekhbet praised as the embodiment of courage and strength, the ideal protector of Kemet, Senmut dismissed as a dedicated soldier but a somewhat foolish and weak individual.

"But how can that be?" she demanded curiously. "Surely it is not the same person of whom you both speak?"

"It is indeed," Senmut said in his quiet voice. "A truly courageous man is one who acts according to Maat at every moment no matter that by doing so he might cause his own discomfort or death, but only a fool seeks danger and hardship for its own sake. Those men who are too weak to conquer their fears sometimes make the bravest soldiers as they strive to display a courage their hearts do not truly feel. A general who seeks adversity in order to prove his mettle is a danger to all the men who serve beneath him."

"Are you the brother of Thoth, Senmut," she said sternly, "that you can so confidently judge a person's heart?"

"I judge a person mainly by their actions, my lady, that reveal how they truly feel despite what they might like to think or admit when they speak."

"If words are of no importance then why are we talking now? Why do we not simply roar like lions or shriek like hyenas?"

"My lady, I did not say words are not important."

"You said words played no part in your way of judging a person."

"Forgive me, my lady, but I did not say that."

"Yes you did!"

He stared back at her silently and how expressionless his face remained threatened to make her even angrier, as did abruptly realizing he was right. She felt a fool but in order to be true to Maat she was obliged to admit her mistake.

"You are correct, Senmut." She held her head up while searching his dark eyes for the gleam of an emotional reaction of any kind. "You did *not* say that. You said you judge a person *mainly* by their actions not *only* by their actions."

"My lady." He inclined his head. "Forgive me for once again being lazy with words. It is my responsibility to make what I mean as clear as possible and I swear that in the future I will strive to do so."

"Never mind, Senmut. I will not ask you now to list all the deeds which have spoken so unfavorably of this candidate to you. What is important is that all of us approve of the man appointed the Great Army Commander."

Her husband was not present in the Seal Room that afternoon and no one mentioned it.

* * * * *

At last, the day came to escort The Horus Ka-nakht Meri-Maat, the king of Upper and Lower Kemet, Akheperkare, the son of Re, Kh-Thutmose-Mi-Re to his House of Eternity. Only a few weeks before the day on which everyone had hoped to celebrate Pharaoh's fiftieth birthday, they were instead mourning his flight into the sky beyond the reach of their eyes.

Hatshesput, her eyes as dry as the land, walked beside her mother behind the oxen drawn cart bearing her father's Master of Life inside a gilded wooden shrine. All the people of Kemet seemed to be crowded into Waset on that miserably hot morning and yet she could somehow still hear the voice of the Lector Priest of Amun. Hapu led the procession as he read from a papyrus filled with prayers older than Mennefer's pyramids.

Behind the cart bearing the gilded boxes containing the king's vital organs, *muu* dancers, all of them women, clapped their hands and tossed their heads back and forth so their long hair rhythmically concealed their grief-contorted features. They repeated this gesture of denial again and again but they were also carefully counting—after every eighty paces they opened their arms toward the sky and smiled joyfully.

The almost entirely naked *muu* dancers were more emotionally expressive than the professional female mourners who walked behind the dead king's body wearing gray-blue dresses and long formal wigs. Their keening laments rose over the steady voice of the Lector Priest as their controlled gestures transformed their bodies into living hieroglyphs. For several weeks after her father died Hatshepsut had everywhere seen women performing the same series of gestures. It had perfectly reflected how she felt when they sank to their knees and with their left hands flung dirt on their heads as their right hands clawed at the earth. *Death is inconceivable*, their gestures said, *the disintegration of life and love into dust is impossible to face!* But they did not remain crouched and defeated on the ground. They picked themselves up and grasped their left arms with their right hands between the elbow and wrist, making the sign of the clenched fist to fight despair by grasping what is true despite what appears to be, thereby mastering the crippling misery of grief. As they crossed their wrists against their chests, Hatshepsut had felt the birth of courage and hope in her own heart faced with the fear of death. And by this awakening, the female mourners were transformed into the Goddess—who enfolds and protects the new Osiris—as they crossed their wrists below their waists directly above their feminine sex where life eternal takes root in mortal flesh. In the final gesture, they had held both hands open at their sides, gracefully accepting a sadness the intelligence of the heart knows is only temporary.

Last night her father had been brought home to the residence in his Master of Life to rest on his gilded lion-head bed one last time. Representing Isis, the wife of Osiris, Ahmose stood at his feet wearing a simple white shift and a long white linen headband. Throughout the night the queen kept opening her arms to spread the magical wings of her love over her husband as she murmured spells which all said essentially the same thing, "Death is an illusion! There is only Life forever!"

Dressed identically to her mother, Hatshepsut stood behind Pharaoh's head. It was easy for her to identify with the goddess Nepthys, married as she was to a man she did not truly care for and desiring another woman's husband.[23] Yet in truth, she rejoiced to feel the Goddess inside her as the very force of the love she felt for her father, a sublime emotion indistinguishable from faith in its power. She kept her eyes on her mother's face as she dreamed of her new palace adjoining the garden of Amun-Re and Hapuseneb. She avoided looking down at the coffin's painted wooden mask. The features resembled Thutmose and yet looked nothing like him. Remembering the great pyramids—and the statues of the immortal pharaohs who had built them carved of imperishable stone—she resented Akheperkare's splendid but corruptible coffin. He deserved much better. He deserved to rest embraced by all the spiritual qualities symbolized by stone protecting and empowering him the way wood, so vulnerably rooted in earthly needs and limitations, could not do. She knew his mummified body lay in the third innermost coffin but she could not feel his presence. The Falcon had flown and been freed into a space beyond her imagining. Pharaoh's right eye was the Bark of Day and his left eye the Bark of Night as his Ka commanded the forces of sun and moonlight—the two Eyes of

Horus united in Atum who exists forever beyond light and dark, space and time, as the One that is All.

The queen and the princess watched all night over Pharaoh's body. When they suffered the need to relieve themselves they crouched down and did so over a golden bowl provided by a servant. For twelve hours, not a drop of liquid passed between their lips. By sunrise Hatshepsut's mouth made her think of a desert cave in which the mummy of her tongue was buried. Her first sip of water, offered by a priest, was such a sensual relief she almost felt resurrected.

The king's mummy was preceded by his son, Thutmose, and followed by the priests of Anubis who had fashioned it. In their wake walked his closest friends, including Ineni, Akheperseneb and Ahmose-Penekhbet, who all wore white sandals that day, as did the dozens of courtiers following behind them bearing in their arms all the beautiful furnishings for Pharaoh's House of Eternity.

The life-sustaining milk poured by priests in front of the two slow-moving carts bearing Pharaoh's body and his organs was immediately absorbed by the parched earth. Hatshepsut felt as though her sadness had also dried up. She was too thirsty to cry and too tired from standing all night over her father's body to feel anything except the desire to lie down and sleep. She scarcely noticed boarding the boat. As it crossed to the west bank, and from there proceeded along the Canal of Akeperkare, the lapping of the oars lulled her into a dream-like state that was enhanced rather than disturbed by the keening of the female mourners kneeling on the cabin roof. It was easy to imagine they were not women at all but a flock of kites flown down from the sky to perch on the gilded wood. Her mother's hand holding tightly onto hers was the only thing that felt real. Her father's death struck her as a mere illusion. Somehow she was sure he was more alive than she was now trapped in a body exhausted by weeks of painfully dry heat aggravated by her salty tears.

She was roused from her reverie when the boat docked with a gentle jolt. She disembarked beside her mother, who finally let go of her hand, at the head of the procession of women following Pharaoh into the cool shade of his Mansion of Millions of Years *Khenmetankh*, One With Life. Wearing the leopard-skin of the *sem* priest, Hapuseneb was awaiting for them inside and all at once her senses felt alert and vibrant again. He had only to glance at her for her to fully relish the life being offered to her by a young priest. She drank the water and smiled at him gratefully. Her face felt strange around her mouth and she realized it was the first time she could actually remember smiling since her father died.

In ancient times, the body of the king made a ritual journey between four holy cities. Sait, in the west, represented the forces of earth, while in the north Buto presided over the Primordial Waters of Nun. Mendes, in the east—its name written by two *djed* pillars—was where the heavy moisture of Tefnut met the airy breath of her brother Shu and the heavenly and terrestrial forces of Re and

Osiris were united. The final stop on the ritual pilgrimage was Iuno, just north of Mennefer, the city of the sun and the holy site of the First Occasion. It was in Iuno that Atum first manifested Himself as the solar disc Re rising and setting between two desert mountains—the hieroglyph *akhet* which meant *horizon*.

Hatshepsut was glad Pharaoh now made the sacred journey only symbolically. After it was lifted off the cart by nine young courtiers, the coffin was removed from its wooden shrine and carried to the four sides of the temple where, closely supervised by Hapuseneb, various priests made offerings of incense, milk, water and wine before carved emblems of the sacred cities. From where she stood she was able to see only the symbol of Sait—a narrow shrine flanked by tall poles flying triangular pennants facing each other.

At first it was cooler in the shade of the temple but the warmth of so many bodies crowded together soon made the air thick and uncomfortable. She longed to run after the High Priest when he finally began leading the procession away from the canal out into the open desert. It was hard not to look impatient as the oxen were freed from their harnesses so Pharaoh's closest friends could take up the ropes and drag him the rest of the way along the sacred route into the Valley of the Gates of the King.

It took a long time to reach the western side of the mountain in which Mentohotep had carved his beautiful monument facing east. As he stood before the coffin of Thutmose where it stood upright before the dark entrance to his tomb, Hapuseneb looked perfectly comfortable in the leopard-skin clinging to his body. In his right hand the *sem* priest held the iron adze of Anubis with which he touched the king's forehead and the bridge of his nose. He then raised his left hand and with Ptah's metal chisel caressed the indentation between the effigy's smiling wooden lips. Passing the sacred instruments of the Opening of the Mouth to a servant of the god, he accepted a *nemset* vase with spouts in the shape of ostrich feathers and slowly poured milk taken from a black cow over Pharaoh's face. Imagining the High Priest's fingertips caressing her features in the same loving way, she started when he abruptly flung the red earthenware vessel against the rock outcropping and it shattered into countless pieces. He then embraced the coffin, surrounding as much of it with his arms as possible, and in obedience to his nod, offering bearers began piling the table beside the king with all manner of food and drink.

"Rise, Osiris!" Hapuseneb's forceful command rose beyond the reach of barren hills and gorges which sought to trap his voice in lifeless echoes. "Rise and take your place before the beautiful gifts of life!"

There were jars of wine and beer, countless loaves of bread, baskets heaped with fruit and platters stacked with meat and fowl. Hatshepsut found the buzzing of the flies magically materializing from the barren landscape oddly stimulating. Any sound was welcome in the desert's crushing silence, even the desperate ring of the queen's voice crying, "Do not leave me!" as she ran forward and flung herself at her dead husband's feet.

"He is here," Hapuseneb told her sternly, "and always will be."

As he helped her up, Ahmose hung her head so the fine braids of her wig fell forward and hid her face. "*Hetep-di-resut!*" She spoke the magical offering formulae which would provide her husband with everything he needed for his journey through the dismembering forces of the Dwat—the power of the love in her heart where he remained strong and healthy.

Meanwhile, the nine young men honored with the difficult task lifted Pharaoh's Master of Life between them. Followed by the officials carrying all its beautiful furnishings, they proceeded down a flower-lined path into the tomb. Hatshepsut recognized most of the objects for they had all stood in her mother's rooms for as long as she could remember. She herself had lovingly given her father eight jars, all shaped like the *nefer* hieroglyph and filled with the finest grape wine, as well as her favorite Senet board, its pieces carved of black and white ivory in the form of *djed* pillars.

Ahmose did not follow the beautiful items, large and small, into the tomb. She remained standing to one side of the entrance with the High Priest and in the merciless sunlight her arms looked thin and dry as twigs, as though she too had slept for months surrounded by natron. Hatshepsut was now as worried about her mother's health as she had once been about her father's. She could not endure another devastating loss, not yet.

"Please, Nepthys," she prayed beneath her breath, "protect what remains of my happiness! Stop my mother's Ba from flying away after my father by gently reminding her how much her daughter still loves her and needs her here on earth!"

Last to enter the tomb were colorful bouquets of flowers silently exclaiming, "Your name will live again!" then the door was closed and sealed by the *sem* priest.

Forever! The word rang terrifyingly in Hatshepsut's head. Emotions burned in her heart like the hot wax impressed with her father's kingly titles by a large stone scarab—*Khefer*, the hieroglyph for Becoming, the symbol of Atum-Re as *Khepri*, He Who Came Into Being. Pharaoh's physical remains were now like the larvae of a scarab beetle gestating in the dark underground tunnels of his tomb, filled with magical nourishment, from which he would hatch into the full range of his Divine creative abilities. The stone scarab also represented the human skull.

"For it is by way of the spiritual faculty of thought shedding light on our feelings," Seni had explained to her long ago, "that we commune with our hearts and make the vital choice to believe in our everlasting nature, which is embodied in the solar disc and its life-sustaining light."

It had seemed strange to her then that a *neter* could take the form of an insect, and now she resented the scarab in Hapuseneb's hand as the transcendent but inflexible laws represented by its legs seemed to separate her from her father forever.

By the time the mourners reached the River the sky behind them was flying luminous red and gold banners announcing the triumphant arrival of the new Osiris Thutmose-Akheperkare into the West. Great quantities of wine would be drunk at the upcoming funeral banquet where only small cakes filled with cheese and fruit would be eaten. Hatshepsut hoped Hapuseneb would still be wearing his leopard-skin cloak.

* * * * *

The Forceful Bull of Powerful Strength, Netjeret-Ka, Wadjet-Renput, King of Upper and Lower Kemet, Lord of the Two Lands, Thutmose-Akheperenre, Protector of Re, became the new bodily son of Amun. In his presence, everyone kissed the earth, including his Great Royal Wife. Hatshepsut did not have to feign the fear and reverence expressed by the crouching position she assumed before her husband in the throne room. Whole-heartedly she respected the fact that he was his father's son, the living *neter*, so that when he ran he was motion itself, and when he shot an arrow he was the very reality of penetration. What she feared, however, was his shallow disposition—the stubborn rocks of vanity and impatience hidden beneath his smooth royal demeanor which threatened to undermine the vessel of kingship currently sailing around them with its own glorious momentum. She hoped that as he grew into manhood his personality would deepen and that greater responsibilities would help him steer away from the idle pleasures of which he was so fond.

Earlier that morning, she had been borne aloft in her litter behind her husband and her mother. A golden cobra reared from Dowger Queen Ahmose's forehead and her vulture headdress was now crowned with Amun's erect double plumes. Mutnofret brought up the rear of the procession. The Crown Prince had proceeded from the ceremonial palace to meet the bark carrying the enshrined image of Amun-Re as it emerged from His temple. From there they had all made their way to the Palace of Maat where Thutmose was officially crowned the Good God Akheperenre. Made especially to fit him, the white *nefer* crown of southern Kemet belonging to Seth and the red *bit* crown of the north belonging to Horus were placed on his head while Songstresses of the God proclaimed:

Oh bit, oh great crown, oh serpent!
Let him be feared as you are feared!

Let him be loved as you are loved!
Let his scepter defend the living!
Let his knife defeat his enemies!

Oh nefer, the Eye of Horus rising in the east!
Oh nefer, descending to illuminate the west!
Make him great that he may conquer the Two Lands
with your love shining from his forehead!
He has set you on his head, oh Mistress of Might,
to bind all his foes with your benevolent power! [24]

Hatshepsut observed the ritual with impatient detachment. She had slept only a handful of hours in the last two nights and reality felt much less vivid than her emotionally charged dreams. When she was awake, her heart could not seem to feel anything at all. She longed only for her bed as it assumed the promising shape of a doorway leading straight into the Dwat where she might actually be able to see her father again. She prayed Anubis would guide her to him through the darkness behind her closed eyelids. Anubis, Ruler of the Nine Bows, conqueror of the enemies of Kemet and of the soul. She remembered the priest of Anubis who had come to the palace to tell her what was being done to Pharaoh in the *Wabet* and wondered if he was one of the Wearers of the Winged Sandals who could meet her in a dream and guide her to her father.

It was not until she stood face-to-face with the High Priest of Amun that her senses awoke and fully rooted her in the moment. At once, her eyes became instruments joyfully playing the subtle tones of Hapuseneb's skin, darker on his head and lighter in his lips, which looked even more softly desirable than the bed she craved. His mouth was a magical portal opening onto his breath and the words it shaped which she knew had the power to both stimulate and comfort her like nothing else. Like sunlight reflecting off the River, the sense of touch burst upon her in flashes of sensation when from two small circular jars he poured cool milk over her breasts. She shivered as her nipples grew stiff and long, poking against the damp mist-linen of her dress that had been scantily cut in an archaic fashion. She pictured his servants rubbing costly oils all over his naked body earlier that morning and the scent of his skin became more intoxicating than ever.

As he placed the vulture crown on her head his voice carried to the farthest corners of the temple's offering court, "Hatshepsut, King's Daughter and King's Sister, Female Chieftain of Upper and Lower Kemet!"

With her heart perched on the High Priest's penetrating stare, the sensation of golden wings slipping behind her ears and embracing her wig felt profoundly sensual. The responsibilities and privileges proffered by the surprisingly light headdress made her pulse quicken in joyful recognition of her true, transcendent nature. Every person in Kemet was a Divine egg she was obliged to nourish and protect with her faith and wisdom. She took an exultant breath, expanding the miraculous instruments of her lungs like a vulture's wings opening to the seminal wind of Hapuseneb's breath announcing to all those present, "Behold God's Wife of Amun, Khnemet-Amun Hatshepsut, the One who is joined with Amun, God's Hand!"

She accepted the staff of her office from him, a staff exactly like the one carried by men who held esteemed and powerful positions. It was made of wood which thickened slightly at the bottom where it was sheathed in silver. Its upper end— carved to look like a living branch with a small protruding twig—was wrapped in precious birch bark. Administrative staffs were not long enough to lean on because power properly wielded never makes a person grow lazy and weak, on the contrary. The God's Wife of Amun was the only woman to whom such a staff was ever awarded.

* * * * *

Enjoying the reassuring company of infinite stars and happily singing frogs, Hatshepsut sat before a small golden shrine in which a candle shaped like a cow—the wick rising from between its curved horns—burned with a steady golden light. When exhaustion at last overcame her, she hoped to see and speak with her father again in a dream. Yet she suspected that her desire, intense as it was, would not bear fruit quite so soon. It seemed she could just as easily reach up and pick one of the stars glimmering in the sky like juicy grapes in Atum's boundless vineyard. Her father now drank only the silver-blue wine of starlight, which poured into her tear-filled eyes in luminous arms like hundreds of Ka hieroglyphs reaching down from heaven in compassionate response to her sadness.

"My lady!"

Nafre's uncharacteristically urgent whisper roused her from her reverie. Reluctantly, she lowered her eyes from the heavens and turned them toward her attendant.

"My lady, you have a visitor!" Nafre crouched down beside her and whispered in her ear, "The High Priest of Amun!"

Rising without assistance, she suppressed the cry, "Why have you kept him waiting?" and said instead, "Tell him it will be my great pleasure to receive him."

"Where shall I tell-?"

Hapuseneb suddenly appeared on the path. "Leave us!" he commanded and Nafre obeyed him instantly.

Never having heard him speak so harshly to anyone, she was almost frightened as he grabbed her arm and led her away from the luminous shrine into the impenetrable shadow of a date palm. He pulled her body hard against his and when he kissed her, thrusting his tongue between her lips, she no longer felt the ground beneath her.

"My lady..."

She moaned in despair as Nafre's whisper abruptly extinguished her dream.

"Come, my queen, it is almost morning and you must rest."

The candle had burned out—the Hathor shrine was cold and dark—but her senses were still under the dream's spell and she perceived the formless lump of wax as the Primeval Mound of Creation holding within it the promise of everything. A priest *had* come to her in her sleep, the High Priest of Amun, and the memory of his demanding kiss—which had tasted so real she could still feel it on her lips—told her that her life, like the day, was only now truly beginning.

BOOK THREE

God's Wife

14

Beloved of Amun

In the festival calendar, Neith rejoined Atum. Akheperkare had gone to his Ka and become one with the forces of Creation. In the hands of his children he had left a much more limited power—over the world, its laws woven by the mother of the gods and men. Spinning light out of darkness, Neith illuminated the first moments of time and space. Neith and Hathor were indistinguishable from each other as the Hand of God but suddenly the oldest form of the Great Mother resonated in Hatshepsut's heart. It helped her fight her fears to evoke the strength of the mother of Sobek. Mistress of the Bow and Ruler of Arrows, Neith would always protect Kemet. Her fierce might glimmering in the scales of all crocodiles and burning in the venom of every cobra, Neith would accompany Re's army south so that when Pharaoh's soldiers raised their bows she would fly through all their arrows straight into the dark and treacherous hearts of the Kushites. Not a single enemy of the Land of the Gods would remain standing.

On the day her husband set forth with his army to help his Viceroy of the Southern Lands crush the uprising, Hatshepsut ordered whole roast perch for her dinner. The fish was delicious washed down with a fine Wine of Bast that helped her embrace the profound calm of Neith, as though she too was floating beyond harm on the Primordial Waters—the bottomless mystery from which she had been born and into which she would once again plunge at the moment of her death. It was foolish to wish that her father lived and was physically journeying south to face the enemy. The calming force of the wine helped her understand that Akheperkare was still alive in the body of the army he had trained and commanded for longer than she could remember. The man who had engendered her was a mummy lying in his tomb and yet he still possessed thousands of eyes and legs and arms with which to see and fight and defeat all those who threatened his children's peace and happiness.

The new Great Army Commander, Nomti, whose name meant *strength*, could be trusted to protect Pharaoh without suffering his own effectiveness to be weakened by the young king's inexperience. She had not needed Senmut's assurance on this point but she was pleased his opinion of the man confirmed her instincts. Like the young Royal Scribe, Nomti had risen far above his parents in position and status. She was beginning to think such men as Nomti and Senmut could be trusted above all others for the quality of their Ka had shone like a golden egg laid in a humble nest. It was entirely possible that a rotten egg could be disguised by expensive perfume and fine linen. She was reminded of the words of the wise King Merikere, *Exalt not the son of one of high degree more than him that is of lowly birth, but take to thyself a man because of his actions.* [25]

It was gratifying if not surprising when word of Pharaoh's victory over the wretched Kushites reached Waset. Raging like a panther, Thutmose had killed and conquered all those who had dared threaten the peace of Maat with their greed for the riches and beauty she protected. A stela was promptly erected in Abu on the road south to commemorate the great victory. The features of the messenger who brought the splendid news were dramatically painted by sweat and dust. If his person had not been sacrosanct because he was on a mission, which meant he was not obliged to kneel before the queen like everyone else, he might not have been able to get up he looked so exhausted. Gasping for breath, he informed Hatshepsut of her husband's glory. The news he brought was good but he smelled bad. Since it was his eagerness to bring her joy that prompted his rude behavior, she forgave him for not purifying himself before entering her presence. She thanked him wholeheartedly then commanded him to take a bath and get some rest so he could fully enjoy the magnificent banquet his news had inspired her to host.

There was one person, however, who would not be attending the celebration. That night, as if realizing she was no longer needed, Mutnofret's heart left the world as she slept. Women keened and performed the ritual gestures of mourning but the light in their eyes spoke of relief and happiness rather than of grief and sadness. Her son's victory over the Kushites completely overshadowed Mutnofret's passive defeat by an enemy no one could hope to defeat. Hatshepsut suffered an unexpected sadness prompted by respect for how politely, without causing a prolonged and inconvenient fuss, the ugly old woman had gone to her Ka. In the end, Mutnofret had behaved with a regal consideration that could too easily be confused with self-effacing timidity.

The Dowager Queen and her daughter sailed across the Nile to *Khenmetankh* to make an offering in the family chapel. The mud-brick rooms seemed too small to house within them the memories and spirits of so many loved ones. After her father, it was Amenmose Hatshepsut missed the most and that afternoon she found her heart devoting most of its thoughts to her beautiful brother. It was pleasantly cool in the shrine where every detail pleased the eye while at the same time reassuring the soul. It was hard to feel sorrowful there. She found herself smiling at the *neters* who protected Amenmose as vivid memories of the happy times they had spent together flowed through her. Outside the temple, there was no longer painfully dry earth, cracked as if with endless reasons to be sad, for the River had risen again to flood the land. In the chapel dedicated to her loved ones an invisible river of sentiment deepened how much Hatshepsut missed them, but in a beautiful way. In the brick-framed plots of dirt saturated with sacred words and images, her heart reacted like a seed planted deep in mystery and bloomed an inexplicable but irrefutable feeling of hope.

Later that day her faith was rewarded by a visit from her brother. A swallow perched on the branch of a tree growing on the western side of her garden and for a magical instant she saw the setting sun resting on its back. *Wer*, the hieroglyph for *great*, was written as the little bird that possessed the power to fly through the Dwat and the twelve hours of darkness, from which it emerged to once more sing the day to life. Whenever she saw a swallow, she wondered if it was someone's Ba-bird and that evening she was certain Amenmose had left the supernatural nest of his tomb and come to visit her. As the swallow flew off her heart happily took wing after it.

When Pharaoh returned victorious to Waset, Hatshepsut sat by his side at another even greater celebratory feast and that night her wifely duty did not feel quite so unpleasant. Thutmose had lived for months surrounded by the virile body of their father's army and some of that noble king's aura still perfumed him. She opened her arms and legs to him with a smile that soon faded when her passive body almost immediately defeated the strength of his desire. As his phallus slipped limply out of her she wondered if Nomti, returned from his first challenge as Great Army Commander, would also expire so quickly inside her. For all she knew every man made love like her brother, yet she could not quite believe that.

After Amenmose became a Westener, she had claimed Shu's brother, Min, for herself. In her affectionate opinion, they were the most beautiful male lions in the world. She adored them and they seemed equally devoted to her. She laughed in delight whenever she witnessed how submissive their potentially ferocious strength was to her gentle caresses. She loved their stimulatingly cold noses and big rough tongues and how muscular and soft they were all at once. However, making direct eye contact with them unnerved her, as they too seemed to experience a similar tension. In those instants she felt uncomfortably like prey as she imagined them sensing, if not quite thinking, how easy it would be to kill her. She wondered if they missed exercising their fearsome vigor and if, deep in their hearts, a profound restlessness threatened their outward contentment. Despite a frisson of fear, she sometimes could not resist the thrill of staring into their light-golden eyes, in the center of which the darkness behind all life was clearly visible.

In an effort to further hone her courage, Hatshepsut instructed their keeper to escort Shu and Min to one of her private banquets. By lamplight, the lions' eyes gleamed a frightening, mindless red even as they sat obediently on either side of her. She enjoyed fantasizing about the even more splendid gatherings she would host in her future palace adjoining the garden of Amun. *I Shall Not Be Far From Him* was currently under construction and already its Pleasure House was being dug and planted. She spent highly enjoyable hours meeting with royal craftsmen and painters discussing all the beautiful furnishings that would grace her new home. She planned on taking her favorite possessions with her, the rest she would give to Seshen and Meresankh to help them decorate the lovely little houses she was giving them as wedding presents. Their husbands both came from noble families and would inherit wealthy estates graced by much larger dwellings but while they were in the city they needed a place to live worthy of their positions. Nebamun had been promoted to Counter of the Grain of Pharaoh and Mentekhenu would soon be anointed Chief of Security charged with the safety and well-being of God's Wife. Seshen and Meresankh still spent most of their time with her but she was not averse to occasionally giving them days off since she had always liked Nafre the best. She depended on Nafre to help the Royal Steward Sinuhe manage all her servants, who were as numerous as the leaves her gardeners dredged out of the pools every morning.

Seven days after he returned from Kush, Hatshepsut accompanied her husband to the Temple of Amun. Her presence was essential to the efficacy of the rituals over which Pharaoh personally presided on select occasions. The sacred rites she participated in as God's Wife were performed together with Hapuseneb or with other high-ranking priests assigned to take his place while he was away. When Thutmose left on campaign she and Hapuseneb, standing side by side in the Temple of Mut, had burned the names of all of Kemet's enemies. For the ritual of Overthrowing Apep she had worn the vulture headdress crowned by a modius—the box-like shape symbolic of the womb of time and space, the House of Horus—from which rose Amun-Re's double plumes fronted by the solar disc. Together they had burned models of the Nine Bows, clearly identifying each one, into featureless pools of wax.

Having returned victorious, Pharaoh now offered the gods all manner of food and drink in gratitude for the physical strength and coordination they endowed him with. Accompanied by three priests, she walked beside the king as he made his way from one *neter* to another in a symbolic circuit of all the different parts and functions of Amun-Re's earthly form. But it was she who received the food from the servants of the god and offered it to her husband who returned it to its Divine source.

It was also her duty as God's Wife to lead newly initiated priests—who followed in a line behind her as obediently as ducklings—into the temple pool to be purified. She stood to one side as they removed their white sandals and their short old-fashioned kilts. Completely naked, they descended the stone steps into water as deep as their hearts where they vigorously scrubbed every part of their bodies. Most new servants of the god were young and she enjoyed studying their faces and physiques. Especially gratifying was observing the unmistakable gesture that meant they were stroking their manhoods clean. However, a handful of the new priests were unappealingly thin. They would soon put on a healthy weight consuming the food provided for them by the Temple, in addition to whatever they grew and produced themselves on the small plots of land granted them. As they walked back up the steps, it pleased her to be surrounded by so many naked men obedient to her slightest gesture. Her eyes were drawn to their curiously delicious-looking buttocks as much as to their male organs, some of which clearly responded to the curious caress of her eyes.

* * * * *

The scepter crowned with a feather stood tall and proud at the gates of Waset, where healthy sounds of construction resonated off the flooded canals into the cloudless sky and alerted God in heaven of His children's joyful industry.

In the Seal Room, Hatshepsut enjoyed going over the plans for her new palace with Ineni as he helped her understand which lines and squares and circles represented porticos, courtyards, columned reception halls, vestibules, dressing rooms, bedrooms, bathrooms and even a staircase leading down into a wine cellar. She was impressed by the ability some men possessed to turn flat lines on paper into actual dimensional structures people could live in. The experiences planted inside her years ago when Seni took her to Ptah's workshops had blossomed into the revelation that she used, admired and took for granted results she could never produce by herself. She relied entirely on the minds and skills of the scribes who drew up the plans for *I Shall Not Be Far From Him* and on the strong bodies of the workmen who actually constructed it. She truly felt like a goddess when she perceived all her subjects—with their fascinatingly varied and specialized talents—as a vital part of herself without which she would never be able to fully express herself. Even the words she used when she spoke had been taught to her by someone else. As scribes and architects and painters, craftsmen, stone masons and wood cutters worked to make real her dream of a palace more beautiful than any other so did all the gods serve to manifest the Hidden One.

"I commend your devotion, sister," was all Thutmose said about the fact that she would soon be moving out of the old palace. "I hope, however, that the empty rooms you leave behind will soon be filled with life again." He clearly disliked the fact that she was not to blame for not yet doing her duty and becoming pregnant since none of his numerous concubines had conceived either. The Festival of Min was months away and even though he did not say so she guessed he was anxiously anticipating it. He considered himself a full grown man who had valiantly defended his country against invasion but she still saw him as her self-indulgent little brother.

In her opinion, it was Nomti who had truly crushed the Kushite rebellion. Pharaoh had dutifully rewarded his Great Army Comander with a lovely golden bowl, its interior decorated with an exqusite relief of six bolti fish swimming around a lotus flower in a papyrus thicket. The design was encircled by a zigzagging line symbolizing water. The king had the bottom of the bowl inscribed with his praise and Hatshepsut made sure Nomti was aware of her own personal respect and gratitude by honoring him with a table at her banquets. Neferkhaut kept a slowly growing list of people who were always to be invited to the queen's private feasts. It all depended on her mood who she would choose for her table companion but more often than not it proved to be Senmut. Puyemra did not seem to mind. He continued making it clear all he

181

wished for was her happiness. It would have been gratifying to see him look at least a little despondent. Instead he showed no sign whatsoever that Senmut's rise in favor upset him. Yet in truth, she was much happier than she would have been if Puyemre had indulged her selfish desire to make him jealous.

Often honored with an invitation to Hatshepsut's parties was the Royal Artisan Ka-hotep, The Soul of Contentment, who she had chosen to create many of the objects that would grace her new home. She had been delighted by a small reddish-brown hedgehog-shaped vase from which she had seen an attendant pouring a special substance over the king's feet purported to prevent snakebites. She loved the adorable little face with the big black ears added to the smooth round body that in reality would have been painfully sharp with protective spines. She had assigned Neferkhaut the task of learning where the unique vessel had been made and by whom, and Ka-hotep had been promptly commissioned to fashion another hedgehog vase for God's Wife in addition to other beautiful things.

* * * * *

Hatshepsut was in *Ipet Sut* with the High Priest of Amun when the winds of Seth suddenly began blowing. The enclosure wall helped shield them from the stinging spears of sand but not completely. He grabbed her arm and pulled her into the nearest shelter—Hathor's sanctuary. The storm's howls were muffled by the stone walls which also served to cool the hateful heat of Seth's breath. Hatshepsut thanked the Goddess for protecting them and for the forceful sensation of the priest's fingers digging into her skin. The army of dust had obscured the sun. Only a faint finger of light pointed the way as he led her into the darkest depths of the shrine, where he pinned her back against a wall and shielded her body with his. It was impossible for her to resist wrapping her arms around him and resting a cheek against his chest. When he did not speak she dared to turn her head and press her lips against his skin, ostensibly to keep the sand out of her mouth even though it had yet to penetrate the inner sanctum. She closed her eyes, breathless with joy and disbelief that what she had wished for more times than there were stars in the sky was finally happening. She would never feel the same way about Seth again. In those moments, she loved the brother of Osiris more than any other god as in her arms she finally held the man she truly loved.

The desolate moaning of the wind sounded sweeter to her than a harpist's voice as Hapuseneb whispered her name "Hatshepsut!" and clutching the braids at the back of her head made her look up at him. It was too dark to see clearly but his lips had no problem finding hers. She fully understood then why the Goddess took the form of a serpent as she slipped her arms around his neck and tasted the reality of all dreams when his tongue forced her mouth open beneath his. It was his hand and not a gust of wind that raised her dress. He gripped the bottom of one of her thighs and lifted it impatiently up against him as his other hand sought Hathor's most intimate sanctuary. With Seth's uncontrolled lust stroking the body of the temple around them, she moaned with joy as his thumb found her holy of holies. He thrust two fingers inside her and almost immediately she felt herself soaring up into the earthly heaven of his kiss where air and moisture, warmth and coolness were no longer separated as she swiftly ascended into Atum's blindingly beautiful power.

She clung to him weakly as he lowered her leg and let her dress fall to her ankles again. Outside the sanctuary, Seth had retreated as abruptly as he had attacked. She kissed his chest, even hungrier for him now than she had been before.

"Our joy must remain hidden for now," he whispered. "But know this, Hatshepsut. I will never leave you, not in this world or in any other."

15

The Great Ones

Three full moons came and went with no bloodshed. Hatshepsut was stunned. Her monthly purification had stopped. Kemet's future Falcon appeared to have made his nest inside her.

Pharaoh had instructed his chefs to prepare him delicacies wrapped in lettuce and his diet had proved effective. Even though it failed to intensify her desire for him, the leafy green plant sacred to Min made his white male sap potent at last. It was the beginning of the season of harvest and Min had come forth in the king.

The Dowger Queen summoned a physician to attend her daughter. Ibenre, Heart of Re, was not the same man who had examined her to determine whether there was something blocking the connection between her womb and the rest of her body. She had spent an uncomfortable night with an onion planted inside her vagina only to discover her breath did not smell bad in the morning. That had not been a good sign, but ever since then she had perfumed her mouth with milk and dates, and her attendants massaged her belly and thighs at least twice daily.

After verbally according her all the respect due her, his left hand resting on his right knee and his right hand grasping his left shoulder, Ibenre straightened from his bowed position. He stared into her eyes for a long moment, and then he lifted her delicately braided hair with the back of his left hand and lightly rested his right hand on the nape of her neck.

"There is no doubt," he said.

Seshen and Meresankh were disappointed the physician left before taking a sample of their mistress' urine to pour over newly planted wheat and barley seeds, for if they sprouted quickly it meant she was carrying a boy.

Nafre was more practical. From that day forward, she applied an oil made from the fruit of the horseradish tree to the queen's belly, so that as the baby grew her distending flesh would remain soft and supple and show no sign afterward of having been stretched.

Hatshepsut was very proud to have conceived before any of her husband's concubines. It was also a relief not to have to endure his amorous attentions almost every evening. She had not believed it was possible she could rise higher in status until she felt the power of the Goddess growing inside her. She was inundated with gifts from her brother and it was wonderful to be able to cut his visits short by complaining she was tired. The truth was she had never felt better and yet he treated her as though she might go to her Ka at any moment and take his precious son with her. She enjoyed worrying him a little, until he tried commanding her not to strain herself with temple duties. She asked Ibenre to speak with Pharaoh and assure him she was strong and healthy.

"If she neglects the sacred responsibilities of God's Wife," her physician told the king, "Amun-Re will not be pleased."

Pretending to conceal a yawn, she hid a smile behind her hand. After that Thutmose left her delightfully alone.

She scarcely dared admit to herself, much less to anyone else, that she was more than a little frightened. Women died in childbirth all the time. Many women gave birth successfully but then—as she knew all too well from her mother's experiences—their babies often died.

In her garden, beside the small altar dedicated to Hathor, there was now another shrine devoted to The Great One, Tawaret. The concubine of Seth took the form of a hippopotamus standing on her two back legs, her large breasts sagging with milk and her belly swollen like a pregnant woman. She wore a long wig topped by the modius of God's Wife and one of her paws rested on an *ankh* while the other sat on the *sa* "protection" hieroglyph. Her lips were drawn back in a snarl, exposing her deadly teeth, beneath two of which the red tip of her tongue protruded. Her expression seemed fierce, until Ahmose explained Tawaret was simply offering sympathy and strength to women suffering through the pain of childbirth, which could cause them to bite their tongues from the strain.

It seemed unreal to Hatshepsut she would soon be a mother. For weeks her belly looked much the same as always. Gazing down at her body she curiously caressed the place where the baby was supposedly growing. It was impossible for her to picture a whole other person living inside her. She had been perfectly happy being Hatshepsut but now she was someone else as well. She wondered if Seth was responsible for the disturbing truth that she felt no love for the Ba nesting in her womb.

She grew heartily bored of her husband's gifts. Fine items like gold and lapis-lazuli bracelets—with slide pieces in the shape of Mut's slender figure standing on a lotus flower and spreading her four wings—degenerated into amulets, vases, beds and other furnishings all shaped like, or including images of, the hideous Tawaret. Thutmose had never before been so obsessed with protecting her and she began to resent it. She recognized the ugly sentiment—she was jealous of the baby—but acknowledging it did not help.

As if her condition was equally problematic for him, Hapuseneb left Waset in his capacity as Governor of the South. Even though she longed for his return she was relieved her lessons in the Temple were temporarily suspended as she felt began to feel increasingly lazy. More than ever she enjoyed spending time in her pool as it relieved the growing weight and pressure of her belly but swimming grew more and more difficult.

Senmut and Puyemre came to see her nearly every evening. If she was not in the mood for company, she simply told Nafre to send them away but that rarely happened. Both men took turns challenging her to Senet. She secretly enjoyed her games with Senmut the most because he always made a real effort to win and often did, which had the effect of making her victories taste truly sweet. Even though he occasionally defeated Senmut, Puyemre continued to lose against her. A more experienced player now, she usually noticed when he deliberately added up his rolls wrong or used them all at once when he should not have done. Occasionally she risked losing in an attempt to force him to win but in the end, he always cheated more skillfully than she did. Both men could add and subtract numbers, relating them to the squares on the board and future moves, more swiftly than she could. Senmut, however, could hold his wine better than Puyemre. Even after six or seven cups, his powers of calculation appeared unaffected. The way he bent over the table, his shoulders hunched forward as he stared down at the board, reminded her of a falcon perched on a rock studying the world below for prey.

"Relax, Senmut!" she commanded. "We are only playing a game but you are making me so nervous I feel we have declared war on each other, or as though the fate of all creation rests upon your next move!"

"I hope not," Puyemre said, "for you are beating him."

Senmut straightened his back, obediently distancing himself from the board a little, but his eyes never left it and his hands gripped his knees with unrelenting concentration.

She sighed.

Puyemre shrugged and rolled his eyes.

Senmut won the match. It was not his superior skill but merely a bad toss of the throw sticks that landed her on the water sign and forced her to go all the way back to the beginning like a soul devoured by Ammit. Nevertheless, her respect for him deepened. A man who applied himself so intently and successfully to whatever he did was to be trusted and admired. At the time, she was too relaxed to examine the budding conviction but she put it away in her heart to take out and pursue later. Her instincts—which told her something was true even though she could not always explain why—were like precious gems mysteriously mined by experiences. Beautiful concepts and enduring beliefs were gradually and painstakingly shaped by the intelligence of her heart. And this process of conscious growth was reflected by the skills of the royal jewelers.

"My lady," Puyemre gently inserted himself into her reverie, "your thoughts are flitting like bolti fish in the lovely golden pools of your eyes and making me hunger for your voice to give them a form I, too, can savor."

She smiled at him fondly." Profound thoughts are not so easy to catch in a net of words, my friend."

"Ah! Well, there is nothing more engaging than watching your face no matter what you are thinking about."

She glanced at Senmut, a little annoyed he had never yet tried to outdo Puyemre's flattering remarks with compliments of his own.

He met her eyes.

Her challenging smile died like a torch dipped into black waters alive with irresistible and, she suddenly sensed, potentially dangerous currents. The effort she had to make to look away almost frightened her.

"I am tired," she declared. It upset her to end the evening with a lie but she was reluctant to once again meet Senmut's eyes.

* * * * *

In Year Three of the Good God Akheperenre, in the first month of Pert when everywhere fields enriched by the River were being sown, Queen Hatshepsut moved to the birthing arbor erected in her garden. The bed she would share with her baby for fourteen days and nights had been prepared using special sheets decorated with red and black stripes invoking the Goddess in her serpent form—the light forever burning in the heart of darkness creating, and flowing through, all living things. Garlands of specially grown flowering vines also evoked snakes where they coiled around the arbor's wooden frame.

The Dowager Queen attended her daughter. The white linen band Ahmose wore over her forehead and tied at the back of her head was reflected by two midwives, summoned all the way from the House of Life in Sait, who represented Heqet and Meskhenet. The gold birthing stool was placed on top of a large rectangular brick which also represented Meskhenet, the goddess who determines the newborn's destiny.

Hatshepsut was scarcely aware of anything except the pain that left her breathless with disbelief every time it blessedly receded. The murderous thrusts of a dagger could not have felt more dreadful. It did not seem possible she could survive such rending agony. Crouching over the birthing stool, she tried desperately to relieve herself of the demon trapped in her belly. Giving birth to another life was terrifyingly akin to fighting for hers.

One of the midwives held a cup to her lips.

She snatched it out of the woman's hand and downed the contents. She would have consumed anything to alleviate the cruelly repetitive torment.

"You will feel better soon," her mother assured her. "You were born on a night much like this one only the moon was full."

The breeze was cool but Hatshepsut was hot beneath the feathered cloak draped open over her bent knees so the midwife crouching before her could reach beneath the birthing stool. The second midwife knelt behind her.

Like a linen cloth wrapped around a sharp knife, what she had drunk only slightly dulled the agony and yet she still managed to feel thrilled when Ahmose said, "The head has appeared, Hatshepsut! Push! Push! Re is being born again between your legs!"

The mouth between her thighs was definitely on fire. She was already pushing with all her might but she took another deep breath and suddenly the relief was so intense she feared she might be going to her Ka. The burden she had carried for so many long months was gone, leaving her utterly exhausted, but strange, high-pitched cries kept her eyes from closing. One of the midwives was holding a bloody squirming shape which looked as if it was being attacked by a reddish-black snake. She realized then that the baby's placenta was still inside her when it abruptly rushed out from between her thighs, glimmering with unfathomable power.

"Pharaoh has a daughter!" the Dowger Queen announced in a voice that sounded not in the least bit disappointed.

"And her name is Beautiful Daughter of Re!" Hatshepsut proclaimed feeling as though she had magically been born twice in one lifetime. She was now both herself *and* this precious little girl. "Behold Princess Neferure, may she live!"

One of the midwifes cut the umbilical cord with an obsidian blade, a dark natural glass created from fire and cooled into form like the newborn soul. She then dipped the tip of her index finger into the placenta and held it close to the infant's lips. Neferure stopped crying and tried to suck it.

Hatshepsut watched with pride as her daughter recognized the magical remnants of her Ka. The princess was perfectly shaped, healthy and wise, just like her mother.

* * * * *

Ah-hotep, one of Senmut's sisters, was appointed wet nurse to the princess. Hatshepsut could appreciate why Inet had been awarded bracelets of honor. Caring for a newborn was surely more exhausting than fighting a battle that soon ended one way or the other. It was a great victory when the infant at last drifted off to sleep and peace descended on the birthing arbor.

She passed the first lazy days of her confinement caressing, enamored, the exquisite little creature she had miraculously fashioned inside her. The power of the gods truly lived in her womb, the mysterious workshop of Khnum. As her strength returned, however, she began feeling as restless as her daughter, whose formidable Ka seemed to be fighting her present physical limitations. It was obvious Neferure longed to speak and communicate her needs and was perpetually frustrated by her inability to do so. By the fourteenth day, Hatshepsut felt more like a helpless subject than like the queen of Kemet. The vines growing around the arbor, pungent with rotting flowers, gave her the impression she had been absorbed into the womb of the Great Mother, from which she was desperate to emerge into her own life again. It was soon apparent that she had not given birth to a fresh little version of herself—Neferure possessed her own infinitely precious, and passionately selfish, personality.

Ahmose-Penekhbet was honored with the position of Tutor to the Princess. Hatshepsut chose him because her own beloved Senimen was still attached to the fourteen-year-old Pharaoh, although Thutmose referred to him as his personal advisor rather than his teacher. Ahmose-Penekhbet was kind and patient by nature, qualities essential for dealing with a royal infant.

Hatshepsut was very happy to have her agile and slender body back. Nafre's special cream had worked; soon the skin of her belly was both smooth and firm again. She was particularly proud of her plump breasts, even though after she stopped nursing Neferure she suffered some serious discomfort for a few days. Ah-hotep had lost her own child, a boy who lived only two months, and her bosom was so full of milk whatever the princess could not drink was saved in clay vessels shaped like women with small holes bored through their nipples.

Ah-hotep's smile was understandably sad but she was a truly gracious young lady. Her eyes were as black as her brother's although not as large and the "falcon" nose was merely unfortunate on a woman. Nafre had recommended Ah-hotep. Apparently, the two had formed a close friendship. Hatshepsut was surprised and a little jealous for she had always pictured her attendant contentedly waiting for her to return from the Temple or the Seal Room but in reality she enjoyed a life of her own.

To celebrate Ah-hotep's new position as Royal Nurse, and her own blessed freedom from Neferure's adorable tyranny, she arranged a banquet to which Senmut's entire family was invited. She was curious to meet the Mistress of the House Hatnefer whose husband, the Honorable Ramose, had already gone to his Ka. From the few references he had made to her, it was obvious Senmut was very fond of his mother. It was natural for a son to feel that way about the woman who bore him and she hoped Hatnefer was truly worthy of his affection. Whenever she was obliged to attend one of her husband's formal banquets, she invariably met proud and haughty women only baby scorpions might consider lovable.

Scorpions—always prepared to strike and render powerless anyone who sought to harm their children—were sacred to *Serket-hetyt*, "she who causes the throat to breathe." Serket the Great, the serpent who nurses the king, had assisted Nepthys and Isis when they were guarding Horus from Seth. Serket was always there to help anyone who was stung by pain and adversity. But who was *she* exactly, this enigmatic goddess also found in the company of Neith?

Hatshepsut's body once again reflected the slender images of herself carved into one of the walls of the new festival court erected by Pharaoh in *Ipet Sut*. In the bas-reliefs she stood behind her husband and the Dowger Queen Ahmose offering the *neters* the gift of enlightened power joining heaven and earth. However, her perceptions felt fuller, as though the forces responsible for shaping another life inside her were now transferring themselves to the mysterious womb of her awareness, which seemed to be developing and growing more swiftly than before. She identified with her daughter's eagerly grasping hands and mouth as reflections of her own increasingly hungry feelings. Every experience felt as desirable as a nipple of the Goddess she savored with a gratitude magically poisoned by the need to experience and discover even more. Suddenly Serket accompanied her everywhere she went as a sense of her own intensifying desire to be truly worthy of the vulture crown.

Neith was behind her. Serket was before her. It was Serket who "stung" her with an even richer appreciation for the world and all it contained. Watching her baby was an education. When Neferure was awake she was alert and curious, challenged and delighted by life. Her passion for new and interesting experiences never abated and she made her displeasure excruciatingly apparent. Hatshepsut knew she could learn much from her daughter, especially now that the proper hierarchy had been restored—the princess affectionately ruled her nurse and worshipped her mother.

* * * * *

Hatnefer turned out to be a short woman with a plump round face, a broad squat nose and thick lips. Her features in no way resembled those of her two oldest sons, who had fortunately inherited only her large and slightly slanted black eyes. Except for Nofret-hor and Pairi, Hatnefer's offspring obviously took after their father Ramose. The lady was extremely polite but Thoth and Seshat must have been busy somewhere else when she was born for she smiled a lot yet spoke hardly a word. She was of common stock—a fact made rather embarrassingly obvious by her timid demeanor and crude features—but her eyes revealed to the world, with endearing frankness, that she loved all her children immensely in addition to being proud of them.

The banquet Hatshepsut arranged for the Royal Nurse Ah-hotep and her family was the last one she would throw in her old Pleasure House. On the following day she was officially moving to her new palace *I Shall Not Be Far From Him*. Everyone responded to the queen's excitement by talking and drinking more exuberantly than usual, except for Hatnefer who entertained herself mainly by smiling happily at her numerous offspring. Watching her, Hatshepsut wondered what it would be like when she herself was old and sitting placidly in a shadowy corner of the pavilion while her lovely daughter enjoyed the admiring company of handsome young noblemen. Immediately she banished the sobering vision by murmuring beneath her breath, "Serket is before me!"

As time passed couples began glancing her way and apparently interpreting her benevolent smile as a secret little hieroglyph giving them permission to caress each other more openly. She enjoyed observing them from the table she shared with Senmut, until she suddenly saw Nafre embracing and kissing another woman. Stung by a confusing jealousy she looked away and caught Senmut studying her face. It occurred to her he might be wondering if she permitted her favorite attendant to take similar liberties with her, a humiliating possibility which transformed into an odd feeling of excitement as he stared silently into her eyes.

"What are you thinking, Senmut?"

"Many things, my lady."

"You can only think about one thing at a time," she pointed out before abruptly realizing that was not true. "Or perhaps a specific thought is like the trunk of a tree branching out endlessly into others and it is, indeed, possible to see more than one at the same time… even if not so clearly as the one thought-branch you are focusing on at the moment."

He smiled. "Yes, that is a very nice was of putting it."

For some reason it gave her immense satisfaction, and made her truly feel like a queen, when how she expressed herself pleased him.

"Many thoughts pondered all at once can also be likened to a flock of birds soaring beneath the firmament of your skull," she went on. "And it would delight me, Senmut, if you would be so kind as to pin a single thought down and share it with me as we are sharing this delicious goose."

"I was thinking about you, Hatshepsut."

When Puyemre flattered her, he was more elaborately subtle, he invariably smiled and he *never* spoke her name.

He added quietly, "I am always thinking about you."

"Even when you are reading important documents Pharaoh trusts you to examine carefully, with the utmost concentration and care?"

"Yes," he confessed, still holding her eyes. "Even then."

His expression forced her to look away as she tried to determine how to react to it. Yet in order to do so she first had to decide how she felt about it and that was strangely impossible. Hatnefer looked over at them and abruptly seeing her own emotions reflected back at her she was forced to face them—elation and fear.

She raised her cup to her lips and took another sip of wine as she waited for Senmut to apologize, as he usually did whenever he had offended her in some way. The longer he remained silent the more a strange pressure began building up in her chest that forced her to turn her head and look at him.

He was still staring at her face. "You should not ask a man what he is thinking, my lady, if you are afraid of the answer."

"I am not afraid of anything!" she whispered furiously even though she understood that by doing so she was proving to be afraid someone might overhear them. "How *dare* you say that to me?"

"You asked me what I was thinking and I told you what was in my heart even though by doing so I put myself in a dangerous position. I knew I risked offending the queen but I hoped Hatshepsut would be pleased I had the courage to be true to Maat."

"Hatshepsut *is* the queen *and* God's Wife. How can you separate us in such a way?" And yet even as she spoke it was happening again—she could not remain indignant with him because she really did know what he meant.

He did not reply.

"Never mind," she said lightly, looking away again and concentrating on Meresankh, who was smiling happily at her new husband. "Naturally I am pleased with you for having the courage to always be true to Maat in your heart as well as with your words and actions. I am not at all offended, Senmut. Honesty can never be offensive even if the truth revealed is sometimes… confusing."

She sensed him lean over the table and then felt his warm breath on her cheek as he whispered, "You are so beautiful!"

Their argument had muted the joyful sounds of the banquet but now they surged back into her ears in vibrant waves of conversation, music and laughter, all accentuated by hands clapping an irresistible rhythm evocative of a man and a woman's naked bodies slapping against each others as they were possessed by Hathor. Her belly was no longer distorted and heavy; she was herself again, slender and beautiful. She could not blame Senmut for seeing what was true and for making her feel even lovelier. It was only natural he was always thinking about her. In fact, if he had confessed to always thinking about another woman in the Seal Room—or anywhere else for that matter—she would have been disappointed by his inability to fully appreciate her. She watched her handsome musician, Harmose, strumming his harp with his eyes closed, and the notes emanating from the sensitive strings responding to the caress of his fingertips expressed how wonderful she was feeling without the need for words. For a few moments, she almost forgot about Senmut, until the silence coming from the other side of the table somehow became louder than all the festive sounds embracing her.

Turning her head slightly she deliberately allowed her gaze to linger on Useramun, who was wearing a particularly flattering wig, before she at last looked back at Senmut.

His chair was empty.

She could not believe it. She suddenly found it hard to breathe. He had walked out on the queen's banquet where he occupied the place of honor beside her! He had left her party without even bothering to say goodbye! It was unthinkably rude. She would *never* forgive him! Then she saw him. He was kneeling in front of his mother—who was apparently not feeling well—holding her hands and gazing at her with a concerned expression that attractively sharpened his already distinguished profile. She was so relieved to see him that the stars pulsing beyond the pavilion all seemed to pierce her heart with their relentlessly ardent light. He had *not* insulted the queen and abandoned Hatshepsut. It did not matter that Hatnefer looked as if she might throw up. Everything was all right.

* * * * *

Hatshepsut crouched down to caress Bubu where he lay curled up asleep but instead of her beloved pet she discovered what felt like a wooden statue covered with hair. She screamed.

Nafre came running. "What is it, my lady?"

"Bubu!" she cried, clinging to her attendant. "My Bubu! He has left me, Nafre! He is dead!"

"Oh my lady, I am so sorry, but no cat could have lived a longer and happier life and now he is with the gods. There is no reason to grieve."

"Of course there is!" She turned away angrily. "He is gone forever! I will never hold him again! I will never pet him or fall asleep listening to him purr *ever* again!"

"He is hunting in a dream which never ends, my queen. His eyes are sharp and his muscles are strong and all the ducks in the celestial pond fear him. He no longer sleeps all day but instead runs happily after mice and pretty cats. His youth has been returned to him."

"But where am *I* in that lovely dream, Nafre? I know he loved me as much as I still love him! How can he be so happy without me? And why does his body not twitch as it often did when he was dreaming? He is *not* dreaming he is simply dead!"

"My lady, what seems like death to us is eternal life to him."

"Oh be quiet! What good is eternity if you cannot share it with those you love?" She flung out her right arm with the thumb held up and summoned one of the pages standing just outside the door. "Send a messenger as swift as his shadow to the Seal Room. Inform the Royal Scribe, Senmut, the queen wishes him to attend her."

Senmut arrived so quickly it seemed as though his sandals had grown wings and he had flown there rather than taken a litter. He strode into the room before the herald had even finished announcing him and the unguarded hope in his eyes told her she was about to disappoint him terribly.

She took a shaky breath and somehow spoke instead of sobbing, "Bubu is gone!"

He held her eyes for a moment before crouching beside the dead cat and gently caressing it.

"He liked you, Senmut. I want you to accompany him to the *Wabet* and to watch over him there for me. Make sure… make sure the priests of Anubis are… make sure they are as gentle with him as possible!"

He cradled the feline in both arms and stood. "I will take care of him for you, my lady."

She stared after him as he left the room, at the smooth skin of his back visible beneath his fine linen shirt, and felt inexplicably better. Nothing had changed, Bubu was still gone, and yet she was no longer quite so miserable. She sent for Neferkhaut to commission a wooden coffin for her beloved pet. She would bury Bubu in the loveliest spot of her new garden and when she went to her Ka he would come running to her again through the fields of Re, his tawny fur made of light and his blue eyes shining fragments of the eternal sky.

16

Seth and Starlight

Hatshepsut loved her new palace. One particular feature of the large limestone bathroom was especially delightful. After her attendants carefully shaved the sparse hair growing on her legs below the knees, the tender lips between her thighs and the skin beneath her arms, she took a shower. Servants stood behind a stone-framed basketwork screen and poured water over her in a steady stream as she rubbed herself clean with soap. She stood in a stone trough through which the water flowed out again without flooding the room.

A small narrow enclosure reminiscent of a shrine offered her a dignified privacy whenever she needed to relieve herself, sitting comfortably on a wooden seat with a hole carved in the center. The commode was held up by two brick pillars between which sat a bowl of sand. Servants emptied and refilled it after every use.

A special paste made from plant roots, which tasted awful, helped her teeth stay white and a liquid made from the ground leaves of the *sem* tree mixed with water kept her gums healthy. She rinsed her mouth every morning remembering what had happened to Amenmose.

She had long been proud of the crimson highlights in her dark-brown hair when the sun shone upon it and desiring this effect to be visible indoors, she had it dyed with henna. The results were not as dramatic as she had hoped and after a few weeks she impatiently abandoned the time-consuming conceit.

Tired of the red color every woman favored, God's Wife had all her finger and toenails painted black. *Kem* was pure power, the source of all light and life. Careful to leave a white crescent above each one, Nafre colored her mistress' nails black with a special absorbent paste into which soot and burned animal bones had been mixed. It pleased Hatshepsut immensely to watch ten crescent moons rise over her whenever she stretched her arms out to perform the gesture of praise and rejoicing. Puyemre dutifully admired her nails but she suspected he did not really like them. Senmut never gave any indication he even noticed them. All that really mattered, however, was that they pleased Hapuseneb. When the High Priest first saw her new polish, he grasped her hands and kissed each of her palms in turn, all the time gazing into her eyes in a way that transcended all possible compliments. Later that night, lying on her bed, she imagined him gripping one of her hands again but this time he lowered it to his kilt and permitted her to reach beneath it so she could stroke the forceful shaft of his phallus with her crescent moon crowned fingertips. Not a single day passed without her remembering, in tantalizing detail, the hot afternoon Seth had attacked when she was alone with Hapuseneb in the

Temple. The enemy of Horus now held a special secret place in her heart. Instead of being horrified by the knowledge that Seth—forever possessed by an unquenchable lust—had sexually molested his young nephew, the story shamefully excited her as she recalled that scorching afternoon in Hathor's sanctuary when the High Priest lifted her dress like an angry gust of wind and thrust his hand between her thighs. Her craving to experience those amazing sensations again became hopelessly confused with her growing respect for Seth, the jealous but undeniably virile brother of the frustratingly virtuous Osiris. Yet she could not bring herself to share these thoughts and feelings with Hapuseneb. He was the cause of her restless longing and no words he spoke, no matter how profound, would be able to make her feel better because it was actions she desired from him.

Thutmose had sailed for Mennefer taking a boatful of concubines with him and over forty additional vessels filled with possessions, body guards, court officials (including Senimen) scribes, priests, personal retainers, chefs, musicians and dancers. Her husband had been disappointed when she failed to produce a boy, but at least his potency had been proven along with her fertility and she suspected that was all he cared about for the moment. Nevertheless, before he left she was obliged to visit his bedchamber every evening for a week. He planted as much of his seed inside her as he could in the hope that when he returned to Waset she would be pregnant again. She rejoiced when, a week after his departure, the onset of her monthly cycle confirmed the feeling in her heart that he had never truly been inside her.

The Dowger Queen was accompanying Pharaoh on his royal progress and Hatshepsut was in charge of the Seal Room. Only Senmut dared express her own conviction the work went more swiftly and efficiently when her husband was not there to question everything. She could have stripped the Royal Scribe of his title and sent him back home to Iuny in disgrace. Instead it pleased her that he rarely referred to Thutmose as Pharaoh but simply called him "your husband" which almost made him sound less important than the queen of Kemet who was also God's, not just the king's; wife.

Akheperseneb, in his capacity as Chief Prophet of Maat, had just returned from judging a difficult case involving the daughter of the Nomarch of the Throne of Horus who had wished to divorce her husband.

"Why did this case require your special attention?" she said curiously. "It is my understanding any woman, rich or poor, may divorce her husband if she so chooses."

"That is so," he confirmed. "Unless she is accused of the Great Sin, then it is more complicated."

"She loses all her legal rights," Senmut explained, "if it can be proven she was unfaithful to her husband."

"I see. And was such proof obtained in this case and, if so, what was your verdict, Vizier?" She concentrated on her calm voice to ignore the anxious beating of her heart. "And please sit down. You look exhausted."

"Thank you, my lady." He raised his robe slightly and lowered his heavy body into a chair. "In this case it could not be proven beyond any doubt that the lady was unfaithful to her spouse, therefore it was my duty to grant her the divorce she requested. All the property she brought with her when she was married was returned to her, and she was permitted to move to a new house in her father's Nome accompanied by her son and daughter."

"I hope she will be happy there but I would like to understand the case completely. What evidence *was* there initially she had been unfaithful?"

"Several servants claimed to have seen her alone with another man, who they could not identify, engaged in the act." His perfunctory tone implied he wished they would move on to other matters that still needed attending to. "However, these servants had belonged to her husband before they were married and their loyalty to her was therefore in question. It was not outside the realm of possibility that her husband, desiring to keep all of her considerable property, either commanded or bribed his servants to lie about what they had seen."

"But is it then not possible this lady *did* in fact commit the Great Sin with another man even though no conclusive evidence could be produced to that effect?"

He gripped his knees as though he was sitting on a boat rocking in the throes of a powerful current. "Yes, it is possible, but not likely."

"Why? Could you see into this lady's heart, Akheperseneb? And what, by the Ka of Ptah, is her name?"

"Her name is Shemei, Desire, and she is the youngest most beloved daughter of the Nomarch of the Throne of Horus. All who know her, including most of her husband's own servants, had nothing but good things to say about her compassion and generosity. From all accounts she has always behaved most virtuously and intelligently. It did not seem in her character to act in the carelessly selfish way her husband accused her of doing. Yet he did not do so until *after* she had initiated a court case against him, a fact I considered quite suspicious and which in the end weighed in her favor."

"You are a wise man, Akheperseneb."

He inclined his head and grasped his left arm with his right hand. "My lady."

A herald entered the room and bowed, his arms crossed against his chest and his hands grasping his shoulders as he announced, "The First Prophet of Amun, the Governor of the South, the Mouth and Ears of the King, Hapuseneb!"

Her heart felt as though it was running toward the High Priest where he suddenly stood on the threshold. "Speak, your name is pronounced," she said, stretching her right arm toward him with her thumb held up.

He entered the Seal Room holding both hands before him, his arms bent slightly at the elbows and his palms facing forward.

She reflected his gesture of praise with her own but deliberately raised her hands slightly above her face to indicate she also rejoiced in his presence.

"Thoth has sent his messengers," he said. "The white ibises have appeared and the River which was green has become red."

She glanced around the room. Everyone except Senmut was smiling. No one looked as if they dreaded the fierce power of the Goddess returning home from Down Below even though her progress—in some places accompanied by crashing avalanches of parched earth—was inevitably accompanied by destructive plagues of insects and fevers of the flesh. But the rising River also promised the renewal of life and another year of natural wealth and abundance, which was indeed cause for happiness.

"Akheperseneb," she said, "your soul is lying in your hand. Please go home. I am sure your wife and children, and all your devoted attendants, miss their beloved master. As for the rest of you, my lords, you are also dismissed for the day with my praise. I would speak with Hapuseneb alone. Everything may be left as it is in preparation for tomorrow's work. When I am ready to leave Pharaoh's southern vizier will impress the door seals with his scarab rings and lock the palace."

Bowing slightly, the officials raised their hands before their faces. "Life, health and strength," they said and left the room followed by four scribes.

She seated herself beside the only large window; the room was primarily ventilated by smaller openings near the ceiling. All were covered by fine screens. Hapuseneb took the chair across from hers while two fan bearers approached to a respectful distance. The air outside was oppressively still and she was grateful for the slight relief from the heat offered by the gently waving ostrich feathers. She was tempted to tell Nafre to cut her hair level with her chin and braid it in a severe ancient style she imagined might please Hapuseneb as well as help keep her cool. She waited for him to speak but instead he smiled as he gazed down at her hands where they rested formally on the semi-transparent linen draping her thighs.

"The color and style you have chosen for your nails, my queen, is interesting indeed."

"You like them?" He had never actually said they pleased him, she had merely assumed they did because of the way he had kissed the palms of her hands the first time he saw them.

"I do like them, very much, for they reveal the depth of your beauty. You have pointed the way for yourself, Hatshepsut. It is time for you to look up and fully recognize the connection between your heart and the stars."

She gazed worshipfully at him before abruptly remembering she had failed to attend to his needs. She gestured to a servant. "Bring water and sesame cakes," she commanded, annoyed by the thought that his wife probably never left him waiting for refreshment when he returned home in the evening.

Looking earnestly into her eyes, he leaned forward in his chair and held out both his hands with the palms facing up.

Willingly, she placed her hands in his.

"There is a direct connection between our consciousness and the universe." He grasped her hands lightly. "As you know, we celebrated the festival of the Opening of the Year when at dawn *Sopdet*, the brightest star in the sky, rose again on the horizon."

"Yes. On that morning we lit new wicks all through the Temple to celebrate the return of Isis in her beautiful cloak of light."

"We did, for *Sopdet*, The Second Sun, serves as a measure of reference by which we track the movements of all the other stars in the sky. The length of the year is determined by *Sopdet*. But as the hieroglyph which spells *Sopdet* tells you, it is much more than just a light in the sky on which our calendar relies." He gave her hands a gentle squeeze then released them and sat back, staring at her in the way that told her he expected her to elaborate.

"The hieroglyph for *Sopdet* represents someone who is prepared, someone who knows the right way of achieving something."

"Correct. And *sba*, the hieroglyph for *star* and for *teaching*, when followed by the determinative of two legs, suggests the concept of crossing a threshold."

"So *Sopdet sba* means someone who is prepared to cross some sort of threshold in their knowledge?"

He nodded. "The stars, the planets, the sun and the moon are all now, in their relationship to each other, indicating the time is propitious for you and for others on the path of Maat to cross another threshold in their training. Tell me, Hatshepsut, do you feel differently about anything? Do you notice a change in your inclinations and dispositions on different days of the week and even at different times during each day?"

"Oh yes! Ever since Neferure was born, I have been feeling as though I can see... I do not know how to describe it really... I seem to see more clearly and vividly, and I feel as if everything has something important to teach me *about* the way I see... but now I sound like a snake swallowing my own tail!"

He smiled. "What happens in the heavens happens inside you, Hatshepsut. There is no actual separation between the earth and the sky, between the terrestrial and the celestial. All our feelings and thoughts are related to the transformative creativity of the stars. That is why, from the beginning of time, the priests of Kemet have studied the heavens."

"Is there nothing you do not know, Hapuseneb?"

His relaxed smile vanished. "I am not yet a god, Hatshepsut."

The presence of the fan bearers and of servants returning with cool water and sesame cakes prevented her from confessing out loud, "You are to me!" Instead, she said, "Is that why the last day of every month is dedicated to Min, because his stars are closest to us then?"

"The simple answer would be 'yes' but the truth is always more complex and we are discussing *Sopdet* and the path on which you are traveling, which relates to the masculine form of the star *Sopdu* linked with Horus. The enlightened person grasps the Laws of Becoming like a ship's rudder because life and death are only as the two shores of one endless River. Have you been thinking of Seth, Hatshepsut?"

She caught her breath. It was always a surprise, even though it had happened dozens of times, when he seemed to read her thoughts without her having to say anything at all. The fact that she sometimes feared him only deepened her attraction to him.

"How did you know that, Hapuseneb?" She dared to reply with a question of her own.

He smiled again, holding her eyes, and the silence between them struck her as so eloquent she had no desire to speak ever again for to do so would only separate them.

"Beware of Seth's forked tail," he warned, but his voice was gentle. "If you are not able to see past the brother of Osiris, but instead always walk blindly behind him, you risk becoming divided from your true nature, Horus-*Sopdu*."

"But how would Seth's tail do that to me?"

"By separating the pleasures of the body from the heart's more profound desires."

"But there is no possible separation," she argued.

"Seth is the enemy of Maat. Seth says the heart merely circulates blood through the body and that our animal appetites are all that matter until we die and cease to exist forever. Seth says a primordial chaos created our minds and bodies by accident and that our gradually decaying physical functions are responsible for everything we think, hope and imagine."

She laughed. "Seth is a fool. No wonder all his wives left him!"

"And yet never forget that by tearing himself away from his cosmic source Seth serves to inspire the birth of Horus inside us—the realization called 'faith' that physical forces are God's body, the eternal reality of Life assuming deliberately fixed and contained forms. Horus is the soul of the world, the triumph of God living and seeing through His own creation. Only when Seth and Horus stop fighting each other does evil cease to exist in the form of crippling destructive fears and hopeless greed. If all men were able to awaken Horus in their hearts the evil and injustice in the world would disappear and Maat would thrive everywhere."

"And that would be truly wonderful!"

"It would, but as we have previously discussed that is not the case, not even here in Kemet. When next I leave Waset, are you prepared to come with me, Hatshepsut?"

The heat suddenly struck her like a god's invisible hand slapping her whole body, forcing her to take a drink of water and to wave the fan bearers closer. She replied with a calm dignity she was far from feeling, "Yes, I am prepared."

"What about Neferure? Will you not be sad to leave her? We may be gone for a long time."

"You speak as if you are warning me yet surely you know your words ring like a beautiful promise in my heart." She hoped he understood she was telling him he meant more to her than anyone else. "No, I will not be sad to leave my daughter. She will be fine without me for a while."

* * * * *

Standing before her in a sanctuary lit only by a single candle, Hapuseneb said quietly, "Why have you not asked me what the stars are, Hatshepsut? Do you not wish to learn more about them?"

"Of course I do, but I feel as if I already know what they are even though it could be said I truly do not know at all."

"Tell me."

"Stars are the way we see." She stared up into the bottomless darkness at the center of his eyes in which the flame of the candle was reflected like two distant stars. "Stars are light. Stars are the eyes of Atum."

"And where is Atum?"

"In your eyes. In *our* eyes. The dark hole in our irises that expands and contracts, responding to different intensities of light, is God's heart beating inside us."

"You do not perceive the darkness between the stars as cold and empty?"

"It appears to be but in my heart I do not feel it is."

"And yet all the stars shining within it cannot brighten the darkness of the night sky."

"That is because darkness is nothing and yet contains everything that can possibly be, which means darkness exists beyond the reach of the stars which are *something*. Stars are the doorways through which the love burning in Atum's heart manifests as light. The space between a woman's thighs is also a doorway and so the sky is depicted as the body of Mother Nut bent over the world. Nut is the Divine womb of all light and life, her arms and legs the four pillars of heaven creating north and south, east and west, time and space, life and death."

"The sun is an Eye of Re. Do you believe the stars are also suns?"

"It is possible."

"Then why can we not feel their heat?"

She glanced at the candle. "This flame gives off warmth I can feel if I stand close to it, especially if I put my hand over it, but when I move away I see only its light without being able to sense its heat. Perhaps the stars are distant suns?"

"Yes." Smiling, he raised his right hand and caressed the air before her face, lovingly stroking her features without actually touching them.

Closing her eyes she inhaled the subtly intoxicating scent of his male flesh.

"You truly see with your heart, Hatshepsut. Kemet is blessed by its queen."

"And I am blessed to have you as my master, Hapuseneb. Without you my heart would not see so clearly for it would not feel so intensely."

"You would be equally bright without me."

"As bright as a star?" she teased.

"Beneath the stars is where all your fellow students are waiting for us on the temple roof."

It filled her with joy that he sounded reluctant to leave the intimacy of the shrine decorated with Nut's starry body.

Reverently, he framed the candle flame with both hands before blowing it out.

She bumped up against him, pretending to be confused by the sudden darkness.

He slipped a hard arm around her waist and whispered in her ear, "We must wait!"

* * * * *

Senmut brought a gift to her one afternoon when she was resting in her garden accompanied only by Nafre. She was in the process of teasing the Royal Scribe about looking like a field-hand who had stolen his rich master's clothing when a tawny bundle of fur with blue eyes perched on the rim of the basket he was holding. She cried out with joy and promptly rescued the kitten from the precarious position its curiosity had put it in.

"Bubu! You have come back to me!" She cradled the creature against her heart not caring that its claws ripped some of the leaves and flower petals of her floral collar as it attempted to climb her chest. "He looks exactly like Bubu did when he was little!"

"I searched for him as the priests search for the *Apis* bull, my lady. Such eyes are hard to come by."

"Indeed they are! Do you believe it is possible Bubu was reborn in the hope I would find him and we could be together again?"

"If such magic is possible it has little, in my opinion, to do with hope. A cat does much more than *hope* when it hunts, during which it employs all its senses and skills. Hoping is pleasant but passive."

"Are you saying that Bubu's Ka—magically able to see in the darkness of the Dwat just as his eyes were able to see on earth at night—hunted the female cat destined to be his mother and pounced into her womb, thereby mysteriously becoming his own prey?"

"You have a way of phrasing things that makes anything seem possible, my lady. I cannot say if the cat in your arms really is Bubu reborn, I only know there is no reason to think it is not, especially if you believe it."

Utterly indifferent to the discussion of its purported powers, the kitten struggled to squirm beneath the solid shadows of her braids.

"But belief is not enough," she argued. "Something has to actually be true in order to matter. If this is not really Bubu then I cannot feel the same way about him."

"Perhaps there is no difference between what is real and what you feel." He stared into her eyes as he added, "Perhaps the limits of reality are determined precisely by what we dare to feel is possible. There is, however, no way to prove that really is Bubu reborn and trying to eat one of your fish ornaments."

"No, Bubu," she scolded gently, prying him off her ruined collar and holding him lovingly at arm's length. "I called him Bubu when I saw him! It *must* truly be him and you have found him for me again!"

She set the kitten back in the basket. "You have made me very happy, Senmut. I will never forget it."

Bowing his head, he grasped one of his shoulders with his free hand. Then he looked at her again and said with quiet intensity, "It seems to me that happiness is very easily forgotten by most people, for when they experience it they do not notice it and only its absence feels remarkable for the pain and emptiness it brings, which are all too easy to recall. And yet, my lady, I have no doubt you will indeed remember how happy you are now and I cherish, as I do nothing else, the joy it brings me to serve you in any way possible. But I want you to realize my devotion to your pleasure is not limited to what is presently in my power to accomplish. Above all things it is my desire to overcome any shortcomings of character and skills, knowledge and wisdom which hinder my ability to always make you happier than you have ever been. These moments of contentment now will seem as nothing compared to the joys I will strive to bring you in the future, my queen."

She exclaimed, "Senmut!" awed by his beautifully phrased promise that did not feel merely like the elaborate compliment of an ambitious courtier. She recalled how he had knelt before his mother's chair and the love on his face. His expression now looked equally genuine.

Tired from his adventure with exciting new landscapes and sensations, Bubu Reborn had curled up in his basket bed. She touched him to feel his warm fur and the gentle rise and fall of his chest. He had fallen suddenly and deeply asleep. Perhaps he was dreaming of the Dwat, where he battled the forces of darkness like the Great Cat of Iuno who protects the sacred Persea tree— symbol of the rising sun—from Apep, the serpent of death and dissolution. And yet Apep, when when magically controlled, serves as the agent of rebirth.

She said, "Perhaps Bubu knew the first time he saw you in the Seal Room, Senmut, that you were the person destined to search for him after he was reborn and return him to me."

"Perhaps he did."

"I am in the mood to go hunting," she announced. "Are you a good hunter, Senmut?"

"I think my family would tell you I am."

"Then you will accompany me. We will make it a festive outing. I will invite my favorite friends and you may also bring whomever you wish." She smiled. "Is there some special lady who desires to show you the color of her bosom?"

He stared into her eyes and did not reply.

Suddenly, she was ashamed of herself for treating his expression of devotion to her happiness as lightly as she had the kitten's adorable curiosity. "It would please me if you would ride in my boat, Senmut."

* * * * *

Large tents were erected near the most favorable entrance to marshes wide enough to accommodate three boats sailing side-by-side. The queen's party arrived at the landing spot shortly before sunset. The River was filled with life but that evening the papyrus thickets lining both banks were utterly still and silent. Marveling at the clarity of the details brought out by the golden light, softly tinged with crimson, she remarked on the dying day's lucid beauty.

"It is a girl's heart suffused with desire," Puyemre described it. "See how her eyes sparkle with expectation in the water and how her hair flows in the shadows?"

"I see." She smiled. "Is this girl thinking of the night's secret pleasures?"

A flock of pintails burst noisily out of a thicket and painted a dark arrowhead against the luminous sky as they flew off.

Puyemre laughed. "Of course she is!"

Senmut added dryly, "What else could she possibly be thinking about."

The queen's gentle army of servants had arrived earlier and made everything ready for them. Before the largest of the four tents, a single chair and several stools had been arranged around a stone hearth in which a fire would be lit should the night prove cold enough to require it. Hatshepsut was well pleased with her make-shift quarters illuminated by eight free-standing alabaster lamps. Her lips did not tire of smiling as she listened to the laughter and voices clearly audible through the cloth walls. It pleased and excited her to know the silhouette of her figure was visible to all the young men waiting for her outside as Nafre undressed her. She was bathed with a wet cloth and a delicately scented cream was massaged into all her limbs. Then from the many garments folded into a cedarwood chest, she selected a short-sleeved tunic made of wool dyed a dark red. To wear over the form-fitting dress she chose a tabard of golden beads that clung to the gentle curves of her body like a net.

"I have been caught, Nafre!" She laughed.

Kneeling at her mistress' feet, onto which she was slipping soft black leather sandals, Nafre looked up at her.

"Are you well, my sister?" The odd expression on her favorite attendant's face—which could not be called pretty except when she smiled—concerned her.

"Yes, my lady, I am well." She stood, crossed her arms over her chest and lowered her head.

Outside the tent, Seshen's bawdy laughter rose above the more delicately expressed amusement of the other women in the party—Senmut's youngest sister Nofret-hor, Meresankh and Useramun's bride to be, Tjuya.

"Why are you being so formal with me, Nafre? Put your arms down and look at me. Do you miss Ah-hotep? I am sorry she could not accompany us but I did not wish to expose Neferure to any fevers the reeds might be concealing." Also fearing Bubu might wander away from his basket and be eaten by a crocodile she had left him safely behind in the palace.

"You are very sweet, my queen, but I do not miss Ah-hotep."

Listening to the stimulating voices of frogs—that never hesitated to express themselves no matter how funny they sounded—a question leapt out from where it lay concealed in the thickets of her thoughts and feelings. "Do you miss the lady I saw you kissing at one of my banquets?"

"No." Nafre smiled slightly. "I do not miss her."

"Then who has entered your heart, sister? Please tell me."

"I cannot, my lady."

She was impatient to make her appearance outside, and to enjoy her first cup of wine, but her attendant's obvious unhappiness felt like mud around her ankles she could not easily walk away from. "*Why* can you not tell me?"

"Please, my lady, do not worry about me. I am perfectly happy here with you."

"You do not *look* perfectly happy," she observed a bit impatiently.

"I am only tired. A cup or two of wine and a little food will restore me."

"Very well." She selfishly embraced that explanation for the moment. "But you should be less restrained with your appetites, Nafre."

"My lady?" She suddenly sounded breathless.

"You may partake of as much wine and food as you desire," she explained cheerfully. "We must please Bes so he remains to protect us from fevers concealed amidst the waterweeds. Ill health plagues those whose hearts do not beat love and joy at every moment. It is happiness that keeps us healthy, Nafre. I wish to see you rejoicing in the knowledge that of all the women in Kemet you are the most beloved by its queen."

When she emerged from her tent, Duaunehe and Useramun were fencing each other with papyrus stalks. Immediately they dropped their makeshift weapons and clasped their shoulders. Illuminated by a full moon and burning torches, their skin shone like a smooth molten mixture of gold and silver yet looked infinitely more precious.

"You should not have stopped," she reprimanded them lightly, "for by doing so you have denied me the pleasure of offering a beautiful gift to the victor."

Useramun promptly retrieved his stick. Duaunehe raised his own weapon just in time to deflect a blow that nearly felled him. He was taller than his opponent but younger, and too considerate by nature to attack as often or as ruthlessly as he should have. Useramun had no such qualms and it was not long before he knocked Duaunehe's weapon out of his hands and emerged victorious. Hatshepsut raised her arms to him in praise without rising from her gilded wooden chair. In the flickering torchlight the duck legs and beaks of the stools her guests occupied seemed actually to clutch their wooden bases as they strained to support the people perched on their backs. Wine was poured, food was served and Useramun sought to win another gift from the queen by standing and challenging Amenhotep to a wrestling match.

The child of Anukis appeared reluctant to accept as his hand rose to the silver amulet that always hung around his neck.

"I will hold the goddess for you, Amenhotep," she said, realizing his opponent could use it against him, "and add my blessing to hers."

Useramun's confident smile deepened for she had implied Amenhotep needed protection from his opponent. He thrust his shoulders back proudly. Two of his attendants had already begun oiling his body.

Amenhotep slipped off the amulet and placed it gently in her cupped hands.

Senmut stood abruptly and whispered something in Amenhotep's ear.

Hatshesput wondered what secret the Royal Scribe had revealed to Amenhotep which gave him the power to win the match, although not until after a considerable and, for her, highly enjoyable struggle. Amenotep was more slightly built than Useramun, whose ideally proportioned muscular body she enjoyed watching the most even as she hoped the future priest of Anukis would win. Tjuya kept jumping up and overturning her stool, oblivious of the servant who quickly righted it for her again each time. Hatshepsut sympathized with the girl's anxious excitement and with the look of mingled relief and disappointment on her pretty face when her betrothed emerged unharmed but defeated.

Senmut had somehow made it possible for Amenhotep to win and Hatshepsut was certain he had done so for her sake. Throughout the night she found herself gazing at him, her eyes drawn to the sight of his face as moths were to the flames. He never caught her staring at him and she suspected that was much more his doing than hers. She sensed he was protecting her feelings, making sure she never had cause to be embarrassed by her interest in him.

She had brought a handful of musicians with her and Useramun and Tjuya responded to the popular love songs they performed by walking off together into the impenetrable shadows of the date palms.

I found my love by the secret canal,

  feet dangling down in the water.

He had made a hushed cell in the thicket, for worship,

  to dedicate this day

To holy elevation of the flesh.

He brings to light what is hidden

    (breast and thigh go bare, go bare),

Now, raised on high toward his altar, exalted,

    Ah!...

A tall man is more than his shoulders![26]

The plan was to wake just before dawn when the moon was setting and the sun preparing to rise. It was hard getting out of bed.

"Was the servant in charge of heating my water eaten by a hippopotamus during the night?" Hatshepsut said testily as Nafre bathed her with a cold wet cloth.

"I thought you might find this invigorating, my lady."

She looked down at her taut breasts and hard nipples. "Well, it certainly *has* roused me."

"My lady, your breasts are round as ripe fruit and yet to the touch they are as soft as a flower's delicate petals!"

"Thank you, Nafre. Do you like touching my breasts?"

"How could I not, my lady?"

"Would you like to kiss them?"

At once Nafre dropped the towel and boldly grasping the queen's hips began sucking on her right nipple much like a starving infant.

Hatshepsut looked down at her curiously. The pleasure she experienced was very subtle but it intensified exquisitely each time Nafre hungrily switched nipples. It felt wonderful to be so worshipped but her friends were waiting for her and she was eager to begin the day's hunt. The prize of ducks and geese, quails and pigeons and, best of all, their beautiful queen's admiration and favor, awaited the hunters. She could scarcely wait to see how Senmut would perform.

"That is enough for now, Nafre."

Her attendant released her and staggered back. "Forgive me!" she gasped.

"Forgive you for what? That was a lovely way to wake me up. I will definitely give you permission to do it again but now you must dress me. The new day is nearly come and I wish to see Re rising above the reeds triumphing over darkness."

Senmut killed more birds than anyone else between teaching her how to use the throwing stick. She managed a few well-aimed tosses but her arm was not strong enough to launch the weapon far enough. It often proved nearly impossible to hear what was being said over the flapping of birds rousted out of the papyrus thickets where they made their nests. The eggs were nearly as delicious as their parents. In the mornings her tongue especially relished the unique texture and flavor of a sun-like yoke not yet solidified into flesh. The magic of Amun-Re was everywhere. Sunlight glittering on the water like millions of tiny spear points was the beautiful force of Re's love flowing with the boats and protecting their occupants from any crocodiles lurking in the shadows cast by the dense flora. The noise of felled birds hitting the water, followed by the more subtle splash of servants diving in after them, kept rhythmically drowning out the sound of human conversation and laughter. All day long the men enjoyed challenging each other's skills.

"Will you kill a hippopotamus for me one day, Senmut?"

"If that is what you wish, my lady, I will try."

"You will *try*?" She turned and called across to another boat. "Useramun! Will you kill a hippopotamus for me one day?"

"In one day I will kill as many hippopotami as you desire, my queen!"

"You see, Senmut? For me he will not only *try*, he will succeed."

"Or he will die, which is highly likely if he tries to kill more than one hippopotamus at a time."

"But of course *you* would never be so foolish."

"I hope not."

"Not even to please me?"

"If I thought it would please you to see me, or anyone else, behaving foolishly, I would not wish to serve you as I desire to do above all things, my queen."

"You are correct, Senmut, I never *really* want someone to do anything foolish or dangerous believing it will please me. I was merely teasing you." She raised her voice, "Useramun, I have changed my mind! The Great One is not to be played with!"

She looked up to adjust her sunshade, avoiding Senmut's complacent smile, and the star-shaped supporting frame attached to the long wooden ray of the handle reminded her of Hapuseneb. Suddenly she missed him so much the sunlit day was swallowed by the luminous darkness always living behind her closed eyelids.

"Is it too hot for you, my lady? Do you wish to embrace the shade until Re becomes Atum?"

Lifting her lids, she gazed at Senmut's face and was awed by the thought that his two eyes also possessed the ability to view the splendor around them—the world animated as if by its own beauty where colorful birds flew, men dove, fish leapt and darkly luminous water flowed around the papyrus boats.

"No, it is not too hot for me, but thank you for your concern, Senmut. I was thinking."

He waited.

"I was thinking how mysterious it is that we must see God in everything to see Him at all."

17

Commanding Chaos

Stepping into *Ipet Sut's* sacred interior, Hatshepsut felt a rush of confidence catching sight of her shadow. Her shade was majestically tall and slender and clearly delineated against the great stones of the forecourt. She could hardly wait to see Hapuseneb again. She had come home to Waset pleasantly relaxed but also possessed by a profound need to return to the consecrated precincts of God's house. Within the Radiant Place of the First Occasion, there existed a reassuring sense of order. Riding in a boat surrounded by the clamor of birds' wings, she had felt less in control of her thoughts and feelings than when she was in the Temple. She could better appreciate now why ducks and other wildfowl were often used to symbolize sensual and emotional chaos. The throwing stick wielded in Senmut's expert hand had begun to feel like the reach of her own heart, with its cathartic ability to conquer fears, doubts and uncertainties. It had aroused her admiration to watch his accuracy with the throwing stick, perhaps because *qema* "throw" also stood for the concepts of creating and begetting. On her hunting trip, the strength and skill of men had constituted a vital part of her pleasure for without them her hunger would have remained unsatisfied. The act of spearing a fish was expressed in the word *seti,* which could also mean "to impregnate." A man's force entered a woman in a similarly direct and violent way, thrusting into the passage between her legs which could become so welcomingly wet. The *medu neters* helped her understand now why her restless frustration had evaporated on the long hot days she spent fowling and fishing with Senmut and other attractive men.

Clutching a fly whisk scepter against her heart, Hatshepsut glanced at her shadow as she walked. Her shade was the reflection of her Ka's unassailable strength. The pillared hall erected by her father had felt too much like the swamp she had just returned from, shadowy and lush with papyrus and lotus stalks. Once created by Hathor—who served her Father Atum-Re as his Eye—substance thrived independent of God, propelled by its own laws and blind momentum. She was beginning to fully comprehend what the High Priest had meant when he said every temple in Kemet kept chaos at bay. Throughout the Two Lands, the First Occasion was ritually reenacted every day to keep the infinite spirit of God alive in the substance generated by the Goddess, and all the forms it assumed as finite projections of a single Divine essence. She was also increasingly aware of how, left to herself—specifically without Hapuseneb—her feelings would degenerate into a chaos of hopeless longings. Hathor's sensual magic could not be separated from the Supreme Being she birthed the universe to please. The God's Wife was always depicted the same size as Amun-Re on the walls of His temple but without His infinite love her heart and her hand would be empty.

A *wab* priest had informed her that the First Prophet of Amun was in Hathor's sanctuary, the very special place where they had taken refuge together on that beautiful afternoon Seth sent a sandstorm into Waset. Her happiness as she anticipated seeing him again grew with every step she took, until she heard the sound of women singing and abruptly understood they would not be alone. Her excitement died completely when she caught sight of the Royal Ornament, Amenhotep, standing beside her husband. It was the prerogative of the High Priest's wife to supervise the Songstresses of the God and the voices of the priestesses—rising with ardent clarity from within the sanctuary—testified to the fact that she was doing an excellent job:

Amun created the Two Lands and set them in place,

the temples and the sanctuaries.

Every city is under his shadow,

so that his heart can live in that which he had loved.

People sing to him under every roof,

every foundation stands firm under his love.

They brew for him on festival days,

they pass the night still wakeful at midnight.

His name is passed around above the roofs,

song is made to him at night when it is dark.

The gods receive sacrificial bread through his life-giving power,

the power of the strong god who protects what is theirs.[27]

Standing in the sunlight Hatshepsut felt the world darken as Amenhotep smiled at Hapuseneb and received the blessing of his approving smile in return. Because she desired to be alone with him, she had dismissed the priests who otherwise would have escorted her through the offering courts but now she felt infuriatingly awkward waiting to be noticed.

As though sensing her presence, Hapuseneb turned his head and saw her hesitating outside the sanctuary accompanied only by her shadow. The smile lingering on his lips vanished like a trick of the light as he raised his right hand to silence the women who had begun talking amongst themselves. "The queen of Kemet and God's Wife!" he announced and held both his arms up to her in praise.

She stepped into the cool shade of the sanctuary feeling her heart burning to ashes in her chest. The conflagration of feelings consuming her made it impossible for her to speak. Staring into his eyes, she silently commanded him with all the force of her Ka to rescue her from the intolerable situation. Amenhotep's secure little smile felt like a throwing stick aimed straight at her pride and power. Her heart beat faster, struggling not to drown in violent emotions. The singers under the Concubine of Amun's supervision—including her two oldest daughters Henut-nefert and Ta-em-resefu—had immediately lowered their heads and crossed their arms over their chests when the queen was announced, but Amenhotep had dared to meet the eyes of God's Wife before clasping her shoulders and looking humbly down at the ground. It was obvious she had borne many children—her breasts were too large and sagged a little—but her hips were becomingly full and her legs were so long she was nearly as tall as her husband.

"Leave us," the High Priest commanded. He held the queen's eyes and did not once glance at his wife as she departed at the head of the long line of songstresses.

Even after the other women were gone, Hatshepsut was unable to find her voice for a moment. She lowered the fly whisk scepter and approached him. "Do you love her?"

He responded quietly, "She has a place in my heart."

"I desired to speak with you alone." She gazed miserably up into his eyes. "Why did you not send for me?"

"I wished to speak with you here in the Temple. I missed it."

"And it missed you, as I have."

The bird of her heart she had feared might be dead suddenly beat swiftly to life again. "You missed me?"

"Yes. You should not be surprised. Did you enjoy yourself?"

"Yes." She looked past him toward the dark corner where he had pressed her back against the wall and lifted her dress what felt like a painfully long time ago. "Would you join me for some refreshment while we converse, Hapuseneb?"

"There is nothing I would rather do, Hatshepsut."

The uncontrolled intensity of his response thrilled her and her happiness was restored. The chaos of jealousy, fear and doubt were averted and in their place love, hope and excitement once more reigned.

They walked together through Amun's garden along the path that would bring them to the gate opening onto her own lavishly landscaped Pleasure House. She did not wait until they reached it to begin sharing her thoughts with him.

"I have just fully understood how the expansion of substance away from the moment of its creation on the First Occasion, and its consequent disassociation from its Divine source, is what causes order to become disorder. Is that not the chaos the temples of Kemet hold at bay?"

He smiled at her. "The riverbanks spoke to your heart while you hunted the creatures which thrive in them."

"They did indeed. I see now that left to itself the substance created by God's Hand becomes more and more disordered until it eventually dissipates like smoke. Maat is the light-creating life and *Isfet* is the darkness of material death.[28] That is why the sacred fires burning in all the temples throughout the Two Lands are never extinguished as a symbol of the Divine creative principle that flows through every living thing."

"Not only as a *symbol*, my queen. A temple truly is the body of God, the home not merely of His image but of the actualizing magic of the Ka which serves to realize His desires."

"That reminds me. I have also been thinking of the five bodies that compose me, specifically my Ba, my Ka and my Akh. Would you please help me better understand them, Hapuseneb?"

"The Ba is the Spirit of Fire that gave birth to the universe. The Ba is depicted as a bird with a human head to symbolize a Divine energy perpetually nesting in corporeal forms and returning to its own boundless essence, a process that gives birth to what we call the Ka. In the Ka elemental forces, and the sensual perceptions they are mysteriously designed to engender, are indistinguishable from each other. The universal Ba is individualized through the Ka that shapes all our bodies and determines the circumstances of our incarnation. The universe is a nest of laws where the Ka lays the eggs of unique worlds, lives and experiences which serve to enhance our creative abilities and nourish God's heart through ours."

"It is very strange to think that my Ka, like the great Persea tree, is home to many Ba-birds. How can I be more than one person at the same time?"

"Are you the same person you were when you were born?"

"Yes... I mean, I am not a baby with pudgy little hands and feet and no teeth, but I still am who I always have been, *Hatshepsut*."

"That sense of self you possess, no matter what you look like, is your Ka that grows and deepens by way of all the forms it takes through endless lifetimes as a falcon feasts on worms and a vulture on carrion. Corruptible flesh is akin to a serpent caught in the beak of Horus."

She voiced her fear, "But then I will not always be Hatshepsut."

"Hatshepsut will live inside you forever just as the child you once were exists in the woman you are now."

"Does that mean that when I am next born on earth I will be even wiser?"

"Perhaps, but the fact is we are often truer to our hearts as children than when we grow older and succumb to pressures which seem more important than our feelings and all their hopes and dreams. I do not mean to confuse you. The path of Maat leads off the easy road of popular beliefs onto what might appear to be dark and twisting passages but you should not feel threatened."

"I do not feel threatened," she assured him even though she was not being entirely true to Maat by saying so.

"Are you afraid you may be reborn in the outermost ring of the circle at the heart of which lives the palace temple?"

"Yes." It was a relief to admit her distress at this thoroughly unappealing prospect. "It would be awful to be born a poor and smelly fisherman's daughter!"

"The only power you truly possess lies in the intelligence of your heart. A smelly fisherman's daughter can be as wise as a queen. The vulture crown confers earthly rule but not true greatness. You, Hatshpsut, are blessed with both." He reached for one of her hands and grasped it urgently in his. "You are truly beautiful!"

Joy at the way he looked at her rendered her speechless for a moment. "But I will not always be beautiful, Hapuseneb. I will grow old. And then, after I die, I may be reborn deformed!"

He laughed. "Your Ka may be forced to actualize your fear in order to help you transcend it. Conquer it now and you will save yourself the trouble of dealing with it in the future."

"You told me once that my Akh came into being when I recognized my Divine nature. Is my Akh what will enable me to travel between this world and the next when I am dead? One of my attendants tried to contact the Akh-spirit of her mother's mother to request her help in becoming pregnant but so far nothing has happened. Does that mean the Akh-spirit she is trying to reach is not powerful enough to help her?"

His smile faded. "My queen, it pains me to see you struggling to rise above the dangerous marshes of superstition. Where there is love there is power and the depth of the heart determines its degree. That is all that can really be said on the matter. When we love, we exercise the only force which truly exists and transcends physical limits. This is why we can still sense the presence of a loved one even after they die."

Turning to face her, he thrust his right hand beneath the heavy fall of her natural hair and gripped the back of her neck. "This is where the magic of the Ka resides, the column linking mind with body, thought with feeling, energy with substance."

Abruptly he slipped his left arm around her waist and lifted her up against him as he lowered his head to kiss the sensitive little hollow of flesh joining her neck with her breastbone. He licked her throat and she parted her lips hopefully for his kiss. She gasped when he bit the side of her neck instead. Closing her eyes she saw in her mind's eye a delicate bird caught in a leopard's jaws as he turned her around, pressed her back against the front of his hard body, and clutching her throat with his left hand completely cut off her breath. She was not frightened. All that mattered was the forceful way the heel of his right hand was rubbing her in the magical place just above her sex. The pleasure was immediate and intense. His erection dug into the small of her back and overwhelmed her with promise. The searing ecstasy felt much more important than breathing. She climaxed so swiftly and with such force, she felt as though the solar disc had plunged from the sky and become trapped between her thighs.

"You see, Hatshepsut," he whispered in her ear, "how the neck is not only a *symbol* of the space between heaven and earth? The neck truly is where the magic of the Ka lives and exerts its control over natural rhythms."

Turning her to face him again, he gripped a fistful of her hair and made her look up into his eyes. "I am very pleased, my queen, by the way you fearlessly embraced the energy you felt rising inside you when, by cutting off your breath, I opened the door between this world and the next."

＊ ＊ ＊ ＊ ＊

Bubu Reborn was as fond of Inet as she was of him. Perhaps the fact that her vision was beginning to surrender to the veil of twilight had something to do with their improved relationship. She could no longer clearly see the shining blue eyes which had made her so superstitiously nervous and Bubu, sensing she was no longer afraid of him, was able to like and respect her. It also seemed possible the magical cat was helping Inet see in ways she never had before. Smiling beatifically, she would gaze vaguely at the queen who had once suckled at her breasts while caressing Bubu with slow rhythmic strokes, sending him into loud raptures of purring. Hatshepsut was glad they would keep each other company while she was away. Neferure, who grew more beautiful and demanding by the day, would also remain in Waset. She would miss her daughter as well as her new palace and Pleasure House and shower. She would miss Puyemre and Senmut. Nevertheless, she could hardly wait to leave. The High Priest had finished building the ship on which they would travel together on her first royal progress as queen. Preparations for their departure had already begun when a messenger from Pharaoh arrived to announce his imminent homecoming. Thutmose would be disappointed he had not received news she was pregnant again but she had no intention of conceiving before she left. Her attendants already knew what to say when the king docked in the Town of

Amun and sent for her—God's Wife had begun her monthly purification and could see no one.

Of her friends in the temple, only Djehuti and Useramun would be traveling with her. Minhotep had become a *wab* servant of Amun and she did not doubt he would soon rise higher in the sacred ranks.

Duauneheh came from a wealthy local family and for the moment had chosen not to serve part-time as a priest. When he was not away at his country estate, he was apprenticed to the Director of the Granary of Amun and to the Overseer of Works in the Temple.

Amenhotep had temporarily returned to Abu to be dedicated as a priest of Anukis and to marry Amenemnopet, the girl who had lived in his heart since they were both children.

Puyemre's heart had also been stolen, by Hapuseneb's youngest daughter. Since her betrothal to the queen's beloved friend, Senseneb had become the only member of the High Priest's family ever to grace one of Hatshepsut's banquets. Senseneb was barely ten-years-old, still too young to wed, but already she fascinated the witty Puyemre into uncharacteristic silence. Her upward slanting deep-brown eyes, glinting with an unusually sharp intelligence, sank like fangs into his heart and paralyzed his tongue. Hatshepsut sympathized with the elation tainted by frustration he obviously suffered whenever he saw his future bride. It was three years in the future but at least the date for their marriage had already been set. Impatiently anticipating it, he channeled his passions into a full-time vocation as a *hmw-neter*, Servant of God, allowed to enter the sanctuaries and to partake of the food in the offering hall. For the youngest son, just turned sixteen, of the Noble Lord Puya and the Royal nurse Neferiah, the income and lands awarded by the Temple were a welcome blessing.

Upon his return to Waset, Pharaoh sent word regretting he would not experience the pleasure of embracing his wife before she left and wishing her a lovely journey. She was relieved and surprised he did not insist on seeing her once her purification ended and before she departed, until she learned he was rumored not to be feeling well. He spent every day in his bedroom attended mainly by a new concubine he had acquired in Tantera whom he favored above all the others. The girl's name was Isis. She was of noble birth and, according to the rumors, extraordinarily beautiful. Hatshepsut pitied her.

* * * * *

The God's Wife and the High Priest of Amun departed in the middle of the month of Epiphi, when the sun and the moon were closest to each other in the heavens, on the Day of the Beautiful Embrace. Dowger Queen Ahmose had sailed south from Tantera with Hathor and together they would remain with their Lord in Djeba for fourteen days and nights. It was a time for feasting and rejoicing. The day before she and Hapuseneb left Waset, Hatshepsut stood on the Temple roof to watch Hathor's great ship *Mistress of Love*—its gilded red oars flashing in the sun—float majestically up the River escorted by five only slightly smaller vessels. The boat flying the emblem of a falcon transported the *naos* housing the statue of Horus, who was attended by all the singers of his most ancient temple in Nekhen and by its High Priest, Tjeni. The Headman of Djeba rode in a separate boat, and Pharaoh's steward and treasurer, Ahmose-Penekhbet, captained the barge honored with towing the Goddess. At the head of the procession, the Nomarch of The Frontier oversaw the opening of the waters by sounding their depths so the Divine couple would not run aground on a sandbank.

Hatshepsut had cried out when she caught sight of the lovely woman's face carved on the prow of Hathor' ship. It was distinguished by bovine ears and a crown of curved horns cradling between them the white-gold disc symbolizing the sun. From that distance, it had been difficult to make out the figure of the Dowger Queen standing before the shrine containing the image of the Goddess hidden from the public eye. She had not seen her mother since she left Waset with Pharaoh nearly a year before. When Thutmose had returned to the Southern Seal Room Ahmose had remained in Tantera to prepare for the festival of The Beautiful Embrace. Hatshepsut missed her very much and knowing it would be a long time before they were together again she had rejoiced at the opportunity to spend at least one precious night in her company.

The River had been crowded with smaller vessels rowing behind the official procession and for as far as she could see both shores teemed with cheering people. Carried aloft on the shoulders of her priests—flanked by soldiers peacefully but effectively forging a path for the Golden One—Hathor had disembarked to visit the Temple of Amun where she resided as God's Hand. That had been Hatshepsut's cue to leave the roof and join Hapuseneb in the shadowy coolness of Akheperkare's hall of pillars. Pharaoh remained indisposed and the High Priest had welcomed the Goddess in his place. When the great copper doors began opening she had blinked wildly as the sunlight of the public offering court flooded her eyes. For a few moments the Dowger Queen's figure had been barely distinguishable from Re's splendor. Conjured and directed by the procession—in which lavishly jeweled priestesses, all of whom wore *menit* necklaces, burned a pungent and peculiar smelling incense—Hatshepsut had felt magic lap in invisible but invigorating waves against her senses, carrying her away on a feeling of profound well-being which almost immediately drowned her ability to think coherently. She had seemed to float rather than to walk behind the Goddess as though it was her own body being borne aloft on the broad shoulders of handsome young priests. Unaware of the ground beneath her sandals she had scarcely noticed the transition from Amun's House to the smaller temple of his consort, where she stood before the sparkling waters of *Isheru*, her ears filled with the high humming vibrations of colors dividing the world into beautifully distinct shapes. Everything she saw, heard, smelled, tasted and touched had suffused her heart with joy. Her body had felt like the center of everything, her heartbeat indistinguishable from the pulsing music played by temple musicians. She had literally seen the earth breathing through the chest of the sky. Her arms raised exultantly in praise had formed part of Hathor's sistrum which at every moment vibrated her perceptions and dimensions into existence.

Hatshepsut did not understand exactly what she had experienced the afternoon Hathor visited Waset. She had lost track of whole stretches of time during which anything might have happened. All she knew was that she had never felt so intensely and invulnerably alive and so in love with the magic of her senses.

She left Waset at dawn enthroned beneath a pavilion set on a pedestal in the center of the majestic vessel, which curved up at prow and stern into tall gilded stems with papyrus-shaped capitals. The High Priest stood behind her right shoulder, his right leg extended and his black staff planted protectively before her.

As they left the shipyard behind, and floated past urban centers where not a single tree grew, Hatshepsut found herself regretting that she had not had the opportunity to bid farewell to Senmut, who was currently in Iuny visiting his mother. He had left a week ago looking morose. She hoped Hatnefer was not ill for she disliked seeing the Royal Scribe distracted by unhappy thoughts. She would not be seeing him at *all*, for a long time.

The wind blew south as the water they rode flowed north and her thoughts and feelings obeyed the same contrary rhythm—excitement quickened her pulse as she anticipated the new places and experiences awaiting her even as she suffered a gentle undertow of sadness thinking about all the people she was leaving behind her.

When only field-hands dotted the shores—their bent bodies straightening from the work of harvesting Geb's bounty as they waved joyfully at the royal progress—Hapuseneb walked around her chair and offered her his hand. She accepted it gladly and as they stepped off the pedestal, the freedom to move about at once dissipated her melancholy. Eight oarsmen sat on both sides of the vessel's broad center but they would not be working very hard until they reached Mennefer. In the back of the ship, behind an open pavilion and two private cabins, sailors manned two larger and longer oars they used to steer the course. Nafre was waiting to divest her of her fly whisk and lotus bud scepters. Platters of dried fruit, sesame cakes and cups of goat's milk had been arranged on a short table set before large and colorfully embroidered cushions stuffed thick with goose feathers.

As one hour led them placidly to another, Hatshepsut lost count of all the southbound ships they passed transporting a variety of cargo, including large stones meant for temples. She did not attempt to keep track of the innumerable fishing vessels drifting slowly with the current, or of all the little reed skiffs flitting swift as fireflies in both directions while steering respectfully around the large pleasure ships of noblemen, which were in turn dwarfed by immense barges transporting harvests of emmer wheat and barely to royal granaries.

She thoroughly enjoyed the subtle exhilaration of conversing and relaxing embraced by a changing landscape which stimulated her senses and perceptions. The River was a luminous skin flowing over the tireless muscle of the life-giving current journeying all the way from its tumultuous birthplace in the south to its peaceful death far to the north, where it was transformed into the Great Green Water.

The captain was a competent man but Hatshepsut did not find him very interesting. She was happy to let him spend the day at the front of the ship, in his own modest shelter constructed of plain wooden poles decorated only with brightly painted papyrus heads. It pleased her to be able to see all around her past the gilded stems of her own comfortably large pavilion, where she was able to forget about Nafre perched attentively on the edge of a cushion as far away from the queen and the High Priest as possible.

When Re was at his most powerful Hapuseneb sat up and asked her permission to retire to one of the private cabins. They had been reclining on their sides facing each other, at first conversing but then simply staring into each other's eyes for long stretches of time, during which she was enveloped by a feeling of contentment deeper than the River. Never before had they relaxed in each other's company as they did on his beautiful new ship the first day of their journey. She had avidly studied his face and feasted on all the nuances of his features. He was wearing a short white linen kilt that tied closed just below his navel. The only detail which occasionally differed was the amulet he selected to protect his belly and sex but it was usually a scarab, each one rendered uniquely potent by the qualities of the material from which it was carved. She was shy about permitting her eyes to travel freely up and down his body even though his soft smile seemed to encourage her hungry exploration. When at last he had looked away and sat up she remained where she was, reluctant to be roused from a wonderful waking dream where she had forgotten about everything except him.

He said tenderly, "Curl up like a cat and take a nap, my queen. I will wake you in the evening."

Gladly she obeyed him and when next she opened her eyes, it was his smiling face she saw again, as though no time had passed at all. Gently he wrapped her fingers around an alabaster cup full of water and she drank it thirstily.

They stood together at the western railing watching the solar disc descending into desert mountains. Above them two falcons were rising and falling together on the wind's invisible currents, the bottoms of their outstretched wings catching the sunset's golden light.

She said, "That is how I feel when I am with you, Hapuseneb."

* * * * *

They spent the first night of their journey in the Nome of the Two Falcons.
The Headman of Gebtu met them at the dock, and then escorted them in a
torch-lit procession to the Temple of Min where they made offerings to the
virile form of Amun. Hatshepsut was not so tired she could not appreciate the
thrill of fully experiencing a temple she had visited twice before but scarcely
remembered. The first time she had been only nine-years-old. The second time
she had been on her way to marry her little brother in Tantera and too sad to
notice much of anything.

Reigning in the sanctuary—all four of its stone walls decorated with herds of
white bulls that seemed to circle her lustfully—the life-size statue of the god
was breathtaking. His handsome black face smiled at her benevolently as she
approached offering him the round stone breasts of two *nw* jars in her
outstretched hands, one filled with milk and the other with water. Illuminated
by alabaster oil lamps, Min stood on a pedestal set before a false door. The door
was engraved with three man-sized heads of lettuce that grew straight up toward
heaven from the hieroglyph symbolizing a garden. His features had been so
expertly carved she could almost feel how much he enjoyed holding his
enormous erection in his left hand. Tall and rigid with Divine virility, his body
was tightly sheathed in white linen bordered by gold from which only his
phallus, and his upraised right arm brandishing a flail, emerged. Min-Amun-ka-
mutef, Bull of his Mother, He Who Conceives Himself, took the form of a man
wearing a golden crown topped by two long stiff plumes—each one divided
into seven sections colored red, green and blue—from which issued a red
streamer that flowed all the way down to the floor. His commanding stance was
in no respect weakened by the pleasure he was forever giving himself. As she
poured life in two streams before him she felt him silently promising her the
fulfillment of all her desires, both sensual and spiritual, for dividing them was
evil and punishable by the flail he perpetually wielded.

The queen and the High Priest of Amun dined with the Overseer of the
Prophets of Min, Ahmose-Ruru, in his beautifully furnished home. The sign for
the Nome of The Falcon was two falcons perched on a pedestal, Horus and
Rahes—Regent of the Land of the South, protector of Pharaoh's mines in the
eastern desert. There Min had once been called Menu, What is Seen, and He
Who Raises His Arm in the East. Hatshepsut was grateful that she was wise and
beautiful enough to merit Amun-Min's full attention through his priests,
especially when they were still virile enough to serve him properly. She knew
Hapuseneb was many years her senior but she could never imagine him growing
old. His Ka was so potent she did not doubt he could imbue his flesh with the
incorruptible strength of stone while still keeping it warm and supple.

As the conversation moved from religious themes to administrative matters her attention wandered. She concentrated on the white wine of Sekhmet, which was as fine as any she could remember tasting. When she expressed her interest in the year of the vintage and its maker, Ahmose-Ruru promptly sent his secretary to speak with hers so Neferkhaut could record the information and order as many jars as she desired. The happiness she felt knowing her journey with Hapuseneb was only just beginning made everything seem even more lovely than usual that evening. The same dishes her chefs prepared for her at home tasted especially delicious. She wondered if it was her excitement flavoring them or a special blend of herbs and spices new to her palate. Even the green beans, which she normally disliked, were made delectable by the sauce enveloping them. The lentil salad was also surprisingly light and refreshing served on a bed of lettuce.

Hapuseneb sat at her table in the center of the room so they could speak privately together whenever they wanted to. Useramun and Djehuti were also present at the small banquet. The soldiers traveling with her, commanded by her Chief of Security Mentekhenu, were staying in the Headman's garrison. Her personal retainers slept in the servant's quarters adjoining the High Priest's villa. It had been a long, lazy, wonderful day on the ship and the evening proved so stimulating Hatshepsut had no trouble falling asleep in a strange room. The furnishings were not as luxurious as the ones back home in her palace but there was, to her immense delight, a shower.

∗ ∗ ∗ ∗ ∗

The queen slept late while the First Prophet of Amun attended to some arcane temple business, then together they boarded the ship again and proceeded toward Hathor's city in the Nome of the Crocodile, reaching Tantera early in the evening. The waning moon was rising as they docked and abruptly Hatshepsut felt her monthly purification arrive more than a week before it was due. She retired to one of the private cabins and suffered the heat of the enclosed space as Nafre bandaged the wound between her legs. The dull ache swiftly radiating from her womb into her lower back seriously depressed her.

"The goddess loves you, my lady," Nafre spoke with confidence. "She loves you so much she wants you to spend more time here in her home city."

The pious observation helped her feel a little better about the fact that she would not be seeing Hapuseneb for five days or more. She decided her attendant was correct, it *was* the Goddess who was delaying her Progress. She could not have chosen a better place to spend her monthly confinement than in The Castle of the *Menit*, also called The House of Incarnation. Hathor was renowned for her ability to revive an ailing Ba by way of a healing sleep, in which the cause of the body's illness was revealed and addressed in dreams. She continued to be fascinated by the doorway of sleep through which all the feelings living in her heart poured out like children to play in a space free of frustrating limits. However, during her prolonged stay in Tantera, Hatshepsut's dreams proved unremarkable. Though she was disappointed, she was not surprised. She had not really known what she hoped to learn while she slept. It had been foolish to expect the Goddess to pay attention to a wish not passionately and properly expressed.

Hatshepsut thought that she was perhaps behaving like a child who plays too close to the River and its bank dwellers. It was entirely possible Hathor was protecting her from all the hostile forces she might encounter in the Dwat. The consort of Horus—who even now was with him in Djeba—bore no love for the crocodile that had threatened her husband's life when he was a baby hiding in the marshes with his mother. Seshen told her how some people in nearby Gebtu crucified hawks merely to annoy the Tantrites, who were themselves famous throughout Kemet for their skill in capturing and killing crocodiles, the symbol of their Nome. The thought of anyone murdering the embodiment of Horus was appalling and Seshen fell into the queen's disfavor for several days merely because she had laughed while describing the gruesome rivalry. Like a crocodile, Seshen no longer seemed to have a tongue as she attended her mistress in silence afraid of incurring her further displeasure.

During her confinement, Hatshepsut found herself missing Neferure. In memory, her daughter's selfish cries for attention sounded admirably ardent and she almost felt guilty about leaving her behind. Her only clear dream was of the River flowing endlessly north, not merely to the great cities and temples of Kemet but much, *much* farther toward places and peoples she could not even begin to imagine. It was a relief to open her eyes and still find herself in her Beloved Earth.

She wondered if, like a crocodile, she was being too greedy, hungering for true dreams. She felt ready to take command of the magical realm of sleep but perhaps she was not. Hapuseneb had told her she would one day be ready to pass through the skin—the mysterious initiation she had been preparing for since she was a little girl. She rejoiced in the confidence he had in her, but not knowing what challenges awaited her also nervously made her wonder if she was truly ready for them. In the end she concluded fear was the main reason she was attempting to so quickly seize and master the otherworldly power of conscious dreaming. All the different ways to write *crocodile*—One Who Seizes, Greedy One, The Enemy, Mouth of Terror—seemed to reflect her own doubts and insecurities, which lay concealed beneath her positive nature in a way that could diminish her Maat if she did not roust them out and kill them. Just as the Tantrites successfully hunted crocodiles, it was essential she become more skillful at exposing and destroying any negativity concealed so deep in her emotions she was scarcely aware it distorted them. It was vital she not become *syntyw-kpw*, the enemy of her own Ka, by permitting hidden fears to manifest as quarrels between the intelligence of her heart and impulses nourished by anxieties. She had the power to defeat the emotional crocodiles bread by her physical body's mortality if she was never foolish enough to pretend they posed no threat to her well-being and happiness.

18

Sensual Foundations

Reverence thou god upon his road, even him that is fashioned of precious stones and formed of copper, even as water that is replaced by water. There is no river that suffereth itself to be concealed; it destroyeth the dam with which it was hidden.[29]

The words of wise men who lived hundreds of years ago made more sense to Hatshepsut now that she was older than they had when she was a child and forced to copy them over and over. Without the education she had received from Seni, and continued to expand in the Temple, she would have found it much more difficult to think about her feelings and understand them.

Many memories flowed through her on the River. Vividly she recalled the dangerous wild waters the *Falcon* and its vast entourage had encountered on the way to Kush. She still marveled at how efficiently the great ships had moved across the land on Pharaoh's command. Thousands of men had obeyed her father without question even though his sandals were no bigger than theirs. It was not fear they had felt when they followed him. They had felt what she still felt for the man who had kept her safe and well fed—love.

He is a master of grace, rich in sweetness, and through love hath he conquered.[30]

Seni and Hapuseneb had both taught her that her thoughts were the soldiers under her command and the greater her knowledge the more she could accomplish with them. Yet no matter how large and well-trained, an army was nothing without its general—her heart, in which the words of the great vizier Ptah-hotep, composed so long ago, rang with ever renewed relevance:

Follow thine heart so long as thou livest and do not more than is said. Diminish not the time in which thou followest the heart, for it is an abhorrence to the Ka if its time is diminished.[31]

Be not arrogant because of thy knowledge and have no confidence in that thou art a learned man. Take counsel with the ignorant as with the wise, for the limits of art cannot be reached, and no artist fully possesseth his skill. A good discourse is more hidden than the precious green stone, and yet is it found with servant-girls over the mill-stones.[32]

If thou art a leader and givest command to the multitude, strive after every excellence, until there be no fault in thy nature. Truth is good and its worth is lasting, and it hath not been disturbed since the day of its creator.[33]

There were no serious faults in her nature which she could see but perhaps that in itself was her greatest fault of all.

She had entirely too much time to think on the ship. At least she was always with Hapuseneb and could share her thoughts with him whenever she wanted to.

"It affected me deeply to meet Min in his sanctuary," she told him. "I saw in the god more things than my attendants and most other people seem to perceive. They believe his face is painted black to represent the fertile soil of the immersion that every year brings life and abundance to Kemet."

"And so it is."

"But I thought his black skin symbolized the infinite darkness from which all light and life emerges."

He smiled. "And so it does."

"Are you teasing me, Hapuseneb?"

"Yes. You are well past the point where you should be tripping yourself up with such thoughts. A symbol has many layers and most hearts see only the obvious ones. Some hearts look deeper and God rejoices in them, for only through passionately discerning Ka's is His potential fully realized."

They were standing at the railing. She looked down at the ship's hull surging through the water and a wish flowed out of her, "More than anything I desire to make Amun-Re rejoice in his daughter by helping everyone see the greatness of His love even if they cannot fully understand the workings of His divinity."

"You will, Hatshepsut. The stars have said it."

She looked at him. "How?"

"On the night you were born priests studied the heavens and drew up the chart of your destiny. Seshat's brush is dipped in the moon's palette. Your body— with all its different phases, from infancy to old age—is a reflection of your Ka's power and subject to the influences of the forces it harnessed to create you."

"Lately I have thought that when the moon is full it resembles a fingertip pointing down at me."

"You are God's Hand. The full moon is *your* fingertip."

"And I feel it prodding me to do beautiful things so I may truly become who I already am, the queen of Kemet and God's Wife... although when I try to pursue such thoughts they become confusing."

"That is when you stop thinking and reverently nurture the feelings blooming from the seeds of your thoughts."

"But it is the desire to express how I feel that leads me to think and say certain things in the first place."

"You have hit upon the heart of the universe, Hatshepsut. The cosmic serpent swallows its own tail perpetually. Just be careful not to bite it off by thinking too much."

"It is sometimes difficult to tell when you are teasing me, Hapuseneb."

He was silent a moment then said, "I noticed the other evening, when we dined with the High Priest of Min in his home, that you lost interest in the conversation when it turned to administrative matters, in this case the trade expedition that had recently left Gebtu for the Great Green Water to the East, and the results of the mining expedition sent out during the last inundation."

"I was listening," she protested, stung by the truth of his accusation for she *had* permitted her mind to wander a bit. "The miners returned with quantities of carnelian and jasper, some garnet and serpentine, and as always there was much wonderful hard stone to be found in the desert sacred to Min."

"You know what they brought back but can you tell me what it cost them?"

"What do you mean? It is the Headman of Gebtu who pays the workers with onions, beer and bread, leather kilts and sandals."

"Seven of the miners were crushed by falling rocks, three were fatally stung by snakes or scorpions, four died of fever and at least ten were too weak to walk home and were borne back in litters, although it is hoped they will soon recover. It is difficult work wresting Geb's treasures from his grasp. Can you better understand now, my queen, the value of the beautiful bracelets you are wearing?"

She looked down at her wrists. The smooth precious stones set in gold were a vital part of her beauty. She knew what their materials and colors symbolized and had earned the right to wear them.

"Every person," she said firmly, "goes to their Ka when they are destined to do so. Seshat and Meskhenet write our fate the moment we are born. The gods rejoice in the splendor of the stones men mine. I am sure those who die in the process are well received in the golden hall of Osiris."

"What about their loved ones? Their sorrow must also be added to the cost."

"All of us lose people we love for one reason or another. Are you suggesting that the most splendid substances generated by Hathor should remain hidden away forever because it is too dangerous to reveal them?"

"You know I am not. If you truly wish for everyone to see the greatness of Amun-Re's love you must first express it and behave compassionately toward all your subjects."

"I can do nothing for the men who died but I *can* see to it that the Headman of their home city supplies their families with headrests for their bodies,[34] and with extra beer and bread so they can joyfully bid their loved ones farewell."

He stared at her intently. "And?"

"And the Overseer of the Work should be questioned," she realized abruptly. "Surely falling rocks can be better avoided. I also think more monuments inscribed with the image of a scorpion should be set up around the work sites and extra jars of water provided so water can be poured over the magical stones and drunk by everyone. That should help protect the miners from deadly bites. Weakness is often caused by not drinking enough water so it would be a good idea to provide more of it to all future expeditions. Fevers are less easy to ward off since you never know where they might come from, but priests of Sekhmet accompanying the miners can help cure those who fall ill. They can also heal minor injuries that might become more serious and weaken the body if not immediately treated. In fact, it seems strange so many men suffered when such simple steps could have been taken to prevent the accidents and illnesses. I repeat, the Overseer of the Work and the men directly beneath him should be questioned, and so too should the Headman of Gebtu who, I assumed, appointed them. He cannot be blamed if the miners themselves behave carelessly but he *should* be held to account for injuries and deaths that occur for potentially preventable reasons. On the return voyage I will have a word with him."

Suddenly it occurred to her that she had just experienced Min-Amun's flail wielded by the High Priest when he accused her of not paying attention when she should have. His rebuke had hurt her and for a hot instant she had been indignant, almost angry with him, but his comment had made her think. Her thoughts had then led her feelings along behind them—like a herd of Hathor's sacred cows—as the sensual pleasure she took in her jewelry was threatened and she was forced to find a way to defend it.

"I wish now," she added, "I had paid more attention to the Headman of Gebtu and all he said. Amun breathes in everything, even in what appears to be a boring conversation. Thank you for helping me understand, Hapuseneb, that whenever I fail to pay attention I not only dishonor God but diminish him. His love and compassion live in my heart and it is my duty to express them whenever possible... always!"

He clutched his right forearm and bowed his head.

Observing the way his fingers dug into his skin she sensed he was making an effort to control himself. More clearly than ever before, she felt how much he desired to take her in his arms. It seemed (she wanted to believe) the effort he made to suppress the urge became greater every time. She fervently hoped so for it meant that one day, possibly soon, he might not succeed.

The royal party arrived in Hut-Sekhem in the seventh Nome of Upper Kemet, The Sistrum, well before sunset. Its principal temple dedicated to Bat had stood on the western shore for more than a thousand years. It was now called The Mansion of the Sistrum for Hathor had merged with the local goddess who was once depicted as a sistrum crowned by a woman's head, her flat bovine ears and curved horns surrounded by stars. At that point, the River flowed east to west from Tantera to Hut-Sekhem where many noble men and women were buried. The city had originally been named after its builder, Kheperkare is Mighty, and ever since then had acted as the heart of the seventh Nome.

Khenti, Leader, the Nomarch of the Sistrum, was a surprisingly young man. One night not long ago both his parents had gone to their Ka together. "Clutched in each others arms like two birds mating in flight," he described it, and for the rest of their stay continued to delight them with the lovely astuteness of his perceptions. A wisdom that seemed too rich for one so poor in years was revealed in the vivid images he conjured with his words. Bat had clearly blessed his birth. Tall and slender, Khenti moved with the confident grace a panther might display if it was able to walk on two legs. His eyes narrowing mischievously, he laughed as often and quietly as a cat purring, without showing any of his teeth. Not long ago his wife had also died, in childbirth. The son she bore him had survived only nine days and yet his faith in the beneficence of the gods remained as strong as the stones of the ancient cemeteries he guarded.

Exceptionally pretty girls worthy of Pharaoh himself served the white wine of Bast and the delicacies which preceded the red wine and richer dishes of the banquet the Nomarch of the Sistrum held in honor of the queen. Khenti's eyes told her he was genuinely pleased to have her there. He slaughtered his fattest cattle for the occasion even though the king and the Dowger Queen's entourage had also visited him recently and considerably taxed his resources. Or perhaps not; Hatshepsut's instincts told her The Sistrum was extremely well-managed for its Nomarch was quick to pounce on the smallest unsatisfactory details. More than one platter of food had to be sent back to the kitchen when Khenti's remarkable sense of smell detected an extra ingredient he declared had spoiled the subtle balance of herbs and spices necessary to create the most truly superior flavors. Such a man was not one to permit loose rocks to crush his workers; he would discern the danger and promptly do something about it.

Hatshepsut was too delighted with their host to leave right away. She chose to stay another night and observe the cattle census scheduled for the following day. In the pavilion erected for the occasion, a lily scepter resting against her heart, she was enthroned to the right of her host. Empowered by Pharaoh, Khenti exercised control over the Nome of the Sistrum and was privileged to hold a golden *kherep*-scepter in his right hand. Hapuseneb sat on her other side grasping the black staff of his priestly office. Her position, she felt, was a very pleasant one to be in.

She was already impressed by the size of the herds and as the day progressed her admiration only grew. In Khenti's domain, the masterful defeat of chaos was invigoratingly evident. Hundreds of fat horned cattle marched past the pavilion on their slender legs, skillfully driven by young herdsmen who still held the coils of rope they used to tether the animals to stones planted in the fields designated for grazing.

After the chief herdsman kissed the ground between the queen and his master, he was given permission to rise and proudly watch the animals he protected trot swiftly by in a single row while four scribes recorded their breed, sex, condition and quantity. The third scribe did not have much to write for every cow, and the less numerous bulls, looked remarkably healthy. The smiles Khenti cast her way—wisely not attempting to speak over the thundering of hundreds of hooves—told her he was happy to pay the considerable tax due to the crown because the more he owed to Pharaoh the wealthier he was. She enjoyed imagining his eyes were also saying he would willingly give even more of everything he possessed to his beautiful queen.

It was with regret that she watched Hut-Sekhem disappear into the shimmering distance like a dream evaporating in the uncomfortably real heat. Barren cliffs gradually encroached upon the shore and reduced it to a narrow strip of greenery where there was depressingly little room to grow anything. She had spent only two evenings and one day in his company and yet already she missed Khenti. She consoled herself knowing she would be seeing him again on the return journey. She had also invited him to visit her at court as soon as she returned to Waset.

"Men such as the Nomarch of the Sistrum are the glory of Kemet," she said to Hapuseneb.

"Indeed. He is very pleasing to the Ka."

"He is remarkably wise for one so young."

"Do you feel that way about your husband?"

The flail of Min struck her again. She fell back across the cushions of their onboard pavilion struggling with the pain it exposed. For some reason she thought of Senmut and realizing how deeply she missed him eclipsed the superficial fancy she had taken to Khenti.

She closed her eyes. "No, I do not feel the same way about Pharaoh." She always told the High Priest of Amun the truth no matter how dangerous it might prove.

She felt his warm breath on her lips as he whispered, "I know you do not. He is not even remotely worthy of you, Hatshepsut. But do not worry. Do not be sad or impatient. You will be fulfilled. Trust me!" He did not kiss her.

* * * * *

Hatshepsut suffered mixed emotions when that afternoon they docked at Abedju. The Nomarch of Great Land actually resided a few miles north in Tjeny but Abedju was the burial place of Osiris, the spiritual heart not only of the eighth Nome but of all Kemet. She remembered the brick temple dedicated to the Foremost of Westerners, but not as vividly as she recalled how impatient she had been at the age of ten to leave behind all the boring revered dead and continue the festive voyage to her new home in Waset. That was before anyone she truly loved had gone to their Ka. The Nile had risen ten more times since then and, inundated by tears of grief, her feelings had become deeper and richer. The last time she walked through the town of Osiris her father had held her hand. That was when he and the queen had always seemed to be together, as they had been on the morning they visited the Temple of the Good God Nebpehtire. The bas-reliefs decorating the white limestone walls were so detailed and colorful that even then she had enjoyed staying to read the stories they told. The battle scenes looked more exciting than frightening filled as they were with handsome young soldiers fighting behind their king, groups of archers shooting arrows and great oared ships being launched into the River. One register was replete with the dead bodies of bearded foreigners wearing long fringed tunics, and still holding the swords with which they had uselessly tried to defend themselves from the speed and efficacy of Pharaoh's horse-drawn chariots. Seni had told her that long ago there had been horses in Kemet but they died out and were not seen again until the Setiu used them to divide the Two Lands. She did not like horses very much. They felt more dangerous to her than valuable for they could bring chaos and destruction on their heels as swiftly as they could be used to defeat it. It was not the cobra but the horse shying away from it too abruptly that had killed her brother Wadjmose.

Visiting the Temple of Ahmose again as Queen of Kemet in the company of Hapuseneb, she was even better able to appreciate the masterful might of her mother's father who had made the woman he loved the first God's Wife.

"I must learn to ride a chariot." She often voiced her thoughts out loud when she was alone with the High Priest. Energy and agility, strength and endurance were all virtues embodied by the horses in Pharaoh's stables, their glossy well-tended coats proudly catching Re's light when they were taken out to be exercised. The fact that even as a grown woman she remained a little afraid of horses indicated she had something to learn only they could teach her. Horses had come from foreign lands but they were mysteriously as much a part of her heart as animals native to Kemet.

The pyramid of Nebpehtire was not as awe-inspiring as those in Mennefer but it still cupped her heart and raised it up its shining slopes, which almost hurt the eyes to look at as though a piece of Re himself lived in the monument's substantial light. The pyramid dedicated to Ahmose-Nefertari was modest enough to be contained within the walls of her temple. Though its dimensions were less elevating it was nevertheless an uplifting expression of her spiritual equality and of the love her brother and husband had felt for her.

The people entering and leaving the large square building at the base of Nebpehtire's pyramid, and the brewery and bakery to its east looked smaller than they actually were. The Ka's of King Ahmose and his queen were revered in Abedju and throughout the Two Lands. Hapuseneb remained in the sacred precinct's administrative center while she and her attendants proceeded farther out into the desert. Ahmose had constructed a false tomb Hatshepsut felt compelled to explore, as though it might actually bring her closer to the next world and its magical powers, but the small door leading into a low-ceilinged passage only made her uncomfortable. The sensation caused her to wonder if that was how she had felt when she was trapped in the tight cleft between her mother's legs during the process of being born in an earthly form. She did not enter the dark unfinished rooms on either side of the passage but she was acutely aware of them for they excited her like possibilities yet to be realized. At the same time they made her nervous, like the chance of choosing a wrong path in life that leads nowhere except to a terrible feeling of emptiness. The hall at the end of the corridor was supported by eighteen pillars and completely empty.

She was happy to leave the sinister demands of the cenotaph and walk once more beneath the sun to the shrine of Queen Tetisheri, the mother of the mother of King Ahmose and of his wife Ahmose-Nefertari. The large mud-brick building, similar to the ancient mastabas of Mennefer, contained an altar on which Hatshepsut's attendants placed her offerings. She then made her way alone down a long and narrow passage to the monument—a large limestone slab engraved with two images of Tetisheri enthroned back to back. Both wore the vulture headdress and received the gifts offered to her by her daughter's son. Decorating the top half-moon shaped part of the stone, a solar disc—adorned with a necklace of erect cobras—spread majestic wings over the hieroglyphs declaring Pharaoh's intention to build Tetisheri a pyramid.

The King himself said, "I remember my mother's mother, my father's mother, the Great King's Wife and King's Mother, Tetisheri the justified... My majesty wants to have made for her a pyramid estate in the necropolis in the neighborhood of the monument of my majesty, its pool dug, its trees planted, its offering loaves established..." Now his majesty spoke of the matter and it was put into action. His majesty did this because he loved her more than anything. Kings of the past never did the like for their mothers.[35]

Hatshepsut gazed at the inscription for a long time wondering if she too was destined to have a son as splendid as Ahmose. He had loved and respected both his sister and his mother's mother so much that they were now worshipped as goddesses even though Tetisheri had been a commoner. She did not sense the promise of such a son in her heart but neither did she feel the need for one. Her mother's father had already given her all she could possibly desire by instituting the position of God's Wife of Amun.

Much as she rejoiced in her family's achievements, it was a relief to board the ship again and relax beneath the pavilion during the brief journey to Tjeny. She did not like being reminded of the Setiu and of how long they had ruled in the north. Meanwhile, in the south, the descendants of the last true king who sat upon the Horus Throne of the Living had wielded a limited authority subject to the invader's whims. It was distressing that Maat had for so long been diminished by people who did not understand her even though outwardly they pretended to respect her. But all during those dark times Amun-Re had held his children close to His heart in *Ipet Sut,* which slowly grew along with the hope, courage and effective force that at last rose on the horizon of Waset in the form of King Ahmose, whose blood flowed through her body.

Setau, the Nomarch of Great Land, was not pleasing to the Ka. His mincing, breathless way of speaking made her think of a wick sputtering as it begins drowning in the wax surrounding it—all his lazy layers of fat. Two attendants had to help him back up onto his feet after he knelt before the queen. The servants of his dressing room had applied too much paint to his eyelids which smudged and ran into the wrinkles around them in a way that made her think of a marsh's dark waters breeding all sorts of unpleasant things. He moved only to command attendants with his staff and to eat and drink. She pitied his litter bearers every time she watched the effort they had to make to hoist the conveyance onto their shoulders. She was happier than ever to board the ship again in the morning. Her room in the obese Nomarch's home had been attractively furnished but she had felt strangely dirty there even after her attendants vigorously bathed and oiled her.

"There is something evil about the Nomarch of Great Land," she told Hapuseneb.

"He does not appear to mistreat his people."

"Yes he does! I am certain his litter bearers suffer from back pains and I cannot imagine how awful it must be to bathe and perfume him everyday while he lies there like a big fat baby. He has only to reach out his hand confident anything he desires will be put into it. It is as though being born is all he has ever troubled himself to do."

"And that is not enough?"

"Of course not!"

"Why?"

"Because it is not enough merely to put a seed in the earth. If the soil is too wet and soft the vessel holding within it the promise of a new life will rot away before it can germinate. The ground surrounding the seed must be firm enough to serve it. I do not see how a man as fat as a baby hippopotamus, and whose eyes remind me of a crocodile's, can ever experience the birth of Horus in his heart."

"Tawaret and Sobek are also gods. Perhaps Setau worships his Divine nature in a different way by throwing his body to Ammit even before it dies to prove that only what lives in the heart truly matters and survives."

"I do not believe that," she argued passionately.

"Why?"

"If you ask me *why* again, Hapuseneb, I am going to become angry with you!"

He smiled.

She looked away, frustrated she could not find the words to justify how she felt about Setau.

"I agree with you, Hatshepsut," he admitted. "The Nomarch of Great Land is not a good person but not because he is fat. In this particular man the neglect of the social proviledges he was born to—which he should have used to cultivate Horus in his heart as he strove to embody the creative generosity of Amun-Re—have indeed manifested as obesity. His lazy self-indulgence dishonors God, who was meant to grow in his heart. But at least his evil is passive. Aggressive evil often manifests in the strongest and most attractive bodies. Followers of Seth are not afraid to lie and often relish doing so. It is a symptom of how, without their realizing it, they are lying to themselves about their own Divine nature, thereby forsaking the responsibilities and joys attending it. This is the worst lie possible and usually the stunted and twisted root of them all."

She nodded. "But if you agree with me that Setau is in many ways a small and petty man despite his considerable size, does that not adversely affect the land and people in his care?"

"Yes."

"Then why is he allowed to remain Nomarch?"

"Why, indeed."

"When the king made his royal progress with my mother they stayed in Tjeny, I know this to be so because Setau boasted proudly of how richly he feasted them. Surely Ahmose dislikes Setau as much as I do and said something to Pharaoh. Thutmose is, I hope, planning to replace him with a better man."

"Setau's family has ruled in the eighth Nome for more than two-hundred years. Great Land contributed many brave soldiers to your mother's father's army and helped make Kemet whole again. He cannot simply be stripped of his rights and titles."

"Then what *can* be done?"

"That is for you to decide, my queen."

She stared over his shoulder at the western desert. It never seemed to change despite how swiftly the ship was coursing through the water.

"Setau must be closely watched," she said. "Closely watched, supervised and, when necessary, firmly controlled. He will be like a fat horse permitted to continue living in its comfortable stable but subject to the king's bridle for it is Pharaoh's justice his actions are meant to carry out."

"And who would you send to be his rider?"

"A good and wise man who would act as his guest for several months out of the year and be granted land and cattle of his own as a reward for his unpleasant but crucial task. The Headman of Tjeny, Satepihu, struck me as an intelligent and tactful person. It was also my impression he too dislikes Setau. I believe we can entrust him to welcome our rider and act as a mediator."

"Setau has two young sons by a concubine who will one day inherit their father's authority. Do you suggest we do something about them as well?"

"Yes! They should be raised at court so we can be sure they are taught to read and write and to behave like true noblemen. They must also learn to value how much the heart appreciates being exercised in every way possible."

She had been so intent on solving the problem of the disgusting Setau she had not noticed how Hapuseneb was smiling at her, until he suddenly looked past her and his expression sobered.

"Shortly after we left Abedju," he said, "we passed a great monument."

"The Fortress of the Gods." She did not like thinking about the time when her Beloved Earth was still struggling to unite itself. "There are other such fortresses farther south in Nekhen and to the north in Iuno."

"The struggle that occurs in the soul was played out here in Kemet on the seemingly empty boards of those mighty fortresses. We are all the Children of Seth and the Followers of Horus. True power lies in eliminating any conflict between the two sides of our nature, lower and higher, for in truth they are one reality in the magic of the embodied god."

"When you speak, Hapuseneb, I can see so clearly…" She lost sight of his face as she found herself in another time and place filled with strong fighting men striding before tall animal-shaped standards symbolizing their power and dominion. Behind them ships loaded down with precious oils and gemstones floated low in the water. The warriors entered the Fortress of the Gods through the southern gate located on the eastern side of the long enclosure wall. One by one they were purified in a small temple palace, from which they emerged into a large open court where their king stood beside his falcon standard on a square pedestal made of brick-framed sand—the Primordial Mound of Creation crowned by Re's bodily son. She was familiar with the symbol of the Horus

Falcon on His Palace but only recently had she come to fully understand the history behind it.

Beyond the lovely painted lotus columns holding up her pavilion, she imagined a dark night intensified by the torches struggling to defeat it and deepened by the blood flowing from sacrificed prisoners. The ritual meetings of Kemet's first leaders lived again in her heart as she became perversely excited wondering what those brutal times had really been like. Then she pictured her husband standing beside the Horus Falcon and returned abruptly to the present, her exhilarating flight into the past felled by the throwing stick of a single thought.

"You were lost to me for a few moments," Hapuseneb observed.

"Not lost… it was more as though in my hand I held the hard and dark but still magical seed of Kemet, which grew into the beautiful flower so pleasing to the nose of God it is now."

"I glimpsed a disappointment in your eyes that returned you to the present."

"I thought of my husband," she admitted flatly.

"A powerful Ka is sometimes concealed in an unremarkable body."

She frowned. "I know you do not really believe that of Thutmose."

"I did not say I was referring to him. I am interested only in protecting you, my queen, from seductive fantasies which might tempt you to commit errors of judgment you are too wise not to avoid more easily."

"The tumultuous meetings held in the Fortresses of the Gods so long ago are still happening inside me," she realized reluctantly. "There are always certain thoughts, fears and blind emotional reactions I must control, fight and sacrifice. Will I ever be able to rule myself more gracefully and peacefully, Hapuseneb?"

"If that is what you truly desire there is no doubt you will, Hatshepsut."

"Yet it will not change how disappointed I am in my husband."

"And it should not. To deny and suppress your feelings is another even more dangerous way of being ruled by them. The last thing you should do is fear the transcendent forces embodied in your passions."

"I know." She gazed at him longingly. "You want me to fully understand my passions so they serve me instead of dominate me. It is why, I think, I suddenly desire to learn to drive a chariot. My passions are like horses to my Ka. That is why it was so stimulating for me to visit the temple of my mother's father. Is it possible he was depicting two kinds of battle, the one he physically fought against chaos in the form of the Setiu and the one we must all fight at times in our lives against fear, unhappiness and despair?"

"What matters is that you perceive this double meaning for only then does it exist."

She saw the captain approaching, undoubtedly to inform them they would soon be arriving in Khent-min. It was time for her to take her place on the throne in the center of the boat. The citizens of the populous and prosperous center of the ninth Nome would all be joyfully anticipating the arrival of their queen.

* * * * *

Desiring a rest after over two weeks of travel—filled with hot public processions to the cool privacy of temple sanctuaries, the stuffy homes of Headmen and the thankfully roomier and breezier residences of governors and Nomarchs—Hatshepsut chose to remain for three days in one of the Mooring Places of Pharaoh located on the east bank of the River in Tjebu. The first night there, she received the Nomarch of the Cobra and his wife in the casual comfort of her own banquet hall. She also invited the governor, the Headman of the city and the senior priest of Min's chapel. The following two days and evenings she relished being alone with her friends while Hapuseneb visited and dined with officials in his capacity as the Mouth and Ears of the King. When they were together back on the ship, he would tell her all that had been said.

Meresankh believed she was pregnant, which was a perfect excuse to celebrate. Djehuty was growing increasingly cheerful the closer they drew to Khmun, his hometown. Watching him made her miss Puyemre, who was equally dark and slight but possessed a much more vigorous wit. Djehuti did not appear comfortable taking entertaining liberties with the truth. Hapuseneb had set him the task of meeting with the scribes in charge of equipping Pharaoh's ports to make sure their records tallied with the actual supplies available to God's Wife during her stay.

Hatshepsut had no complaints. She dined on harvest pigeons fattened in the fields, succulent quails stuffed with dried fruits, finely sliced raw beef and whole fish steamed in palm leaves. She drank wine and milk out of gold and silver cups, licked her fingers clean of goose grease, dipped her bread in a garlicky chickpea and sesame paste thinned with the oil of the flaxseed, and indulged in countless honey cakes. Outside the temporary palace coarser loaves of bread were stacked high by the royal bakers and Djehuty—freshly bathed and oiled so he shone like a statue in a fresh white linen kilt and floral collar—supervised their distribution to the queen's staff and soldiers. Her private guard, commanded by the proud father to be Mentekhenu, ate inside with his wife and other favored attendants.

On the night before they left Tjebu, after she had been undressed, Hatshepsut dismissed Seshen and Meresankh. Lying back across a gilded couch formed by the elongated bodies of two Hathor cows—their curved tails framing the backboard decorated with *djed* pillars and Isis Knots—she told Nafre to massage her breasts.

239

Her attendant obeyed silently.

"I enjoyed it when you perfumed your mouth with my nipples that morning in our hunting tent, Nafre," she said, and smiled with satisfaction as the other woman promptly captured one between her lips.

"Suck on it harder," she urged, resting her right hand between her thighs as she parted them slightly. "Pull on it, Nafre. Do not be afraid you might hurt me. And keep moving from one to the other as you did that morning."

Nafre moaned and cupped her mistress' bosom hungrily in both hands, pressing the tender mounds together so she could more easily flick the tip of her tongue from one stiff peak to the other.

Hatshepsut felt her nipples hardening like seeds mysteriously linked to the breathtakingly wonderful sensation which could only be cultivated between her legs. She hesitated for a few moments but then could not resist closing her eyes and vigorously caressing herself in that special place.

"Oh my lady," Nafre said urgently, "please let me to do that for you!"

She opened her eyes again, as shocked and offended as if her attendant had asked to be allowed into a temple's holy of holies. But her body was hungry for pleasure and she saw no reason not to indulge it. "You may not touch me there in that way," she said firmly, "but I did not give you permission to stop what you were doing."

With Nafre alternately sucking on her nipples, rubbing them between her thumb and forefinger and gently nipping them with her teeth, Hatshepsut brought herself to a climax thinking about Hapuseneb.

19

Primordial Magic

In the thirteenth Nome of the Upper Pomegranate, Sycamore and Viper, in the city of Zauty sacred to Wepwawet, Anubis of the South, Hatshepsut dreamed with her father. She was wandering through a palace filled with so much light the colorful paintings and furnishings were only luminous shadows, unless she concentrated on them and attempted to discern the objects they defined. Then she experienced a sensation like warm water rushing up through her head and realized she was dreaming. A surge of joy made her conscious of her closed eyelids where she lay asleep in bed and passionately she thought, *No, I must not wake up! I will not wake up!* She knew she was in the Palace of the Other World near her father's tomb and the weight of sadness threatened to pull her back into her body. Determined not to give into the pressure, she walked to a window open to a profusion of colors and suddenly her father was beside her. She saw him clearly for an instant before he embraced her and became only a beloved darkness she could distinctly feel against her. He said, "Everything you do is so beautiful!" and she laughed as he held onto her so tightly she began falling backwards. She ended up lying on the floor feeling only his arms around her as Hapuseneb's voice said directly in her head, "Love is the light in the Fields of Re" and abruptly she found herself standing alone outside the palace in a night blacker than any she had ever known. There was no moon and she could see no stars beyond the palace's silhouette looming to her right. She knew she had to walk around it but she feared encountering something. When she suddenly saw Bubu and his magically reflective eyes waiting for her, it was easier to force herself to be brave and not to try and wake up. With a cat following just behind her, she began walking. Her courage received a further boost when a white dog-like creature emerged from the night on her left and trotted along beside her. Recognizing the animal of Seth, she rested her left hand welcomingly on his head. Continuing along the invisible path, she summoned a small grey jackal to run ahead and open the way for her. She sensed herself approaching the open space beyond the palace where she would be able to fully claim her powers if she dared to face encountering all her fears there. Then suddenly the veil of her eyelids lifted and she woke to the safely confining light of the solar disc.

* * * * *

In the fourteenth Nome of the Lower Pomegranate, Sycamore and Viper, the queen and the High Priest of Amun walked together through the ruins of Hathor's temple. The warm desert wind blowing through cracks in the walls made a low moaning sound as if the place was possessed by the Akhs of women lamenting the neglect of the Goddess. Nearby lay the tombs of a distinguished family that for hundreds of years had passed the power and title of Nomarch from father to son. Their successors, not as spiritually virile, had been unable to fight off the Setiu and the lifeless sands of ignorance had swiftly consumed Hathor's sanctuary. The normally lovely sound of children laughing sounded uncanny coming from the desecrated holy of holies, where the flame symbolizing the Divine creative fire had been extinguished years ago. Hatshepsut turned away from it. Those were all *her* little boys and girls growing up without a temple in which to make offerings inspiring to their hearts, a temple that might have rescued them from harsh lives their beautiful Ka's were not meant to suffer. Since leaving Khent-min Hathor's was the third abandoned sanctuary she had seen.

She could not hear his footfalls on the soft sand but she was confident Hapuseneb was following behind her as she hurried back to where their litters were waiting. A soft rustling sound entered her ears significantly but she ignored it. She stepped onto a large stone lying in her path and Hapuseneb immediately joined her there. He placed his body in front of hers but not before she saw what he was protecting her from. Resting her hands on his shoulders, she peered around him. In the center of an abandoned offering court three large cobras were mating. They were standing perilously close to the serpents twining around each other in a way that made it difficult to tell where one began and the other ended.

He whispered, "Leave very slowly."

She longed to continue watching the sinuous coupling. In all her life she had never seen anything so terribly exciting. It was not until she stepped off the stone that her body reacted to the danger it was in by making her legs so weak, it felt strange to be walking on two feet instead of undulating sensually and fearlessly across the ground.

* * * * *

In the fifteenth Nome of the Hare, Hatshepsut stayed in another temporary palace and honored Djehuty's family with an invitation to a banquet. It took her mind off ruined temples—where children played without fear of the sacred cobras copulating in the empty offering court—to watch Djehuty laughing with his siblings, four sisters and three brothers, who obviously bore him much affection. She too was happy to be in Khemnu, Eight Town, the home of the god for whom her beloved father had been named. The High Priest of the Temple of Thoth, The Great One of the Five, was a special friend of Hapuseneb. Although he was considerably older than the First Prophet of Amun, Patehuti was distinguishingly tall and his shoulders were still broad.

When he spoke, he chose his words carefully and pronounced them precisely. His eyes were fascinating. By lamplight, they were gray but in the sunlight they looked made of silver.

"Patehuti's eyes are the color of the moon," Meresankh said in wonder as she braided her mistress' hair. "He must be a truly powerful priest!"

Hatshepsut did not argue with her attendant's assessment of the man. She had felt, and she had seen, that he was indeed a powerful priest. Patehuti knew of the angry despair she had suffered in Hathor's abandoned sanctuary and of her intention to rebuild it and others like it. On the roof of his home, he had shown her the fruit of her desire in a bowl of water in which the full moon was reflected and formed part of the future temple's luminous white walls. He carried a black staff like Hapuseneb's and her longing for the High Priest of Amun intensified as she wondered if he was as great of magic as Patehuti. Lord of The Ka's, the god Heka was the personification of magic's Divine force and to Hatshepsut he wore her master's face. Heka accompanied Re in his bark and protected Osiris in the netherworld just as Hapuseneb rode on her ship, which he had built, and his voice in the dream where she embraced her father had helped shape it around her. Heka enabled every person to eventually become a god. She had been crowned queen and God's Wife years ago but Hapuseneb was still helping her grow into her titles. If he were to die all the magic would go out of her life. Empty of his presence, she feared the world would fall into meaningless ruin around her like a temple robbed of its *neter*.

On the night she glimpsed a fragment of the future floating in a moonlit bowl of water, she stayed up until sunrise talking with the two High Priests on a cool rooftop. Although his silence always felt encouraging, Hapsueneb's gaze remained inscrutably dark in the light of a single oil lamp, while Patehuti's eyes seemed to gleam an intense interest in every word she said.

In an attempt to define the nature of magic, she remarked, "Substance can be physically manipulated and altered but it is a different matter to influence it using the power of our heart in which Re burns."

Patehuti's smile deepened as the tips of his fingertips and thumbs lightly touched to form a pyramid, the pinnacle of which gently tapped his chin as he said, "If for some reason a person believes he is ill and imagines himself in that condition, he soon will be." "We are all of us magicians. It is Thoth's power of thought that makes it possible not only to perceive what our eyes do not see but to manifest what we desire and believe."

"I do not understand. How can we perceive what our eyes do not see?"

"Our senses are part of the created world but it is only our ability to think which enables us to make sense of the information they provide."

"You are speaking in riddles," she protested.

"He is not," Hapuseneb said mildly, his right ankle coming to rest on his left knee as he relaxed in his chair and took another sip of wine.

"A pyramid when seen from a great distance appears small to our eyes and yet we know it is not," Patehuti went on, "because we can *think* about the fact that it is far away. It is because we can think we are able to see a plant in a seed. Inseparable from time and space, motion and growth, backward and forward, is the ability of thought to perceive them. Only the intelligence of the heart can recognize a loaf of bread in grains of wheat. The seed, the stalk of wheat and the bread into which it transforms, all exist in space and are subject to time whereas thought, a Divine faculty, is not. A seed only produces more manifestations of its virtual form, but because we can think about our feelings we are capable of vision—of seeing beyond elements blindly reproducing themselves to the infinite creativity responsible for every finite process."

Hapuseneb said, "The most powerful magic lies in the study of Number. Numbers are the body of God. It is Number that gives substance to the form assumed by the desire in Atum's heart. Hathor, God's Hand, has five fingers which doubled become ten."

"The value of God is infinite," Patehuti explained. "Only what is infinite can hold within it all possibilities."

Hapuseneb spoke again, "*Khemt*, written by a man's phallus, denotes the number Three and the act of reflecting, as upon our feelings and desires, through our ability to think."

She looked shyly away from him. She did not need to be reminded he possessed a phallus she longed to feel inside her.

The priest of Thoth signaled to his servant to refill all their cups before he continued. "The Word spoken by Thoth is Number, which is how a single word uttered at the beginning of time said it all. Everything is the experience of One. The division of One into Two created the dimensions of Three—the sun rising between the two lions of the horizon—which means the mystery of Two completes itself in Four—the primary elements of space and time and the four cardinal directions. The number Five is the soul of all forms that in Six are born into substance, taking on a defined appearance and function through the power of Three plus Four—Seven, the perfected finite cycle transcended in the conscious heart of Eight. Eight, the Divine Ogdoad, is the vessel become aware of the eternal fire that forged it and which it contains. Eight leads directly to the greatness of Nine—the magic of Three forever multiplied—and to the power of the Ka expressed in Ten—the individual reunited with his infinite source and strength."

"Is that why Eight is sacred to Thoth, because Eight represents the intelligence of the heart?" Glancing at Hapuseneb she quickly corrected herself by adding,

"Not only represents but *is*, meaning the intelligence of the heart actually *is* the power of eight?"

"That is why," Patehuti replied, his smile deepening. "All elements can be defined as numbers and their combinations. Four is the stage where the possibility of experience in Three is specifically realized and played. Seven is the reality of decay which promotes the spirit of growth. Eight is the consciousness of the Creator in the created, the intelligence of the heart, the power of thought and the number of Thoth, scribe of the gods.

"Infinity, darkness, water and the forces hidden in the wind are the four gods," he went on, "Heh, Kek, Nun and Amun, and they are wed to the knowledge of themselves—Hauhet, Kauket, Naunet and Amaunet—realized through Horus, son of Osiris."

"You mean through Pharaoh?" She could not keep a note of incredulous scorn out of her voice.

Hapuseneb said, "Through the spiritual awareness represented by Pharaoh."

"But not, in this case, actually embodied in him?" She could not resist expressing the sacrilegious sentiment. She realized then she had drunk too much wine when her true feelings slipped out of her as smoothly and irresistibly as the serpent she suddenly saw coiled and rearing its head between her and the two priests. She wanted to banish it but she could not, for once spoken words could never be destroyed only remembered or forgotten. And yet she did not wish to forget she had said what she did because she meant it.

His smile gone, the High Priest of Thoth stared down at the spot where she thought she saw the venomous cobra of her frustration and just as abruptly it was no longer there. It vanished so completely she was possessed by the certainty she had not merely imagined it.

* * * * *

Hatshepsut arrived in the southernmost end of the Nome of the Oryx on the feast day of Raet. It was late in the month of Mesore. By mid afternoon the sunlight was so searing, and the shadows it cast so sharp, venturing outside felt like being attacked by Pakhet the lioness. Nevertheless, there were hundreds of people crowding the eastern shore waiting for her. In the remorselessly dry air, she scarcely perspired beneath her heavy ceremonial wig. It was gratifying to know that, lavishly adorned in gold, she shone and flashed in everyone's eyes like a true daughter of Re. She was Queen of Kemet but, even more importantly, she was God's Wife and Hand, Hathor-Raet incarnate. Aspects of the Supreme Goddess, Pakhet, Isis and Selket embodied qualities innate to the Divine made flesh and she recognized them all in herself. More than ever, she felt she had the right to hold the fly whisk scepter against her heart. She was increasingly aware of—and as a consequence more quickly and decisively able to swat away—the finite fears hovering around her boundless imagination, which never tired of feasting on desires and dreams and sipping the stellar vintage of infinity.

The soldiers marching on the outskirts of her personal guard—flanking the royal litter seven rows deep—suffered minor juries inflicted by women who tried to scratch their way closer to the living Goddess. Like the sudden sensation of a great cat's whiskers brushing her skin, idle worries of something going wrong made Hatshepsut tense in her high seat. At times, she wished she was not so close to the crowd's wild devotion but in truth she did not for an instant doubt the ability of Mentekhenu and his men to protect her.

Later that evening her anger was fiercer than the abating heat when Hapuseneb took her to Pakhet's abandoned temple.

"But how can this be?" She was deeply disturbed by the lifeless silence inhabiting the Divine lioness' rock cut chapel. "The women of this city still clearly worship their goddess."

"Yes."

"We have much to do, Hapuseneb!"

"Yes."

She turned to him. "Do you love me?"

"Yes."

She clutched her dress tightly over her thighs, digging her nails into her skin to resist the overwhelming desire to throw her arms around his neck. "You will not always say 'yes' to me because I am the queen, will you, Hapuseneb?"

"Did you truly feel it necessary to ask me that?"

The hardness of his mouth, and the unfamiliar look of anger in his eyes, excited her. His displeasure should have distressed her but Pakhet was possessing her and she was angry too—angry that her arms remained as empty as the temple in which they stood, angry she was forced to endure a desire which grew debilitating sharper by the hour with no fulfillment in sight, angry her heart felt trapped in Pakhet's jaws and that no thoughts could free her from the need burning in her blood to feel the High Priest's naked body against hers.

"You know what I feel, Hapuseneb." She looked away from him in an effort to control herself. "I will restore Pakhet's temple and make it even more splendid than before. I intend for all the goddesses of Kemet to rejoice in their sanctuaries and to be fulfilled, for it seems that perhaps only then will I be!"

* * * * *

Two days journey with one night's rest in a Mooring Place of Pharaoh brought them to Henen-nesu, the capital of the twentieth Nome of the Upper Laurel and the Southern Sycamore. The queen's mood had not improved since her stay in the town of Pakhet and the early arrival of her monthly purification did not make life any easier for her attendants. Only Nafre was not afraid to speak to her. Wherever she went, Hatshepsut felt mysteriously subject to the influence of the local god or goddess. Pahket's claws had reached into her womb and drawn her blood. She was inundated by feelings that made her profound thoughts feel less important than the young men who dove into the River and swam after her ship, yelling and waving in an effort to win her attention. Younger boys and girls ran along the shore, their joyful cries carrying on the wind making her feel as though hundreds of beautiful Ba birds had brushed her skin with their invisible wings.

She regretted her little fight with Hapuseneb even as she kept remembering how much it had excited her to feel his anger. She longed to tear through the frustrating control he exercised over his desires and to bite him, his chest and his neck, then to lick him lingeringly, running her tongue along his hard belly and the firm insides of his thighs, anywhere and everywhere. There was no one to whom she could have confided her fierce longing except Nafre, who she suspected would not understand anyway. Nor would Seshen and Meresankh, who were both happily married to men they loved in every sense.

In the end, her purification made her feel better. It was with pure pleasure she anticipated once again enjoying the High Priest's stimulating company, and the River's refreshing breezes caressing them, as they reclined together on feather-stuffed cushions.

Henen-nesu was located on the slender arm of the River that flowed north-west to The Southern Lake through a large expanse of fertile land. But the realm of Sobek—dominated by the pyramid of Senwosret and its populous town—was not their destination. Another day's journey at last brought them to the first Nome of Lower Kemet, White Wall, and the city of Itjtawy, once a royal capital, located south of Mennefer.

She had been introduced to dozens of Nomarchs on her progress but had been seriously impressed by only two of them—Khenti, Nomarch of the Sistrum, and Rasui, whose name meant *dream*, Nomarch of the Oryx. More than once, Hapuseneb had told her, the Oryx had played a vital role in ridding the Two Lands of corruption, whether it was brought by the Setiu or was an even more foul kind festering within Kemet itself. She was intrigued by how many noble men and women of the Oryx had been awarded a necklace of golden flies. Temple scribes kept records of this special gift given only to the most valuable royal spies. Bravery that seemed long forgotten was in truth forever remembered. Rasui was as pleasing to the Ka as Khenti but more solidly built and possessed of an attractively sober demeanor. From the moment she met him, she had liked and trusted him. She was looking forward to seeing him during her stay in Mennefer when he visited his oldest son there, a priest of Ptah.

* * * * *

A chamber in the Temple of Sokar was dedicated to the vibratory magic of sound. For the nocturnal ritual—which he had said was impossible to describe to her beforehand—Hapuseneb had instructed her to wear a short wig over a plain white tunic and not to eat anything after she had perfumed her mouth in the morning.

Feeling very hungry and a little irritable because for some reason she was nervous, Hatshepsut followed the silent priests walking before, beside and behind her. Hapuseneb was not one of them and disappointment contributed to her unease. She could not stop thinking of food as her tongue and her heart both thirsted for wine.

The chapel was lit by bronze oil lamps in the shape of bolti fish interspersed with candles made of animal fat molded into the form of mummified falcons. Four men wearing short white kilts and blue skull caps sat against one of the undecorated walls with their right legs bent before them. One rested a flute against his chest like a scepter. Another held a small drum and their companions simply sat with their hands on their thighs.

She was surprised when the priests left her alone with the musicians. Then Hapuseneb strode into the room and her heart seemed to take wing. The flickering illumination lapped like water against the bare stones of the floor, walls and ceiling but suddenly the absence of a god's figure no longer felt oppressive. The High Priest of Amun was holding a *Menit* necklace. Draping it over her chest, he stepped behind her and fastened the clasp just below the nape of her neck. She shivered slightly as the cool metal counterpoise, evocative of a man's erect sex, kissed her warm flesh. She was no longer thinking of food.

One of the seated men placed his left hand between his jaw and his right ear and in a deep, curiously flat voice began chanting while a second man clapped in rhythm. They did not look at the queen as the High Priest took her left hand and led her into a small dark room not much larger than a shrine.

In the close unlit space, the chanting and clapping in the adjoining chapel reverberated around them. She watched, her mouth expectantly dry, as Hapusuneb turned toward a niche in the wall and poured liquid into a cup. He offered it to her and she accepted it with both hands.

"Drink it all at once," he commanded.

The cool red wine flowed down her throat to her heart and when it reached her belly sent an intoxicating warmth rushing straight up into her head. As though her pulse was conducting him, the drummer in the next room began beating his instrument swiftly and urgently. It was too dark for her to see Hapuseneb's face as he took the cup from her but she gazed longingly at his silhouette as he put it back in its place. The breathy notes of the flute blended with her gasp as he stepped behind her and kissed the base of her neck. A series of high-pitched notes reflected the sensation aroused in her by the tip of his tongue flicking against her skin directly above the necklace's metal counterweight resting between her shoulder blades.

The urgent pulse of the drum and the flute's soaring emotion felt concentrated in her body as the High Priest gripped her right wrist and drew her hand back toward him. His kilt was gone. Feeling only flesh, firm and warm, she grasped him hungrily.

His right hand took hold of her throat as his left hand clutched her possessively between the legs. He was the man she desired but he was also much more than that—he was Atum-Re, a potent darkness all around her, and she was Hathor, his Hand. They were the cosmic duality opening onto the dimensions of the room beyond them in which the sound of the first Word, which was music and Number, created the world where they stood.

He whispered in her ear, "Stroke me!"

She complied willingly, in awe of how thick and long his phallus was, nothing like her husband's modest little organ. He slid his erection back and forth in her hand and a tingling heat began rising up her spine that made her heart and the drums pound faster.

"Do you feel it, Hatshepsut?"

"Yes!"

He slapped the crown of her sex.

She somehow stifled cries of pleasure as he spanked her there repeatedly while the man clapping in the next room mysteriously obeyed the rhythm of his hand.

"This is where the energy of the Ka enters the heart," he said, the sensation of his breath against the nape of her neck telling her exactly where he meant. "This is where Ptah-Sokar-Osiris gives your body life by spreading his wings in your lungs. The millions of red serpents inside you are ruled by the Lord of the Netherworld. Sokar is the captain of the *henu* bark that journeys between this world and the next, our lungs the expanding and contracting sails of his Divine breath."

The heel of his left palm began firmly caressing the crown of her sex as he pressed his right thumb and index finger into the sides of her neck and cut off her breath. "Do you feel yourself being raised onto his bark now, Hatshepsut? Join me there!"

The chanting, drumming and clapping all ceased abruptly, replaced by a weightless silence alive with precisely cut, jewel-like patterns of colors like the feathers of imperishable wings stretching for as far as she could see...

Sound and air abruptly caught her again in their net and flung her back down into the temple. Her heart was beating like a bird struggling to break free of her rib cage and her right hand was slick with primordial magic.

* * * * *

Nafre dug her thumbs into the soles of the queen's feet, her eyes intent on her expression.

Hatshepsut pretended not to notice how her moans and gasps of pleasure affected her attendant. There were few things she enjoyed more than an excruciatingly good foot massage. Experiences like the one in the Temple of Sokar were too exceptional to be counted amongst normal daily pleasures.

She was in the old residence in Mennefer where she had grown up but she did not feel at home there. She was not staying in her former rooms, which were smaller and plainer than she remembered them. She had felt better only after she instructed Neferkhaut to have them brightly painted with ducks and fish swimming in a marsh full of frogs and dragonflies. The colorful scenes would also delight Neferure when she brought her there with her one day.

Sleeping in the apartments Ahmose had always inhabited—and still occupied whenever she was in the city—made Hatshepsut miss her mother even more than she already did. Surrounding herself with her own possessions—all of them inscribed with her name and her title *God's Wife of Amun*—gave her little pleasure. Their luxurious wall did nothing to keep out memories brought by the breeze wafting in from the garden that spoke silently of years past as if they had happened only yesterday. She kept hoping to dream with her father again but her nights remained a senseless confusion of images set in a darkness that swallowed her awareness of anything meaningful she might have experienced.

Even though she was reluctant to do so, she granted Meresankh's request to summon a magician who could divine whether she was carrying a boy or a girl. She charged Neferkhaut with the task of finding the appropriate man, ostensibly because Hapuseneb had more important things to do but in truth because she worried he might think less of her for indulging her attendant's superstitions.

The magician selected by her secretary was a man of indeterminate age whose dark-skinned face was so scored with deep lines they looked more like marks left by a knife than wrinkles. She mistrusted him at once and the ensuing ritual deepened her instinctive dislike. The angry buzzing of the large scarab beetle he brought with him in a small stone jar sickened her. She sympathized with the insect that served as the symbol of Becoming and rebirth, and then suffered both anger and guilt as she allowed it to be drowned in milk purportedly taken from a black cow. The magician placed the bowl on a mound of smoldering cow dung and when its contents began simmering summoned Khepri to answer the lady's question.

"Is there a boy growing in my womb?" Meresankh said timidly and then glanced around the room as if she feared the god might actually walk in.

The magician stirred the hot milk six times with his index finger without wincing.

Hatshepsut was not surprised he did not seem to feel any pain for his dry skin looked disturbingly insensitive.

"Yes," he pronounced Khepri's silent reply.

Meresank grinned.

Hatshepsut frowned and gestured to an attendant.

The magician and his paraphernalia were quickly escorted out of her presence.

Later that evening she told Hapuseneb about the disgusting event and was relieved when he laughed. Ever since the night in the Temple of Sokar, he seemed more relaxed in her presence. In her heart, she thanked Pakhet for those angry moments in her abandoned chapel where she had communicated the urgency of her need to him and compelled him to react. However, she also believed the High Priest would have done what he did, exactly where and when he did it, no matter what. The superb wine he had given her to drink during the ritual—into which he had mixed an extract of the blue lotus—had come from the western desert and the oases of Bahriya. Nearby Kawa also produced truly delectable vintages. Neferkhaut and his assistant scribes were kept busy writing letters arranging for the shipment of hundreds of jars of wine to Waset destined for the storage rooms beneath her palace. Her steward would be delighted. She had chosen a man named Dhout for the position mainly because he was nothing like Sinuhe. The much younger and thinner Dhout delighted in walking briskly back and forth through the residence dozens of times a day, lashing everyone with his untiringly cheerful smile as he arranged intimate parties and large banquets with equal zest and attention to detail. He also kept a particularly close eye on the royal laundry and all the queen's beautiful dresses.

When she was alone at night, she missed Dhout along with everyone else she had left behind in the city of Amun. With growing frequency, she found herself wondering what Senmut would think of this or that. She had especially missed him during the magician's performance imagining the amusing sarcastic remarks he might have made.

* * * * *

251

While she was in Mennefer, Hatshepsut met with various officials. Hapuseneb was always present. As the Great Royal Wife she walked behind Pharaoh and the Dowger Queen Ahmose, therefore she wished it to be known she was traveling in her capacity as God's Wife of Amun who wielded a power all her own. Her journey with the High Priest was helping her define what she desired to do with her immense wealth. She dictated a letter to her husband:

The Great Royal Wife and God's Wife of Amun, Hatshepsut, Foremost of Noble Women, inquires after her husband, the Horus of Fine Gold, Lord of the Two Lands, Thutmose, Born of Thoth.

I wish you life, prosperity and health and the grace of Amun-Re, King of the Gods.

I pray to Re, to Seth and to Nepthys that you may live and prosper daily until I see you again and fold you in my embrace.

When my letter reaches you then will you know I am in good health, but likewise will you learn I have suffered great distress on my journey bearing witness to so many lifeless Mansions of Eternity. My sadness is the sorrow of Maat who is left to languish in barren offering courts and empty sanctuaries. When I united with the Lower Pomegranate, Sycamore and Viper, my heart especially grieved in Hathor's great temple where the "the ground had swallowed up its august sanctuary, children played upon its house, and the uraeus caused no fear.

My heart searches for the sake of the future and truth is the bright bread"[36] on which I live. In my heart I know my beautiful brother will agree with me that the Goddess, by whose grace every life is conceived, must be well pleased with all her beautiful temples where "Feasts of Light"[37] are celebrated without end.

Furthermore, all goes well with your wife and with Pharaoh's realm. Do not be anxious about me.

Fare well!

Hatshepsut approved of the Overseer of the Works in the Red Mountain. His men—divided into two groups symbolic of the Two Lands—were well-fed and healthy. They suffered only those occasional accidents ordained by the Mistress of the Mountain, who sometimes desired payment in blood for all the dark-red stone she allowed them to wrest from her home.

The port in Mennefer was even busier than the one in Waset. Ptah's workshops always hungered for materials, in particular the fine cedar wood from Byblos where the jeweled coffin of Osiris had washed ashore. It seemed a fair exchange for the wheat and barely, dried fish, linen cloth and papyrus parchments Kemet possessed in abundance.

She could scarcely imagine a land where trees grew as tall as pyramids, numerous as papyrus in the marshes, and where water poured down from heaven much more often. She wondered if when the moon disappeared from the sky in Kemet if it was visiting the Land of the Two Rivers and turning its mountains to silver. She still recalled the torrid sunlight of Kush which had always seemed to explain to her why it was so rich in gold. The curiosity inspired in her by a foreign face was just as soon curbed by distaste and yet she genuinely liked Ruiu—the Viceroy of Kush whose skin was as black as Min's—and his son, Amenemhat, who was being educated at court. When persons born in wretched Kush were physically clean, and behaved in a civilized manner, she did not hesitate to call them brother or sister. It was possible then that not all northern foreigners were as bad as the Setiu. The ships docking in Mennefer were filled with the beautiful gifts—copper, precious oils, silver and wood—sent by neighboring peoples to Pharaoh, who disciplined them whenever they misbehaved much as a father does his children.

"A good father also loves his children and does not consider them inferior simply because they are not yet as wise as he is," Hapuseneb said when she expressed her thoughts to him.

She recalled a man she had recently seen in the market with a beard and hair like black snakes clinging to his face and head. He was clad in a filthy robe with long wide sleeves that would trap even more dirt and food in addition to harboring all sorts of vermin. He was Fenkhu and probably worked in the nearby limestone quarry.

"It would be easier to love them," she said with feeling, "if they would learn how much more pleasing to Maat they would be if they were clean."

"Indeed," Hapuseneb replied, "and many of them learn to appreciate that. But whether they do or not, anyone who wishes to enter even the humblest home in Kemet is obliged to remove his sandals and bathe his feet, his hands and his face."

"I cannot imagine what their countries smell like!"

"Not all foreigners are unclean, as you will see when you meet the royal ambassador of the Keftiu in Perunefer. Kallikrates is as clean as a lotus leaf."

"The Keftiu are not one of the Nine Bows."

"No, but the Kushites are and yet you are quite fond of Ruiu's son, Amenemhat."

"How do you know that?"

"I have been observing you closely for a long time, Hatshepsut."

She was so pleased to hear that she nearly forgot what they were talking about.

"When you speak of your feelings to me," he went on, "you express them in images that evoke the land of Kemet and all its plants and creatures. If you lived in the Land of the Two Rivers, the way you described your feelings would paint a different picture. There, craftsmen fashion more vessels of wood and copper and silver than they do vessels of stone and gold, obeying the qualities and properties of the materials available to them to express their creativity and skill. And yet in the end all vessels, no matter what they are made of or where, hold essentially the same substances, which can be likened to the feelings contained in all persons wherever they are from."

"But some vessels are not as fine as others or hold contents as pleasing to the heart."

"That is true of vessels made even here in Kemet."

"The world is not the same everywhere," she insisted. "It seems to me that the farther away it gets from the primordial mound of the First Occasion in Iuno, marked by the *ben-ben* stone, the less perfect it is and the more chaotic it becomes."

"Re shines on everyone and Atum lives in everything and his Hand is everywhere, although in the Land of the Two Rivers she is not called Hathor. There her name is Astarte."

"*Astarte.*" She savored the unfamiliar syllables on her tongue and found them pleasing. "Then, if I am the embodiment of Hathor-Raet, does that not mean I am also *Astarte* made flesh?"

He smiled. "Yes."

Hatshepsut met with the commander in charge of the soldiers sent to the Auxiliaries of the Well, fortified well-stations located along the route to the Land of the Two Rivers. Not one of the various officials to whom he had sent several letters—complaining supplies were scarce and did not reach their destinations in a timely fashion when they were sent at all—had responded to his communications. When he had heard God's Wife was in the city he had decided to appeal to her directly.

"You were wise to do so," she told him. "You and your men surely miss your loved ones when you are stationed so far away from home helping protect us from predatory peoples who flew unfinished from Khnum's wheel. It is an offense to Maat that you suffer a shortage of the supplies you require to perform your duties with a joyful heart, confident you will return to your families strong and healthy and perfumed with honor. Let it be known that from this day forward two of my own scribes will supervise the officials in charge of administering to your needs. Should these men continue proving ineffective in the discharging of their duties they will be stripped of their positions. From now on you will write directly to me and I will see to it you want for nothing."

It was becoming increasingly obvious to her that when anything went wrong there was usually a lazy or a greedy and dishonest individual involved. It was true supplies traveling across the desert could suffer from the unstoppable wrath of Seth, but such misadventures were expected and compensated for. The order essential to the success of any process unraveled only when men who did not faithfully cut Maat were in charge of it. A problem could never be completely solved if the persons responsible for it were not either disciplined and shown the error of their ways or removed from office.

She recalled what Meri had said to her long ago, that if she wanted to help her husband rule effectively she had to be a good judge of character. She had been God's Wife for some time yet only now did she appreciate the full value of the army of scribes and administrators under her command.

Tai, her Overseer of the Seal Bearers, became even more important to her than Neferkhaut. To Tai she entrusted the onerous task of determining who was responsible for the messy wounds caused by selfish inefficiency so they could be healed.

"Injuries to Maat are not like some illnesses of the body which can be diagnosed and treated even if their cause remains a mystery," she said to him. "Maat can only be healed when the source of her ailment is revealed and eliminated by whatever means necessary."

"Majesty, your words and your countenance both shine like the Golden One," Tai responded, his open hands raised before his face, "but I will not permit myself to be blinded by your beauty and wisdom, for then I would not be able to serve you effectively as I desire to do with all my being."

She was well pleased with Tai, who Hapuseneb agreed would be as relentless as a royal cat in rooting out avaricious rats playing the parts of important men.

"I am reminded of the words of Ptah-hotep, True of Voice," she said. "*You may recognize a noble man by his good deeds.* No matter his title, a man's true value can be assessed by his actions."

She thought of Senmut searching for a kitten with blue eyes in the hope it would make her happy and felt sad because she could not immediately send for him to thank him again.

20

The Ba's of Re

The High Priest of Iuno, Greatest of Seers, wore a sash of white leather stars all stitched together and attached to a belt of golden *shen* rings. In Hatshepsut's eyes, he was even more magnificent than the temples he served in. Ptah-Sokar was a true Ba of Re, an honor popularly accorded to Mer-Wer, the black bull of Iuno famous for the wisdom of its oracles. Obviously, it was a priest who made known Re's wishes and opinions but many people were like children and believed an animal actually served as the god's herald. Mer-Wer had three wives, gorgeous cows representing the goddesses Hathor, Iusaas and Nebet-hetepet.

Ptah-Sokar treated her with all the dignified respect due the God's Hand and Pharaoh's Great Royal Wife, but once they had spoken for a time his stiff demeanour relaxed into a smiling appreciation even more pleasing to her heart. She felt perfectly at home and happy in Iuno, where temple forecourts were planted with an abundance of beautiful flowers and Hathor was worshipped as the wife of Atum-Re. Iusaas, She Comes Who is Great, was Hathor's name in the darkness where One had not yet become Two. The moment Iusaas gripped Atum's cosmic phallus and brought the universe into existence she became Hathor. The Divine sperm of stars issued from an infinite power defining itself through Creation, where Hathor lived in the magical seed of everyone's heart as Nebet-hetepet, Mistress of Contentment.

In Iuno, the City of the Sun, Monuments of Heh symbolizing rays of light drew the eyes straight up toward heaven and reminded Hatshepsut not of dead kings but of her own inspiringly personal Father, Amun-Re.

Hail to you, Re, perfect each day,

Who rises at dawn without failing...

In a brief day you race a course,

Hundreds, thousands, millions of miles.[38]

Re was Atum in the Midst of His Eye and if it was true that stars were all suns then it was true Atum had hundreds, thousands, millions of eyes. Thinking of Re's unimaginable power was like trying to look directly at the solar disc when it was high in the sky. In those moments, her heart sought the comfort of the One hidden in her heart, Amun, who caressed her flesh with cooling breezes, and who had the same soothing effect on her thoughts when they became too focused on the inscrutable. Looking down from the blinding pinnacles of gold-tipped monuments it was a profound relief to experience The Hidden One through the pleasures of her senses—in everything her eyes beheld, her hands touched, her ears heard, her nose smelled and her tongue tasted. Contemplating the infinite power of Atum-Re was exalting but exhausting. She was learning to know when it was wise to look away and, as Hapuseneb had said, to feel instead of think. Amun was the Divine Ram, The Flesh of Re, therefore it could truly be said Waset was the Southern Iuno.

Her days were filled with splendorous responsibilities and emanations of Re— the dedication of an offering table to each of the solar *neter's* three temples, the unavoidable public processions after she left God's Houses which were all protected by tall mud-brick walls, and the perusal of ancient books with Ptah-Sokar and Hapuseneb. But it was evening she favored over all other times of the day. When Re became Atum and prepared to enter the netherworld in his bark, she returned to the ancient palace where freely flowing wine carried her away on its profoundly relaxing current as she steered the course through stimulating conversations, her lips and fingertips shining with the flavorful juices of earth's most delectable offerings.

On the feast of *Per Sopdet*, The Coming Forth of the Goddess, when in the morning sky just before sunrise Isis appeared on the horizon in her cloak of light, God's Wife helped the High Priest of Re light the new wicks for the temple fires. It was *Wept Renpet*, the Opening of the Year, the beginning of Akhet, the season of inundation, and traditionally Pharaoh's birthday. Geese, ibises, horned oxen and baskets filled with the first fruits of the season were offered to Re. She was not at all upset to be away from Waset on the joyful occasion. As the embodiment of Osiris, Thutmose-Akheperenre would be wielding a plow today instead of the crook and flail, breaking up dry mounds of earth and symbolically preparing all of Kemet for the flood and the seeds that would be sown when the waters receded. The sun was born again on New Year's Day to begin another twelve month cycle, and so too the king's spiritual energies were renewed when he was sprinkled with water from the River. She had not fully understood why six *heset* jars were used for the ritual, and why Pharaoh was anointed with the sacred water of Isis seven times, until Hapuseneb and Patehuti helped her fully grasp the power of Number. The numbers *six* and *seven*—Re being born again into an earthly form subject to the cycle of death and renewal—was celebrated on *Wept Renpet*.

Even after her monthly purification ended and she was free to travel again, Hatshepsut was reluctant to leave Iuno. Yet she was excited because their next destination was Bast, the domain of the cat goddess. Discussing the sacred writings in various Houses of Life with the High Priests of Re and of Amun had proved as frustrating as it had been fascinating. Her Ka and her body had come to feel almost painfully separated as the former feasted on the profound truths expressed by the unimaginably old hieroglyphs, while the latter cared only for the present in which she stood between two handsome virile men. She suffered a thrill each time Ptah-Sokar's fingers brushed hers as he helped her unroll delicate scrolls. In those moments it felt significant, in a highly arousing way, that Hapuseneb's arm was always lightly but distinctly touching hers. She sensed a stimulating tension in the room that had nothing to do with the wisdom buried, and magically still living, in hundreds of alcoves reminiscent of a hive. Sacred to Re, bees were the symbol of kingship for they always knew where they were in relation to the sun and could find their way home by its light. Some of the best honey came from Iuno.

Imagining the House of Bast would be filled with restful shadows, she wondered if its First Prophet would appreciate the subtle joy of a caress better than Ptah-Sokar did. The High Priest of Re appeared unaware of the effect his touch had on her. He worshipped the sun's obvious penetrating force yet left her feeling hot and frustrated by how blind he was to his own power over her. The High Priest of Amun, she knew, saw her much more clearly. The sensitivity of his perceptions was the most special kind of magic and he practiced it on her everyday, without the aid of his black staff or any other kind of implement.

The High Priest of Bast, Hathor of the North, was called The Great One of Physicians, reinforcing the goddess' connection to the physical forms which house the Divine creative fire. As it turned out, Hatshepsut did not like him very much. His eyes rarely met hers; reason enough to distrust him. Bast's sanctuary—much smaller than the temples dedicated to the sun in Iuno—was embraced by the two arms of a sacred lake. It gave her the impression of a basket woven from stone in which the fierce lioness Sekhmet enjoyed curling up in her benign form of a domestic cat. Trees cast a refreshing shade over the water as she and Hapuseneb approached the temple. They stood together at the railing of a small pleasure barge—they had left their ship at the dock when they entered the city—and the tall trees planted along both shores deepened the green color sacred to Bast of her faience bracelets and matching collar. Her fingernails and toenails were all painted red, the color of Sekhmet.

She had never been that far north before and perhaps it was the presence of so many cats—none as special as her beloved Bubu Reborn—that suddenly made her miss Waset so much. Iuno had been much more to her liking with its phallic monuments penetrating the clear mystery of the sky, and its flocks of sacred grey herons lining the banks of the River and perching on the *ben-ben* stone that marked the Primordial Mound of Creation. She was not surprised that her attendants preferred Bast to any other city they had visited so far. It was true the wine was delicious and even more intoxicating than the sweeter vintages of the south. The light felt gentler there in the mornings and night seemed to fall more swiftly, like a black cat silently pouncing on the scurrying activities of the day, the shushing of hundreds of sistrums its contented purr. Hathor's sacred instrument was shaken by both priests and priestesses as the dying sun, like a feline's cool pink tongue, was swallowed by the dangerous mouth of darkness.

They left Bast early one morning for Perunefer and arrived late the same afternoon. Thanks to her family, the great harbor city was no longer the reigning capital of the Setiu but Pharaoh's second most important military headquarters. It was from there that her mother's father had continued to push the invaders away from Kemet by pursuing them into their own lands. The Great Army Commander was currently far away in Wawat but she was met by three of his highest ranking officers who, along with their best men, joined her personal escort for the procession to the palace.

Hatshepsut looked around her curiously. Dozens of granaries dotted the gently undulating landscape like massive piles of hay soaring over the long mud-brick barracks built between them. It was reassuring to see just how large Pharaoh's army truly was. More interesting than anything else, however, were the large foreign ships floating in the River like exotic birds. A strange creature adorned the prows of several vessels, its head resembling a snake's and its yellow body covered with what appeared to be a repetitive pattern of more snakes swallowing their tails. The figurehead merged with a wooden pavilion which was closed in on all sides, its undulating gilded edges repeating the serpent motif. Four red poles supported a flat cloth sunshade. The numerous oars were also a dark-red, in striking contrast to the top part of the hull painted bright blue and decorated with a black line rhythmically cresting like a tide. The bottom half of the hull, partially visible above the water, was painted white and divided from to the blue upper half by a red line—the ships of the Keftiu.

A royal page had been sent ahead to give the city time to prepare for her arrival and hundreds of people had gathered to see their queen. The crowd was dominated by her own native brothers and sisters but she also saw men and women wearing bright red and yellow clothing. The men's faces were darkened by close-cropped beards and she could not help staring at the strange circular black growths on their heads she realized must be their hair. She could not understand why they would allow it to grow long as a woman's and then pin it up in that unsightly fashion. These people looked disturbingly related to the Setiu but their fine clothing indicated they were respectable citizens, most likely high-ranking carpenters. The outer edges of her own escort were dominated by the slender black figures of archers from The Land of the Bow—former Kushite prisoners of war wisely recruited by her father, and her mother's father before him, for their useful skill. Once the spear of Re struck their heart Kushites proved strong and loyal allies of Pharaoh. It was a pity so many of them chose to continue existing in darkness.

The plainness of the small palace was relieved only by pretty and unusually shiny yellow tiles festooned with blue lotus buds and flowers. They lined the bottoms of the otherwise undecorated white walls. There had not been time for her father, or for her mother's brother and father, always so busy fighting, to concentrate on the strength and vitality imparted to the Ka by Ptah's skilled artisans. Seth ruled in Perunefer. She valued and respected the brother of Osiris, lord of physical strength and aggressive mastery, and was excited to be in his city (where its foreign residents called him Baal) but she saw no reason why beauty had to be neglected there.

The royal residence was large enough to accommodate only her personal attendants and servants. Mentekhenu and his men would sleep in an adjoining building. Hapuseneb, as usual, would stay with the High Priest of the principal temple. Neferkhaut met with the headman of the city and assigned temporary homes for himself and for all her other scribes, either in houses designed for that purpose or with noble families. Djehuty and Useramun had been honored with an invitation from Prince Kallikrates to stay with him in his palatial home where she planned to join them the following evening for a banquet held in her honor.

On their way to Perunefer, Hapuseneb had told her all he knew of the Keftiu and now that she had seen their lovely ships, she was even more intrigued by them. Far away in a land surrounded on all sides by the Great Green Water, Re was venerated very much as he was in Iuno—in the form of a black bull with golden horns—but it was the Great Goddess they primarily worshipped there; the Keftiu loved and revered God's Hand even more than God Himself. Their priestesses handled live serpents and, equally astonishing, young men and women ran straight toward mighty bulls, gripped them fearlessly by the horns and somersaulted over their backs. It made her feel awkward that priestesses of the Keftiu were greater of magic than the God's Wife of Amun and she confessed as much to the High Priest.

"It is not magic," he assured her. "Either the serpents are milked of their venom beforehand or harmless snakes are used for the rituals. The bull dancers are trained from childhood and many die practicing the art. Those who excel in the dangerous performance are greatly honored but they must continue dancing with the bulls even after their strength naturally begins ebbing."

"They offer their bodies to the gods as we offer loaves of bread and jars of water and wine?"

"Yes, but they have no temples as we do, only sacred caves symbolizing the womb of the Goddess. The Keftiu are very pleasing to the Ka, they are in love with life's pleasures and laugh as often as happy children but their hearts can be sad and dark. Over their heads hangs the double axe of life and death and they do not believe they will survive its blow. They are convinced that when they die they return to the earth, where they remember nothing of who they were even if they are reborn as a tree, a butterfly or a bird."

She was appalled. "They believe everyone is devoured by Ammit no matter how they live?"

"They do not see it that way for they believe only in the physical body."

"That is truly frightening, Hapuseneb. They do not worship Seth and yet he rules them."

"They value the beauty of life and enjoy every moment even if in the end their personal awareness must be sacrificed. The sacred bull dancers face the double axe every day. Those who survive are provided with all they desire."

"Unless what they desire is to live forever. Surely at least the king and queen of the Keftiu believe the double axe is a weapon wielded by their own Divine natures?"

"Perhaps, but our relationship with them has nothing to do with death and everything to do with earthly life and its pleasures, so it does not matter."

She was inclined to disagree until she met Kallikrates, then she was determined to believe there were exceptions to the rule and that not all the Keftiu were content to think that when they died they returned to the dark and unconscious womb of a Goddess who did not truly love them. The vibrant paintings gracing the foreign prince's palace defied such a depressing scenario. The ambassador was fluent in the language of Kemet but no hieroglyphs or writing of any kind filled the space between plants and animals drawn in ways she had never seen before. Two birds facing each other, their spread wings shown from different perspectives, seemed actually to be hovering above her as they kissed rapturously in mid air. Rendered against a white background like everything else, tall flowers similar to lotus blossoms rose from leafy bushes in all four corners of the reception room. Gazelle-like creatures with long horns were brought almost effortlessly to life by a few flowing black lines. White columns—their bases and capitals rimmed in black—grew slightly broader as they rose toward the undecorated ceiling.

The prince was as striking as his residence. When Hatshepsut entered the receiving room flanked by her personal guard, Kallikrates showed his respect for the queen, and offered his praise to the God's Wife of Amun, just like a courtier of Kemet by sinking to one knee and extending his right arm with the hand held open. He then beat his chest four times before raising his clenched right hand over his head and resting his left fist against his heart.

It was oddly gratifying to witness the gesture of praise and rejoicing performed by a foreigner. His black hair undulated down his bare chest and back in groups of three finger-thick strands reminiscent of flails. His headdress was an astonishing profusion of golden cylinders from which reared the stylized golden head of a strange creature with a blindly open mouth, its elaborate tail formed by tall red, blue and white plumes that drooped backwards from their own weight. The prince's white kilt—concealing his manhood while leaving one thigh provocatively exposed—was adorned by a blue animal skin. The odd creature's tail curled over his hidden sex and its limp body hung down the side of his bare leg, reminding her of the Anubis Emblem.[39] The prince wore another smaller golden belt, inlaid with blue stones, which did not support his kilt but merely called attention to the narrowness of his waist compared to the broadness of his shoulders. Two plain golden bands adorned his forearms and his feet were bare. He looked like a handsome man but he smelled more like an exotic animal for he was not anointed with any of the costly oils with which she was familiar. Perhaps it was the natural scent of his skin that intrigued rather than repelled her for he did indeed appear to be as clean as a lotus leaf.

The deeper she progressed into the ambassador's home the more impressed she became with its lively beauty. Everywhere there were golden circles resembling coiling snakes flowing into and out of each other, a black disc at their centers. She especially liked the banquet hall with its red columns and big blue-and-white fish swimming over all the doorways.

"Those are dolphins," Kallikrates informed her. "They are as smart as people and much wiser."

She laughed even though he did not sound as if he was joking.

"Dolphins spend their whole lives happily making love and eating, playing with their children and leaping toward the sun. They have no need of hands because everything they desire flows straight into their mouths."

She laughed again and said, "Tell me more about these *dolphins*."

He grinned. "When I was a young boy, I leaned too far over the railing of my father's ship, fascinated by the strange chirping sounds a group of dolphins was making as they all looked up at me just as curiously. I fell into the water and drowned and suddenly I could understand what they were saying to each other with their eerie songs."

"You are telling me, prince, that in the Great Green there are fish who speak?"

"Yes, but not with words. They communicate purely with sounds."

Perhaps dolphins were creatures sacred to Thoth, she thought, for as Hapuseneb had told her the gods were everywhere even if in other lands they were known by different names. "I would love to see your dolphins, Kallikrates."

"And I would love to show them to you, Majesty."

Abruptly she realized exactly what he had said. "Excuse me, but did I hear you tell me you *drowned*?"

"Yes. I was dead when my father's men dragged me from the water after a dolphin pulled me by my hair to the surface, or so they told me later. They pumped the water out of my chest and with their fists made my heart begin beating again. I have never felt more wretched."

She asked softly, "When you were dead?"

"Oh no, it was awful being alive again! It was wonderful being dead and swimming with the dolphins. It is something to look forward to."

She rewarded him for that statement with what she felt to be her most radiant smile.

He seemed appropriately dazzled for he turned his head away almost shyly and gestured to an attendant.

Two young boys wearing scanty red loincloths held up by tight black belts, their coiling long black hair sprouting in patches from their shaved heads, entertained their lord's guests with a boxing match.

Hatshepsut did not enjoy the violent sport but she smiled politely even while permitting her attention to wander. Kallikrates was the youngest son of the queen of the Keftiu and a true prince. Everything he said, and the way he expressed himself, proved it.

Sharing a table with Djehuty, Useramun ignored his long-time friend and asked Kallikrates questions whenever she silently indicated to him he had her permission to speak, which was often. She wanted to know as much as possible about their gracious host and his distant home.

All the ambassador's servants were boys or older men. Their heads were almost completely shaved except for a few tufts of hair erupting from their scalps in what appeared to be a half hazard fashion. Useramun, silently encouraged by her smile, remarked on the regrettable absence of women in the prince's otherwise lovely palace.

Kallikrates grinned. "My wife prefers to remain at home when I travel." He gazed into Hatshepsut's eyes and added quietly "I miss her" in a way that implied just the opposite.

Djehuty blurted, "But why do you not have any female servants?"

"Because I prefer to be served by boys."

She remembered the way Amenmose had caressed his serving girls and understood that although Kallikrates worshipped the Goddess he had a secret place in his heart for Seth.

Useramun looked away and fell into a disapproving silence. Djehuty looked embarrassed to have asked a question that produced an answer potentially displeasing to the queen.

Her smile deepened as she found herself entertained by the discomfiture of her courtiers. What probably bothered Useramun was the fact that the prince was older than he was and outranked him, putting him in a position similar to Horus, who as a youth had been seduced by his father's brother. It was the man who weakly allowed himself to be penetrated by another man who was looked down upon and dishonored.

Even though Hapuseneb was not present, Hatshesput thoroughly enjoyed the evening. When she returned to the palace, her attendants were full of questions.

"The Keftiu worship the Goddess and their priestesses handle dangerous snakes as casually as we do kittens." She permitted herself some entertaining liberties with the truth. "Their women hold the same honorable positions at court as the men and they sometimes wear dresses left completely open in front to expose their breasts. Their hills are filled with copper and silver and magical fish swim around their island. These fished, called *dolphins*, speak to any who are wise enough to listen to the wisdom they bring as offerings from the deep, for there is no bottom to the Greet Green."

It was of less interest to Seshen and Meresankh that the Keftiu were master ship builders and that their presence in Perunefer enhanced Kemet's ability to build even larger and stronger vessels, for which a vast quantity of wood was needed, wood that came mostly from the Land of the Two Rivers.

"Their houses are decorated with paintings almost as beautiful as ours but they depict strange plants which do no grow here and fantastic winged creatures."

She looked around her at the white walls, their plainness relieved only by the decorated yellow tiles at their base. She wanted more of these tiles painted with a greater variety of designs, including the Keftiu pattern evocative of serpents flowing and curving into themselves. She had been especially impressed by the precise symmetry of large white, blue and red flowers that resembled sideways floral collars and rested on black beds separated from each other by black-and-white lines drawn on a blue background.

It was from Perunefer that Pharaoh's troops set off along the Paths of Horus to frontier fortresses helping guard Kemet's northernmost border. It was a very important city populated by people who wore garish clothing and called the gods by strange names but whose lands were rich in substances she and her subjects coveted. Hatshepsut could not distinguish the mild feeling of anxiety she suffered in Perunefer from a strong sense of excitement. She sensed her heart trying to tell her something important. At first, she could not understand what it was, almost as though her own heart was mysteriously speaking to her in a foreign tongue.

The sun and God's Hand ruled the Keftiu, who were like distant brothers and sisters conceived by the same supreme Father but born to a different mother whose name was not Hathor. And even though in the Land of the Two Rivers he was called Baal, Seth was a mighty god there. She found herself feeling sorry for persons in whose hearts Horus had not yet taken wing and, reluctantly, compassion poured like water over the smoldering fear stoked by her thoughts whenever she remembered how much Maat had suffered in the hands of the Setiu. But she was Pharaoh's Great Royal Wife, Queen of Kemet and God's Wife of Amun—it was unacceptable for her to be afraid of anything or anyone.

She thought of her menagerie back in Waset full of exotic pets that gave her much pleasure because the men who served as their keepers had helped her tame them. When kept in their place with a strong arm, barbarous foreigners were not very different from animals, and if they possessed commodities she desired then they were worth the effort of controlling as well as the cost of feeding. There were, of course, people as bad as hyenas that possessed no redeeming qualities whatsoever. She suspected souls devoured by Ammit were often reborn as hyenas for they were disturbingly intelligent and stole things merely for the sake of doing so, whether or not they could actually use the objects. She would never forget the screams that had issued from a lady's tent during the long journey into Kush when a hyena slipped into her temporary dressing room and snatched her precious copper mirror. There were people who lived in the desert west of the River who deserved only an arrow through the heart to put them out of their misery but they were nothing like the Keftiu, or even like craftsmen and artisans from the Land of the Two Rivers, many of whom had been touched by Ptah. A quantity of the fine furnishings gracing Kallikrates' residence had been acquired in foreign ports. Seeing them had stimulated her imagination into trying to picture where they had come from and what other beautiful things might be found there.

She could not imagine boarding a ship that would take her to the end of the River and the Great Green Water flowing around islands where no one believed in the Ka or the Akh, and the black entrances to caves dotted the hillsides like mouths silently screaming in terror of eternal death. She could understand why every year Kallikrates made the journey, because it was Kemet he was returning to, as anyone whose heart possessed a modicum of intelligence would desire to do. She would never leave her Beloved Earth but she *would* see to it that everything she and her people needed was brought to them, preferably in even greater quantities than at present. It might even be that, along the shores of the Great Green Water, Ptah had deliberately dropped desirable luxuries intending for his daughter to find them, thereby enhancing both his glory and hers.

She hoped Kallikrates would make her a present of some of those magical talking fish. She intended to ask him more about dolphins the next time she saw him. She did not know when that would be for a letter had reached her from Waset. The Dowger Queen was ill. It was time to go home.

BOOK FOUR

Mistress of the Two Lands

21

The Double Axe

So death is before me now –

    the healthy state of sick man –

    like coming out in the air after suffering.

So death is before me now –

    like the fragrance of myrrh

    or sailing at ease on a breezy day…

So death is before me now

    like a clearing sky,

    like understanding what perplexed us before…

So death is before me now

    like one longing to see his home

    after long years in prison.[40]

During the long journey from Perunefer to Waset, a letter reached Hatshepsut from Senmut, who dared tell her more than Pharaoh. The Dowger Queen Ahmose had slipped on wet tiles decorating the edges of her favorite pool and broken a bone in her hip and another in her right wrist. Her physicians had bound the fractures but feared there was little chance of them ever healing completely.

More than ever, sunlight glimmering in the corner of her eye felt like her father speaking to her silently, and encouraging her to be happy no matter how sad she was. The loving approval of the solar disc felt as real to her heart as the world it revealed to her eyes, where nothing was more important than the people she herself loved. Love was too powerful to care if its subjects were still living on this side of the River or if, like her mother, they were impatiently waiting to make the mysterious crossing. At least Akheperkare had not lingered long in his broken body. Watching Ahmose slowly dying was the hardest thing she had ever done. She thanked the gods for being kind enough to balance the scales of her emotions with the joy she also experienced watching her daughter swiftly growing. After leaving her mother's bedroom, she always bathed and went to see Neferure.

Ahmose was so thin and her skin was so dry it seemed the priests of Anubis had already begun filling her with natron. That horrible thought was only one of dozens Hatshepsut was forced to shoo away every day like invisible hordes of flies. She was glad her father was not there to see his wise and beautiful wife mumbling irritably and wetting her bed like an infant. Her physician, Imhotep, had seen this slow wasting away before but still could not explain or prevent it. All he could do for his patient was regularly dose her with a tea made from acacia seeds mixed with pomegranate juice. For the pain in her hip and wrist, and in the hope of settling her stomach, he also prescribed strong infusions of lotus root sweetened with honey. Both medicinal drinks were poured into a libation jar made from a grayish-black stone in the form of the Ka hieroglyph— a pair of open arms cradling an *ankh* sign. The form imbued the liquids it contained with the eternal life-force of Atum-Re, passed to every person through the embrace of a physical body shaped by the Ka. By way of three openings, the fluid flowed into the bowl formed by the top of the *ankh*, absorbing the power of Life before emerging through an open spout at the base into a waiting cup.

Hatshepsut dearly wished the sacred libation jar would give Ahmose the strength and desire to talk with her more often but her mother gazed up at her almost indifferently. Then one day she finally spoke.

"I love you, Hatshepsut," she said, "and my heart is content knowing I leave you in excellent hands, but I am jealous of your youth and beauty. Bring your daughter to see me. Her life is just beginning as mine is ending. Neferure is closer to the magic of her Ka than any of us. When I look at her I see the promise of my rebirth and the new life soon to begin for me in the dark cradle of the Dwat, from which I will rise to walk in the fields of Re."

She complied with her mother's request and brought the princess to see her more often. Ahmose actually smiled when Neferure perched on the edge of her bed and described to her everything she had already done that morning. Then, very gently, the little girl stroked the old woman's forehead and said, "Do not be sad, mother. You know magic lives in the sand and does not need people to see it. If you want magic you have to dig really deep, night and day. Sometimes magic lives in people's hands and sometimes in a stone jar. There is magic in trees. When magic falls from a tree and no one catches it, magic disappears and flies up to the stars to be friends with the stars. Inside seeds there is lots of magic. It makes trees grow. Magic knows where God lives. Magic knows what God looks like."[41]

It was a relief to Hatshepsut that during her mother's illness her husband left her respectfully alone. Perhaps he feared the Dowger Queen's ailment might be contagious for it was rumored he was not feeling very well himself. She could always count on Seshen to tell her what people were saying. Meresankh was temporarily relieved of her duties and comfortably awaiting the birth of her baby boy at home. Hatshepsut felt as if all she did herself for long months was anxiously wait—for her mother to be born to a higher life where she would no longer be old and plain, sick and suffering. In all her feelings and thoughts, she carried the hope of her mother's eternal life and she found herself longing for the moment when Ahmose's Ba-bird would fly off, leaving her shriveled body behind like afterbirth.

Her steward, Dhout, looked unhappy about all the food his mistress sent back to the kitchen but wisely refrained from commenting on it. She ate less and drank more grape wine than usual. The hundreds of jars she had ordered while on her royal progress had arrived. The cellars beneath her palace were filled with vintages all bearing the seal of the highest quality. Only Nafre dared to scold her for not eating enough. Her head felt heavier than normal in the mornings but a brisk swim quickly took care of that. And everyday, before she went to see Ahmose, she visited the royal stables where lived the beautiful black horse she had claimed for herself and named Nomti in honor of the Great Army Commander. Stroking his sleek muscles reinforced the vibrant health of her own young body and gave her the strength she needed to face her mother's sickbed. She wanted to run away from the sight of death the way a horse bolts when spooked but she was not an animal, she had to be braver, and all her hopes for Ahmose's soul seemed related to the courage she herself was able to muster before entering the chamber that smelled of urine, boiled roots and decay. She began to see the sickroom as the stable of her mother's Ka, which was gradually dismissing all the organs that maintained and nourished its physical mount. The Dowger Queen's body was like an old dying horse but she, Ahmose, was so much more—the Divine rider of the long and slender limbs which could no longer properly serve her.

These thoughts comforted Hatshepsut but she was not inclined to share them with Hapuseneb or anyone else for they meant too much to her. Such feelings were like butterfly's wings—if anyone touched them with the fingers of their own thoughts, they might lose their effectiveness. The concepts and images would still be there but they would no longer have quite the same ability to lift her heart away from grief and sadness.

She would always be grateful to Senmut for the letter he sent her which had enabled her to prepare herself to face the severity of her mother's condition. If she had relied on Pharaoh's communication alone the shock she received upon arriving in Waset would have been great indeed. Instead, the surprise she got was a pleasant one. Neferure had grown extremely fond of the Royal Scribe, who had spent a great deal of time with the princess while her mother was away. He was apparently very good at telling stories for she invariably demanded one from him whenever he visited. If a particular ending failed to gratify her, she did not hesitate to change it and she often requested the same story. She was particularly enamored of the tale of Sinuhe, the courtier who, according to her, had fled Kemet by mistake. "For surely Pharaoh did not mean to make him so unhappy," she said firmly. She never tired of listening to the part where Sinuhe returned home and was restored to all his former glory:

I was put in the house of a prince. In this house were luxuries including a bathroom and mirrors. In it were riches from the treasury; garments made of royal linen...Years were removed from my body. I was shaved and my hair was combed. In this way was my squalor returned to the foreign land, my dress to the Sandfarers. I was dressed in the finest linen, I was anointed with perfumed oil and I slept on a real bed. I had returned the sand to those who dwell in it.[42]

Neferure also loved the story about the fish that fell in love with a little boy. Hatshepsut recalled that day long ago on the River when Inet told her the same sweet tale right after Ahmose explained to her about Tawaret and the destruction necessary for transformation. She longed for the return of the beautiful smiling woman who was caught now in the jaws of the crocodile which had already killed her beauty and continued cruelly devouring her health and happiness. Listening to Senmut tell the wise yet light-hearted child's tale, Hatshepsut was able to forget, at least for a little while, the profoundly demanding image of Tawaret wearing a crocodile on her back in the magical womb of the burial chamber. Yet she discovered she could spend no more time with her growing daughter than she did with her dying mother. Both visits ended up exhausting her, one with an excess of hope and happiness, the other with fear and sadness. Neferure's boundless energy and radiant health contrasted so strikingly with Ahmose's condition that Hatshepsut became uncomfortably aware of her own body's age and position in the relentless march of time. She remembered the symbol of the double axe sacred to the Keftiu and felt rather like the handle supporting the heavy blades of a sick mother and a blossoming daughter. She told both of them about the talking fish which lived in the Great Green knowing the princess would be delighted, and hoping the Dowger Queen would find comfort in Kallikrates' opinion that dying and swimming with the dolphins was something to look forward to.

It was the middle of the night and the door to the Dwat was wide open when the heart of Ahmose, King's Sister, King's Wife, departed.

* * * * *

Neferure performed her Sprouting Flowers dance for Senmut. The group of sacred dancers consisted of the princess and two of her favorite friends, Meri and Isis. Kneeling on the floor looking intently up at her playmates, Nefrure hugged her upper body and lowered her head making herself small enough to fit beneath the basket with which they quickly covered her.

"Begin!" came the princess' muffled command.

Meri and Isis lifted their arms over their heads and circled the primordial mound seven times, all the while turning their bodies around and around faster and faster. Just when it seemed they should have spun off from their own momentum they stopped abruptly, swaying slightly, and clapped their hands together. Bending at the waist like flowers blowing in the wind, they walked around the basket watering it with the spout formed by their joined palms. When Neferure's smiling face appeared, they quickly lifted the basket and the princess surged up to her full diminutive height, her hands reaching for the sky with her fingers spread wide. The three girls then danced joyously around the primordial mound. In the end, obeying some hidden signal, they draped their arms around each other's shoulders and collapsed dramatically across the floor, where they lay giggling.

Hatshepsut smiled proudly. Her daughter's body was barely four-years-old but her Ka was obviously ancient. It seemed to her that Neferure possessed an innate grasp of the most profound concepts. She glanced at Senmut, wondering if he was thinking the same thing. She would be disappointed in him if he was not.

"My lady, that was truly lovely," he said to the princess who had risen to her feet between her friends and, holding their hands, awaited his praise. "Trained temple dancers could not have displayed more skill and grace."

Grinning, she ran to him, perched herself on his lap and flung her arms around his neck. "I love you!" she whispered loudly in his ear.

"Nefi," Hatshepsut said quickly, "come here."

She went and stood dutifully before the queen. "Did you like my dance, too, Mami?"

"Of course I did. It was beautiful. What made you think of it?"

"I did not think of it, it just felt right."

"Has Ah-hotep told you about the Primordial Mound of Creation?"

She shook her head.

"Has anyone mentioned it to you, Nefi?"

She shook her head again.

"You are very wise, my daughter. Now run off and play with Meri and Isis, but first give me a kiss."

When the children had gone she remarked, "Ahmose-Penekhbet is away a great deal on royal business. My old teacher, Senimen, is still attached to Pharaoh as his personal advisor and will—regrettably for my daughter but fortunately for Kemet—remain so indefinitely. Neferure will soon be of an age to begin her lessons and I wish for her to have a teacher worthy of her intelligence. You have already won a place in her heart, Senmut. It would please me to honor you with the position of Royal Tutor to the Princess."

Rising, he sank to one knee before her and grasping both his shoulders lowered his head. "Majesty, my heart rejoices! Gladly I accept the most honorable position you are offering me."

He looked up into her eyes and added quietly, "Everything I do, I weave for Hatshepsut, Foremost of Noble Women, whom I adore in the morning for her wisdom and beauty. The only thing I desire is to bring the love flowing through my heart into any harbor it pleases her."

Holding his eyes she permitted her feelings to speak as she said, "You need not be afraid to let Neferure show her affection for you, Senmut. She is far braver than I was at her age. Her Ka already knows everything but her Ba still has much to learn from you… as does mine."

✴ ✴ ✴ ✴ ✴

The Lady Isis, Pharaoh's favorite concubine, was elevated to the position of minor wife.

Hatshepsut was grateful to the girl for consuming so much of her brother's attention. Unfortunately, she could not entirely avoid it. Thutmose was a fully grown man and pleasing to look at, she did not suffer distaste when he entered her, what she felt was simply nothing. The only aspect of the experience she enjoyed was exercising the power she possessed to clench her innermost flesh around his phallus. When he was spearing her with his erection, she practiced opening and closing the fish-like mouth between her thighs, intrigued by the obvious breathtaking effect it had on him. The exercise also enabled her to catch a glimpse of the beautiful sensation she was able to give herself, and which the High Priest of Amun had blessed her with on occasion. However, with her husband the pleasure was never more than a feather teasingly brushing the top of her sex as his seed continually failed to germinate inside her.

In the month of Hethara, obeying Pharaoh's command, Ibenre came to see her again but he did not examine her. Men and trained monkeys were climbing the date palms to reap their harvest and she was able to offer her physician baked dates coated with cinnamon-flavored chickpea flour. The pomegranates growing in the royal gardens were also finally ripening. Her Receiving Room was decorated with bouquets of scarlet flowers and wherever she went there was always a bowl filled with the pale golden orbs. When sliced open they revealed strikingly red seeds.

"Do not feel obliged to keep eating them, my lady." Ibenre said with a smile as he caught her eyeing the fruit with distaste. "In fact, I would counsel against excessive consumption of pomegranates. It will have the effect of purging you much more certainly than it will help you conceive."

"I fear there may be something wrong with me," she confessed reluctantly.

Since Neferure's birth, Pharaoh had fathered three more children by two different concubines and though the babies were all girls they served to prove he was virile.

Ibenre held his hands up for a serving girl to wipe clean as he said, "There is nothing wrong with you, my lady."

She regarded him skeptically, wondering if Hapuseneb had told him how she felt about her husband.

"I know," he said abruptly.

She dared to believe he was answering her unspoken question. "And you do not think how I feel may be affecting my ability to conceive?"

"I did not say that. I said there was nothing wrong with you."

"But I cannot change how I feel."

"That is not possible," he agreed, helping himself to another date. "We can only change how we think in the hope our feelings will eventually follow."

"If the subject does not alter its nature, then I see no reason why I should change my thoughts concerning it, which leaves me feeling exactly the same as I do now."

"Indeed." He smiled at her appreciatively. "I am not suggesting you do that, Maat forbid. It is only that sometimes we think we want something when we really do not and, if that is case, the more powerful our Ka the more certain it is we will never get it."

He was telling her she believed she wanted to conceive but that in truth she did not. His gentle prod forced her to face the emotional source of her barrenness. How she felt about Thutmose was creating a blockage inside her body his sperm was powerless to overcome. It was a rather gratifying thought.

* * * * *

The Good God Akheperenre officially anointed his Royal Scribe, Senmut, Brother of Mut, Royal Tutor to Princess Neferure and steward of her estate.

His young charge, not permitted to attend the investiture, insisted he tell her all about it afterward.

Hatshepsut smiled at him sympathetically. "It is quite a task you are taking upon yourself, Senmut. My daughter is more curious than a cat and as energetic as a dragonfly. You never know what subject she will land upon and ask you all about."

"I will strive to make my answers as true to Maat as possible without boring her."

"Have no fear of that. She finds *everything* interesting."

"A sign of true wisdom."

Smiling contentedly, Neferure studied their faces as they discussed her and when they fell silent she said, "What will you do with my estate, Senmut?"

"I will take care of it for you, my lady."

"But what *is* my *estate?*"

"Your estate is all the land and animals, administrators, scribes and servants who belong to you."

"Oh! I want to see my *estate*, especially the animals!"

Hatshepsut said firmly, "You will, my love, but not today. Senmut belongs to me this evening for I am holding a banquet in his honor. Go now with Ah-hotep. It is time for your bath."

Recalling how much it had frustrated her when Ahmose quenched the flow of her questions with that statement, she gestured to a waiting attendant. "But first I have a present for you. After you are clean, nurse will show you how to use it."

Keeping her eyes respectfully lowered, the servant presented the princess with a green eye paint tube decorated with carved figures of Bes on both sides.

"One of the openings is for black and the other for green," Hatshepsut explained as her daughter avidly studied the object.

"What an ugly little man!" the princess declared. "He almost looks more like an animal for his tongue is sticking out, the way my cat's sometimes does, and he has a mane and a tail and even ears like a lion's."

"Bes will help protect you."

"From what?"

Hatshepsut glanced at Senmut. All those in close contact with Neferurfe were forbidden to speak to her of demons.

"The paint my sister puts around your eyes everyday," he said, "repels flies and other insects. The fierce look on the face of Bes also helps frighten away the agents of disease."

Neferure continued curiously examining her present. "But why are flies so hungry for my eyes?"

Reminded of the golden necklaces hung with three golden flies awarded to royal spies who went everywhere reading men's hearts and minds, her mother replied, "The way Atum-Re lives in your vision attracts them for our eyes still glimmer with traces of the Primordial Waters. Mami brought it for you all the way from Perunefer near the Great Green Water. And speaking of water, it is definitely time now for your bath."

The artisan who fashioned the eye paint tube had clearly been influenced by the paintings of the Keftiu. On either side of Bes rose two slender columns composed of the circles resembling rows of serpents coiling in on themselves. Hatshepsut found it both a pleasing and a magically potent design evoking as it did the One who is everything.

* * * * *

The north-eastern boundary of Kemet was being threatened by organized bands of raiders. Accompanied by his Great Army Commander, Pharaoh set forth from Waset bound for the Paths of Horus.

Hatshepsut was left in charge of the Seal Room where she received regular reports from Tai, the "royal cat" she had left in Mennefer to hunt out corruption. Various officials had been stripped of their titles and sent into exile along the same route the supplies they regularly failed to deliver to the Auxiliaries of the Well now safely traveled. Justice was being done in a fashion she considered very pleasing to Maat.

Meanwhile, Raab, the youngest son of Rasui, Nomarch of the Oryx, had been received by Satepihu, the Headman of Tjeny, who politely forced Setau, the grotesque Nomarch of Great Land, to accept the youth's presence in his home and to heed the wisdom of his advice whenever he chose to give it. The success of Setau's "rider" went more smoothly than expected because—Satepihu informed her in one of his letters—Raab was extremely handsome and well-spoken. It was not necessary for him to write more. The thought of Setau in love was oddly gratifying. Once more, she felt Maat was smiling upon the justice worked by her daughter.

Khenti, the Nomarch of the Sistrum she had taken such a liking to, had attended the Dowger Queen's funeral but she had spoken to him only briefly. At the time, her heavy heart had remembered the pleasure she took in his company as superficial, not worthy of her attention during such a sorrowful and momentous occasion. She felt better now and regretted the dismissive way she had treated him. She dictated a letter inviting him to visit Waset again and assuring him of a much warmer welcome whenever he chose to grace her palace with his presence.

The well-being of the Servants of the Place of Truth became a priority in the Seal Room. She was distressed to learn their lives could be much more difficult than she had permitted herself to believe. Men who for years worked deep in tombs lit only by candlelight often paid for the beautiful paintings they produced with failing eyesight and occasionally blindness. Many professions, it seemed, could prove dangerous. Beekeepers were stung senseless, butchers died of a wasting illness and the bowels of fishermen turned to liquid.

The Great One of the Crew, Nekhetmut, a foreman of the left side of the Ship's Crew—the diggers, draftsmen and painters who had recently begun working on Pharaoh's tomb—met with Akheperseneb and Ineni in the Seal Room to recommend a handful of skilled young men for positions which had recently become vacant due to injury, old age and death. The men being replaced either had no living offspring to inherit their posts or their sons were still too young to rise from the ranks of the *semedet*. It was also possible the youths had chosen to seek another profession for all male children born in The Place of Truth were taught to write and draw. Those less artistically inclined and more ambitious could grow up to become civil servants or even officers in the army.

Hatshepsut did not much care for the Foreman Nekhetmut, who after performing the ritual greetings did his best to pretend she was not present as he conferred with Akheperseneb and Ineni. She learned later from her vizier that Nekhetmut was suspected of accepting bribes and of recommending boys for positions based mainly on the generosity of their relatives.

"However, it has yet to be proven he is actually dishonest," he concluded.

"You have only to see his face and look into his eyes," she retorted mildly, "to know Maat is suffering inside him."

"Unfortunately," Senmut said, "evidence produced by the intelligence of the heart cannot be presented in court."

"In any case, no damage is being done that we can see," Ineni added while unrolling another scroll in the obvious hope of moving the business forward.

"The fever which robs a body of strength and life cannot be *seen* and yet it does very real damage, as does greed," she said sternly. "Greed cares only for itself and so eventually begins destroying everything it comes into contact with. Greed is a dangerous fever, my lords, for it erodes truth, which is the spirit of health. It is wise to diagnose greed before the persons in which it festers are seen to thrive by others lazy enough to make their beds with them. Such people secretly live weak and miserable lives because no one obliges them to realize they are sick at heart."

After she spoke the only sound and movement in the room came from a fly which had escaped the royal whisks and landed safely on a papyrus lying on the table beside her scarab-ringed fingers.

"The effects of a fatal fever are at first so subtle they may scarcely be noticed but they quickly get worse," she continued, feeling passionate about the subject. "The men recommended by Nekhetmut will be working on the eternal homes of my loved ones and on mine as well. If those who render the gods with red and black ink, and then give them life with incorruptible colors, are chosen not because they are touched by Ptah but because those who raised them are corrupt, Maat will not fully inhabit their creations."

She smiled down at the fly which was rubbing its two front legs together with intense satisfaction.

"Spies must be placed on the Ship to observe its crew before I begin work on my queen's tomb, which I intend to do very soon. Senmut?"

"My lady!"

"Will you see to that for me?"

"In my hands, Majesty, the will of your heart may always be considered realized. Were I a god, I would conquer the two lions of the horizon so no time would need pass from the instant you expressed your wish to the moment of its fulfillment."

She smiled at him before turning a more sober countenance toward Akheperseneb and Ineni. Two of Pharaoh's greatest officials were staring at her in a way that suddenly made her feel she had sprouted horns from her head. She thought they almost looked a little frightened.

"There must be no doubt whatsoever that The Great One of the Crew, the one who assigns the task to each man under his command in the Place of Truth, has faith in Maat and always behaves accordingly," she concluded.

Ineni's back straightened. "The Deputy who speaks into the ears of the Great One with the voice of the people, the man who supplies the workers with all their needs and answers for their behavior, was elected to his position. It is Kamut who voiced his doubts as to Nekhetmut's integrity."

Senmut spoke decisively, "Kamut will be the jar from which the life of the queen's investigation will pour."

The business of the day then proceeded on another course.

A report had arrived from Djehutihotep, the Deputy of the King's Son who had replaced his father, Ruiu. She had grieved for Amenemhat—serving now as a scribe in all matters related to Pharaoh's southern lands—when news of his father's death reached Waset. Although he had kept his delicate features free of all emotion, his slanted eyes had been rimmed with red for days afterward. She could not really imagine how he felt. He had lived at court most of his life far away from his father, who had visited Waset on only a handful of occasions. Perhaps what he missed most was the time had had not spent with the man who gave him life.

On that afternoon all traces of grief had long since vanished from Amenemhat's eyes when he was admitted into the Seal Room to read the letter sent by his brother. Amongst his other duties, Djehutihotep was in charge of policing Kemet's southernmost roads and mines. There were no problems to address. The peace imposed by Pharaoh remained unchallenged. In one of the mines, a shaft had collapsed but no workers had been present at the time.

Hatshepsut was outwardly gratified by the report sent by the Deputy of the King's Son and inwardly relieved. The bulk of the army was currently as far away from Kush as it could get. There were always troops stationed in the southern fortresses but with Nomti occupied elsewhere, she felt better knowing there was nothing to worry about in Wawat. She kept reminding herself that her father was still present in the limbs of the army he had commanded and strengthened, yet the truth was she did not feel quite as safe as she had when he was alive. Her lack of faith in her brother and husband contributed to her unease. Like a snake's jaws, the southern borders would not remain safely sealed forever. The venomous fangs of Kushite lances would dare to bite Kemet again one day. It was vital never to cease expecting the threat and always to be prepared to crush it. Her Beloved Earth required as many diligent guardians as her Pleasure House needed the gardeners who kept it free of destructive vermin.

The workshops in Mennefer had been expanded to include the manufacture of more chariots, produced in even greater numbers in Waset by the Temple of Amun. An enormous amount of leather and of high-quality wood was required. It was somewhat distressing to think that much of the wood needed to make the chariots used to fight off invaders came primarily from potentially hostile countries. Once again, she remembered the double axe of the Keftiu, who were wise enough to recognize the relentless duality of life.

The Royal Treasury was in charge of equipping the army. One of Senmut's tasks as the Superior Royal Scribe was to go over the different lists of supplies required by the various workshops, and to either question or approve them based on careful monitoring of the rate of production and a precise inventory of all the items produced. He in turn was under the direct supervision of the Overseer of the Seal Bearers, the Royal Treasurer Nehesj. Like Hapuseneb, Nehesj rarely wore the wigs adopted by men of his status. He reminded her of the High Priest of Amun, not as a result of any marked physical resemblance but because they both emanated the same quiet aura of authority. Even when they did not speak, their silence felt more filled with meaning than the most eloquent discourse. The office held by Nehesj administered all the wealth of the Kingdom. For that reason he traveled a great deal and was seldom in the Southern Seal Room but it was to him she would first have to speak about increasing the size of the army.

22

Queen's Tomb

Hatshepsut conceived again but Pharaoh's joy was short lived. One morning she woke and discovered her bed sheets stained with blood in which solid clots were sinisterly visible. There was a dull ache in her lower back but other than that, she felt in good health. Ibenre was summoned immediately and Thutmose sent three of his own priests of Sekhmet to attend her.

"The God's Wife is in no danger," Ibenre informed them. "The baby's Ka simply chose to abandon the body it had begun weaving in the magical loom of her womb."

His fellow physicians looked skeptical, in addition to extremely annoyed that no less than six priests of Amun were preventing them from getting any closer to the queen.

"Ibenre is correct," she said, avoiding Hapuseneb's eyes for fear they would weaken her with the need to feel his arms around her. "I dreamed of a baby falcon pushed out of the nest by its own father because it was too small and frail to please him."

One of Sekhmet's scribes spoke in a strained voice, "Perhaps because the mother failed to give her child the nourishment it needed?"

She knew he dared proffer that diagnosis because he had been sent to her bedside by the king, to whom he was reluctant to give any news that threw the potency of the royal sperm into question. It was much safer to blame the queen for the loss of Pharaoh's heir. Until the baby was born and proved otherwise, it was assumed a boy.

Hapuseneb lifted his right arm slightly. His fingers were curled into a fist but his thumb was held up and erect.

At once eight of the queen's personal guardsmen, headed by Mentekhenu—whose own little boy had survived his first year of life—surrounded the priests of Sekhmet.

"What? What is this?" One of them sputtered indignantly. "We are here on Pharaoh's behalf and by his command!"

After a quick glance at the High Priest of Amun, Mentekhenu drew his dagger and said shortly, "You will come with us, please. Now."

The room smelled much better after they left. She was able to take a relaxed breath and sit up more comfortably against the pillows Nafre had propped up behind her.

"I will come to see you again this evening, my lady." Ibenre held his hands up to her in praise as he departed.

Her attendants were silently directed out of the room by all the priests of Amun except Hapuseneb, who remained standing until the door closed behind them. He then seated himself on the edge of her bed and grasped both her hands in his. "How do you feel?" he said gently.

If he had been anyone else she would have fished for the proper fiction and served it to him as the truth but with him that was impossible to do. "I feel relieved."

"Good. I was afraid you might feel guilty. I am sorry, Hatshepsut."

"I told you, I am not sad."

"I am sorry you must continue giving yourself to a man you do not love."

"He is my husband," she reminded him bitterly, wishing her hands could rest in his like that forever.

"You are married to him, but he is not truly your husband."

Despite the linen cloths stuffed between her thighs and tied closed around her waist, she suddenly felt better then she had in months.

"You will not conceive again, my lady. It is written in the stars you will not bear Pharaoh a male child and heir. It is not your destiny."

She was stunned. "But then who will rule on the Horus Throne after the Good God Akheperenre flies to heaven?" She thought of her mother's father and of his great wife and son and could not bear the thought of being the cause of their Divine bloodline drying up.

"Many great pharaohs will reign for centuries after your brother," he assured her. "The rule of Maat will reach farther than before and the Falcon will bring back in his talons riches yet to be imagined."

"But the future king will not be my son."

"No. That is not your destiny," he repeated firmly, holding her eyes as if willing her to glimpse in them what he already saw.

"You can tell me what my destiny is not, but you cannot tell me what it is?"

"Only you and your heart can determine that."

"I thought everything was already written in the stars, Hapuseneb."

"The stars are the possible seeds of the future, but like seeds they must be properly cared for to reach their full potential."

"So many feelings flow through my heart it seems my thoughts are canals necessary to contain and direct them. Is it my feelings that somehow nourish the seeds of the stars, which speak of what might be through me?"

He smiled. "Yes, and that is why it is vital you not dam any of your deepest feelings for fear their power will wash away all that is irrelevant, and yet might seem important when perceived through the eyes of souls smaller than a townhouse garden."

She giggled. "How awful!"

"It is good to see you laugh."

She looked away and said wistfully, "I wish we could take another journey together, Hapuseneb."

"We will enjoy many more journeys together, Hatshepsut. Did you really think I built that ship just to take one trip with you?"

She looked at him in surprise. "You built that ship for us?"

"Of course I did, and you already knew that in your heart."

"I feel my heart knows everything that is truly important but my mind too often questions from where that certainty arises."

"I understand, but you are not thinking deep enough. What you feel is always true and yet sometimes, for one reason or another, we do not clearly recognize what we feel or choose to accept it. Only by taking full command of our thoughts can we be true to the intelligence of our heart that never fails us. Only our thoughts fail us by choosing to serve selfish fears instead of the truth revealed through our feelings, which is always much clearer than thinking about it might lead us to believe."

"But why should I be afraid to believe you built your ship for us? Surely no thought could be more pleasing to my heart."

"You did not realize I built my ship for us because you are afraid I do not truly love you."

"I-"

"You fear that even if it is true I love you," he interrupted her sternly, "that I can never do anything about it because circumstances will not permit it. You must confess you are afraid of that, Hatshepsut."

"To hear you say you love me, I will confess to anything, Hapuseneb."

* * * * *

Now that he was finally wed to Senseneb and expecting his first child, Hatshepsut did not see as much of Puyemre as she used to.

Useramun, who had married Tjuyu, was serving as a scribe of the Treasury of Amun. The importance of the work suited him. It was obvious he did not find it at all dull assisting his fellow administrators in keeping an accurate account of the Hidden One's ever growing wealth. In the presence of great boards of cedar wood, bundles of elm, fir, oak and yew, sacks of copper nuggets, crates of silver vessels and neatly bound piles of fine leather hides, Useramun wielded his scribe's pen with the same proud concentration he hunted, bowled and wrestled.

Serving as a Steward of Amun, Amenhotep divided his time between Waset and Abu, where his wife and baby girl still were. In the future, he hoped to bring his family north.

Min-hotep was acquitting himself admirably as a *wab* priest in *Ipet Sut*.

Upon the queen's recommendation, Pharaoh had made Djehuti a scribe of the Royal Treasury.

Hatshepsut had begun planning her eternal home. Normally it was Pharaoh's vizier who determined the best place for the Great Royal Wife to be buried, but Akheperseneb did not appear offended when she informed him the High Priest of Amun would be helping her select the location of her tomb. She was not surprised by the relief she glimpsed in his eyes before he carefully hid it. He was no longer a young man. She had suspected he would not relish the prospect of spending hours in the western desert.

She honored Hapuseneb with the task of supervising all aspects of her tomb's construction. The project would take years. It was wonderful to think about. She was literally placing her soul in his hands by putting him in command of the stone nest her Ba-bird would use to fly between this world and the next. It was a profoundly intimate act and the ultimate expression of trust.

They chose the nineteenth day of Mechir, in the peaceful season of Immersion when all the seeds had been planted and begun growing, to cross the River together. It was still night when their boat rowed away from the eastern shore. They stood together at the prow and out on the starlit water, accompanied by only four carefully picked oarsmen, it was almost like being alone. The vessel rowing ahead of theris was crowded with guardsmen, litter bearers, personal attendants and scribes. Djehuty was amongst the latter, supervised by a senior scribe from whom he was learning the skill of calculating and recording precise measurements.

Disembarking on the west bank, they paused on the landing stage to gaze across the milky-white River at the red-gold disc of the sun slowly rising over the Temple of Amun-Re.

They followed the processional route to the small mud-brick House of Amun erected over the first mounds of earth to be left behind after the Primordial Waters of Nun, rich with the unfathomable currents of creative forces, receded. They stopped there to make a libation to Amun-Kematef, He Who Creates Himself. Behind the monument stretched a seemingly endless expanse of desert, in which the vast powers responsible for the world's formation had left their mark in the form of treacherously deep and shadowy canyons winding between soaring cliffs. Hapuseneb had warned her they could only travel so far by litter but she was more than willing to walk to see the location he had chosen for her eternal home.

She was glad he was holding her hand, officially to prevent her from tripping, because the remoteness of the place made her heart grow cold even beneath Re's intensifying warmth. Her mother and Meri, and their mother and her mother's mother, were all buried far from there. She would rest all alone in Seth's lifeless embrace but her body would be safe. She carried a sunshade, since it was impossible for their attendants to hold a cooling canopy steadily over them, and her feet were beginning to hurt when they finally reached the desolate spot Hapuseneb had chosen.

"The tomb will be situated high up in the rock face and will not be visible." He pointed up at a section where the cliff ascended straight toward heaven, its bottom lost in the mottled light and darkness of the narrow canyon undulating serpent-like below them. "And at certain times of the year the rising sun will shine directly upon its door."

"But I will be so lonely out here," she protested before she could stop herself.

Gently he brushed her hair aside and whispered in her ear, "You will not be here."

"Only my body will rest here," she agreed, trying to believe it, "but I will wish to come and visit it."

"If that is what you desire, my lady, we will fly here together, for the Ba's of Hatshepsut and Hapuseneb will continue to exist beyond time. Perched on the porch of your tomb, we will gaze out over that hill all the way across the valley to the River and watch the sun forever rising over the House of Amun."

"You make me want to move in right away," she said with a smile. "I will inform my steward. He will be delighted."

His laughter echoed below them in the dead canyon, through which a river of life had once flowed, and resounded against the rugged face of the cliff that looked impossible to climb much less penetrate.

* * * * *

After she sanctioned Hapuseneb's suggestion for the location of her tomb, they consulted on the design. It would be the largest ever constructed for a queen in Waset's western desert. A scribe drew up the plan they agreed upon, which was further approved by Ineni and then carefully studied by Djehuty, who was proving remarkably adept at the arcane science of ropes, cubits, fractions and everything else related to the art of measure.

From the entrance—which would be bored into a natural cleft in the rock face—a handful of steps would lead down to a second door opening onto a long corridor thrusting straight east. The first passage would end in a small chamber where her Ba would enter the presence of the *neters*—the forces conducted by her Ka to compose the beautiful music of incarnation currently playing the unique melody of Hatshepsut. Another door would lead into a shorter and slightly wider corridor descending south to the magical throne room of her Ka, although it was not so labeled on the plan drawn up by the scribe. From an opening in the center of the floor of the final room, a ramp would plunge down into a narrow passage terminating in the actual burial chamber. Her Ba's stone nest, as she liked to think of it, was laid out in a similar fashion to her mother's and Meri's, except for this last south-eastern facing shaft descending into a short corridor which ended in the intimate space where her mummy would rest. She suffered a perverse thrill every time she wondered how her Ba-bird would be able to escape the dark and solid stone depths. It was impossible to imagine, yet not for an instant did she doubt her power to be born to a superior form of life from the mysterious womb of her tomb, its narrow passages the supernatural equivalent of a birth canal.

She looked forward to being reunited with her integral Ka and its boundless creativity, but she would always be very fond of the form she presently inhabited. She did not want to lose anything she had already felt and would continue to experience and learn throughout her earthly existence. She desired the person she was now to always be there for her Ka to remember and reap magical nourishment from. Her Ba would return and perch on her mummified limbs whenever her Akh felt nostalgic for the inimitable beauty of Hatshepsut.

Furniture and chariots were made from high quality wood and so too were Master's of Life. Wood, however, was not imperishable. Trees symbolized corporeal existence and their products served the needs and pleasures of the flesh. Even when inlaid with precious stones and painted with incorruptible colors, wood, like the physical body, did not last forever.

She said to Hapuseneb one afternoon, "I desire a container for my Master of Life that will not eventually decay and expose my mummy's wooden bed to vermin and possible decomposition."

She was once more recalling the day Seni had taught her the symbolism of stone.

"The bed in which my Master of Life will rest must be made of stone like the eternal home that will house it," she went on. "Rocks are the strong enduring bones of the created world. Stone can be shaped by the sensual caress of water and yet it is never corrupted. Stone perfectly symbolizes both my embodied and immortal natures and how they cannot truly be distinguished from each other."

"My lady, if what you desire is a stone repository for your Master of Life, then that is what you will have," the High Priest replied. "You need only choose the stone that pleases you most."

She lost no time in bringing the subject up with Senmut and the information he provided her with helped her decide on a sandstone rock that had transformed itself into a much harder and stronger stone called *biat,* "wonderful."[43] However, the size of the grain and the color could vary greatly. Letters were sent to the quarry near Mennefer as well as to the two quarries west of Abu. In the end, she chose a fine-grained variety with a yellowish tinge, which made it seem as if the rock had managed to trap some of the sun's light while buried in the dark earth. The symbolism pleased her. Even though the stone called *wonderful* was often used for important thresholds, and to line the walls of tombs, hers would be the first receptacle for a Master of Life made from *biat* to be buried in Waset's western desert.

After searching her heart for the right words to express her feelings, Hatshepsut wrote them down to show Hapuseneb and no one else, until the time came for superior craftsmen to inscribe them on the golden stone in the embrace of which she would live forever:

Great Princess, great of popularity and charm, Lady of the Two Lands, King's Daughter, King's Sister, God's Wife, Great Royal Wife, Hatshepsut.[44]

She says, "O *my mother Nut, stretch thyself over me, that thou mayest place me among the imperishable stars which are in thee, and that I may not die.*"[45]

The lid would be decorated with an image of Nut, her arms outstretched where she stood protectively over the name, *Hatshepsut,* contained in the first *shenu* ring ever to be carved in that location. On one side of her stone bed, to the left of the sacred inscriptions, two *wedjat* Eyes of Horus would see into the darkness for her.

* * * * *

Pharaoh dedicated two bulls and two calves to Amun-Re and Amun-Min, and then commemorated the offering in a new shrine he erected to house the bark of the god. Hatshepsut, who had stood behind him during the rite, was pleased with the delicate beauty of the bas-relief immortalizing her smiling profile. She was portrayed as the king's equal, her slender figure as tall as his. She could not be certain if her husband was in any way responsible for that vital stylistic detail. The artists who carved the images were servants of the temple and under the direct supervision of its senior priests as well as of Ineni, Overseer of the Double Granary of Amun and Supervisor of all the works of the King. She strongly suspected the respect Thutmose felt for her was more passive than profound. When the design was presented to him, she imagined he approved her equal stature in order not to offend Amun-Min, who also claimed her as his wife and whose assistance he clearly needed to impregnate her again.

One of the calves offered to Amun represented the male heir the royal couple was still waiting for. The other calf was Neferure, the beautiful daughter with which they were already blessed. Heavy with symbolism, the two bulls represented the flesh of Re—the celestial muscle of all terrestrial forms—as well as the eternal Ka's of the King, his queen and of their offspring, born and yet to be conceived. Because air could only be depicted by the object that moved it, drawn behind Hatshepsut was the *shut* hieroglyph—a fan in the shape of a blue lotus leaf held up by an *ankh* sign and wafting the power of life over the royal family.

Pharaoh's features were faithfully rendered on the walls of the new bark shrine but in reality he was not as broad of shoulder, nor were his legs that long and strong. The artist had captured her brother at his most magnificent—wearing the double crown and a floral collar enhanced by two gold falcon wings crossing downward over his chest, the bird's claws grasping the *shen* symbol for eternity encircling his navel. A phallic sheath was attached to his belt beneath the traditional short ritual kilt and stiffly pleated royal apron. After the ceremony, when she returned to his palace with him, she watched two of his pretty attendants reverently remove the red ribbon attaching the fine leather pouch to his belt. She concealed her disappointment when he chose to undress completely before possessing her. The hard kiss of gold against her breasts and the *shen* ring beating gently against her belly might have proved stimulating.

Hatshepsut kept such thoughts to herself. Much more exciting than her brother's thankfully brief amorous attentions was standing in a chariot beside a soldier named Inebni. Quite often, he was forced to drape his left arm over her shoulders or to slip it around her waist to keep her from losing her balance. She was impressed by the skill with which he swiftly transferred the reigns into one hand, attending to her safety while at the same time controlling the horses with no apparent effort. She was mesmerized by the muscular strength of Nomti's shining black buttocks galloping before them in perfect stride with his brown companion. She laughed in delight even when she genuinely feared being thrown from the light-weight vehicle. However, she quickly grew impatient with the safe trot she suspected Inebni would never have taken the animals beyond without her express command. She had been forced to make it clear to him she was not to be treated like a helpless child.

"Very well, my lady," he had replied soberly, "but in that case you must give me permission to touch you in any way necessary, for I would sooner face life-long exile than permit you to be hurt. In fact, I would find it difficult ever to forgive myself if even the smallest scratch was to mar your beautiful skin."

She laughed, thrilled by his boldness. "You have my permission!" she said, and in the end she was so pleased with Inebni she made him a troop commander.

The morning she took the reigns into her own hands was one she would never forget. Inebni stood directly behind her, his distinctly firm manhood cradled in the small of her back as he held the leather straps along with her. He did not release them until she ordered him to, then he stepped aside and all she felt was the warm desert wind, the smooth reigns in her grasp, the hard hide beneath her sandals and the energy of the horses. The joy Nomti and his partner were obviously taking in the exercise flowed up her arms into her heart and made her gasp exultantly.

"Turn to the right!" Inebni spoke directly into her ear so she could hear him over the chariot wheels hissing and the horse's hooves thudding across the packed sand of the training grounds.

Overwhelmed by the sensual intensity of the experience, at first she could not remember how to execute the turn, until she felt Inebni positioning himself to take over again. "No!" she cried, and the horses began veering to the right as her arms and hands sought to emulate the subtle motion she had seen him execute dozens of times.

"Very good, my queen! Now run a tight circle around that rock for me!"

She obeyed him, the animals obeyed her and she laughed, lost her balance and fell against Inebni as he helped her complete the maneuver.

That night Hatshepsut dreamed she was standing in a chariot driven by a man she did not recognize. She held a bow already strung with an arrow she let fly with a feeling akin to sexual desire. They seemed to be riding through a sky filled with black clouds through which her arrow flashed like lightning and revealed that the deep rumbling sound she heard was not thunder but hordes of marching Kushite soldiers. Her arousal gave way to terror and she ordered herself to wake up. But then she realized she was not alone and her courage returned as more and more shafts of light began flashing through the invading hordes. Hundreds of chariots like the one in which she rode were following behind her where she raced at the head of Re's army in the name of Maat. The power of God beating in her heart thundered in the hooves of all the horses under her command. The chariot wheels hissing across the sand were the magic of the Goddess living inside her and spinning across the battlefield like the spiraling serpentine designs of the Keftiu. Her fear was conquered by elation as she anticipated a victory that would always be, no matter what, if she believed in it—the triumph of light over darkness, life over death, hope over fear, compassion over corruption, wisdom over ignorance, beauty over ugliness.

When she walked out into her garden that morning she smiled with surprise and joy when she saw stars shining in the trees. It had rained during the night. For the first time in countless months, water from heaven had poured from the sky.

Perhaps Nut's triumphant laughter had entered her ears as she slept and shaped her dream around her. The messages the Ba brought back from the Ka to its physical nest were often as symbolically complex as hieroglyphs but this one was clear—it was necessary she speak with the king and with Nehesj about increasing the size of the army, beginning with the divisions stationed in Kush. Yet when a few days later the opportunity to bring up the subject presented itself in the Seal Room, she let it slip away.

Hatshepsut was disappointed with herself for not speaking when she felt she should have, but she had feared her dream would not carry much weight with officials who were not also priests. It made her stomach hurt to swallow urgent words sent up to her mouth from her heart, which refused to take them back. The business of the Seal Room was in some ways like standing in a swiftly moving chariot constantly turning from one issue to another. In the rare instances when both she and Pharaoh were present in the administrative palace, she never took the reigns of the day's affairs in her own hands as she sometimes did when she was alone with his advisors. She felt her husband would not listen to her the way Ineni, Akheperseneb, Ahmose-Penekhbet, Senimen and even Nehesj always did. She had observed, on innumerable occasions, that her wisdom was beyond the grasp of her brother's intelligence and so she chose not to waste her breath on him.

Amenhotep, at least, was well pleased with the king, who had recently begun enlarging the Temple of Khemnu and his Divine family in Abu. The priest of Anukis was very happy his goddess was being so honored. Thutmose was also planning the expansion of an ancient temple in Wawat and would soon be sailing south for the consecration ceremony. She approved of her brother honoring the gods and of seeking to make their splendor and might more visible to the Kushites. Unfortunately, restoring the ruined Temple of Hathor in the north was not a priority for him, and Pakhet's abandoned rock-cut chapel seemed beneath his notice. Pakhet was merely a local goddess he had never even heard of until Senimen explained to him who she was. Instead, he commissioned another statue of their father for the Temple of Amun-Re and put her in charge of the project.

In her heart, Hatshepsut longed for a statue of Akheperkare similar to that of Menkaure the Divine—near life-sized and approachable compared to the colossal Osiris figures he had commissioned of himself before he died. She continued to feel his love in the sunlight but a more faithful representation of his smiling face would have been nice to have as well. She met with the sculptor who had modeled her father's features for his colonnade and knew he would not be able to fulfill her dream. His hands, spotted with age, no longer deftly obeyed him. She doubted he still possessed the skill to recapture the special quality of her father's grin. The work that eventually resulted, although somewhat smaller, was no different from the others, impressive but impersonal.

Like his Ka, Akheperkare's new statue would live forever yet his daughter was selfishly disappointed by it.

Prompted by her dream of battle, and in an effort to relieve a restless frustration, Hatshepsut began spending her days with Troop Commander Inebni again. He was teaching her how to shoot an arrow from a bow, and he was visibly impressed when only on her third attempt she hit the target dead center.

✷ ✷ ✷ ✷ ✷

Puyemre's beloved Senseneb gave him a baby boy they named Menkheper. Surprisingly, Hatshepsut saw more of her friend after the birth of his son than she had in months.

"The choicest place on earth has been stolen from me by my own offspring." He sighed with mock sadness. "Senseneb's beautiful breasts now belong to a crude and insatiable infant."

"I am surprised your wife chose to nurse the child herself," she remarked.

"I am not," Senmut said. "She is wise to naturally postpone a much greater and often dangerous discomfort."

Puyemre was not about to argue with that even in jest. The stress of his wife's long confinement had drawn dark circles under his eyes his consequent happiness had yet to lighten. Senseneb had nearly died in childbirth. For the sake of both Puyemre and Hapuseneb, Hatshepsut was glad the gods had spared the girl. The High Priest never spoke of his children to her but she did not doubt that, like his wife, they all held a special place in his heart. She wondered if Senseneb had been named after the Great Royal Wife Senebsen. Her husband, King Neferhotep, had erected several monuments near Abu recording the names of his family members as well as the identities of all those who served him. Neferhotep had been born in Waset, the son of a temple priest, and he never tired of immortalizing his loved ones and the friends dearest to him. She had seen his monument in Abedju where he described, in enlightening detail, how his desire to have a statue made was expressed and realized. Like her father, Neferhotep had not been born to royal parents.

Gazing at Senmut's profile as he turned his head to say something to Puyemre, she thought it much more noble and reflective of Ptah's expressive fire than her brother's complacently stubborn countenance. It was the quality of a man's Ka that made him great and a commoner's body could be as virile as any other…

Abruptly she realized Puyemre was studying her face as she stared at Senmut. He said nothing and she guessed he had seen in her eyes the feelings that had long lived in her heart finally daring to spread their wings in her thoughts.

"How is the Lady Inet?" Senmut asked her gently.

"My beloved nurse no longer recognizes me," she was grateful to him for rescuing them from an awkward silence. "The veil of twilight is working a strange magic on her vision. She believes Neferure is her little Hatshepsut and sometimes confuses me with my mother. The only thing that has not changed about her is the love in her heart."

"I am sorry," he said with quiet firmness, as though he was angered by anything that caused her pain and by the fact he was not always able to do something about it.

"I think one of the main reasons Bubu was reborn was to keep Inet happy in her old age," she added brightly. "He sits on her lap for hours purring contentedly. Watching them, I feel as if time is only a dream I am still having while my beloved nurse sees only what is real. I sit beside her and feel the past has been returned to her through a cat and that all the happiness we shared has not vanished but is forever present."

"And so it is," Senmut agreed, "and always will be in her heart."

"In *both* our hearts. It does not matter to Bubu that the hand stroking his fur is gnarled and wrinkled with age for he does not notice such things."

"I am sorry as well," Puyemre said, "that I must leave your shining company, my queen, but I wish to kiss Menkheper goodnight before he goes to sleep."

A moment later, she was alone with Senmut in one of the pavilions decorating her Pleasure House. Her attendants and guardsmen knew she enjoyed the illusion of privacy and were careful to stay out of sight though in reality they were as much a part of her as the toes on her feet, which she admired now for their slenderness and to avoid Senmut's eyes.

He whispered, "Hatshepsut!"

"Yes, my lord?" she said almost as softly, daring to look at him. She could no longer pretend to be interested in the Senet table sitting between them. The strangely earnest and expectant look Puyemre had given her as he left had wiped away all her carefully planned strategies.

Whatever words were in his heart, Senmut did not speak them. He sat straight-backed and unsmiling on the stool, tensely gripping his knees.

The River was rising and the frogs were singing ecstatically and the longer he stared into her eyes the more she was aware of an emotion swelling inside her she could neither accept nor fight. The feeling was dangerously powerful and she had done nothing to prepare for its inevitable and irresistible momentum. Like canals directing the inundation, circumstances had to be quickly created that would accommodate the sentiment and fulfill its need to flourish somewhere safe and private.

"You are my unique friend, Senmut," she heard herself say decisively, "and to your list of honorable titles—Superior Royal Scribe, Superior Steward, Chief Male Nurse and Tutor of Princess Neferure—I would like to add two more positions—Superintendent of the Private Apartments of the Queen and Superintendent of the Royal Bedroom."

23

Min Comes Forth

The height of the grain growing throughout the Two Lands was measured and the size of the harvest that could be expected estimated and recorded. As had been predicted by the level of the River—carefully observed at the first wild waters during the arrival of Hapi—the lord of the fishes and birds had once again blessed Kemet. Amongst the scribes working out in the fields of Amun were Nebamun, Seshen's husband, and Djehuty, who carried the illustrious weight of the surveyor's rope for the first time. Hatshepsut remained fascinated by the power of Number. Everything could be measured with numbers because they were the soul of substance. Numbers were the firmament—the body of Nut who gave birth to the universe when her cosmic waters broke and spread open the legs of heaven and earth.

Ever since the morning when she stained her bed sheets red and Hapuseneb came to her room, no life had taken root in her womb. She understood the earnest, rigidly concealed desperation with which Thutmose celebrated the harvest festival in the ninth month of the year. The day before the silver mirror of the moon went black—in the magical space when what existed married everything yet to be—Pharaoh was carried forth from his palace by favored courtiers, honored soldiers and priests. His Great Royal Wife stood directly behind his gilded throne. Hatshepsut wore an ostrich feather in her long wig, sewn into the white headband of Isis and Nepthys, and the curves of her body were delineated by a blood-red sheathe dress. A pair of colorful wings was attached to her arms by golden bracelets and she held them spread protectively forward around her brother's throne.

All the nobility of Waset accompanied the king and his queen to God's Stairway. The shrine containing the statue of Min, Lord of the Snakes, had been erected in a threshing area on the edge of the god's fields where the great royal litter was carefully set down. Forty sun-crowned golden cobras—individual flames of a single Divine fire—decorated the top of the King's portable pavilion and were dazzlingly reflected by Min's own shrine. After four young men wearing the feather of Maat erected the ceremonial mast, Pharaoh stepped forth toward the god. Meanwhile, two priests divested Hatshepsut of her ritual wings and replaced her feathered headband with the vulture headdress crowned by the double plumes of Amun.

Hatshepsut cupped her breasts in her hands as the High Priest of Amun handed the king a copper sickle, with which he quickly cut a sheaf of wheat brought to him by a servant of the god. The impatience in her brother's gesture was obvious but her pride forced her to hope no one noticed it. She would have liked to make Thutmose happy by giving him the son he desired but in her heart, she knew that would never happen. Because she trusted Hapuseneb with her life and with the future of Kemet, she was able to accept her barrenness without worrying it would adversely affect the fertility of the land. There was still hope for the king. The priestess dancing around him was one of his favorite concubines and her hips were promisingly full, her breasts round and firm. She hoped the girl would be pleasing to Amun-Min so He would grant his son the same productive potency with which every year he sowed his eternally vigorous seed into the body of the earth.

Standing behind Pharaoh, the Chief Lector Priest of Amun sang an ancient hymn:

Hail Min

who fecundates his Mother,

How secret is that

which you have done to her

In the darkness,

Divine One, Sole One...[46]

Thutmose stepped forward again to offer an ear of grain to the god, the symbolic seed of the coming year. His every move was observed by his ancestors who were carried high on the shoulders of priests. One of the statues bore the name of his father but their faces looked the same for they represented the Ba's of a single Divine Ka.

The statue of Min—flail held high in his right hand—was slowly lifted out of its shrine by priests wearing knee-length white kilts tied closed above their navels. The poles resting on their shoulders and carrying the god aloft were partially draped in a crimson cloth studded with circular pieces of the sacred dark-silver metal, *bia-en-pet*, which fell to earth from heaven.[47] Pharaoh walked ahead of Min and behind a large white bull wearing a red cloth version of the *sa* "protection" hieroglyph around its virile neck. Hapuseneb had shown her more than once how the neck was, indeed where heaven and earth met. When that vital link was severed, death immediately resulted because flesh, no matter how healthy and strong, was nothing without the force animating it. The *sa* amulet necklace he had recently given her made of gold and lapis-lazuli was her most treasured possession.

Personifying the mysterious muscle of Divine creativity become fully conscious of itself in Pharaoh, the bull was led forward by twelve priests. The one walking at the end of the line, directly in front of the magnificent beast, held a incense burner in the shape of an arm ending in an open hand. The body of the priest before him was deliberately made formless by a long white cloak from which only his right arm emerged extended high and erect, so that he seemed to silently conduct the ten priests walking ahead of him. They carried a variety of symbols, including a crook, a flail, the *was* scepter of dominion and power and a large ceremonial *naos* sistrum. Three priests—also draped from shoulder to toe in white cloaks—supported a pole on which perched two falcon statues of Horus and another of Thoth in his form of a baboon. Holding a falcon standard, the First Prophet of Amun led the procession in a broad circle symbolic of the lunar disc and the cycle of birth and death obeyed by all incarnate life.

When the moon-white bull reached the place in the field directly across from the god's vacant shrine, three sacrificial priests approached it and Hatshepsut closed her eyes. An instant later, she opened them again fearing the gods, and everyone else, would observe her reluctance to see the splendid animal killed. Turning her head slightly she caught sight of Senmut. His tall figure and uncovered head stood out in the crowd of noblemen who all wore semi-transparent short-sleeved shirts of mist linen over knee-length kilts. Looking away from her favorite courtier her eyes perched even more hungrily on Hapuseneb. The bare skin of the priest's chest, lavishly oiled, gleamed in a way that almost enabled her to taste the luscious truth of his immortality.

The metallic smell of blood cut through the sweet clouds of incense like a knife as the bull was killed swiftly and mercifully. Nevertheless, the note of a trumpet failed to drown out the animal's rebellious bellow, which was quickly cut off, for pain and suffering were not pleasing to the gods. The magically potent offering of the bull's blood was not made bitter and ineffectual by cruelty. Min's priests would dine well that night.

Her relief was intense when the procession began moving again. The heat pressing against her skin, combined with the weighty pressure of the vulture crown clinging to her long wig, was distracting her from pious thoughts. It was increasingly difficult to resist indulging in daydreams of her pool and the joy she would take in the cool water when she completely submerged herself in it. She was tired of holding the backs of her hands together against her chest in imitation of a bird's wings. She walked to one side of Pharaoh and slightly behind him in the wake of the Lector Priest of Amun. She wished the three priests refreshing the painted statue of Amun-Min with ostrich feather fans would kindly shift their attention to her living body instead. She could not see the sacred lettuce plants but she could smell them beginning to wilt.

Min was returned to the celestial space of his shrine where Pharaoh made him another offering of the incense through which his breath mingled with that of the Supreme Being renewing his life-force and the fertility of Kemet for another year. Four birds were released toward the four cardinal directions and the festival was complete, except of course for the feasting and drinking to follow later in the cool of evening.

* * * * *

God's Wife embarked on a royal progress south. Her fleet consisted of eight vessels—the ship in which she rode with the High Priest of Amun and seven transport barges. The six-year-old princess—accompanied by her tutor and steward, her nurse and her favorite cat, Sekhy—had a barge with a double roofed cabin all to herself. Hatshepsut smiled as she imagined her daughter running eagerly from one window to another in a joyous effort to see everything. She trusted Senmut to keep Neferure focused on her lessons in the mornings, after which she imagined he would accompany his ward out on deck and enjoy a well-earned rest by letting the captain answer her endless questions.

Djehuty, Amenhotep, Useramun and the black-skinned cat-eyed Amenemhat shared another barge. She wished for the younger brother of the Deputy of the King's Son to become better acquainted with her other dearest friends and hopefully learn from their relaxed confidence. She admired Amenemhat's intelligence, which was expressed by his attentive silences and the carefully considered words that followed them, but he tended to make other people nervous. In that respect, as in so many others, Neferure was superior to the most esteemed ladies of the court. Not only was she not intimidated by her mother's Kushite friend, she had immediately recognized the quality of his heart and rewarded it by honoring him with dances and gifts of flowers whenever she saw him.

The eight ships of God's Wife rowed by Iuny, Senmut's birthplace, and soon after passed Djerty. Both cities were devoted to Horus of the Strong Arm, the falcon god Montu dear to the heart of the great Mentuhotep, whose beautiful temple would soon no longer stand alone across the River from Waset. Thutmose-Akheperenre had declared his intention to create his own Mansion of Millions of Years beside it.

Before the sun set, they reached the edge of the third and fourth Nomes of Upper Kemet and docked in the port of The Two Hills on the west bank. While her scribes and attendants prepared the temporary residence on the edge of town at the foot of the easternmost hill, the queen, the princess and Hapuseneb, accompanied by Useramun, Amenemhat and Senmut, made offerings in the temple. The Domain of Hathor crowned the eastern hill. It was the golden breasts of the goddess, swelling up in their earthly garment toward the naked luminosity of the sky, for which the city had been named.

Leaving her small entourage behind in the second offering court, Hatshepsut took her daughter's hand and led her into the innermost shrine. The High Priest of Amun and the High Priest of Hathor walked behind them. Her second royal progress was enabling her to fulfill some of her desires, not the least of which was for Hapuseneb to spend more time with Neferure. She wished for him to verify her belief that her beautiful daughter was especially gifted because every god was in her.

A strangely knowing little smile on her lips, the princess dammed her flow of questions as she watched her mother make offerings to the Goddess. Hathor graced her sanctuary in the form of a beautiful woman wearing a long wig beneath a red headband, a form-fitting red dress adorned with turquoise borders and straps, and a floral collar rimmed with golden leaves. In her right fist she gripped the *was* scepter of dominion and power and with her left hand she rested a gilded metal sistrum against her heart.

In the temporary palace later that evening, alone in her private apartments with Senmut and Neferure, Hatshepsut asked her daughter what she had felt during her visit to Hathor's House.

"She looks like you, Mami. She is very beautiful."

"She looks like me because I *am* her." She caressed the skin of her arms and then raised her hands to her cheeks. "This is the flesh of the Goddess."

"Then why do the priests not worship *you*?"

"Priests worship the creative force of God's Hand which manifests in all women."

"Does that mean all men are God?"

"That is a complex question but, essentially, yes. Atum-Re's infinite power can only be comprehended through love and Hathor helps Him express it in any way he chooses."

The princess looked from her mother's face to her tutor's. "Then why do you never let Senmut express *his* love?"

Fortunately, she did not wait for a reply, having an even more important question to ask. "Do I look like you, Mami?"

"Like your mother you are beautiful," Senmut told her, "but you look like yourself."

"Am I a goddess too?"

"You will be when you grow up." Hatshepsut smiled. "Right now you are still just a dirty little princess in need of a bath."

It did not help her to realize that when she began growing weary of her daughter's relentless questions she sounded just like Ahmose, True of Voice. Invariably she echoed her own mother's words to her whenever she felt annoyed or uncomfortable. The only problem was that if she sent Neferure away she would also have to dismiss Senmut and she had no desire to do that. Hapuseneb was staying with the High Priest of Hathor and she was too tired to host a banquet. She felt like eating by herself, with Senmut.

She addressed the two royal pages. "Take my daughter to her nurse and tell my Steward I desire enough wine and food for two people brought here to my room and tell my personal attendants I will not be requiring their presence for a few hours. You are both also dismissed for the time being."

Neferure smiled. "Does that mean you are finally going to let Senmut express-"

"Nefi, go now!" she commanded, and then added more gently, "I am sure Sekhy misses you. Cats do not like water or ships and to make matters worse she now finds herself in unfamiliar territory. She will be craving the familiar safety of your arms."

Outside the door, four of her personal guardsmen stood watch. Nevertheless, she was alone with Senmut for the first time. She did not dare look at him.

"I see your attendants have set up the Senet table," he remarked. "Or would you perhaps find Twenty Squares more relaxing tonight, my lady?"

She walked over to the board and seated herself before it. "You know I do not much like that Setiu game. They ruled without Re and played without heart. Senet is much more meaningful."

"I agree." He seated himself on the leopard-skin stool across from her. "But that is precisely why Twenty Squares can sometimes prove more relaxing."

"Very well, Senmut." She pretended to admire the delicate papyrus plants carved into the sides of her chair. "If that is what you wish, we will play Twenty Squares."

She waited for him to remind her that he always wished whatever she desired, but instead of responding like Puyemre or any other courtier he simply opened the drawer at the base of the Senet box and pulled out the smaller Twenty Square's game. She continued avoiding his eyes as he set the red and white playing pieces on the board. The red tokens were squat circles while the white ones were taller and more slender, with a thick base and a rounded head.

"I will play with the white pieces tonight," she said even though they were normally assigned to men.

He did not comment as he offered her the knucklebones for the first throw.

She reached out for them.

He placed them gently in her open palm and grazed her fingertips with his as he drew his hand away.

The door opened and her chief steward entered the room bowing low. His long and slender fingers rested lightly on his shoulders, which were not much broader than a woman's even though he was exceptionally tall. "Majesty, I bring you the wine you requested, which I have tasted and am pleased to say is excellent. As for the food my lady, I did my best, but the kitchen was not as prepared for your arrival as it should have been. Djehuty has taken the... *individuals* in charge aside and is, I hope, dealing with them appropriately."

"Raise your head, Dhout, before you get a crook in your neck," she teased him, "and I am forced to hear you complain about it for weeks."

The servants bearing the wine and cups and the platters of food were permitted to enter the room and just as quickly ushered out, for Dhout was always sensitive to her mood.

Once more, she found herself alone with Senmut. She was not the least bit interested in playing Twenty Squares and her appetite had deserted her. Fortunately, her steward had poured them each a cup of wine before leaving.

Senmut drank his down in two hearty swallows.

"Well, you are certainly thirsty this evening, my lord!"

He replied with quiet intensity, "I am also starving."

She could feel him staring at her face and was obliged to finally meet his eyes. "Then eat." She waved her hand toward the food dismissively.

He set his cup down next to the neglected board game and rose.

Enjoying another civilized sip of wine, she watched him, admiring how tall he was.

He bent over her chair and turned it away from the table.

She gasped as wine spilled across her lap.

He whispered, "Put it down!"

His face was so close to hers she felt the warmth of his breath, which smelled pleasantly of myrrh and grape wine. She could not believe a commoner had just given her a command. It was so shocking she actually obeyed him.

He took hold of her hands and pulled her to her feet so forcefully she was obliged to cling to his shoulders as her body fell against his. Then he kissed her the way Hapuseneb did, thrusting his tongue between her lips. Yet the experience was not exactly the same and she found the differences quite stimulating. She decided the High Priest possessed more control over his desire; he made her feel as if they were two birds mating in mid flight, their tongues the powerful muscles of their wings always in swirling, soaring rhythm with each other. In contrast, Senmut licked her teeth like pomegranate seeds and groaned as though her tongue was the fruit's succulent flesh and he had not eaten in weeks. Selfishly he devoured her mouth with his while holding her so tightly against him she could not even be tempted to pull away and deprive him of the great joy he was taking in the taste and feel of her.

"Hatshepsut!" He cupped her face in his hands and gazed earnestly into her eyes.

"Forgive me, Senmut, for making you wait so long."

"I forgive you!"

"And yet, my unique friend, I fear you must find yourself another lady if you wish to fully satisfy your desires."

"There are priestesses for that," he said dismissively, "but I will never love or marry another woman, Hatshepsut. Never!"

She placed her hands tenderly over his and moved them down to her breasts. His eyes closed and his mouth twisted as if her firm nipples had stabbed him and he could scarcely bear the pain of how long he had waited to feel them. At once he grew impatient with the linen separating her skin from his. He clutched the straps of her dress and ripped them as he yanked the material down to her waist.

She feared the exaltation she experienced as he fondled and feasted on her bosom would be impossible to fight if she allowed it to continue intensifying. Yet it was already too late, she could not find her voice to protest as he moaned and sucked her nipples with such ardor she was obliged to hold on to his head as her knees threatened to buckle. Consumed by the need to discover how much longer he would last inside her than Thutmose, she was seriously tempted to collapse across the couch and pull him down on top of her.

"Stop," she begged. "Please!"

Breathing hard he took three steps back and gripping his left shoulder lowered his head.

"Let us drink together, Senmut, and eat what my steward has taken such great pains to prepare for us." She was relieved yet also disappointed he had permitted her to escape his lust. "But first promise me that you will never forget you are my one unique friend and always will be."

* * * * *

Neferure scraped both her knees running after Sekhy, who was determined not to get back on the ship. As he gently dressed the wounds with linen bandages soaked in honey, Ibenre spoke sternly to the cat, explaining to her that she had nothing to fear from transport barges. Hatshepsut was not surprised Sekhy seemed to understand him but suddenly she feared for her daughter. In addition to cowrie shells, and girdles strung with little golden *nefer* signs, she made sure the princess now also wore a small leather pouch around her neck containing protective amulets—an *ankh*, a *djed* pillar and a piece of serpentine to protect her from snake bites. She herself had taken to wearing a clenched fist amulet around her neck made of *bia-en-pet*, metal from heaven. She wanted to hold on to the happiness she was blessed with even as she reached for something more inside herself. The God's Fist also helped her control her desires and her new more sensual relationship with Senmut.

Hapuseneb told her with his eyes—and with the patient but demanding length of his silences as they reclined together beneath the pavilion on his ship—that he knew she was trying to keep a secret from him. She sensed he was waiting for her to confide in him but she was still too frightened and elated by the discovery that there was room in her heart for more than one man. The only difference was the High Priest also possessed her soul.

"You will always be my master, Hapuseneb," she said for it was the only way she could think of to broach the forbidden subject.

"Are you in love with him?"

Softly she threw his own words back at him, "He holds a place in my heart."

He smiled slightly but his eyes were darker than she had ever seen them.

"I cannot deny you a true friend and companion, Hatshepsut. Senmut is a good man. He will serve you well and help me take care of you. Our love is like the amulet you are wearing around your neck made of metal fallen from heaven."

She thought of the few times he had touched her and that she had touched him and understood what he meant. On the rare occasions they came together, she felt as though heaven fell to earth.

Their second afternoon traveling southward brought them to Tasenet, where they stayed the night and dined on Lates fish accompanied by a white wine of Bast.

The following evening they arrived in Nekheb, the heart of the third southern Nome. Hatshepsut had slept most of the afternoon on the ship and she was feeling pleasantly relaxed when, riding high on the shoulders of her strong and handsome litter bearers, she entered the town through the main gate in the walls. She wore the vulture crown by itself, without the solar disc and plumes, in honor of Nekhbet, The White One of Nekhen, Nekheb's western counterpart. Smiling past Kanefer's shoulders at the cheering crowd, she decided to honor him with a promotion, including a little house of his own.

The following morning she crossed the River and met with the High Priest of Horus in the temple from which hailed so many Prophets of Maat. Tjeni was an amiable man who never ceased to smile even when he opened his mouth to speak, which was not often. He seemed to prefer using his keenly observant eyes more than his tongue, with which he knew many people tripped themselves up and revealed the lies in their hearts. She brought Senmut with her, awarding him a reprieve from Neferure's exhausting energy, for she desired his company in the House of Life filled with the scrolls of Kemet's Prophets. Many of the cases they had judged, going back hundreds of years, were recorded.

She expressed her surprise and dismay at how often people stole from each other.

Senmut muttered, "You have never been hungry."

"I can understand why a man would steal a pig if he was hungry but not why he would steal his brother's wife," she retorted mildly.

"That is a different kind of hunger but hunger nonetheless," was his grim reply.

She suffered a thrill that forced her to move away from him.

Men and women were constantly lodging formal complaints heard by local magistrates. More serious offenses required that a group of citizens be convened to help judge the case. More exhausting than spending a whole day with Neferure was reading about the blindly selfish ways people behaved. It would have seemed childish if they had not all been adults. Later that afternoon she made offerings in Maat's chapel and apologized to her for the way her subjects comported themselves.

"Their cruelty is born of pain," she told the goddess, "but they are not yet wise enough to realize that causing others to suffer in an effort to relieve their own misery will only make everything worse."

When they docked in Djeba, capital of the Nome of the Throne of Horus, the memory of the morning she had visited the Temple of the falcon god with her father came back to her so vividly she felt he was actually there with her. Suddenly she missed him again so much she had to struggle not to cry in front of the hundreds of people who had come to see their queen for the first time. She wore a crimson dress in honor of Hathor's local title, Mistress of the Red Cloth—the flesh and the blood that weaves it.

Neferure, perhaps upset by her mother's pensive detachment, refused to eat anything except honey cakes, distressing Dhout, who spent more time than he should have in the kitchen with the chefs striving to create irresistibly delectable dishes for the princess.

"Why are you so sad, Mami?" Neferure finally demanded, climbing onto her lap and slipping her arms around her neck.

"I am sad because I miss my father's voice and smile even though I still feel his love and, I hope with all my heart, always will."

"Is he a tall man with a little mark in his chin, you know, like when you press your finger into mud?"

"Yes, he is! How did you know that, Nefi?"

"I saw him last night when I was sleeping. He told me to tell you something but I forgot what it was."

Hatshepsut was silent for fear the sound of her voice would push the words her daughter had heard in her dream forever beyond their reach.

"I think it was something about skin... I remember! He told me to tell you that it would soon be time for you to *pass through the skin*. Do you know what that means?"

* * * * *

They left Djeba before dawn in the hope of reaching Nebet by evening. Even though winds from the north swelled the sails, the oarsmen would have to work hard. She had already arranged it with Djehuty and Dhout to provide the crews with extra beer and bread and, if enough could be caught in time, fish and wildfowl.

Torchlight reflecting off the River formed long shimmering golden columns across the water's black depths, which was full of invisible fish like the souls of the dead traveling between the two shores of life and death. Fish evoked the wet and magical vulva of the Goddess through which the soul slipped into form and out of it again. Fish and their watery element symbolized pure substance speared by the will of the Ka and netted by the Laws of Becoming. Her heart was a red bolti fish filled with desire and it beat faster every time she thought about passing through the skin, which she knew would entail facing the darkness at the bottom of the red river of her life. She was afraid of deliberately shedding her flesh and diving into the black space beyond it, alive with unimaginable forces, like a gazelle fallen into wild waters.

It was early afternoon when the two banks gradually began drawing closer to each other as the River narrowed between tall cliffs. They had reached *Khenu*, The Place of Rowing, where the eastern sands were rich with gold and copper and the western desert yielded a variety of hard stones, including the one she would be using to enclose her Master of Life. Several vessels traveling northward had risked running aground on sandbanks as they respectfully hugged the shore to let the queen's ships pass.

Hatshepsut stood with Hapuseneb at the railing looking west.

He pointed. "There."

Shielding her eyes with one hand, she found the entrance to her father's rock-cut shrine—a gaping black hole in the sandstone cliff rising just behind the reeds growing along the shore. She could see the winged solar disc carved above the *shenu* ring containing his name, *Akheperkare*. The River rose higher there than anywhere else in Kemet and every year rushed into her father's chapel, where the life-giving water caressed and submerged his stone statue.

"*The inundation rises above your chest,*" she quoted an ancient text beneath her breath, "*and this is more effective than any carved monument.*"

Embraced by the Primordial Waters of Nun—the infinite potential flowing through the heart of Atum and symbolized by the River—Akheperkare would survive the disintegration of the substances composing his physical body and rise from the dead, like the sun in the morning, to live forever as a unique spark of the Divine creative fire.

"Would you like to go ashore, my lady?"

"No. There is no false door to which I might direct offerings. It is enough to have seen the place. My father is here and yet he is not for he is everywhere."

They arrived in Nebet at sunset and it was wonderful to see the happy smiles on the faces of its citizens, relaxing after a joyful day of gathering the harvest to watch the queen's procession. She headed directly to the Temple of Sobek and Horus the Elder. The High Priest Sobekmose—who wore a carnelian amulet in the shape of a crocodile around his neck—insisted she admire the pool of sacred crocodiles behind God's House. He was obviously proud of the well fed and placid creatures honored with mummification when they died.

As Sobekmose consulted with one of the numerous servants of the god assigned the dangerous task of feeding the crocodiles, and of making sure they did not escape to terrorize the citizens of Nebet, she glanced significantly at Hapuseneb. A few moments later they were alone together in the temple's cool dark sanctuary.

"It is interesting that here Hathor is Sobek's consort," she said. "I can easily believe crocodiles were the first creatures to emerge from the Primordial Waters, but Sobek himself is not actually a crocodile. Sobekmose is very silly. He does not seem to understand that Sobek takes the form of a man with a crocodile's head, which is in turn crowned by a solar disc and plumes, because he symbolizes the same spiritual transcendence Horus embodies, which is why they share a temple. Is it true, Hapuseneb, that Sobek steals women from their husbands whenever he desires?"

He pulled her to him and wordlessly responded to her question in a way that left her in no doubt whatsoever about the answer.

24

Passing Through the Skin

The final destination of the queen's southern royal progress was the island of Abu and the city of trade, Swenet, at the northern end of the first wild waters. Amenhotep, having arrived earlier, accepted the queen's hand as she disembarked and escorted her up the landing steps. In a few weeks, when the River began to rise, how high the water climbed over those steps would help foretell the richness of the coming year's harvest. Together they entered the Temple of Khnum erected at the water's edge. The addition to the chapel, still under construction, gave the sacred place an unfinished look Hatshepsut found unsettling. Amenhotep, on the other hand, was as happy as if the Divine couple and their child were members of his own family soon to enjoy an even finer home. Her friend's joy pleased her but her sense of well-being was intimately linked to the rule of Maat and her inner peace felt strained in Abu, which had once been Kemet's southernmost boundary. Or perhaps how nervous she was had more to do with the fact that in the adjoining Temple of Satis, Khnum's consort, she was at last destined to undergo the initiation she had long feared and anticipated. The rite was to take place that very night. Hapuseneb had proceeded straight to the house of the goddess to supervise the preparations.

When she told the High Priest about Neferure's dream, he had said it was time she took her courage in hand and passed through the skin. "That is why you have been wearing a clenched fist amulet around your neck since we left Waset, Hatshepsut. Your Ka knows it is time but your Ba keeps flying away from the knowledge like a lapwing intimidated by a falcon."

If it had not been for Amenhotep, she would have felt disturbingly alone in Khnum's shadow-filled sanctuary. The ships following behind hers had turned into a nearby channel with the intention of docking alongside Abu's ancient fortress. The adjoining palace and barracks had been enlarged by her father. It would be a brief journey from the Temple of Satis back to her loved ones and yet already she felt as though she was in another world apart from theirs. If she failed the test she was to undergo that night she would never find her way back to Neferure or Senmut or anyone else dear to her heart.

She wished, as she made offerings to the ram-headed Khnum, that she was home in the Temple of Amun, who was always fully a man even though he could also take the form of a ram. Amun was the Divine muscle of her own hopeful heart and every breeze was the caress of his compassionate love. Khnum felt darker and heavier, a deity of the primeval mud he had spun on his cosmic wheel to fashion all birds and animals and their mysterious masters, human beings. She kept thinking of Senmut. He did not know what Hapuseneb had planned for her and she regretted not telling him. Selfishly, it would have helped her feel better to know he was worrying about her. Tomorrow, in the name of Pharaoh, he would inspect the northern granite quarries in the eastern desert. Her father's two Monuments of Heh had been carved there, loaded onto ships in the busy port and rowed down the River to Waset.

If I survive the night, I will do as my father before me, she vowed. *I will fashion rays of light from incorruptible stone and unite heaven with earth. The transcendent power that resides in God's House will enter me through the sublime monuments I erect and I will never die.*

Hardly anything grew on the island. Swenet's citizens were principally soldiers, miners and traders. They were fed and clothed by their northern neighbors who, like the rest of Kemet, coveted the exotic luxury goods arriving there from Kush that included white and black ivory, ostrich feathers and eggs, pygmies, baboons and leopard skins. It was a prosperous yet barren place, the home of stone. When, still accompanied by Amenhotep, she emerged from the temple through a side door she saw gardeners watering groups of date palms but no other workers were present for it was a festival day—The Conception of Horus. A short processional route led north-west to the home of Khnum's consort. Visible in the distance was a modest step pyramid and desert cliffs looming behind it concealed the other side of the River.

Satis was Mistress of Abu, the consort not only of Khnum but also of Montu. Like Hathor, Satis was an Eye of Re, Mistress of the Inundation and, like Isis, she shone in the star Sopdet, which would soon return to the sky and herald the imminent rising of the River. Hapuseneb considered the Temple of Satis the ideal location for her initiation. She would not be surprised if he had somehow known all along that when they reached Abu she would at last be ready to pass through the skin. The High Priest of Amun was so great of magic she felt it was entirely possible he had played some mysterious part in Neferure's dream.

"My lady, are you certain you do not wish me to accompany you as far as-"

"No, Amenhotep. You know I must walk this road alone."

He looked worried, and then ashamed of letting her see it.

"Leave me, my friend."

He grasped his shoulders resolutely, lowered his head and turned away.

She did not wait to see him reenter the temple before she took her first steps toward the challenge awaiting her. The old men watering the palm trees paused in their task to watch her pass. She wore a crimson sheathe dress over leather sandals adorned with turquoise beads. No wig or ceremonial crown covered her head, exposing her finely braided shoulder length hair. The only jewelry she wore was a delicate little *djed* pillar made of obsidian that hung from a black leather cord around her neck.

She smiled at the temples' faithful servants wondering if they knew who she was or if they merely saw her as another beautiful lady come to make offerings to the Divine couple in the hope of conceiving. Or perhaps they thought she had come to enlist the aid of the goddess in retaining her beauty so her husband would not bring a lovely young concubine into their house. It was both intriguing and insulting to feel so anonymous.

The ancient temple devoted to Satis had been rebuilt by numerous pharaohs. The three granite boulders which once formed a natural holy of holies were buried now under several foundations, making the location even more sacred. By the time she reached the entrance located on the north-east side of the enclosure wall, the edge of the solar disc was kissing the desert hills. As she stared at them, they began resembling the naked hips and shoulders of women sleeping with their backs to her. Before knocking the requisite seven times, she narrowed her eyes and opening her heart listened to her father speaking to her in silent sentences of light, which love's mysterious faculty translated into words of encouragement and absolute confidence in her ability to triumph over all adversities.

A young priest opened the wooden door. He kept his eyes on her feet as she crossed the threshold. Silently he escorted her down a narrow passage open to the sky. She had not perfumed her mouth that morning. She had not eaten anything since the previous evening. Her head and body both felt lighter than normal. The sedate pace he set helped her reign in her emotions. She knew Hapuseneb was in the temple but she was anxious to see him again for the wrong reasons—because she was nervous, even afraid. Two priests waiting for her at the end of the corridor removed her sandals. The flagstones were hot beneath her feet. The water poured over each of them in turn was welcomingly cool. Holding her hands out to receive the libation, for a few invigorating moments she felt cleansed of all her doubts and anxieties as Satis purified her Ba.

It was already dark in the vestibule. The torches burning in the corners of the covered offering court left the faces of the priests lining all four walls mostly in shadow. Reflected by their oiled skin, the trembling light caressing them almost made them look like dark bodies of water magically standing upright, and transformed their white kilts into substantial moonbeams embracing their hips.

She turned north, away from the holy of holies, and at last saw Hapuseneb standing between two columns holding a silver cup in both hands. She went and stood before him and accepted what he dared to offer her. Bracing herself for the bitter taste, she emptied the chalice of its contents. She returned the empty vessel to him, suspecting an extract of the blue lotus had been blended into the wine, and watched him set it down on a table piled high with offerings of food and flowers.

A priestess emerged from the shadows, an old woman with a thin unsmiling mouth that was nearly indistinguishable from her numerous wrinkles. Her withered breasts sagged beneath a long-sleeved white sheathe dress. Hatshepsut suffered the impression the woman's skin had already dried up and left nothing but bones. She suppressed a protest when the awful creature held up an obsidian knife resembling the kind used by midwives to cut the newborn's umbilical cord. She glanced uncertainly at Hapuseneb but his eyes were on the priestess of Satis. He had not described to her the rite she was about to undergo. She knew only she would spend the night completely alone. That was all she had been worried about until the hideous woman reached out, clutched her dress between her breasts to pull it away from her body, and thrust the knife into the fine linen, following the sharp blade all the way down to her ankles. She was the queen of Kemet and yet she silently suffered the indignity of permitting her garment to be stripped from her as if she was merely an animal being skinned. She would have felt angry and insulted if she had not also been God's Wife and understood the symbolism. The ancient sign for Satis was an animal skin pierced by an arrow. She had come to the goddess' house to hunt down all her mortal fears and to kill them.

The old priestess disappeared into the darkness from which she had come clutching the dead skin of the younger woman's dress against her heart. For the first time in all the many years she had loved him, Hatshepsut stood naked before Hapuseneb. She had never imagined it would happen this way and suddenly all she felt was hurt and disappointed. Then she met his eyes and realized how foolish she was being as they silently revealed to her the fullness of her beauty.

Obeying his unspoken command, she turned east. It was necessary for her to make a complete circuit of the vestibule in all four of the cardinal directions before she entered the holy of holies. Surrounded as she was by men, excitement eclipsed her fear. Acutely aware of her soft young body caressed by torchlight, she stared straight before her pretending not to be aware of all the hard and smoothly shaved heads turning to watch her pass. The doors of the sanctuary stood open and a single candle flickered within. She crossed the threshold and prostrated herself before the golden shrine that housed a small statue of the goddess wearing the royal cobra and the white crown pierced by horns. She was aroused, it was impossible not to be as the devotional position she had assumed offered up her naked buttocks to Hapuseneb and the other priests entering the chapel behind her.

She was too surprised to suppress a cry when both her arms were gripped and she was pulled to her feet. Ashamed of her outburst, she stood with her chin held high as two priests knelt before her and began wrapping her body in red and white linen bandages. They wound the alternating strips of cloth tightly around both her feet, bound her ankles together and then began moving slowly up her legs. When they reached her waist, Hapuseneb grasped her wrists and crossed them between her breasts. She smiled up at him trying desperately not to be afraid. Once they were finished with her, she would be as helpless as a mummy. Willingly she was becoming an Osiris and facing death at the height of her life. She thought longingly of Neferure and prayed to Satis, Isis and Hathor to give her the strength she needed to once again see her daughter and everyone else she loved. As the priests of Anubis pinned her arms against her chest and approached her neck with the cocooning linen, she was under no illusions that the rite she was about to undergo would be as easy as she had foolishly hoped.

The pressure of the bandages lessened a little over her nose. She would be able to breathe freely but she would not be able to see or even open her eyes. With her feet bound it was difficult maintaining her balance but every time she swayed Hapuseneb caught her and held her up. In the end the two openings in her nose, the seat of life, were the only part of her left exposed.

Blinded, she could no longer be sure if the High Priest of Amun was one of the men supporting her between them as they carried her into the Chamber of the Other World. There was no need for her to try and relax; she felt as trustingly languid as her limbs were stiff. It was almost a relief not being able to see the room hidden behind the holy of holies where she would rest like a mummy for the twelve hours of the night. Realizing she would be unable to relieve herself without humiliation forced her to exercise her trust in Hapuseneb as never before. She was certain the drink he had given her was formulated to aid rather than hinder her.

She felt herself gently laid across a soft bed. She was in a Master of Life, she could sense its enclosing walls, but they smelled dank, like stone not wood, and abruptly she understood it was not linen cushioning her body but dirt. Her hearing was muffled but she thought she heard the heavy lid slide into place as the darkness behind her closed eyes seemed to become even more impenetrable. She resisted the temptation to increase her discomfort by crying. The truth was she felt calmer than she had in days while anticipating and dreading the moment which was at last upon her. She had no choice now but to face what could not reasonably *be* faced.

It was a mistake to think of the bugs potentially living in the dirt she was resting on like a germinating Osiris. The silence was so absolute it was easy to imagine she could hear insects buzzing hungrily. She was glad of the bandages protecting her skin until she realized they might not be able to save her from a scorpion's sting. Scarabs were symbols of Becoming, of light and life emanating from darkness and emptiness, but she did not relish the idea of beetles, sacred or not, crawling all over her. The more she thought about the worms and unpleasant insects she might be spending the night with the more itches she was powerless to scratch asserted themselves, most of them concentrated around her nose. There was nothing to prevent a small spider, for example, from crawling up inside her through the opening left in the bandages so she could breathe. The thought was so disgusting she exhaled furiously, and then feared to take another breath.

She could not have been lying in the dark more than a few moments and already she longed to be set free. Time seemed to be slowing down, and all throughout her ordeal she would not be able to know with certainty how many hours had actually passed...

Perhaps her entombment would never end. It almost seemed possible she had actually died and been mummified and was only imagining she was undergoing a rite under Hapuseneb's guidance because she did not want to face what had really happened. In her heart she knew that was not true but it was frighteningly easy for her thoughts to be seduced by the horrifying possibility. She was in the Temple of Satis lying in the Chamber of the Other World, she was *not* in her tomb... and yet it was possible her brother had conspired with the priests to leave her there until she starved to death in order to rid himself of a wife who could not give him a son. Perhaps Hapuseneb did not truly love her and he had told her husband what the stars had foretold—that she was destined never to conceive again—and they had agreed it was best for Kemet to do away with her. There were no ventilation shafts in the stone container and she would soon begin suffocating...

Hatshepsut was appalled by the fears and doubts rearing venomously inside her. Her emotions seemed to have become the insects she imagined crawling all over her. It filled her with despair that Senmut did not know where she was. Only Amenhotep had been privy to her plans and surely he would tell everyone if she failed to appear in the morning...

Stop it!

She clung to the strong clear sound of her true voice rising over the crazy clamor of her insecurities.

I am allowing myself to be devoured by fears that are not real!

She felt better for a while, and then abruptly the silence was populated by hideous faces taking shape directly behind her closed eyelids. Demonic countenances, male and female and something in between formed and dissolved into even more hideous visages as though competing for her attention. Some of them even stared straight at her grinning demonically. Unwillingly fascinated, she allowed the gruesome pageant to go on until she could bear it no longer and focused her inner vision away from it. She was not imagining the gruesomely deformed people who coalesced and faded without her making any effort to perceive them. Even when she refused to look at them they continued to haunt the darkness so it felt like an endless black body of water swimming with nightmares... crocodiles surrounded her with open jaws, she was about to suffer the experience of being devoured...

Somehow, she succeeded in escaping the evil black depths only to abruptly find herself standing in a sunlit but equally vulnerable position on a rock in the middle of the desert, clearly visible to the male lion hunting her. She had nothing with which to defend herself and there was absolutely nowhere to run and hide. She had no choice but to let the beast pounce on her and sink its teeth into her throat as it claws ripped her face off. She did not suffer any pain witnessing the brutal attack on her features only a sinking despair...

It does not matter. Even if I am killed and eaten by a lion only my body will die and be unrecognizable. My Ba will fly away and join my Ka, which is infinitely more powerful than any beast. My Ka is the lion, the Divine lion of light feasting on all my incarnations. I may seem like a helpless victim but only for an instant no more real than a bad dream.

Hatshepsut took firm hold of the reigns of her imagination and steered her vision toward beautiful memories that were much more vivid than the images generated by her emotional insecurities and visceral terrors. She was sailing on the sunlit River, reclining beneath a shaded pavilion with Hapuseneb, and his soft smile was silently telling her how much he loved and respected her. She could see his face clearly and rejoiced at the ordeal she was undergoing because it was helping her kill those parts of herself which could still so easily doubt the reality of his love. His smile was like a shaft of light shining into the sealed chamber and flooding her heart with a happiness so intense it cast away the shadows of all doubts and fears. Her body was isolated from others but in truth she had never been alone and never would be for everyone she loved was a Divine company.

With her senses blinded and muffled, it was impressed upon Hatshepsut how vibrantly real and accessible the feeling of love remained. Not only was love not crippled, it was mysteriously enhanced by her mummified condition. More than ever she loved Hapuseneb and Neferure and Senmut and Nafre and everyone else dear to her. To be able to continue feeling and expressing love was the reason she looked forward to the dawn when she would rise from the crypt and take possession of her body again in the splendor of the sensual world. The insects she was making her bed with that night were sustained by light just as she was. The light burning as love in her heart could only be consumed by the Divine darkness of Atum-Re from which it blossoms as universes and worlds without end.

Imprisoned in a red and white cocoon, she began feeling like the small and vulnerable yet magically potent seed of every conceivable reality. Then she experienced a familiar shift in her inner vision—the sensation which mysteriously woke her to the fact that she was asleep and dreaming. An indescribable joy possessed her as she broke through some indefinable barrier and found herself in a place of infinite possibilities limited only by her imagination. Distinctly she sensed creative powers germinating in the husk of her flesh. The darkness behind her eyelids was like rich black soil where she could plant any images and experiences she desired... she thought of the cliff where she was building her eternal home and immediately found herself perched at the summit. The stars and a half moon illuminated the ropes used by the men working on it. She could see the scaffolding and everything around her clearly, as if she was truly there. Her Ba-bird had escaped the Chamber of the Other World and brought her home to Waset in a single heart beat. She stood on her own two feet but her wings were not merely attached to her arms by golden bracelets, they were real. Exultantly, she opened her arms to the wind like a vulture and plunged off the cliff. A violent gust carried her upward so swiftly she feared it might take her too far from earth for her ever to return but then suddenly another current tugged her forcibly back down. She soared across the desert sacred to Hathor, directly over the monument of Mentuhotep and Djeserkare's Mansion of Millions of Years, all the way to the River. The joy flooding her was indistinguishable from the air supporting her. She was no longer lying in a stone container on a bed of dirt she was flying over the silver serpent of water more swiftly than was physically possible toward Abu and Hapuseneb. The High Priest of Amun was waiting for her. She could sense his expectation like the very atmosphere embracing her in which she heard no sounds and experienced no sensations. She knew only the elation of flight and the wonder of watching Kemet unfold far below her. Featureless dry fields, and the desert stretching endlessly beyond them, were punctuated by miniature pyramids and temples that caught and trapped the moon's light with their magically mathematical slopes and lines. Countless moth-like sails were still unfurled over the River but she left them all behind as swiftly as an arrow shot from the bow of the Goddess.

She saw the island of Abu and in the same heartbeat she was there looking down upon the Temple of Satis. She dove down to the enclosure wall and perched her awareness on it. Hapuseneb was standing just outside the entrance. He was staring east but sensing her presence he looked up and saw her. Only then did she realize the form she had assumed was that of a falcon. Across the River, the horizon was growing more luminous and suddenly the desire to return to her body possessed her with an intensity impossible to distinguish from the rising of the sun. Just before Khepri blinded her, she saw Hapuseneb running into the temple. A moment later she understood it was not the sun she was seeing but a lamp as the High Priest ripped open the bandages covering her face. Light pierced her vision like the arrow of Satis. *Love* was that arrow, her heart was the bow, and death was powerless against them.

She smiled up at Hapuseneb and said, "Is it morning already?"

He laughed. "Yes, it is morning already, my lady, and you will never forget it! No matter what happens to you in this life or in any other, you will never in your heart forget this morning."

* * * * *

Hatshepsut was in awe of everything, even the most seemingly insignificant details. The word *insignificant* had in fact lost its meaning. Nothing was insignificant, except perhaps the thoughts and aspirations of people blind to what truly mattered. Most ladies of the court and their illustrious husbands soon discovered she was even less inclined than before to grace their banquets and invite them to her palace. She preferred walking through her garden with Neferure reading the hearts of flowers. The story of the First Occasion was written everywhere. The manner in which colors, lines and shapes both emanated from and converged in the center of every blossom created hieroglyphs alive with meaning.

Isis, Pharaoh's secondary wife, was with child. All of Waset was in suspense, except for the Lady Inet, who was bedridden. The queen's beloved nurse had herself returned to infancy and yet instead of developing, her senses were swiftly wilting. When Hatshepsut spoke to her, Inet sometimes seemed to listen, but only briefly. The glimmer of cognizance soon vanished from her eyes. She swallowed dutifully when water and milk were gently tipped into her mouth, and laboriously chewed each small bite of food with the few teeth remaining to her, seeming to remember it was important to make the effort but obviously taking no pleasure in it.

Once Inet's attendants had bathed her and propped her up in a chair to receive the queen, Hatshepsut spent an hour with her every morning. The only time Inet moved of her own volition was when Bubu Reborn leapt onto her lap, then a smile touched her lips and she stroked him once or twice before simply resting both her hands on his purring body.

"I wish you could have accompanied me on my progress south, Iny," Hatshesput told her brightly. "You would have loved to see how much Neferure enjoyed watching young fishermen jousting with sticks as they sought to impress us with their fighting skills. More than once both combatants fell into the water, undone by their eagerness to catch a glimpse of the queen and the young princess, not to mention all the beautiful ladies traveling in their entourage."

Thutmose had taken Isis north to Mennefer where her baby would be born. Hatshepsut was in control of the Southern Seal Room and despite the shell Inet had become she was happier than ever. After an hour spent with her utterly passive old nurse, it was an indescribable pleasure to work. Surrounded by Pharaoh's intelligent and receptive advisors, she felt increasingly like the Ka of Kemet. The Royal Treasury was the heart through which flowed the red river of life sustaining and nourishing the living body of the Two Lands. It was vital the connection between the effective intelligence of the Seal Room and the vital organs of the Nomes serving it never be strangled by greed or lazy inefficiency. Even the smallest injury to the system of taxation could affect the health of Kemet and all its children if not immediately cleaned up and healed.

During her two royal progresses, one of the topics she had broached with the High Priests of every temple where she made offerings to the resident *neter* was the need to recruit more bright young men into the Corp of Pages.

"It is your responsibility to see and hear for Pharaoh," she told them. "It offends and injures God when a noble man born to poor and ineffectual parents is not recognized and assisted in advancing his lot in life by becoming a scribe, a priest or, should Montu beat stronger in his heart than Thoth and Horus, a soldier."

The God's Wife personally commanded an army of scribes and administrators but it was taking more men than she would have imagined necessary to help implement and enforce her wishes. For example, it was her opinion the High Priest of Sobek in Nebet spent too much time admiring his crocodiles and tossing them choice bits from his own table. It was obvious to her that, in his eyes, the creatures were not symbolic of transformative powers—it was their deadly strength and insatiable hunger he admired and consequently reflected with his own behavior. When young girls and boys disappeared in Nebet their parents believed they had fallen into the River and drowned or been eaten by crocodiles. Those were real dangers, of course, but so too were priests in which the light of Re had been extinguished or never burned at all. For her it was enough that Hapuseneb had reason to suspect Sobekmose secretly enjoyed feeding small children to his fierce pets, although not until after he had satisfied his perverse hungers with their helpless bodies.

She could easily believe it when the High Priest of Amun said, "The more dead a man is inside the more sexually attracted he will be to children, and suffer the need to penetrate them in order to feast on the positive energy contained in their blooming flesh, still so fresh from its Divine source. The older a body becomes, no matter how beautiful it is the less desirable such men find it for it is not beauty to which they are drawn. They crave the promise of what is new and still radiant with the hope which has died in their hearts or not yet taken root there at all. Murderously perverse individuals are so terrified they will cease to exist when they die they cannot look forward but only backward to their childhood, a time when they innocently believed they would live forever. This beautiful promise lives in every little boy and girl and they are repeatedly compelled to betray it as revenge for the horrible suffering they impose upon themselves believing they too are being betrayed, by their own decaying bodies."

Sobekmose was carried away in the middle of the night by soldiers of the God's Wife, one of whom was instructed to throw the amulet the priest wore around his neck to the crocodiles. His fellow priests had either been asleep or pretended to be when the arrest occured. A new First Prophet of Sobek was appointed and the citizens of Nebet rejoiced when their children stopped disappearing, which meant the gods were no longer displeased with them. Sobekmose was never again seen by anyone who knew him. He had been exiled to Wawat and condemned to work as a slave in the gold mines, until he died and realized how foolish he had been to permit his spiritual cowardice to cause other people so much harm.

"Why did you not simply have him killed?" Amenemhat asked her one afternoon when he was playing marbles with Neferure, and kindly allowing her to succeed in rolling more of them between the goal posts.

"Because he needs time to think about the terrible things he did to himself and to others and to hopefully repent and learn from his mistakes."

"Men like that never repent or learn anything!" Incensed, he forgot not to be accurate with his next roll. "He will be devoured by Ammit the instant he dies!"

Neferure looked up from the marbles remaining to her. "Who will be devoured by Ammit?"

Amenemhat's face turned to black ivory, indicating he could not think how to respond because he was too busy regretting the words he had already spoken.

"A very bad man," Hatshepsut replied lightly. "I see you are winning, my dear. You are very good at marbles."

"Ameny is *letting* me win but I do not care because I like winning."

One of the queen's pages entered the room and informed her that a messenger from the Nome of the Sistrum respectfully sought an audience with her.

"If he has properly purified himself," she said, "you may pronounce his name."

A smiling, very clean and personable young man entered the room. After performing the gesture of praise he announced, "Majesty, I bring you a gift from the Nomarch of the Sistrum, my Lord Khenti, who sends you his undying devotion and hopes with all his heart his offering will please you."

Neferure abandoned her marbles, indifferently relinquishing her certain victory to go stand beside her mother's chair. Any mention of gifts excited her.

"Lord Khenti's offering was delivered straight to the Pleasure House of your palace *I Shall Not Be Far From Him* for it was too... large to bring here, my lady."

"Oh Mami, please, I want to go see what it is!"

"Very well, my love, you may ride with Amenemhat in his litter for I am sure he is also curious what has been sent to me by one of my favorite Nomarchs."

The gift was a full grown female cheetah named Satis.

* * * * *

The Lady Isis gave birth to a small but well shaped and healthy boy named Thutmose in honor of Pharaoh and of his father before him. All of Kemet rejoiced, including Hatshepsut. She did not care if most of the ladies of the court did not believe her smile was genuine. Even Seshen, who still longed for a family of her own, seemed to think her joy was feigned. Nafre knew her mistress better and understood what she felt was primarily relief.

The Superintendent of the Private Apartments of the queen inspected the royal bedroom and bathroom every evening to make sure their cleanliness and beauty remained worthy of a goddess. On the occasions when Senmut, after performing his duties, remained to dine with the queen and her principal attendant, Nafre secretly left the royal chambers through a back door leading to a storeroom converted by Dhout into a lovely little receiving room. There Ahhotep joined her after the princess went to bed. Nafre had long been close with Neferure's nurse and their friendship had grown into love.

Only a handful of people Hatshepsut trusted implicitly, including her Chief of Security Mentekhenu, were privy to the fact that she was sometimes alone with Senmut. But the privacy they occasionally enjoyed was always dangerous and required they spend much more time apart than together. Highborn ladies had become even more interested in the Superior Royal Scribe when he became Tutor to the Princess and they were constantly courting him, either for themselves or for their daughters. Hatshepsut ordered him to accept their invitations and to pretend he was considering their offers. It amused her to listen to him describe the excruciatingly dull gatherings he was obliged to attend.

"But surely you behave as if you are enjoying yourself, Senmut?"

"I do my best, Majesty."

"How do you go about pretending to be interested in a lady?" Her curiosity was peaked by a touch of jealousy.

"I do not seem to be required to do anything." He frowned. "They desire to marry my titles, not me. I need only sit, drink and eat. I do not even need to remember to nod in agreement when they speak because listening to them immediately begins putting me to sleep. My head keeps falling forward and snapping back of its own accord as I struggle not to fall asleep."

She laughed. "My poor Senmut! Perhaps these will make you feel better?" She undid the straps of her dress and offered him her breasts.

Her faith in his self-control had grown slowly. It was several months before she was able to relax and surrender to the exaltation spreading through her body in response to his hungrily wandering hands and mouth. Even though she regularly cradled it longingly in her hand through his kilt, she had not yet caressed his penis. Often he bit the side of her neck growling like a leopard intensely frustrated by the cage of the rules he was forced to obey even when they were alone together. She did not ask him how often he visited a priestess of Hathor after he left her.

* * * * *

After granting Pharaoh's wish for a son, Amun-Min seemed to abandon him. The king's strength ebbed as if his Ka had directed all its power into his sperm, which thrived now in the form of a one-year-old boy. His decline was so sudden and swift it seemed more like a bad dream to Hatshepsut from which she would soon wake than a reality she had to face. She strove to forget her brother was spending most of his time being coldly examined by priests of Sekhmet instead of with nubile young concubines who wrapped themselves warmly around him and made him feel truly divine. But sometimes—usually when she was walking from her litter to the Seal Room—her legs felt weak. Then one day she addressed Kanefer from her high seat, commanding him to change course and take her to the ceremonial palace located inside *Ipet Sut*.

Her chief litter bearer communicated her wish to his subordinates without giving any indication whatsoever that he was either surprised or happy she had spoken to him directly. For years she had anticipated witnessing his expression in that special moment but, in the end, she had missed it. Filled with regret, she told herself there were more important things to worry about than a litter bearer's feelings but she did not quite believe it.

Once inside the ecclesiastical palace she dismissed the priests flocking around her and waited until she was alone before stepping up onto the dais. She seated herself on the throne and at once felt better as all the wealth and beauty of Kemet embraced her. Gold-plate, inlaid with semiprecious stones and pieces of colored glass, supported her back. The curved wooden seat, decorated with fragments of ivory carved in the shape of a leopard's markings, at once made her feel comfortable with the power and authority she possessed but not so much so that she was tempted to feel lazy and neglect any of the responsibilities attendant with it. The legs of the chair were formed by intersecting ducks' heads, their golden eyes framed by delicate black lashes, and between them the gilded wood was carved in the shape of the *sema* hieroglyph—entwined papyrus and lily plants representing the union of the Two Lands. Behind her she could feel the presence of the vulture Nekhbet spreading her gold and lapis-lazuli wings between her shoulder blades.

Hatshepsut stared down at the wooden footstool decorated with the ugly figures and faces of the Nine Bows. Their constricting foreign garments were gilded and their black-ivory and cedar-brown countenances stood out against the blue faience background. Gripping the arms of the throne, she gently pinned Kemet's enemies beneath her feet.

25

The Powers of Waset

Hatshepsut had neglected Nomti for some time but she began visiting the royal stables again. It pleased her he was happy to see her, a fact he expressed by dipping his head and nudging her with such force she had to cling to his mane to prevent herself from falling. She respected him even more for daring to reproach her.

"I am ashamed of myself for neglecting you, Nomti." She caressed his sleek virile neck. "We will go riding in the desert again soon, I promise. Commander Inebni is taking you out regularly?"

He nodded.

"Good." She reached up and whispered in his ear, "One day I will need you to help me fight for the light, so stay strong and healthy!"

The two lions of her personal horizon, Shu and Min, had died. At first, she missed them terribly but in truth no animal had ever been as dear to her heart as Satis. She spoiled her cheetah with baby oryxes and wild birds caught especially for her. Satis was one of four cubs the Nomarch of the Sistrum had rescued and raised himself after he saw their mother killed by the male lion he was hunting.

The cheetah's slender but ideally muscular body reminded her of Khenti and the pleasure she took in his company. She sent him a letter thanking him for his present and asking him to spend the coming season of the inundation in Waset as her guest. He immediately accepted her invitation.

The first time she had heard Satis purr she looked up at the cloudless sky amazed to hear what she at first thought was the rumbling sound of Nut laughing. Heaven and earth had magically come together in the cheetah, an animal that seemed to fly across the ground and chirped like a bird when it was happy but hissed and spat like a snake when it was angry. When Satis purred Hatshepsut could no longer hear her thoughts; she felt only a joyful awe inspired by the splendid creature submissively resting its head on her feet. As the queen of Kemet, she exercised the powers of her perceptions in the Seal Room to hunt out dangerous corruption and keep her people well-fed and happy very much like a female cheetah enthroned on her playtree.

Satis seemed content enough where she lived in a special area of the Pleasure House redesigned to accommodate her, but Hatshepsut hated parting from her and leaving her confined in the same limited space all the time. One afternoon she declared impulsively, "I wish to bring her with me."

Without comment, Sati's principal keeper slipped a leather leash adorned with semi precious stones around the cheetah's neck.

"I will lead her myself," she said. "You may walk behind us and restrain her should she misbehave."

Kanefer's eyes widened when he saw them approaching.

"It is all right," she assured him, flattered by the fear in his eyes. "She is completely tame and obedient to my will."

Curiously sniffing Kanefer's feet, Satis chirped approvingly. She seemed to enjoy riding in a litter for she purred loudly as she sat gazing down at everything.

When they reached the administrative palace, Hatshepsut, a mischievous smile on her lips, instructed the herald not to announce her by placing a finger over her lips and shaking her head.

As she entered the Seal Room, the Royal Treasurer Nehesj glanced up from the document he was reviewing.

Ineni looked up an instant later.

"Good afternoon, my lords." She obliged the cheetah to walk directly beside her by holding almost the entire length of the leash wrapped around her hand and pressed against her heart. "I would like you to meet my beloved pet, Satis."

Nehesj stepped around the table, knelt before her and offered her his praise. A moment later Ineni did the same, half shielding his body with that of the Royal Treasurer's.

Satis attempted to approach Nehesj and when the leash held her back, she emitted a hoarse bark in protest.

Hatshepsut stroked her head.

The cheetah promptly sat down and began purring as she surveyed her new surroundings.

The look in Nehesj's eyes provoked the same deeply content response in Hatshepsut. The soft smile on his mouth, so similar to Hapuseneb's in its enigmatic eloquence, clearly told her the time had come to give a voice to the dream that still haunted her.

"My lords, I have sent a letter to the King's Son to join us here in the Southern Seal Room to discuss increasing the number of divisions stationed in Kush. The gods spoke to me through a dream and made it clear Kemet's army must grow even larger and stronger than it already is. The Royal Treasury is the heart of the forces that maintain Maat throughout the Two Lands and protect her when she is attacked. I am hoping you will tell me, my Lord Nehesj that our heart is strong enough to sustain the hundreds, even the thousands of additional bodies needed to obey the Divine will expressed through the message the god's sent me."

She reached down and stroked the cheetah's head before concluding, "As Mistress of the Two Lands, I desire above all things to protect my children from predatory peoples."

* * * * *

While her attendants spent a merry day with their husbands, Seshen desperately still trying for her first baby, Hatshepsut sat with her sick brother. When she saw his eyes, she knew at once that his physicians sacrificed Maat every day in order to spare his feelings. Stubborn hope and helpless fear battled on his face as obviously as a vulture's circling shadow. She wondered if he knew The Servants of the Place of Truth had been instructed to abandon all other projects and work only on his tomb.

Her compassion for her husband vied with her interest in the beautiful Isis, who sat on the other side of his bed. Unfortunately, her curiosity was all too quickly satisfied. Vanity, pride and selfish ambition emanated from Pharaoh's minor wife like the stench of something dead doused with sweet-smelling oils that fail to mask its soulless nature. Restlessly, Isis admired her rings and fingernails, glanced challengingly at the Great Royal Wife and smiled sweetly at the king, in that order. She spoke only when addressed but it was not necessary she speak for Hatshepsut to hear her thoughts—the title "King's Mother" was within her grasp and she wanted it much more intensely than she desired her husband to live. Her eyes revealed how little she truly loved him.

"Leave us, Isis," Thutmose commanded gently. "I would speak with my sister alone."

Once the other woman had gone, Hatshepsut said, "What is it, brother?" He was so thin she could easily imagine the skull beneath his skin.

"It is the wish of my heart to commission two Monuments of Heh such as those erected by our father in the house of Amun-Re."

She smiled, surprised and pleased. "That would be a splendorous thing, brother!"

"I fear the Mansion of Millions of years I am planning beside the monument of the great Mentohotep may take too long but I might yet live to see my offerings to Amun shining like the first rays of light which illuminated the darkness at the beginning of time. And if the god is well pleased with them, if they help show him the great love I feel for him, he may decide to spare his son's life."

Tears welled in her eyes and she reached blindly for his hand.

"I do not trust Ineni to work quickly enough," he went on breathlessly. "He is always making excuses for why things take more time than they should. You are God's Wife and Pharaoh's beloved sister. You will do this for me?"

She suspected he had intended that as a command and his vulnerability nearly felled her control but if he saw her crying, he would suspect there was no hope. "The desire of your heart is one with mine, brother. It will be done as swiftly as the falcon flies. Amun will see how much his son loves him and be merciful, I promise."

* * * * *

Hatshepsut put Senmut in charge of ordering and supervising the initial production of her two Monuments of Heh. So she thought of them, so they were and so they would be. Her brother's wish was behind their commissioning but before he expressed it she had already vowed in her heart to erect them. She trusted Senmut to make certain the most favorable location for quarrying them was selected. The birth of each monument would be painstakingly slow for the perfect marriage of skill and patience was essential to prevent cracking the rock and killing the magic. Each solid shaft of light would be shaped from a single block of stone. Its unblemished wholeness would make it a pure and potent reflection of Atum-Re, the One from which all light and life emanates. When at last they stood side-by-side in the temple, the two monuments would embody the duality of life as they united heaven and earth through the fearlessly loving heart of their creator—Hatshepsut, God's Wife.

Wearing the wigs and jewels of a nobleman, Hapuseneb suddenly began accepting invitations to banquets. His wife never accompanied him. The Royal Ornament Amenhotep was far away from Waset visiting one of her daughters, who had married a son of the Oryx and was expecting her first baby. Hatshepsut stopped being surprised to see the High Priest in public and instead rejoiced whenever his presence transformed a tedious party into an exciting affair as together they controlled the flow of the conversation. It was stimulating to casually toss profound concepts between them, and to watch people caught in their net struggling to produce a comment sharp and witty enough to save them from stinking with ignorance. She saw Hapuseneb more often than ever outside the temple. It was like being on a journey together except for the fact that they had not left Waset. She felt as though the city itself was their ship as with their eyes they silently expressed the ever expanding joy they took in each other's company.

The town of Amun was not in mourning. Pharaoh wanted everyone to think he would soon recover because this was what he himself wished to believe. There was no doubt his son was healthy. Little Thutmose was entering his second year of life, a cause for great rejoicing. Only the priests of Amun, Hatshepsut knew, were preparing for the change foretold by the heavens. Within the confines of *Ipset Sut*, Hapuseneb still wore only a short old-fashioned kilt and white sandals but in the homes of nobles and high-ranking officials, he donned a slightly longer more fashionable kilt with a double waistband. He wore the Divine set of jewelry reserved for gods and First Prophets. His rigid cuff bracelets, his anklets and his belt were made from alternating rows of green and gold beads that matched his decorative collar, and the fine braids comprising his shoulder-length wig were so black it shone a heavenly blue in the lamplight. When his shaved head was covered, it was possible to forget he was the First Prophet of Amun and to see only the Governor of the South, the Mouth and Ears of the King.

The Good God Akheperenre was increasingly weak but his heart continued to beat sure and strong in the stone House of Amun where he had commanded a new chapel be constructed. Pharaoh and his Great Royal Wife would be worshipped there and receive offerings of Life made by the priests that would nourish their Ka's perpetually. Whenever she was in the Temple, Hatshepsut stopped to observe the progress of the work. The two principal artists had both been especially blessed by Ptah and were always so engrossed in their task they rarely noticed her standing behind them, her living lips reflecting the smile one of them was carefully shaping on her stone face. Her brother had permitted her to choose the deities in whose company she wished to be depicted. Seth, the One Who Rules Over the South, stood before the queen offering her Life in the form of an *ankh* crowned by a *was* scepter held up to her nose. Nepthys, She Who Rules The House of God, stood behind her, her right hand resting on the queen's right shoulder and her left hand cradling her left elbow. On the other side of the stone wall, in the adjoining chapel, Thutmose was shown receiving the red crown from Osiris and Isis.

Hatshepsut felt the combination of Seth and Nepthys was magically appropriate for that moment in her life. At the age of twenty-five, the power of her Ka resided fully in her body. Providing she lived to be as old as her father she was as far from her Divine birth and death as she could get. She might yet suffer the same fate as her brother and suddenly begin wasting away at the height of her beauty, but it was wrong to tempt the gods by admitting to any doubt whatsoever about her destiny even if it seemed reasonable to do so. Her heart told her what was happening to her husband would not happen to her and so she chose to believe it was not even a possibility.

Osiris ruled the other world. Seth commanded the forces of earth that fashioned attractive bodies which relished indulging the sensual appetites it was such a pleasure to satisfy. Nepthys smiled whenever people lived life so joyfully they forgot to dread the future and Anubis. Hatshepsut no longer feared the jackal born to Seth and Nepthys. One night it would come to guide her through the Dwat, but not yet. She controlled her feelings like chariot horses even while giving them full reign and the power of thought enabled her to steer around any obstacles in her path because the future was hers to command.

* * * * *

The Nomarch of the Sistrum arrived in Waset and Hatshepsut arranged for him to stay in the Temple of Amun-Re. She honored Khenti with the privilege of strolling leisurely through the beautiful gardens of the god straight into her Pleasure House. When Satis saw him she tested her keeper's strength by straining on the end of her leash, chirping ecstatically. Every time Khenti visited the queen, her cheetah purred so loudly it was difficult for human beings to hear themselves speak, but there was no doubt they were all pleased with each other's company. Dhout kept popping into the pavilion to make sure his mistress and her guest had everything they needed, always bringing another plate of delicacies with him just incase. It was obvious to Hatshepsut her steward had fallen in love with the Nomarch of the Sistrum, who also seemed to realize it judging by the narrow-eyed way he smiled up at Dhout. Khenti's feral grin seemed to affect everyone's heartbeat. Seshen and Meresankh literally tripped over each other in an effort to be the first to refill his wine cup. Only Nafre was immune to his charm.

"I regret my new bride was not able to accompany me," he remarked lightly, dipping his fingertips into the blue water lily shaped bowl offered him by one of the handsome male servants the God's Wife preferred over young girls. "It is my fault, really. My great affection for her has made it dangerous for her to travel."

"She is with child?" Seshen said wistfully.

"Indeed. And speaking of children, I am anxious to pay my respects to the lovely young princess."

"I am afraid you may have to wait," Hatshepsut informed him with a smile. "Her side-lock of youth was shaved off yesterday. She is too busy admiring her presents and, I imagine, making a mess of her face with some of them to grant anyone an audience."

"I am delighted to hear she is thriving, my lady, although, and I hope you will forgive me for saying so, it is impossible she can ever be as beautiful as her mother."

"You are forgiven, my Lord Khenti, although there is no reason for you to slight my daughter in order to compliment me. I am not jealous of her now and nor will I ever be for she is part of me even though she walks on her own two feet."

"You speak the truth, Majesty. Beauty is beauty and can never be greater or lesser than itself. It would be more accurate to say that no matter how beautiful Neferure becomes she will never possess her mother's beauty, which is uniquely her own and dearer to my heart than any other form Maat takes on earth."

An appreciative silence followed the Nomarch's lovely compliment and suddenly the distant voices of women shrieking and wailing became audible.

The unmistakable sound of mourning was coming from the direction of Pharaoh's residence and could mean only one thing. The Falcon had flown.

Hatshepsut stood but then abruptly discovered she was sitting down again. Her little brother was dead! Of all her father's children, she was the only one left living.

"My lady?"

She looked down in response to a man's concerned voice and realized Khenti was kneeling beside her chair. Standing just behind him, their wrists crossed over their hearts and their hands clenched into fists, her attendants resembled life-size *shwabtis* of themselves waiting for her to tell them what to do next.

"My lady," Khenti repeated softly, "I am sorry."

"But I saw Pharaoh this morning and he seemed better," she protested. "There was actually a little color in his cheeks and he smiled at me for the first time in weeks. He told me he was not feeling quite so weak. 'The gods are helping me recover' he said, that was what he believed. Was it cruel or merciful of the *neters* to disguise the joy of dying and going to his Ka as renewed health?"

"The gods are always merciful," Khenti assured her firmly.

Something was soothing her. Looking down she realized it was the strong and cradling warmth of his hands holding both of hers. He was daring to touch the queen of Kemet and God's Wife. He could receive lifelong exile for that. The thought was so ridiculous she laughed.

Nafre spoke, "Majesty, the High Priest of Amun approaches."

Khenti hesitated a moment before letting go of her.

Sensing how reluctant he was to relinquish his intimate position beside her, she vowed to reward him for it as soon as possible.

* * * * *

The Good God Akheperenre went to his Ka on the full moon before the festival honoring the Lament of Isis.

Hatshepsut traveled to Abedju. Her thoughts and feelings were strangely quiet as she circled the Temple of Osiris seven times, walking directly behind the heavy bier on which lay a dead white bull covered with a sheet of black linen. Two young priestesses—their bodies not yet opened by men or children—led the procession in the guise of Isis and Nepthys, the wife and sisters of the ascended king.

Hatshepsut was mostly sad for Neferure, who had lost one of her parents at such a young age. Yet the princess had spent little time with the man who engendered her. His loss did not appear to cause her the intensity of grief her mother had experienced when her own father went to his Ka.

For nine whole days that each felt as long as a week, Hatshepsut forced herself to sleep while the sun was up. At night, she made offerings of milk and water to the statue of Osiris, until at last a shaft of moonlight signaling his resurrection shone directly into the sanctuary. Flesh decayed like the moon returning to darkness every month but life's Divine force was never diminished. Life always created a new form designed to serve it.

It was like waking from death herself when she was once again allowed to rise with the solar disc in the morning. The sorrowful laments performed by the priestesses, followed by transcendent hymns of rebirth, had exposed all the feelings of her heart to the sympathetically pulsing stars. The subtle caress of magic cooled the more obvious heat of grief and her Ba felt fresh and cleansed of mortal fears and sadness. Joyfully she boarded the ship that would take her home to Waset and all those she loved still living on this side of the River. She was happy anywhere in the Two Lands but the city named after The Powerful Female One was her home. Like the goddess Waset, she was prepared to wield the *was* scepter of dominion and power inextricably linked in her heart with the divinely compassionate feather of Amun. As soon as Akheperenre was buried the double crown would be placed on the little head of his son but it was she, Hatshepsut, God's Wife, who would hold the crook and flail while the Falcon was still a fledgling in the nest. The Oracle of Amun had come true.

Her brother's tomb was hastily painted. It was smaller than he had planned. In contrast, the ambitions of his minor wife kept getting bigger. Her title was now King's Mother and after Hatshepsut—King's Daughter, King's Sister, King's Wife and God's Wife—Isis was the most revered woman in the Two Lands. But that was not enough for the lady from Tantera who also sought to be named King's Guardian, a position that would give her the power to choose his tutors and to remain always by his side. Even the queen would have to go through the King's Guardian whenever she desired an audience with him.

Long time friends of her family, the Nomarch of the Crocodile stood behind Isis. Sobekmut made his opinion on the matter known to his fellow Nomarchs as they arrived in Waset for the funeral. It was not surprising to Hatshepsut that most of the men who sided with him had all, in one form or another, felt the displeasure of God's Wife and been obliged to accept the justice her men enforced.

"Only a fool would fail to see your wisdom and not wish to bless her son with it," she told her beloved Senimen after he was dismissed by Isis. Her former tutor looked very distinguished in his old age. He had taken to shaving his head and, because his hair was entirely white, the moon sacred to Thoth, scribe of the gods, seemed always to be shining directly down on his skull.

"Fools can be dangerous, my lady." His stern warning was softened by an affectionate smile.

For a moment they were silent and she felt them remembering together those days long ago in the garden of the residence in Mennefer when he taught her how to write her first word.

"Do not worry, Seni. I have no intention of letting anyone hinder the fledgling falcon's growth by seeking to control him. However, it is dangerous to fight a serpent head-on. I believe it would be wiser to feed the King's Mother the titles she covets. They will fatten her pride and make her complacently lazy."

Many Nomarchs proved indifferent to Lord Sobekmut's influence, including Khenti of the Sistrum and Rasui of the Oryx. They granted the King's Mother the respect due to her and no more.

For one very long night, Isis stood behind Pharaoh's Master of Life while Hatshepsut occupied the position at his feet. The transcendent sentiments of the prayers she intoned, like her mother before her, tasted disturbingly lifeless in her mouth in the presence of a woman who at first looked bored and then, as she grew increasingly tired and thirsty, openly skeptical.

I am the soul of Re who issued from the Abyss, that soul of the god who created authority. Wrong-doing is my detestation, and I will not see it; I think about righteousness, and I live by it; I am Authority which will never perish in this my name of 'Soul.' I came into being of myself with the Abyss in this my name of Khepri, and I come into being in it daily.

I am the Lord of Light; death is my detestation...

I am Nun, the doers of wrong cannot harm me. I am the eldest of the primeval gods, the soul of the souls of the eternal gods, my body is everlasting, my shape is eternity, Lord of Years, Ruler of Everlasting. I am he who created darkness and who made his seat in the limits of the sky. I desire to reach their limits, and I walk afoot, I go ahead with my staff, I cross the firmament...[48]

As the hours dragged by, Isis ceased to appear beautiful and assumed her true form. Instead of a lovely figure, Hatshepsut began to see a dimly luminous skeleton sickeningly embraced by writhing black serpents that constricted the red bird of her heart between them until it seemed hopelessly dead. The attractive power possessed by the King's Mother was of the most superficial kind and it was precisely by such magic that she could be undone. Hatshepsut found herself fantasizing about assigning a beautiful young nobleman the task of thrusting the weapon of his profound charm through the festering mass of Isis' cynical and selfish thoughts. He would take hold of her small heart and rest it in his hands and so gently would he caress it with loving words that her feelings would flutter irresistibly to life. In the end of her daydream the King's

Mother was caught in the arms of her lover and completely disgraced but in the process her soul was saved. It was a very gratifying daydream.

Like her brother's life, the following day passed more quickly than it should have. Despite her nightlong vigil over the mummy, hidden inside its smiling Master of Life, Hatshepsut's senses were all keenly alive. When in front of the tomb Hapuseneb performed the ritual of the Opening of the Mouth—using an adze made of metal from heaven—she almost seemed to taste the instrument herself. Watching his muscles flex around a leopard-skin cloak it was hard to turn her thoughts to the next word.

Banners of gold and crimson light streamed across the western sky as Akheperenre was joyfully welcomed into the afterlife. In the meantime, his subjects and loved ones sailed back to their side of the River. Splendid as they were, Hatshepsut observed that the colors of the sunset were not as vivid as those which had been lovingly mixed by the gods the evening her father was laid to rest.

The funeral banquet was held in the residence where Thutmose had resided while in Waset, in the same hall where she was first officially introduced to all the great lords and ladies of Kemet. Neferure shared a table with Senmut, who had returned from the quarry in Abu. He traveled back and forth regularly to inspect the progress of her Monuments of Heh. Throughout the night, she smiled over at him, attempting to tell him with her eyes that she had a great surprise for him. Very soon, many of her friends would know how dear they were to her and in what high esteem she held them.

The youngest son of the Nomarch of the Oryx was seated at a table with the toad-like Nomarch of Great Land, Setau. Raab was indeed beautiful and might yet prove even more helpful to her in the future. She was thinking of the King's Mother.

Whenever she shared a table with Hapuseneb, food did not interest her as much as their conversation.

"Eat," he commanded gently, "or you will not sleep well tonight."

"Are you my nurse?" she teased him.

"No, I am your master."

She felt as if he had stabbed her directly between the thighs with a weapon forged of Divine light. Shyly she avoided his eyes by studying the plates of delectable finger-foods resting on the table between them.

He selected a boiled quail's egg and offered it to her.

She parted her lips and accepted it, eager for the chance to taste his skin.

The King's Mother, sitting on the royal dais with them and sharing a table with her loyal relative, Sobekmut, was watching them.

Hatshepsut smiled at her and then laughed softly to herself when Isis immediately looked away.

"I have thought of a way to deal with that poisonous snake," she told Hapuseneb. "We will make her desire something more than titles."

He fed her a baked fig dipped in cream and once again permitted her to lick his fingertips clean. "What could she possibly desire more than the honor and wealth titles bestow?"

"A man, of course."

She slept well that night, pulled deep into dreams by royal women whose faces and names eluded her they had lived so long ago. When they spoke to her she understood everything they said even though, afterward, she could not remember a word. She woke feeling as if she had taken a long River journey during the night back in time to palaces, now buried beneath the sands, which had once stood beside Mansions of Millions of Years where the spirit of the great people who built them still lived. Like her mother's mother, Ahmose-Nefertari, she was charged with the task of caring for the Two Lands in the name of an infant pharaoh. There had been other queen regents before her but only one, Neferusobek, had dared to wear the king's *nemes* head cloth over her dress.

Her mind could not remember the night's dreams but her heart seemed to have absorbed the advice and encouragement offered to her by the queens whose voices all rang true. She felt profoundly calm and confident, as if the reins of her thoughts had been grasped by invisible hands and pulled taut, steering her in the right direction—the path of her destiny. She would rescue the fledgling falcon from his mother's ambitious talons and make sure the wings of his Ba spread to the full potential of his Ka without being clipped by selfish courtiers posing as knowledgeable men. Thutmose would be taught how to fight for the light by growing and strengthening his heart in the temple and his body in the army, where he would receive the training necessary to become the Great Army Commander like his father's father. Wherever he was, she knew Akheperkare would be well pleased with the daughter of his heart as the son of his son thrived in her care along with the Two Lands. That very morning Thutmose would be crowned and assume his throne name, Menkheperre, but Kemet would not yet be his. For a few years at least, just as the Oracle of Amun had foreseen, the Land of the Gods would belong entirely to her, God's Wife.

Perhaps it was the luxurious new wig, woven especially for the august occasion and glistening with fresh beeswax, that made the full vulture headdress feel lighter. Or perhaps she had at last become the person she truly needed to be to wear the crown without feeling the weight of responsibility it entailed as anything but a supreme blessing.

The edges of the canal were thick with the humble brown-and-white reeds of Waset's citizens while the courtyard fronting the ceremonial palace bloomed with the colorfully jeweled figures of noblemen. When Thutmose emerged the joy of the spectators was so great Hatshepsut imagined it crashing through the darkness of the Dwat like a wave which was the very sound of light. She was nearly deafened by the roar of rejoicing where she rode in her litter behind her brother's son in front of the King's Mother, who had made it clear she was not happy with the position allotted to her in the procession.

The royal family and their noble entourage proceeded to the Temple of Maat where, with becoming gravity, Thutmose accepted the double crown made especially to fit him. It seemed only yesterday her brother had stood in the same place. It was frightening how quickly the years passed. But she did not want to think about that. From now on, she vowed, she would make more excellent use of every moment Seshat had allotted to her by fully exercising the wisdom Thoth had blessed her with in the beautiful service of Maat.

She was pleased by the young falcon's composure. He was either remarkably mature for his age or his mother had frightened him to death with tales of the awful things that would happen to him if he did not behave properly. It was reassuring when he forgot himself and waved happily at the jubilating crowd as the procession emerged from the temple and proceeded slowly back the way it had come to *Ipet Sut,* where Amun-Re embraced his new bodily son and gave him all his names, chosen by the High Priests—He of the Sedge and the Bee, Menkheperre, The Being of Re is Established, Strong Bull Arising in Waset, Enduring of Kingship like Re in Heaven, Powerful of Strength, Sacred of Appearance, King of Upper and Lower Kemet, Lord of the Two Lands, Son of Re, Thutmose, Beautiful of Forms.

Three days later Hatshepsut, now officially Queen Regent, held a more private ceremony of investiture. The King's Mother attempted to insist Pharaoh be present.

"I am God's Wife," Hatshepsut reminded her. "The priests and officials I will honor belong to me. While he is still too young to care about anything except his nurse's breasts and his pets, Pharaoh must trust me to do what is best for Kemet."

"Everyone belongs to Pharaoh and Pharaoh is *my* son not yours, Majesty."

"You forget yourself, lady. Pharaoh is my *brother's* son and I am the sister and the daughter of kings. You are the boy's bodily mother but you are his guardian only because I permit you to be."

Hapuseneb was not present at the interview. It was not necessary. All of Kemet had seen the Governor of the South share the queen's table at the funeral banquet. Her husband was dead but the King's Mouth and Ears still sat beside her.

Hatshepsut spent a long time at her dressing table while her attendants made her body as beautiful as her heart. The lengthy process of applying gold-leaf to her fingernails and toenails was worth an exercise in patience. On that special day she was indeed the Golden One, alive with love and the power to make all those closest to her grow in happiness. Over a simple sheath dress as white as the moon, its straps barely broad enough to conceal her breasts, she wore four chokers, each one slightly larger than the other, made of tiny gold ring beads strung on plant fibers. Her earlobes were weighed down with ribbed gold hoop earrings. On her wrists were slipped a pair of rigid cuff bracelets made from sheets of fused gold decorated with alternating rows of red and blue beads for a touch of color. Her white leather sandals were strung with golden beads. Her hair was cut short so it was a simple matter to brush it back and set a long wig over it topped by the full vulture headdress.

The God's Wife was met outside her apartments by the First Prophet of Amun heading a retinue of high-ranking priests and scribes brought to witness and record the investitures. She led the way to the audience hall—entered by way of a small door concealed behind the dais—and without hesitating seated herself on the throne her brother and her father had both occupied before her. Her right hand held the staff of God's Wife planted firmly against the dais next to her gilded foot and her left hand rested the queen's lily scepter against her heart. Hapuseneb came to stand behind her right shoulder wearing the splendid clothes and jewels worthy of the Governor of the South. She smiled as she attempted to picture the expressions on the faces of her friends as they waited outside in the courtyard. The first courtier to be summoned into her Divine presence would approach the doorway leading into the palace portico and from there he would be guided along the secret path to the audience hall.

When Puyemre entered and beheld her golden radiance on the lamp lit dais, he collapsed as if wounded by a spear of light and kissed the floor.

"My Lord Puyemre," she said, "please rise and let me look upon your face, which is as dear to me as my own, for we are all one in the heart of God who smiles through our lips and sees His beauty with our eyes. Amun-Re is well pleased with his servant, Puyemre, whose thoughts race swift as cheetahs through his head to catch the profoundly succulent concepts so pleasing to the gods, and whose heart is as a vulture's nest where the feelings and confidences of his friends are always safe, lovingly protected and nourished by his wisdom.

"The faithful servant of the Mistress of The Two Lands and the beloved friend of God's Wife, Puyemre is hereby named Supervisor of the Treasury of Amun."

The honored official was anointed by a priest who touched his body's five centers of energy, beginning with his forehead and ending with his genitals. The divine-smelling unguent symbolically helped unite all his faculties and imbue him with the wisdom necessary to hold the office awarded him. He then took his place beside the dais.

Duauneheh was next. She made him a Herald of God's Wife and Director of the Granary and Fields of Amun, positions which would enable him to move about freely and exercise his talent for supervising a variety of processes.

Amenhotep's sensitive reserve and respect for the feelings of others earned him the position of Royal Butler.

One of Hapuseneb's sons was awarded the life-long position of High Priest and Supervisor of the *hemu-Kas* in Akheperenre's Mansion of Millions of years.

Djehuty was made Overseer of the Treasury of God's Wife.

Hatshepsut could not recall a more wonderful day.

She saved Senmut for last. Throughout his investiture, his face remained expressionless but his eyes spoke to her more eloquently than ever. As he gazed boldly up at her, she could believe he truly saw her for what and who she was—a being of Divine light transformed into a beautiful woman through the mysterious magic of God's Hand. Senmut's ardent regard abruptly penetrated her heart with a stunning thought—she was both Atum *and* his Hand, Re *and* his Eye, God *and* his Mother. Men and women, like all dualities, were the pillars of creation, but the part of her which was eternal—the part of her that exercised her Ka's powers the way she used her imagination and muscles—had existed before the First Occasion as part of the infinite heart of Atum-Re. Her true being was beyond nature, beyond male and female…

"My Lord Senmut!" She was almost angry with him for arousing in her such profound thoughts and distracting her from the simple but intense pleasure of making him happy. "I hereby name you Superior Steward of God's Wife and Superior Steward of the Lady of the Two Lands. From this day forward you will serve as the chief spokesman of my household."

26

Intelligence of the Heart

In addition to her lessons with Senmut, Neferure began studying in the temple. Her principal tutors were Senimen and the Second Prophet of Amun, Amenhotep, who had outlived three Pharaohs. On rare occasions, Hapuseneb spent a day with the princess but he did not give her the regular undivided attention he had bestowed on her mother. Hatshepsut suffered mixed feelings about that. Her pride was stroked like Nomti's glossy coat by the High Priest's special regard even as she was upset for her daughter. She decided not to let the matter trouble her. Neferure was blessed by Senimen, who had grown even richer in knowledge, patience and understanding, which he exercised with his usual gentle firmness.

She recalled remarking to Lord Khenti she would never be jealous of her daughter but, she admitted to herself, that might not have proved true if Hapuseneb had suddenly begun spending time with Neferure instead of with her. Instead, she saw more of him than ever. Her happiness was so great it mirrored the inundation as the enriching depth of his company brought every feeling in her heart, and every moment of her life, into full flower. His wife remained in the Nome of the Oryx and one of their daughters, Henut-nefert, had been appointed to direct the Songstresses of Amun in her mother's absence. Hatshepsut approved.

During the fifteen days of the month Neferure studied in the temple, her Superior Steward Senmut spent much of his time in the queen's palace and presence. Officially, he was still the Superior Royal Scribe but she had provided him with even more assistants. The King's Mother had recommended one of her younger brothers for a position as a scribe in the administrative palace but after discussing the youth with Senimen, who had been in charge of his education, Hatshepsut refused the request. Isis was not happy about it yet there was little she could do besides complain by way of letters to her most powerful relative, Sobekmut, who had returned to his home in the Nome of the Crocodile.

During one of his routine sojourns south to inspect the progress of her two Monuments of Heh, Senmut wrote and asked her permission to bring home a quantity of the same stone she was using to build the container for her Master of Life. He desired to have an image carved of himself for God's House. She immediately granted his request. Although she preferred the golden hue she had chosen for herself, the reddish-brown color he selected also evoked the sun. He had himself depicted in the sitting position, with his legs bent before him and his body concealed beneath a long cloak. There was only the suggestion of his shoulders and of his hands crossed at the wrists resting on his knees. She had seen many such statues of devotees in the offering courts of temples throughout the Two Lands that enabled their owners to always remain in the Divine presence no matter where they were. The box-like form from which only the head emerged symbolized the physical body of God shaped by the four cardinal elements and directions.

Hatshepsut gave her Superior Steward permission to place his statue in *Ipet Sut*. He had drawn up the texts of the inscriptions himself and told the artist exactly where he wanted them to appear. Even though she was only mentioned on the base, she was well pleased with what he had written:

The God's Wife, Hatshepsut, "the king made me great; the king enhanced me, so that I was advanced before the other courtiers: and having realized my excellence in her heart, she appointed me Chief Spokesman of her household."[49]

All across the cloak concealing his body, Senmut documented his relationship to the Good God Menkheperre, who he had followed on his journeys, describing himself as *"one who has access to the marvelous character of the Lord of the Two Lands,"* and as *"the Chamberlain who speaks in privacy, one vigilant concerning what is brought to his attention, one who finds a solution every single day, Overseer of All Works of the King."*[50] Her name was not mentioned but Hatshepsut could easily guess it was to her Senmut actually referred. Thutmose spoke privately only to his nurse and mother, the one journey he had taken was to Waset from Mennefer shortly after he was born, and he had not yet personally commissioned any works. Senmut did, indeed speak in privacy with the king for it was she who held the crook and flail while her brother's son was still too young to understand who he was.

"Your ears are not so big," she teased him one evening when they were alone, "but the wig is faithfully rendered. You should wear it more often for it makes you look even more distinguished."

"I am content with your pleasure, Majesty, but wish to give you much more. Perhaps the next time I journey to Abu you will grant me permission to return with an even greater quantity and variety of stone. It is the desire of my heart to have made statues the like of which haver never before been seen in the Two Lands."

"I approve of your Divine impulse, Senmut, and admit to being excited by the thought of the Hidden One revealing even more of His heart through you."

"Many people will find the work shocking," he warned. "I can scarcely imagine what they will think when I dare to have my deepest feelings rendered in stone for the gods and everyone to behold."

"I am even more intrigued. We both know I do not find your feelings shocking and what others think is of no consequence. You have my permission to order made whatever your Ka so greatly desires to see take form here on earth."

"My lady, are you now granting me, a commoner, the power to emulate Divine creativity, which is traditionally only the prerogative of royalty and the highest nobility?"

"Yes, Senmut, that is precisely what I am doing. And please do not insult me by referring to yourself as a commoner. The titles you have honorably earned raise you above your birth like wings, with which you would be wise to aspire to even greater heights. Would the Queen Regent and God's Wife consort so intimately with a common man?"

His voice was barely audible, "*Consort?*"

She immediately felt ashamed of her evasiveness. "Would the Queen Regent and God's Wife *love* a common man?"

* * * * *

The Overseer of the Double Granary of Amun, Headman of Waset and Supervisor of all the works of Pharaoh, Ineni, went to his Ka.

The news was brought to the queen by her Royal Butler, Amenhotep. Stroking the amulet of Anukis he still wore around his neck, he bowed after delivering the sad message and left her alone. He was wise enough to realize no amount of words could dam her tears and that it was wrong to try to use them for that purpose. When someone died, the happiness of the people left behind reached its lowest point. Those who did not cry were as dead inside as the earth when the River failed to rise. Sorrow's uncontrollable flood became a blessing as it drowned hopelessly miserable thoughts. Only when the heart was inundated with grief as it faced the darkness of death and felt itself breaking like a seed could hope and joy take root in it again with magical swiftness.

Hatshepsut had loved the slightly built man who was the first to smile at her kindly and make her feel welcome in the Seal Room. It felt like such a long time ago; the years seemed to pass as swiftly as she blinked. She scarcely noticed their going until death reminded her that what she saw and felt would not always be there. She was comforted by the fact that while he lived she had shown Ineni how much she respected and cared for him by presenting him with lovely gifts for his home, many of them made from gold and silver, so his wealth increased beyond measure and his honor was magnified in everyone's eyes. She had spent many enjoyable hours in his Pleasure House, which rivaled even Pharaoh's in magnificence. Ineni was so proud of his garden he had instructed the Servants of the Place of Truth to depict it in his tomb. Since space was limited, and only certain varieties of trees and plants could be represented, he made sure they included an inventory of everything which actually grew there. The tally was impressive—thirty-one Persea trees, seventy-three sycamores, one-hundred-and-seventy date palms, five figs, five pomegranates, sixteen carobs, eight willows, ten tamarisks, two myrtles and many others all planted in neat rows.

Hatshepsut occasionally visited the royal workshops to watch the craftsmen at work. To the homes of the men she had promoted she had recently sent a variety of gifts inscribed with their names and titles. It was a source of continuing satisfaction to her that her dear friends now enjoyed even more generous access to the wealth of Amun-Re and his bodily son. The most talented jewelers, carpenters, stone masons, sculptors, artists and even glass blowers no longer worked exclusively in Mennefer. Her brother had not objected to her bringing several of them down with her when she returned home from her first royal progress. The town of Amun was as dear to her heart, or even more so, than the city of Ptah in the north. It was her desire to see God's southern home made even more beautiful with splendid offerings.

She permitted Puyemre to borrow Satnem, her favorite painter, when after his promotion to Supervisor of the Treasury of Amun he chose to build a second larger home in the countryside. It was no secret he had fallen in love with a lady named Tanefert. Apparently, Senseneb had spent too much time in the temple as a Divine Adoratice and Songstress of the God and unwisely permitted her husband's eye to wander. Hatshepsut was pleased Puyemre could now easily support two wives. She wanted everyone she loved to be as happy as possible. She awarded Senmut his own ship and skipper, the Honorable Nebiri, so he could travel to and from Abu in comfortable luxury.

No one could ever take Ineni's place in her heart but it was necessary to fill the positions emptied by his loss. Ahmose-Penekhbet, who had worked closely with Ineni for a long time, slipped naturally into the role of Headman of Waset. She had the pleasure of once again promoting Djehuty, this time to Director of Works. His growing love of numbers and the art of measure would find life-long fulfillment.

Shortly before he died, Akheperenre had begun building another family monument in God's House. Only two of the six chambers had been completed in which she appeared alongside her brother as his Great Royal Wife making offerings before Amun-Re and Amun-Min. In one scene Neferure, her body already that of a woman, was shown standing behind her parents. In the new raised reliefs, the queen and God's Wife was depicted alongside Menkheperre, also rendered as he would appear years from then. Together they offered the water of Life to the Hidden One in two identical round vessels symbolic of the unity behind all duality. True of Voice, Akheperenre sat enthroned behind them.

Hatshepsut often found herself contemplating the profound reassurance of art. Gazing at beautiful and incorruptible representations of her face and figure flattered her on all levels. Her carved images defying the ravages of time in God's carnal home reflected her Ka's creative immortality. All the copies of herself decorating temple walls represented the multitude of Ba-birds nesting in her ever developing Ka, which never grew old and undesirable. When Neferure asked her why people were drawn in that funny way—always in profile but with their eyes and shoulders facing forward—she replied, "Because it is the only way a dynamic wholeness independent of past and future can be expressed. Artistic conventions are actually spiritual truths and that is why Kemet's artists will always remain faithful to them. Drawn in such a fashion the human figure, even though it appears motionless and confined to the moment, is never limited by the perspective of the senses but instead reveals the ever flowing energy behind them. It is a way of showing the whole person at once and defying the constraints of space and time."

She doubted the princess fully understood her reply but she was confident all the words she spoke to her daughter would germinate in her mind and eventually blossom into understanding through the intelligence of her heart. Neferure would become God's Wife one day and, like her mother, she was destined to marry her little brother. Hatshepsut fervently hoped Thutmose would grow up to be more like his father's father.

Senmut requested that the princess accompany her mother to the royal workshop to view his new statue, which had not yet been seen by anyone except the sculptor who fashioned it. Hatshepsut was even more intrigued than her daughter was by the aura of mystery surrounding her Steward's new project. The radiance of the smile she cast him was visible to her in the mysterious mirror of his eyes, which both darkened and shone with emotion. The intensity of his love filled her with such wonder and happiness she scarcely noticed it until she said or did something that hurt him, then she became fully aware of how vital his joy was to her own. She relied on him for so much it might have worried her if she had not trusted him with her life. Neferure and her tutor were curiously alike in many ways and she enjoyed listening to them talk. It was quite entertaining how they could go on and on about something, dredging up more and more minutely detailed observations on a single subject often without reaching any meaningful conclusion. She found it a little disturbing they did not desire to explore, or even touch upon, the profound symbolism she herself needed to see in everything in order to enjoy a conversation. They seemed to relish the intricacies of the world for their own sake without seeming to recall that everything was part of a single awe inspiring mystery—existence itself. And yet she knew Senmut's love of facts was not superficial and she continued learning from him how the hunger of curiosity, and the knowledge it attains, sharpens the faculty of awe and nourishes the intelligence of the heart. She had often thought that if she were Amun-Re she would relish seeing through Senmut's eyes, which perceived and admired the complex splendors of Creation in a way that made priests who never looked up from crumbling old papyri appear blind.

The room containing Senmut's new statue was small and hot but she forgot her discomfort. Even though it only reached as high as her hips, the carved stone dominated the stuffy space with a cool and peaceful authority. To anyone else, Neferure's gasp might have sounded like one of shock but her mother recognized the delight so eloquently expressed by that single passionate intake of breath.

Wearing the wide shoulder-length wig she had admired, Senmut's image sat on a narrow stone pedestal that rested on a thick and solid base, but this time he was not alone. Neferure sat on his lap, her body completely concealed by his cloak flowing tightly over their bodies down to his ankles. His left hand lay protectively over her heart while his right fist rested gently on her lap. His narrow beard merged with her shaved head which still wore the side-lock of youth. Her childishness was further expressed by the finger she held up to her lips. The polished stone was a dark-gray approaching black that made their eyes and their smiles shine with a depth transcending life's sad evanescence. The inscription between his legs, running down the length of his cloak, identified the seated man as the Chief Steward of the princess Neferure, Senmut.

As Hatsheput deliberately kept him in suspense about her reaction, Neferure tugged on his kilt. He lifted her obligingly up against his chest so she could wrap her arms around his neck but his eyes never left her mother's face.

Never in all the long history of Kemet had a royal and a non royal appeared together as they did in Senmut's creation. A commoner was never permitted to touch a member of the royal family, much less have himself depicted holding one of them intimately in his arms. It was also unheard of that the princess be represented smaller than her tutor for a royal person was always drawn or sculpted on a larger scale than a non-royal to stress his or her divinity. The statue was completely shocking.

The approval of the Hidden One could be felt in the breeze wafting in from the River through the windows. Her Superior Steward had indeed created something new and she felt in her heart that the gods were well pleased with it. The princess and her tutor—whose affection for each other would now live forever—were both waiting for her to say something but she was finding it difficult to find the right words to express how immensely gratified she was by the work. The fact that it also made her nervous added the excitement of a challenge to the pleasure she took in it. She truly felt she was in the presence of a part of Amun-Re's heart revealing itself for the first time.

"My lord Senmut," when she finally spoke the tone of her voice prompted him to set Neferure down even as he kept hold of her hand, "Ptah smiles more deeply today and Amun is well pleased by your offering, as I am. Tell me what it is you wish for so I may give it to you as a gift."

"If you are truly pleased, my queen, then what I most wish for I already possess, but I do have one request. 'Grant that there be made for me many statues of every type of precious hard stone for the Temple of Amun in *Ipet Sut*, and for every place where the majesty of this god proceeds, like every favored ancestor. Then they will be in the following of your majesty in this temple.'"[51]

Neferure had remained respectfully silent for too long. "You mean I cannot take it home with me?" she exclaimed.

"No, my dear," Hatshepsut replied gently. "The princess and her beloved tutor will sit forever in the Temple, where your love for each other, openly and fearlessly expressed, will nourish God's heart and make a fair memory with people."

* * * * *

Whenever Hatshepsut performed the gesture of praise and rejoicing before Hapuseneb, and he reflected it, she distinctly felt a warm current flowing between them. When his palms came close to hers, the sensation of invigorating resistance was as real as when she lightly pressed her hands against the surface of water. In the presence of the High Priest, she literally felt herself to be the body of energy serving as the mold for her physical form—she feared and worried about nothing and was completely happy. Whenever she was alone with Senmut, however, she did not always feel so confident and in control. It was becoming increasingly difficult to deny her Superior Steward what she wanted as much as he did. It was impossible for her to accept that simply because her husband was dead she would never again be permitted to spread her legs for a man. When Hapuseneb said to her one evening at a banquet held by the King's Mother, "You are waiting for my permission" she somehow knew what he meant. When she was in Senmut's arms, she sometimes wondered if she was letting him go too far, in every sense, and the thought cooled her ardor with anxiety, making it possible for her to resist the melting desire aroused in her by his kisses and caresses. Waset was aflame with conversations, all revolving around the statue of the princess and her tutor. That Senmut must have had the permission of the Queen Regent to produce the shockingly unconventional work was not mentioned by anyone in her presence but she suspected the King's Mother never tired of stressing this fact in private to anyone who cared to listen. She was growing heartily tired of the woman. The sooner Thutmose was removed from her venomous influence the better. She could not allow Pharaoh's heart to be turned against his father's sister, who was striving to rule the Two Lands in his stead with love and wisdom, even if it meant not being blindly faithful to every tradition.

"You have not answered me, Hatshepsut."

The High Priest of Amun was the only person who still addressed her by the name given to her at birth and a feeling was brewing inside her… there was something not quite right about the fact that he could still call her *Hatshepsut*. She certainly *was* Foremost of Noble Women but she was much more. She was God's Wife, Hatshepsut United with Amun, and Queen Regent. Her heart could fully embrace her new greater identity only through the sound of another name serving to contain its power. Only then would she be able to walk the earth with the profound confidence necessary to effectively wield the crook and flail.

"I have not answered you, Hapuseneb, because there is nothing to say. You know I will forever obey you for your wisdom is the Divine space between my heartbeats without which they would be meaningless. Besides, I was already thinking about something else. You told me yourself never to walk blindly behind Seth. There is, I realize now, another important matter I must address, one that may, because all things are related, affect how you feel about what I can or cannot do."

His penetrating stare made her forgot all about the banquet hall and the people in it.

"I require a new name, Hapuseneb, to express and contain my power as Queen Regent, and my heart is telling me that name must, and will be, *Maatkare*."

"Truth is, indeed, the soul of the sun, my lady. Truth is beauty, and it is true there is no woman in all of the Two Lands who is remotely as beautiful as you are in every way, Hathepsut-Maatkare."

"Do you recall the evening we stood together before the abandoned chapel of Pakhet?"

"I will never forget it. You asked me there if I loved you."

"And you said 'yes', such a simple word but the most marvelous of them all. Ever since then your reply has sustained me and made me happy enough to become who I am, Maatkare, Mistress of the Two Lands, who understands it is wrong to set aside the desires of our heart, whether it be out of fear or from the mistaken belief—reasonable as it may seem—that we do not have the means to fulfill them. I should have expressed my wishes more firmly to my brother but, too easily, I surrendered to his indifference. I must rebuild the Temple of Hathor in the Nome of the Lower Pomegranate, Sycamore and Viper and the Chapel of Pakhet in the Oryx."

"Where we witnessed three cobras mating," he reminded her, "a female and two males."

The insinuating way he spoke the seemingly innocent words rendered her speechless for a moment, during which she both resented and was grateful for the distraction of a serving girl pausing by their table to replenish their wine cups.

"My new name, Maatkare," she went on breathlessly, "will be made public here in Waset and throughout the Two Lands as once again we take a journey together, Hapuseneb." Stunned to realize she had not asked him to come with her but simply told him they were going, the candle flames reflected in his eyes trembled just as she did inside awaiting his reply.

A harpist strummed her instrument, preparing to sing, as Hapuseneb said quietly, "I am well pleased with my student *Hatshepsut*, and for a long time that will stretch into forever my heart has belonged to her, God's Wife. Now I rejoice beyond measure at the opportunity to act strictly in the name of the Mistress of the Two Lands, *Maatkare*."

All conversation in the great hall was silenced by a woman's lovely voice proclaiming:

Whenever I leave you, I go out of breath
  (death must be lonely like I am);
I dream lying dreams of your love lost,
  and my heart stands still inside me.
I stare at my favorite datecakes-
  they would be salt to me now-
And pomegranate wine (once sweet to our lips)
  bitter, bitter as bird gall.

Touching noses with you, love, your kiss alone,
  and my stuttering heart speaks clear:
Breathe me more of your breath, let me live!
  Man meant for me,
God himself gave you as his holy gift,
  my love to outlast forever.[52]

* * * * *

Senmut oversaw the raising of statues of Akheperenre in the newly expanded Temple of Khnum dedicated by his sister, Hatshepsut-Maatkare. Her brother, Thutmose-Protector of Re, was also to be worshipped as a god just north of the second wild waters in another new temple dedicated to the falcon god Horus. Stars shining in the feathers of his chest and his great wings giving birth to the winds, The Lord of the Sky had always helped protect Kemet from her enemies. The first reliefs would soon be carved in which she would appear alongside her brother wearing a form-fitting dress but with one leg extended in front of the other. Women were invariably depicted with their feet positioned passively together. In the border temple of Horus, Maatkare was shown striding forward like a man. She believed her new stance more accurately reflected reality, for even though her flesh was still adorned by feminine dress and ornaments she was, in fact, the king of Kemet.

Acting on behalf of Menkheperre, Hatshepsut had also begun restoring and expanding the Temple of Senwosret in Wawat dedicated to the Lord of Incense. The chapel of Dedwen—the god who personified Pharaoh's sovereignty over the southern lands—was located inside one of the border fortresses she had stayed in with her parents all those years ago when they journeyed together into Kush. She would never forget its reassuring embrace. In honor of the memory, she had ordered the bark shrine enlarged and Senmut had overseen the project's completion.

She relied heavily on her Superior Steward, who kept her abreast of the progress being made on her two Monuments of Heh. In his letters, he described to her in detail how after the most promising expanse of rock was selected it was shaped by stakes thrust into strategically drilled holes. When the wooden stakes were soaked in water, they expanded and gently cracked the stone free of the mountain. Fires were then ignited and almost immediately quenched, which had the effect of cracking the surface of the rock so it could be more easily worked. The front was smoothed and then the sides were shaped by repeatedly striking them with small balls made from a rock even harder than *biat*. As the monument took form, it gradually assumed its own identity distinct from the forces that created it. The mother rock continued to support it in key places but these bonds would eventually be severed. Every time she received a letter from Senmut she dreaded he might be writing to tell her one of the monuments had cracked and been ruined but so far the news had always been good.

The Superior Steward of the queen and God's Wife returned to Waset for a few days, before he left for the north to oversee preparations for the ceremony of Stretching the Cord at the ruined Temple of Hathor she was replacing with an entirely new structure. Before work could begin it was necessary the king perform a series of foundation rituals accompanied by the spirit of Seshat, Mistress of Builders, the wife of Thoth who, like her husband, personified the Divine will contained in the art of writing and measure. As Queen Regent, Hatshepsut-Maatkare would be standing in for Menkheperre at the ceremonies. Her presence alone embodied the goddess and sanctified the actions carried out by skilled priests and workmen.

The most important part of the rite took place at night in the darkness of the new moon. The four corners of the future temple were aligned using a notched palm stick called a *merkhet* and two plumb lines. Representing Pharaoh, the High

Priest held the *merkhet* and one end of the line while another priest, standing on the north side, held the other end. The First Prophet looked through the hole bored into one end of the *merkhet* to locate the imperishable star marking the location of true north, and then the Keeper of the Hours raised the slightly wider V-shaped end of the notched palm stick and fixed its position. When the plumb lines were properly aligned, posts were driven into the ground at the four corners and the cord marking the outline of the temple was stretched between them then permitted to fall to the ground. Where it came to rest was where the builders would dig the trenches for the foundation.

The following day, before building of the structural walls could commence, the water table—representing the Primordial Waters of Nun from which everything emerged, including the future temple—had to be symbolically tapped. Hatshepsut decided to perform the next step in the rite herself by using a wooden mold to form the first brick. It was curiously satisfying to darken her hands with mud and to let it cover her scarab rings so they seemed to return to their damp dark homes.

The final stages of the ceremony involved the burial of foundation deposits in a circular pit symbolizing the seemingly empty wholeness from which the Laws of Becoming emerged. The first items added to the pit were four faience plaques inscribed with Pharaoh's name and his intention to construct a monument for eternity. The second deposit was the ribs and vertebrae of a female cow. Hatshepsut offered ten scarabs made of different materials inscribed with her name and title of God's Wife, and the Overseer of the Work buried a variety of model wooden tools. Finally the High Priest of Hathor, acting on behalf of the King, picked up a wooden lever and heaved a large stone into place at one of the temple's four corners. Construction could now begin.

Hatshepsut spent a stimulating evening on the southern boundary of the Nome of the Oryx in the company of Hapuseneb, Senmut and Djehuty designing her new temple to Pakhet. She had decided it would not be enough to merely restore the goddess' small chapel. The Divine lioness, one of the fierce faces of Hathor, deserved an even larger home. The new sanctuary, aligned on a north-south axis, would be cut into the living rock of a desert mountain that towered over the mouth of an arid valley and overlooked the verdant land watered by the River. The open entrance would consist of a row of four columns mirrored by an additional four pillars erected behind them to hold up the ceiling of the entrance hall. In the center of the back wall, a narrow doorway would lead into a small antechamber and the holy of holies.

Hatshepsut sacrificed a goat before the abandoned Temple of She Who Scratches and offered it to the goddess whose aid she sought every day to keep confusion and disorder at bay in her thoughts and feelings and, therefore, throughout all Kemet. She chose the cool of evening for her personal ritual and preserved the desert's mysteriously eloquent silence by bringing only Hapuseneb and three other priests with her.

The tension between Senmut and the First Prophet of Amun whenever they spent a prolonged amount of time in the same room had her thirsting for the stress-relieving sight of hot red blood gleaming on cool metal knives and staining pure white linen. It felt as natural to love two men as it did for her heart to beat. She could no more choose between them than she could control her pulse. Hapuseneb was married and yet if he ever told her to give up Senmut she would do so no matter how much distress it caused her. Fortunately he was wise enough to know it would be like commanding her to cut off a part of her own body and that she would suffer much more than the sacrificial goat, which was swiftly dispatched.

The problem was not with Hapuseneb but with Senmut who she knew would have greatly preferred not to share her love with the High Priest of Amun. It was rigorously concealed but the jealousy he suffered was as palpable to her as the smell of the goat's blood. There was nothing she could do about that except sacrifice her own happiness by attempting to change how she felt about Hapuseneb and that was impossible. She was incapable of lying to herself in an effort to satisfy someone else was. It seemed to her this was one of the most serious crimes a person could commit against his heart and Maat.

Hatshepsut-Maatkare spent several moons in the Northern Seal Room after sending Senmut and Neferure back home to Waset. She felt it was time her daughter, who had been thoroughly enjoying her first royal progress, continue her lessons in the temple. She herself intended to travel further north to Perunefer, where she was looking forward to seeing Kallikrates again and hopefully hearing more dolphin stories. It was also her intention to begin building a series of new palaces in Seth's city. Nehesj had raised no objections to the army's expansion. One of the new residences would serve as his home when he was in Perunefer and be available for use by other high ranking officials. The small residence erected by her father's father would be torn down and replaced by a much larger and beautifully decorated palace fronting a ceremonial building where foreign delegations could be received in more impressive splendor. The Great Army Commander's quarters would be expanded and adjoin a public structure where the business of the military, including promotions, could be more regally and comfortably conducted.

It was her wish to have parts of the new ceremonial palace decorated in the style of the Keftiu. She trusted their ambassador would be flattered and that Kemet's ties with the people of the Great Green would grow even stronger. Kallikrates had never been farther south than Mennefer. She would invite him to Waset and ask him to bring some of his artists with him so their creative magic could be placed in the service of the Hidden One, who she firmly believed never tired of seeing more and more of His heart revealed in works of beauty.

Close to the great palace where she herself would reside whenever she visited Perunefer it was also her intention to build a smaller residence for Pharaoh where he could live while receiving his military training. The thought of sending the King's Mother as far from Waset as possible was extremely appealing and one of the reasons she had not resisted her demand to also be named King's Guardian. For as long as Thutmose was a child, Isis would be obliged to travel with him wherever he went. If she could not succeed in disgracing the lady then she could at least get her out of the way. It would remain necessary, however, to surround Pharaoh with men wise enough to handle the serpent who bred him. It was imperative the King's Mother not weaken her son's character with the cynicism responsible for her painful selfishness.

While in Mennefer, Hatshepsut received word that the Deputy of the King' Son of Kush, Djehutihotep, had gone to his Ka. She immediately sent a letter to the Southern Seal Room appointing Amenemhat in his brother's place and indicating he was to depart at once for Wawat. It was fortunate the young lady he had married was not the type to pine away after court life. The Mistress of the House, Hatshepsut, would undoubtedly organize a remote court of her own and, for a while at least, reign as queen amongst the wives of officers hungering for the latest news and gossip.

The Queen Regent enjoyed her time in Mennefer more than ever because even when they were relaxing Hapuseneb was always by her side. She especially liked it when he took her hunting with his favorite falcon. Observing the skill with which he handled the beautiful predator, she could not help thinking how much like a king he looked. She wondered if Thutmose would grow up to be as tall and strong as the High Priest of Amun. But her brother's son was only a child; when he was a man, she would be an old woman. His time would not be hers. The sacred time of Hatshepsut United with Amun and of the Queen Regent Maatkare was now. Watching the High Priest's falcon—a female named Hathor—descending from heaven onto his wrist, she sensed it was vital she not hesitate to fully grasp the power she possessed.

She thought about the journey she had taken out of her body while it lay wrapped up like a mummy in the Chamber of the Other World in the Temple of Satis. She did not doubt Hapuseneb had meant to remind her of how, in the final moments of her ordeal, she had assumed the form of a falcon. The intent way he glanced at her each time he sent Hathor flying made her heart beat as hard as the bird's wings.

She said, "I wish the King's Mother was a fat pigeon we could command Hathor to bring down."

He smiled and replied, "Together there is nothing we cannot do, Maatkare-Hatshepsut. You need only believe that for it to be true."

27

The Royal Ka

The day after Maatkare returned to her palace in Waset, the First Prophet of Amun sought an audience with her. Surprised and delighted she would see him again so soon, she ordered him admitted into the most intimate of her receiving rooms.

Hapuseneb did not sit down. "Eight days from now," he announced, "the sun and the moon will become one."

She gripped the arms of her chair. "The Two Eyes of Horus will cross? The night sun and the day sun will rule in heaven on a single throne?"

"Yes. When Re and Thoth, the Two Companions who cross the sky, become one for a few moments, day will turn to night here in the Town of Amun. Elsewhere the solar disc will only be partially obscured."

"What does it mean?" she said in awe. "Surely it portends an event of great importance!"

He did not respond.

"Hathor-Sekhmet is the Eye of Re who travels with Thoth on his wing through the heavens…" She felt like a little girl again back in the temple obliged to answer her own profoundly difficult question. "What you are telling me is that, for a few moments, Hathor and Thoth will merge and seem to return us to the magical darkness in which Atum and his Hand were One, before Thoth spoke the Word that separated them through Creation?"

"Yes."

"It will be a most exciting event, Hapuseneb!"

"I agree, but most people must not be allowed to see it. If they look upon the celestial union for too long they will be blinded. A decree must be issued by the king commanding everyone to remain indoors that afternoon. Those who cannot do so must be warned it is dangerous to look up as the darkness falls."

"But surely *we* will be able to behold the Divine union!"

"We will observe it from the temple rooftop but only for a minute or two, while the darkness is absolute."

A thrill of fear stoked her excitement and she could scarcely catch hold of her emotions. "But you still have not told me, Hapuseneb, what you think it means that the moon and the sun have chosen to become one directly over Waset."

"It is not for me to say, *Maatkare.*"

"The meaning lies in my name?"

"The name you chose for yourself as the Mistress of the Two Lands who holds the crook and flail in her hands."

"Maatkare is the name given to me by my heart. My Ba is wise enough to hear my Ka when it speaks and to obey its decrees. The health and vitality of my body rely on the solar disc, but my mysterious growth and joy depends on always being true to Maat with all my thoughts and feelings. I am part of the sun's Divine life force, the Ka of Re which perpetually caresses the One immutable truth of Beauty with loving fingers of creative light."

He said, "In eight days time a Divine darkness will fall upon Waset where God's Wife holds in her hands the power of Pharaoh. When the moon completely covers the solar disc, a ring of light will surround it. The Eye of Re will hold the moon child Khonsu against her breast and her light will glow and flare, revealing all its life-giving beauty."

Like Khonsu—the child of Amun-Re and the Great Mother Mut— Menkheperre was still a child at the breast, the efficacy of his Royal Ka darkened by the youth of his Ba. On the other hand she, Hatshepsut-Maatkare, was at the height of her powers, God's Hand and God's Wife, the Eye of Re, Mistress of the Two Lands, Hathor embodied. In eight days time the heavens would reflect earthly events—the sun and the moon would rule together.

Hapuseneb said firmly, "Do you understand and are you prepared?"

Dismissing the frightening possibility that she might be mistaking his meaning she replied, "I believe I do, and that I am. There is a part of me that exists forever beyond duality. My body is that of a woman but my Ka is neither male nor female for it can create Ba's of either sex. When a man and a woman sit together on the Horus Throne of the Living, as they do now, then does the heart of the Hidden One rejoice as cosmic unity and created duality are perfectly reflected on earth."

"My lady, Pharaoh must possess the Attractive Power which holds the world together and is thus vital to the health and prosperity of the Two Lands. Not everywhere will the moon completely obscure the sun. In the lands ruled by the Nine Bows the moon, like a hungry predator, will take a large bite out of the sun and the power of Re will appear to be weakened. Our enemies will believe that because a child sits on the throne we are vulnerable. They will not believe that a queen, a mere woman, can stand against them. They will very likely interpret the celestial event as an omen encouraging them to invade us again."

She stood. "That must not happen!"

"And even here, in our Beloved Earth, what has been reunited by your great family may once again become divided," he went on relentlessly. "Already the selfish ambition of the King's Mother spreads a debilitating poison throughout Kemet by encouraging its Nomarchs to take sides against each other. As long as you are merely Queen Regent you will be within swiping distance of the King's Guardian, and though the cuts to your supremacy may be minor, you will continue to bleed authority in the eyes of others. You are right. You must not let that happen, Hatshepsut-Maatkare. At this moment, in this Sacred Time, your Attractive Power is great enough to keep the Two Lands united and strong. The Royal Ka lives in each king and when he dies takes a new form. Until he is anointed, the man who is Pharaoh is not Divine. The double crown represents the inner awakening that makes him one with his eternal nature and bestows the ultimate power of creation and destruction."

Fearing her legs might fail to support her, she sat down again. "Are you, the First Prophet of Amun, saying the Royal Ka lives in me even though my body is that of a woman?"

"Amun-Re has not forgotten the last words spoken by your father. With his dying breath Akheperkare said, 'My daughter, the Female Falcon'. I think you know it is true that in that moment his Royal Ka passed to you even though his bodily son sat in the same room."

She said softly, "Do you truly believe, Hapuseneb, that I am destined to rule, not on behalf of my brother's son but *with* him, like God and His Hand?"

"Even if I personally did not believe that was your destiny, it would still be possible."

"What you believe is of the utmost importance to me, Hapuseneb."

"Do not underestimate yourself, Maatkare. I say no more than I do because I know there is no need for me to."

Eight days later most of Waset's citizens remained indoors to protect themselves from the great celestial event the priests of Amun had prophesized would take place that afternoon. On the temple rooftop, Hatshepsut stood surrounded by her friends. Puyemre and Amenhotep, Duauneheh and Min-Hotep, Useramun, Djehuty and Senmut all seemed torn between staring up at the sky and looking down at her face. What was about to happen in the heavens over Waset threatened their eyesight for only a few moments. The earthly event soon to take place beneath the starry ceiling of the ceremonial palace would challenge their vision of tradition forever. The caution expressed by the tense set of their mouths was softened by the reverent excitement shining in their dark irises. They had all studied with her in the Temple and since then she had been well served by them. The oracle years ago where Amun declared Princess Hatshepsut would one day hold the crook and flail in her hands had come true, and so too would her father's final words. When she had communicated her decision to each of her favored courtiers in private, she had watched their faces carefully. She had been very pleased to note that not one of them had looked shocked or even much surprised.

Nehesj, Ahmose-Penekhbet, Senimen and Akheperseneb were also present on the temple rooftop that day. She had worked with them in the Seal Room while her father was still alive and during her brother's reign. When she became Queen Regent, nothing really changed. Three Pharaohs had come and two had gone but God's Wife remained and continued having an important influence in the affairs of state. As far as the governance of the Two Lands was concerned, it was a small matter to make her power officially absolute. The old vizier and the new headman of Waset had not verbally expressed it but she had sensed their initial resistance to the concept. It had been quickly overcome, however, by the support of the Royal Treasurer. Nehesj was a close friend of the First Prophet of Amun and everyone knew in what high esteem Hapuseneb held God's Wife. The Governor of the South acted as the fledgling falcon's Mouth and Ears but it was the Queen Regent for whom he spoke and to whom he listened.

In a single day, nothing and yet everything would change forever. Fear and confusion might darken parts of the land, just as the light was dimming now on the temple rooftop, but the ensuing glory would reveal the truth—the power of Re, and the wisdom that perceived the solar disc's Divine source, was stronger in Kemet than ever, strong enough to see beyond tradition and to look directly upon the spiritual truths it reflected.

The priest who oversaw all the other prophets devoted to the study of the heavens indicated it would soon be time to look up. When she smiled with excitement, the men surrounding her grinned in response and she felt them all bound together by that special moment. The sun was still high in the sky but the day was indeed turning to night.

"The god has kissed the goddess," the priest's quiet voice intensified the suspenseful silence, "and she is slowly taking him in her golden arms."

The sky over the western desert sacred to Hathor was alive with radiantly soft colors and Hatshepsut gazed at them, entranced, as the shadow of Thoth's vast wing swiftly began falling over the land and the River. Flooding the city, darkness lapped against the palaces and all the other buildings below them as though the Celestial Waterway was overflowing. She wondered if her pulse would come to a stop when night fell in the very heart of day but she was truly much more in awe than afraid.

The priest announced, "You may look up now."

Useramun exclaimed beneath his breath, "By the Ka of Ptah!"

The moon had become the pupil in the Eye of Re, which glowed in magically visible splendor all around it. Hatshepsut's joy was boundless. She was looking directly at the solar disc and it was speaking to her heart more clearly than ever.

The sun was her father's heart and her own heart, it was everyone's Divine heart, and the death of the fleshly body symbolized by the moon could never totally eclipse it. Faith and gratitude flaring in her breast, she reached for Senmut's hand.

"Look away now!" the priest commanded.

She did not obey. She never wanted to look away!

"If you see with your heart," Hapuseneb said as he covered her eyes with his hand, "you can witness the same magic every time you look straight into a mirror."

A handful of people, who either had not heard or foolishly disregarded the royal decree, looked up in dread when day suddenly turned to night, fearing the sun was dying, and were blinded. God's Wife made arrangements for the unfortunate victims and their families to be taken care of for life.

...In her hand by night as by day

To see the darkness you create

The day-time darkness thou hast made

To see day like night![53]

* * * * *

"You said once, long ago, I had entered your heart, Seni, and that you could never be angry with me," Hatshepsut told her old tutor one afternoon when he came to visit her.

"And I am not angry with you, Hatshepsut-Maatkare, only concerned some people will fail to see the obvious—that your father lives in your heart and it is his wish you will be fulfilling when you accept the weight of the double crown."

She could still scarcely believe what she had agreed—what she had decided—to do. It was impossible to distinguish between her feelings and Hapuseneb's desires. All the power of Amun was behind her and so too were the most influential men in Kemet—the Great Army Commander Nomti, the Royal Treasurer Nehesj, and the Vizier Akhepersenecb. She had believed herself prepared for the opposition of Sobekmut and other allies of the King's Mother, until they began hurling insults at her using the cowardly forces of gossip while never challenging her directly. It was disturbing living with the image of herself they were circulating of a female hyena flaunting a false penis. They said she was robbing her brother's son of his rights and claiming them for herself like a hyena stealing a baby away in the night with the purpose of devouring it.

In contrast, those Nomarchs who retained a reverent connection to the Ka's of their ancestors, and eschewed hearsay, all supported Maatkare. Also standing behind her with their extremely meaningful silences were the High Priests of Kemet's most ancient temples, including the High Priest of Re in Iuno and Patehuti, High Priest of Thoth in Khemnu. The Temple of Osiris in Abedju—beside which her mother's father had erected a pyramid to his Great Royal Wife, the first God's Wife—openly defended the claims of Ahmose-Nefertari's direct descendent, who was also passionately supported by the Headman of Tyjeny, her good friend Satepihu. Paheri, the Headman of Nekheb, and the First Prophet of Horus in the temple her father had made even more splendid in Nekhen, let it be known they were the sacred guardians of documents proving the situation was not unprecedented. Queen Neferusobek had worn the *nemes* headdress, and long before the great pyramids of White Wall were erected five female Pharaohs had helped shaped the destiny of the Two Lands with their wisdom. In Mennefer itself, Maatkare had one of her most important allies of all—the son of Rasui, Nomarch of the Oryx, Ptah-Hotep, who had recently been anointed High Priest of Ptah.

"Supporters of the King and his mother argue that Queen Neferusobek's brother died without leaving behind a male heir," Seni went on, "which is not the situation now. They say what you intend to do goes completely against tradition and all that is right and good."

"I know what is being said of me, Seni, but you need not worry. In the form of their First Prophets, Amun-Re, Ptah and Thoth, Osiris and Horus are all behind me. I do not plan to usurp the rights and powers of my brother's son, I merely intend to share them as his equal, claiming the larger share of responsibilities while he is young and his Ba is occupied growing into the wisdom of his Ka, as mine has already done."

"Once, long ago, at the beginning of Kemet's history, a brother and a sister ruled jointly as Pharaoh, but since then the like has not been seen in the Two Lands."

"I feel, Seni, it is time that memory was fully revived in our hearts and minds. The reason for its loss is not clear to me, but I am certain the chaotic dust kicked up by the horses of the Setiu buried the glory of sacred times long past even more deeply beneath the sands. It is time to recover and revere the wisdom of the past. It is time for Osiris and Isis, Horus and Hathor, to rule the Two Lands together, side-by-side and hand-in-hand."

Hatshepsut woke often in the night, her feelings suffering a fever of chill dread and flushed excitement that made her too restless to sleep. She longed for her father to appear to her in a dream and reassure her she was doing the right thing, so naturally he did not. He was a god and she was his daughter, it was not fitting he indulge her weakness.

Senmut's statues haunted her in the darkness. In the third carving, he commissioned—in which he was depicted with the princess in the ancient pose of a mother and child—he seamlessly merged tradition with innovation, the acceptable with the shocking. He wore the formal wig she had admired but he was shown in a more casual pose, sitting on the ground with his left leg bent before him. Perched sideways across his lap, the smaller figure of Neferure rested against his upraised knee as his large hands held her close against his chest. A mother and her child were often portrayed in this fashion but Senmut was not a woman, he was a man and a commoner who had risen to the position of royal tutor and the princess was not his child, she was his Divine mistress. In Senmut's statues, the conventional and the unconventional lived as in a single heartbeat.

Hatshepsut felt the heart of the Hidden One beating more strongly than ever in her breast and, through her, in all of Kemet. That all the gods were pleased with her she did not for a moment doubt for she had the full support of their king, Amun-Re. The High Priests of the Two Lands were bound for Waset, as were all its Nomarchs. The Black Dog, the Falcon, the Knife, the Hare and the Viper, the Throne of Horus, the Cobra, the Sistrum, the Crocodile and the Oryx... she lay awake mentally reciting the names of all the Nomes and putting a face to each one. Khenti and Rasui had arrived weeks ago and were lodging in the Temple. Recalling the whole-hearted and passionate support of the Sistrum and the Oryx helped her relax and slip back into sleep, but not until she had lain awake for much too long, doubts and fears hovering like shadows around the lamp she lit to keep her heart company. Demons lived in her head where she either gave them the power to injure her Divine self-assurance or she killed them by showing no mercy whatsoever to feelings of anxiety, timidity and insecurity. In the dead of night, when the door to the Dwat was wide open, her Ba trembled in the fragile nest of its flesh but allied to dreams, her Ka feared only not being able to sleep. Sleep was as death, a blessing during which her strength and beauty—her Attractive Powers—were all replenished, preparing her for the coming days of light and life and all their splendors.

Hatshepsut was already awake when her attendants arrived to prepare her. She forced herself to drink a cup of milk and eat a piece of bread but she waved away the platters of dried fruit in distaste. She craved nothing sweet that day. Later she would feast on bloody meat like a female cheetah and drink as much red wine as Sekhmet had indulged in human blood before Thoth and Geb tamed her.

She wore the vulture crown without the modius of God's Wife or the double plumes of Amun. A strange silence had fallen over the palace and beyond it throughout the entire city. Even Seshen did not speak as she slipped golden sandals onto the queen's feet while around her neck Nafre draped a clenched fist amulet. At last, she was prepared to grasp the destiny written for her by Seshat at the moment of her birth.

The Mistress of the Two Lands appeared at the western gate of her palace *I Shall Not Be Far From Him* and raised her arms in praise when she saw the golden shrine of Amun-Re emerging from His temple. The god was carried aloft on the shoulders of priests and the First Prophet of Amun—a leopard-skin cloak draped over his shoulder—headed the procession, his black staff held high before him. She sank to the ground as he approached, her knees buckling beneath the impact of a wave of magic so powerful the pounding of her heart suddenly seemed to fill the world and strain against the chest of heaven. For a terrifying instant, she feared her senses were escaping her grasp, but her faith in the High Priest saved her as the love they felt for each other somehow held her together. Picking herself up she raised both her arms in praise and to defend herself from the overwhelming force she felt rushing like an invisible river straight toward her.

"How vast is the plan of your Majesty's creation!" Her voice was muffled in her ears as if she was miraculously talking under water. She suffered the dizzying impression that Geb and Tefnut were changing places as heaven poured down to earth through the supernatural canal of Hapuseneb's black staff.

"Oh you my Father!" she gasped. "He has invented all existence! What is it that you love so much it should be done?"

She ceased to be aware of the Nomarchs standing in the palace courtyard because she was abruptly surrounded by animals and birds, trees and serpents. It was like dreaming in daylight. Colors flowed into shapes which expanded and contracted shimmering like sunlit water. A huge cobra rearing menacingly before her was caught in the beak of a giant falcon that soared away with it. A crocodile materialized with open jaws intent on devouring her but was immediately defeated by a spear driven into its mouth. Silent battles were fought around her that lasted mere seconds and yet she knew she was not imagining them as she struggled not to collapse beneath the impact of the force emanating from Hapuseneb's staff. In her heart, she was certain he was influencing the outcomes of the spectral confrontations by challenging a priest who stood beside the Normach of the Crocodile with his right hand extended and two fingers held together. She realized this priest was attempting to direct his own power against the High Priest of Amun but instead of terror, she experienced a transcendent excitement watching her champion defend her.

"I do everything according to what you have ordered!" she cried, her eyes riveted on Hapuseneb's expression, which had never been so intent, so determined, so unbearably arousing. The golden shrine carried behind him ascended like a solid shaft of light from the shadow of his shaved head. Its doors were closed, concealing the god's true form from the multitudes she suspected were being held back more by fear and awe than by her soldiers. She had no idea what everyone else could actually see but to her the magical forces flowing through the great courtyard were as breathtakingly palpable as floodwaters overflowing the canal.

The god's bark stopped before her and the empty litter being carried behind him was brought forward. The silence in Waset had become absolute, as though Thoth in his ibis form was muffling all their ears with his celestial feathers. She suffered the impression that no one dared speak for fear the Divine energy contained in sounds and words would burn the tongues right out of their mouths. Continuing to hold the black branch of his staff up toward heaven, the High Priest of Amun took hold of her right hand with such force she feared her fingers might break in his grasp. She did not care. He led her over to the waiting litter. As she sat down, she glanced over her shoulder. The priest who had been standing beside the Nomarch of the Crocodile was on his knees and cradling his head in his hands as though it suddenly weighed too much for him to hold up.

Hatshepsut-Maatkare was lifted aloft onto shoulders so slick with precious oils they shone like copper. No one and nothing blocked her path as she was borne forward in front of the god. Nomarchs, priests and privileged courtiers following on foot, she felt the journey to the Palace of Maat took far too long as her body began making demands like a traumatized child. She was thirsty. She was hungry. She should have eaten more for breakfast. There should have been ritual pauses along the processional route, where she could reconnect with the High Priest and partake of the water of life before they offered it back to the *neters* sustaining their senses through the enchantment of manifestation. A silence pregnant with wonder followed her all the way from *Ipet Sut* to the Palace of Maat. When her litter was set down, Hapuseneb gripped her hand again to help her up and the heat of his palm made her want him so much she could barely resist the urge to fall into his arms. She gazed at him longingly and the smile with which he responded to the naked desire in her eyes promised her everything. His mouth was hard as he concentrated on the power he was conducting that prevented anyone from speaking a single word against her.

It was blessedly cool inside the temple where she received the jewelry of her Majesty and her jewels of God's Wife. The reason her attendants had left her mostly unadorned that morning was so the First Prophet of Amun could dress her himself in the gold and precious gems symbolizing her spiritual discernment. In the presence of her Mother who created her beauty, Hathor—the First Lady of Waset, the Lady of Heaven and the Lady of the Two Shores—the Majesty of her Overlord Amun embraced her and penetrated her with the miracle of her being. Only a handful of men were present in the innermost sanctuary when the vulture crown was removed from her head. It seemed to her the stone of the False Door was breathing ever so slightly as she looked around her in growing awe. The papyrus columns risen in the body of Hathor—the bones supporting and forming the portico of incarnation—were swaying gently, like the hips of sacred dancers, while deep in the earth beneath her feet a sistrum made of metal and stone and all the elements of the First Occasion hummed and vibrated without respite so she could see and feel, taste, touch and smell. Everything was a part of her body nourishing it with life and joy. The

Great Name was *her* name, Hatshepsut-Maatkare. *She* was the shape of Becoming, both its Divine source and its sensual form.

Standing in the hall erected by Akheperkare where he had made sacrifices to the powers that transformed him into the Lord of the Two Lands, his daughter, Hatshepsut United with Amun, fully awoke to the presence of the Royal Ka in her heart as upon her head was set the Double Crown. Red and white, blood and bone, flesh and light, death and life, all duality was One Authority perceivable only through the magic of Creation.

She took three steps toward the False Door then stopped and turned to face the men who all raised their arms to her in praise. Accepting the *heka* crook of the south and the *nekhekh* flail of the North from Hapuseneb, she crossed her wrists and rested them against her heart as she cast the radiance of her smile upon the High Priests of Ptah and Thoth, of Osiris, Horus and Seth, of Amun and Re, all bearing witness to her second birth and her new name—The Powerful of Ka, Flourishing of Years, Female Horus of Fine Gold, Divine of Appearances, King of Upper and Lower Kemet, Maatkare, Son of Re, Khenmet-Amun Hatshepsut, United with Amun.

As Pharaoh Maatkare, Hatshepsut was borne back to *Ipet Sut* on a roaring wave of exultation that drowned all other sounds and made it seem as if the Celestial River truly had flooded the world. Her co-ruler, Menkheperre, rode behind her in his own litter. He wore a miniature version of the double crown but his little hands were empty of the crook and flail. Hatshepsut-Maatkare had become the Female Falcon and in the throne room of the ceremonial palace, the great lords of Kemet kissed the floor in her presence. Satis observed their obeisance from where she reclined beside her mistress on the dais purring happily.

BOOK FIVE

The Female Falcon

28

Re In His Eye

Maatkare's two monuments of Heh were ready to be transported to Waset. Before her coronation by Amun-Re, she had commissioned the building of a great ship. The tallest sycamore trees throughout the Two Lands were cut down and sent to Abu where they were received by Senmut, her Master of Works. He had promised her the shafts of embodied light would arrive in time to glorify the ascension of Maatkare onto the Horus Throne of the Living, and she believed him. Her trust in her Superior Steward was so great her appetite was unaffected by any serious concerns, but she still suffered the occasional nightmare. Should one of her monuments crack or sink en route to *Ipet Sut* or, even worse, if either one or both of them should fall while they were being erected, the disaster would seriously injure her confidence. She did not permit herself to imagine what the men who had opposed her kingship would say about it. It was simply inconceivable her first act as Pharaoh not proceed as smoothly as her whole-hearted devotion to Maat warranted.

Senmut wrote her nearly everyday, informing her in detail of the work's progress. He let her know he had commemorated the great task she had entrusted to him in an inscription cut into a rock on the island of Sehel:

Hereditary princess, great of praise and charm, great of love, one to whom Re has given the kingship, righteously in the opinion of the Ennead of Gods, King's Daughter, King's Sister, God's Wife, Great King's Wife, Hatshepsut, may she live, beloved of Satis, Lady of Abu, Beloved of Khnum, Lord of the first wild waters.

Presentation of this work to God's Wife, Mistress of the Two Lands by the Seal Bearer of the King, a great and beloved friend, the Great Steward Senmut, True of Voice.

The coming done by a Hereditary Prince, a great confidant of God's Wife, one with whose utterance the Lady of the Two Lands is content, Great Steward of the King's Daughter, Neferure, may she live, Senmut, in order to lead the works on the two great Monuments of Millions of Years. Then it happened as that which was ordered was made, and it was because of the power of her Majesty that it happened.[54]

Once her monuments had been freed from the earth the 'people of the entire Two Lands were gathered in one place, the young men were mustered'[55] and a canal was carefully dug beneath the stone shafts until only their top and bottom ends rested on the two banks. When the River rose and the sluice gate was opened the floodwaters rushed into the canal. The great double ship she had had built was loaded down with stones and pushed and towed until it floated directly beneath the monuments. The blocks weighing the vessel down were then removed. As it rose gradually into the light, its massive loads came gently to rest on a bed of sledges. Wrapped in protective bandages and secured with ropes, her offerings to Heh began their joyful journey to the River, on which they sailed downstream with gladness of heart. They were towed by three rows of nine boats directed by three master barges manned by thirty-two oarsmen. The great vessel bearing the monuments was escorted by three ships—captained by Senmut, Nehesj and Satepihu respectively—where offerings were made and prayers spoken. As a reward for his fervent loyalty, she had honored the Headman of Tjeny with a prominent place in the great procession. Satepihu's long and narrow face was characterized by prominent features and his ears were the largest she had ever seen on a man—fleshly flags indicating he was a very good listener who heard all that was said and reported it to her whenever necessary.

When her two Monuments of Heh landed in peace in Waset, Maatkare could feel the wonder and joy beating in the hearts of all her people as they beheld her gloriously effective piety. Once the massive pillars were dragged off the ship, it would take some time to erect and decorate them, but their presence had the effect of making everyone feel as hopefully lighthearted as they themselves were heavy. Pleasure barges of all sizes rowed and sailed into the crowded dock as everyone who was able traveled to Waset in order to join the festivities and offer bulls and oxen to the king of the gods, Amun-Re. The carefree and often bawdy revelry the multitudes indulged in during the inundation was muted by a reverent sense of expectation on the afternoon the Monuments of Heh—their tops pointing earthward—began moving slowly up the ramps of sand towering on either side of the eastern entrance to the temple.

Hatshepsut was more impressed than ever by the power of Number and the calculations making what seemed impossible actually happen. Scribes of every age remained cool and clean as they directed the work of healthy young men chosen to weigh the ropes down with stones, and then to pull on them with all their strength. The soldiers of Heh labored in the fierce sun for hours without respite and come nightfall were well rewarded by the king with as much goat stew, loaves of bread and sweet onions as they could consume and all the beer they could drink.

The moment the bottom of her first monument made contact with its stone base, she caught her breath and held it in a torment of suspense. The groove chiseled into the support, Senmut had told her, was fitted with a semi-circular copper rod. The flat side rested in the slot while the rounded end faced up and received the triangular socket cut into the rear edge of the monument. Understanding how it worked helped calm her but she still found it hard to breathe as, with excruciating slowness, the stone shaft suspended on the edge of the man-made mountain of sand was pulled up by ropes wrapped tightly around its upper half. When it finally made contact with the base the socket bored into its back edge helped it roll smoothly up into place, and yet the final moments were the most harrowing of all. If the monument's momentum was too great it would plunge forward and crush the rope tower before smashing against its mirror image resting on the opposite ramp. If that happened, she would go to her Ka on the spot. Smiling to conceal her anxiety, she watched the straining muscles of the men pulling on the ropes and vowed to reward them all with lovely little town homes if their efforts proved successful, which they absolutely had to.

Maatkare truly felt herself to be in the company of kings as her first Monument of Heh landed gently on its stone base and remained solidly planted there, its unadorned pyramidion pointing toward heaven. She let out her breath and her small public smile broadened into one of true joy. She was completely confident now the erection of her second monument would go just as smoothly, after which scaffolding would quickly be built around them both and sheets of gold-leaf applied to all four of their sides. Only then would they come to life and receive their names as they reflected the sun's light. On their pyramidions she would live forever receiving the double drown and the power of Life from Amun-Re. She could not wait to see them gradually begin glowing as the sun rose until they shone so brightly everyone would be blinded with joy witnessing heaven descending to earth every morning.

Weeks later, after the scaffolding was removed from around the monuments and the achievement of her Majesty was fully visible to gods and men, Maatkare addressed the *rekhyt*.[56] She stood in her palace's Window of Appearance[57] framed in gold and lapis-lazuli wearing a white sheathe dress of mist-linen through which the dusky buds of her nipples were visible, a golden collar with falcon-head terminals and the green-striped *nemes* headdress of Pharaoh. Her wrists were crossed over her chest and in her fists she grasped the crook and the flail.

"Behold the sacred elevation of the First Occasion!" she proclaimed. "Behold the Eye of the Lord to the Limit—His favorite place, which bears His perfection and gathers His followers!"[58]

Then she repeated the words spoken by his father to King Merikare, True of Voice:

"People, the flock of the god, are provided for!

"He has made the sky and the earth for their heart!

"He has made the heart's air so that they may live when they breathe!

"They are his likenesses, who came from his body!

"He rises in the sky for their hearts!

"He has made for them the plants, flocks and fish that feed them!

"He makes sunlight for their hearts and sails across the sky to see them!

"He has raised a shrine about them: when they weep he is hearing…

"The god knows every name!⁵⁹

"Behold your Father living in His Mother, Re in his Eye! Behold your King Maatkare, Hathor-Raet!"

The roar of rejoicing drowned out any other words she might have spoken.

Maatkare erected a shrine inside the eastern entrance to Amun's-Re's temple. Every morning for a whole month, she made an offering to the sun as it rose over the horizon embraced by the two great Ka arms of her shining monuments of Millions of Years.

* * * * *

The fledgling falcon's two wet nurse's had both been appointed by Maatkare—the wife of Ahmose-Pennekhbet, the Mistress of the House Ipu, and the wife of her dear friend Satepihu, the Mistress of the House Tinet-iunet. Both women served as her Eyes and Ears in the palace ruled by the King's Mother. Ipu had recently borne a daughter named Satioh and her breasts were filled with milk. Unlike Tinet-iunet, Ipu was not really her friend, but Hatshepsut knew she was devoted to her husband, who fully supported the female king, and would never think to question his position on anything. Normally she preferred less blindly dutiful and more whole-hearted subjects but in this case it was necessary to make due with Ipu.

Maatkare's two Monuments of Heh breathed energy and purpose into her every day. The heart of the southern Seal Room never stopped pumping heralds and scribes, Nomarchs and governors, priests and headmen and myriad other officials. Every morning she traveled to the administrative palace in a new litter carried on the shoulders of eight magnificent Kushites brought to her as a gift by the King's Son of Kush, Seni. She had finally retired Kanefer and awarded him a fine little house in town. Sitting enthroned behind a sky-blue curtain decorated with gold and silver stars, she sometimes missed the familiar site of her favorite litter bearer but did not permit herself to indulge the sentiment. She was the Female Falcon—she saw things differently now as her boundless power gave her a new perspective on almost everything. It was difficult not to resent how long she had lived with clipped wings as she felt them opening wide and lifting her up inside so she knew there was nothing she could not do.

She encouraged the King's Son to recruit more Kushites into the royal service as bowmen and foot soldiers. It seemed imminently sensible to conquer as many foreigners as possible with the beautiful efficacy of believing in Maat before enlisting the forces of Seth to deal with the rest of them. Currently on its way to Waset was a delegation of the Keftiu headed by Prince Kallikrates. She was looking forward to seeing him again. His splendid ships were reputedly so weighed down with gifts his oarsmen never rested. Work was progressing on the new palaces and governmental buildings she had ordered constructed in Perunefer. When they were finished she would maker her first royal progress north as king.

Though she held the crook and flail only on ceremonial occasions she never ceased to exercise the responsibilities they symbolized. With the crook, she fed and protected the *rekhyt* and with the flail, she would smite their enemies whenever necessary. On the day the moon had taken a bite out of the sun, whatever hostile thoughts they might have entertained in the Land of the Inverted Water—where one of the Two Rivers flowed unnaturally south instead of north—they kept to themselves. Kemet's northern and southern borders were peaceful and secure but they would not always remain so for all manifested life obeyed cycles by which it was ruled. When the agents of chaos inevitably attacked again, she would be ready for them. Foreign lands paid a just tribute to Pharaoh for it was the Son of Re who kept God alive in all his creations. Nowhere else on earth was the Divine force embodied in the sun—Maat— served with such relentless and successful devotion. Not even on the island of the Keftiu surrounded by magical dolphins did Maat thrive as she did in the Two Lands.

Officials who had served her faithfully when she was God's Wife and Queen Regent—such as the "royal cat" Tai who remained in Mennefer rooting out destructively selfish rats masquerading as noble men—were rewarded with gifts of land and oxen, jars of wine and bolts of the softest linen, ivory boxes in which to store their seals and rings, pleasure barges complete with oarsmen, and tame gazelles for their gardens. The gifts were distributed according to the officials' needs and dispositions. Yet even the king's generosity was subject to limits—the heartfelt balance which maintained the health of her Beloved Earth and dictated it was wrong to impoverish anyone to make someone else rich.

Maatkare spent long months meeting personally with every Nomarch, with the governors of provinces and their overseers and even with the headmen of obscure villages. In the heat of summer, the stench of greed and dishonesty were even more noxious. It was disturbing how many powerful men were amazed to learn Pharaoh cared about the health and well-being of all the souls living in their Nomes, whether they were priests, fishermen, wealthy ladies or the low-born women who serviced soldiers. People with painfully small hearts were incapable of imagining how much love could fit inside human beings true to Maat with all their thoughts and feelings. She was grimly amused by the spectacle of provincial scribes, who served their masters like dogs, attempting to overwhelm the royal overseers with cartfuls of clay tablets and papyrus parchments—an impressive display of clerical diligence designed to bury their corruption. But there was no masking the smell of lies with the oil of the desert date or any other perfume. Senmut and his assistants, increased to eighteen men, were inundated by the quantity of official records they were entrusted to examine.

Even though paper was no substitute for her soft skin, ever since her coronation official documents were all she put in Senmut's hands. The way he made her feel when he took her in his arms made it impossible for her to concentrate, therefore she saw to it they were never alone together anymore. In public, she constantly sought to assure him with her eyes and her smiles that he had not fallen into her disfavor and his exile from her bedchamber was only temporary. She believed—she desperately hoped—he understood. She had become the Son of Re and, for the moment, could not behave like a woman. But she was also Hathor-Raet, she knew she would return to her body one day—she *had* to—and when she did there was nothing she would not be able to do. She was the Female Falcon—no one had the right to deny her anything she desired. She savored the proximity of her sexual freedom like a drop of frankincense without biting into it or even trying to picture it in distracting detail. There was a great deal of important work to be done before she could relax into her new position and once again wear earrings.[60]

Over a dozen headmen, six governors and two Nomarchs were stripped of their titles and possessions and forever banished from the Two Lands along with the scribes who had been foolish enough to serve them instead of Maat. The decision was easy to make for the men in question were so foul not even the fat of the white hippo could have rubbed them clean of their sins. Setau, the Nomarch of Great Land—at least outwardly reformed by the presence of Rasui's son in his household—was not amongst those sent into exile. Maatkare sat in judgment wearing the blue crown and holding against her heart the flail with which she punished evil doers. She was performing the cleansing *sen shem shem* on her kingdom as she did every morning on her mouth. To represent the will of Pharaoh it was necessary a man speak with a true voice. The breath of his heart could not reek of lies, nor could his deeds be as ineffective as rotten molars when it came to nourishing the contentment of all the people living in his realm. Ahmose-Pennekhbet had cautioned her against being too harsh on influential men but she had not listened. She was the heart of Kemet's body—if her actions did not beat sure and strong from the very first moment she assumed the Horus Throne of the Living the country would become vulnerable to the diseases of greed and fear and grow weaker rather than stronger and healthier. It was vital, she told her officials that the power of the Female Falcon be felt everywhere. Her determination to root out corruption had to be as obvious as a raptor's ability to dive to earth and capture snakes and rodents in its talons.

Wearing an old-fashioned cylinder seal around his neck engraved with spirals surrounding the hieroglyphs spelling his name, a symbol of prestige, Senmut oversaw the production of new scarab seals in which Hathor-Sekhmet spread her wings protectively over the *shenu* ring containing Hatshepsut's throne name,

Maatkare. There were many more scarabs being produced for use in the Seal Room in addition to decorative scarabs—worn by Kemet's nobility as a sign of devotion to the Female Horus—on which her name appeared alongside the images of protective deities. Scarabs inscribed with *God's Wife, Neferure* had also gone under production. The king's daughter had recently begun her purification and was ready to join with Amun.

Together Maatkare and Senmut designed many of the amulets daily pressed into wet clay and hot wax to seal documents, jars of costly unguents and boxes of all shapes and sizes used to store royal records as well as taxes in the form of earthly treasures brought to the palace from across the Two Lands and beyond. With an Eye of Horus amulet—its base inscribed with *Maatkare, Beloved of Amun*—she sealed the scrolls on which were recorded the list of supplies and the names of the men constituting the expedition she sent northeast into the Land of Turquoise in search of untapped mines rich in the stone sacred to Hathor. An intelligent and energetic young military scribe named Kheruef, recommended to her by Troop Commander Inebni, was honored with the task of exploring the mysterious valleys watched over by Sopdu, Lord of the East, in search of additional and hopefully even richer sources of the precious blue stone.

* * * * *

The arrival of a prince of the Keftiu in Waset was a joyful event. Seshen and Meresankh talked about it for weeks afterward as did Neferure, who had fallen half in love with Kallikrates and with a Keftiu courtier whose hair was as red as Seth's and whose eyes were bluer than the summer River. Hatshepsut felt sorry for her daughter. There was no equivalent of Hapuseneb in Neferure's life and her future husband was barely four-years-old. Thutmose would eventually be leaving for Mennefer, where he would be educated in the Temple of Ptah until he began his military training in Perunefer. Tinet-iunet had informed her the King's Mother was planning to build herself a tomb in Kemet's most ancient city of eternity and that her mind was entirely occupied with the project. Hatshepsut was glad to hear this and made arrangements with the High Priest of Ptah, and with her passionately loyal Tai, to keep Isis busy with religious and secular duties so she spent as little time with her son as possible.

Like her mother, Neferure loved animals, but her tastes tended more toward mischievous monkeys than regal cheetahs. She was also very fond of dwarfs. As soon as she became God's Wife, she surrounded herself with miniature attendants. Although Hatshepsut could not understand her daughter's predilection for squat-legged men and women with unnaturally large heads, she did not question it. After all, Bes was Hathor's devoted companion. The affectionate respect the princess showed distorted people could also be regarded as admirably profound. She wanted to believe Nefi was making an important statement with the courtly trend she was setting—that the Ka is much more important than the physical vessel containing it, which Khnum shapes according to everyone's individual destiny. To look down on dwarfs was to question the Divine impulse of the *neters* who made them for reasons only love might fathom.

The Prince of the Keftiu presented Neferure with so many presents it took two fully loaded oxen-drawn carts to transport them to her apartments. The princess was especially enamored of a vase Hatshepsut would certainly not have liked to see in her own rooms. Kallikrates explained the ghastly creature adorning both sides of the vessel lived deep in the Great Green.

"Do they eat dolphins?" Neferure asked with an eagerness her mother did not approve of.

"No, they do not eat dolphins." He smiled as he spoke but abruptly his expression sobered. "At least I do not believe they do…"

"But such a creature as this could easily catch any fish it wanted to with those eight serpent-like arms and those huge eyes surely nothing can escape being seen by! Why does it have another head on top of the first one? Is that where its mouth is, on the back of its second head?"

Hatshepsut put two fingers together and made the sign for protection toward her daughter. "The Keftiu would not decorate their homes with images of evil spirits," she stated firmly.

"My sincere apologies, Prince Kallikrates," Neferure said but the little smile on her face belied the regret she expressed.

Maatkare made gifts of portions of the Keftiu's tribute to her most beloved friends and devoted officials. Mentekhenu, her Chief of Security, received a fine dagger, its blade inlaid with the exquisitely detailed scenes of a lion hunt. Hapuseneb was permitted to take whatever he desired. She chose Senmut's presents herself, including over a dozen vessels painted with the running spiral decoration she herself favored. She had never visited her unique friend's home but it had been described to her by Nafre, who sometimes met Ah-hotep there.

"His house is modestly small but his garden is large and beautifully landscaped. His servants say he knows exactly what all the bushes and trees need in order to be happy, how often they should be watered and trimmed and everything else involved with caring for them so they flourish. They also believe he holds converse with the gods at night for he spends hours gazing up at the heavens and drawing on sheets of papyrus he himself lovingly burnishes. He stores them in a special little room which is jealously guarded by his steward."

"He is mapping the stars? He never told me he had such priestly inclinations, although I suppose it is not surprising considering no less than three of his brothers serve in the temple. Are his personal attendants very pretty?"

"Yes, *very* pretty," Nafre replied with more relish than her mistress felt was strictly necessary. "But he does not lie down with them."

"How can you possibly know that?"

"Merely by looking at the girls' faces when they serve him food and drink, my lady. It is obvious they long to do much more for him and that their desires have not yet been satisfied. As you know, Majesty, he has greatly offended all the ladies of Waset by refusing to choose a wife from amongst them. It is rumored he is seeking a concubine instead, at least for the moment."

"Is there any truth to this rumor?"

"I do not believe so. The most beautiful concubines have attempted to become better acquainted with him and he has ignored them all, even the famous singer and conductor, Heset. Soon it will be said he prefers boys to women."

That last remark made Hatshepsut angry but she did not show it. The joy of the future depended on the patience of the present. Whenever her feelings threatened to run away from her, she reminded herself of this and deliberately changed the subject.

Jewelry, stone figurines, metal axes and copper cauldrons brought as tribute by the Keftiu crowded the Royal Storerooms alongside an abundance of jars, large and small, holding special infusions reputed to possess medicinal and beautifying uses. Hapuseneb, Senmut and Ibenre were some of the noblemen present at one of the banquets she held for Kallikrates, during which he intrigued them all with his herbal lore. Stubborn coughs could be treated, he said, with a distillation of laurel, sage and lavender. Kemet's physicians also extracted the essential oils of many herbs, such as cumin and coriander, to treat illnesses but it was intriguing to learn some plants had been introduced into the Two Lands long ago by the Keftiu, including rosemary, one of her favorites. Her attendants frequently washed her hair with warm water infused with rosemary and gave her hot rosemary tea to drink on the rare occasions she suffered from a headache. Amidst the many personal gifts the foreign prince offered her were gilded wooden boxes containing the sorts of cosmetics used by the highest ranking ladies on his island. He explained they were made from mixtures of anise and beeswax, honey, olive oil, carnations and resin.

During the conversation on medicinal herbs, on more than one occasion Hapuseneb looked long and hard at her in a way that almost made her forget what she had been about to say. She distracted herself from the effect his penetrating stare had on her by thinking about the priestesses of the Keftiu who allowed their bodies to be caressed by snakes, wore dresses completely exposing their breasts and were served by handsome young men. The only women in the Keftiu delegation were pretty young females who would remain in Waset as part of Pharaoh's tribute. She gave one of these girls to Senmut in the hope of assuaging his frustration by tempting him with an exotic bloom.

Her Superior Steward continued producing extremely interesting statues of himself and Neferure. The three most recent pieces were all similar to each other. He was depicted in the traditional seated pose but with the added touch of Neferure's little head emerging from the center of his cloak-enfolded lap. The princess looked as though she might drown in all the hieroglyphs flowing around her. One of these statues sat in his home while the other two graced an offering court in the Temple of Amun. Largely due to Senmut, the block statue was once again becoming popular. It was a good thing she was planning to expand God's house for soon there would not be enough room to accommodate all the officials who desired to sit forever in the Divine presence. Hatshepsut believed the power of a feeling grew the more it was expressed. She understood why her unique friend continued producing images of himself with the princess, who loved him as deeply as she ever had even though she was no longer the child he depicted and her lessons with him had ended.

Senmut's most recent statues intrigued and pleased her as much as his first two because they incorporated profoundly meaningful elements into the traditional design. On either side of Neferure's head, strange and never before seen hieroglyphs spelled *Maatkare, Khenemet Amun, United with Amun.* Her throne name *Maatkare* was written by an Eye of Horus which formed part of the body of a flying vulture—its head and beak flowing from the eyebrow—that grasped a pair of Ka arms in its talons. The figure of a man—an *ankh* fused with a *was* scepter rising from between his shoulders in place of his head—strode forward holding an *ankh* in his left hand and a *was* scepter in his right fist to spell *Khenemet Amun.* Senmut had created an entirely new way of writing her name. The inscriptions flanking Neferure's head on the two statues read:

Images which I have made from the devising of my own heart and from my own labor; they have not been found in the writing of the ancestors.[81]

Senmut's creations were fresh and new, they invigorated her like a swim in her pool on a hot afternoon after which everything looked even more beautiful and anything felt possible. Stone storage vessels, wooden linen chests and cosmetic boxes, alabaster eye paint tubes and unguent jars, faience amulets, copper lamps and ivory-legged couches—everything inscribed with her titles *God's Wife* and *Great Royal Wife* was removed from her rooms in the palace *I Shall Not Be Far From Him* and put into storage. She would give everything away eventually to anyone deserving of her generosity. Her personal attendants naturally received those objects they most admired and coveted, as did the Royal Nurse Ah-hotep and Inet's faithful attendants, who continued to care for their mindless mistress with sweet smiles and amazingly positive dispositions.

Ka-hotep and other royal artisans had designed the lovely new objects gracing her apartments inscribed with her King's titles. Ivory, bronze, copper, wood, stone, gold and white-gold, silver, glass, bone, faience, clay and turquoise—all substances possessed a uniquely symbolic beauty that expressed subtly profound truths to her heart. But first it was necessary she know as much as she could about each substance and how it was transformed by craftsmen. Duauneheh was more than happy to describe the different processes to her. For example, her favorite flask and stand had been hammered from a single sheet of bronze and then scraped smooth. The tapered end of the flask—reminiscent of the *heart* hieroglyph—could not stand on its own but needed the spool-shaped base which reflected its lovely curves but was broader and firmly planted on the floor. *She* was like this vase and the men around her fully supported her.

Her steward, Dhout, was ecstatic when she ordered three large chests full of new dresses even finer than those she already owned all hemmed with gold thread and designed to flare open around her ankles so she could walk as freely as a man. She also commissioned mirrors with fully gilded wooden handles in the shape of a papyrus plant from which Hathor's small head emerged crowned by a large silver disc. She had been better able to appreciate why the goddess was depicted with the prominent ears of a cow ever since she suffered from a head cold and Ibenre explained to her how the inner ear still contains traces of the Primordial Waters.

"It is the ear that roots us in space," he told her, "orienting us to the four directions of earth and the celestial horizon beyond them. The ears experience the Word which at every moment gives a specific form to God's infinite potential."

The reflection in all her mirrors remained essentially the same—her smiling face was as lovely as ever—yet she felt herself changing inside as everything she perceived took deeper root in her thoughts and feelings. It was necessary to own many mirrors in order to reflect her different moods but most important of all was the one that showed her Maatkare, King of Kemet. For this very special see-face, she chose a more archaic design and had it fashioned of bronze. Bronze was harder than silver, gold or copper and the color of the sun blended with the darkness of the Dwat. The base of the slender handle was engraved with four wavy lines reminiscent of the Primordial Waters and at the top it curved open and down like the horns of a cow. On the "horns" perched two falcons facing away from each other, representing the One dividing into Two and forming the bosom of the eastern horizon, between which Atum-Re's eternal life-force rose every morning as the solar disc reflecting her face. The mirror she gazed into as Maatkare reminded her every day was a magical occasion and that God smiled through her lips.

The workhouse attached to *Ipet Sut*—where bread was baked and beer brewed for offerings as well as to feed lower-ranking servants of the god—was being expanded. It was the foremost desire of Maatkare's heart to make God's House much larger and greater than it already was. To that end, she met with Hapuseneb in the temple garden in the cool of early morning in the season of

Immersion. They sat facing each other on a bed of leopard skins, spread out beneath a blue-and-yellow striped canopy supported by black ivory posts with ends carved in the form of lion's paws.

"This pavilion is new," she observed.

"Does it please you?"

"Naturally it does."

"I had it made for us."

"Then it pleases me even more, Hapuseneb."

The personal scribe and steward of the High Priest, Amenhotep, sat cross-legged in a corner.

"It is my desire," she said, signaling to Amenhotep that he should begin writing, "to rebuild those parts of Ipset-Sut beginning to show their age in a way disgraceful to Amun-Re's eternal nature. There are ancient but still rich quarries near my father's River chapel in The Place of Rowing I intend to re-open for the purpose of restoring God's house in stone, so it truly stands for Millions of Years as it was meant to."

She paused, giving the scribe time to catch up with her.

"Portions of the temple floors, and the lower half of the walls, will be painted black, for it is from Atum's infinite darkness that all light and life emerges. It is also my wish," she reached up and caressed the *heart* amulet hanging between her breasts carved in the shape of a cluster of grapes, "to offer you, the First Prophet of Amun and Governor of the South, a rock-cut chapel near Akheperkhare's. Every time the River rises your statue will be embraced by the floodwaters and imbued with Nun's timeless essence and creative powers."

Amenhotep recorded everything she said as Hapuseneb sat staring into space over her head, his expression unreadable.

She was compelled to ask, "Is something wrong, master?"

"No," he said, meeting her eyes, "but there is something missing."

"Tell me what it is and I will build it."

He made a brief slicing gesture with his right hand. "We are offending Min."

Amenhotep stopped writing.

"On the night of the full moon in the month of Pamenot," he went on quietly, "Ibenre will bring you what we need, Hatshepsut-Maatkare, to properly and safely worship Amun-Kamutef together."

As he stared into her eyes, Min's invisible lightning struck directly between her thighs and rendered her speechless.

"As you know, my lady, Amun created many different plants and herbs, some of them especially designed to serve and enhance Min's blessing. Ibenre will instruct your attendants on how to administer the substance he will deliver to your bedroom."

* * * * *

In the month of Pamenot, Hatshepsut awaited the full moon of as if on that night the gods would once again walk on earth. The fact that she was a little frightened only intensified her excitement.

The sandstone quarries near The Place of Rowing were re-opened and would soon begin transporting the material to Waset on a regular basis. While awaiting its arrival she set the temple artists the task of re-carving her husband's bark shrine. The image of herself as The Great Royal Wife no longer reflected reality and had to be altered. The *shenu* ring was the first to be reworked so it embraced her throne name *Maatkre*. Her shoulders were broadened, indicating she was strong enough to bear the weight of kingship, her wig was transformed into the *nemes* headdress and her queen's scepter became the crook of Pharaoh. Her submissive femininity, expressed by the close placement of her feet, was altered by extending her right leg so she strode purposefully forward. But even though the outlines of a royal kilt were drawn above her knees, traces of her form-fitting dress were deliberately left in tact around her ankles and shoulder strap. She was both the daughter and the Son of Re because the Royal Ka lived in her heart not her genitals.

The Monument of Akheperenre, Amun Divine by his Monuments, erected in *Ipet Sut* had been completed but was now modified in select places. Because it served as a family history, she did not alter any of the images and she changed her name from *Hatshepsut* to *Maatkare* in only one of the *shenu* rings identifying her. The figure of the princess Neferure standing behind her mother—who at the time was the Great Royal Wife offering life to Amun-Re while receiving it from Him—was enhanced to show her current status of God's Wife. Akheperenre's name was also in some places superimposed over that of his son. Menkheperre had for a time been his father's direct successor but that had ceased to be the case—it was Hatshepsut-Maatkare who truly ruled after her brother and husband.

The responsibilities of queen had all fallen upon Neferure. Hatshepsut often wondered what her daughter was thinking. The princess had many friends she enjoyed spending time with but how much she actually cared for them was a mystery. When Neferure was not in the mood to talk not even Thoth and Seshat holding her upside down by the ankles would be able to get a word out of her.

"She simply likes people no matter how wise and beautiful or ugly and foolish they are," Senmut explained to her in a tone that implied Neferure was superior to her mother in this regard. They were relaxing together in her Pleasure House accompanied by Nafre.

She took no offense because she felt guilty about how badly she was treating him lately. They saw each other nearly every day in the Seal Room but her attendants were always conspicuously present in the evening when he arrived at the palace to perform his duty as Superintendent of the Royal Bedroom.

"I do not have a problem with her liking people, Senmut, but there are times when her..." she searched for the right word, "*disposition* does not strike me as appropriately reverent. The other day, when we were giving the seventeen deities of *Ipet Sut* their dinner, she seemed to be rushing through the offerings simply because Useramun had challenged her to another game of bowling and she did not want to be late."

"She roles the small ball into the hole every time," he sounded proud, "and when it is her turn to block his rolls with the larger ball she is just as skillful. She makes it impossible for him to score higher and he hates that."

"Useramun is very proud," she agreed.

"And you approve."

"Naturally I do." She resented his flat, almost judgmental tone. "A man who does not cultivate pride in himself offends God who created him."

"I agree, my lady. But true a man does not run away from a challenge merely to spare his pride."

Suddenly she desired him so much she was forced to avoid his eyes.

Nafre abruptly went and sat behind her harp. She ran her fingertips urgently across the strings and made further conversation impossible as she sang:

Ho, what she's done to me—that girl!
  And I'm to grin and just bear it?
Letting me stand there huge in her door
  while she goes catfoot inside
Not even a word: "Have a quiet walk home!"
  (dear god give me relief)
Stopping her ears the whole damned night
  and me only whispering, "Share!"[62]

29

Leopard in the Reeds

It was the evening of the full moon in the month of Pamenot in year three of the Good Goddess Maatkare, Flourishing of Years, and the Good God Menkheperre, Given Life. The king's attendants worked in devoted silence to make her as beautiful as Hathor. They cleaned the skin beneath her fingernails and toenails with an ivory splinter. They rubbed her entire body with a cleansing cream made from safflower oil and lime juice, and then washed it off with water taken from a copper jar in which floated a blue lotus flower. Hatshepsut endured the routine standing, her eyes partially blinded to everything around her by visions of the coming night. Nafre massaged *hekenu* perfume into all her mistress' limbs and beneath her arms rubbed a little crushed frankincense gum mixed with sesame oil. Meresankh offered her a low chair. Seating herself on it, she spread her thighs and Seshen applied a warm salve to the delicate lips of her sex. The special mixture was made from the boiled and crushed bones of birds blended with sesame oil, cucumber, sycamore and gum tree juice. As her attendant liberally applied the cream, the decoration of the unguent dish became visible beneath her fingertips—frogs and ducks greeting the sun rising over lotus buds. While she waited for the paste to dry, her fingers and toenails were painted red.

Pain woke her to the present when the exfoliating cream was quickly stripped off her labia, taking most of her pubic hair with it. The rest was carefully shaved off. Her sex was soothingly perfumed with an extract of the blue lotus while her shoulder-length hair was brushed back away from her face with an ivory comb.

The setting sun—perched for a moment on one of the walls of her garden—gazed ardently into her dressing room through a window from which the screen had been removed for the afternoon. A green copper ore imported from the mountainous regions of Roshawet, malachite was applied to her upper eyelids and used to lengthen the corners of her eyes. Made from galena ground into a fine dark-grey powder, Khol was smoothed with a moistened bronze applicator directly above both her upper and lower lashes. After a red gloss made from duck fat and ochre was brushed onto her lips, she was ready to receive her wig. Hatshepsut chose the longest one she owned, its mass of fine braids falling below her breasts and tapering into waving, snake-like ends. To adorn the wig she selected a fillet made of precious stones in the form of mandrake fruits interspersed with lotus and poppy petals to which a freshly picked lotus flower was attached so it hung down over her forehead.

Gently, her scented body was wrapped in a sky-blue linen dress embroidered with tiny daisies, its straps just broad enough to cover her breasts. A collar reflecting the design of her fillet was draped over her chest and a duck ring made of glazed blue steatite was slipped onto the middle finger of her left hand. Her earlobes were decorated with earrings made from hollow gold hoops all soldered together. Leather sandals dyed a dark-red were slipped onto her feet and a *Menit* necklace, its counterpoise crowned by a woman's head, was solemnly offered to her by Nafre. Hatshepsut accepted the vulva of the goddess as servants silently began lighting lamps throughout the room. The solar disc had disappeared behind the garden wall and night was swiftly falling.

The mixture Ibenre had delivered to her bedroom had already been given to her. Her pleasure litter was waiting. Behind a dark-green curtain embroidered with mandrake bushes, she reclined comfortably on woolen blankets smoothed by a lion's skin. She had not made use of this particular litter since the death of her husband. She did not attempt to conceal her destination but traveled openly. Everyone would know she was on her way to properly serve her Father and Husband Amun-Min with her woman's body. She was bound for the High Priest's private retreat on the north-eastern shore of the River. She had never been there before and the closer she got the faster her heart beat in her breast like a festival drum.

Pharaoh's personal guard walked on all four sides of her litter. Her traveling couch was set gently down on the stone of the royal road after every eight-hundred paces and Nafre, traveling in a separate litter behind her, dismounted to offer her mistress refreshment from a well. She sipped the cool water gratefully but impatiently, the vivid colors of the sunset reflecting her excitement. The western sky, streaked with dark-red clouds, evoked the lips of the Goddess as the dying light gave the Divine vein of the River the appearance of silver slowly being tarnished by darkness.

"Raise my curtain, Nafre. I wish to feel the north wind on my skin."

Torches had been lit on either side of the narrow road leading to the High Priest's home. The oiled flesh of her Kushite litter bearers gleamed like black ivory as the burning path guided them directly to a small open court where Hapuseneb stood waiting for her. When her conveyance was lowered, he offered her his hand to help her up and as his fingers slipped away they caressed hers lingeringly. Walking in a conscious dream, she preceded him into the house he had built for himself and no one else. His wife and his children had never been there, it was his special place, and now it would be theirs.

The main entrance led into an intimate space completely open on one side to the moonlit River and supported by four blue-and-yellow papyrus bud pillars. Wine jars—sealed with herbal stoppers and decorated with garlands of lotus flowers—flanked two gilded couches supported by bulls' hooves placed close together at the western end of the room facing the River. Triple translucent alabaster lamps, their flowering buds burning a delicately scented oil, provided a soft golden light. To the north and south closed doors concealed four more chambers.

She was surprised when a steward failed to greet them as they entered.

Somewhat insulted by the lack of formality with which he had chosen to entertain his king, she held the *Menit* necklace firmly beneath her left breast and turned to face him. The foolish sentiment died the instant she met his eyes. Suddenly all she remembered was that he was a man and she was a woman.

Beneath a collar strung with alternating rows of red, blue and gold beads, Hapuseneb wore a shirt made from a leopard's skin molded to his firm chest and abdomen. The animal's front paws draped over each of his shoulders, its claws resting against the skin of his forearms, and two deliberate narrow rips in the fabric exposed his nipples. The leopard's hind paws rested against the backs of his thighs beneath a short old-fashioned kilt. He had donned a formal wig and his leather sandals were adorned with golden beads.

He said quietly, "We have waited a very long time for this, Hatshepsut."

"Yes…" Hathor's overwhelming presence made speech feel almost impossible.

Extending her right arm, she offered him the *Menit* necklace.

He took it from her and, holding her eyes, kissed the face of the woman whose head crowned the counterpoise four times.

No night on earth had ever felt like that one. The moment Hapuseneb set the necklace down on a table and pulled her into his arms, the two lions of the horizon suddenly seemed to turn and face each other. Space and time as she had always experienced them ceased to exist. The first thing he did was wrestle her body into submission with a long deep kiss. Then he lifted her up in his arms and spread her across one of the couches. A cool breeze from the west replaced the warmth of his flesh and she trembled. Seating himself beside her, he held a narrow stone container to her face in which something smoldered.

"Inhale," he commanded.

She obeyed him and the room spun around her. When dimensions settled back into place, she saw him holding the vessel beneath his own nose. His eyes, staring challengingly into hers, were as black as the heart of the Dwat. Silently, he encouraged her take three more deep breaths of the intoxicating substance. A hand she vaguely realized was attached to the body of a girl wearing only a colorful bead girdle and a shoulder-length wig took the container from her. Then she vanished, leaving her alone with Hapuseneb and all the gods abruptly crowding the room in her senses. A faience bowl resting on the table beside the couch—its interior decorated with lotus flowers and bolti fish—had come to life and was gently undulating as if actually made of water. She might have gazed at the magical bowl for hours if the priest's strong and demanding arms had not come around her. The next thing she knew, he was lying beside her on the couch kissing her. Her arms and legs began to feel as long as the four horizons merging as she clung to him in a passionate effort to consume him absolutely. He made a sound like a growl and for a frightening moment, she thought she was actually embracing a leopard. Quickly she slipped her hands up into his shirt and was reassured by the unmistakable sensation of his human skin. Running her nails hungrily up and down his back, she greedily inhaled the deep musky scent of a man no amount of perfume could mask.

Abruptly pinning both her wrists over her head with one hand, he pushed himself up with the other and looked down into her eyes. "You are not the king of Kemet tonight, Hatshepsut! I will do whatever I wish with you and not ask your permission!"

Her dress was bunched up around her waist and he had long since tugged the straps aside to expose her breasts. Continuing to hold her down by the wrists, he caught her left nipple between his lips and sucked on it ravenously while quickly unwinding his kilt.

She cried out as Amun-Min himself entered her body. Fire flared between her legs and yet she still managed to tighten her sex around him, fervently striving to please him by squeezing and caressing his erection, which felt much larger and harder than her brother's. At long last, she had a real man inside her and the joy she experienced with all of herself was almost unbearable.

Reaching down with his free hand, he gripped one of her ass cheeks for the leverage he needed to thrust even more fiercely. It thrilled her how his groans of pleasure evoked the growls of a lion feasting on its kill as the sharp ache in her neck where he was biting her mysteriously intensified the luminous sensation blooming between her legs. He released her wrists, but only so he could transfer his hand to her throat. He met her eyes as he cut off her breath and the vessel of her flesh overflowed as all the power of her Ka plunged to earth and poured into her body.

A timeless while later, when they were half sitting up with her head resting against his chest, the same pretty servant appeared holding a cup reverently in both hands. Hapuseneb took it from her and Hatshepsut raised her head so he could hold it to her lips. She sipped the sweet liquid, then returning the cup to him reached out and caressed the naked hip of the girl standing before her, the way she had so often seen Amenmose do. The attendant's skin was remarkably soft, very much like hers and yet enticingly unknown.

Holding the empty cup, the girl turned to go.

Hapuseneb said, "Put that down, Meri, and come here."

She obeyed him at once, with unconcealed eagerness.

He gripped one of her wrists and pulled her onto the couch.

Hatshepsut drew the girl curiously into her arms, and then giggled she was so delighted by the sensation of firm little breasts pressing against her fuller and softer bosom. She discovered that kissing another woman was like slipping a lush moist flower between her lips. The girl's mouth was as small and delicate as hers own, very different from a man's demanding teeth and tongue which had the power to stoke the flame of desire deep inside her. The experience was purely sweet, especially when the girl moaned and, forgetting herself, rolled them both eagerly over onto their sides.

Hatshepsut stopped laughing and tensed with anticipation as Hapuseneb pressed his body up against hers from behind. Gripping her behind the knee, he raised one of her legs.

"Caress her, Meri," he instructed. "You know where."

Fingertips firmly stroking the crown of her labia, combined with the sensation of the High Priest slowly penetrating her, almost immediately pushed Hatshepsut over yet another horizon hidden inside her. Such beautiful sensations were concealed beneath the veil of her skin she fervently regretted how long it had taken for her body to bloom in a true man's hands. This time Hapuseneb possessed her with long and slow, excruciatingly patient strokes as his attendant, still kissing her, polished the sublime gem secreted away in her flesh. Pinned between them, the climax she soon suffered was different from any other. The blinding joy that flooded her barely subsided long enough for her to catch her breath before it crested again as Hapuseneb suddenly began thrusting so hard she felt him reach the very core of her being where the magic of her Ka still smoldered in all its devastating glory.

Hatshepsut does not remember the girl leaving. Food was delivered and she found herself happily licking her lover's fingertips as he fed her bite-size morsels of lamb seasoned with rosemary. Gently, he encouraged her to eat and to take sips of cool water. She worried their evening was drawing to an end but soon discovered he was far from finished with her.

By the time they were sated the full moon had set. Never had she lived a more beautiful and precious twelve hours of darkness during which some of the flowing magic of the Dwat was channeled by the High Priest's erotic skills to their side of the River.

Wearing white linen robes to ward off the early morning chill, they walked down to the water's edge.

"I believe there are leopards concealed in these reeds," she teased, "for one of them attacked me last night as I was sleeping. I suffered from the most marvelously violent dreams!"

"Centuries ago," he draped an arm over her shoulders but did not look at her as he spoke, "priestesses of Kemet could gaze upon the surface of still water and see distant parts of the earth. We have lost that ability, as we have lost many others. Although blessedly not in our lifetime, there will come a day when we will not be together like this, Hatshepsut, when a darkness will divide us which will prove much harder to fight than the Setiu. But I will always love you, Maatkare, remember that. Never forget that love is infinitely more powerful than fear. If you sacrifice the intelligence of your heart to Seth, seduced into thinking his selfish greed is stronger, the door through which we can meet in dreams will close and Amun-Re's heart will break with woe."

* * * * *

Word reached Waset the Kushites were invading. The magical barrier of Akheperkare's monument had been breeched and chaos in the form of enemy soldiers was flowing north in dark currents.

"The gods are with us," she told the officials present with her in the Seal Room. "Together Horus and Sekhmet will make them regret the day they so foolishly chose to ignore my father's warning."

The Great Army Commander was in Perunefer. She sent a message telling him to remain there and guard the north. When Commander Inebni strode into the room, in a single heartbeat she relived all the hours they had spent together racing across the desert in a chariot. The exhilaration she had experienced then, and the pride she had taken in her growing skill with the bow, would be as nothing, she realized, compared to the thrill of an actual battle. Her dread was so intense she could scarcely distinguish it from an excitement experienced directly by her Ka even as her vulnerable body struggled not to tremble.

"Make my horse and his partner ready," she said to the troop commander. "Pharaoh will lead Kemet's forces."

Five companies of two-hundred-and-fifty men, divided into platoons of fifty soldiers each, left Waset to join an additional five companies already stationed in the south under the command of the King's Son, Seni, and his Deputy, her close friend Amenemhet. During the journey to Kush, she would meet with the captains of the southernmost Nomes who were all presently mustering their men and preparing to join the campaign. Wearing white linen sailors' circlets, the oarsmen worked in shifts as Amun-Re accompanied them in the north wind which blew steady and strong, lifting her spirits and cooling her skin. But her heart felt so impatiently hot in her chest, she could easily believe it was a portion of the sun fallen to earth burning within the horizons of her flesh.

Hapuseneb remained in Waset to serve as her Eyes and Ears. She brought Senmut with her. Nehesj also remained in the Seal Room but his chief scribe and assistant, Ty, traveled south to record the victory and the rich spoils attendant with it. The faces of the officials surrounding her revealed not the slightest doubt Maatkare would emerge victorious from the battle. Never before had she felt so close to her father in her heart, not even while he still lived on her side of the River. The body of the army he had commanded surrounded her like a potent extension of her own delicate limbs. Her eyes never tired of admiring the firm bodies and shining weapons of the soldiers crowding the military transports sailing around and behind her. The glorious sight left her feeling breathless, as if she was lying on a vast bed with hundreds of men and all their virile strength was intent on serving her. Remembering how fiercely the High Priest had stabbed her with the Divine weapon of his erection, she suffered no fear of enemy spears and arrows. She was transformed into Sekhmet journeying Down Below to feast on the blood of her enemies. Yet she also found herself hoping that, in a future so distant it could scarcely be imagined, the number of people who lived in darkness and chaos would diminish as the beautiful rule of Maat extended to the ends of the earth in all directions...

She indulged in a beautiful dream of peace but did not permit it to weaken her resolve. She was prepared to be as merciless as necessary with anyone who threatened the safety and happiness of her people. She desired company during the long days on the ship and it was provided by, amongst others, Senmut, Djehuty, Amenhotep and Puyemre, one of the priests of Amun representing God's presence on the campaign. Amenhotep and Djehuty supervised the daily allotment of bread, beer and fish to the soldiers. Wherever possible the army's diet was supplemented with meat provided by local headmen. Troop Commander Inebni was honored with a seat at her table every evening but the rich banquets of a royal progress were replaced by satisfyingly brief meals so everyone could get as much sleep as possible and be fully rested for the coming conflict.

Comforted by Nafre's presence in the adjoining room wherever they passed the night, every morning Hatshepsut made offerings in the local temple. Not for an instant did she doubt the gods were with her. She knew in her heart she was true to Maat and that all the deities to whom she offered life as she received it from them knew it also.

During the entire voyage, Senmut remained almost as silent as the statues of the *neters* she communed with, but his eyes were so much more eloquent it was hard to catch all the feelings she saw in them with a net of words. Like everyone else, Senmut knew about the night she had spent with the High Priest of Amun. She had suffered a cowardly sense of relief when news of the Kushite invasion provided her with an excuse to ignore her unique friend's reaction. Until Kemet was safe again she was not obliged to face her Superior Steward's emotions and the power they possessed over hers, which sometimes unnerved her into treating them like her enemies even though she knew in her heart they were not.

At close quarters, Pharaoh's soldiers would fight with axes, flint knives and maces. Commanders carried daggers. Enemies could be dispatched from a distance with spears, boomerangs and bows and arrows. Tough leather hides stretched tightly over wooden frames was all that served to shield flesh left almost entirely exposed by leather loincloths designed for freedom of movement. The only adornment worn by the troops was the feather of Maat and despite its ineffectiveness as a weapon or as protection it was their greatest strength.

When Maatkare at last stood in a chariot beside her driver, Thutmose, she yelled as loudly as she could, "Never forget you are soldiers of Re and fight for the light!"

Cheers rising from the ranks filled the vast sky of that desolate place. Perhaps all the Kushites she killed would be reborn in Kemet, where they stood a much better chance of becoming enlightened. The mere possibility would make dispatching as many of them as possible all that much more gratifying.

She glanced at Inebni, who was driving the chariot flanking her left, and then at General Amenhotep stationed on her right. She had deferred to her commanders when it came time to discussing strategy and choosing the time and the place where they would confront the barbarians. Behind them, the solar disc was burning only a hand's breadth above the eastern horizon and the advancing horde was partially blinded by it. Scouts sent by the King's Son had kept Pharaoh and her officers informed of the invader's location. The Kushites were traveling by land and their progress was slowed by heavily laden supply carts. One of her father's fortresses had also held the enemy up for some time. When word was brought that the foreign army—such as it was—had reached the southernmost bend in the River between the third and the fourth wild waters, the decision was made to march eastward away from the water. As the King's Son attacked from the River they would swiftly double back and pin the enemy between them.

The trip out into the eastern desert felt longer to Hatshepsut than all the days she had spent on the ship as she worried the Kushites would move north faster than expected and elude them. The whirring of chariot wheels and the soft thudding of horses' hoofs across the sand only accentuated the oppressive silence. No breeze defended them from Re glaring remorselessly down upon the Children of Horus and their enemies indiscriminately, as if God did not care one way or the other which side won the coming conflict. Lest it weaken her resolve, Hatshepsut firmly banished the disturbing thought from her heart. She would not fail her people when they most needed her.

After the sun set she slept for a brief time in a tent by herself while the bulk of the army of Horus rested beneath the stars. Exhausted from standing in a chariot all day she did not dream and woke eager for action. They stopped for only three hours in the cool of darkness before rising and doubling back toward the River. The light of a half moon offered no reassuring omen about the future. Four royal scouts arrived as silently as jackals, their presence and identity announced by eerie whistles anyone who did not know they were pre-arranged signals would undoubtedly have believed to be supernatural in origin. The Kushites were exactly where they were expected to be. Even as they began setting their tents up for the day, Seni and Amenemhet would attack and begin herding them away from the River toward Maatkare and her army.

So far, everything had gone as planned.

His right hand clutching the hilt of his dagger, Inebni said, "The King's Son has done his job. Now it is up to you, Majesty, to finish the job!"

She smiled exultantly. The passivity of dread was a nightmare—reality and joy were confident and passionate action. She wore the soft white kerchief of the Khat headdress over her hair and a matching kilt, its gilded hem cut just above her knees. A short-sleeved yellow linen shirt covered her breasts and a falcon collar forged of white-gold protected her chest. On her feet were leather sandals colorfully embroidered with figures of Kushite chiefs she crushed with her every step. The stars had faded and the rising sun was suffusing her heart with courage.

The confrontation proceeded just as in her dream but for the fact that she had never felt more awake in her life. The sounding of the trumpets accompanying the rumble of earthly thunder produced by hundreds of horses and foot soldiers made her heart beast so fast she felt it taking wing. Thutmose steered the chariot with one hand while holding a shield protectively before her with the other. She raised her bow and loosed the first arrow, aiming for a garishly plumed and painted man running straight toward her who was clearly a chief. She imagined the gilded wood of her chariot flashing with menacing beauty in his eyes and half blinding him with the power of Re fighting on the side of Kemet and the light.

Her driver shouted, "You got him!"

Her delight was eclipsed as Thutmose deflected a spear with his shield and the force of the impact caused him to ram his forearm against her chest. But Inebni had put her through that test dozens of times and she managed to keep her balance. The intense satisfaction she had experienced when her arrow lodged itself in the Kushite's neck and promptly felled him was perversely erotic. She quickly drew another arrow from the leather pouch hanging down her back, notched it, and let it fly. She missed her target but a mere heartbeat later, another arrow shot by a soldier of Maat killed the man for her. The solid black cloud of enemy soldiers was already dispersing. With Montu on their side—his presence heralded by a large falcon soaring overhead observing the battle—Amenhotep and Seni were effortlessly taking great bites out of the sides and rear of the screaming horde while her own troops, led by Inebni, dealt with the rest of the enemy.

Maatkare distinctly felt Sekhmet possess her. The din of the fighting was oddly muted in her ears and yet at the same time she seemed to hear every scream of pain and every shout of rage or triumph as if she was seeing and feeling with her Ka as much as with her physical senses. Neith and Satis were also invisibly present in her chariot helping drive the arrows she shot straight into their targets. The air was filled with the buzzing of deadly mosquitoes—the sound of Kushite arrows being constantly launched in her direction—yet not one of them stung her. Re was fighting behind her, embracing the beautiful daughter who fought in his name with luminous arms and making it impossible for anyone to see her clearly enough to kill her. Thutmose and his shield also did their part. Soon the greatest danger came from fallen enemy bodies threatening to trip up their horses. Many of Kemet's soldiers had also perished, it was inevitable, but she did not dwell on their loss for she was confident Isis and Nepthys were already welcoming them with loving smiles into the beautiful land beyond the sunset.

She ran out of arrows just as Thutmose shouted, "It is over, Majesty! You are victorious!"

The sudden quiet tugged her fully back into her body as Kushites running for their lives stopped emitting their hideous battle cries. She saw Inebni's chariot make a sharp turn and come racing toward hers.

"Stop!" she commanded.

Thutmose expertly coaxed Nomti and his companion to a standstill. Her horse's black body gleamed with sweat as he tossed his head exultantly and chewed thirstily on his reigns. She would thank him later. She leapt onto the sand and knelt beside a fallen Kushite chief who appeared merely to have fallen asleep with his eyes open.

"You should not have been so foolish as to believe you could defeat me for I act in the name of Maat," she told him gently even while wresting a gold band from his wrist.

As she straightened Inebni strode toward her and signaled to a soldier to take the booty from her. Healer priests, and their assistants carrying litters, were already moving around the battlefield separating the wounded from the dead as vultures circled patiently overhead.

"All those Kushites who are still alive are to be given a choice," she told Inebni. "They can either fight for Pharaoh and Maat or they can serve as slaves in the gold mines. As always, the hands of the dead will be severed from their bodies so their owners are rendered powerless to raise arms against Kemet in future lifetimes. First, however, a great tent will be erected on the River's edge where all the chiefs who were not killed in the fighting will to be brought before me."

"Majesty, everything shall be done exactly as you wish it!" He stared at her the way Hapuseneb had done the night she entered his home—as if he longed to take her in his arms and wrestle her into submission with a kiss. She was very pleased with Troop Commander Inebni and she would let him know it. A lovely little villa in the country and two beautiful concubines to distract him from the boredom of marriage should please him.

Before Atum set that evening the Kushite chiefs who refused to kiss the earth at Maatkare's feet, and to rest their foreheads submissively against her toes, were executed, she did not care to be told how. When any sons they might have left behind in their towns and villages were located, they would be bound hand and foot, loaded onto transport barges and brought to Kemet to be re-educated. Hopefully they would come to understand how fortunate they were the Good Goddess Maatkare had taken them under her wing. Those Kushites archers in whose hearts the wings of Horus had suddenly begun beating were given to Seni. The men who refused to fight for Pharaoh were shackled and taken away by Amenemhet. For the rest of their lives they would regret the mistake they had made in underestimating the Female Falcon. However, on the return journey, she would refrain from hanging the headless corpse of one of her enemies from the prow of her ship as her father had done before her. The decomposing body would have looked and smelled terrible and she had already proved her strength. Ty would be kept busy for months tallying the booty soon to be brought back from conquered villages rich in ivory, gold and other desirable luxuries.

The hands severed from the bodies of dead enemies were the first things to be counted and recorded. Much less pleasant was the task of compiling a list of the wounded and slain soldiers of Horus. She was impressed with the skills of Sekhmet's priests and by how calm they remained when confronted by the gravest injuries. Two of her transport barges were loaded with jars of honey, oil and alum in addition to rolls of linen for bandages. Fresh meat was caught to eat as well as to treat wounds requiring it. She marveled at the delicate resilience of the human body. Split cheeks, crushed noses, dislocated collar bones, broken ribs and limbs could all be treated. More difficult to heal were open wounds that tended to fester and dangerously weaken the body if the bleeding was not stopped immediately. A separate tent was erected for those men not expected to live and Maatkare honored them all with a personal visit. Wearing a gray-blue dress, she knelt beside each soldier and whether he was asleep or awake she whispered in his ear, "Isis and Nepthys are longing to embrace you! Do not keep them waiting too long for they hate to see you suffer, my brave and beautiful brother! Slip joyfully back into the womb of the Goddess confident your loving Father Amun-Re is waiting for you!"

On the way home, the Female Falcon presided over the foundation ceremonies of a new rock-cut chapel dedicated to Hathor. The Eye of Re and the wife of Horus had made her power known to the Kushites through her daughter, Hatshepsut-Maatkare, and the temple in Ibshek would perpetually serve to remind them of it.

While in Wawat she met with the High Priest of the House of Horus she was also building 'as a pious daughter does for her father, establishing a shrine for him who formed her, that caused she should appear on the Horus throne like Re forever'.[63] In the sanctuaries she and her brother—to whose Divine Ka she was dedicating the temple—were represented in raised and painted reliefs making offerings to the falcon god. Maatkare was also depicted in the presence of Seshat, who appeared clad in the skin of a panther, and in the company of Satis. The section depicting her coronation by Amun-Re had nearly been completed. Dressed in the formal kilt and stiffly pleated apron of the King, she knelt with her back to the enthroned *neter* as he rested his hand protectively on her right shoulder. Before her stood the High Priest of Amun cloaked in a leopard skin, his left hand gripping one of the animal's legs and his right arm extended toward the dais, which was supported by hawk-headed deities. Behind him the vertical inscription read: *He gives life to Maatkare who lives. Appearing in the white crown, receiving the red crown.*[64]

Behind Amun-Re, hieroglyphs proclaimed his daughter's victory over the Kushites. In part of the long inscription, she said to her Father: *I have put thy terror in the bodies of them that know thee not.*[65]

30

Bull of her Mother

Pharaoh brought her daughter a special present from Kush—four dancing pygmies who had belonged to one of the tribal chiefs she executed. The princess was delighted with her gift and showed them off to everyone, beginning with Senmut.

Hatshepsut kept her eyes on his face as he watched the performance. She was feeling the strain imposed on her contentment by his unsmiling mouth. He never looked happy anymore and it was beginning to have a detrimental effect on her appetite for food and everything else. On the journey home, she had favored the companionship of her army commanders at celebratory banquets. Inebni looked particularly handsome in the *shebiu* collar and *a'a* armlets she awarded him for the crucial part he played in her victory over the Kushites. The double choker made of thick golden beads, worn tightly around the neck, drew attention to the troop commander's broad shoulders, and the narrow golden bands embracing his forearms enhanced their muscular strength. Eventually, however, Inebni's conversation began to bore her and she realized she was making a futile attempt to recapture the erotic elation of battle. During the fighting, her body and her Ka had come together as during a sexual climax but for a much longer and acutely conscious stretch of time. As a result she had subjected her true unique friend Senmut to even more humiliation as it began to be rumored the king had taken Troop Commander Inebni as her lover.

Suppressing a sigh, she turned her head and gazed at Neferure's profile. Her daughter's nose remained small and delicate but her mouth was beginning to bloom into a woman's, catching up with her eyes which for a long time had seemed to know things they should not. The princess was smiling at her pygmies for reasons her mother could not begin to fathom. At best, she found the spectacle of miniature men jumping wildly up and down and throwing each other around boring. At worst, she perceived it as an insult to the sacred command of motion perfected by temple dancers who were all pleasing to look at.

She glanced at Senmut again and caught him staring at her. She wanted to smile at him but found she could not bring herself to do so as his eyes held hers more eloquently than ever.

Neferure abruptly clapped her hands and ended the performance as her pygmies immediately fell facedown across the floor. To Hatshepsut, the colorful feathers they wore around their ebony wrists and ankles evoked the charred logs of a pyre where exotic birds had been horribly murdered.

The princess clapped her hands again.

The pygmies sprang to their feet and ran from the room. She had them well trained already.

"Well, what do you think of them?" Neferure demanded of Senmut.

"I do not think much of them at all," he replied frankly. "They are what they are."

"And what about you, mother?"

"I think they are ghastly, my love. You know that."

"Then you are not really looking at them and truly seeing them," the princess retorted mildly but her smile stiffened.

Rising, Hatshepsut cooled her face and her indignation with an ostrich feather fan. The handle was made of black ivory and the feathers had been dyed red. The heavy fall of her hair was coolly confined in a *khat* headdress and she was never troubled by the light pressure of gold against her flesh. She walked over to the window, impatiently shooing away a royal fly swatter following too closely behind her. Outside in Neferure's Pleasure House fat bees droned lazily from flower to flower, their golden bodies heavy with the nectar priests of Sekhmet transformed into the lotion that kept wounds from festering. Honey was one of the ingredients in the concoction Ibenre supplied her with every week.

Behind her, she heard Senmut say something quietly and Neferure laugh softly, almost as if they were keeping a secret from her.

"My daughter," she turned to face them, "I have been thinking about what you just said. Perhaps you are correct, in a sense. Perhaps it is because I do not find male pygmies and dwarfs desirable as men that I perceive them as ugly. If I were to look at them as I look at children or animals I might not consider them so hideous, but as *men* I simply cannot take them seriously."

"Oh mother!" Neferure laughed as she inspected a bowl of dates. "Do you really think Hathor never lets Bes have his way with her? Of course she does, when she is in the mood for someone delightfully obedient. Sometimes Horus can be such a commanding bore. Bes is Hathor's devoted friend and very amusing too, so why should she not lie with him when she chooses? My male dwarfs all have full sizes penises, you know. Do you not agree with me, Senmut?"

"Bes is not so much Hathor's friend as her servant," he replied soberly, "and as a spirit he does not possess a man's pride, which is why he is content to be his mistress' plaything and does not abhor it when she chooses to give the color of her bosom to another. But pygmies and dwarfs are not gods, they are people with hearts which can be wounded. What disturbs her Majesty is that she can never feel for dwarfs or pygmies what she does for men who are tall and strong and capable of wrestling her body into submission beneath theirs."

Hatshepsut approached him. "It seems to me dwarfs are reflections of ourselves distorted by God's Hand for some mysterious purpose."

"The purpose is not so mysterious," Neferure said with her mouth full of fruit. "The gods are telling us we should not take ourselves so seriously and be so vain of our beauty, which fades so quickly. In my opinion, Anubis does not howl like a jackal but rather laughs like a hyena at our pompous profundity. The gods never save anyone from dying no matter how much bull's blood we offer them."

Hatshepsut stared at her daughter in horror. "Neferure, what are you saying?" She glanced at Senmut, hoping he would be able to rescue the afternoon that suddenly seemed to have darkened even though Re still ruled in heaven.

The God's Wife shrugged and gestured to a servant to remove the bowl of dates she had grown tired of. Her expression indicated she was beginning to feel the same way about the conversation.

Senmut looked up at Hatshepsut even while ostensibly addressing her daughter. "Believing Beauty itself is eternal is very different from the vanity that focuses merely on the petals of the flesh, which fade and fall into the grave even as the sensual joy of flowering forever remains."

Hatshepsut stared gratefully down into his eyes and added, "All physical seeds are manifestations of Atum's heart that broke with longing in the darkness."

"And breaks everywhere everyday at every moment." His eyes never left hers. "Without his beautiful Hand, Atum-Re is everything and yet also nothing, for it is the Goddess who realizes all his desires."

"Yes…"

"Well!" Neferure stood and embraced her mother. "Thank you again for my delightful presents but now I must wash. It is time to feed the gods again. Their desire is boundless and they are always hungry for more."

Hatshepsut realized they were being dismissed. It was a relief because, she admitted, it was definitely time to give Senmut what he needed. She suspected they had both been expertly manipulated by God's Wife, a possibility that went some way toward defining the determined quality of Neferure's smile.

Senmut had risen and was preparing to take his leave.

"My friend," she said quickly, "I would like you to return with me to my residence… unless you have a previous engagement."

"If I did I would immediately cancel it, Majesty. The pleasure of your company transcends all other possible activities."

She permitted him the liberty of a little sarcasm blended with the truth for she *had* treated him terribly. But no longer. If there was room in her heart for more than one man then there was room in her bed as well. Neferure had forced her to face why she had been hesitating to fully embrace Senmut even though it was obvious she loved him—because he was a commoner. But their Superior Steward possessed the face and figure, the mind and heart of a god and her reticence was only hurting them both. She kissed her daughter on both cheeks and smiled into her eyes, silently thanking her. She never would have thought dancing pygmies could be so enlightening.

* * * * *

Hapuseneb, Governor of the South and First Prophet of Amun, was anointed Treasurer of the King of Upper and Lower Kemet and Overseer of all the Works of Pharaoh. Maatkare also placed him at the head of the entire priesthood and effectively made him the most powerful man in the Two Lands. It was only fitting that in the same ceremony Senmut, Steward of Princess Neferure and Superior Steward to the King, was further anointed Great Steward of Amun and put in charge not only of Amun-Re's estates but of all God's worldly possessions. The Overseer of the Treasury of Amun, Puyemre, would enjoy working with his long-time friend but he would also have other important duties to attend to as the new Second Prophet of Amun for the ancient Amenhotep had at last gone to his Ka. She felt Puyemre's positive sense of humor would prove very pleasing to Amun. She was not privy to what Puyemre had undergone when he was initiated in the sanctuary adjoining the temple's herb garden. How the Hidden One had revealed himself to her friend was between God and his heart in the same way she never spoke to anyone (except, of course, Hapuseneb) about what she had experienced in the Temple of Satis.

Hatshepsut felt the scales of Maat balance perfectly. Hapuseneb and Senmut ruled in *Ipet Sut* as they did in her heart. The High Priest was lord of the Temple's Divine dimension while Senmut oversaw all the needs and pleasures of God's earthly form. Whenever she let her Superior Steward delight in her body, they invariably lay talking afterward, sometimes for hours. What she shared with Hapuseneb was very different, a formal banquet of the flesh that usually lasted all night and left her profoundly exhausted. Together she and the High Priest worshipped Min with such intensity it burned away the more subtle pleasures of intimacy in a violent sacrifice of their personal identities. The experience was impossible to sustain on a regular basis and might even have proved dangerous. The things Hapuseneb did to her required he keep his strength and skills perfectly honed by resting several weeks between each of their carnal offerings to Amun-Kamutef.

"You are now so weighed down with titles, Senmut," Neferure teased him one afternoon when he and the king once again visited her in her palace, "it is a marvel you can get out of bed in the morning."

He did not reply as he moved one of his pieces across the Twenty Square's board resting on a table between them.

She frowned. "You beat me!"

He smiled.

She laughed. "I do not mind it so much when you win because you are the smartest man in Kemet, Overseer of the Fields of Amun!" She rose and hugged him fondly before gesturing to one of her female dwarf attendants.

Grinning mischievously, the woman ran up to her mistress.

Neferure grabbed her hands and began spinning them both around and around, moving faster and faster as she recited all of Senmut's titles, "Chief Steward of the Estates of Amun! Overseer of the Cattle of Amun! Chief of the House of Amun! Steward of the Bark of Amun! Chief of the Weapons of Amun! Overseer of the Double Gold House of Amun! Overseer of the Treasury of Amun! Overseer of the Gold and Silver Foundry of Amun! Inspector of the Servants of Amun!"

She stopped abruptly and looked as if she might have fallen had her dwarf not clung to her legs.

"But I believe I am forgetting one... oh, yes! Overseers of the Beauties of Amun! That must be a particularly smelly duty tending to all the young cows the bulls lust after!"

"He is also Overseer of the Jewelry and Decoration of the King," Hatshepsut reminded her as she rose to take her leave, "and it is time for him to help me dress for tonight's banquet. We will see you there later."

The dwarf prostrated herself by spreading her little body facedown across the floor. Her nose and mouth pressed against a painted tile, her voice was grossly muffled as she exclaimed, "Majesty, your beauty is already blinding!"

The princess smiled down at her attendant and then looked at her mother, at which point her dimples deepened challengingly.

Hatshepsut gazed back at her soberly. "You will be the Great Royal Wife one day, Neferure, and for the sake of Kemet and all her people, not just the amusing little ones, I hope you will take the responsibilities of a queen more seriously than you do your duties as God's Wife."

* * * * *

Senmut was in charge of supervising the delivery of the sandstone blocks being used to restore parts of *Ipet Sut*. The stone was wrested out of its birthplace from the quarry near the Place of Rowing, where she had granted the Great Steward of Amun permission to excavate a River shrine near the ones being prepared for Hapuseneb and herself. The name of the King who had given him the chapel as a sign of her favor, *Maatkare*, was the first inscription to be made on the lintel over the doorway beneath a winged solar disc. Inside the sanctuary, Senmut did not intend to limit himself to the traditional symbolic banquet, purification and offering scenes. The single room would contain his statue—cut directly into the back wall—and every available surface would be covered with bas-reliefs, even the ceiling.

It was not images of tables piled high with food he needed to nourish his soul for all eternity. Instead, he wanted to see her, Hatshepsut-Maatkare, standing before him embraced by Sobek in the form of a man with the head of a crocodile, and by Nekhbet standing behind her as a woman wearing the queen's vulture crown. The theme he selected of transformation and transcendence pleased her, as did knowing she was the one who so beautifully embodied these metaphysical principles in his personal universe. The choice of Sobek-Re was appropriate for a River shrine and profoundly flattered her because Sobek could also serve to symbolize Pharaoh's might, which the accompanying inscriptions affirmed she possessed in full even though she was a woman. The figure of Nekhbet was particularly rich in significance linked as she was with the white crown of the south where the chapel was located, and with the Great Mother who gives birth to and nurses the king in the form of the white celestial cow associated with Hathor. Standing between the two *neters*, Maatkare was the undisputed King of the Two Lands and more than that—the tableau could be simply translated to read *God and his Hand*.

Senmut's provocative originality also remained evident in the statues he kept producing. His latest offering to *Ipet Sut* was a small but unique figure. Similar works existed but they all invariably depicted a king sitting on the lap of a deity. Once again Senmut was portrayed in the company of Neferure but instead of sitting he strode forward holding the princess in his arms, his large left hand serving as her seat while his right hand rested just below her bent knees. Hatshepsut was not impressed by their expressions—which failed to capture the attractive dynamic quality of their living features—but this was easy to forget in the face of the palpable feeling of affection communicated by Neferure's arm raised to embrace her tutor as her right hand rested on his right shoulder. In her left hand, the princess held a lily scepter, a royal cobra crowned her forehead, and the Ka's power over time was expressed by the side-lock of youth she no longer wore in life. Hieroglyphs ran in horizontal lines all around Senmut's ankle-length cloak, as well as across the base on which his bare feet were planted. The inscriptions described how the work had been given as a blessing to the High Official and Steward of Amun by the Lord of the Thrones of the Two Lands, Maatkare, as a reward for nurturing the King's Daughter, God's Wife, Neferure.

The Good God Menkheperre was six-years-old and leaving for Mennefer. Maatkare met formally with the junior pharaoh and his mother in the throne room where she was attended by her most beloved courtiers, including the Nomarchs of the Sistrum and of the Oryx. It was her wish that Khenti and Rasui accompany the fledgling falcon on his journey north. It was clear the Lady Isis did not know whether to mistrust her escorts or to be pleased by them. For the moment, her greedy nature appeared satisfied by the plans for her prestigious tomb. The young king would spend six months in the Sistrum and six months in the Oryx, where their Nomarchs would begin his education. By observing Khenti and his courtiers hunting, the future king would become acquainted with the bow and arrow and learn to ride a horse. In the Oryx, Rasui would show the boy the day to day work of a Nomarch as he met with local headmen, inspected fields and herds and every ten days sat in judgment. It was her desire that Thutmose spend as much time as possible around truly noble men who lived by the intelligence of their heart and honored the gods not just with offerings but with all their thoughts and actions.

It was at this time that a new term, *per-aa*, was devised by the royal scribes which meant "Great House." It was not bound to either a feminine or a masculine determinative and could therefore be used to refer to either one of the two reigning pharaohs, Maatkare and Menkheperre.

Satisfied her brother's son and the future of Kemet was proceeding on the proper path, Hatshepsut was able to concentrate on the matters most dear to her. In his capacity as High Priest of Amun and Overseer of all Works of Pharaoh, she met regularly with Hapuseneb. He had approved of her wish to erect a series of bark shrines extending all the way from *Ipet Sut* to the Palace of Maat. Based on the distance between the temples, and the metaphysical principles expressed by each number, it was decided six bark shrines would be erected along the processional route. However, the foundations could not be laid until a mansion dedicated to Amun-Kamutef was built outside the enclosure wall leading into the temple of his consort. Mut's modest mud-brick house was being torn down and reconstructed on a larger scale in imperishable stone.

At first she had almost been shy about expressing her wishes to Hapuseneb, suspecting he would realize her piety also encompassed the desire to immortalize the beautiful power of their erotic relationship. The Temple of Amun-Kamutef would become the first stop on the processional route and, like the head of the god's phallus, directly adjoin the entrance to Mut's expanded complex. The House of Mut and its sacred lake, *Isheru*, symbolized the vulva and womb of the Goddess. In the future, there would be seven stops, representative of the seven-fold nature of the First Occasion, extending from the seat of Divinity in *Ipet Sut* to conception in Mut's enclave and birth in God's Favored Place, the Palace of Maat. The first bark shrine would sit directly across from the monument to Amun-Kamutef, and the avenue leading to it from *Ipet Sut* would be as straight as the shaft of His cosmic phallus through which He begat himself on his Mother as he ejaculated the glimmering life-filled universe.

She should have known Hapuseneb would appreciate her way of thinking and privately reward her for it.

In Hatshepsut's heart, Kemet's goddesses were all aspects of God's Hand. Mut was the wife of Amun and the mother of the moon god Khonsu, the southern Sekhmet-Bast, yet another form of Hathor. Mut was present at the splitting of the Sacred *Ished* Tree—another way of expressing the First Occasion when One became Two through the sensual magic of God's Hand engendering Creation. She wanted to make it clear that Mut was the Hidden One's magical mirror. Mut was the mother of the moon through which Amun-Kamutef, her Father and Husband, manifested as Khonsu—the physical body born from the womb of time and space. Through his son Khonsu, Amun-Re traveled from east to west and from west to east—from life to death and from death to life—subject to the forces of incarnation commanded by the Divine Ka. Currently the temple of the Mistress of Isheru was unacceptably modest and composed of corruptible substances. Maatkare determined it was of vital importance Mut be given a larger home made of imperishable stone where her connection with Hathor-Sekhmet would be stressed by a columned porch of drunkenness.

Presently, the processional route to the Palace of Maat began at the southern entrance to God's house and was accessed by a gateway built by Djserkare. A greater, much more profoundly imposing facade was required to do justice to the splendor of her six bark shrines and the new Temple of Amun-Kamutef linked to Mut's sacred complex. She spent more than one sleepless night worrying she was being too ambitious and impatient with her building projects and straining the royal treasury, which was still channeling considerable resources into her goal of expanding the army, but then the sun rose and reminded her she was Pharaoh—it was her duty to emulate Divine creativity and to use all the means at her disposal to do so. She was ashamed of the timidity which sometimes possessed her when she was alone in the dark and made her think more like Hatshepsut than Maatkare, the Son of Re.

Hapuseneb and Senmut, Puyemre and Djehuty all agreed with her another entrance to *Ipet Sut* was needed to show that God's heart is always growing in his earthly body. She named the new pylon *The Place of the Sunrise*. It would be decorated with large bas-reliefs of winged solar discs carved into the sandstone facade built in the shape of the *horizon* hieroglyph. The massive gateway would conceal a stairway leading up to the roof, from which priests and privileged officials would be able to view the ceremonies performed in the courtyards below, made private by a low limestone wall. Three colossal figures would sit enthroned on both sides of the entrance, which symbolized the doorway into Incarnation of the First Occasion. Fashioned of limestone and *biat*, the statues would embody the Royal Ka—Amun-Re fully conscious of Himself in his earthly form through the spiritual enlightenment that ultimately makes a person Lord of the Two Lands—of life and death, creation and destruction.

The two colossi directly flanking the pylon would be the largest, their male bodies crowned by the symbolic lion's mane of the *nemes* headdress, and both would be inscribed with her throne name *Maatkare*. To the right of her westernmost statue would sit her direct ancestors—her mother's brother, Djeserkare, and her mother's father, Nebpehtire. To the east her successor, Menkheperre, and his father, Akheperenre, would be represented. God's Hand would also guard the portal into and out of physical existence in the form of two much smaller standing figures, one inscribed for Neferure and placed beside Maatkare's right leg, and another dedicated to Ahmose-Nefertari, the first God's Wife, placed between her son and her husband. Also to be honored with inclusion in the new pylon was Mutnofret. Her statue would be larger and more noticeable than she herself had been in life.

All the additions planned for *Ipet Sut* and its environs constituted a great undertaking requiring the skills and labor of hundreds of men, many of whom would be conscripted during the coming inundation. Hatshepsut rejoiced in her heart and was plagued only by regret she had not begun the work sooner. In retrospect, she resented how long her husband had lingered on the throne without accomplishing much of anything. She was still beautiful—all her see-faces told her so—but she was no longer a young woman. Suddenly there seemed little time to actualize everything her heart insisted she was destined to accomplish. She was healthy, she sensed many more years of life stretching before her, but Hapuseneb was thirteen years older. The passage of time was revealed by the fine lines around his eyes and mouth but otherwise he looked no older than when she first met him. The high priest's chest and stomach were as firm as ever, a result of the vigorous afternoon swims they both enjoyed, although seldom together. Hapuseneb required no statues of himself in which his youthful self was restored to him. Of all the people she knew he was the most in touch with the timeless powers of his Ka. In that respect, as in so many others, she sought to emulate him. Senmut, on the other hand, did not seem to notice that his chest and belly were both growing as tender as a woman's. The Great Steward of Amun had broad shoulders, and he was so tall the weight he had gained was scarcely noticeable when he was clothed, but in her bedroom, when he stood naked before her, she could see his thickening middle and it displeased her.

Neferure occasionally teased Senmut about his burgeoning belly but he appeared to take it as a compliment since a nobleman's rolls of fat were akin to papyruses proclaiming his prestige and wealth. In the distant past, such an attitude would have been frowned upon as decadent but in contemporary Waset body fat was now synonymous with success in a man. Hapuseneb's dress and behavior were often deliberately archaic, one of the things, she had come to realize, which had attracted her to him from the moment she met him. The high priest not only shared her reverence for the past, he embodied its wisdom.

Together they recalibrated the festival calendars, which had suffered some adulteration when the Setiu, ignorant of religious matters, ruled in the north.

With the input of Hapuseneb, Senmut and Puyemre, Maatkare designed her new temple dedicated to Mut, the Mistress of Isheru. To the Second Prophet of Amun—who was also the principal Overseer of the Treasury of Amun—she awarded the honor of supervising the erection of a shrine made of black ivory worked with electrum. The marriage of silver and gold was visually as beautiful as it was symbolically meaningful and her victory over the Kushites meant the treasury was full of her favorite material. The doors to the shrine would be carved from the finest limestone and show Maatkare standing before Mut in her form of a woman wearing the vulture headdress. The door jams would be inscribed with her throne name and her male counterpart's—*Maatkare* and *Menkheperre*. The entire monument—including the pillars of the courtyard and the columns supporting the porch of drunkenness—would be made of sandstone.

The monument to Amun-Kamutef posed an even greater challenge to her imagination. The Great House of Amun on his Stairway she considered her very personal monument to the magic of manifestation and the part played in the Divine creative process by love and desire. An offering court leading into a sanctuary with a false door would not suffice to express all the subtle and complex feelings her heart had experienced throughout her life and continued entertaining. She desired to express in stone the power of Number—the forces of incarnation symbolized by the *neters*.

Amun-Kamutef was also Amun-Kematef, *Amun who has completed his moment*, the forefather of the great Ogdoad of Iuno. Amun-Kematef was inseparable from the Goddess who gave his desire substance as the serpent of light and life. Inspired by Senmut, she was possessed by the idea of fashioning something never before seen in the Two Lands. His statues with Neferure had helped her realize it was her wish to express, through innovative works of her own, the direct connection she felt to the celestial forces flowing through her heart's four doorways.

In order to reflect what it felt like for her Ka to be caught in the net of her senses, the temple she was erecting to the sexual soul of Amun needed many small dark rooms and intimate chapels all contained in a larger space. Some of the chambers would be open to the sky while others would be hidden deep inside the structure, the flux of illumination and darkness mirroring the emotions of love and loss, desire and despair, hope and fear—the relentless rhythm of duality. Two rows of chapels—flanking a complex of rooms accessible only from the entrance court—would evoke playing squares in the game of Incarnation. Victory demanded the exercise of faith's magical muscle to defeat the opponent of mortality and achieve eternity.

In addition to raised reliefs, she would place statues of herself in the temple showing her in the company of the *neters* actively creating a uniquely beautiful blossom in Amun-Re's sensual garden by shaping her body and breathing life into her heart. Amenhotep was present the evening she voiced the idea of the group statues to Senmut. The priest of Anukis was so excited by the concept the conversation quickly progressed to the gods and goddesses she desired represented and the types of stone which would be used to carve them. Not able to make up her mind about certain details, she sought the opinion of Hapuseneb, who with a few incisive comments helped her make her final decisions. Senmut, however, often confused her by presenting her with too many general options. The Great Steward of Amun approached her project more from the angle of the materials themselves—where they came from, their physical properties, their availability and so on—in a way that almost struck her as insensible to spiritual concerns. He seemed to admire and approve of her initiative more than he empathized with the sacred perspective motivating it. She knew he understood and respected her but she was not entirely sure he shared her fascination with numbers for quite the same reasons. Senmut was as skilled in the art of measuring and calculating as Djehuty. The star charts he showed her rivaled those of the temple scribes except for the fact that he ascribed no meaning to the configuration of lights in the sky.

"But you must agree the stars form specific shapes," she insisted.

"I agree they appear to do so, which proves useful for recording their positions and mapping different sections of the heavens."

"But you do not believe these figures are truly there and mean something?"

"I did not say that, my lady."

"Then what *are* you saying, my lord?"

His answer was a long time in coming. "I believe in possibilities."

"But if something is possible then it is also *not* possible. If I were to think like you, I would have to consider the terrible *possibility* my father has vanished forever, like everyone else I love who has died or will die, including myself, and I absolutely refuse to do that!"

"That is not what I am implying, my lady," he insisted a little desperately.

"Yes it is!" She almost wanted to cry.

"I think it is much more possible—in fact, I believe it is highly likely—there is much more to us than the body we inhabit. When cut off from its source a fruit fallen from a tree and a flower plucked from a garden immediately begins withering. When the heart ceases to beat the same thing happens to animals and people, as though they have been cut off from their source—the mysterious force of life itself flowing through the heart and animating it. If I must define what I believe then I will tell you this—I believe in life. Life has always been there and always will be, in one form or another."

She had no desire to pursue the troubling conversation and that afternoon she dismissed him early. Even when they worshipped Min together, she did not usually desire to spend the entire night with Senmut. He was a selfish sleeper and she had quickly come to feel her bed was not big enough for both of them. His unconscious body lying beside hers made her feel hot and uncomfortable, until she almost began resenting the indifferent silence emanating from it. When he was asleep he no longer seemed alive as his Ba-bird flew in dreams through the Dwat, leaving behind the physical limbs, beside which she lay awake disturbingly conscious that only the corruptible part of him remained to accompany her. She much preferred sleeping alone.

With the assistance of Amenhotep, her Royal Butler and a priest of Anukis, of Hapuseneb and of the High Priest of Thoth, Maatkare completed her designs for the Great House consecrated to Amun-Kamutef. Patehuti had traveled to Waset to pay his respects to the Female Falcon and to visit his long-time friend, Hapuseneb. She wondered if he had glimpsed the finished structure in a moonlit bowl of water. He now served in the new temple she had consecrated to Thoth which was even larger and more richly appointed than the old one. Patehuti's arrival felt like a good omen and imbued her with the last bit of courage she needed to commission her innovative group statues.

Senwosret, the founder of *Ipet Sut*, was honored with a seat beside her in several of the chapels. It was her fervent hope the great Pharaoh's long-lived strength and wisdom would permeate her own reign. She sought to emulate Senwosret in many ways and she was off to a good start with her successful campaign in Kush, the mining expeditions she had sent to the Land of Turquoise, the diplomatic envoys presently traveling to the Land of the Two Rivers, and particularly with her policy of supporting and rewarding Nomarchs true to Maat, thereby strengthening the health and unity of the Two Lands.

No less than seven group statues displayed Maatkare in the company of select *neters*. In a triad made of golden stone, evocative of sunlight and immortality, she perched on the lap of the southern Hathor who sat across from her father Khnum. Anukis was the daughter of the cosmic potter and the mother of the King—life's Divine force embraced by a physical container become fully conscious of its eternal nature. Anukis was essentially indistinguishable from her mother Satis, a goddess personally dear to Hatshepsut.

Also sculpted of yellow travertine was another threesome where Maatkare knelt between Atum and Amun as their daughter and wife, both gods within reach of her hands. Atum-Re and Amum-Kamutef were different forms of the Supreme Being, one of them revered for centuries in the north while the other had come to power more recently in the south.

The most important tableau showed Amun enthroned behind Pharaoh where she knelt on the dais with her back to him as she received life from Weret-hekau, *Great of Magic*. The serpent-headed goddess held an *ankh* to the female king's nose with her left hand and rested her right hand on her forehead while Thoth marked the number of years she was destined to live and reign on a palm rib.

Four of the group statues depicted the ritual of Maatkare's coronation by Amun-Re in which he conferred upon her the Divine status of his bodily son.

31

Hathor's Human Herd

The Seal Room lost one of its vital limbs when Ahmose-Penekhbet left for the Field of Reeds. His tomb had long been finished. Kemet would dearly miss his devoted efficiency.

Kemet's beloved vizier, Akheperseneb, had already gone down into the west, it was only a matter of time before his physical heart followed.

Both men had become ill during the time of the green water when Hapi first began rising and the stench was hard to abide. Maatkare sacrificed seven black bulls but without much hope the gods would spare her old friends' lives. Ripening dates were turning red in the palm trees when Ahmose-Penekhbet coughed up blood, as though his body had become a channel for the red waters of Sekhmet rushing up the River's mighty vein. Too easily, Hatshepsut could foresee the day when all the officials who had worked with her father would be dead. The thought saddened but did not trouble her for she was blessed by the friendship of many noble men worthy of replacing them. Rats, snakes and scorpions, their nests and homes flooded, were scurrying openly onto fields and roads when she summoned Useramun to her private receiving room.

"I regret your beloved father will soon become one of the blessed dead," she began gently, and then proceeded more firmly, "Begin preparing yourself, Useramun, for the honor I will do you. Your intelligence and passionate drive to excel are too often wasted on idle pastimes. Clearly, your duties as a scribe of the treasury of Amun do not sufficiently engage you. When you are vizier, I trust your Ka will shine as brightly as it was meant to. Together you and Hapuseneb will be the two supporting posts of the whole land. The forty leather thongs of your vizier's staff will demand you give the best of yourself while exacting the same from others as the earthly representative of the Forty-Two Assessors."

The administrative palace was like a field where the old crop had been harvested and a new one was being planted. Maat would not languish after the great men who had so long served her departed. Inet, however, seemed intent on merely existing forever. Her attendants fed her too well and her breasts, always generously large, now hung large and limp as cow udders against her chest. The hair on her head was thinning like a nest being dismantled by her Ba-bird who no longer used it; behind her eyes no thoughts or desires seemed to fly. Hatshepsut rarely visited her anymore, it was too depressing, and Inet did not recognize her anyway.

Before embarking on her first royal progress as Pharaoh, Maatkare officiated at the rite of Hauling the *Meret* Chests. She wore a knee-length kilt beneath the stiffly pleated royal apron. The crossed wings of her golden falcon collar covered her breasts and her head was embraced by a short wig secured by a red sash and topped by the *Atef* crown. The tall headdress, similar to the white crown of Upper Kemet, was decorated with red, green, blue and gold vertical bands flanked by two equally colorful ostrich plumes rising out of the waving horizontal horns of Khnum. The royal cobra protecting her forehead, she held the *Kherep* scepter of *control* in her right hand. The ritual began when she raised her right arm and extended her left arm, the hand held up and open, to offer Amun-Re her life and the world he had created. She stood before the god's enshrined image in the temple's innermost offering court as four large chests, each one resting on its own sledge, were dragged between them four times by four young priests. It was a difficult pose to sustain and the muscles in her arms began to ache as the procession slowly circled her once, twice, and three times until at last, on the fourth circuit, the chests were left sitting before her. The wooden containers were wrapped in yellow linen bandages and crowned on all four corners by the ostrich feather of Maat dyed the color of the cloth each box contained—green, white, blue and red.

"My Lord, I bring you Kemet! Your bodily son and the daughter who serves as your Eye, Maatkare offers you the Two Lands unified! Receive from me *Ta-meri*, your Beloved Earth!"

The different colored cloths symbolized the forces that wove the universe into existence on the First Occasion. Embodying the four principal elements of the physical world and the four cardinal directions, the chests and what they contained also represented all the peoples of earth spun by Khnum and their spiritual heart, the source of all true power—Pharaoh.

Maatkare had only yesterday sent a fleet of ships to the Great Green bound for the land of the Fenkhu to trade linen and food for more precious cedar wood and to invite their princes to enter into her presence in Mennefer. It was her desire to nourish Maat by revealing her beauty to others at every opportunity. At the same time she would be further enriching the treasury for the purpose of emulating Divine creativity vigorously and joyfully without being limited by a scarcity of all the materials she needed to do so.

Also before leaving the Town of Amun, she ordered the god's much smaller temple in the western desert restored. Sections of the chapel were refurbished with mud-brick and an enclosure wall built around the entire sacred district. It was called the Holy Place because when the primeval waters of Nun receded it was one of the first spots on earth to emerge. The Divine forces behind the First Occasion could still be felt in *Djser Set* and their power tapped into by those initiated into The Mysteries as normal men draw water from a well.

The king's barge was now at her disposal and she felt obliged to make use of it even though she would have preferred the intimacy of Hapuseneb's ship. Despite her protests, the princess remained in Waset.

"The God's Wife is needed here while I am away," her mother explained, "and it is you who must travel from Tantera to Djeba when Hathor next visits her husband."

Neferure's sullen expression vanished. "I am planning to dress all my male dwarfs up as Bes for the procession!"

Hatshepsut was secretly relieved she would not be there.

Senmut traveled with her on the magnificent vessel in which the fan bearers waved ostrich feather fans in perfect rhythm with the rowers obeying the beat of a golden gong. The gilded oars moving as one resembled the wings of a great bird flown down from heaven to float on the water, and every evening it glided regally toward a dock crowded with people waiting to greet her.

Everywhere she went Maatkare was welcomed with processions of oxen—their horns gilded for the occasion—and fat cows draped with garlands of flowers all walking docilely into the arms of the royal butchers. Even the poorest farmers and fishermen and their wives and children wore kilts and dresses dyed festive colors. Everyone showed off whatever jewelry they possessed even if it was only a single faience bracelet. Dancing to music played by the priests and priestesses of Hathor traveling with Pharaoh, even the humblest of her people drank sweet fruit juices in the morning and beer in the afternoon. The High Priest of Amun was Treasurer of the King of Upper and Lower Kemet and his generosity proved as great as his wisdom for everywhere they went he extended his hand as though there was no limit to how much he could give. Hapuseneb's scribes everyday proved the power of Thoth by efficiently procuring and distributing as many loaves of bread and barrels of beer as were needed to fulfill the needs of the multitudes.

Cakes of incense, jars of wine, alabaster vessels filled with unguents, gold plates and silver cups—all the luxuries required by Maatkare and her entourage traveled with her on over fifty transport barges. When there was not enough room to accommodate all the members of her court in the homes of nobles, priests and Nomarchs, they slept in pavilions erected beneath the stars and raised above the ground to protect them from rodents.

The Female Falcon spent seven weeks in *Ta-wer*, the Eldest Land, in the presence of the seven gods of Abedju ruled by Osiris. She made offerings to the Great Sekhem, the Foremost of Powers, on behalf of her dear friends Ahmose-Penekhbet, Akheperseneb and Seni. A letter had reached her in Tantera, sent by Amenemhet from Wawat, regretfully informing her The King's Son had died, not in a border skirmish but peacefully in his sleep one night. She lamented the loss of the Viceroy who had served her father and helped her secure her own victory in the Southern Lands but she lost no time in replacing him with one of his senior men. She had been impressed by the taut strength of Amenemnekhu's slender body and by his remarkably penetrating mind. His appointment had been approved in advance by her senior military officials. She had recently awarded Troop Commander Inebni a block statue dedicated to him by the Good Goddess, Lady of the Two Lands, Maatkare, and her brother's son, the Good God, Lord of Action, Menkheperre. Inebni longed for a son himself but his wife remained barren. She hoped the two lovely young women she had also awarded him would help distract him while perhaps fulfilling his desire for a family in the future. A boy born from a concubine was better than no son at all.

Maatkare presided over the symbolic embalming of a figure of Osiris carved from stone that rested in his temple for seven days before being buried in the earth, through which he was reborn into form through the starry womb of Mother Nut. When mounted on a long pole for public processions, the reliquary purported to contain the head of Osiris was unabashedly phallic. A gilded wooden shrine secured on a sled was erected around the towering monument and borne through the city on the shoulders of six priests led by a seventh. The ancient fetish, as tall as ten men, was crowned by the plumed solar disc and the royal cobra headband of the King from which streamed colorful ribbons. Smoothly rounded at the top and divided into four sections by silver bands, the golden reliquary resembled the head of a man's erection and, although thinner, the pole supporting it was clearly evocative of the shaft.

The evening after the *Ta-wer* was paraded through town Seshen said, "Every woman knows which one of his heads truly rules a man and the gods are no different." She had never been granted her desire for a child and her bitter disappointment tended to take the form of irreverent comments.

Hatshepsut worried her attendant had lost her faith but knew there was nothing she could say to reawaken it in her. Only the Lord of the Universe, buried alive in everyone's heart, had the power to do so.

Osiris was the body of Re. Wearing the white crown of Upper Kemet, his body wrapped in white bandages exposing only his green face and hands gripping the crook and flail, Osiris represented the world of flesh sustained by earthly energies subject to the cycles of birth and decay which in their turn were inseparable from time. The black skin with which he could also be depicted represented the power of transcendence. Hatshepsut felt the flail of Osiris strike her heart every time she thought of death, and the promise of eternal life was the loving crook of his arm in which all her hopes rested.

She regretted that Menkheperre was currently staying with Khenti. The boy went to bed early but the presence of the King's Mother dampened the pleasure she was able to take in the banquets held for her by her beloved Nomarch. Khenti's wife, Nefertari, was nearly as tall as her husband and so fine-boned that her full breasts and hips were even more lusciously prominent. It soon became apparent she was not his equal mentally, but she had borne him three children successfully and was sweet and soften spoken. Despite having to put up with Isis, her stay in Hut-Sekhem was quite pleasurable and every day Khenti took her hunting. Hapuseneb had brought his falcon with him and Hathor seemed determined to make more kills than Khenti's smaller and darker partner, although in the end Bat acquitted herself nicely. Senmut was apparently more comfortable wielding throwing sticks than commanding predatory birds. Pharaoh was able to show off her skill with the bow by killing an oryx with the help of her chariot driver Thutmose, who was now also her Sandal Bearer and Chamberlain. It was not as thrilling as defeating Kushites together but she enjoyed herself.

While in the eighth Nome, she spent time with Satepihu as a guest in the new and much roomier home her generosity had enabled him to build. The Overseer of the Priests of Tjeny had begun working on his Ba-bird's eternal home in Abedju, the burial place of Osiris and of Kemet's most ancient kings. His tomb was prestigiously situated on the great processional route leading from the sacred precincts of God's House to the holy City of Eternity. She found her conversations with him stimulating because like her he understood that Osiris was only another form of Atum, the self-created Great God, King of Heaven, also known in the Nome of the Sistrum as Onuris, the Royal Huntsman.

Continuing north, Maatakre presided at the foundation ceremonies for her new temple to Pakhet. She was particularly pleased with the door-leaves made of acacia wood inlaid with bronze. All the chambers were perfumed with incense, and balls of natron were arranged in a perfect circle in the innermost chapel. Holding the *sekhem* scepter of *power* in her right hand, she faced the statue of Pakhet where it stood restlessly caressed by shadows in the holy of holies lit only by flickering candles molded from animal fat. On behalf of the King, eight priests presented the *neter* with loaves of bread, the haunches of cows and jugs filled with beer dyed blood-red. The rich pungent scents of costly unguents and freshly slaughtered animals helped stimulate and magically awaken the figure's wooden senses while reaffirming the direct link between physical existence and a Divine dimension. She urged the goddess to protect the throne of her Father and at the end of the rite her Majesty ceded the great seat of the new temple to its Lord.

The Hathor heads crowning the columns lining the entrance were deliberately left unfinished because Pakhet embodied the fierce untamed aspect of the Goddess. Every night the wild lions sacred to She Who Scratches hunted in the desert behind her house while its entrance faced the civilized and cultivated land of Hathor.

On the left wall of the inner corridor leading from the vestibule into the chapel, Maatkare knelt before Amun-Re while behind her the lion-headed goddess proclaimed:

I place your terror in all lands,

I rear up between your eyebrows,

On the right wall Pakhet became the fully human Hathor offering the king the *menit* necklace and a snake-entwined scepter.

On her first royal progress, it became obvious the Female Falcon had everywhere captured the hearts of the *rekhyt*. Many of her subjects had felt her touch in the form of the scribes and officials who served as her Eyes and Ears and were charged with the task of rooting out wrong-doers and healing injustice wherever they discovered it. Local temples were once again becoming the heart of the people whose bodies and souls they were meant to protect and help nourish. In too many Nomes, the house of the *neter* had become nothing more than a voracious mouth demanding more and more offerings while providing nothing in exchange.

Everywhere she went Maatkare repeated the words of King Khety spoken to his son Merikare as she addressed Nomarchs and headmen, priests, farmers and fishermen, anyone who came to listen so they would know that, rich or poor, noble or commoner, hereditary lord or *rekhyt*, they all played a vital role in the worhsip of Maat:

"Let your voice be just on the side of God. The heaven of a man is his good nature; but the slanders of an angry man are shameful.

"Be skilled in words that you may be strong. Words are more powerful than any fighting.

"Respect the living man who is sharp-sighted; it is the naïve man who shall be miserable.

"You must speak truth within your household. The foremost house must earn respect from those who serve it.

"Be just that you may prosper upon earth; soothe the weeper, do not oppress the widow; do not deprive a man of his father's goods nor interfere with high officials in their functions. Beware of punishing unfairly, and cause no injury—that will not help you!

"A man lives on after his final mooring, and his deeds are heaped beside him. Existence over There is certainly forever, and one who takes it lightly is a fool; but one who reaches there free of wrongdoing—he shall live on like a god, wide-striding like the Lords of all eternity.

"Honor your high officials, advance your trusted men, give gifts freely to the young troops; equip with knowledge, furnish fields, provide with cattle. Do not prefer the rich man's son over the humble—you should pick a man according to his deeds.

"A man shall do what benefits his soul, hallowing the Mysteries and breaking bread in the House of God. A single day contributes to eternity, an hour embellishes the future. Through service to Him, one is known to God."[67]

For the vital task of making certain Maat did not suffer anywhere in the Two Lands, Hatshepsut sacrificed the profound pleasure of Hapuseneb's company more often than she would have liked to. But even when they were not physically together she basked in the joy of knowing they were fulfilling the dream they shared of enlarging the Houses of Amun, Osiris and Ptah while building new monuments, restoring those fallen into ruin and sweeping clean temples that had degenerated into nothing more than foul stables for the cult statues of animals. The House of Hathor where they had witnessed three cobras mating had been reconstructed in brilliant white limestone and the confining decay reigning in that desolate place driven away by the shaking of dozens of sistrums. All that lived moved, exercising the power to create which kept death and decay forever at bay. She entered the temple for the first time vigorously shaking a *naos* sistrum with her right hand and a *loop* sistrum with her left, stimulating the renewal of earthly cycles by striding forward between the dimensional pillars of the First Occasion as God and his Hand vibrating the universe into existence.

When Hapuseneb rejoined her in Itjtawy, she sent Senmut, the rest of her courtiers and the bulk of her household ahead of her to Mennefer. It was the gentle month of Mechir, an ideal time to spend hours in the desert admiring the works of some of her great ancestors ostensibly to make certain their chapels were being properly managed and furnished with offerings. The *hemu-ka* in charge of the pyramid complex of Senwosret met them in the entrance hall. He had inherited the position from his father, who had inherited it from his father and so on in an unbroken line stretching all the way back to the king's lifetime.

The outer enclosure wall encompassed nine small queen's pyramids erected around the towering monument of their husband, Kheperkare. Her father had chosen essentially the same throne name but that was not the only reason she felt such a deep affinity with the Horus of Fine Gold Ankhmesut, named Senwosret by his parents. Another wall, built entirely of limestone blocks, surrounded his great pyramid as well as the much smaller pyramid rising from its southeastern corner where he was actively worshipped by the priests devoted to the service of his Ka. After they made their offerings there, Hapuseneb took her arm and with a single gesture dismissed their attendants. Then he slipped his hand into hers and led her out of the narrow precinct of the last Mansion of Millions of Years to be constructed in the form of a pyramid. Instead of heading back the way they had come, they walked around the enclosed cult center between the base of Senwosret's eternal home and the inner wall separating it from the tombs of his queens.

Gazing directly up one of the soaring slopes forming the mysterious cradle of Kheperkare's Ka filled Hatshepsut with awe at how close the sky felt even as to her eyes it looked farther away than ever. She was obliged to squint against the blinding power of Re reflected by the limestone casing as the silence seemed to vibrate with meaning. She remembered what her mother had told her long ago, that Thoth was Re's servant, as her mind could find no words to express the beautiful feeling flowing through her heart. When she looked down, Hapuseneb's features were shadowed by the dark veil temporarily fallen over her eyes. She tried to blink it away and her breath caught as she seemed to glimpse in his face the ever-changing features of all the people he had been and was yet to be.

As though sensing she needed to move away from that moment, he gripped her hand more firmly and led her forward. He wanted to show her the exquisite bas-reliefs carved into the enclosure wall every few paces, the images and hieroglyphs confined to narrow panels. In all of them the River god Hapi—distinguished by his sagging breasts and belly and a woman's long wig worn over the phallic beard of a king—offered life, power and dominion to the pharaoh whose Horus name, Ankhmesut, was written above them and combined either with his throne name, Kheperkare, or with his birth name, Senwosret. Every panel was crowned by Horus in his falcon form wearing the double crown.

Detailed scenes decorated the walls of Senwosret's domain and recorded important moments in his reign, including the transportation of the Monument he erected in honor of Heh. It was not as tall as the two she herself had dedicated to the Lord of Eternity but that was only fitting for the creative power of every king, as of every human being, was meant to grow through successive incarnations. It troubled her that Nafre and Meresankh and many others dear to her did not believe they would ever live on earth again. She herself had once been shocked when Hapuseneb told her that her Ka's flock of Ba-birds was potentially endless in number. As she gazed at an image of Seshat wearing a long wig crowned by a seven-pointed star, it seemed obvious the tablet she balanced on her lap was large enough to hold many birth names and not merely the one she was currently inscribing. Seshat was the spirit of the Integral Ka that kept a record of all the bodies and lifetimes it had fashioned and all the things, good and bad, each Ba had done while contributing by way of growth to the whole. When the stones of old temples were given life again in new monuments, and when the *shenu* ring of a statue was re-inscribed with another name, the reality of many lifetimes was symbolically expressed and affirmed. Everyone she had once been was part of who she was now, all the names she once answered to replaced by a new one. The belief that Pharaoh was the same Royal Ka born again and again served to symbolize the reality of every soul's endless incarnations. It was obvious to anyone who could see that Maatkare was neither her brother nor her father and yet she sat on the Horus Throne of the Living.

Pyramids, and the temples embracing them, were Cradles of the Ka and she never tired of admiring them from a distance or of walking directly beneath them. Another reason she was so particularly fond of Senwosret was because he had honored his Great Royal Wife, Nofret, by placing her name inside a *shenu* ring, a privilege until then reserved only for kings.

* * * * *

In Mennefer, Pharaoh presided over the annual reception of foreign tribute. Princes of the Retenu kissed the floor before her and filled the royal storerooms with treasures. In her presence men who lived like kings at home were forced to remain on all fours, their eyes lowered. They scarcely had the chance to confirm Pharaoh was indeed a woman before they were suddenly able to see only the floor and the feet of her soldiers. If the envoys hesitated for even a heartbeat to prostrate themselves, Mentekhenu relished shoving them roughly to their knees, and then forcing them down with the point of a lance coldly kissing the napes of their necks. All bearers of tribute were obliged to bathe their hands, faces and feet before entering the Divine presence, but the skin of the bearded men from the Land of Turquoise—bringing gifts sent by tribal chiefs for the privilege of grazing their herds in the eastern mountains—still retained traces of hopelessly ingrained dirt.

A delegation of Asiatics made a more favorable impression in long-sleeved ankle-length white tunics almost entirely covering their hairy chests. A long strip of cloth with silver edges was wound decoratively around their waists and fell to their knees. Their shoulder-length black hair was confined by a thin white headband and their neatly trimmed beards jutted from their chins into sharp points. The ambassador knelt before Pharaoh, his head and eyes lowered, as his courtiers filed into the throne room. Each one held two gifts they placed at the foot of the dais. Predominant amongst the offerings were ivory horn containers, their broad bases rimmed in gold and their narrow ends tapering into the painted head of woman wearing a feather in her hair—an apparent tribute to Maat that impressed her. Also pleasing were corded leather necklaces hung with silver crescent moon pendants, colorful fringed shawls, and clay vessels in the shape of a woman sitting with a child on her lap or standing and holding a variety of objects, amongst them musical instruments, baskets and birds. Pottery vessels designed to hold wine and carved in the form of bejeweled male and female dwarfs would make splendid gifts to take home to the princess. Even more useful were quantities of arrows, bows and javelins, an endless assortment of drinking vessels and great copper cauldrons her chefs would certainly appreciate. Many lovely objects were brought before the female king and laid at her feet in addition to baskets brimming with raw silver and gemstones.

After he had performed the required obeisance, the Fenkhu ambassador was allowed to remain standing. His people had long traded with Kemet and with their good friends the Keftiu, and it was in her heart to strengthen the friendship between them. All the men in the Fenkhu delegation were elegantly dressed in short-sleeved shirts matching their *shentis*—a close-fitting tunic extending to just above their knees made either of a single piece of linen or of a material called cotton. The ambassador was dressed slightly differently in an ankle-length tunic and a cloak draped elegantly over his left shoulder. Both garments were dyed a striking shade somewhere between gold and red and divided by black lines into sections filled with little black and crimson circles. His oiled hair clung to his skull in serpent-like tendrils, four of which had escaped the confines of his golden diadem to fall in tight spirals around his ears. It if it had not been for his beard, which resembled a row of coiling black asps clinging to his chin and cheeks, the Fenkhu ambassador might almost have been considered handsome. He walked in his bare feet wearing armlets and bracelets of gold twisted three times around his forearms and wrists, and his fingers were adorned with silver rings set with dark gems she had been told served as his seals.

The Fenkhu delegation presented Pharaoh with beautiful furnishings for her palace fashioned entirely of bronze, not only cups, dishes, bowls, lamps and vases but also chairs and chests and couches adorned with fierce-looking animal heads. The seats of the chairs, the edges of the beds and the tops of the chests were made of smooth ivory carved with patterns pleasing to the eye. She was well satisfied with the gifts offered to her by the Fenkhu. Although his manner remained intensely reserved throughout the duration of the formal audience, later that evening, at the banquet she held in his honor, the ambassador was soon smiling and laughing where he sat at a table with the Great Steward of Amun. She was pleased Senmut was able to coax the foreigner out of his shell with the genuine curiosity he felt about his country. Coached for merely a few days by a scribe, her brilliant Steward was already half fluent in the language of the Fenkhu. She was confident he was making a mental list of interesting and important things to tell her when they were alone together.

While in Mennefer, Maatkare made it clear to all the foreign envoys that she gave priority to peace but whoever desired war would find her well prepared. Those who lived in the Land of the Two Rivers were daily reminded of the superior strength of Kemet's army by the monument her father had erected on the shores of the backward flowing water.

✳ ✳ ✳ ✳ ✳

The new palaces in Perunefer were as beautiful and comfortable as she had imagined they would be. The governor's home, serving as the administrative center, was both magnificent and efficiently structured, more receptive to cooling breezes with its open columned courts and numerous windows than the previous much smaller building. A ramp led up from the landing dock directly into her spacious new residence. She was especially gratified by the Keftiu-style paintings adorning the walls of interior courtyards in the smaller ceremonial palace, until Senmut ruined it for her.

"They are lovely," he agreed, "but I am concerned they will not last very long."

"Why?" she demanded, feeling personally offended for it had been her idea to employ foreign artists.

"Because it is my understanding the Keftiu, as we often do, use as the base for their pigments a plaster made of lime which continues to harden for a long time even though it looks perfectly dry. I fear that as it begins shrinking it will not permanently adhere to mud brick walls erected on soil containing large quantities of sand and silt, as it does here on the shores of the River."

"But then what will happen to the paintings?"

"The plaster beneath them will crumble and they will fall off the walls," he replied bluntly.

"What? Why did you not mention this sooner, Senmut?"

"It was not until I met Prince Kallikrates, and spent time conversing with him, that I learned more about the building practices of the Keftiu. Besides, I could be wrong."

"I doubt it, but I hope so!"

He laughed and pulled her into his arms.

She rested her hands on his chest, intending to push him away after one kiss because she was not in the mood for intimacies.

He released her abruptly.

Suddenly it worried her he was no longer smiling. "Will you stay with me tonight, Senmut?"

"I got the impression you felt like being alone."

"Did I say that?"

"Not with words, but your eyes reveal more than you know, as does your body when I hold it against my own."

She turned away from him and sat down. "You simply upset me for a moment, that is all."

'Forgive me, my lady, it is never my intention to upset you."

"I know." She sighed and patted the tops of her thighs. "Come here, my unique friend."

At once, he knelt at her feet and rested his cheek on her lap.

Gently she stroked the prickly down of hair covering his head which he had neglected to shave for several days. He looked more handsome without a wig, like a falcon with his hooked nose and large eyes that saw everything; nothing seemed to escape the talons of his thoughts. It was not his fault some of the facts he dropped devotedly in her lap upset her. Only his sinuous mouth, revealing as it did a vulnerable tenderness, did not belong on the otherwise predatory countenance she found so attractive.

"You are my beloved brother, Senmut. Please never doubt I love you. It is my fault, not yours, if sometimes you distress me by forcing me to realize there are so many things I still am not aware of even though in my heart I feel I know everything that is truly important. It puts me in a strange position, you see, for to love and believe in Amun-Re does not seem like enough when I am constantly confronted by all the hidden intricacies of Creation causing me to question how much I really know. Sometimes you make it all seem so complicated, I am tempted to despair at what a daunting task it is to seek to fully reveal The Hidden One and truly know what He expects of us. When I seem angry with you I am actually upset with myself for feeling lazy and overwhelmed instead of stimulated and intrigued.

"Since the afternoon you spoke of proof I have been avoiding you, Senmut. And yet I know everything my heart tells me is true even though I cannot prove it. I believe God employs His own mysterious strategy with us as we do with playing pieces in Senet and it is in great part due to you, my unique friend, that I am wiser and stronger now than I have ever been. Because of you, I am more determined than ever to achieve the ultimate victory of faith free of fear, and confident I will do so because of, and not despite, all the challenges placed before me. In many ways, you are one of those challenges as well as my sweetest happiness. Because I love you so much, I feel closer to the heart of God than I did before we met. I thank you for that, my brother, and for everything else that you do for me everyday. I must definitely think of more ways to repay you."

He raised his head and his eyes were luminous with unshed tears as he said, "I desire no more titles."

She smiled. "I know what you desire, Senmut, and you know it is yours, now and always, but I will award you more honorable positions as often as I want to."

* * * * *

The day after Akheperseneb was buried the installation of the new vizier took place in Waset. The court was admitted to the audience hall of Pharaoh, the newly appointed vizier was ushered in, and his Majesty said to him:

"Look to the office of the vizier, be vigilant concerning all that is done in it, for it is the mainstay of the entire land. Now as for the vizierate, it certainly is not pleasant; indeed it is as bitter as gall. See, he is copper enclosing the gold of his master's house; he is one who does not turn his face to magistrates or counsels, and who does not make for himself a partisan of anyone. You should see that everything is done in accordance with what is in the law and that everything is done exactly right. Do not judge unfairly for God abhors partiality. Regard him who you know like him you do not know, him who is near you like him who is far. Do not pass over a petitioner before you have attended to his pleas. Dismiss him only when you have caused him to hear why you dismiss him. Do not wrongfully show anger with a man, but be angry over that over which one should be angry; inspire respect for yourself that men may respect you. Men say of the vizier's chief scribe 'Scribe of Justice'. Do not do your own will in matters whereof the law is known. If you are absent from an investigation, you shall send the overseers of lands and chief sheriffs to investigate. If there is anyone who shall have made investigation before you, you shall question him; thus shall you act in respect of what has been laid to your charge."[68]

After the ceremony, Hatshepsut returned directly to her private apartments where she was divested of her ceremonial attire by Nafre and Meresankh. Seshen, crooning happily, was holding in her arms the baby boy she and her husband had adopted in the Nome of the Hare during the journey home. Both the child's parents had died in a pestilence which spread through the poorer villages of the district but left the more affluent homes unmolested, in large part due to the efforts of the healer priests sent by the Nome of the Oryx. She had honored Rasui with her company for several days even though by then she was homesick for Waset and seriously missing Neferure. Her daughter's expression when she saw the Asiatic dwarf-shaped vessels her mother had brought her was curiously disappointing. Surprisingly, she seemed less pleased by them than by the brightly patterned and delicately fringed shawls. She was especially enamored of the Fenkhu jewelry. She exclaimed over the bracelets where both ends were left open and terminated in exquisitely detailed animal heads facing each other—male and female lions, short-horned bulls, goats and rams. The earrings also captivated her, particularly a pair made of gold and composed of separate parts joined by chains as fine as spider webs woven elegantly together. The central rosette was surrounded by spirals from which flowed five separate chains hung with a variety of tiny objects—human heads, bottles, vases and other furnishings. For weeks, Neferure wore only her new foreign jewelry, showing it off to everyone, including her new special friend Tusi, Overseer of the Cultivators of Amun, one of Senmut's numerous assistants.

Tusi was twenty-years-old and dangerous. He made Hatshepsut think of a young Khenti but only for an instant because in truth his masculine beauty defied comparison. She could understand why the princess had lost interest in dwarfs and replaced most of her miniature servants with normal-sized young attendants pretty enough to please her handsome friend without competing with her own blossoming powers of attraction. She surprised herself by being distressed rather than relieved by the change in her daughter's tastes and temperament, which had suddenly become more conventionally submissive than uniquely assertive. She was worried, and confessed as much to Senmut.

"I am afraid Neferure will fall in love with Tusi," she said.

"She already has."

Her heart was flooded by emotions she had succeeded in rising above only because her husband had died and left her free to set the course of her life— longing and frustration and inexperience vying with curiosity stoked by a painfully intensifying sexual appetite which was never truly satisfied. Yet there was nothing she could do to rescue her daughter from the coming inundation of feelings no one had the power to set themselves above no matter how great their position was. Neferure had finally heard the trembling call of the *menit* but she was not free to dance. Even though her heart undoubtedly beat like an ivory clapper whenever Tusi entered the room, it was necessary for her to behave as if she was deaf to the attractive forces holding the universe together. It was an imperfect world which issued from between Nut's thighs, her body burning with desires, many of which, for one reason or another, could never be satisfied.

32

The Ka's Cradle

Bubu Reborn vanished one night and Hatshepsut was certain he had returned to the Dwat. She did not expect him to come back. She believed the next time she saw her beloved cat would be in the Field of Reeds. She was not surprised Bubu left no body behind the second time for he had already been mummified. His second death reminded her she would not live forever and that it was necessary that she choose the place where her Ba-bird would nest eternally as Maatkare. Her queen's tomb was finished but she would not be using it. She understood now why she had never been able to imagine herself forever lying in that desolate place so far from everyone she loved. She now had the right to build an eternal home in her father's newly established Royal Necropolis—The Valley of the Gates of the King.

The River had risen to its highest point and the sound of construction echoed off the still waters. Work had begun on her new pylon and on the first bark shrine. Elsewhere, two of the colossal statues planned for the southern entrance of *Ipet Sut* were slowly being born from a mountainside. Next year the House of Mut would be torn down and completely rebuilt. Amun-Kamutef would have to wait until his consort was prepared to receive him before his own temple was erected even though work had already begun on the first of her group statues.

"It all goes so slowly," she complained to Hapuseneb one afternoon when they were alone together in her Pleasure House. "Yet every day and every year seems to pass more and more quickly than before."

"All the more reason not to be impatient. Whenever the seed of an idea is born on earth it immediately flowers in the realm of the Ka."

"Then why is it necessary for us to be born in a place so inferior to the one from which we came?"

"For the same reason merely imagining something is not enough. Were I to spend my entire life dreaming of making love to you, and picturing the event in endless detail, it would not be the same because I would never truly feel and experience it. Actualization fulfills even as it teaches. Divine creativity hones itself on the stones of earth and the bones of our body, supporting as they do the eyes through which it sees in ways it never has before."

She gazed at him sadly. "The experience you use as an example seems to be one you are growing tired of."

"You may as well accuse me of growing tired of life and weary of beauty, Hatshepsut."

"I did not mean-"

"Do you doubt my love?"

"Of course not," she whispered, unable to meet his eyes.

"Then why do you question my desire?"

"Because..." She was forced to utter the humiliating concept, "Because sometimes, for men, it is not the same."

"If I had known you were going to spend the afternoon insulting me, I would not have requested the pleasure of your company."

"I know you are not like other men, and the last thing I meant to do was insult you, Hapuseneb, although of course I have. I realize that now and I beg your forgiveness." He was sitting beside her on the leopard skin and yet she dared not touch him. "Please do not be angry with me."

"I am not angry."

She was relieved but only slightly. Not knowing what else to say she remained desperately silent gazing at his beloved countenance.

"I understand." Abruptly, he reached for the water jug and refilled their cups. "I apologize for speaking to you so harshly."

"I deserved it!"

He smiled and she drained her cup feeling she had been given life again.

"It troubled me, Maatkare, to see you doubt your beauty, and I speak not only of your body but of your Ka, wherein truly reside all your powers of attraction that never age or die. Our flesh will one day cease to arouse lust and yet at night, by the light of the moon and the stars, we will always have the power to caress away time with our love. It will be many years before we are unable to burn away decay with Min's fire, and until the day I die there will be no place on earth more wonderful and desirable to me than inside you. The passage between your thighs leads out from the womb to my present happiness and back into my tomb, where my youth will be returned to me."

He set his cup down, took hers from her and pushed her back across the leopard skin rug. Spreading himself on top of her, he supported himself on his elbows and stared down into her eyes. "Although the stars have said I will cross the River before you, I promise I will not leave you alone for long, Hatshepsut."

For a while, his body thrusting into hers managed to drive what he had said out of her mind as the emotional pain caused by the thought of their inevitable separation became indistinguishable from the physical joy he made her suffer.

When he had recovered his breath he said, "You would agree, my lady, that I seemed most interested in that experience."

She smiled even as she suddenly wondered where Senmut and the Royal Ornament Amenhotep would be when she and the High Priest were together like this in the Field of Reeds.

"Do not fear," he said as though responding to her unspoken question. "Our hearts are larger than thoughts can comprehend. But it is true, Hatshepsut, that to no one else will we ever feel so close for your Ka and mine have known each other since the beginning of time."

His arms tightened around her as he whispered in her ear, "You and I were born together from Atum, brother and sister like Shu and Tefnut, Geb and Nut, separate and yet one forever!"

She clung to him and sighed, "I know!"

* * * * *

The workings of the heart were too mysterious to be fully grasped even by Thoth. Hatshepsut gave Senmut another gift, not because she felt guilty about the time she spent in another man's arms but because she adored him and constantly sought to reassure him of the fact in case he sometimes doubted it. She slipped the amulet, hanging from a leather cord, around his neck and from that day forward, he wore the carnelian Hathor-head inscribed for him by the king on which her name was engraved just above his:

Maatkare (Hatshepsut),

beloved of Iuny;

the hereditary prince and Great Steward

of Amun,

Senmut[69]

She presented him with the intimate gift on the ship she had given him while his skipper, Nebiri, lustily cracked his whip to keep the oarsmen in perfect rhythm. The rowers never actually felt the hot kiss of the lash, which served merely to encourage them, its slapping sound echoing the lapping of the water against the hull. The whip's wooden handle was delicately inscribed with blue hieroglyphs and Nebiri was obviously proud of the fine gift he had received from his lord, Senmut. The Great Steward of Amun was now in charge of dozens of barges. On that particular morning, they were traveling a few miles south to Iuny. His mother, Hatnefer, was mortally ill and it was Maatkare's desire to show the lady how much she respected her son by accompanying him. In the next world, Hatnefer would undoubtedly relish telling the story of how she was personally honored by a visit from Pharaoh. She would tell all the loved ones waiting for her there, beginning with her husband, Ramose, from whom she had too long been parted. Hatshepsut wanted to be by Senmut's side as he began facing the loss of the woman who bore him and loved him like no one else. A mother's unconditional affection could never be replaced but she would do her best to assuage its absence with hers.

Senmut left Tusi in charge of supervising Amun's flax crop, two-thirds of which was harvested when it was in bloom because only then did it produce the exceptionally fine thread needed to make the mist-linen prized by the king, priests and nobility. The fields of the god were a lovely sight rippling with what remained of the bright blue flowers, which were permitted to wither and produce the seeds for next year's planting. Senmut supervised dozens of administrators but Hatshepsut was particularly aware of Tusi who carried a vital part of her daughter with him everywhere he went. She was afraid some misfortune would befall him and that Neferure would be devastated. Men as young and strong as the Overseer of the Cultivators of Amun had perished unexpectedly and she worried for her daughter's happiness as she did not think to do for her own. When Senmut and Hapuseneb traveled, she knew in her heart they would return to her unharmed. The fact that Tusi could never marry God's Wife was irrelevant. She herself had been wed to one man while loving another, *two* others. Neferure had been as pleased as Tusi himself when Senmut awarded him a fine staff of office made from wood embellished with precious birch bark and silver.

Among the gifts Maatkare gave to the Mistress of the House Hatnefer was a gilded wooden box containing several cakes of *khyphi*, incense made from sixteen different ingredients the gods preferred above all others. It was a gift worthy of a queen and the woman still had energy enough to appreciate it. Judging from the lines etched into her face, Hatnefer was in great pain but she never complained or seemed to tire of smiling at her son, who could not possibly have made a mother prouder. Also present in the sick room with their sisters Nofret-hor, Ahmose and Ah-hotep were Amenemhet, recently promoted to a Priest of the Bark of Amun, and Pairi, working with his older brother as an Overseer of the Cattle of Amun.

Hatshepsut did not stay long with the dying woman but left her in the loving arms of her family while she made an offering in the Temple of Iunit, the local form of Hathor-Raet. Later that evening Senmut rejoined her in the High Priest's Riverside home, where the private apartment reserved for honored guests looked out on the water toward the golden hills of the western desert. The sun was setting when he was announced into her presence. Immediately she rose, slipped her arms around his neck and rested her cheek against his chest, seeking to comfort herself as well as him. Listening to his heart, she recalled how she had once imagined a tiny man who never needed to rest living inside everyone tirelessly beating his drum. She knew now the drummer was the Ka, the imperishable director of the mortal body's sensual orchestra.

"I am sorry," she said.

Senmut was silent and even though his arms returned her embrace, she sensed he was not yet truly present. Disengaging herself from him gently, she dismissed the hovering attendants by making a slicing gesture with her right hand and pouring red wine into a cup offered it to him herself.

He drained it thirstily.

"Now sit down, please." She indicated two chairs placed before the open window.

He obeyed her.

She refilled his cup, and then sat down beside him. Staring out at the sunset, she remarked, "Re is at his most beautiful when he becomes Atum and prepares for his journey through the darkness of the Dwat. Look at all the colorful sails flying from his mast, so vibrant and yet so delicate, their hues as ever changing and subtle as the breath of the Goddess."

"Hmm."

She glanced at him. "I am sorry," she repeated helplessly, and once more focused on the inspiring view that helped her forget the emotional anguish of death and to feel its mysterious promise instead.

"She wishes to be buried with my father."

"That is natural. I am sure he is waiting impatiently for her."

"The tomb of the Honorable Ramose is not worthy of the mother of the Great Steward of Amun."

Turning her head, she saw he was looking at her and not at the sunset. "I agree completely, Senmut. When the time comes you must bring your parents' bodies home to Waset, where they will lie together in a stone nest their Ba-birds will not be ashamed to enter whenever they choose to visit their loved ones in the offering chamber."

* * * * *

Back in Waset, Ibenre attended the king, who was suffering from a head cold.

"I feel miserable!" she told her physician. "Is there nothing you can give me besides milk mixed with honey and egg yolks?"

"You could not be healthier, Majesty. The unpleasantness will soon pass."

"My nose seems to be blocked with limestone! Not being able to breathe is not only unpleasant, it fills me with despair, as if I am cut off from life even though

I still exist. Not to mention it makes my throat feel as dry as a tomb's entrance shaft!"

"This tea should help a little."

She accepted the cup from him hopefully.

"Careful," he urged. "It is still quite hot and I do not wish to add a burned tongue to your list of discomforts."

She smiled up at him. "You think I am behaving like a child but the truth is I would rather go into battle against the Kushites than feel so awful for very much longer."

She braved a sip of the odd smelling beverage. "I cannot imagine what it must be like to be truly ill and in pain, Ibenre. I do not think I would be able to tolerate it. Better to die swiftly in battle than to perish slowly from the betrayal of one's own body."

"You may be sitting down and resting at the moment but in truth you are fighting the invasion of chaotic elements, Majesty. What is making you so miserable are the side effects of this battle, which is affecting your body's Maat. Your blood is a river upon which sail millions of soldiers commanded by your Ka in much the same way Pharaoh, wearer of the white and the red crowns, rules over the Two Lands and the vital organs of its Nomarchs."

She smiled at him again. "Suddenly I find myself almost happy to be indisposed since it is giving me the opportunity to speak with you so."

"My lady, it is a source of great happiness to me how infrequently you have need of my services."

"Thank you, Ibenre." She hesitated a moment before saying, "You are Hapuseneb's personal physician as well. Tell me, does it not seem to you the High Priest possesses a direct link to the magical healing powers of his Ka?"

His right dimple deepened as he half smiled. "Perhaps." He removed another leather pouch from a small wooden box decorated with golden *ankhs*.

She chose not to take offense at his reticence. She felt bad enough already. "I understand, Ibenre that you spend much of your time engaged in research. What do you do, exactly?"

"I observe."

"That is all?"

"That is everything."

"But the eyes, as the High Priest of Thoth has pointed out to me, cannot truly see anything by themselves for they require the intelligence of the heart to make sense of what they observe."

"I engage in research, Majesty, a system of carefully documented observations through which it is possible to come to a greater understanding of all aspects of manifested life and how they work, or fail to work, together. How our eyesight and all the other senses serving our awareness function is a vital part of my studies even as it inevitably provides the initial premise—that the observer and the observed are in essence inseparable. We are none of us truly divided from the world which makes it possible for us to see and be."

"Would it not be more accurate to say that to *feel* is to be?"

"Feeling is, indeed, the music of the cosmos but there is no higher pursuit than the mastery of consciousness. Creation is a complex instrument and the more we study its nuances and subtleties the more accomplished players we empower ourselves to become."

"Right now I feel as if only sour notes are emanating from my physical instrument." She forced herself to finish the bitter tea. "I do not want the royal embalmers to put plugs in my mummy's nose! Although I realize my Ka will no longer be breathing the air of life into my body, it would still be awful to look congested forever."

He laughed. "I see you are feeling better. Humor and health walk hand in hand. Every time we laugh the magic of our Ka flows out of us and energizes others even as it cleanses us, if only for a few moments, of all illusory anxieties."

"I have heard it said that when we laugh we defy death."

"I believe we are able to laugh because nothing is permanent, including death, which is only a transition, and deep in our hearts we know that. Illness invariably results when we fail to heed the intelligence of our heart. Diseases are all too often the self-fulfilling prophecy of unconquered fears. And whether directed inward at ourselves or outward toward others, hatred is a dangerously infectious sore."

She still could not breathe through her nose after Ibenre departed, leaving behind another pouch of the foul-tasting tea for Nafre to prepare later, but she felt better. In four days she was fully recovered, but while she was indisposed she thought entirely too much about her mummy and the new stone Master of Life she had ordered from one of the southern quarries. The one carved for her as queen was no longer suitable. When the miracle of breathing freely was restored to her she almost felt reborn, and suddenly she was less than satisfied with the plans she was making for her afterlife. She relived her flight from the Chamber of the Other World in the Temple of Satis to the now abandoned entrance of her queen's tomb and how she had soared across Mentuhotep's luminous Mansion of Millions of Years. Remembering that her brother had desired to erect a similar sanctuary for his Ka, she summoned the scribes who had drawn up the initial plans and studied them in the company of Hapuseneb and Puyemre.

"There is not much here," she observed.

The prophets of Amun were standing on either side of her at a table in the library of the *per-ankh*. She rolled the papyrus back up and handed it to the scribe waiting behind her.

"Destroy it," she commanded. "Burn it. I do not want my brother's Akh teased and saddened by the evidence of dreams he was never meant to realize in that lifetime."

The scribe hurried from the room.

"I will begin anew," she declared. "I feel my heart taking wing and urging me to erect a truly magnificent Mansion of Millions of Years."

"And the treasury will be the wind beneath your wings," Hapuseneb said firmly. "Do not worry about the cost. It is for your Ka, which exists beyond all such concerns, to determine the monument's design and the truths it will express. Ideas must emanate freely from your heart without material constraints."

"You are the River," Puyemre added. "It would be wrong for you to worry about things like dykes and canals not being able to support you. To give splendorous life to the seed of your dream is all you need be concerned with. We will handle the rest for you, Majesty, and that is as it should be, otherwise we risk offending Amun-Re whose creative spirit you embody."

"Well said, my friends." She smiled at each of them in turn. "My heart tells me it is doubtful any other Pharaoh has ever been so well served by his advisors. In the western desert sacred to Hathor, I will build a Mansion in honor of God's Hand and the magical steps she fashioned for Amun-Kamutef. The monument will also serve as the Cradle of my Ka and directly face the Great House of my Father and Husband, Amun."

She paused, suddenly wishing that Patehuti and his magical bowl of water were there so he could give her a glimpse of the splendid building taking shape in her heart.

"I will most certainly need your help to give birth to what has been conceived in me today," she told the priests. "In truth it is your love and friendship which have brought me to this moment. As Ibenre recently reminded me, nothing and no one is separate from anything or anyone else and I especially know that to be true when I am with the First Prophets of Amun."

And with Senmut. She did not need to speak his name for the room to suddenly be filled with his presence. The Great Steward of Amun was still in Iuny attending his dying mother. Her physicians did not expect Mutnofret to live much longer.

Waiting for her unique friend to return to Waset, she thought about the beautiful temple she would erect beside the Mansion of her great ancestor. Almost directly across from where construction would commence, on the western side of the mountain, lay her father's tomb. One night she had been thinking about it before she fell asleep so she was not surprised to find herself perched on a rock just across from the entrance conscious of being awake in a dream. She discerned her father's silhouette outlined by moonlight where he stood before the door and joy propelled her toward him. She was unaware of a bodily form and yet she clearly saw and felt her hands as he grasped them with both of his. "Come, Hatshepsut," he spoke without moving his lips, "and rejoice at the beauty within." The stone door felt no more substantial than air as they walked through it together. She marveled at the golden skin of his face, which wore an expression of such profound contentment it mysteriously served to illuminate the entrance corridor. He turned away and though she wanted to follow him, she suddenly found herself in bed on the other side of the River.

"Father!" she whispered, and knew she would never forget the silently eloquent hieroglyph of his smile and all she wonderful things she could still feel it telling her.

✴ ✴ ✴ ✴ ✴

The Lady Inet finally went to her Ka. Expecting to be relieved, Hatshepsut was unprepared for the terrible sense of loss she suffered. She had seriously underestimated the comfort of Inet's continued physical presence. Abruptly she was forced to come to terms with the depth of the sadness she had avoided by channeling it into the responsibilities of kingship and her great building projects. The moment her nurse took her final breath, she simply became Hatshepsut. As if it had happened only yesterday, she recalled sitting on her lap vowing to commission a statue of them together to prove she would never forget her. She had thought about this promise every time Senmut showed her a new carving of himself with Neferure, but she had felt obliged to wait until Inet departed and could actually recognize herself in the monument. Now at last the old woman's Ba-bird had flown away and in the midst of its magical flights between the shores of death and life was free to perch on imperishable stone image of who she had once been. As a transfigured Akh, Inet would once again be able to feel the love Hatshepsut had felt for her and always would.

"I will build her a tomb near my own," she told Seni, who had known Inet even longer than she had.

"She would like that very much, I think."

"And her Ka will be revered along with Pharaoh's in my Mansion of Millions of Years for I intend to commission a statue of us us as we were on the afternoon I promised her I would never forget her. Even though I will be king, I will also be the little girl who sat on her lap attempting to comfort her because she was sad I was growing up so fast. I remember what she said, 'the journey was too

423

short', and she was right, Seni. Time is our friend when we are young but the older we get the more it becomes our enemy."

"It may feel that way, my lady, but time is no more your enemy than Inet was when she insisted it was time for you to go to bed, where you enjoyed having adventures in your dreams instead of out in your garden."

"You are right, my friend." She smiled at him gratefully. "Each lifetime is but a day to the Ka, merely another egg laid with Re's magical yoke burning inside it."

She wrote out the inscription to be carved on the sandstone statue of Inet and herself:

May the king, Maatkare-Hatshepsut, and Osiris, First of the Westerners, the great god Lord of Abedju, be gracious and give a mortuary offering of cakes and beer, beef and fowl, and thousands of everything good and pure, and the sweet breath of the north wind to the spirit of the chief nurse who suckled the Mistress of the Two Lands, Sit-Re, called Inet, True of Voice.[70]

She apologized to Sit-Re, known as Inet by all those who loved her, for how long her mummy would have to wait before being taken to its final resting place, but the delay would be worth it. She tried to imagine her nurse's surprise and happiness when she discovered her body was buried beside a king, an honor never before accorded a royal wet nurse.

* * * * *

Life clasped hands with death. The forbidding contours of the western desert became as familiar to Hatshepsut as the relaxing confines of her Pleasure House.

For an entire moon, Djehuty listened to what she and the First Prophets of Amun had to say before he finally drew up a rough outline and, after several revisions, she approved the initial design for her Mansion of Millions of Years. As soon as the consecrated foundation deposits were buried, her dream of a monument embodying all her deepest thoughts and feelings would begin taking root in reality.

Satisfied with the progress of her building projects, Hatshepsut crossed the River with Senmut to view the location he had chosen for his tomb. She had long since given him permission to excavate wherever he wanted to. His mother and father were to be buried directly beneath him in a rather cramped room serving as the site of a joyous family reunion. Two wooden Master's of Life, carved and painted in the likeness of Ramose and Hatnefer, would rest beside two featureless containers embracing the six bodies of their parents and siblings.

The burial chamber would be hidden behind a door located beneath the terrace, in its turn safely blocked from view by the rocky debris due to rain down from above when their illustrious relative began digging his own resting place.

Hatshepsut was glad Hatnefer had lived long enough to enjoy her son's astonishing success and all the wealth attending it. She hoped it went some way toward comforting Senmut for his mother's loss to be able to provide her with a rich burial. From his expression, she gleaned how much it meant to him when the king herself made offerings to the Mistress of the House Hatnefer. Maatkare gave the lady a magnificent golden funeral mask in addition to one of her own heart scarabs carved of serpentine mounted in gold and hung from a chain of four golden wires plaited tightly together. The king's name was erased from the amulet and replaced with Hatnefer's above lines of text taken from *The Book of Coming Forth By Day and Opening the Tomb*, excerpts from which were also copied onto two rolls of papyrus and onto a third scroll, made of leather, placed beside the scarab beneath one of the outer layers of linen embracing the lady's body. The spells were all based on ancient versions but in recent years many of them had been elaborated upon, either partially or extensively, and collected into a single document. Jars of wine inscribed with *Gods Wife, Hatshepsut* were taken out of storage and found life again in the funeral procession boasting luxury items Hatnefer had enjoyed while she still lived as gifts from her son—a silver bowl and two matching pitchers, scarab rings, chests of fine linen and boxes filled with cosmetics she could magically use in the Dwat to make herself beautiful again.

In Year Seven of the Good Goddess Maatkare, on the second day of the fourth month in the season of Immersion, the Great Steward of Amun, Senmut, began work on his tomb. He had been preoccupied with the plans for months and as soon as construction commenced she rarely saw him. Before that time, he had also been away from Waset a great deal choosing and acquiring the stone for the imperishable container she had given him permission to acquire for his wooden Master of Life. She was beginning to feel he was somewhat too obsessed with his personal affairs. He spent more time around his dead mother, at the summit of the hill beneath which she was buried, than he did with the living woman who loved him and missed his input in the Seal Room. Initially she listened patiently to the difficulties he encountered in the prestigiously visible area of the western desert he had selected for his resting place. The slope of the mountain was so steep he was forced to build an artificial terrace leading to the tomb's entrance but, clever as ever, he solved the problem by tunneling into the rock and using the resulting debris to fashion the buttressed porch on which the public forecourt would rest.

"Need you spend so much time out there, Senmut?" she asked him one evening when they were dining alone. "Surely you trust the Workers of the Place of Truth to follow your plans scrupulously."

"They are trained to dig, not to think. Once the terrace is finished my presence will not be required quite so often."

"I am pleased to hear it for you are needed in the Seal Room… I also miss you."

"Do you? I am pleased to hear it," he echoed, "although I am surprised since you are always with Hapuseneb."

"And with Puyemre and Djehuty and-"

"You know what I mean."

She was silent for a time as she searched his eyes and her heart for the right thing to say because it also had to be the truth.

"I understand you miss your mother, Senmut, but I never heard you complain about having to share her love with your brothers and sisters."

"That is different."

"Why? Do not men sometimes have two wives?"

"Yes, but the women are never equal in status. There is normally the chief wife and the minor wife or concubine. You know that."

"Are you not in the least bit interested in the Mansion of Millions of Years I will soon begin building?" She changed the subject.

"You know I am. It will serve as the cradle of your Ka and for that reason it is my wish to be buried as close to it as possible."

"But your Master of Life was just the other day hauled all the way up to the tomb you have already begun digging!"

"It has. Nevertheless, I have discovered my mummy is not destined to rest above my parents as I intended. The gods have appropriately rewarded me for my foolishness. The stone of the mountain is unstable and will not permit extensive tunneling without collapsing. Yet that is not the only reason I have determined that location will merely serve as the chapel where offerings will be made to my Ka by priests and any loved ones who survive me."

She felt him reminding her of the children he would never have because he loved her exclusively and refused to marry another woman.

"Why do you say you were being foolish, Senmut?"

"Because it is always foolish to lie, especially to yourself. I thought I could bear to distance myself from you but the truth is I desire to be buried as close to my beautiful king as possible."

"I would also like that," she said softly. "You need only tell me where you wish to dig and I will permit it. Separating the offering chapel from the actual burial chamber is becoming quite fashionable. However, I would be grateful if in the future you would spend less time in the western desert while we both still live and can take joy in each other's company as Hatshepsut and Senmut, before the Dwat transforms us and, after we have relaxed for a time in the golden fields of Osiris, we are born as other people."

The sudden silence seemed to ring with his skepticism.

"You do not believe we will one day be forced to say farewell forever, do you Senmut?"

"No," his expression softened, "for your beauty awakened my faith, Maatkare. When I was young, I confess I did not believe in the gods much, but Seshat had other plans for me. The sharp intelligence that caused me to cut my heart with doubts led me to Amun, and to you. I thought I was able to see more clearly than anyone until you made me realize I was foolishly taking pride in being blind to the truth only because it seemed too easy, too simple, like loving someone. Then I met you and I never wanted how I felt to end. Hathor smiled at me with your lips and the gods entered my heart. I knew then how stupid I had been even while imagining myself one of the special few faithful to the miserable illusion that life begins and ends with the flesh. I always felt a great affection for my parents and my brothers and sisters but I never truly loved anyone until I met you, Hatshepsut."

33

Master of Life

Year eight of the Good Goddess Maatkare and the God God Menkheperre, the fourth month of Akhet, day sixteen, saw the beginning of opening the doorway of the temple in the western mountain sacred to Hathor. Fourteen brick-lined pits filled with consecrated objects marked the future location of the north and south walls, the central ramp and the eastern courtyard. Scarabs and other amulets inscribed with the throne names of the two pharaohs were ceremoniously buried alongside jars of food, cakes of perfume and hundreds of model tools, everything needed to translate dreams into reality. Some of the scarabs serving to sign the monument, and to draw the power of good fortune down upon it, were inscribed with the name *Akheperkare* for it was his daughter's intention to dedicate a chapel to him in her Million Years Mansion where his Ka would be revered alongside hers. Hapuseneb and Senmut, Nehesj, Djehuty and Puyemre all began accepting Name Stones donated by the citizens of Waset to the glorious project. Each rough-hewn block was inscribed with the name of the donor, the name of the official who received it and the date it was sent to the building site.

Dejehuty, her Overseer of Works, acted as chief of construction. Senmut acquired another title, Controller of Works, empowering him to command the crews should he spot a problem and feel it necessary to intervene. Naturally, she wanted Senmut intimately associated with her Mansion. To further link his burial chamber with the chapel of her Ka, she gave him a quantity of the amulets and objects originally intended for her foundation deposits so he could bury them wherever he chose to dig. He had not yet selected the location for the second half of his tomb and she did not press him because she liked to think there were still many years of life left to them. Nevertheless, she now knew where she wanted to be buried and she lost no time in broaching the subject with Hapuseneb. One stimulatingly cold evening, she invited the High Priest to dine alone with her. She was as filled with a sense of profound purpose as the earth was with seeds. Many of her workers had gone home for the sowing but had now returned and renewed their efforts to make beautiful monuments bloom from the sand on both sides of the River. Nothing gladdened her heart as much as watching the brightly painted walls of bark shrines and temples unfurl like the petals of imperishable flowers. The harvest would once again slow down the progress of her various building projects, but not for long.

"Do you recall, Hapuseneb, the dream I recently had with my father?"

"Of course I do."

They were sitting across from each other on colorful woolen rugs spread across the floor of her most private apartment. The windows looking out onto her garden were open and it was sometimes hard to hear each other talk over the rapturous singing of frogs. Heqet's creatures were courting each other and laying their eggs in the palace ponds even though their offspring—the tadpoles used in the *medu neters* to write 100,000 years—would all mostly be eaten by the pretty fish which helped keep the water clean.

"I know you believe a single dream may hold many meanings," she continued, "and I agree with you. In this dream, my father's smile was so eloquent I truly feel it has a positive effect on my feelings every time I remember it. But it can only mean one thing he invited me into his eternal home... I believe he wishes me to share it with him."

"I also believe that is what Akheperkare wishes. As to what else he may have meant to tell you through the dream I cannot venture to guess. That is between your heart and his."

"His tomb must be enlarged," she said decisively, "and it would give me great joy, Hapuseneb, if you would take charge of the project."

"I would be honored," he replied, "but delicious as their contents are, I wish we were not separated by all these dishes."

She fell forward onto her hands and knees and, watching his face, crawled around the food laden platters. The way he eyed her gently swaying hips pleased her so much she felt her breasts tightening and the long nipples he often complimented press impatiently against her tunic. She was not wearing a wig and the moment she was close enough he clutched a fistful of hair at the nape of her neck, treating her like the feline she was pretending to be as he kissed her hungrily.

Her servants knew better than to disturb her when she was dining alone with someone but Satis—who had been asleep on her pillow in a corner of the room—was not quite so disciplined. Hatshepsut was still on all fours and moaning shamelessly as the High Priest possessed her from behind when Satis purred loudly in her ear. Startled, she raised her head and a rough tongue eagerly licked her face.

Hapuseneb laughed as the cheetah rubbed against them both with increasing ardor but he did not permit the animal to rush him. On the contrary, Hatshepsut could feel how aroused he was by this wild and potentially dangerous addition to their erotic activity. In the end, the frustrated cheetah had to settle for a platter of raw duck meat.

As she lay in the High Priest's arms on a couch before one of the windows, it did not feel strange to talk about her tomb. They had just shared one of life's greatest pleasures but all earthly joys would pale in comparison with the sensual magic of the Dwat and the boundless creative powers they would possess there.

When she expressed this thought out loud Hapuseneb said, "That is true. What I can do to you here is only a dim reflection of the amazing things I will be able to make you feel in the next world, so be prepared."

She smiled. "You are teasing me again, my lord, and yet I feel you are also serious." Her cheek resting against his chest, she gazed contentedly up at the night sky. Between the leaves of fig trees, infinitely juicy stars glimmered like fruits forged of electrum.

She sighed. "The universe feels like an endless banquet spread out just for us!"

"Every universe *is* a unique feast," he agreed. "The mysteriously delicious ingredients of incarnation served by our Ka can be combined in countless different realities pleasing to the palate of God."

"How everything comes together when I am with you, Hapuseneb, is excelled by nothing else. There are many people I dearly love and yet I do not feel they are an inseparable part of me. It *must* be true that you and I are like Shu and Tefnut, brother and sister forever."

He stroked her hair. "I am sorry, Hatshepsut, that in this life you could not be my wife."

"Perhaps it is just as well," she forced herself to speak lightly as his tenderness threatened to make her cry. "I could never have borne you as many children as Amenhotep. I do not know how she did it. I thought it terribly annoying being pregnant, and giving birth was even worse."

"I am fond of all my sons and daughters but it was Amenhotep who desired so many offspring. I would have been content to act as father to one or two souls I was bound to by the much deeper affection that comes from having lived other lifetimes together. None of my children are familiar to me. If you and I had formed a child I believe the three of us would have shared a more meaningful bond."

"I understand... I sometimes feel there is someone inside Neferure I do not really know and yet it does not affect how much I love her."

He fell silent and for some reason this worried her. She raised her head and gazed up at his face. "Are you aware of something concerning Neferure's destiny you are not sharing with me, Hapuseneb? Does it have something to do with Tusi? You know they are hopelessly in love."

"I know."

It further worried her he did not meet her eyes but kept staring out the window as if the stars told him something he did not wish to share with her. Even though she dreaded pressing him on the subject, she was compelled to do so. "*Tell* me!" she begged softly.

"I am afraid there is nothing to say."

Only after he had left did it occur to her to wonder, and the possibility filled her with dread, if he had, in fact, confessed what the priests who read the heavens had said about her daughter. And her unease only deepened when she suddenly realized that was the first time she had ever heard the High Priest utter the words, "I am afraid."

* * * * *

Before work began and his rest was disturbed, Hatshepsut visited her father in his eternal home. Hapuseneb went with her. Akheperkare's *hemu* Ka led the way holding a yellow candle shaped like a falcon perched on a golden pedestal serving as the handle. Mentekhenu and four of his strongest men walked behind the king and the High Priest. They would not be able to protect them should a section of the roof and walls collapse around them, but her chief of security had looked less concerned about her plan to venture deep into one of the mountains of the Necropolis when she gave him permission to attend her.

At the base of the rockface, work was progressing on the tomb of Sit-Re, known as Inet, and on the east bank a statue of the King sitting on her nurse's lap was taking shape in one of the royal workshops.

Hatshepsut felt her heart rise into her throat, reminding her of the ultimate inadequacy of words, when the seal protecting her father's tomb from potential intruders was easily broken. She recalled the awful feeling she had suffered on that afternoon years ago watching this same door close for what she had believed would be forever. She had not foreseen how, on her command, the separation between the living and the dead would one day be breached by love, which remained as strong as ever in the heart and in the dreams flowing from it. She experienced a thrill inseparable from the chilly stillness that greeted them in the entrance corridor. She was very glad her father's *hemu* Ka lit the way with the burning light of life emanating from the body of Horus—the spirit's ability to rise above physical death and dissolution. The hot and beautiful flame reminded her that the man named Thutmose by his parents was not truly there. Only his mummy lay in the burial chamber, its brittle limbs a mere handful of branches in the Divine tree of his Ka. For an instant, the possibility of glimpsing her father's Ba in flight between this world and the next filled her with exciting horror, until she remembered the Ba-bird was only a symbol of transcendence. Or so Hapuseneb had told her.

The tomb's entrance looked exactly as she remembered it from her dream. The passage turned slightly to the right, aligning itself with the eastern horizon before beginning its steep descent. However, actually being there felt very different because she was not safely asleep in bed; her body anxiously registered the floor's demanding angle and the oppressively lifeless silence. Two of Mentekhenu's men carried oil lamps but the deeper they went the more fervently the flames spurted in protest and the weaker they became. When the corridor began curving south, Hapuseneb gripped one of her arms as she preceded him down the steps cut into the northern wall. The stairway was flanked by the smooth ramp along which Akheperkare's wooden Master of Life had been pushed all the way from the entrance above them to its resting place far below. When they finally entered the first chamber, she stopped and took a deep breath. The room was small, roughly hewn and unpainted, but after the cloying embrace of the descending passage, it offered the space she needed to breathe more freely. Flowing south like the rippling waters of Nun, the stairway divided the left wall from the right wall along which the corridor plunged.

The farther they progressed into what had once been seemingly impenetrable rock, the happier Hatshepsut felt at the prospect of being with her father again. Although her eyes would behold only a wooden countenance not truly resembling him, she was certain her heart would feel his presence and silently commune with his Ka in a fashion even Thoth and Seshat could not express with words.

Their pace was slowed when the steps ended and the solid limestone floor gave way to a grainy gray slate. As she tripped on the uneven surface, Hapuseneb and Mentekhenu both caught one of her arms and for an invigorating moment she was pinned between two strong men.

A gradual eastward curve in the corridor brought them to a second chamber. Grooves in the walls had once held supporting rods used to slow the progress of the heavy Master of Life where the passage abruptly angled down even more steeply. She let Hapuseneb know with her eyes that she did not think she could manage the descent. He motioned to Mentekhenu and they braced her between them. It was necessary to walk swiftly and she struggled not to become dizzy as the rising ceiling made her feel disturbingly uprooted from the world of the living outside. She knew from studying the plans of the tomb that they had entered the final passage and her physical body was very glad. A Ba-bird would have no problem flying down to its nest but the muscles in her legs were protesting and her chilled flesh was letting her know it had no desire to remain there much longer.

The corridor turned sharply west before they finally reached the richly furnished burial chamber. The warm glimmer of gold was mysteriously reassuring to the heart, as was the presence of materials other than stone, which represented all the beautiful colors and forms of life embraced by the sun. Positioning himself at the head of Akheperkare's wooden bed, the *hemu* Ka murmured unintelligible prayers while Maatkare took her place at her father's feet. Mentekhenu and his men did not enter the room. The High Priest of Amun stood level with the dead Pharaoh's heart, his eyes closed and his head lowered. His arms were crossed over his chest and his hands respectfully grasped his shoulders.

Father, forgive me for disturbing you, she spoke to him silently with her heart, *but I remember the dream in which you invited me to enter your eternal home. I love you, father. I love you even more now than I did while you lived on earth. I rejoice in the belief that you have joined with your true self again, the magical Ka that fashioned the beautiful Ba of Thutmose. I have become what you proclaimed me to be the moment before you crossed the River—the Female Falcon, your successor—and it is her desire to embrace your wooden Master of Life with imperishable stone and provide your mummy with a resting place more worthy of the great Pharaoh you were.*

It was determined that from the north-western corner of the room an additional stairway would descend directly west. The new and larger burial chamber, supported by three pillars, would face north-east toward heaven and the eternal light of Life. Adjoining the space where the mummies would rest, two small rooms furnished only with magical inscriptions would act as gateways between terrestrial and celestial existence. The double portal would serve her father and herself.

The new stone container she had commissioned to hold her King's Master of Life—its brownish-red hue evoking the color of the solar disc setting in the west—was re-worked and enlarged to accommodate Akheperkare. She had no intention of waiting for the new burial chamber to be finished before she surrounded him with the potent spiritual symbolism of an incorruptible substance carved inside and out with magical words and images. All four external sides of the container, in addition to the head and the base of the lid, had already been inscribed for *Maatkare* in even more detail than the one made for her as queen. In order to enlarge it to accommodate her father's taller mummy it was necessary to smooth away all the painstakingly etched figures and hieroglyphs as if they had never been. Fortunately, the bottom of the lid and the four inner walls had not yet been decorated when she made her decision to order another container for herself and to give the current one to her father. With the assistance of the Lector Priest of Amun and of his son, Hapuseneb, she selected the sixty-nine texts and the nineteen divinities that would embrace and protect Akheperkare. Thirty-six magical recitations were decided upon in which twenty *neters* were mentioned and nine were represented.

Inside the grooves made by the bas-reliefs, the rock's red color became more strikingly visible and the result was quite beautiful after the entire surface was washed with a special solution before being polished. Even after the wash was removed, deep traces of red remained in the lines of the hieroglyphs and in the figures of the gods and goddesses. The exterior west side of the container was inscribed with her dedication:

May the Horus, Weseret-kau, Powerful of Kas, the Two Ladies, Wadjet-renput (Flourishing of Years), Horus of Gold, Divine of Appearances, King of Upper and Lower Kemet, Maatkare, Son of Re, Hatshepsut United with Amun. May she live forever. She made it as her monument to her beloved father, the perfect god, Lord of the Two Lands, King of Upper and Lower Kemet, Akheperkare, Son of Re, Thutmose, True of Voice.[71]

The exterior east side of the container was dedicated to Re and Life. The west side belonged to Anubis and other deities of the Dwat. *Shenu* rings—symbolizing the successful completion of an earthly cycle and the Ka's magical protection—surrounded several of the horizontal and vertical rows of hieroglyphs. Longer inscriptions were divided by straight lines. The interior of the lid had originally been decorated with an image of the celestial Mother Nut but now it reflected the outside of the lid devoted to the gods Hapi, Imset, Duamutef and Qebh-senuf. Wearing long wigs, the royal beard and the short ritual kilt, the Four Sons of Horus guarded the king's mummified vital organs.

Imset, with his human head, is linked with the liver, *merset*, the mysterious reservoir of the fiery water of Seth through which the Divine becomes incarnate. It is in the liver that the Ba makes its nest and leads his brethren—the blind functions of the flesh commanded and purified by spiritual consciousness.

The jackal, Dwamutef, watches over the stomach. Anubis was called the Opener of the Way because a jackal, like the vulture of Mut, converts rotting substances into the vital nourishment that sustains and creates life. Food decomposes in the stomach like mortal flesh in the tomb. The *wa* hieroglyph, written as a knot coming untied, symbolizes one form giving way to another—in the burial chamber as in the stomach—through the Gate of the Heart opened by Dwamutef.

Hapi, the baboon, guards the life-giving flow of the blood and its cyclical renewal. As the River rises and recedes every year, rushing into canals and tributaries, so the lungs expand and contract to harbor a Divine life force within a physical vessel.

The hawk-headed Qebsenuf feeds the flesh and the bones through the large intestine. The many folds of Qeb resemble a coiling serpent—the cobra rearing from the royal forehead behind which thoughts fly as they arise from the substance of incarnate life. What is destroyed in the stomach becomes energy and inspiration in the large intestine, promoting continued growth and creation.

Hatshepsut determined that a chest made of *biat*, divided into four compartments by wooden cross walls, would hold four stone jars containing her vital organs. The head of her new Master of Life would face north. The canopic chest—inscribed on all four sides with a horizontal row of hieroglyphs at the top and two vertical lines of text on each edge—would be placed directly east of her mummy's feet and read:

Oh Children of Horus, go carrying your daughter, this Osiris Maatkare who is inside—she is retired in you.

Neith, join your arms about that which is in you, delimit your protection about this Lord of the Two Lands, this Foremost of Noble Women, United with Amun.

Nepthys, unite your arms about that which is in you, extend your protection over the Lord of the Two Lands, this Maatkare.[72]

Freed of the brain, which the royal embalmers either ignored or discarded, the ability of the Ba-bird to pass through solid rock was affirmed by how the inscriptions on the interior and exterior of her stone Master of Life mirrored each other with only minor but meaningful variations. Inside, the figure of Nut lay ready to embrace and protect the mummy, her open arms stretching along both inner walls, on the exterior side of which two Eyes of Horus were etched so the deceased could use them to watch the sun rise and to see through the darkness to a new life. It was not necessary, as they had believed in the past, to turn the body on its side so it was actually facing the Eyes of Horus, for such literalness was shed with the flesh.

Inside her father's new stone bed the artist managed to fit one of Hatshepsut's favorite prayers from *The Book of Coming Forth By Day and Opening the Tomb*:

Recitation by King Akheperkare: Hail to you, owners of Kas, who are free of evil and who exist forever to the end of eternity. I have gained access to you, for I am a spirit in my own form, and powerful in my magic, and I am recognized as a spirit. Rescue me from the aggression of this land of the righteous; give me my mouth that I may speak with it. My arms are extended in your presence because I know you, I know your names, and I know the name of the Great God to whom you give offerings as he gains access to the eastern horizon of heaven, and as he alights in the western horizon of heaven. As he departs, so do I depart; and I flourish as he flourishes. I will not be driven from the Milky Way. Rebels will have no power over me. I will not be turned back from your gates. You will not seal your doors against me. There shall be given to me my father Atum, there shall be established for me my houses in the sky and on earth, with barley and emmer therein without number. My festivals will be made for me there by my bodily son, and you will give me invocation-offerings of incense, unguent, and every good and pure thing by which the god lives, to exist and be established forever, in every form beloved of Akheperkare, that he might travel downstream in the Field of Reeds, and that he might reach the two fields of divine oblations. Akheperkare, True of Voice, is the Double Lion, the Ruty of the horizon.[73]

✳ ✳ ✳ ✳ ✳

The new Temple of Mut was nearing completion. Maatkare gave Hapuseneb, Useramun and Senmut permission to order portrait statues for the inner courtyard. She was not surprised Senmut's offering was the most impressive of all, the reddish yellow color he chose worthy of a Pharaoh. The figure of the

Great Steward of Amun kneeling behind a large sistrum was as tall as she was. She had expected it to be big for he had requested permission to quarry a considerable amount of stone for himself while he supervised the excavation of her new stone Master of Life in which she would place her wooden Master of Life.

Irreverent as ever, except for when Tusi was present, Neferure said, "Senmut's statue *had* to be big, mother. Otherwise he would not have had enough room to inscribe all the titles you have loaded him down with!" She seemed to prefer the small copy he had commissioned to the much larger public monument. The two works were not identical, however, for on the right shoulder of the copy, carved from a polished black stone, a *shenu* ring embraced the name *Hatshepsut*. There was also a hole in the neck of the cobra—seen rearing in a temple doorway between two Ka arms—designed to hold interchangeable heads made of different materials. When Senmut offered the miniature piece to Neferure as a gift, she hugged him with the same unaffected passion she had displayed when she was a little girl. She had ignored her mother's suggestion she travel to Mennefer to become better acquainted with her half brother. The God's Wife left Waset to preside at certain festivals but she refused to travel north merely to spend time with Thutmose. In short, she refused to leave Tusi. She did not say as much but the obstinate set of her jaw and the look in her eyes told Hatshepsut all she needed, and did not want, to know.

Senmut's offering to Mut, when viewed head-on, had three levels that could be seen to either begin or end with his face rising above the life-sized sistrum—a temple gateway with a door in the center occupied by a cobra and supported by a base carved in the shape of Hathor's face. The goddess' features replaced the usual featureless loop of the *tiet* knot and her bovine ears stood out prominently against her shoulder-length wig. Senmut knew the king believed Mut was another form of Hathor, God's Hand, and his inscriptions, referring as they did to both female deities, made it obvious he agreed with her. His short beard merged with the sacred instrument, which from the side also appeared to be part of his body rather than to simply rest on his lap. He wore a short kilt and no jewelry or sign of rank except for his beard and wig, its braids rendered in exquisite detail. Inscriptions crowded the sides, the back and the base. Senmut's appeal to the priests of Mut to make offerings to the Goddess on his behalf, so she would continue granting him the gift of life, health and strength, struck her as somewhat unnecessary because the statue itself, and where it would be placed, embodied this request and guaranteed its fulfillment. She wondered if her unique friend was betraying the insecurity of a commoner awarded the privileges of the highest nobility. It saddened her to think he secretly feared the cult of his Ka might be ignored after he died. Perhaps that was why he inscribed nearly all of his titles on the monument and remarked on how satisfied Pharaoh was with him, so people would forget where he had come from and remember only the Overseer of the Cattle of Amun, the great official who cut Maat with all his actions and with whose words the Lord of the Two Lands was content.

Goregmennefer, Maatkare's Northern Herald, sent her regular reports on the taxes levied from district heads acting on behalf of their Nomarch while also keeping her abreast of the young pharaoh's developing character. Thutmose would soon be ten-years-old. The boy king was so short he looked younger but his accuracy with the bow and arrow was already legendary. He could drive a chariot almost as well as a man and would gladly have spent all his time hunting if the High Priest of Ptah had not strongly counseled him to spend at least five days a week studying in the *per ankh*. Rasui often visited the city to see the fledgling falcon and regularly invited him to spend time with him in the Oryx. The young king was apparently as fond of the Nomarch as he might have been of his father had he lived. The King's Mother rarely saw her son for it seemed not even he could tolerate her company for long. Hatshepsut worried Thutmose might be developing an unfavorable opinion of women. In a series of letters, she expressed this concern to Rasui, to his son the High Priest of Ptah, to Goregmennefer and a few others. She told them it was imperative Menkheperre learn to respect the Goddess by spending time around women of noble character and temperament.

Her longtime personal secretary, Neferkhaut, was suffering from an infirmity that caused his hands to tremble uncontrollably and he could therefore no longer serve her. She would miss his familiar face reminding her of a time when she was young and all of life lay before her. It was much too easy to apply an idealistic wash to the difficulties of the past just as the royal stone cutters applied a smoothing wash to her third stone Master of Life. As she watched them carefully grinding away any rough areas, she understood it was necessary to sometimes behave abrasively with her own emotions, which for some reason made particular memories to stand out as vividly as the rock's reddish color where the sacred hieroglyphs and images were incised. For several weeks, as Nafre was dressing her in the morning, Hatshepsut selected a *wedjat* Eye of Horus amulet to wear around her neck to remind herself it was important to see both the past and the present clearly. If she behaved like a ship failing to heed the two banks of the River and their true features, often hidden from view, her heart risked running aground in the mud of self-indulgence and prolonging the mysterious journey of her growth. Fulfilling the future Seshat had written for her demanded she read all her thoughts and feelings as accurately as possible because each and everyone, drawn by circumstances and events, was a hieroglyph alive with meaning. How her mind and heart reacted to everything at every second shaped her destiny as surely as her feet propelled her through space. The meaning of healthy, *wedjat*, was the ability to see through the mist of false sentiment, the obscurity of doubt and the cold darkness of fear into her true luminous nature and the loving responsibilities inherent in it.

Amenhotep and Senmut both recommended the same man to replace Neferkahut as Maatkare's chancellor. She summoned Lord Neshi to her private receiving room and interviewed him for the position. When she asked him why he was not yet married he hesitated a moment before replying, "I prefer the conversation and company of concubines, Majesty. They are more interesting than women who can talk only of children."

"If babies stopped being born because all men felt as you do, Neshi, Kemet would soon be a lonely place."

He was wise enough to remain silent. If he had pretended to change his mind and declared he would find a woman to marry the moment he left her presence she would have ceased to respect him. Instead, she found his honesty admirable.

"But there is no danger of *that* happening," she concluded mildly. "If you become my Chancellor, Neshi, you must promise to share with me some of the conversations you enjoy with concubines. I admit to being curious about these beautiful women who rule their own lives and attach themselves to one man only for a limited amount of time."

Apparently surprised by the request, he forgot himself and glanced up at her.

"Neshi, it will be impossible for us to work together if you are afraid to look at me. Uncross your arms, please. Your heart is now a part of Pharaoh's, whom you will serve with earnest devotion, cutting Maat with your every breath, for she will accept no less."

"Majesty!" Holding her eyes, he sank to one knee and raised his hands to her in praise. "My body and my shade, my Ba and my Ka, all belong to the Son of Re, Maatkare!"

Her smile deepened. He was much more attractive than dear old Neferkhaut. Neshi's gleaming oiled skin was so black it fascinated her to look at him. She had been disposed to like him from the moment he told her he went for a swim in his pool every afternoon. Waset was entirely too crowded with noblemen and women who did nothing but eat and drink, disregarding the fact that they were destroying their attractive powers in the process. Like the candles by whose light they feasted at banquets, many of them were melting away into undesirable folds of fat. She had always believed the heart needed to be exercised in every manner possible. Essential to a healthy life, in her passionate opinion, was the joyful mental, spiritual and physical activity which made a person beautiful to others in every sense.

"I will award you a more generous plot of land, Neshi, three more bulls and twenty-four cows to serve them, in addition to increasing your offerings of bread and beer, for it is my understanding concubines are expensive."

Useramun, meanwhile, spent much less time in Waset. As she had suspected, the viziership was serving to hone and focus the noble qualities she had always admired in him. His wife was one of the few ladies of the court whose company Hatshepsut did not merely tolerate. She enjoyed recalling how the prestigious noblewoman had once been just a pretty young girl jumping anxiously off her stool as she watched her betrothed wrestling another man by moonlight. Tjuyu behaved less exuberantly now, but behind her carefully painted eyes, her feelings still flowed freely, escaping as breathless giggles in formal settings and as a lovely rippling laughter at private gatherings. Tjuyu was very good for Useramun. Whenever he returned to Waset, his wife reminded the great vizier he was a husband with equally important duties. Hatshepsut thought it touching the way Tjuyu consoled herself in her husband's absence by planning what they would do together when he returned. And so it happened that she found herself on a pleasure barge one afternoon accompanied by said lady and Senmut. Useramun had not forgotten he had promised to kill a hippopotamus for his queen, who was now the king, which meant he was obliged to find a really big one.

They watched from a safe distance as Kemet's vizier hunted a large male hippo. Senmut soothed Tjuyu's nerves by telling her the animal was known to be old and not as vicious as a female protecting her offspring. Acting as the soldiers of Maat, the hunters—Useramun and his friends Amenhotep, Antef and Duauneheh—simultaneously launched harpoons from four papyrus boats. As the weapons penetrated their target, the blades at the top separated from the shaft but remained attached to strong ropes. In this way, the animal was wrestled into submission and hauled onto the Riverbank. By the time it had been dragged out of the water the hippo was exhausted and mortally wounded but he was still dangerous. Tjuyu covered her face with her hands when Useramun leapt off his skiff and strode right up to it. Maatkare did not look away. She had no doubt her vizier would defeat chaos wherever he faced it.

"You can open your eyes now, Tjuyu," she said. "It is over and your husband is victorious."

Hatshepsut distracted herself with all the pleasures God's Hand made possible from the knowledge that Hapuseneb's tomb was almost finished. Several of the walls would remain unpainted until after he went to his Ka, for it would have been foolish to tempt Anubis to open the way for him before Seshat and Meskhenet had planned. She could not forget what he had told her—that the stars had indicated he was destined to cross the River before her—and was grateful he had not mentioned when. It was much better to imagine they would both be so old by then it would be a relief to shed their wrinkled flesh as a snake does its skin. She could scarcely imagine how handsome the High Priest would be as a transfigured Akh. She had witnessed the extent of the powers he possessed the morning of her coronation but they had never spoken of them. She doubted that in all of Kemet there was a man greater of magic than Hapuseneb. He had begun excavating his eternal home years ago and since then other nobles of Waset, including Senmut and Senimen, had added their tombs to his in the prestigiously prominent mountain overlooking the eastern side of the western desert. Senimen had so greatly admired Senmut's statues with Neferure he chose to immortalize himself with her in an identical manner over the entrance to his offering chapel. The Great Steward of Amun had set more than one trend. Maatkare noticed her older male courtiers had begun adopting the ankle length kilt her unique friend now favored beneath a short-sleeved shirt. Adorned by a colorful stone and bead collar, and carrying his silver handled staff of office, Senmut looked at once strikingly handsome and royally affluent. The shirt concealed the soft flesh of his chest and belly and his face did not seem to age.

She was honored when Hapuseneb requested she visit his eternal home with him. He wanted her to see it and to familiarize herself with its location, almost as if he was worried her Ba-bird might get lost should she decide to fly there from her own supernatural nest in the Necropolis. She knew the High Priest was of the opinion Ba-birds were merely symbols but she could not quite bring herself to believe that, and she told him as much when they were standing just inside the entrance of his tomb. She was much impressed by the long and elegant façade with its numerous large windows open to the sun and sky. Six columns held up the offering hall and a doorway, cut into the center of the western wall, opened onto a long straight corridor leading into the slightly smaller burial chamber supported by four pillars. The ceiling was decorated with a version of the Keftiu spirals she so admired—open-ended circles emerging from diamond shapes crowned by a bud divided into three sections. It was exactly the same design she had chosen for the cabin of her new ship.

"When I escaped the chamber of Satis, I flew just like a bird even though I saw with human eyes," she reminded him.

"In the Dwat we can all fly no matter what we look like, if we believe we can, and frankly I much prefer your woman's body to a falcon's."

"But what if I choose to appear to you as a man in the afterlife?" she teased him.

"Then I would promptly become a beautiful woman and greet you appropriately."

She laughed.

"You have now blessed this space, Hatshepsut. Thank you. After I leave my physical body the resonance of your joy will surround me and protect me from all negative forces."

34

Mistress of Isheru

Maatkare's arrow was amongst the northerners. Her Great Army Commander had no trouble defeating the foreigners seeking to cross the border established by her father. Asiatic princes did not willingly bow to a central authority even in their own country and ambitious tribal leaders sometimes made the mistake of thinking that Seth—or Baal as they called him—had favored them with special powers guaranteeing they would be victorious in battle no matter the odds. It was impossible to comprehend how men could be so foolish. The invaders had made a grave mistake underestimating Akheperkare's daughter. A woman sat on the Horus Throne but Kemet's army was stronger than ever, and very well fed. Hapi's approval of the Female Falcon was blatantly apparent in the bountiful harvests swelling the royal granaries. There was an even greater abundance of grain, linen and dried fish available for export in exchange for foreign goods and luxuries. Newly reopened mines in Roshawet sent home cartloads of turquoise and copper. Routes once blocked were now trodden on both ends of the Two Lands. Fenkhu vessels loaded with wood were almost as common a sight in Perunefer and Mennefer as the ships of the Keftiu and Kemet's own navy was growing as rapidly as papyrus in the marshes.

The King's Superior Steward presented her with another statue for the newly completed House of Mut in which he was portrayed kneeling with a cobra rising before him from a pair of Ka arms and crowned by Hathor's curved horns and solar disc. At first, she thought he intended the work as a tribute to Renenutet, goddess of the harvest and the Mistress of Food who protects all granaries from hungry rodents. The Ka arms could be used to denote *offerings* and to serve as the word for *food*. It took her a few moments—during which Senmut silently watched her face—to realize he had once again written *Maatkare* in a new and meaningful way by referring to her Horus name, *Wosretkaw*, Powerful of Ka's. When combined with the *Ka* arms and the solar disc *Re*, the cobra representing her royal identity spelled *Maatkare*. The front and the back of the statue presented the viewer with strong straight lines, but when viewed from the side sensual curves predominated in the cobra's coiling body and in the exaggerated rolls of fat over Senmut's belly—a deliberate synthesis of masculine and feminine principles. His plump unlined cheeks and childishly wide eyes had already undergone the eternal rejuvenation his offering to the Goddess would reward him with in the afterlife. His lavish wig and larger-than-life ears also struck her as a tribute to Hathor.

Maatkare was so pleased with the cryptogram of her name she chose to incorporate it into the decoration of her new bark shrine dedicated to Amun-Kamutef in front of his temple on which construction had begun. The double-winged door on the east side of the shrine led into the front of the sanctuary where the god would rest while on procession. Interior walls made of individual stone blocks rose to the north and south, protectively enclosing the bark as its prow and stern faced east and west. The first chamber on the east was held up by fourteen pillars and from it two narrow doorways led into the western half of the building. In one of the small back rooms, Maatkare sat on either side of Amun-Kamutef in the first of her completed group statues expressive of the threefold nature of the First Occasion. An alcove adjoining the tableau served to store incense and oils, water and linen, lamps and fire sticks all symbolizing the elements the Divine uses to assume a sensual form. The room in the southwest corner of the monument provided a private place to worship Amun-Kamutef in the manner he most favored—sexual intercourse.

The Gardener of the Divine Offerings of Amun and his assistants worked late into the evenings picking flowers for the beautiful bouquets destined to grace the offering tables in the newly consecrated Temple of Mut. Senmut—Overseer of the Gardens of Amun as of everything pertaining to the Hidden One's earthly manifestations—had been permitted by the king to order an image of himself carved in low relief on the left side of the doorway leading into the Goddess' sanctuary in which he knelt forever offering praise and receiving Divine grace.

Mut's ancient roots stretched south to the vulture Nekhbet and north to the cobra Wadjet. Mut was the Mother of all the gods, the serpent who with her luminous caresses stimulated the eruption of stars that created the universe out of Amun's desire to be born in an earthly form—their son Khonsu. Like a vulture preying on dead flesh, Nekhbet took a bite out of the moon every night until there was nothing left and yet every month it was born again. Hatshepsut wondered if the moon was where her Ka stored all the Ba-birds it had ever fashioned. It would explain why she felt the moon was linked with her womb through the blood which every month was mysteriously compelled to escape the confines of her flesh. The dark areas on the moon were the ink in Seshat's palette where she dipped her reed as she recorded the destiny of each individual life blessed by Thoth with a fragment of Divine consciousness.

In Tantera, a Festival of Drunkenness was celebrated every year in the first month of Akhet and from now on, it would be honored in Waset on the columned porch erected before the House of Mut specifically for that purpose. On the joyous feast day of Hathor-Sekhmet's inebriation, everyone was called upon to rid themselves of unpleasant thoughts and feelings and to satisfy all their heart's desires, provided of course they did not hurt anyone else in the process. The insecure timidity responsible for so much unhappiness was despised by all the gods but it was especially abhorrent to Sekhmet. Burning frustration and destructive behavior were sometimes symptoms of suppressed desires—the claws of the lioness no one could escape. Sekhmet was not restrained by the maternal compassion of Bast or the tenderness love inspires.

Sekhmet was driven purely by sexual hunger and the thrill of its satisfaction. And yet, in the presence of women who had ceased their monthly purification, Sekhmet behaved as docilely as a domestic cat. It was believed the older a woman grew the wiser she became, as the life-giving force of her blood was turned inward to nurture her own mystical growth. Hatshepsut was thirty-four-years-old. It comforted her to know the loss of her youth would at least bring her a deeper rapor with the Hidden One, and by then her ever growing creativity would have borne ample fruit in the form of beautiful monuments.

From that year forward, Sekhmet would be properly worshipped in Waset on Maatkare's columned porch of drunkenness. On the afternoon of the event her attendants were so excited she felt as though the years were stripped away and they were all girls again. She wanted to wear a vulture crown to the festivities but not a stiff one made of gold impossible to relax in. Real, light and sensually soft feathers were required for a rite which began at sunset and did not end until dawn. Only the beak and claws of the vulture headdress she chose were made of gold and its carnelian eyes wone shine a piercing red by lamplight.

Dhout lovingly delivered the dress she had ordered made for the occasion. Seshen and Meresankh eagerly took it from the steward, whose wistful expression indicated he was reluctant to surrender it.

"You may stay, Dhout," Hatshepsut told him. "In your heart you are also a woman, therefore I see no harm in you watching as my attendants dress me."

After a shocked silence the room was flooded with the unrestrained laughter Sekhmet respects as the echo of her own fiercely joyful purrs.

Nevertheless, Dhout kept his eyes respectfully averted as his mistress slipped out of her robe and stood with her arms outstretched while the crimson tunic was wrapped around her body to just below her breasts. It was secured by thin multiple straps strung with tiny gold beads that felt stimulatingly cool and firm against her nipples. Gold hoop earrings, and broad golden bracelets inlaid with turquoise, were the only jewels she elected to wear. Her leather sandals were dyed red to match her dress. The mist-fine linen clung tightly to her torso, accentuating the soft swell of her belly and the erotic curves of her buttocks. Her fingernails and toenails had been painted red to match her lips.

The king's attendants all looked especially lovely themselves that evening. Meresankh was resplendent in a garment the color of clear water decorated with little golden fish magically seeming to swim out of the fabric's gentle ripples into the matching fish girdle she wore beneath it. Seshen's slighter figure and darker skin were not quite as suited to the green dress she had selected embroidered with miniature white oryxes—her skinny arms evoked a fence corralling them—but her cheerful grin was more impossible to resist than ever. Nafre and Ah-hotep, Djehuti, Duauneheh, Nehesj, Useramun and Tjuyu, Senmut and all his brothers and sisters and their spouses, Amenhotep and his wife, Inebni and his favorite concubine, her sandal bearer Thutmose, her new chancellor Neshi, Puyemre escorting Senseneb on one arm and Tanefert on the other, Khenti and Nefertari just arrived from the Sistrum, the royal artisan Ka-hotep and her favorite painter Satnem—almost everyone dear to Maatkare had been invited to worship and await the Goddess on her columned porch of drunkenness. Yet if Hapuseneb had not also promised her he would be there, and that he would not bring his wife, she would have felt lonely even surrounded by her most beloved friends.

The royal chefs had risen before Khepri to begin baking the pastries filled with meat and fowl that were to be served with the blood-red beer. Her long-time harpist Harmose, accompanied by the musicians of his choosing, would provide the music to which scantily clad young men and women would take turns dancing. Twenty-four females, a handful of them related to Maatkare through her brother's concubines—amongst them Meritre-Hatshepsut, an extraordinarily sweet and pretty girl who had recently begun her purification—were chosen to stand in the shadows of the forecourt and take turns shaking the sistrums and *menits* of Hathor. Maatkare had secured honorable homes for a handful of her brother's oldest daughters as the wives of officials eager to add a touch of royal blood to their lineage. Her father's offspring by women of the harem were not so numerous, only a handful still lived and resided in Waset, and she had never felt any affection for them.

A new stone statue of Mut sat enthroned in its shrine in the heart of her House. The Goddess would not appear before her children until morning but the two limestone gates leading into the temple were left open so she could feast on the sounds of rejoicing. Erected in the first offering court before the entrance gates, the slender grooved columns supporting the porch were painted the primary colors of creation and supported by square black crowns and bases. The jambs of the four polished limestone doors opening into the temple were decorated with images of Mut in her vulture headdress offering life in the form of an *ankh* to Maatkare, who wore the double crown and the royal beard above her masculine shoulders. But it was the living Goddess everyone saw when the Female Falcon parted her litter's star-embroidered curtains and stepped directly out onto the porch of drunkenness. All conversation ceased and in the sudden silence, Hatshepsut felt her voice reach all the way up to the profoundly intoxicating foam of stars left behind in the wake of Atum's barge. "Only when we do something to excess do we touch upon the Divine within us that knows no boundaries or limits! Welcome, my friends, to Hathor-Sekhmet's first Festival of Drunkenness in Waset! Tonight no hunger must go unsatisfied lest we risk offending the Goddess and drawing her terrible anger down upon us!"

Low tables surrounded by animal-head stools were laden with platters of small meat pastries designed to take the edge off everyone's appetite without diminishing the inebriating effects of the beer. The sistrums hidden in the shadows vibrated ceaselessly as Harmose strummed his harp in a slow relaxed rhythm. The guests remained standing at first, too excited to sit down and preferring to mingle. Useramun entertained all those in his immediate proximity by emptying four full cups of beer in as many breaths. On that night, even the vizier of Kemet was not obliged to keep a clear head.

From where he stood with his brothers and sisters, Senmut caught her eye but did not approach her. His sideways glance told her he was not happy Hapuseneb was already by her side and would undoubtedly remain so all night. She smiled at him, ignoring the guilt she imagined he was attempting to burden her with. He had taken her advice and was making better use of his pool. His chest and upper arms were firmer and his stomach no longer hung so softly over the belt of the knee-length kilt he had chosen to wear beneath a fresh floral collar. And yet as handsome as her Superior Steward looked that night he could not compare to Hapuseneb. The High Priest of Amun was resplendent in a shirt made from a panther's skin sewn together at his shoulders, and down both sides of his torso, with bright red thread. Three of the animal's claws hung from a black leather cord around his neck. His forearms and wrists were embraced by broad bands of solid gold and his short crimson kilt matched her dress. His black sandals, strung with turquoise beads, reflected the deep shining tones of his blue-black wig.

As she gazed at him appreciatively, he emptied his third cup of beer and said, "Even though it scarcely seems possible, you look more beautiful than ever, Maatkare."

Smiling, she gestured to a pretty attendant wearing only a garland of lotus flowers around her hips to refill the lord's cup. She could not drink quite as quickly as he could but she had every intention of trying to catch up.

"I understand, Hapuseneb, that many people when they become drunk remember nothing of what they did or said and yet, though I have often indulged to excess, I recall everything quite clearly." She emptied her cup. "But then again it is entirely possible I only *think* I remember everything when in fact I have forgotten quite a bit!"

"You will not forget tonight, Hatshepsut, I can promise you that."

Following the direction of his fixed stare, she was surprised to discover he was looking at Senmut and that her unique friend was staring back at him. She suffered the impression they were communicating with each other. She had observed prize bulls regarding each other in a similar fashion. Then suddenly a flash of heat between her legs told her it was *her* they were fighting over without moving a muscle.

It was not long before she felt as if the relentless purring of sistrums—blending with the more subtle trembling vibration of *menit* necklaces—was emanating from inside her as the mysterious sound of her blood rushing through her body as red beer flowed endlessly from vases all shaped like the hieroglyph for beauty and joy, happiness and good fortune. The magic of fermentation transformed her mortal flesh into the shining limbs of the Goddess as she walked amongst her subjects talking and laughing with them and even embracing them as her sensual appetite inexorably deepened. Entertained by how Tjuya giggled and squirmed when her husband tried to kiss her, she assisted him in holding her still. She does not remember falling but suddenly she was on her back half drowning in a wonderfully fragrant marsh of flowers all blooming in her mouth as one woman after the other fought for the pleasure of kissing the embodiment of Hathor and tasting her divinity. She kept her eyes closed, curious to see if she could recognize each lady by the feel and taste of her, but she soon gave up trying and surrendered to the delectable experience. Her legs longed to spread open past the confines of her dress as the feel of soft breasts and lips, cool hands and tongues saturated her senses. She became Nekhbet writhing in the vast nest of the cosmos with her sister serpents, until she distinctly felt a man's hard, warm hand grip one of her wrists and the next thing she knew she was on her feet.

Like a panther making a kill, the High Priest was leading her away from everyone to feast on her in private. Submitting to his will like helpless prey, she glanced over her shoulder and saw Senmut stepping around some of the bodies littering the temple floor as he followed them.

In the deepest and darkest section of the portico, Hapuseneb shoved her in front of him and pinned her back against a wall with his hard body. "I said you would never forget this night, Hatshepsut." He kissed her hungrily for a moment, then abruptly stepped back and pushed her away from him.

Senmut caught her in his arms and subjected her to an equally demanding kiss, crushing her body possessively against his.

Grabbing her by the hair at the nape of her neck, Hapuseneb turned her to face him again.

Trapped between two demanding men, she moaned in the throes of an excitement indistinguishable from dread.

The High Priest whispered in her ear, "Where do you want us? I will let you choose!"

She knew what he meant but could scarcely believe it.

He tugged painfully on the roots of her hair. "Answer me."

"I cannot!"

Senmut interjected uncertainly, "She does not seem to-"

"Do not be a fool, steward." Hapuseneb interrupted him impatiently. "We are waiting, my lady."

"I choose what would be most pleasing to you, my lord…"

The two men seemed to forget all their differences as they worked together to get her dress up out of their way. Then Senmut gripped the backs of her thighs and she clung to him as he lifted her up against him. She had not realized how strong he was, or perhaps it was Sekhmet's fire burning in his blood. She could not understand why it had taken the three of them so long to come together like that. It felt so natural, so perfect, she passionately regretted the time they had wasted.

Senmut was the first to penetrate her but he was forced to remain motionless, impatiently buried in her sex, as with one hand Hapuseneb covered her mouth to keep her from crying out and with the other slowly forced his erection into her anus. She feared she would not be able to endure the rending pain but gradually the agony transformed into an almost unbearable pleasure. The two men had *not* settled their differences; they were battling inside her now, their rigid weapons separated only by the infinitely sensitive wall of her innermost flesh.

Hapuseneb clutched her throat. "Feel *this*, steward."

Her sex at once tightened and deepened as he made it harder for her to breathe and easier for both men to thrust violently into her body, which began to feel magically bottomless.

✳ ✳ ✳ ✳ ✳

Hapuseneb and Senmut both accompanied the Female Falcon to Tantera to celebrate the Festival of Offering the Phallus Which Makes All That Exists Fertile. The rite of Hathor and Min was as old as time and yet to Hatshepsut it had never felt more immediate and alive and vital to her happiness. Her deepening sensuality was mirrored by the rising of the River. At first she worried the flood, like her joy, would be too strong and destroy the structures designed to control it. Fear was one of the invisible diseases bread by the turgid green waters, but she was much too strong to succumb to it. At long last she felt the Goddess fully living in her body as she openly honored the Divine force of her sexuality. Her subjects were not suffering as a result, on the contrary. As Amun-Re's bodily son thrived so did the land. More than ever she was certain cosmic currents of endless Becoming were being channeled by her heart and flowing out across Kemet as a nourishing positive energy.

Wearing the horned headdress, during the rite of Hathor and Min she acted the part of both Pharaoh and the Goddess—Atum-Re and his Hand, the Self Created One. As she emerged from the cosmic womb of the temple, the sight of her drove her human herd wild. The statues of Min and Hathor preceding her were hidden away in their shrines but everyone could see the god and the goddess in the female king's dark-golden eyes and blooming red smile. Men and women copulated openly in the streets as she passed riding high on the shoulders of priests, flanked four rows deep by her personal guard. Her eyes were irresistibly drawn to the rhythmically undulating bodies even though, in truth, she was a little repelled by the crude public displays of intimacy. Many of the *rekhyt* were still living on the lowest step of Min's Stairway. She could not empathize with the thrill of intercourse in the dirt within reach of so many feet, which at the very least could uncomfortably interrupt the proceedings. Nevertheless, wherever Min and Hathor came together there was always a seductive glimmer of magic.

What happened inside the temple in the quiet of the holy of holies beneath the smiling approval of the *neters* was very different from what took place out on the streets, where wooden clappers played too enthusiastically by women seeking to emulate the sensual skill of priestesses sounded more like locust wings dangerously devouring the good sense of the crowd. The party in the town grew progressively rowdier to the discordant music of drums beaten out of rhythm by drunken revelers. Deep in the temple, in the private sanctuary filled with trembling shadows, only the controlled rhythm of sistrums shaken in the interior offering court was audible, and mysteriously enhanced the wordless eloquence of her soft cry as the High Priest penetrated her. No physical life would be conceived, a fact she had worried was sacrilegious until he helped her understand it made their unions even more magically potent. Min was well served by Hapuseneb, who had long ago established his sovereignty over her mind, heart and body. But Hathor was certainly not passive, she was Mistress of the Vulva, and Hatshepsut prided herself on the number and quality of his groans as she enjoyed milking his erection by tightening and relaxing her sex around him. He lifted her up around him like Horus soaring away with her body trapped in his talons but in the end it was she who supported him as he clung to her, his breathing ragged, as though he was struggling to pull himself out of the Primordial Waters threatening to drown him. Holding his head gently against her breasts, there was no doubt in her heart she was the woman destined for him by the Goddess as she saw in him both her Horus and her Seth.

The following evening Hapuseneb invited Senmut to join them in the apartments he and the king were sharing in one of her temporary palaces. Outside the enclosure wall, the festivities were as loud and joyful as ever. After what had happened on the columned porch of drunkenness on the night Sekhmet ripped through Waset, Senmut's behavior toward her had changed. He had learned from the priest not to be as gentle and hesitant with her when they were alone together. She did not think she was imagining that his tenderness toward her was growing even as he behaved more forcefully with her in the bedroom. Every day she thanked Hathor and made offerings in her temple for the wonderful turn of events which had so deepened her contentment. And yet *hotep* was not the word she would have used to describe how she felt when Hapuseneb and Senmut were both inside her.

One of the lovely musicians who always traveled in the High Priest's entourage—her pet monkey cavorting around her as she played a delicate long-handled lute—smiled knowingly at the female king where she knelt pinned between two strong and relentlessly ardent men. On the outside of the musician's right thigh, a figure of Bes was tattooed in blue-black ink, a decoration favored by priestesses of Hathor. It aroused Hatshepsut to be watched by a woman who also knew what it was like to surrender all control over her body, and to reap a harvest of overwhelmingly intense sensations through which her flesh caught blinding glimpses of the Divine energy it served to contain.

She was crouched on all fours over Senmut, bracing herself on his shoulders. He fondled her breasts while intently observing her expressions and occasionally raising his head to kiss her. Hapuseneb was kneeling behind her and she moaned when his erection abruptly slipped out of her bowels, the experience of its loss strangely more distressing than its rending presence. She realized he had gestured to the lute player when the woman set her instrument aside, crawled across the rug toward them, lay down on her back and spread her legs for him. Looking significantly at Senmut, he prepared to enter her.

Hatshepsut suddenly found herself on her back with one side of her body pressed against the musician. She watched, enthralled against her will, as Hapuseneb's god-like phallus disappeared into another woman at the same time that Senmut raised her own thighs around him and penetrated her. She moaned in wordless protest as the High Priest leaned forward and thrust his tongue into her mouth, urging her to kiss him back even as her heart despaired that the best part of him was lost to her. The more passionately Senmut thrust into her body the more she lost herself in the dreadful vision of a lesser female being blessed by what she desired more than anything else. She was stunned to suddenly feel the boundaries of her flesh dissolving. Despite her emotional anguish there was no damming the physical ecstasy overwhelming her as Hapuseneb smiled at her even while lifting another woman's legs against his chest. She was only vaguely aware of Senmut slipping out of her...

When she opened her eyes, the High Priest was kneeling between her thighs. She felt her heart restored to her as he drove his shining erection into her slick sex, claiming the vulva of the living Goddess for the culmination of his pleasure. Meanwhile, the priestess of Hathor to whom Senmut had been demoted sounded as though she was very much enjoying his anger.

* * * * *

On the day when Neith went forth to Atum, Maatkare sacrificed sexual pleasures, drank only water and ate no beef because God had sacrificed parts of Himself to become flesh. The soul of Neith resided in the cows sacred to

Hathor and as the goddess joined the dying sun in the west, it was impossible for Hatshepsut to forget the years of her life were passing as swiftly as hours. All too soon, she would be old and forced to shed her mortal flesh. Yet Hapuseneb had said that even when they left their physical bodies a very real form would remain to them with perceptions much like the ones they now possessed. When she asked him how he could be so sure of what happened in the Dwat, he replied matter-of-factly, "Because I remember dying. Violent demises are always unpleasant, especially if you fail to realize you are no longer encumbered by a mortal vessel, but crossing the River is normally no more stressful than falling asleep at night, when we pass from so-called real life into the space of dreams, where our Ka nourishes and educates our Ba and shapes our lives more than we realize."

"Did I really hear you say you, Hapuseneb, that you remember dying?"

"You did. Patehuti also recalls going to his Ka on several occasions and he agrees with me it is much more traumatic to be born."

"I can well believe that! Birth is such a messy and painful business."

He drew her to him. "But it is worth it," he said and before she could ask him any more questions kissed her more tenderly than ever.

BOOK SIX

FACING THE HORIZON

35

God's Land

Pharaoh was laughing so hard she could barely breathe. She was not the only one so affected by Chancellor Neshi's descriptions. The ships Maatkare had sent to the Land of God, ruled by Hathor, had returned laden with treasures. The celebrations, both outside and within the palace precincts, had achieved unprecedented levels of intensity. The royal chefs had not slept in an effort to do justice to the achievement of their mistress, who could now, like the living goddess she was, also be called the Lady of Punt. No restraint was exercised in preparing the nightly feasts. His chin held high, her steward supervised the preparations for the banquet with an expression reminiscent of sexual pleasure as his most extravagant desires were all satisfied.

"But surely, my Lord Chancellor, you exaggerate!" Puyemre was the first to pull his voice out of the laughter flooding the room. "If what you say is true, the queen of Punt could not have been shaped by the hands of Khnum. Such a grotesque woman could only have emerged from between the god's buttocks, the result of a bad case of cosmic indigestion!"

People at the point of recovering themselves from crippling attacks of laughter doubled over again, clutching their stomachs and each other.

Hatshepsut clamped a hand over her mouth, making a supreme effort to control herself, but the image of the foreign queen as a divine turd was almost too much for her. When Puyemre opened his mouth to speak again—his eyes narrowed to darkly gleamung slits as a wildly mischievous grin consumed half his face—she cried, "Stop!" genuinely fearing for her life because if she laughed any harder she might suffocate.

In the sudden silence punctuated by gasps for breath, Neshi resumed his narrative. "The men of Punt obviously consider short and grotesquely obese women the pinnacle of beauty. The queen was clad in a transparent dress through which all her rolls of fat were clearly visible."

Useramun said, "How you endured the sight I cannot imagine!" and attempted to clear his mental palate with a long draft of wine.

His expression soberings lightly, Puyemre spoke again, "Are you certain the Puntites are peaceful people, Chancellor? Their queen sounds more like a weapon than a woman for with just one look she would have shriveled *my* manhood."

"Her young daughter was with her," Neshi ignored the remark, "and she was already more than plump. It is obvious the people of Punt spend a great deal of their time and resources feeding their royal females."

Neferure said lightly, "Force-feeding them like cows, you mean?" but her mother knew her well enough to notice her smile was strained and that she was probably refraining from making a more caustic comment only because Tusi was her table companion.

"So it would appear," Senmut's voice was heard for the first time that evening, "but it is only our particular concept of beauty that is slaughtered."

"Beauty is not a concept, my lord, it is a reality." Hatshepsut was annoyed, almost insulted, by the way Senmut and her daughter smiled at each other. "Beauty is a balm to our vision because it is a truth our hearts recognize."

"Every heart is different." God's Wife dared to argue with Pharaoh, her mother.

"The truth of that statement can easily be contested," the priest of Anukis and Royal Butler, Amenhotep, politely entered the converation. "Every heart is unique but not essentially *different* for its nature and function is the same in everyone, to sustain and nourish life."

"Even fat and ugly life," Neferure retorted with a smile, "which some hearts have the ability to perceive as beautiful. If it is beautiful to eat, then why is it not beautiful to be fat? If flesh is beautiful, then why is it not beautiful to be rich in folds of skin? The queen of Punt must have a very tender body that would provide a hardworking man with a nice soft cushion. The fact that she is both small and huge might prove an intriguing combination to her husband, who can easily conquer her and yet also feel lost in her, making his every plunge both an adventure and a victory. What could possibly be more appealing to a man?"

"I enjoy hunting hippos in the marshes," Useramun said firmly, "not the bedroom!"

Everyone laughed again except for the king. She stared soberly at her daughter, who was speaking as boldly as a married woman even though, or perhaps because, she was still a virgin and longed to sacrifice this frustrating condition to Tusi, who proved Neferure was not as immune to traditional beauty as she pretended to be.

"However, the Chief of Punt was almost as tall as I am." Wearing the golden collar awarded him by Pharaoh, Neshi went on as if he had not been interrupted, his eyes resting on Maatkare's face as he addressed her directly even while speaking loudly enough so everyone else could hear. "His short hair was divided into neat plaits and his black beard thrust sharply from his chin. In the belt of his knee-length kilt he wore a dagger and his skin was the light-red of Horus. The whole of his left leg was embraced by rings made from precious metals. I am not sure if they were meant as decoration or if he had injured himself, but whether the rings were the cause or the result he walked with a limp.

"The king of Punt greeted Pharaoh Maatkare through me, her representative, most graciously. 'How did you reach here, this country unknown to men'? he said. 'Did you come down on the ways of heaven, or did you travel by land or by sea? How happy is God's Land that you now tread like Re'![74]

"My men had set up a table with the gifts her Majesty had entrusted me to deliver to show the people of Punt we meant them no harm. As they approached us, they did indeed seem more in awe of us, and of our five great ships, than afraid of the eight armed men and their companies who had disembarked with me. The queen, having been hoisted off her donkey, walked—or it would be more accurate to say *waddled*—behind her husband. She and her daughter both gazed ardently at the bracelets and necklaces lying on the table next to baskets filled with beads. The daggers and axes clearly interested her husband, as well as the two young men in his company I later learned were his offspring. Several attendants walking behind them bore offerings of gold forged into large rings, bushels of boomerangs and a plate piled high with frankincense.

"After the gifts were exchanged and received, I commanded a tent to be raised for myself and my soldiers 'in the harbors of frankincense of Punt, on the shore of the sea, in order to receive the chiefs of this land, and to present them with bread, beer, wine, meat, fruits, and all the good things of the land of Kemet, as had been ordered by the sovereign'."[75]

Chancellor Neshi entertained the company with the story of his journey even more effectively than the performers Dhout had arranged for. Girls spinning over each other like human balls, and bending over backwards to walk on their arms, was entertaining but Maatkare preferred the men who danced in a more archaic fashion, relying not on the superficial thrill of acrobatics but on dramatically precise movements filled with meaning. Fear and courage, desire and restraint, weakness and strength, pain and pleasure—all emotions could be wordlessly expressed by way of gestures.

If Hapuseneb had been present at the celebratory banquet her happiness would have been complete but the day before he had left for the north, accompanying Menkheperre back to Mennefer. At least he had witnessed the successful return of the expedition. The High Priest of Amun who had urged her to make real her dream of bringing the riches of God's Land to Kemet. God spoke to her through him and when he assured her the venture would be successful, she set aside her fear the vessels might sink or suffer some other misfortune. Great Pharaohs of the past had sent envoys to the distant land rich in the incense beloved of the Hidden One and so too, acting on behalf of Amun, had the Female Falcon. She would never forget the moment one of her herald's ran unannounced into her garden and informed her that the fleet captained by Chancellor Neshi had returned safely to the port of Quseir in the Green Water to the east.

By the time the glorious news reached her the ships would already have been unloaded and disassembled and, slowed down by treasures and living riches, begun the slow trip across the desert. In Gebtu, the boats were once again put together for the journey home to Waset. The detailed descriptions of their cargo brought to her by her heralds only intensified how impatiently she awaited Neshi's arrival. Her chancellor would now be able to afford a small army of concubines for she had promised him even more land and cattle if his mission was successful. He had been gone for nearly a year and she had secretly begun to worry that he and all the men in his company had perished. She had felt better when Senmut explained it would take weeks to collect trees and exotic animals and then to prepare them for transport while waiting for the wind to turn.

"The people in Punt live in huts raised up on poles," Neshi went on, "even the king and his rotund queen, although I never actually saw her climbing the ladder. Their elevated houses are made of plaited palm stalks and surrounded by a natural colonnade of ebony and frankincense trees interspersed with date palms. The Puntites own many tame dogs that warn them when dangerous wild animals approach the village."

"The little fat queen would make a tasty snack for a panther." No one laughed at Duauneheh's remark; they were too enthralled by the Chancellor's descriptions to interrupt him further.

"I saw men with skin even blacker than mine who live further inland and only travel to the shore of the Green Water to trade. It is they who breed the large white dogs with the floppy ears."

Hatshepsut smiled. She was quite fond of the puppies Neshi had brought her, which were rapidly revising her negative opinion of the species. He had also returned with live black panthers in addition to piles of their skins, a quantity of apes and monkeys, birds complete with their nests and eggs and a fantastic creature that proved Amun-Re had a sense of humor. Neferure insisted giraffes were perfectly beautiful. "Many a great lady would sacrifice all sorts of unsavory rodents to retain such a smooth and elegant neck into her old age," she pointed out. Her mother had been disturbed to hear her casually mention the practice of black magic, and had once again wondered how successful she had actually been in protecting her daughter from negative influences.

Everyone present at the banquet that night had witnessed the triumphant arrival of the ships laden with luxuries from the Land of God, a truly intoxicating sight the grape wine they were drinking helped them recall as they listened to Neshi describe how he and his men had furnished the ships on a distant shore alive with exotic people and creatures. Frankincense trees, planted in large baskets and pots, were the most precious cargo and were loaded first followed by sacks of incense, ostrich eggs and feathers, malachite, elephant tusks and black ivory, jars brimming with precious unguents, blocks of resin, wooden boxes filled with silver and lapis lazuli, "all the good woods of the divine land, heaps of pieces of *ani* and trees of green *ani,* green gold of the land of Amu, cinnamon wood, balsam, resin, antimony and inhabitants of the country and their children."[76]

When the ships docked in Waset great chiefs wearing colorful feathers in their hair all kissed the earth before Pharaoh. The exotic ambassadors were currently residing in the Town of Amun as honored guests. Hatshepsut had not invited them to her banquets for their manners and eating habits could not be considered sophisticated by any standards, and their language was a series of strange guttural sounds it offended her to listen to for long. Most of the chiefs, accompanied by a handful of their wives and offspring, would return home with the caravans she had been assured were currently on their way north. The world was so large it filled her with awe and deepened her reverence for God. Over three-thousand long-horned bulls would soon swell the herds of Amun. Already Djehuty had spent days calculating the quantity of incense piled up in sacks in front of him, in addition to recording all the other tributes offered to King Maatkare. The incense trees were immediately planted in the temple and palace gardens and Pharaoh herself presided over the weighing of white-gold on the scales of Thoth and Seshat—measured out in rings, powder and blocks—which took place in *Ipet Sut's* innermost offering court. All the highest officials of Kemet were present as she "stretched forth her hand to measure the heaps for the first time. It was a cause for great rejoicing to also measure the fresh *ani* offered to Amun, the Lord of the Throne of the Two Lands, the Lord of the Sky. It was the first day of summer and the River was rising when all the good things of the land of Punt flowed into Waset. His Majesty herself caressed oil of *ani* onto all her limbs.[77] She had never felt more beautiful as into her nose her own fragrance wafted like a Divine breath. In view of the entire land through the eyes of its greatest noblemen, her skin shone as though made of gold.

Afterward—enthroned in her palace on a dais supported by the two lions of the horizon—Maatkare addressed the highest officials of the Two Lands. She wanted them all to understand on whose behalf she acted and where the true source of her power lay—in God, who revealed Himself through her heart.

With Senmut, in his capacity as the Great Steward of Amun, and Chancellor Neshi standing behind her, Maatkare addressed the assembled company:

"My Majesty made petition at the stairs of the Lord of the Gods and a command was heard from The Great Throne, an oracle of the god himself, to search out ways to Punt and explore the roads to the terraces of myrrh. And so my Majesty set before her eyes the goal of reaching the harbor of incense, to open the way and the roads to the Land of God according to the orders of my Father, Amun. It was Amun who led my soldiers by land and by water on mysterious shores in His abode of pleasure. I was obedient to my Father, who put before me the joyous task of establishing life in His house by digging up fruit trees in the divine land for the two sides of His earthly garden. As He ordered, so it was done, and I even increased the offerings which I had promised Him. I never neglect to obey my Father's orders, which are all accomplished according to my prescriptions, and never will I transgress against what my mouth says on this subject. Amun-Re has opened a place in His heart for me who knows all He loves, and what He loves He takes hold of. I brought Punt to God as he commanded. I enlarged His garden and now He walks in it."[78]

During the ceremony Menkheperre, a very short eleven-year-old, offered Amun-Re's statue the first fruits of trees in whose barks flowed the rich resins of myrrh and frankincense. The young falcon was present later in the palace when Maatkare, sitting enthroned on the dais alone, addressed the nobility of Kemet. Afterward she met with her brother's son in her private receiving room, dismissing all her attendants so they could be alone together. Thutmose was a handsome boy, his brown eyes full of a clear and engaging light but he had unfortunately inherited his mother's slight stature. She had received glowing reports of his intelligence from the High Priest of Ptah, Rasui and others, so at least in that respect he had already excelled his father. He spent five days a week studying in the *Per Ankh* of Ptah's temple in Mennefer for he very much enjoyed reading and history fascinated him. Standing before her he leaned forward slightly. At first his eager posture seemed caused by an avid curiosity but as their conversation progressed she began to perceive it as the outward evidence of a deeply stubborn personality. Thutmose was a young bull, there was no doubt about that, and his determination would only intensify along with his military training. He had recently begun dividing his time equally between Mennefer and Perunefer, where the Great Army Commander was himself in charge of the young falcon's education in the arts of warfare. When she had offered him a seat, he had declined it, declaring he preferred to stand before Pharoah.

"You are also Pharaoh," she reminded him.

"Not really, Majesty." His voice had not yet changed but already there was a bracingly serious ring to it. "Not yet."

"And what is the first thing you intend to do when you are *really* Pharaoh?"

"I will do as my father's father before me," he replied without hesitation. "I will take the army north into the land of the Two Rivers and put an end to the border skirmishes Nomti is constantly forced to deal with. I will lead the troops past Akheperkare's monument on the shores of the backward flowing water and make Kemet larger and stronger and richer than ever!"

"It is admirable you wish to emulate my great father by expanding and strengthening Kemet's borders, but you risk neglecting the happiness and well-being of your own people if you think only of war."

"I do not see how, Majesty, for surely our subjects will be enriched by my conquests."

"Those people you conquer will also be your subjects, which means you will have even more bodies to care for and require even more resources."

"Those people I conquer will serve Pharaoh and provide Kemet with every resource it requires and all the luxuries it desires."

"In return for what? If you truly believe in Maat you cannot force her upon anyone."

"Whether or not the people I conquer worship the *neters* is of no concern to me as long as they obey the laws of Pharaoh who will help protect and feed them." His impatience with her reasoning became even more visible as he shifted from one foot to the other and clenched his hands into fists. "I do not see how the greater glory of Kemet can possibly be an offense against Maat."

"Beware, Menkheperre, for I fear that nourishing people's bodies by force will only starve their hearts, until it is your destruction they hunger for more than anything else."

"Those who desire Pharaoh's destruction will all die on the point of his lance and be rendered powerless!"

"A strong man is different from a bully, Thutmose, and the stench of slain enemies is not as pleasing to the gods as the perfume of friendly commerce. For the sake of Kemet, I pray you remember that."

Hatshepsut did not succeed in getting her daughter to spend more than a few hours with her half-brother.

"He is so short it could almost be said Isis slept with a dwarf instead of my father," Neferure joked, but the bitterness in her voice made her mother cringe.

"Then you should find him quite attractive," she retorted, and once again wondered why love and concern so often emerged as sarcasm. But she knew the answer to that—how powerless she was to do anything about her daughter's unhappiness made her angry.

The princess said very quietly, "I will *never* marry him."

At that moment, Hatshepsut could not bring herself to argue with her. She did not say "You have to" she did not speak at all, and the silence which bloomed in the room mysteriously went a long way toward healing the emotional rift between them. When she felt Neferure would not push her away, she sat down beside her on the couch and took her gently but determinedly in her arms. Her heart seemed to break beneath the gentle impact of her daughter's sudden sob.

"I am sorry, Nefi!" she whispered desperately. "I am so sorry!"

"You will not force me to marry him, will you, Mami?"

"No."

She felt the answer surprise them both as they clung to each other. Hatshepsut wondered at the fact that it had taken years for her to realize she could never make Neferure do anything which made her truly unhappy. She prided herself on the clarity of her thinking, on her ability to look straight at all her feelings, and yet it seemed the success of her inward vigilance was only an illusion; emotions and desires she was not aware of hid deceptively and successfully inside her. She not only believed that her daughter, already God's Wife, was also destined to be the Great Royal Wife and queen of Kemet, she *wanted* her to be, and because of this she had failed to question tradition and made the special beautiful person born to her miserable. But no matter how hard she held onto her body, the princess was not a part of her she could manipulate into acting exactly as she expected her to in order to satisfy her own ideas of what was necessary and good.

Neferure's voice was barely audible as she said, "I am eighteen-years-old, mother."

"I know, my love, but you must wait just a little longer. That is all I ask of you. I promise I will not make you do anything you do not truly want to."

"Tusi says he will wait for me forever… if he has to."

"That is admirable."

"Do you think it is true?"

"It is you who love him, my dear. I cannot see into his heart as you have the power to."

"I believe him!"

"Good, then you have something to look forward to and nothing to dread. Perhaps, knowing that, you will be able to consider your future with a clearer head. You still have time to decide if you truly wish to give away the splendorous responsibilities Seshat recorded on her palette as forming part of your destiny. Perhaps knowing you are no longer obliged to marry Thutmose will enable you to look at him more kindly and objectively as he grows into a man rich in wisdom and strong of body, the son of your father and your half-brother, Kemet's future Falcon."

"He will not be as good a king as you are, mother. That is already apparent. He may prove to be a great Pharaoh but the Two Lands will never again be as peaceful and happy as they are now, in the embrace of Maatkare."

* * * * *

The Temple of Montu-Re in Iuny, Senmut's hometown, was restored and enlarged. It was one of four abodes of the god located around Waset and in *Ipet Sut*. Mont-Re, Horus of the Strong Arm, was inseparable from the king of the

Gods Amun-Re, whose double plumes he wore behind the solar disc and cobra crowning his falcon's head. Hatshepsut was constantly sensible of the need to be strong and merciless in the task of maintaining and strengthening the flow of Maat throughout the Two Lands. It distressed her how much injustice Useramun encountered in his travels. Too many of her *rekhyt* still went hungry and suffered other ills because of greedy and foolish people in positions of power. It was impossible to root them all out at once; it was a slow and tedious process. Tired by the long meetings with her vizier, she turned her mind to the more inspiring and gratifying progress reports on the Divine Houses she was refurbishing and enlarging because their enlightened beauty directly affected how she felt about herself. It did not matter that she had begun to notice fine lines radiating from the corners of her eyes, like desert dunes seen from Montu's point of view when he took the form of a falcon flying through the sky. The vital moisture of youth was being leached from her skin by the years marching relentlessly toward a battle she could not win. The mortality of her Ba was a fact she had accepted long ago, yet more than ever she was reluctant to surrender her Attractive Powers or to permit them to seriously diminish. When she went to her Ka, she wanted it to be suddenly in her sleep. Ideally, she would not even notice the transition as death merely became the extension of a dream and not having to return to her aging body a blessed reprieve.

To preserve her physical beauty she had long ago enlisted the help of her attendants. Oil of fenugreek was applied daily to her face, neck and chest to eliminate existing and potential wrinkles. When she consulted Ibenre, he suggested she try a solution made of frankincense gum, wax, fresh oil of balanites and rush-nut.

"That is the traditional salve applied to the skin of women who have been scarred by a disease," he said. "You, Majesty, are hardly in need of such drastic measures. However, if you believe it will help replenish your radiance then it most certainly will. When you hold an old piece of linen near the light of a lamp, it appears smooth and luminous again. It is the creative intensity of your Ka, burning inside you, that keeps your skin looking young much more effectively than any unguent."

"I agree, Ibenre, but I also feel it is best to help my Ka in its magical effort to sustain the vessel of my flesh, which all my mirrors tell me is beginning to crack a little in places."

He left her presence smiling and yet there was no denying her own lips were thinner than they used to be. Her mouth had lost its lush bloom but younger women were no more beautiful than she was, they were simply in a different place in time, and she would not have returned to the past for all the gold in Punt. She had never been so fulfilled and in command of herself and of the Two Lands. At least she still had all her teeth, unlike Meresankh who had recently suffered the trauma of having one removed because it was costing her even greater discomfort to keep it. Fortunately, it was only one of her back molars and the disfigurement was not visible.

When Patehuti, the First Prophet of Thoth, went to his Ka, and Iamnefer, the Headman of Nefrusy, took his place, Hatshepsut found herself comparing all the people she dearly loved to the teeth of a single mouth. Eventually, if she lived too long, they would all fall out, and with the loss of each one, her ability to savor the pleasures of life would be seriously compromised.

Frog amulets had the power to grant their owner many years of life but Hatshepsut did not feel the need to wear one surrounded as she was in her Pleasure House by so many of Heqet's creatures. She regularly met with Senmut and Djehuty in the shade of a pavilion where she received their reports, and it was always a pleasure to be able to dismiss her fan bearers when Amun blessed them with a cool breeze from the north. Puyemre sometimes joined them there, as did Duauneheh, who she had recently promoted to Chief of the Factories at the Temple of Amun and Director of the Business. As they talked, Dhout served them the small baked pastries she favored before dinner filled with spinach and a variety of cheeses blended with garlic. A fine white wine was the perfect accompaniment and she often waved away musicians sent by Harmose as the conversation became sufficient to entertain her.

"I have always wanted to play Seth in the Mystery Plays," Puyemre confessed, "but I am too small. The crowd would never take me seriously."

She laughed. "You are right about that! A more unlikely candidate for the role of Seth I can scarcely imagine. However, your son, Menkheper, would make a fine young Horus."

"You think so?" He grinned. "Really?"

It pleased her to see she had surprised him, something she rarely ever succeeded in doing with Senmut.

On that particular afternoon, the Royal Painter, Satnem, was present at the king's informal gathering. Even Ty had uncharacteristically turned his back on his tablets and papyrus scrolls to grace the company. In the last few years Nehesj, the aging Overseer of the Seal, had delegated many of his duties to Ty, in whose hands the taxation of Kemet now mostly lay. She did not like to think about the fact that Nehesj seemed to be gradually preparing to take his leave of life even though he was only a litter older than Hapuseneb. Ty, a thoroughly competent man, relished trapping, in the complex net of his meticulous records, anyone who failed to pay their full tribute to the crown even more than he enjoyed hunting birds and hippos.

Also present was her principal southern herald, Antef, and his brother, Ahmose, a royal scribe and Overseer of Horns, Hoofs, Feathers and Scales, the Counter of the Bread of Upper and Lower Kemet. Ahmose oversaw the herds of cattle belonging to Amun and Pharaoh that never did a day's work, for their only role in life was to grace the tables of those people the gods had blessed. The cows of the *neter* were fed as much bread as they could eat and slaughtered only when they had become almost too fat to walk. Maatkare had made it clear to Ahmose that the less choice cuts of beef were to be distributed to the citizens of Waset according to their needs. No part of a cow was thrown out for even their tongues and brains, their ears and their entrails were delectable to some, and their feet could be boiled in stew while their blood was made into a pudding. Female widows who had no children to care for them were supplied first, followed by families whose father had been crippled in some way or another. Such people regularly received baskets of bread and lentils, cucumbers and leeks, the distribution of which was overseen by the Great Steward of Amun, Senmut, who delegated the actual task to some of his numerous assistants. Life was harder in the city than in villages, where people tended to care for each other better. In the countryside, houses and their vegetable gardens were not as small as they were in town and the hearts of their owners were mysteriously larger. In Waset, the Priests of Horus were flooded with complaints filed by people whose gardens had all been devoured by a neighbor's goat when it broke free of its post. Pigs roamed the streets consuming rubbish until they were eaten by their owners. Priests and nobles never touched pork for it was obviously unclean. Hatshepsut enjoyed lamb as much as beef but while she was in residence in Waset, she refrained from consuming the ram sacred to Amun.

Antef and Ahmose were both intelligent men she could trust to do their jobs, but their wit and imagination combined could not compare to that of her old friends' from the temple. The two brothers were also much younger than her most beloved courtiers. It was sobering how many people had not lived as long as she already had. At Meritre-Hatshepsut's age she had felt like a woman ready to experience all the joys of Hathor even though she had still been only a girl. Of the numerous children born to her brother, Meritre-Hatshepsut was by far the loveliest in every way. The Female Falcon never visited the harem palace—she felt an aversion to the place—but she received regular reports on what went on there. When Menkheperre had last visited Waset, the harem palace had become a dangerous place for Meritre, the youngest and prettiest of Akheperenre's offspring, all of whom longed to become his son's wives or concubines. Meritre grew painfully sick to her stomach and the physician who attended her suspected the dates offered to her by someone's pet monkey were responsible. The adorable little creature had made its way into her room and into her heart but the fruits that he brought her were tainted with arsenic. As a result, she was not able to attend the rituals that would have made her visible to the young pharaoh. She was lucky to have lived.

Once the identity of the perpetrator was discovered by forceful questioning, and confirmed by her weeping confession, she was severely punished. Hatshepsut enjoyed watching the girl flogged much more than she had believed she would. Afterward, one man held the culprit's naked body firmly against his as another man force-fed her dates, until her stomach was visibly swollen and she nearly perished a few hours later from the length and intensity of her bowel movements. Unfortunately, she failed to speak the name of the individual who had provided her with the poison, probably because she feared this person's retribution much more than she did the king's harsh but non-lethal discipline.

Meritre-Hatshepsut was no longer living in the harem palace. When Neferure heard what had happened she made her half sister one of her personal attendants. Meritre could play the lute and sing with engaging skill and convincing sincerity, but it was the quiet intensity with which she appreciated everything that won the affection and protection of God's Wife and Pharaoh. Meritre accepted a gift, no matter how trivial, with as much joy as if it was a golden collar, and she behaved so compassionately toward all life that even the despicable creature who had tried to kill her received her pity instead of her hatred…

When silence fell beneath the pavilion, Hatshepsut realized she had forgotten to listen to Ty. She smiled at him. "Forgive me, my lord, for allowing my mind to wander onto other subjects. I was so interested in what you were saying it reminded me of other important things."

He inclined his head, graciously accepting her apology.

Puyemre and Satnem exchanged a smiling glance. Ty tended to bore everyone.

Hatshepsut was very glad the hands of her favorite painter were still steady. Satnem was working exclusively in her Mansion of Millions of Years. Each time he drew a god's long, strong legs, broad shoulders and powerfully elegant stance, he perfectly captured the virile wisdom of the lord of her heart, Hapuseneb. Maatkare's artists merged the precise proportions and formal style of ancient times with the somewhat more relaxed sensuality of the present in a manner she felt was very pleasing to Amun. The enrichment of reality in any conceivable fashion was her abiding passion. Her ability to appreciate beauty, she had discovered, could deepen and grow in ways she would never have been able to imagine only a few years ago, and the skills of her favorite Servants of Ptah had developed in tandem with her powers of perception.

Satnem was not himself a very tall or attractive man but that hardly mattered. It was his ability to capture the detailed splendor of the world she valued and admired. She was surrounded by other handsome men, many of whom had been recruited from the outermost rings of society, the sons of poor farmers and fishermen. Though she found them pleasing to look at, and enjoyed being served by them, only a handful possessed the Attractive Power inseparable from wisdom that distinguishes a person and makes it possible for him to rise to higher positions. Sharpness of perception could give even irregular features an appealing edge less enlightened countenances did not possess, and generosity of heart imbued its owner with a luminous aura not quite visible to the eyes that nevertheless succeeded in drawing and holding them.

Amenhotep inquired with his usual quiet respect, "What are you thinking about, Majesty?" and the curiosity in his voice was flattering.

"I am thinking about you, and you, and you." She smiled at each of her friends in turn. "I am thinking about how much I love you all and how much I will miss us being together like this."

It was fortunate Dhout chose that moment to reappear—supervising the delivery of more wine and pastries—because her eyes had filled with tears and not even Puyemre seemed inclined to help her brush them away with a light-hearted remark.

It was Senmut who said, "Wherever you are, Maatkare, I will be also. It does not matter if you are next born on the other side of the earth or on a far away world given life by a different sun. Wherever you go I will follow because your smile is the bark of my heart, without which it would sink into a meaningless darkness. The lights of thoughts and feelings shining in your eyes are more beautiful to me than all the stars in the universe!"

Even Dhout—who had bent over a plate and begun fastidiously repairing a toppled pyramid of pastries—did not move for a long moment, as though Senmut's passion was a Divine presence demanding their silent reverence.

Amenhotep was the first to push himself off his stool and onto his knees before his sovereign. Bending forward, his hands planted on either side of her sandals, he kissed the top of both her feet one after the other. As he rose, Useramun quickly took his place followed by Puyemre and Djehuty, Duauneheh and Satnem, Ahmose and Atef, by every man present.

The sadness she had been possessed by was magically dispelled and Dhout—seemingly frantic at the change of plans but, she sensed, secretly elated—ordered the royal chefs to prepare enough food for the feast Pharaoh had suddenly decided to host. Her married courtiers sent for their wives, Senmut summoned a handful of his brothers and sisters, Neferure and Meritre were invited, Harmose brought out his harp and soon a large portion of the garden was lit up by lamps and candles, their golden light gilding pomegranate trees, date palms, sycamores and lotus flowers. But laughter bloomed more freely than anything else, reminding Hatshepsut that indulging in the fear of death and the grief of loss was a foolish waste of time for the dangers of the Dwat could only be fought and conquered by the joyful power of love.

The morning after her impromptu banquet, she vividly recalled the first time she had indulged in the fruit of the vine, and how awful she was feeling when her father came to her room and rested his hands on her throbbing head. Now she was a grown woman and walking alone to her favorite pool. Nafre had not yet awakened and she always sent Senmut away before daybreak. She shooed away four young women recently sent to the palace by noble families who hoped their daughters would find favor with the king. Everyone knew

Maatkare's most beloved attendant was suffering from a swelling of the joints that caused her great pain and made it impossible for her to braid the king's hair herself or to perform many of the other tasks she had once been so skilled at. Hatshepsut missed Nafre's knowledgeable hands when she was being massaged but Seshen and Meresankh still did a good job and she much preferred their company and conversation to that of young strangers. Nafre's physician had recommended she eat more celery but it did not seem to help her.

The water was colder than she liked but it woke her up completely and cleared her head somewhat. She did not know if Senmut had slept when he returned to his home but she was sure he was not going for a swim as she was. Propelling her body toward the other side of the pool, she wondered why she still felt compelled to distance herself from him. Remembering what he had said to her in front of everyone, her heart ached with regret he was not there to share the splendor of the new day with her.

She was pleased when Nafre—appearing on the path with a linen towel draped over her arms—once more transported her back to that morning so long ago when she was miserable with her first hangover but her father still lived.

"Thank you, Nafre." She accepted the towel and wrapped it around her upper body. It was entirely possible her Superior Steward was already in the royal workshop supervising the creation of another of his remarkable statues. She knew he had dedicated two of them to the recently refurbished Temple of Montu in Iuny. The monuments showed him kneeling behind a cobra, crowned by the bovine horns and solar disc of Hathor, which rose before him from between a pair of Ka arms—his unique way of spelling her throne name *Maatkare*. He had mentioned he was also working on another group of statues for the chapel of Iunit in his home town in which he knelt holding a sistrum in front of him crowned by the head of Hathor, who it represented. She took it as a personal compliment he spent so much of his time causing to appear and displaying the beauty of the Goddess "so that her place was elevated more than those of the other gods."[79]

A cup of warm goat's milk, lavishly buttered bread and a soft-boiled duck egg were waiting for her inside, simple but delicious pleasures she never tired of.

36

Goddesses of the Hours

The three women who had nourished kings in recent history—Neferiah, beloved mother of Puyemre, Sitre, known as Inet, and Ipu, wife of Ahmose-Penekhbet—were all now sleeping forever in the western desert. Maatkare strove to forget how old she was only to be continually reminded of it by the death of those dear to her. It was particularly hard for her when her beloved old tutor, Senimen, went to his Ka. She was comforted imagining he suffered no pain; he simply went to bed one night and never woke up. Persons who died thus were truly blessed by the gods. For as long as the High Priest of Amun and her Superior Steward, Senmut, continued to live she could face the greatest adversity. The possibility that she might have to continue breathing and ruling without them was one she refused to reflect upon. Both men were healthy and strong; it was easy to hold on to the dream they would all die immediately one after the other in the distant future.

The daughter of Ahmose Penekhbet and Ipu, Satioh, was fourteen-years-old and a close friend of Thutmose. Her mother had been the young falcon's nurse and the grief in his eyes during Ipu's funeral had been real and endearing. Though he was still short, Menkheperre had begun to speak with a man's voice. He managed to keep it from cracking as he informed his father's sister he wished to marry Satioh as soon as possible.

"She is all alone in the world now," he said. "Her mother had a younger brother but she hardly knows him. I want to take care of her."

"You do not have to marry her to do that."

"She is the sister of my heart and of noble birth. There is no reason why she should not be my wife."

"I can think of *one* reason—Neferure, your true sister and the daughter of two kings, the Crown Princess and God's Wife, the direct descendant of the great Nebpehtire who defeated the Setiu and made the Two Lands one again."

He looked away. "I do not believe she likes me."

"You may marry whomever you wish," she heard herself pronounce. "You are king."

Six months later, Thutmose wed Satioh in Mennefer even though Maatkare's northern Herald, Goregmennefer, informed her that the King's Mother had done her best to talk him out of it. As if by way of compromise, Menkheperre refrained from making Satioh his Great Royal Wife. Apparently, he was wise enough to realize he was still too young to be certain she deserved the title and that it was best to hold it in reserve.

Even though in public she made it impossible for anyone to know what she was feeling, in private Neferure appeared torn between relief and disappointment. "At least Satioh will serve to break him in for me," she said morosely.

"Does that mean you have reconsidered your position?" her mother asked quickly, scarcely daring to believe it.

"No, I am simply tired of swimming against the current. I feel that if I do not reach one shore or the other soon I will be devoured by the crocodile of my own frustration. Besides, Tusi is growing tired of priestesses of Hathor who cannot give him the son he desires. I fear he will soon marry someone else even though he swears he will love only me for as long as he lives." Her smile was cynical.

Senmut was in the room and Hatshepsut cast him a desperate look. He had always had the power to make Neferure feel better. On that occasion, however, even he seemed at a loss for words.

"How long must I wait, mother?"

"That is up to you, my love." She thought this response would make her daughter feel better but it seemed to have the opposite effect.

Neferure stood and left the room without bothering to excuse herself. She had never done anything so rude.

Senmut said, "She wants your permission."

"I cannot give it to her! It is enough I have permitted her to question the will of the *neters*."

"You wish for her to marry Thutmose."

"No. What I want is for her to be happy. Yet I fear that a few years from now she will realize she made a mistake marrying Tusi, and regret the loss of the power she was meant to possess, which will make her even more miserable in the future than she is in the present."

"It is always a mistake to sacrifice the present for the sake of a future that may not exist. We can none of us know how many years the goddesses of the hours have allotted us. Neferure is unhappy, and has been that way for a long time, which you continue prolonging by pretending to understand what the gods intend for her. Perhaps Mistress of the House is the only title to which she aspires, despite the fact that she is the daughter of two pharaohs."

"I cannot believe that! And she is already God's Wife. Her Ka is much too developed to be content with such a modest fate for the extraordinarily wise and beautiful Ba it created."

"You are confusing her with you, Hatshepsut. Neferure's Ka is very strong, I agree, but her Ba is weak enough to be plagued by doubts which never swayed you. She has confessed to me that every day she suffers a crisis of faith when she makes her offerings to Amun and the seventeen deities of *Ipet Sut*. I see her battling the same demons I wrestled with when I was her age, for demons thrive on our fears and doubts. I might have lost the struggle with my heart, and walked in darkness all my life, if I had not been fortunate enough to fall in love with you, Maatkare."

They stared into each other's eyes for a time before he concluded, "I fear Neferure is not as blessed by Tusi as I am by you. Tusi always honored the gods and accepted his responsibilities without questioning them, until he met Neferure. His inability to live according to tradition is having a detrimental effect on him. Because he always did the right thing, he cannot understand why his life is not turning out as he planned, which was simply to live just as his parents and all their revered ancestors did."

"Is he truly so simple?"

"Intelligence and wisdom do not always share the same table."

She smiled at him, grateful he was making an effort to lighten their somber mood a little.

"Perhaps I should not have been so lax with her, Senmut. Perhaps you are right, as usual, and I should tell her what to do instead of leaving the matter in her hands. If what you say is true it is unlikely she will make a decision that will not have a detrimental effect on her future."

"The question is *what* will you decide and by what criteria will you determine you are right?"

"You will not help me in this, my unique friend? You know how much I value your opinion on everything."

"On this matter I do not feel comfortable playing Thoth to your Seshat."

"That is not fair, Senmut. Neferure was your student and in many ways you know her better than I do."

"I know her well enough to understand if you command her to marry Thutmose she will make herself miserable missing and pining for Tusi, and that the same thing will happen in reverse if you permit her to defy tradition and wed the man of her choosing. She will not regret giving up her half-brother but I am sure she will become bored with Tusi eventually. She will realize that as the Great Royal Wife and Queen of Kemet she could have done more important things than wash her husbands hands and feet every evening."

"Who washes your hands and feet when you return home, Senmut?" she said curiously, exhausted with the hopeless subject of her daughter's happiness, which like a bolti fish eluded the nets of her thoughts and any plans she might conceive to secure it.

He answered dismissively, "One of my all too numerous attendants."

"Are they all very pretty?"

"I usually do not notice."

"Ah, but that means you sometimes *do* notice."

"My steward enjoys procuring attractive women to serve in my household and every year they seem to grow younger, a fact that is definitely not arousing."

She smiled. "You prefer older women?"

"I prefer one very special old woman." Grasping her hands, he stood and pulled her up into his arms.

"Old?" She attempted to push him away, enjoying the struggle she always lost and that excited her by reminding her how strong he was. "I am not *old!*"

"No, you are not," he agreed, turning her around and forcing her to bend over the couch. "Not to me."

Truly indignant now, she tried to push herself up. "I am not old to anyone!"

He held her down. "You are beautiful, Maatkare, you know that."

Relaxing somewhat, she permitted him to lift her dress.

"You will always be beautiful to me, Hatshepsut, no matter how old and decrepit you get."

"Stop!" The insult made it impossible for her to take any pleasure from his penetration.

He promptly slipped out of her.

She straightened and smoothed her dress back down to her ankles before turning to face him.

"I am sorry." His voice was cold. "I thought you wanted me."

"You say you are sorry but you do not *sound* it. I did want you, until you insulted me."

"You find the truth insulting, *Maat*kare?"

She stared up at his face in despair. "Why are you being so hostile, Senmut? Obviously I will grow old, if I am fortunate, but I will *never* be decrepit!"

"I am sorry," he repeated, this time much more convincingly. "I believed, quite wrongly I see, that I was flattering you, for it is the truth I will always think you are beautiful no matter how you look."

"The tone in which you delivered what you continue insisting was a compliment was more aggressive than loving."

"You often enjoy it when I am rough with you."

"You are confused, my lord, seriously so. I find it impossible to understand how you could believe talk like that would inspire me toward deeper intimacies."

"It will not happen again," he promised, but his voice was hard.

"I hope not!" They had not only failed to resolve the problem of Neferure, they had created a rift between them more unexpectedly sudden than the ones forming in the parched earth outside as everyone waited, on the edge of despair, for the River to begin rising.

* * * * *

On the night following her argument with Senmut, in the hour of the Slicer of Souls, Hatshepsut saw a turtle in her garden and cried out in alarm, unable to control her reaction. Malevolent forces often found homes inside the shells of turtles and seeing one could imply she needed protection from something. She was feeling upset enough to worry she had not paid enough attention to the minor divinities who served the *neters*. The Hidden One commanded many servants he sent out to do his work and, depending on her own behavior, they could either hurt or help her. It was possible she had somehow offended a demi-god with the attitude she had taken toward some matter, just as Senmut had insulted her pride even while ostensibly flattering her...

Abruptly realizing she was letting superstitious thoughts shatter her heart's Divine confidence, she sought a conference with the High Priest. Hapuseneb had recently returned from the north, where he had spent several months in the Oryx with his wife. The Royal Ornament, Amenhotep, had been ill for a long time but had at last made a full recovery. At first, Hatshepsut did not feel jealous. However, as the weeks passed she was less successful at controlling the painful feeling, which forced her to exercise her patience and compassion to an exhausting degree in an effort to defeat it.

It seemed there were as many places inside her—where emotions she was less than proud of hid from the light of Re—as there were dark caverns in the Dwat. At least it was in her power to mysteriously behead those parts of herself and render them impotent. Her spiritual growth would be slowed if she did not confront every one of her thoughts and the circumstances from which they arose. Feelings, straightforward as they seemed, could have secret names very much like the guardians of the Twelve Gates of the Underworld, each one of which was protected by a fiery serpent and guarded by a *neter*. Despair was often only another name for fear, impatience for greed, laziness for spiritual doubts, and so on indefinitely.

While she waited for Hapuseneb—all the time thinking about what had happened with Senmut in a vain attempt to determine who had been at fault or if they had both behaved badly—Sahekek attacked her. The minor divinity— who was depicted as a naked child suffering from such a terrible headache he

473

was forced to hold his arm over his face—abruptly made her feel her heart had caught fire as the muscles between her shoulder blades seized up painfully.

"Nafre, I feel terrible!" she declared, and an embarrassingly loud belch was wrenched out of her mouth by the gross discomfort.

Her attendant immediately sent for Ibenre.

"Something you have eaten recently did not agree with you," he said. Excusing himself, he returned a few minutes later with something for her to drink—a cup of warm milk strongly flavored with mint and more subtly spiced with other ingredients she could not identify.

She took three quick sips and felt better almost at once. "It is strange, Ibenre. I have suffered from an upset stomach before but I have never felt as if my heart was burning up in my chest."

"You are very fortunate to be able to say that, Majesty."

It was the tenth hour of the day—named after Heka, Lord of Magic—when Hapuseneb was announced and admitted into her presence.

The High Priest listened in silence as she made an effort to convey to him what she had been feeling and thinking during his absence. She refrained from mentioning he had been gone much too long.

When she finished talking he said, "It is in our nature to grow blindly comfortable with our habits, like all animals. Although it is right to embrace our sensuality, it is also vital to consciously transcend it. All too often only adverse circumstances can affect changes within us by challenging us and forcing us to once again see clearly."

"But I believe all of my habits are good and positive," she argued.

"When something becomes a habit it tends to lose its magic. It is natural to enjoy many of the same things everyday but we must never take them for granted. We must truly appreciate everything for what it is—a sublime mystery."

"I do not believe I am guilty of a lack of appreciation, Hapuseneb." She was becoming offended. "I practice discipline, not indifference."

"We all fall into habits in some form or another," he insisted.

"I feel as though I was attacked today by Sahekek, who felt very much like a demon to me."

"My lady, you are regressing to a way of thinking you have not indulged in since you were young and did not know better."

She was so hurt by his impatient comment that she suddenly felt numb. "Are you telling me, my lord that I am growing old and foolish?"

"It is precisely this insecure and self-defensive attitude that attacked you today, Hatshepsut. What you choose to call Sahekek was actually your Ka exerting its influence on the physical vessel it created in order to wake you up to the destructive path your thoughts and emotions have been taking because you are afraid."

She clutched the arms of her chair. "It is true, Hapuseneb. I am not afraid of going to my Ka and facing all the magical challenges awaiting me in the Dwat. What I dread is suffering the unflattering decline of my body as it slowly ages, until one day it no longer obeys me. Dying is easy but growing old and ugly is not."

Leaning forward, he gently wrenched her hands free of the armrests and held them in his own as he commanded gently, "Look at me, Maatkare."

She obeyed, and found all the solace and courage she needed in his stern but loving gaze.

"As a person grows older," he told her, "who they truly are inside rises to the surface. For that reason, and many others, there is no doubt in my heart you will age gracefully. What is causing you so much suffering is your concept of beauty, which must grow and deepen. Beauty, *nefer*, is the Divine will behind all physical processes become visible through their creative potency. No matter how small and wrinkled, every newborn is beautiful because it literally glows with the magical forces of growth. Old people are equally splendorous, if you perceive in them the fulfillment of a cycle containing within it the celestial seed of its own transcendence."

She sighed. "Hapuseneb!" and lowering her head rested her forehead on their joined hands. "It is hard for me to really feel that is true when you are absent."

"It is something you need to work on, Hatshepsut, for though I will always be with you, there will be times when we will not be able to speak together like this. You will need to find the strength that comes from truly believing what you know in your heart is true."

"Because Thoth is only Re's servant." She rarely thought of her mother and she was beginning to understand why—she feared dying in that slow and ignominious fashion. She raised her head and fixed her eyes hungrily on the High Priest's face in an effort to brand it straight into her Ka so she would never forget it, not for a hundred million years and beyond. "You are right when you say my concept of *nefer* must deepen, Hapuseneb, for I feel that when people cease to arouse sexual desire in others they are no longer truly beautiful. You know I have always had a secret place in my heart for Seth."

"Seth definitely has his place in the adventure of incarnation, but the power of the body to conceive and create another physical life is only a reflection of our Ka's much greater magic. Latent in our hearts is the spiritual ability to command the laws contained in the substance of the Golden One, who serves as the House of God and provides Ptah with the tools he uses to give form to the Hidden One."

"I know this to be true in my heart, Hapuseneb, but it is impossible to imagine what lies beyond the uterine boat of Hathor, in which Atum sails across waves of darkness every night beyond the reach of our physical vision."

"Thoughts are like fish flopping from one concept to another on the shores of mystery."

"But when the powerful waves of my Ka stop flowing through my heart my mind will also expire. I hope that then I can dive back into the Primordial Waters and be free of the weight of reason. In the Dwat whatever I can imagine will be realized around me in obedience to endless currents of love!"

"That is a lovely thought, Hatshepsut-Maatkare, and yet you yourself are more beautiful than anything you can conceive of. You always will be, and not only to me because I love you. What you really are is the very breath of Beauty flowing through the body of which we are both so fond. You are beginning to feel imprisoned by your flesh but it will not betray you, not if you truly identify with your Ka and do not let it."

* * * * *

Just beyond the holy district, at the base of the sacred mountain—in the western corner of a shallow desert valley that would soon begin supplying stone for the processional route from Maatkare's offering chapel to her Monument of Millions of Years—the Great Steward of Amun, Senmut, began excavating the second half of his tomb. He had apologized to her again for the way he had behaved the last time they were together, but briefly and with so little grace, it had almost given her new cause for complaint. She forgave him because she loved him and because she missed the unique blend of mental stimulation and emotional contentment she enjoyed in his presence.

Maatkare made it clear to her Superior Steward that he was fully in her favor again and accompanied by Neferure, she crossed the River and paid a visit to the first public half of his tomb. Hathor heads and cobras lined the walls of the interior pillared offering hall, where a delegation of the Keftiu bearing gifts was magnificently rendered. The tile-like decoration of the ceiling also evoked that distant island.

"When I am queen," Neferure's voice rebounded with a disturbingly trapped energy against the stone walls, "I will cross the Great Green with Prince Kallikrates and see for myself those magical fish he is so fond of called *dolphins.*"

Hatshepsut smiled at her as though she had not said anything of great import, for it was entirely possible she was only jesting.

The figures of two soldiers guarded texts commemorating Maatkare's victory over the Kushites and described how Senmut had accompanied the king on her campaign. The name of his parents was written on the ceiling along with a curse:

Concerning any man, who will cause damage to my statue,
he may not follow the king of his time;
he may not be buried in the western cemetery;
he may not be given any lifetime on earth.[80]

Erected at the end of a long and narrow corridor opening off the back wall of the Offering Hall was a monument made of red *biat*. In its center—above the carved façade of a false door guarded by the two Eyes of Horus—Senmut was shown at a banquet with his parents. Seated behind his son, Ramose rested an arm around his shoulders while Hatnefer sat before him holding a Lotus flower to his nose. The monument was inscribed with a prayer from *The Book of Coming Forth by Day and Opening the Tomb*. Above it—in a niche carved directly into the rock—a block statue of Senmut, the head of princess Neferure emerging from his cloaked lap, looked out from the Dwat to the world of the living and the offerings of life which magically continued nourishing his Ka. Hatshepsut suffered a stab of jealousy. Not only was it unusual to incorporate someone else into the statue of your Ba, it had never been done. She strongly suspected her daughter already knew about her intimate inclusion in Senmut's tomb for she displayed no emotion whatsoever when she saw the carving. But what truly upset her was the fact that neither one of them had mentioned it to her.

She spent a great deal of time formally admiring Senmut's monument, which included the plans for its construction, in an effort to ignore her turbulent emotions. He had chosen a spell which was believed to have been discovered on a block of *biat*, one reason, she supposed, he had employed a stone so difficult to work. The size and quality of his tomb proclaimed that even though his Ba had been born to commoners the power of his Ka was comparable to pharaoh's. She had no quarrel with that. Senmut was one of the most intelligent and noble men she had ever met and it was she who had given him permission to use whatever materials he wished when exercising Divine creativity. He did not need to say so for her to know he had designed the monument himself. The spell began on the left side and proceeded toward the central panel of the door to just below the Eyes of Horus. From there the hieroglyphs flowed to the outermost edges of the right-hand frame before once again moving inward and drawing the eyes back to the false door—the threshold between life and death and the mentally incomprehensible transformation between one state of being and the next. Red plaster was used to cover up small flaws in the rock, against which the blue pigment of the images stood out with contrasting vividness. By lamplight, the hieroglyphs resembled the sky outside the tomb glimpsed through their miniature but vastly meaningful windows. They brought an uplifting sense of heaven into the darkness. The room, dug deep in the earth, was transformed by the beautiful monument into a magical womb. The narrow corridor leading back out into the sunlit Offering Hall symbolized the passage between a woman's legs. The reddish hue of the stone itself evoked the solar disc as well as the life-giving blood that congeals and hardens after death.

As they were leaving, Hatshepsut remarked on the nine small panels hung in unexpected places close to the entrance—six on the south wall and three on the north. Blue hieroglyphs stood vividly out against a white background and spelled Senmut's name, the name of the man who engendered him and the name of the woman who bore him. Also inscribed on the panels were a handful of his titles, including Great Steward of Amun and Chief of the Granaries and Barns of Amun. Around them a ritual pilgrimage to Abedju, the city of Osiris, ran alongside a scene from the future day of the funeral, which included scribes and officials towing shrines and other treasures to the tomb. She would have asked Senmut to explain the curious monuments if she had not been feeling so hurt by the knowledge he had kept something from her.

Later that evening, when Nafre was combing her hair, she was able to think more clearly. Neferure was the child Senmut had never had. She had always known he was fond of her daughter but she had not realized, though she should have, that he loved her like a father. The mysterious ways Amun-Min worked was to thank for that. And yet, perhaps, if Neferure had received a more traditional education from priests—many of whom did not think for themselves as Senmut most certainly did—she would not be so troubled now by doubts concerning her destiny. And yet that was a foolish thought for she had no desire to change anything about Nefi. In fact, she had great cause to be happy the man her daughter loved like a father still lived.

"And because of Nefi he is not as lonely as he might have been," she said beneath her breath, "because of me."

"Majesty?"

"It is nothing, Nafre. I was merely thinking out loud."

"I see."

"And sometimes *I* do not see, not as clearly and truthfully as I believe."

"Well, Majesty, at least you realize that eventually, unlike most people who have no idea how blind they are."

"Thank you, Nafre. Since our first morning together, you have always been able to make me feel better even while telling the truth, a remarkable feat indeed."

* * * * *

When next she met with Djehuty, in the room serving as his office in the administrative palace, he was engaged in the task of reviewing a letter he was writing to the High Priest of Iuno. Ptah-Soker—the handsome man who years ago had proved so insensible to the effect his touch had on her—was apparently more apt to react to what he perceived as an insult. The Greatest of Seers had, very generously, sent a company of temple workmen to Waset to assist Maatkare's architects in the building of her Million Years Mansion. Djehuty had insulted them by not being sufficiently impressed with their suggestions.

"I regret you must waste your time with this matter," she told him. "Should you find your progress slowed in the future by more officials supposedly sent to assist you, let me know and I will handle them personally."

"Thank you, Majesty, but I would not dream of troubling you! Goregmennefer will deliver my apology to Ptah-Soker and everyone will be happy again... I hope. Your Northern Herald is very clever. He helped me compose the letter." He looked admiringly down at the papyrus covered with small, neat and boldly outlined hieroglyphs. "He has made it sound as though I intend to heed the advice of the temple workmen sent by the Greatest of Seers without actually saying I will do so. He states several times how grateful we are for his generous contribution to the beautiful work, which I suppose is true, in theory at least. Nowhere does he offend Maat by actually lying and yet I believe Ptah-Soker will be satisfied."

"Goregmennefer has proved most useful to me," she agreed, smiling at the man who still reminded her of a serious little boy. Djehuty was more impressed by a scribe's way with words than by his own remarkable skills, which enabled him to picture the walls and rooms, the shrines and colonnades of a three-dimensional building merely by drawing lines and numbers on a papyrus. Djehuty was a priest of measure, the expression of Number. Embodied by Thoth—Lord of Time and the scribe of Atum-Re—measure served as the 'determination of potentiality, the order-producing gesture by which substance manifests as form'.[81]

Hatshepsut felt compelled to assure herself almost daily that the growth of her beautiful Mansion was not being slowed down by anything. She was not able to depend so much on Senmut now that he had begun working on the second half of his tomb. Not since before the first wave of darkness flooded Kemet in the form of the Setiu had a Pharaoh ordered to be constructed such a uniquely magnificent structure to cradle his Ka. Hathor and Anubis would each command their own sanctuary on opposite ends of Maatkare's temple. An ancient cave shrine to the Goddess was in the process of being replaced with rock-cut chambers, to be fronted by an open court supported by pillars carved in the shape of sistrums crowned with Hathor-head capitals. The three-fold nature of Amun-Re would be embodied in her Mansion, its three spacious terraces forming part of a single flowing whole by way of a central unifying ramp, something that had never been done before. As more columned passages and courts stretched forth their gleaming white limestone limbs—the material which most resembled embodied light supporting the vital organs of interior rooms devoted to the forces of incarnation—Maatkare named her temple *Djser-Djeseru*, Holiest of the Holy and Purest of the Pure. Its design embodied the first words Hapuseneb had spoken to her, "Three in one, One in Three" and faced its Lord, the House of Amun rising in the east across the River.

Construction had begun on the uppermost terrace, from which the eternal life-force contained in the solar disc descended into corporeal form. When the Mansion was complete, it would be possible for her to walk freely up and down between the three levels along a unifying path, an act symbolic of grasping the full creative power of her Ka and its source—the Divine heart of the universe. Djehuty had calculated all the complicated measurements but Senmut had been instrumental in helping him apply them to the actual space. Superior Steward navigated any constraints that became apparent while facilitating the changes they dictated. Though the occasional deviations from the original plans were minimal, Hatshepsut took them very seriously, for she felt they meant something. The result of questioning her metaphysical reasoning was invariably to deepen it. As the work progressed, she discovered that materials—and all the details involved in shaping and fitting them within a limited amount of space and in specific locations—had the ability to speak to her silently about how complex was the process her Ka had gone through while creating her body. She developed an even deeper appreciation for the magical work of incarnation.

Hathor's chapel would occupy the southern end of the central terrace, part of, and emerging from, the mountain long sacred to her. The sanctuary of the Goddess was located below the celestial level on the floor devoted to the forces of manifestation, its southern orientation expressing the Golden One's sovereignty over the realm of the physical senses and all the pleasures they make possible. The ancient cave consecrated to the Lady of Life was located in just the right place for Maatkare's Mansion to embrace it while also adjoining the temple of Mentuhotep. This was just one of the many facts which strengthened her belief that Amun-Re, the Lord of her heart, had meant for her to become king and build *Djser-Djseru*. The sanctuary of Anubis would be constructed directly across from Hathor's chapel, where she would appear alongside him, her life-giving forces joining with his in the realm of the Dwat—the dangerous place where physical decay and dissolution are faced and transcended as the Ba rejoins its Ka.

"All life is conceived in the heart of God and born through the Goddess," she told Hapuseneb. "It is this truth I wish to express between the chapels of Anubis and Hathor on the central terrace of my temple."

He was silent, wise enough to realize she was thinking out loud and did not require his input.

"Because I believe in life's Divine conception, Anubis will walk beside me after I die and protect me from the forces of destruction to which only the physical body is subject. But if I were to identify only with my flesh this same jackal, the son of Seth, would rip me to shreds and only faint traces of my awareness would remain. Whether or not I was able to recover my senses would depend on how many people I loved who could help my lost shade by enlightening me in dreams, until I was finally strong enough to walk on my own again toward the Golden Hall of Osiris."

Hapuseneb looked down at his hands, which were spread open on his knees as if he was reading his fingers like sentences. "There will come a time," he said, "when people will believe that when they die they will either cease to exist forever or achieve eternal life without having to make any effort whatsoever."

"But that is as foolish as believing that once babies drop out of their mothers they will all die or, if they survive, that they must do nothing to achieve the lives they grow to desire."

"Indeed."

"What terrible time is this of which you speak, Hapuseneb? Surely such a thing could never happen here in Kemet."

"It is a time you need not concern yourself with, Maatkare."

"Is this something the priests of Amun who read the stars have foreseen?"

"Perhaps, I have not asked them, I know only that I have glimpsed it in my dreams."

"They sound like nightmares to me."

He smiled. "I did not mean to interrupt you. Forgive me. You were talking of your Mansion of Millions of Years, that will continue to stand long after the time I mention and illuminate futures which cannot yet be fathomed."

"Alongside the sanctuary of Anubis," she continued eagerly, "images expressing life's Divine origin, and the vital part played by the Goddess, will decorate the walls."

He said, "It is also important to show there is a purpose to existence as we know it. Why did Atum-Re's heart break into time and space?"

She replied without hesitation, "To experience love and desire, joy and pleasure."

"Fear and pain, doubt and hopelessness?"

"Merely illusions of the flesh we must all suffer as we grow into our true nature. Hathor is called the Golden One because as the womb of Substance, God's Hand, she too is Divine. The sensual pleasures she makes possible depend on our incarnation but Life itself does not. It is the power to spiritually command the *neters* which constitute the House of Horus that is personified in Pharaoh and guarded by him for all his subjects—from those nearest to him in wisdom to all those who have yet to travel far on the path of enlightenment paved all along the way for us by the Intelligence of the Heart.

"On the middle terrace of my temple, I will record my Divine conception and birth alongside images expressive of incarnate life's joys and pleasures. My coronation will also be inscribed, for as king I am the efficient seed of God on earth, His bodily son in command of the Two Lands—the cycle of life and death and the Divine unity from which it issues. When Pharaoh wears the *khat* headdress, he fully assumes the power of the Ka, which gives a corporeal form to God's boundless life-force through the ultimate act of creation."

"And unlike many of your predecessors, Maatkare, you have truly earned the right to wear it." He raised his hands to her in praise.

She reflected his gesture and more distinctly than ever felt the warm resistance of an invisible force that both separated and joined them.

"Hatshepsut!" he whispered, and pressed his hands firmly against hers. "Beloved of Amun!"

37

Hathor's Kisses

The Royal sculptors—closely supervised by Amenhotep, Hapuseneb, Puyemre and Senmut—were hard at work. Amun-Re had provided Maatkare with men blessed by Ptah who could understand exactly what she wanted and make it happen. There was no greater magic. The images of herself carved when she was queen, and those made after she became regent, no longer completely pleased her for they failed to fully capture her uniqueness. Even the statues she had commissioned for the House of Amun after she became king, on which her name and titles were all written with masculine determinatives, resembled her immediate predecessors more than they did her. This was no longer acceptable, and *Djser-Djeseru* was the perfect venue in which to express everything her heart was telling her.

She stayed up late into the night conversing with Senmut and Amenhotep, who was currently overseeing the creation of two group statues for her River shrine. All the mirrors she possessed everyday reflected her face slowly but remorselessly aging. They failed to preserve her beauty and personality, two inseparable qualities. The best stone carvers in Kemet now lived in Waset because only statues could capture who she was forever. She valued the wisdom embodied in tradition, but innovation was an essential element of creativity, without which it failed to live up to its Divine nature and became mere replication.

"Every infant is essentially the same and yet different from every other baby," she commented to Senmut and Puyemre one day. "And so too every Pharaoh who has ever lived, and will be born in the future, is a unique incarnation of Amun-Re. My Million Years Mansion will honor the knowledge and wisdom of my ancestors without being a blind copy, for it is through the eyes that the Ka shines and reveals its exceptional beauty. How I think and feel is part of the ancient knowledge which shaped and enlightened me. But this same glorious tradition also empowered my perceptions to such a degree that I am able to elaborate upon it, and make it an even sharper reflection of the Hidden One's magical workings."

She could never be satisfied with merely altering the inscriptions on existing monuments. Hapuseneb agreed she was not displaying the weakness of vanity by showing respect and reverence for her individuality, on the contrary. The High Priest encouraged her to exercise her imagination as a tool used by Amun-Re to further reveal Himself through her temples and statuary.

Four images of Pharaoh Maatkare—to be placed on either side of the granite gateway leading into the upper terrace of her temple—were modeled after those in the adjoining Monument of Mentuhotep but carved on a much larger scale. She wanted to show that with every ruler the heart of Amun mysteriously grew. The king was carved in a striding pose, her left leg extended and her hands resting before her at the edges of her stiff pyramid-shaped royal apron. Her thumbs and fingers clearly delineated—and held tightly together at the western and eastern sides of her outward thrusting kilt—represented the Divine Void that divided to become Number and the creative process embodied in the digits One through Ten. The pose was one commonly used to express reverence toward God. The fact that her statue was more massive, and cut along even more imposing lines than those of her predecessors, showed how much more powerful Amun-Re had become through his daughter's heart, the most recent embodiment of the Royal Ka and His bodily son. On each statue her belt, the supporting pillar and the base were inscribed with its intended location in *Djser-Djeseru* alongside her name and king's titles, in which both male and female determinatives were used. In keeping with the monument's ritual and symbolic nature, less care was taken with her individual features but they were still finely carved. She felt it was important the hint of a smile lighten her colossal countenance and touch upon the joy that is an indelible part of adoring God.

It fascinated Hatshepsut to see her identity reflected dozens of times over in the royal workshops crowded with towering figures of herself. Never before had a woman's face crowned a statue of Pharaoh portrayed as Osiris, the embodiment of eternal Divine kingship. Though she had been inspired by the images of Mentuhotep where the king's cloaked figure took the place of columns—as well as by the statues of her mother's brother in which his linen-wrapped body was supported by pillars—she had incorporated meaningful new elements into her representations. She expressed her love for her family, and all her revered royal ancestors, by adopting the jubilee cloak of Mentuhotep even though her legs were carved to look like those of a bandaged mummy. She was one with her beloved father, Akheperkare, when she was portrayed holding the crook and flail, but she revealed the mysterious growth of Amun-Re's heart through her unique incarnation by grasping two additional symbols. In her right hand she gripped both a flail and an *ankh*, and in her left she held a crook as well as a *was* scepter. Not only was the combination of sacred objects rich in significance, the number Four was also important as a symbol of containment and the completion of God's original intent to manifest a fragment of His infinite potential.

The power of Number and its direct relationship to the void of Atum—the seemingly empty darkness that is latently everything—would be expressed everywhere in *Djser-Djeseru*. Four of Maatkare's Osiris figures would be placed on the topmost terrace and an additional ten would be embraced by niches in the western wall. No less than twenty-six statues of eternal Divine kingship, crowned by her smiling face, would line the upper portico, all of them fashioned of limestone. No matter its size or the ritual nature dictating its style, Maatkare's face was recognizable on every statue being produced for her Mansion of Millions of Years.

The image of the King as a lion with a man's head was as old as history but never before had similar monuments been produced in sufficient quantities to line an entire avenue. Hatshepsut could not imagine a more spiritually significant and impressive approach to the summit of her Mansion. The statues' copious numbers served to represent the great prosperity the Two Lands was enjoying during her reign, which made it possible for her to exercise her Divine creativity to its maximum potential. Two rows of leonine figures would line the avenue leading to her temple and an additional six—the *shenu* ring containing her throne name engraved on their chests—would be arranged in two east-west facing rows directly across from each other along the processional route from the middle to the upper terrace of her temple. Though the statues would all be carved of *biat*, and each one would wear the *nemes* headdress and beard of Pharaoh, they would not merely be identical reflections of each other. Their expressions, and the color of the stone they were carved from, would vary slightly along with their proportions and sizes. However, on all of them would be inscribed the name of Amun, Preeminent at *Djser-Djeseru*.

Between the lower and middle terraces, crowning the posts at the head of the ramp ascending between them, two additional images of the King as a lion with a human head would sit gazing east in the direction of the River. Though smaller in scale than her other leonine statues, they were even richer in detail and while they were being created consumed a larger portion of her attention and affection. An animal's tail wrapped elegantly around her right haunch, a solar mane and four lion-like ears framed her human face, and jagged lines carved into her chest evoked a hairy pelt. Though a peaceful smile softened even her most colossal works, on these two vividly painted limestone statues her countenance was particularly friendly and approachable. Senmut described them as "paradoxes set in stone."

"In them you possess the body of a male lion and the face of a lovely young girl," he observed. "You are obviously powerful enough to devour all your adversaries and yet instead you appear to be welcoming them, reassuring them of your gentleness and compassion with your benevolent expression. And even though on both statues is written *Maatkare, beloved of Amun, given life forever*, on one of them your name is followed by a feminine ending and on the other by a masculine determinative."

"Because my Ka has the power to create both male and female bodies," she explained even though she knew it was not necessary. "I understand better than ever how the image of Pharaoh as a lion with the head of a man represents how the Ka is linked directly to God, from whom it derives the power to command the sensual substance generated by the Goddess. Every Ka is a part of Atum-Re, and yet at the same time it cannot be separated from the magical act of creating a sensual home for the Divine life-force. Before I understood this, I was always confused by the fact that the Ka sustains life yet also requires sustenance in the form of offerings. Those who blindly follow Seth by thinking there is only one beginning for them and death is the end dangerously cripple their Ka simply by not believing in it."

"That danger does indeed exist," Senmut agreed soberly, perhaps remembering when he himself had felt that way before he met her.

The small painted human-lion hybrids, symbolizing as they did the creative power of every individual Ka, naturally belonged on the middle terrace of her temple at the head of the ramp leading up to, as well as down from, the Divine upper level. Both statues were brightly painted with all the colors of creation— their animal manes were a celestial blue, their bodies a tawny gold evoking the sun, their faces were the reddish brown of earth and blood, their black eyes were surrounded by the shining white of embodied light, and the green borders of their *nemes* headdresses rose up into the royal cobra.

* * * * * *

In order to call upon the power of Sekhmet to protect Maatkare from her enemies, the Priest of Amun, Senenu, had been responsible for erecting a monument in the heart of God's temple. It seemed to be working. The great quantity of cattle herded to Kemet all the way from Punt had arrived safely. The northern borders were not so quiet, but in a sense that was a good thing—the occasional skirmishes served to keep Pharaoh's soldiers from growing bored with the peace of prosperity and helped hone their skills. Heavily guarded oxen-drawn carts, loaded with turquoise and copper, traveled peacefully down from the mountains of Roshawet. In Mennefer as well as in Perunefer the ships of the Fenkhu now regularly docked alongside those of the Keftiu.

Senenu, like many other priests, had elected not to shave his head. The soft dark curls of his natural hair were so heavy they stayed in place almost as neatly as a wig even when the north wind blew. Only the shorter strands would respond to the caress of Shu's invisible fingers, or curl against his temples and forehead like black hieroglyphs whenever his skin was damp with holy water. Senenu was currently Hapuseneb's only student and Hatshepsut could not fail to notice that the First Prophet of Amun spent almost as much time with the young man as he once had with her. Senenu's beauty was not like a bird's egg that cracked, ruining its flawless effect, when you attempted to tap his depths. A true incorruptible metal was forged into his long and slender bones. His thighs and calves were well formed and his shoulders were broad. Senenu was so handsome, Hatshepsut expected Neferure to forget Tusi the moment she saw him but instead she did not even seem to like him.

"Not everyone shares their thoughts and feelings with others as freely as you do, my lady," Senmut told her on one of the many occasions they discussed Neferure together. "Many people keep secrets even from themselves."

"But if she does not completely understand herself then how can anyone else expect to fully know the color of her heart? Is that what you mean?" She did not wait for him to speak. "She will be twenty-one-years old soon and Thutmose is fourteen, a man fully grown who will soon marry again. The Fenkhu king has offered him one of his youngest daughters. Actually, he brought all of them with him the last time he visited Mennefer so the young Pharaoh could choose between them, and accept more than one if it pleased him. I am beginning to despair that Neferure will never decide between her brother and that foolish Tusi!"

"'Since the days of old, no daughter of Pharaoh has been given to anyone in marriage'," he quoted.

"That statement refers to unclean foreigners, not to princes of Kemet," she said impatiently and yet, as he had undoubtedly known it would, the thought gave her pause. She had accepted the fact that she could not oblige Neferure to do anything if it made her unhappy, but she had not realized how hard it would be to merely observe as her daughter did nothing for herself except live as she had for years—perfunctorily performing her duties as God's Wife and challenging male courtiers to the archery matches that truly aroused her passions. Now that Satioh was officially queen, Neferure did not even need to leave Waset to preside at festivals as much as she once had. Tusi continued to share her table at banquets and to ignore offers of marriage. The issue might have been resolved by Menkheperre himself if he had not behaved with utter indifference toward his half sister. Yet he could hardly be blamed for not asking a woman who did not even like him to become his wife. Isis had probably not helped matters much by continuing to insist he wed the Crown Princess. The young falcon was stubborn and Hatshepsut suspected the more his mother told him to do something the less chance there was it would ever happen.

She found herself thinking, more than once, that if she were Neferure she would have been very pleased to have a priest of Amun like Senenu washing her hands and feet with water taken from the sacred lake, and then assisting her in other ways as she performed her duties in *Ipet Sut.* But naturally, her daughter would not be attracted to someone who looked serious even when he smiled. Tusi laughed a great deal and perhaps that was what Neferure loved the most about the Overseer of the Cultivators of Amun, his sense of humor. If Tusi had not behaved quite so nobly, the woman who adored him might not have been so unhappy. More than once Hatshepsut considered asking Ibenre to tell Neferure about the special brew which permitted a woman to serve Hathor freely and without fear, but for some reason she had not translated that thought into action.

The gardens of Amun provided a beautiful distraction from the responsibilities of the Seal Room and troublesome thoughts of the princess. She was intensely disappointed when a handful of the exotic trees and plants brought back from Punt did not survive despite how lovingly they were tended. Even though it was not one of his responsibilities, Senenu often helped the gardeners. He lived alone in one of the small houses inside the enclosure wall, a great honor for a young man born to poor farmers. His presence in the House of Amun reassured Maatkare that the Eyes of Horus—opened all throughout the Two Lands by true priests—were seeing clearly and far and spotting radiant Ka's no matter where they lived or how dirt-encrusted they happened to be. The tenderness with which Senenu cared for a dying tree from the Land of God, and nursed it back to health after all the other temple servants had abandoned it, inspired Pharaoh to address him directly. She had seen him whispering loving encouragements to the leafless branches as if the warmth and moisture of his breath would help them sprout again.

"Thank you, Senenu," she said, "for restoring one of Amun-Re's offerings to its full beauty. I truly believe everything we see is a part of the Hidden One's heart. Therefore, in a very real sense, it is God Himself you nursed back to health."

He sank to his knees with the thoughtful grace that distinguished him and crawled slowly toward her. Very lightly, so she scarcely felt the touch of his lips, he kissed both her big toes one after the other. Seshen had recently painted all her nails red and suddenly the vivid color felt hot against her body as if Sekhmet had entered the garden. Senenu's splendid physique crouching submissively at her feet made her think of her pet cheetahs. His young body was similarly taught with muscles, no doubt developed during the years he had spent helping his father in the fields.

As she remained silent, enjoying the act of gazing down at him, he dared to glance up at her. Instinctively, she took a step back. His black eyes shining with thoughts felt dangerously deep.

Hatshepsut found herself thinking about those moments in Amun-Re's garden more than they warranted. Men and women both kissed her feet every day, it was a matter of routine, but for some reason she had especially noticed the way Senenu performed the gesture—with a slow and sensual reverence that captured her special attention and continued mysteriously holding it. She often experienced distaste when a mouth whose owner she did not particularly care for left a moist imprint on her skin. In those instances, it was a relief to come home and immediately have one of her attendant's wash and oil her feet. She felt very different remembering the sensation of Senenu's lips barely brushing her skin, which had the effect of leaving her wanting more from him. At the time, his obeisance had seemed full of a flattering depth of emotion, but she began to wonder if he had actually insulted her by how briefly he had kept his mouth in contact with her body. Maybe the reason he had kissed her toes instead of the tops of her feet was because he had not wanted to come any closer to her than necessary.

She banished the disturbing thought as foolish and irrelevant; she did not care at all what minor priests or anyone else thought of her. But Senenu was not just any young man, he was Hapuseneb's prize student, which was the reason she had noticed him to begin with. It was natural for someone with a strong Ka to have an affect on her flesh when he touched it. There was no question the young priest possessed Attractive Power. It was a sobering to know that when Senenu was an old man she would have been resting from life for a long time. The position of First Prophet of Amun in her Million Years Mansion was one she would have offered to Hapuseneb, had he not been older than she was. There could have been no one better than the man she loved serving as her *hemu-ka*. Perhaps she had become so aware of Senenu because he was destined to hold that office, and to be the first priest to serve in *Djser-Djseru*, where her Ka would forever be lovingly nourished.

* * * * *

Thutmose and Satioh sailed south for the festival of *Apet-Aset*. Maatkare's great north-south facing pylon, creating a new entrance into *Ipet Sut*, had been completed along with her six bark shrines. Pharaoh and Amun-Re's priests could now stop along the processional route to reconnect with their Divine source, invigorating their Ka's by inhaling the sweet breath of the *neters*, then refreshing their bodies by drinking, and offering back to God, the Primordial Waters magically flowing through them all. Outside every shrine stood two figures of Osiris, the crook and flail crossed against his chest, inscribed with a *shenu* ring protecting her name *Maatkare*. Menkheperre greeted the bark of the god on its first stop, *Amun in Front of the Stairs*, and escorted it into the cool shadows of the building, while the Female Falcon offered Maat to the images of eternal Divine kingship she embodied. Each sacred station had been named according to its place on the processional route symbolizing the journey from the dark heart of Atum into the magical womb of the Goddess—the *Station of Amun in Front of the Steps of His House*, the *Station of Maatkare Who is Strong of Monuments in the House of Amun*, the *Station of Maatkare Who is United with the Beauties of Amun*, the *Station of Maatkare Who Cools the Oar of Amun*, the *Station of Maatkare who Receives the Beauties of Amun*, and the *Station of Maatkare Amun Holy of Steps*.

The magnificent north-south entrance into *Ipet Sut*, the new House of Amun-Kamutef erected just outside Mut's complex, and the six bark shrines providing ritual stops along the route to God's Favored Place, were not the only changes Maatkare had made to the sacred celebration of *Apet-Aset*. From that year forward, Amun-Re and his entourage would sail back to His temple instead of being carried on the shoulders of priests the way He had come. The River represented the birth waters upon which every child glides between the two shores of a woman's thighs. It was appropriate for Amun-Re, when he emerged from the Palace of Maat, to flow back home to his celestial abode accompanied by his bodily son. The two kings, male and female, embarked on the beautiful ship 'worked in gold of the best of the desert'.[82] *Userhat-Amun* rowed downstream with Maatkare standing at the prow and Menkheperre at the stern. Both kings wore the *khepresh* headdress made of leather dyed a deep blue and decorated with tiny golden solar discs—the crown representing absolute power and the infinite heart of Atum beating sun-filled universes into existence without ever being confined by any of them. When Pharaoh wore the *khepresh* crown into battle, he became Atum, impervious to all obstacles.

The doors of God's golden house were closed and protected on all sides by four rows of alternating gold *tiet* knots and *djed* pillars. The *tiets* were arranged in three groups of two, and the *djeds* into two groups of two each, totalling ten symbols on each row. The shrine stood on its own small bark, *Wetjes Neferu*, and rested on the splendid ship—given life and health by the guiding Eye of Horus painted on its prow—which was towed by another boat. Two tall papyrus poles—one crowned by the Horus falcon on his pedestal and the other by a golden *shenu* ring formed by the bodies of two serpents protecting the name *Maatkare*—stood beside her. Both standards were also topped by the god's double plumes. Menkheperre held an oar with which he kept the great boat on a straight course.

That night, at the first of ten scheduled banquets, Hatshepsut studied Satioh where she sat at a table with her husband. The girl had always been pleasant but she remained unremarkable. She suspected Thutmose cared for her more as a friend than as a woman. She considered it a blessing that Satioh had not yet become pregnant for she still stubbornly continued to hope Neferure would suddenly wake up one morning and decide she wanted to marry her half-brother after all. It was not lost on her that she was much more realistic in the Seal Room, where she was confident of her judgments and behaved more forcefully than she did with her daughter.

She no longer completely trusted Senmut's opinion where the princess was concerned for he was much too fond of her. In many respects, he behaved like a doting father. It was conceivable he had spoiled Neferure in ways she wanted to believe she could not have foreseen or prevented. The Great Steward of Amun was away from Waset and it was Useramun sharing the king's table. Kemet's vizier was a few years older than she was, but as often happened with handsome men it did not show in a negative sense. The lines around his mouth and eyes seemed the evidence of loving caresses left by the goddesses of the hours, who only grew fonder of him as the years passed and devoted themselves to distinguishing his person with their sensual magic. She inquired as to the health of his sister's son, Rekhmire, and then they discussed the progress he was making on the River shrine she had awarded him. Despite the singing and laughter rippling around the dais, they ended up discussing business for most of the evening.

On the second night of feasting, she chose the more heart-warming companionship of Puyemre. At once, he commented on the ardent glances Thutmose was casting Meritre-Hatshepsut, who modestly kept her own lovely eyes downcast.

"When a girl looks so innocent it only stokes a man's ardor and she knows it," he remarked indulgently. "She is acting like a tame little gazelle pretending not to notice the lion which has spotted her, and fully intends to bring her down beneath him. It is only a matter of time."

She smiled briefly and then sighed, "Oh Puyemre, what am I going to do about Neferure?"

At that moment, a serving girl tripped and fell over something, most likely a young man's mischievously extended leg. The *nefer*-shaped vase she was carrying cracked on impact with the floor and red wine flowed in all directions.

Hatshepsut suffered a stab of dread. She looked at Puyemre, silently begging him to pull the knife of superstition out of her heart and rescue her, but instead he made her feel even worse by looking equally disturbed. Her question concerning Neferure had happened simultaneously with the accident, a fact a priest was certain to notice and a mother would be foolish to ignore. Yet in truth there was nothing she could do to protect her daughter if that was indeed Seshat's ink shimmering in the lamplight with a menacingly dark magic. Servants were already beginning to wipe the mess up but it was too late. Maatkare heard Sekhmet speaking to her with a silent yet terrifyingly clear voice: *If Neferure's life does not flow as I intended it too, I will shatter the vessel of her Ba and return her to her Ka, where her present journey will end and a new one begin, without you.*

* * * * *

Hatshepsut caressed Senmut's chest where they lay together on one of her beds and buried her face in the delicious harbor formed by his neck and shoulder. With her eyes closed, surrounded by the warmth and tenderness indistinguishable from his strength, she felt content. Yet whenever she fell asleep in his arms, she always woke abruptly feeling hot and restless. At that point, the same thing inevitably happened—she disengaged herself from him and got up. Years ago, she had used the excuse of needing to empty her bladder. After she became Pharaoh, it was no longer necessary to explain her actions and he did not ask her to. She sensed he had grown accustomed to the manner in which she detached herself from him after they worshiped Hathor together. She did not always dismiss him, in fact she usually sent for wine and whatever savory pastries Dhout had been inspired to order baked that day. The deeper intimacy she craved after sex could only be fulfilled by conversation, and

Senmut certainly did not seem to have a problem with that. Still, she was increasingly plagued by a mild but persistent feeling of guilt. She knew she was not giving him everything he really wanted, even though he was richer in titles than any other man in Kemet and many of the privileges of royalty had also been granted him.

One afternoon they were standing naked before each other when he voiced his desire to carve images of himself in *Djser-Djeseru*. Gently, he extended both her arms toward him and said, "I will put the panels in secret hidden places like these…" He kissed the inner crease of her elbows one after the other. "And like these…" He brushed the space between her breasts with his lips, and then turning her around caressed her hair out of the way so he could kiss the nape of her neck.

"I will be everywhere in the body of your Mansion of Millions of Years," he whispered, "and in every monument you erect for the Hidden One, forever giving praise to Amun-Re for creating beauty so great in the form of Hatshepsut-Maatkare." He made her face him again and passionately claimed her mouth with his.

A few days later, after thinking about what Senmut desired and growing increasingly excited, she granted his request to penetrate *Djser-Djeseru*, the Purest of the Pure, with images and inscriptions of his own devising. There was magic in repetition. God's power knew no limits and by producing dozens, seemingly endless numbers of panels inscribed with the words of his choosing, Senmut was openly claiming and expressing his Divine creativity exactly like a king. It did not matter to her there were still those who were shocked and angered by the immense privileges she granted a former commoner. People who were slaves to the superficial supremacy of social status enjoyed only by the body were to be pitied. They failed to grasp the transcendent power of love, which was experienced directly by the Ka and in the end was the only true measure of an individual's worth—the intelligence of his heart.

While Senmut was occupied in designing—and then in overseeing the production of the stone panels through which his Ka would forever rain kisses down upon the body of her temple—Hatshepsut desired him almost as much as she had when they were both younger. It seemed the older she got the less her sexuality had to do with her flesh and the more she responded to the stimulating caress of thoughts, words and actions which in themselves might not appear erotic. Growing old was a curse and yet becoming more mature was a blessing as she saw things more and more clearly, until it almost hurt how intensely she appreciated everything and everyone. The feeling of arousal, once primarily concentrated between her thighs, was spreading up to her heart and mysteriously deepening her sense of wonder. The majestic statues of the female pharaoh being produced for *Djser-Djeseru* filled her with reverence for Ptah and the men through which he worked. A block of crystalline limestone—that when highly polished would shine like embodied light—was gradually assuming the shape of her figure and face. The statue would show her as she had appeared at the pinnacle of her beauty, and as she always would be when she was transformed into a radiant Akh reunited with her Ka.

Carved with nine different kinds of inscriptions and all of them stating they had been made on behalf of the life, prosperity and health of the King of Upper and Lower Kemet, Maatkare living forever, Senmut's panels crowded a royal workshop. Two of the sanctuaries where they would be placed in *Djser-Djser*— the chapels dedicated to Hathor and Anubis—were not yet ready to receive them. However, the upper terrace was finished and Senmut was beginning to take his place there inside the granite gateways, behind all the doorways opening onto sacred chambers, and in the eight intimately deep niches penetrating the western wall. Only two of his monuments would be openly displayed on the reveals of the doorway leading into the Hall of Offerings. Whereas in most of the secret panels Senmut was shown kneeling with his arms raised in praise, in the public versions he appeared standing above five columns of hieroglyphs as he faced north into the hall, his arms raised in the gesture of adoration:

Giving Praise to Amun and smelling the ground to the Lord of the Gods on behalf of the life, prosperity, and health of the King of Upper and Lower Kemet, Maatkare, May he live forever! by the Hereditary Prince and Count, the Treasurer of the King of Lower Kemet, the Sole Companion, the Steward of Amun, Senmut, in accordance with a favour of the King's bounty which was extended to this servant in letting his name be established on every wall, in the following of the King, in Djser-djeseru and likewise in the temples of the gods of Upper and Lower Kemet. Thus spoke the king.[83]

By so sensually requesting the privilege to exist forever alongside her in her Mansion of Millions of Years, Senmut insinuated himself even more deeply into Hatshepsut's heart. Or perhaps it was the accumulation of all the beautiful things he had said to her throughout the years, combined with the relentless devotion of his actions, that finally broke the dam of her resistance and permitted the flood waters of her love to flow more freely and generously. Now whenever he left Waset on business she missed him more than ever before, but instead of resisting the emotion she surrendered to it joyfully.

Amenhotep, who always found time to add meaningful little details to her daily pleasures, instructed the royal chefs to bake sweet cakes stamped with images of Tawaret to celebrate the season of Immersion. Everywhere in Kemet, seeds were being sown in the womb of the Goddess. In the festival calendar, Isis was returning from Byblos with the body of her husband Osiris wrapped in the trunk of a Tamarisk tree. Wood, and its life-giving sap, was an apt symbol for the flesh and the Divine force flowing through it which never dries up no matter how many times it seems to die through the forms it inhabits.

Hatshepsut was pleased when Senmut returned to Waset on the nineteenth day of Pachons in time to share Amenhotep's Tawaret cakes with her. After the rites celebrated in the chapels of Isis and Osiris, they were joined in her Pleasure House by Neferure and Meritre. The latter was wearing a girdle made of white calcite beads interspersed with seventeen groups of four carnelian beads each. Red and white was a popular color combination with young women who had not yet been opened by a man. Hatshepsut more than suspected this would not be the case much longer with Meritre for Thutmose was obviously infatuated with her. He would most likely make her his wife soon and not only because Satioh still had not conceived an heir. The small gathering was informal otherwise Meritre would undoubtedly have delighted in wearing one of the many other girdles, bracelets, necklaces and anklets—all made of gold and precious stones—given to her as gifts by the king. Judging from how many times she had appeared in public with them, Meritre was particularly fond of her cowrie shell girdle, forged of gold and lapis-lazuli, and of her necklace hung with golden *nefer* amulets.

Neferure was wearing her favorite leopard-head blue-and-gold necklace, and the contented smile on her face—combined with the long silences during which she seemed completely unaware of the conversation—led her mother to suspect something had changed. Hatshepsut was hopeful rather than worried because she had finally asked Ibenre to speak to her daughter about the sexually liberating substance he prepared for the king every week. Dreamily returning her gaze to the pavilion, the princess caught her mother staring at her and smiled.

Hatshepsut glanced at Senmut and understood he had already noticed the subtle yet profound change in Neferure's demeanor and that he had reached the same conclusion. She relaxed, confident he would speak with Tusi immediately and make sure the young man—who had proved he could behave quite foolishly— did not regret what he had done and make matters even worse than before.

The hours passed lazily, the conversation no more profound than the sound of frogs diving into the ponds. Then Neferure asked Senmut to recite passages from *The Tale of Sinuhe*, knowing it was his favorite story as well as hers, so much so he had included it in his tomb. Hatshepsut listened with one ear while musing about everything and nothing. Her daughter at last looked truly happy and it made her own heart swell with contentment. She recalled the first time she had heard her baby's voice—a surprisingly strong cry of protest—followed soon after by the inexpressible joy of smiling into each other's eyes for the first time. It was hard to understand why she had believed Nefi could eventually be happy without Tusi when she herself still found it impossible to imagine living without the two men she loved. She prided herself on the objective veracity of all her memories and yet she had chosen to forget, where Neferure was concerned, what it was like to be young and in love with someone she could not have. But in truth, it was possible for God's Wife to do all she desired for Kemet without marrying her brother.

Smiling at her daughter, she returned her full attention to the story just as Senmut was saying:

"And may the king of Kemet be at peace with me
        that I may live within the heartland of his mercy,
And greet my Lady who is in his palace,
        and hear tidings of her children.
Then would my very self grow young again!
        For now old age is come,
And misery, alone it drives me on;
        my eyelids fall, my arms are heavy,
                feet fail to follow the exhausted heart.
Oh God, be near me for the final journey
        that they may guide me to the City of Forever
                to follow faithfully the Mistress of Us All.
Then would she tell me it is well with all her children,
        that she will while away eternity with me.'[84]

38

Great of Magic

Many of Maatkare's pets and exotic animals were interred in a small section of the western desert. Her beloved Satis was mummified and buried there. The cheetah's offspring, two girls and a boy, continued to give her much joy. The giraffes brought back from Punt did not live long as if, like people, they missed their homes and families so much they chose not to go on living without them. Senmut believed it had more to do with what the fantastic creatures had been accustomed to eating. Neferure thought both explanations seemed reasonable. The king's prized horse, Nomti, had been accorded the honor of his own grave in the highly prestigious Necropolis where many noblemen had excavated their eternal homes. When the Kushites inevitably rebelled again, Pharaoh sent her generals and soldiers south but did not accompany them. Kemet's forces were larger and stronger than ever, her fortresses well-equipped. The King's Son Amenemnekhu, and his Deputy, the True Royal Confident Amenemhat, could handle the uprising without her. Maatkare had already proved her courage and her prowess with the bow and arrow. It did not matter that her glorious victory had happened years ago for it would live forever, eternally present in the body of her monuments and in the hearts of all who beheld them.

In private Hatshesput admitted to her daughter, "When I was fighting the Kushites it was as if I left the earth even as I saw and felt through my senses more vividly than ever. What I felt was akin to the ecstasy I experience at the climax of festivals where the magical incense is burned—a sense of union with all Creation during which I seem to become the joyously invulnerable center of everything. Do you know what I mean, Nefi?"

The God's Wife concentrated on petting the dog sitting beside her chair. "Not really," she admitted finally.

Nepthys emitted a high-pitched yelp when her mistress scratched the back of one of her ears too vigorously.

"You have never felt that, Nefi?"

"I have felt quite wonderful," she replied more brightly, kissing the canine's mouth to apologize for her roughness. She was rewarded with a passionate lick that made her laugh. "Perhaps I simply do not think of that feeling the way you do, mother. But if you truly feel so, why did you not lead the army into battle again?"

Hatshepsut regretted bringing up the subject with a healthy young woman who worshipped Hathor with her lover as often as possible. Neferure could not possibly understand yet, the Goddess be blessed, what it was like to see moonlight sinisterly threading itself through her dark hair. The profound confidence with which she had once faced screaming Kushite chiefs was stronger than ever but her physical body was growing ever weaker. It was only because her Ba consciously heeded the advice and the warnings of her Ka that she was still so remarkably healthy. She was increasingly aware of the connection between all her bodies. On the glorious morning she had led Kemet's army into battle, the energy of her Ka had flowed effortlessly into its corporeal container through the invisible ostrich feather spout of Maat, in whose name she fought. But now the *nemset* vessel of her flesh showed signs of wear in the fine lines spreading like sinister cracks around her eyes and mouth, making her more vulnerable to enemy arrows. And so she stayed home in Waset while her troop commanders handled the sad nuisance of half formed men who kept fighting the rule of Re which was as foolish as preferring sickness over health.

"Dogs are as magical as cats, you know." Neferure changed the subject. "Dogs can smell sickness. One of my attendants was suffering from an infection of the bladder and little Nepthys here-"

The dog barked at the sound of her name.

"Nepthys could smell there was something wrong with the woman. She kept circling her and whimpering and looking up at me if she expected me to do something about it."

"That is fascinating, Nefi. Have you mentioned this to Ibenre? He would surely be interested."

"I did, and naturally he was not surprised. He seems to know everything already."

"There are a handful of men in the Two Lands whose Ka's are older than the pyramids and who know things the rest of us have forgotten, to our detriment."

"But surely they tell *you* everything mother. You are the king."

"To be told something is not the same thing as knowing it. In many respects I still feel like a puppy suckling at the breast of the High Priest."

Neferure giggled. "Tusi was quite surprised when he discovered I liked licking his nipples as much as he relishes feasting on mine."

Hatshepsut smiled and surrendered to her daughter's merry mood, which prevented any overly serious conversations from entering the room. Nevertheless, she said, "The Puntites keep these dogs to warn them when dangerous animals approach the village. If it is true dogs can also smell disease, it would seem Amun-Re designed the creatures to be our special protectors. All sickness is caused by an imbalance in *whedew* resulting either from a mysterious blockage or too much of one particular substance. Perhaps it is that unnatural excess dogs can smell."

"I have never quite understood what *whedew* is," Neferure admitted. She had left the comfort of her chair to crouch beside Nepthys, who was lying blissfully on her back getting her belly scratched.

"*Whedew* is the energy flowing into our body from our Ka that animates and sustains it."

The princess said absently, "Then all illness results from a lack of communication?"

Hatshepsut laughed. "That is a very succinct way of putting it, Nefi. Yes, it could truly be said illness results from a lack of communication. I believe if we were fully in touch with the Divine power of our Ka that our Ba would no longer be obliged to fly back up to the sky from its physical nest because heaven and earth would no longer be separate. We would be transformed into radiant *akhs* right here on earth."

"You mean Geb would at long last catch hold of Nut—as he is always shown striving to do with his erect manhood—pull her down around him and crush everything between them?" She smiled mischievously up at her mother. "Perhaps each of us is merely a drop of Divine sweat created by the friction of Min and Hathor spending a merry eternity together."

"Oh Nefi!" Hatshepsut laughed again. "There is such great wisdom in your humor. You truly are God's Wife."

"Senmut says all dogs were wild once." She changed the subject again. "He says it is people who have made them so tame and nice to us."

"I am not surprised since this reflects a process which occurs in all of us as we tame the chaos of our emotions with disciplined thoughts, and thereby make our feelings serve instead of hurt us. We cannot allow the fears that hunt us every day, following the scent of our physical decay, to devour the intelligence of our heart—the only thing capable of taming our dread and conquering all limitations in death."

Neferure looked pensively up at her just as Nepthys, her limp paws up in the air, heaved a contented sigh. "When I go to my Ka, I will conquer the demons of the caverns by telling each one a joke. They will laugh so hard they will not notice as I pass. Imagine how surprised they will be when I regale them with amusing tales instead of reciting the same boring old spells."

"Oh Nefi! I believe you will succeed!"

* * * * *

For as long as she continued feeling strong and healthy, Hatshepsut found the process of aging strangely pleasant. Substance divorced from its Divine source was the enemy, a trap of endlessly repeating cycles that never went anywhere except back into themselves. To age gracefully it was necessary, as Neferure had pointed out, to communicate with her Ka at every moment of the day. She lived by the ancient saying "You must be like the scales."[85] She never forgot that the free flow of *whedew* through her body was directly linked to the health of her heart, which received Maat—the life-giving power of her faith in Amun-Re, the Hidden One become visible in her—and offered it back to God mysteriously enhanced by all her positive thoughts, words and actions.[86]

It was also essential she make use of material elements beneficial to her physical body. Pomegranate juice was not only delicious, it served as an astringent her attendants used to clean the skin of her face and neck everyday before gently applying a variety of moisturizing unguents. There was nothing to be done, however, about the fact that her monthly cycle was becoming irregular, no longer obeying the phases of the moon as it always used to. It was very inconvenient not knowing exactly when to expect her purification for it was unthinkable she should appear in public while she was bleeding. She was also discovering she could not eat and drink quite so much without suffering from a mild but still annoying discomfort afterward. If, for some reason, she missed her daily swim she grew tired more easily and was ill-tempered in the Seal Room. More than ever, she loved the luxury of being Pharaoh so that when she traveled she was not obliged to sacrifice any comforts or pleasures.

Wherever Maatkare went, everything and almost everyone she loved accompanied her. No matter where she docked, a freshly cleaned pool awaited her. An entire transport barge was loaded with dozens of unguent jars and *nefer*-shaped vases containing, amidst other substances, a pain-relieving liquid made from water lilies. Tall-necked vessels filled with the magical extract of poppies were especially precious. She offered the intoxicating juice as a gift to favored officials but herself indulged in it only on rare occasions, usually with Hapuseneb. The drug made her feel so wonderful she did not feel the need to talk. Lying on a couch beside the High Priest as they both gazed out at the stars, his occasional lamp-lit smile and caress felt like the sun rising and the horizon embracing her. The rhythmic beat of his heart against her cheek was infinitely more eloquent than speech. His pulse transformed the darkness behind her closed eyelids into the very heart of the cosmos. Her arms became those of the Goddess slipping around Atum as the power of his desire entered and filled her.

If Hapuseneb and Ibenre had not both warned her against it, she would have been tempted to indulge in poppy juice more often. Senmut never touched it. He said it had no effect on him. She found this hard to believe for at the very least it could serve to alleviate severe pain. An extract of water lilies was good for more minor discomforts, such as soothing her sore muscles if she swam too long, and for alleviating the sweet aches she suffered after spending a night with the High Priest in his private retreat on the River. From his sitting room, she had once been able to see every individual reed growing along the water but now they all blended into each other. Her vision was not as sharp as it used to be and sometimes, when she was alone, she feared the veil of twilight was slowly but inexorably beginning to fall over her eyes. She crushed the dread like a scorpion and evoked both Sekhmet and Tawaret to help protect her from the dangerous imbalance created inside her by negative thoughts. She whisked fears away like disease bearing flies threatening to blind her to her true unassailable nature.

Whenever she appeared in the gold and lapis-lazuli window of her palace, the crook and flail gripped against her chest, Maatkare reminded the multitudes that Amun-Re was King of the Gods because He lived and ruled in their hearts. She assured them that Amun listened to all their prayers. They had only to truly believe in it, she said, to experience God's love and compassion. She told them the food they ate, the beer they drank and the North Wind which cooled their faces were all blessings given as gifts to his children by the Hidden One so they could see Him and know He was with them at every moment and in every breath.

"Do not let Seth strangle you with dreads that in the end are only illusions of the flesh! The virile brother of Osiris can enrich our life as long as our heart commands him to assume the crouching position before Maat. The Beautiful daughter of Re lovingly accepts all your offerings and blesses them with pleasures that are perfectly reflected, only a hundred times more splendidly, in the Land Beyond the Sunset."

She remarked to Senmut one evening, "Have you ever noticed that even when there is no wind blowing there is almost always one leaf in the garden twirling around and around as though dancing to an invisible music?"

"Yes, I have, but it does not mean there is no breeze simply because *we* cannot feel it."

"By why does that one particular leaf feel the wind, as if it has been mysteriously singled out?"

"I cannot answer that, I only know there is a reason for everything even if we cannot yet perceive it."

"I agree with you, Senmut, there *is* a reason for everything. It also pleases me to hear you say *yet*, for it means you believe that in the future we will be better able to understand how Amun-Re works his magic. And yet I believe, as does the High Priest, that we have forgotten a great deal. When a tree's greatest branch is cut off others remain but much is still lost which must grow back again."

"Because of you, Maatkare, the Two Lands are in full and beautiful bloom."

"Thank you, Senmut, wisdom *is* once again flowering freely in the form of priests who truly believe in Maat and obey the intelligence of their heart. To the benefit of all those who live beneath them, Nomarchs and headmen, high officials and wealthy courtiers all at least behave as if they truly honor Re's daughter. And yet I am increasingly plagued by the feeling that knowledge and abilities we once possessed have failed to bloom even now during my reign, and that once Menkheperre takes my place on the Horus Throne there will be no opportunity for them to do so ever again."

"When a great tree dies many of its seeds remain. Though they must lie in darkness for a time one of them, at least, will take root and flower again."

At the time, she found Senmut's response to her concern soothing, until she realized he had essentially agreed with her about Thutmose, and Kemet's future, without actually saying so. The young falcon was sixteen-years-old and she could feel he was growing impatient to fly from her wrist. She took responsibility for the lack of affection between them for she had always deliberately kept her distance from him. There were still those who believed Maatkare did not wish to be reminded of Menkheperre's existence because she had stolen his birthright from him. Her Ears and Eyes were everywhere; she commanded as many loyal spies as there were flies in the markets. No one openly opposed her and all the truly great men in Kemet served the Female Falcon with unfeigned devotion. Her see-faces clearly told her that though her lips were a little thinner—which made her mouth appear smaller and her nose seem somewhat larger—she was still the beautiful embodiment of Hathor.

Like the Goddess, Maatkare fed and cared for the *rekhyt* through her vizier, who journeyed up and down the River making sure no injustice was done to anyone. Her wisdom illuminated the darkness of abandoned temples and of hearts living in fear and despair. The Son of Re conquered her enemies by blinding them with Maat's beauty. As a result, foreign princes swelled Kemet's coffers with offerings. Gold and cattle, copper and turquoise, exotic fabrics and intricate jewelry, vessels forged into strange shapes and decorated with colorful designs, black and white ivory, animals both skinned and alive, rare oils and unguents, cakes of the sublime incense so pleasing to Amun-Re, impossibly thick and long tree trunks strapped onto the decks of ships which somehow managed not to sink beneath them, copper for temple doors, white-gold for divine statues—the wealth of the Two Lands knew no bounds in the embrace of The Clarified One, Maatkare. The tribute offered to the Hidden One every year steadily increased as Hapi blessed Kemet with Rivers that rose just far enough to bring abundance and avoid destruction. That the gods were pleased with her no one could doubt, not even those who continued secretly opposing her. Now and then an official—whose intelligence and heart were as small as his mouth and his belly were large—was stripped of his linen and wigs and sent into exile along The Paths of Horus. She doubted any of them would find a place with the Retenu like the legendary Sinuhe for they *had* done wrong and earned Pharaoh's wrath by talking disrespectfully about her.

Proud of all she had accomplished, Maatkare inscribed a list of her achievements in a place dear to her heart—the Temple of Pakhet, She Who Scratches, the lioness who continued giving her the strength she needed to defeat her enemies and to rip through fear and corruption with the Divine claws of faith and courage. Above the unfinished Hathor-heads of the columns were carved words of her own devising:

The favored places of all the gods had their fires lit and their chapels broadened, each deity possessed the sanctuary it desired, its life-force was content with its throne and its statue fashioned of white-gold. The festivals of the gods are stable in their totality in adherence to the system of my making, the rites of their arrangement having been made firm as Re created them.

My Divine mind is looking out for posterity, my king's heart has thought of eternal continuity because of the utterance of Him who parts the ished-tree, Amun. I have magnified the Order He has desired, for it is known to me that He lives in my bread and it is His dew I drink. I was in one body with Him, and He has brought me up to make the awe of Him powerful throughout the land. I am one with Atum-Khepri, who made what is, who made me knowledgable as one whom Re has fated and established for Himself.

The shores are united under my supervision and foreign lands bow down, for the cobra on my brow pacifies them all. Punt has swollen forth for me on all its fields, its trees bearing fresh myrrh. The roads that were blocked in both lanes are now trodden. Since great Thoth, who came from the Sun, has been revealing things to me, I have consecrated to him an altar of silver and gold and chests of cloth, every vessel set in its proper place. My incarnation's vision gives clarity of vision to those who shoulder the god. I have constructed his great Temple of white stone, its gateways of alabaster, the doorleaves of bronze, the reliefs on them in white-gold, holy with the image of him of high plumes. I have magnified the incarnation of this god with a double festival which I set for him anew. I have multiplied the god's offerings for him, for Khnum in his forms and for Heqet, Renenutet and Meshkenet, who united to build my body; for Nekhbet, She of Whom it is Said that the Sky and Earth are Hers.

So listen, all you elite and multitude of commoners—I have done this by the plan of my mind. I do not sleep forgetting but have made form from what was ruined. I have raised up what was dismembered from the time when the Setiu were in Perunnefer with vagrants in their midst destroying what had been. They ruled without Re, and did not act by God's decree down to my own royal incarnation. Now I am set on Re's throne, having been foretold from ages of years as one born to take possession. I am come as Horus, the sole cobra spitting fire at my enemies. I have banished the gods' abomination and removed their footprint from the earth.

This is the system of the Father of my fathers, the Sun who now comes. Damage will not happen again, for Amun has decreed that my decree remain like the mountains. My Father, Amun, made my boundary at the limits of heaven. All that the sun encompasses works for me. When the sun-disk shines it will spread rays over the titulary of my incarnation, and my falcon will be high on the top of the serekh for the course of eternity.[87]

* * * * *

It did not matter how long she studied the plans Djehuty had drawn up of her Mansion of Millions of Years, Hatshepsut could not see it on papyrus as she did in her heart and mind. Staring at lines enclosing spaces dotted with little squares and circles that represented columns and pillars was intensely frustrating. And yet the flat featureless design was essential for merging the limited physical space available with the boundless realm of her imagination, and for helping her communicate where she wanted to put everything. On the burnished scrolls the chapel of Amun, dug straight into the mountain, resembled a *djed* pillar and made her think of a disproportionately small head set on top of a vast square body. The sanctuary cradling her Ka and the Ka of her father, Akheperkare, was located south-east of Amun-Re's shrine, its offering hall modeled on the ones built by great pharaohs of old alongside their soaring pyramids. The north-east end of the upper terrace was dominated by the sanctuary of Atum-Re.

It was necessary for her to visit the building site regularly to reassure herself of the monument's actual magnificence as it bloomed from the mountain and flowed down in rays of embodied light to the desert below. She was not satisfied with how slowly it was growing despite the fact that Senmut, Hapuseneb, Puyemre and everyone closely involved in its construction assured her the glorious work was being given absolute priority. Senmut showed her the lists of conscripted labor brought in to assist the more skilled stone masons and painters. The amount of debris that resulted from the process of creation was sobering. Hundreds of men were needed to carry off baskets of gravel and to haul arduously cut stones to their allotted destinations. The unimaginably heavy blocks were rolled across the ground on logs and drawn up temporary ramps of packed sand. Processions of freshly polished and painted statues were an impressive sight as they made their slow regal way from workshops to the River and from there to the building site in the western desert.

Whenever he visited Waset, Menkheperre seemed impressed. Maatkare had always given him a prominent place in all her monuments, where he appeared standing behind her. She sensed he was looking forward to that order being reversed as she grew older and officially began ceding more responsibilities to him. It was gratifying to note how her splendorous appearance and unrelenting good health both aroused his admiration and annoyed him; the emotional battle played itself out on his face more clearly than he seemed to realize. However, his conduct toward her was almost painfully respectful.

In private, Puyemre irreverently and succinctly described the young Pharaoh's expression whenever she was around, "He looks constipated."

That Menkheperre was able to understand her architects' plans was evident by the questions he asked. Neferure thought he was jealous but Hatshepsut did not quite trust her daughter's opinions where Thutmose was concerned. There could be no doubt he knew the Crown Princess had a lover and his disapproval was silently communicated by the set of his mouth whenever Neferure was present. Tusi considered it prudent to visit distant relatives in the Nome of the Hare whenever his beloved's half brother came to town.

It was a source of deep regret to Hatshepsut when Rasui, the Nomarch of the Oryx, went to his Ka. Both pharaohs honored him and his relatives by attending the funeral. Standing in the ancient cemetery where so many great men were buried, she suffered a profound sadness listening to the wind blow with a low and desolate voice. And as Rasui's son, the High Priest of Ptah, symbolically opened the mouth of his father's mummy, more forcibly than ever before she was gripped by the terrible conviction that she had forgotten vitally important things she *should* have been able to remember and made live again in the present. The impression was almost as tangible as the warm breeze wafting the gilded hem of her dress around her ankles. As though the adze of Anubis was working its magic on her as well, her senses were mysteriously heightened and she actually seemed to feel the seductive caress of a more spiritually virile past against her skin—a glorious time where wisdom, honor and joy achieved such beautiful heights in the Nome of the Oryx it seduced heaven down to earth for a precious time lost now forever to the lifeless sands. Inside the tomb the mummy's head, embraced by the wooden arms of its Master of Life, was positioned due south in the direction of the horizon where the shining star of Isis had risen again that morning—the luminous heart of the Goddess opening the door to the next world to receive the Hereditary Prince Rasui into her loving arms.

After the desert's unrelieved emptiness, the sight of black cows grazing in green fields soothed her vision. She looked into an empty sky the deep blue of Ptah's skull-cap, and then back down at the River sparkling an infinity of fallen stars and teeming with invisible life. It depressed her to feel her body was merely part of the substance engendered by Divine forces that, for as long as she lived on earth, she had the power to command only with her heart. Fat cows embodied the pleasures of the sensual world even as they also reflected the heaviness of her heart whenever she grew tired of swatting the flies of mortal fears with the spiritual tail of her wisdom. Life-giving milk, cheese, butter and beef, leather hides and lush cream—all the things offered to her children by Hathor were made simply of sunlight and grass that had been chewed in a cow's mouth and digested in its stomach. It was miraculous and incomprehensible, an obvious and constant reminder of the transformations which make physical life possible and death both inevitable and irrelevant.

She remained for a few weeks in Mennefer, something she later bitterly came to regret. She returned to the Town of Amun at night. On that occasion, she preferred the privacy of disembarking observed only by the silent multitude of stars overhead instead of by a loudly cheering crowd. The High Priest of Amun was there to greet her, and to escort her to the palace, where they parted formally before members of her household gathered to welcome her. A short time later she fell asleep not realizing, somehow not even sensing, that before the new day was come she would wake with only half a heart.

Shrieks emanating from unbearable grief yanked her out of a bad dream she was foolishly glad to leave because reality was to prove much worse. She had not heard such violent sounds of anguish since her brother died. She got out of bed just as the door opened and Senmut staggered across the threshold. She was vaguely aware of her body sinking to its knees as her heart deciphered his contorted expression before her mind could possibly even dare to try.

He strode toward her and grabbed her hands so fiercely she cried out. He pulled her up into his arms and clung to her.

His silence filled her with such dread she could not catch her breath to utter the question it already seemed to answer. Only the desperate hope she might be wrong gave her the courage to ask, "Nefi?"

Nafre appeared in the doorway, stepped unsteadily into the room and brought an invisible river with her—the force of the grief that struck Hatshepsut was as great as if she had been standing before a sluice gate when it was opened and the rising water rushed through it. She pushed Senmut away. "Tell me it is not Nefi!" she pleaded with him. "Tell me it is not Nefi!"

"She is…" His voice sounded as if it was buried at the bottom of a shaft filled with gravel and required all his strength to pull out. "She is dead!"

She was so shocked, so appalled by the immensity of her loss, she suddenly felt blessedly calm. "Dress me," she commanded Nafre, and in the same breath said almost lightly, as if it did not really matter, "How did she die?"

Senmut sank into a chair. "The Goddess found her way into the residence through a cobra whose home was probably flooded by the rising River." His head looked so heavy as it fell into his hands it seemed impossible he would ever be able to lift it again.

"Ibenre says she died instantly!" Nafre added desperately. "She felt no pain, my lady, he is sure of it. She was asleep when the snake bit her and you know how deeply Nefi sleeps!"

"Hathor has blessed her by opening the door to the other world for her in a dream," she agreed, raising her arms so her attendant could slip a dress on over her head. To adorn herself she chose the bracelets and anklets Neferure had most recently admired. It was not until her hair had been pinned up and a wig placed over her head that she collapsed as if from its weight but actually because her legs refused to continue supporting her. A pain infinitely worse than that of childbirth ripped through every part of her. Gasping for breath, she was mildly surprised to discover Senmut still had the strength to lift her up in his arms.

She thought, *Grief is a wild beast!* as it sank its teeth into her chest and swiped its claws across her head so she found it nearly impossible to breathe and think at the same time. *Grief is devouring my heart!* "Make it stop! Make it stop or there will nothing left! Nefi! My love! My heart! I love you, Nefi! I love you! Do not be afraid!"

She became conscious of struggling to free herself from Senmut's grasp when he abruptly set her down and slapped her. "She is gone!" He said angrily.

"She is in a better place, my lady!" Nafre insisted even though she too was weeping.

She ignored her attendant and addressed the man whose grief, by perfectly mirroring her own, offered her a mysterious comfort even though it should have made her feel even worse. "Neferure, King's Daughter, King's Sister, God's Wife, will be buried with *The Book of Coming Forth by Day and Opening the Tomb* but it is the amusing tales she will tell the demons of the caverns that will save her. She will not wander long in the company of Anubis for the love in my heart burns hot and bright enough to light up even the darkest reaches of the Dwat for her!"

* * * * *

According to the trails it left behind in the palace garden, the cobra that killed Princess Neferure was eight feet long. The events of that dreadful night did indeed seem choreographed by unseen forces. The God's Wife was sleeping with her windows open to the garden but the removable screens were in place. If they had all been completely secure she might have been safe, but a gap at the south-west corner of the window nearest the bed made it sinisterly apparent one of the screens had been loose enough to be pushed open. How the serpent gained entry into the palace grounds was impossible to say and yet there was no doubt it had found its way to the bed where Neferure lay. Hatshepsut wanted to believe her daughter had never even felt the deadly fangs that pierced her throat. Ibenre insisted the cobra had aimed its attack with supernatural accuracy. It was his firm opinion the princess had died instantly. No one who saw the blood-drenched sheets doubted the great serpent had been acting on behalf of the Goddess. Their awe-struck horror was communicated to everyone in the residence, and from there the conviction spread throughout all of Kemet that the princess had been personally escorted back to her Ka by Hathor-Sekhmet.

If it was true that Neferure had slept through the gruesome event then it could very well be said she was blessed. The venomous fangs sank directly into the most important path used by her heart in its tireless task of pumping blood through her body. According to Ibenre, the bite had killed her long before the poison could do its fatal work. Hatshepsut thought that if she could only be sure he was right she might be able to experience a measure of peace and, eventually perhaps, even a mysterious contentment knowing the gods had paid such close attention to her daughter and the manner of her death. She had no illusions she would ever truly be happy again. The world would never feel—and therefore would never be—the same without Nefi. The princess' dog Nepthys, who had slept on a mat outside her mistress' room, had been the first to alert her attendants to the fact that something was amiss. She barked hysterically, scratching at the closed door, and when someone at last opened it she ran whimpering into the room. Hatshepsut could hear in her mind—as vividly as if she had been there herself—the devoted animal's high-pitched yelp of pain and surprise when the cobra bit her as well. Neferure's attendants all swore they had risen from their beds the moment they heard Nepthys whining and barking, which argued favorably for Ibenre's opinion the princess had died between one breath and the next. Nepthys was slowly recovering in the king's own bedroom. For as long as she lived, Hatshepsut would keep the dog close to her knowing Nefi would have wanted her to. Fortunately, for Nepthys the cobra had already injected most of its venom into Neferure, who had been shoved into the Dwat without any warning as the door between the worlds suddenly swung open through the serpent's jaws.

Senmut also seemed to have gone to his Ka even while considerately leaving his body behind. They sat together for hours as she endlessly recalled her daughter's smiles and laughter and bitterly regretted the years she had dampened them with the stubborn desire she marry Thutmose. Foolishly, she had dared to hope that if Menkheperre proved to be as short-lived as his father that Neferure would take the crook and flail into her hands just as her mother had done before her. That would never happen now and when Maatkare flew to heaven, the Two Lands would once again fall exclusively into the hands of kings who were only men. The tradition she had initiated of assigning feminine royal titles even to Pharaohs whose bodies were male would not survive her. Thutmose would make sure of that. She kept remembering his expression when he saw a painting of his father's father, Akheperkare, commanding a space in the chapel of Anubis in *Djser-Djeseru* where *The Good Goddess* was included in the list of all his kingly titles. He had swallowed his thoughts but she had seen them in his eyes. The future she had conceived of and was daring to gestate in the body of her monuments—where male and female pharaohs ruled side by side as the two sexual halves of a single Divine Being—had most likely died with Neferure, the Beautiful Daughter of Re.

39

Spearing the Crocodile

Useramun and Ty did not seem surprised to see Maatkare waiting for them when they parted the gates of the royal house, preparatory to performing the ritual that opened the administrative palace in the morning and secured it in the evening. She waited impatiently as various overseers, pages and scribes lined up behind two of Kemet's most important men. She suspected they were all thinking the same thing. Instead of being crippled by grief and hopelessly distracted from her duties, more than ever Pharaoh was acting as Horus—the bodily son of Osiris, king of heaven—by ruling on earth with a hawk-like clarity of vision and a relentless grasp of issues. She distinctly sensed how much her officials respected and admired her. The organs of the body all had to function in harmony to maintain its life, health and strength, and so too the efficiency and effectiveness of the Seal Room depended on men with different skill sets whose hearts were all faithfully open to Maat. Intelligence of the heart could not be taught but it could definitely be sharpened by a proper education. The more scribes there were in Kemet the better.

As a result of how much more time she was spending in the Seal Room, Ahmose, First King's Son of Amun, was now taking Maatkare's place in the temple three times a day for the ritual prayers. He was even standing in for the king during important festivals held in the environs of *Ipet Sut*, something he had previously done only when she was away on a royal progress. Pharaoh had recently awarded Ahmose a full-length staff with a handle of white-gold for he was getting old and required its support.

Hatshepsut could see in Useramun's eyes (and deeply appreciated it) that he understood how much she needed to keep busy. The complex details of earthly life, and the unique personalities and abilities of the individuals who assisted her in dealing with them, had never seemed more interesting. Even though her beloved daughter was now traveling its dark roads, she thought less about the Dwat and all its perils, married to magical possibilities, than ever before. It was as if she was truly seeing the world through Neferure's eyes for the first time. The sudden and absolute absence of God's Wife had the effect of blessing Hatshepsut with the gift of how her daughter had experienced life—as a joy in itself no matter what happened after you died.

She spent whole days in the Seal Room savoring the work more than the wine and food she enjoyed after her daily swim, during which the obstacles she had encountered and overcome, and all she had managed to accomplish, mysteriously invigorated her muscles and made her feel younger. The water offered her body both support and resistance, very much like her officials— their intelligence and their often profound wisdom was the element in which she swam, exercising her own strength and joyful determination so there was almost nothing she did not feel able to accomplish. The distant borders of the Two Lands and all they encompassed felt as manageable as the two ends of her pool.

Menkheperre would be seventeen-years-old soon. Fortunately, all those he chose to appoint to positions of power in the northern Seal Room—whenever death or old age made them available—were invariably officials she approved of for she had always been careful to surround the young falcon with good men. Her heralds traveled from the Town of Amun to the Mansion of the Ka of Ptah, and from there to the City of the Sun and beyond, as her Eyes, Ears and Mouth, seeing, hearing and speaking for her. Maatkare's heralds were as numerous as duckling and she used each one according to his special talents. Antef, for example, was kept busy at home in Waset performing the march of the *ruyt*. His ability to make people feel relaxed, even when they were kept waiting for hours, was invaluable. Antef constantly won subtle battles, positively affecting the atmosphere of the palace by conquering desperate impatience and establishing in its place the rule of hopeful reverence. Only a master of human emotions, with a keen eye for the workings of the heart, could excel in the onerous task of not ruffling any noble feathers in the close quarters where people waited to be admitted into the presence of the Female Falcon to make their petitions. Antef successfully encouraged all those 'who were disaffected to make rule, law, and precision out of the hatred of his heart.'[88]

Only the most important disputes reached the king. All witnesses swore the oath "As Amun endures, and as the Ruler endures, we speak in truth"[89] but there was no doubt many of them took liberties with it. Especially trying were cases involving a slave who had come to be embraced by a household as someone deserving the respect and rights of a free person. Quite often family members disagreed with each other on the matter, and when one of them passed away, those who remained contested the dying wishes of their relative. Numerous complaints were brought by women whose husbands had left a portion of their wealth and possessions to a slave, usually a female (although sometimes a male) he had grown to love. The slaves in question were sometimes Kushites captured in skirmishes and shipped north, but more often than not were ordinary citizens who, for one reason or another, were left bereft and obliged to sell themselves into lifelong service to others. It was a source of great satisfaction to Hatshepsut that at the beginning of her reign such cases had appeared before her much more often. When the affair was obviously one of genuine respect and affection felt for a slave, she ruled in their favor, granting them the right to be admitted into the presence of free and noble people and to own whatever property had been given or willed to them. It was depressingly easy to discern when pretty males and females had manipulated their owners into believing they cared for them, in which case she sided with the outraged family.

More boring to listen to were land disputes where the borders between two properties had been obscured by time, or by the rising River wiping away the landmarks used to determine them. Such cases reached her ears only when an extremely important man did not agree with a ruling and insisted on presenting the matter to the king, the true owner of all the land everywhere.

Three mornings after the burial of Princess Neferure—in a tomb very near the one her mother had excavated for herself as queen and consequently abandoned—Hatshepsut relished watching the hierarchy of the Seal Room in action when she announced her intention to erect two additional Monuments of Heh. She longed to stretch her arms further toward heaven so Neferure could look down and see how much her mother loved her and longed to embrace her again. She would place her massive stone Ka arms at the western entrance to the Temple of Amun-Re so they mirrored their eastern counterparts. The first pair marked the beginning of her reign while the second would celebrate its splendid effectiveness.

"And they will both be covered entirely in white-gold," she informed Useramun.

As though he could already see them, a reverent light entered his eyes and he inclined his head. "Majesty," was all he said. They knew each other well enough to understand what that meant.

Nehesj spoke in a matter-of-fact voice which indicated he was clarifying what she desired rather than questioning it, "Not merely the pyramidions but all four of their sides, from top to bottom, will be sheathed in white-gold?"

"Yes, my lord," she replied.

He asked no more questions and when the time came, she knew he would set his seal to the document authorizing the Overseer of the Gold and Silver Houses to withdraw the necessary materials. More immediately involved was the Overseer of the Workshops in charge of mustering the men most skilled in the task. He would work closely with the Overseer of the Storehouses, who was in charge of supplying the workers with bread and beer and everything else they needed. On this occasion, it would not be Senmut supervising their labor for she could no longer bear to be parted from him for such long stretches of time. She desired to honor her Royal Butler and Priest of Anukis, Amenhotep, with a sacred project worthy of his pious nature and personal devotion to her. Her high officials approved his appointment along with that of Djehuty, who she also wished to reward for the invaluable part he was playing in realizing the dream of her Million Years Mansion.

It was with the High Priest of Amun-Re, however, that she consulted in private about where exactly she intended to erect her two new Monuments of Heh.

"There is only one place for them," she said, "behind my father's. Yet they must create their own gateway into the Divine realm, they cannot simply mirror his, and this spiritual truth will be expressed in stone at the principal entrance to *Ipet Sut*. The pain of Neferure's death is making me feel as though my Ka is in labor, Hapuseneb. The shadowy hall ribbed with pillars that leads from the sunlit outer courtyard into God's house… it feels too small now, too dark. It was erected by my father but now it must be expanded so something new can be born and my own powers continue to grow. The ceiling covered with flying birds and stars must break open and reveal the actual sky so the Celestial River, like Divine birth waters, can on those special occasions when Nut laughs pour down from heaven between the luminous legs of my two monuments.

She concluded, "My heart directs for me to make for Amun-Re two monuments of white-gold, their pyramidions merged with the sky, in the august pillared hall between the great pylons of my father, King Akheperkare."[90]

He inquired softly, "And what names will you give them?"

"*Djet*, Eternal Sameness, and *Neheh*, Eternal Recurrence."

"The Divine power of love *is* always the same and yet its experience is eternally new in every heart through which it manifests."

"I knew you would understand, Hapuseneb. You always do."

"There are many who understand but there is only one other who loves you as I do." The corners of his mouth turned up in an oddly dark smile. "Almost."

"I fear Senmut's heart has suffered a wound from which it will never fully recover."

"To hear them speak was like listening to a single heart beat."

She understood he was referring to Senmut and Neferure and was shocked by the remark even though she realized it was absolutely true—on occasions too numerous to remember this fact had deeply annoyed her. "He loved my daughter like a father," was all she could think to say.

"There were many who loved her."

She suffered the impression he was changing the subject. However, there was no doubt God's Wife had left a huge current of desolation behind her in the form of servants and attendants, scribes, heralds and pages whose hearts all suddenly beat without purpose. Their bodies had walked forlornly through rooms emptied of her vital presence like fish swimming aimlessly back and forth in a pool where there is no food to sustain them. Maatkare had rescued them all by finding them positions in her own palace. Occasionally one of them would say something, or use a turn of phrase, that reminded her painfully of her daughter's way of speaking. Maiherperi, the son of a slain Kushite chief raised at court, had especially absorbed many of his mistress' mannerisms for, like Dhout, he fancied himself a woman in a man's body. Hatshepsut kept Maiherperi beside her as one of her fan bearers even though he sometimes sounded uncannily like her daughter. It touched her that he wore only the earrings the princess had given him. It was as though Nefi, mischievous as always, amused herself by possessing the effeminate fan bearer with her after-life body merely to disturb her mother, who was so confident she knew just how everything worked both on earth and in the next world.

As the months marched on—and that terrible bloody night was relegated to the past on the calendar even though it was forever present in her heart—Hatshepsut spent less time silently talking to her daughter and desperately hoping to dream with her when she went to sleep. At first, she had sensed Neferure's presence. After the funeral she had even heard her daughter's voice say with an almost audible joy, "Mami, you were right! You were right, Mami!" Whether or not she had imagined it she had felt almost happy for a few weeks, until the memory inevitably began fading. Each day fell like a drop of water deepening the darkness between them and drowning all words in unfathomable depths, where only the heart stubbornly dares to swim.

She was not surprised, nor did she care, when Tusi eventually married one of the young ladies determinedly courting him. His sense of humor seemed to have died with Nefi for he was rarely seen smiling or heard laughing anymore. The special and irreplaceable beauty of God's Wife would haunt him for the rest of his life.

The need for a sacred place where she could visit privately with Neferure—and hopefully re-experience the transcendent elation of those moments when she *knew* she heard her daughter's voice joyfully confirming her faith—was not satisfied by the rare and arduous trek out to her tomb with its desolate little offering chapel. The wind moaning through the desert canyons spoke only of loss and absence so that thirst seemed indistinguishable from a despair not so easily quenched. The God's Wife and the Beautiful Daughter of Re deserved to have a temple built in her name. The western desert was a sacred location, a holy place shimmering with the boundless energy contained in light that blinds the reason just as the solar disc burns the eyes. It was as foolish to look straight up at the sun as it was to try and completely grasp the Divine with thoughts. In *Djser-set*, Holy is the Place, all the forces commanded by Atum-Re had first emerged and were now buried in the body of the earth to which they gave birth on The First Occasion. *Djser-set* was both a mysterious womb and the tomb of the eight gods revered in Khemnu as the mothers and fathers of Re. The eight primordial deities—four male and four female—were the seeds buried in the black heart of the cosmos containing within them all the complimentary and opposing forces needed for Creation—Amun and Amaunet, Heh and Hauhet, Kek and Kauket, Nun and Naunet. All the beauties of Re were hidden in the darkness wherein flowed infinite waves of pure life perpetually becoming incarnate.

The multitude of commoners believed the eight primordial *neters* were actually buried in *Djser-set* but Hatshepsut knew what it all really meant. Neferure had undergone a similar transformation—by ceasing to exist physically, she had become everything. She felt her daughter's presence everywhere at every moment even though she seemed to be nowhere forever. She had felt the same way when her father went to his Ka, and she still did, but the sadness she suffered was deeper as she thought about how her beautiful child was snatched from life so suddenly and violently. The veil between the worlds was believed to be woven of serpents that both protected and destroyed, like Tawaret and Sobek—the agents of transformation so terrifying to the mind. Only the strength of love, wielding the heart's weapon of faith, could hope to defeat the reasonable fear they inspired.

It was to Senmut she voiced these thoughts. He listened in silence, his eyes resting on her face even while somehow looking beyond her.

"What are you staring at?" she demanded at last. "You appear to be seeing something else even though you are looking straight at me."

"I see darkness."

"Darkness cannot be *seen* only experienced," she pointed out desperately. "Nefi is with the gods, Senmut. She is not lost to us forever. You *must* believe that."

Surprise lightened his somber expression. "I *do* believe that. I could not continue living if I did not believe that. The darkness I see exists within me, not in the next world, where I am confident Neferure is much happier than I am. I fear my Ka is growing tired of this body and will soon discard it. I would not mind so much if it did not mean leaving you behind, Hatshepsut."

Rising, she sank to her knees before his chair and planted her hands on his thighs as if she could force him to remain sitting there for the rest of their lives. "Do not say that, Senmut," she begged. "You *must* stay with me!"

He cradled her face tenderly in his hands. "I will strive to obey you, Maatkare, even though my body has already begun betraying me with tightness in my chest that hints at a much greater discomfort to come."

"Have you seen Ibenre?"

"Yes. He supplied my steward with a list of the things I can eat, which is much shorter than the list of what I must no longer consume. He has also encouraged me, as you keep doing, to swim in my pool more often."

"I trust you are obeying him?"

He kissed her and effectively changed the subject.

It was to Puyemre that Maatkare delegated the glorious work of building a temple on the west bank dedicated to Neferure in her heart and officially to Amun-Re and Hathor—God and his Hand. The second Prophet of Amun knew exactly what she meant when she said, "The Void is the heart of God forever becoming everything." Construction began on the Mansion of Maatkare Kha-Akhet-Amun on the edge of the fertile land, where every year the rising

River would flow between its papyrus-shaped columns into the inner and outer sanctuaries, Kha and Akhet—potential and realization. Hapuseneb's former student, Senenu, was made High Priest of Amun in Kha-Akhet, until he assumed his duties as Maatkare's *hemu-Ka* in *Djser-Djseru*. Appointing him to the position helped Hatshepsut understand why Neferure had never liked the handsome young priest. She must have glimpsed her death in his eyes.

❋ ❋ ❋ ❋ ❋

Hatshepsut gave Senmut a small pouch—made from the hide of a black bull offered to Ptah—that she had personally filled with protective amulets carved from seven different materials. The pouch was attached to a leather cord so he could wear it around his neck. She asked him to never take it off.

He smiled. "You want me to bathe and sleep with it as well?"

"That is for you to decide."

"I will wear it until the day I die," he vowed, "except in bed to avoid the danger of it strangling me as I sleep and defeating its intended purpose of protecting me."

She would have laughed if she had not remembered again how Nefi had died in the eighth hour of the night. Her daughter had not known when she retired to her room that the gods had already decided her life had reached its perfect completion even though she was only twenty-two.

Senmut gently grasped her arms. "Your love gives me the will and the strength to go on living, Hatshepsut. You know that. But if it makes you feel better, I will gladly wear as many amulets around my neck as I can support without stooping like a decrepit old man. So do not look so sad. That makes me feel far worse than any physical discomfort."

"I was merely pondering the relentless reality of numbers, for we are all subject to the forces they measure and manifest in the form of all our joys and complaints."

"I would like you to visit my eternal home with me," he said abruptly. "The decorations of the first chamber have been completed but for me they will not truly be finished until you see them."

Three days later, a multitude of Waset's citizens watched the Great Steward of Amun cross the River in the company of the Female Falcon. The intensity of his devotion to Pharaoh was revealed by all the gold he wore that reflected the sun, and by the silver staff of office he gripped in his right hand which in the full light of Re shone like a moonbeam. Hatshepsut wondered how many of her more humble subjects knew the Keeper of the Seal of the King of Upper and Lower Kemet had once been a commoner. Outside the palace and temple precincts, she behaved as coldly toward him as a smiling statue. It was a relief to reach the intimate confines of his tomb, where only a handful of attendants accompanied them past the entrance.

Whenever she crossed the River, it elated her to witness the swift progress being made on her avenue of seated sandstone lions crowned with the head of Pharaoh. Two rows mirroring each other would extend all the way from the small but beautiful temple of her unique incarnation, erected just beyond the fertile land at the edge of the desert, to the gate leading into the sacred precinct of her Million Years Mansion. Her excitement was further heightened by the sight of *Djser-Djseru's* shining white limestone ramps. Its courtyards and porticos, cut as precisely as her thoughts, shone in the sun like an embodiment of the joy and awe that filled her heart whenever she beheld what she had conceived of and ordered made real.

The king's party stood for a long moment at the dark mouth of the passage which thrust deep into Geb's body. They were all gazing up at *Djser-Djseru,* visible beyond the wall of the quarry supplying the stones for the processional causeway. Senmut had excavated his tomb as close to the cradle of her Ka as he possibly could and yet, in those moments, it looked depressingly far away. The men working in the quarry had all been temporarily dismissed in preparation for Pharaoh's visit and the stillness immediately surrounding them was broken only by Seshen's persistent coughing. The distant sounds of construction were mysteriously reassuring. Very soon, Amun-Re would journey from *Ipet Sut,* his Divine cradle in the east, to *Djser-Djseru,* his magical home in the west.

"You should remain out here, Seshen," Hatshepsut said. "I do not think the air in the tomb will be good for you. Go and rest beneath the pavilion. When we return to the palace I will call for your physician. Your cough seems to be getting worse and I am concerned."

"Oh my lady, thank you, but I am fine, *really!*" Yet how rigid her smile looked made it obvious she was trying hard not to cough again.

Although they were steep and roughly cut, Senmut had furnished the corridor with steps which made it much easier to descend. The first passage of the solar bark—on which the Ba-bird of the deceased traveled with Re through the darkness—had begun to feel endless to Hatshepsut when the lamp her Superior Steward was holding suddenly revealed a surprisingly casual portrait of himself. His profile and shoulders were sketched in black ink on white stone and around his neck she distinguished the leather pouch she had given him.

"In reality," she whispered, "you are much more distinguished looking."

"I believe it is a faithful representation."

"How can you possibly know that? You have never seen your profile, Senmut. I am a much better judge of your appearance than you are."

"I am confident my Ba will recognize me."

They stepped into the first chamber but it was not until their attendants entered behind them carrying more lamps that she was able to see the decorations. The ceiling amazed her. At once, she recognized the hippopotamus Tawaret with a crocodile draped across her back—the agents of transformation. The five-pointed stars made it obvious she was looking up at the sky but not as she actually saw it with her eyes. A quick glance told her everyone in the room was staring up in wonder, except for Senmut, who was looking at her. Smiling at him, she returned her attention to the map of heaven he had created.

Five rows of hieroglyphs divided the sky into north and south. Twelve large circles, each one segmented into twenty-four sections, undoubtedly represented the twelve months of the year ruled by the moon. She recognized four of the five brightest points in the sky as they all gathered around Sopdet, the brilliant veil of Isis. Seven deities—crowned by solar discs and facing eight of their mirror images—added up to fifteen, which doubled symbolized the thirty days of the month. Personified as gods in the southern sky were the imperishable stars used to calculate the hours of the night. In the north, located between two rows of deities weaving each year of his life with the days of the month—directly in front of Tawaret bracing herself on a crocodile-shaped staff—Senmut himself confronted a crocodile rearing up toward him. The creature was smaller than he was, lessening its destructive powers.

She returned her gaze to the room and his earnest expression. "One of the brightest lights in the sky appears to be missing," she said

"Not so. It is represented in the southern sky by the empty boat in the west that sometimes moves backward."[91]

"You have created a window to the sky deep in the earth, Senmut. Geb is pleased you have made it possible for him to see the other half of himself even from here, where the light of the stars burning in the womb of Mother Nut would not reach if it was not for you. The love of the Divine brother and sister will live forever in your heart even after it ceases to beat the life you know now, which is only one of many more to come through millions of years."

He said softly, "I would like you to see something else."

Intrigued, she followed him to a corner of the room where, following his example, she crouched down to view something on the wall. The light from his lamp trembled over two figures facing each other. She thought it was Senmut in the presence of a goddess, even though it was extremely odd they were both so small, until she read the accompanying text and understood the reason for their secret location: *His servant in the place of her heart, who makes pleasure for the Lord of the Two Lands.* She understood then that the man and the woman were Senmut and Hatshepsut.

As they straightened he spoke so that only she could hear him, "This chamber lies outside the sacred perimeter of your temple, therefore I have tunneled deeper and farther into the earth for I desire to exist forever only if I can be as close to you as possible."

She longed to embrace him and yet with others watching she was not free to touch him.

* * * * *

The night after visiting Senmut's tomb, Hatshesput dreamed with the Fields of Hotep. Her father was giving her a ride somewhere in a chariot made of solid gold that shone so brightly it was hard to distinguish anything around it. He was smiling and happy, as though he had completely forgotten he was dying. She dared to hope the gods would answer her prayers and spare his life for he looked fit and strong and his laughter was as healthy as ever. They raced across fields as green as a gemstone while she looked eagerly around her for Neferure but she could not find her. Her father let her off beside the River, which was so wide it merged with the sky. She was surprised to see Seshen standing thigh-deep in the water wearing one of her finest dresses and the most beautiful jewels Pharaoh had given her. She called out to her attendant but her voice did not carry. Seshen turned away from the shore and walked deeper into the River even as a crocodile glided purposefully toward her. She tried screaming a warning to her friend but only Menkheperre seemed to hear her because he suddenly appeared before her holding a knife in his right hand. Smiling pleasantly, he raised the weapon and with a determined stroke severed her head from her neck. The shock woke her.

Hatshepsut discovered the sounds she had made while she slept, though ineffectual in the dream, had been clearly audible in the palace. When she opened her eyes, Nafre was already in her room. Behind her stood a handful of servants who all kept their distance from the bed as if they feared seeing the same cobra that had killed the princess.

Dismissing everyone, she lay awake thinking about the myth which had its roots in one of Kemet's most ancient cities. Horus and Seth once battled each other in the form of two great hippos. Isis, fearing for her son's life, threw a copper harpoon into the River. The weapon missed its target and instead of killing Seth lodged itself in Horus whose cry of pain betrayed her error. She commanded the blade to let go and the second time it struck Seth as she had intended, but when her brother also cried out in anguish she suffered a change of heart and spared him. Horus was so furious with his mother that he climbed out of the water and with the same knife he had battled Seth promptly cut off her head. He then stormed away into desert mountains nursing his rage, as she wandered, robbed of all but one of her senses, along the water's edge. Thoth found her there and it was he who, on Re's command, cut off the head of a horned cow and set it between her shoulders. To Hatshepsut the tale had always seemed to explain, in a childish way, how Isis and Hathor were merely aspects of one supreme Goddess but her dream now forced her to focus on the highly disturbing way the merger took place. Horus loved his mother and yet he had not hesitated to mutilate her and deprive her of almost all her senses. Thutmose invariably showed her the utmost respect but she would never be able to forget how, in her dream, his thin smile had reflected the edge of the blade he used to cut off her head. She was confident she had nothing to fear from him but the dream deepened her suspicion that he was growing increasingly impatient with her continued health and well-being. It also troubled her—and she could not dismiss the feeling—there were other ways he could hurt her and destroy all she had worked for.

Nafre had lit a candle before she left and staring into its blue heart she felt comforted recalling the images of Senmut—carved on both sides of the entrance to his tomb—where he stood wearing the long kilt he favored and adoring her name. *Maatkare* was precisely cut inside the *shenu* ring protecting her unique identity and giving her life forever through the serpent of substance that swallows its own Divine tail. On the ceiling of the passage just outside the first and, at the moment only decorated chamber in his eternal home, her magnificent Steward had commissioned a depiction of the Fields of Hotep. She had been so pleased with his rendering of the land of peace and contentment it had become the seed of her dream, where her father's love and approval had been as the life-giving River. She had not been prepared for the hot-tempered hostility of her brother's son, whose heart was as empty of affection for her as the desert. She knew she had to be careful not to confuse the real Thutmose with the young man in her dream, but in her heart she did not doubt there was at least a kernel of truth in all she had experienced in the Dwat.

She was tempted to walk out into her Pleasure House to see if she could determine exactly what hour of the night it was by looking up at the stars but her body had no desire to get out of bed. Like her father before her, she would not live to celebrate her thirty-year jubilee. That glory would most likely belong to Menkheperre alone. The thought almost angered her. It certainly succeeded in upsetting her, robbing her of sleep long enough that when the new day was come no cosmetics would be able to completely hide the dark half moons under her eyes. But ever since Nefi's death, she did not resent her life as Hatshepsut-Maatkare was waning. Every year more people she cared for went to their Ka and forced her to look forward to the moment when she too would make the inevitable crossing.

Her brother's sun, an avid historian, would surely know about the Oracle of Amun where the god proclaimed Princess Hatshepsut would one day hold the crook and the flail in her hands, and about her father's final words. Akheperkare's voice had been distorted but all her life it had continued to ring in her head, clear and strong as he said, "My daughter, the Female Falcon!" Even though his youngest son had succeeded him, *she* was the successor of his heart. She believed that now more than ever remembering how, in his last moments on earth, he had looked only at her. It had all begun on the afternoon fire from heaven struck the Persea tree in her garden. It still thrilled her to recall the way Hapuseneb and her mother had looked at each other when she entered the audience hall…

Hatshepsut finally fell asleep, but the moment she woke in the morning she understood where her thoughts had all been leading.

Completely naked, her graying but still stubbornly thick hair restrained in a braid, she raised her arms over her head in a luxurious stretch, walked out into her garden and dove into her pool. She knew what she had to do. The two Monuments of Heh she had commissioned for the Temple of Amun-Re would act as her arms reaching toward heaven to embrace Neferure, and they would also serve to commemorate the first sixteen years of her reign, exactly thirty years after her father took her under his wing in the Seal Room.

It soon became painfully clear, however, that she had ignored an even more obvious message relayed to her while she slept. Much too late she remembered how Seshen had turned away from her and walked deeper into the River dressed as if for a celebratory feast. One of her best friends since they were children in Mennefer, and her intimate attendant for more than thirty years, had gone to her Ka before the time decreed for her by the goddesses of the hours. Seshen, she was horrified to learn, had killed herself.

"Her physician told her she was dying and there was nothing he could do for her," Nafre attempted to explain the unthinkable.

"It was cruel of him to be so blunt and hopeless in his diagnosis!"

"It is worse to be lied to, my lady, and not to have time to prepare yourself."

"Clearly she did not *want* any time!"

"She was afraid of dying."

"We are all afraid."

Her attendant did not look surprised by the confession even though she should have been for it was the Son of Re she was talking to.

"I fear for her, Nafre," she went on earnestly. "What will happen to her in the Dwat? How will she find her way? Will her Ba be as a baby bird not yet ready to fly out of its nest forever falling into darkness, completely vulnerable to the forces of incarnation that might crush it as inadvertently and yet as fatally as a gardener's foot?"

"I cannot say, my lady."

"You cannot say? You have always comforted me with your calm and steady faith, Nafre."

"I have always *tried* to comfort you, Majesty, but it was never really necessary. You always rise above the abyss of loss, soaring on a current of wisdom and faith the rest of us find humbling. I do not know what will happen when I die but I cannot imagine myself simply ceasing to exist. I believe the spells in *The Book of Coming Forth By Day* will help me. I am grateful they are there because I would not know what to say to all those gates, demons and deities which for some reason feel compelled to bar my way to the Field of Reeds."

Hatshepsut had not perfumed her mouth—news of Seshen's death had killed her appetite—and her stomach felt queasy as she silently swallowed Nafre's literal interpretation of metaphysical truths impossible to explain to a heart that had not yet grasped them.

She did not permit grief to affect her performance in the Seal Room even though she suffered the loss of one of her beloved attendants like the gap left by a missing tooth. The pleasurable routines of her dressing room would never taste quite as rich and joyfully fulfilling again without Seshen. Nehesj set his seal to the document authorizing another expedition to Punt, the third since Chancellor's Neshi's successful return. Neshi, unfortunately, would not be leading the ships again. He too had become a passenger on the bark of the sun that unfurled its magical sails at twilight, and followed the current of darkness flowing over the earth into the next world.

40

The Heart of Amun

The years were swept away from Maatkare. The Divine sap rising up the stem of her spine bloomed in her smile and shone in her eyes as she pulled on the ropes, slowly raising the *djed* pillar. Made of gold and ebony, lapis lazuli and electrum, carnelian and green feldspar, the backbone of Osiris—taller and heavier than any mortal man—glowed all the colors of Creation. Her smile deepened as she remembered Seni using the *djed* as an example the day he first explained to her the complex nature of symbols. The lifeless body of Osiris, trapped in the roots of a tamarisk tree, was freed by Isis who realigned all his parts and made him whole again. Everyone watching the ritual of Raising the *Djed* was familiar with the myth, but few would see the pillar's four rungs as the horizons of north, south, east and west existing as one in God's heart, from which issued the four major forces required to manifest the universe—a mere fragment of His infinite potential. Pharaoh, and the priests assisting her, could read everything the *djed* silently said and their wisdom brought stability to the Two Lands. The essence of life was incorruptible, only temporarily contained in a fleshly bark that cracks with wrinkles before returning to the earth and freeing the eternal Osiris within.

The hearts of all those assembled in and around the palace courtyard ascended into heaven on cries of exultation, creating a current of joy in the Celestial River that flowed beyond the moments containing it to enrich all life in the future. Maatkare scarcely felt the weight of her body. Her bones were light as a bird's, her pulse the beating of imperishable wings soaring above the horizons of life and death. She was Horus transcending the branches of her mortal limbs even as she dove down into the nest of her heart to feed her hungry senses. She rejoiced that her confidence and wisdom, once tentative and fledgling, had grown and matured and would give her the power, when she went to her Ka, to command the *neters* of incarnation as she rejoined her Father, Amun-Re, whose bodily son and daughter she was. All of Kemet was celebrating the festival of Maatkare's *heb-sed* sixteen years from the day the double crown was placed on her head, thirty years since lightning struck the Persea tree outside her room and her father, the Horus of Fine Gold, Akheperkare, took her under his wing in the Seal Room.

It was the first day of the season of Immersion and the air was bracingly warm as she ran ahead of four young white bulls. The animals, led by four priests, symbolized both the completion of one cycle and the beginning of another. Beneath the stiff royal kilt her legs felt long and strong. Her new steward, Wadjrenput, had personally supervised the gilding of the pliant leather sandals she was wearing that enabled her to run as swiftly as humanly possible. She deeply regretted that Dhout had missed the opportunity to arrange all the feasts being held during her jubilee. Wherever he was in the Dwat, she imagined he was letting all seven Hathors know how inconveniently they had timed his death—less than three months before the king's *heb-sed*, during which his skills as Royal Steward would have shone as never before. The thought made her laugh as, holding the sealed papyrus scroll providing her with ownership of the Two Lands, she ran around the sacred circle for the fourth and final time.

Throughout the day, the only part of her that ached were her cheeks every time her smile stiffened a little as she wished Neferure could have been there to witness her mother's triumph. Menkheperre also smiled as he stood behind her on Amun-Re's barge sailing back to *Ipet Sut* from the Palace of Maat, but more than ever, she sensed his growing impatience. He was eighteen-years-old, a man fully grown, and yet a forty-two-year-old woman still ruled Kemet instead of him. She felt so magnificent, it perversely amused her to imagine he was wondering how long she could possibly live, and how old he would be before she was at last considerate enough to go to her Ka and leave him completely in charge. The military was already under his command. When Nomti retired, Thutmose appointed the Overseer of the Garrison and Royal Scribe, Djehuty, the new Great Army Commander.

The unique nature of Maatkare's reign became most evident when, wearing the red crown of the north she stepped up into a pavilion built in the shape of the hieroglyph for *sky* that represented Lower Kemet. At the same time, Menkheperre took his place in an adjoining pavilion wearing the white crown of the south. They seated themselves on their respective thrones, the crook and flail crossed against their hearts, and the most powerful men in the Two Lands kissed the ground as beyond them the multitudes cheered until they grew hoarse from the intensity of their joy. Eventually the roaring ecstasy of the *rekhyt* hushed to a rumbling purr of contentment as everyone refilled their cups with either beer or wine and drank to the Good God Menkheperre and to the Good Goddess Maatkare—the double beat of a single Divine heart, God and his Hand, Re and Eye.

Foreign chiefs had been invited to the jubilee and Thutmose's smile looked less strained as their daughters approached the throne two at a time to offer the pharaohs libations of water and wine. The girls had adopted native attire for the occasion and the mist-linen exposed all their charms. A few of them wore short wigs but most preferred longer and more elaborate coiffures. By far the most striking was a princess of the Retenu. Her green eyes outlined by malachite and galena, she looked up at the young king's face for a bold instant and Hatshepsut could easily guess the effect her beauty had on him. If she had been born a man she would undoubtedly have enjoyed collecting women as her brother and her father once had, and as the High Priest of Amun continued to do. Whenever she visited him in his private home on the River, a lovely girl she had never seen before attended them. Curious, she asked him what he did with his female servants when he grew tired of their limited charms. "Because the living Goddess is the sister of your heart," she told him with a smile, "and pretty girls are merely honey cakes serving to sweeten the feast of our love."

"I only keep a girl for as long as it takes me to assess her character and determine where she would be most happy on the tree of life as she grows toward her Ka," he replied soberly. "Some I marry off, others are appointed to serve in various households, a select number become priestesses and a few are merely sent home."

"Do you enjoy all of them before they go?"

"No," he said, and she believed him for he always spoke the truth. However, wondering what exactly he did with some of his lovely attendants stimulated her imagination. Her sexuality had begun to feel like an old horse she had to coax along. That ceased to be the case during her *heb-sed* when her youth, and its intense erotic appetites, was magically restored to her by the unbridled rejoicing of her subjects. Listening to the festivities lapping all night long against the palace walls like a supernatural river mysteriously invigorated her. Hapuseneb shared her table at the banquets where sacred dancers invoked The Golden One—the fiery serpent of substance whose fangs were the first rays of light to illuminate the darkness as its jaws parted to form heaven and earth. The young female performers wore mist-linen skirts beneath red and white sashes crossed tightly between their breasts and around their waists. The lower halves of their long fine braids were adorned with golden beads, and as they swung their heads passionately back and forth throughout the dance their hair hissed like broods of black serpents with luminous tails. They gyrated their hips and assumed erotically inviting positions, expressing with their remarkably limber bodies how motion through space and time, backward and forward, past and future, is made possible by the supreme sexual act of Creation

The lithe young females were followed by eight young men chosen to embody Ihy, Hathor's son. The youths wore green *menit* necklaces against their bare chests. Four of them shook copper sistrums and four played clappers shaped like a woman's hands. With their abrupt yet precisely choreographed motions, the male dancers evoked the struggle undergone by every child as it emerges in a messy pool of blood and fluids from between its mother's thighs. The birth of dimensions on The First Occasion—which set the stage for sensual experience through the physical senses—was a magical but far from effortless affair. During the performance, Hatshesput once again found herself thinking about Neferure and hoping that Ihy, the Jackal of Light, had come to her daughter's room and helped her quickly move past the fear and pain she might have felt during the process of leaving her Ka's earthly womb. Ihy would surely have blessed Nefi with his help for she had been so passionate about life's pleasures she had never hesitated to incite emotional turbulence, in herself as well as in others, by questioning and challenging anything that interfered with the sheer joy of living. Neferure had been born a girl but she had been as stubborn as a bull-calf and everyday her mother's thoughts and feelings—Hathor's mysterious herd—followed her across the River to the Land Beyond the Sunset.

Herons lined the shores, and flew in formations across the sky, as on the final day of her jubilee Maatkare, enthroned on her great ship, headed north toward Mennefer. For as long as they were in sight, she kept her eyes on her two new Monuments of Heh thrusting toward heaven like naturally existing things and channeling Divine power directly into the world. Nothing quite so splendid had been made since the beginning of time as her two soaring mountains covered entirely in white-gold. When Re was high in the sky it was painful to look at them for very long even as they suffused the heart with hope and awe. The sight of them was especially uplifting because one of their precursors had abruptly cracked and been ruined just when it was about to fully emerge from the mountain. The disaster had made her sick to her stomach, after which she embraced the humility necessary to blame herself for being overly ambitious with the monuments' dimensions. She accepted the reprimand sent from God and instructed Djehuty and Amenhotep to scale down the size she had originally commissioned. In the end her tributes to Heh were still even more magnificent than those her father had erected outside *Ipet Sut's* western entrance. They were cradled within the sacred space itself, only partially visible to the multitudes. In a niche below the foundation pits she had buried two statues of Neferhotep, the king whose especially creative spirit, strength and wisdom were now joined with hers, the seed of his reign having fully flowered through her own glorious incarnation. Just as every earthly body had to die in order for the Ka to create a new one—in which the knowledge and accumulated experiences of the others continued to live—so too were parts of buildings and statues erected by former kings sacrificed to give birth to new and even more awe-inspiring monuments. A Temple built by her mother's brother, Djeserkare, had been torn down and some of its blocks re-used to make way for the lower terrace of her Mansion of Millions of Years, *Djser-Djseru,* in obedience to the Divine rhythm of creation and destruction.

Dressed in a gown of mist-linen, and adorned purely in gold and turquoise, more than ever Maatkare felt like the Golden Flame, Beloved of Horus, whose arms were around God's neck in the black depths of space. The magic of The First Occasion was visible everywhere and was also buried deep in the earth's bowels, where everyday miners split rocks and exposed Hathor's radiant beauty in the form of the blue stone named after the Lady of Life, goddess of the earth and sky. Enthroned beneath a pavilion erected in the center of the royal barge—her Monuments of Heh, *Djet* and *Neheh,* drifting slowly out of sight as the Town of Amun was left behind—the words with which they were inscribed reflected how she felt in those quiet moments. The sound of her *rekhyt* rejoicing was fading into the distance. The indifferent lapping of the water against the hull began sounding louder and both vigorous and sluggish, like the blood flowing through her old heart which still felt so young. Honored officials and priests, fan bearers, attendants, sailors and oarsmen surrounded her and yet she felt strangely alone with the River. The water beneath her was swiftly flowing toward another time when she would no longer be there. It was frightening to think that when she was born again she might not remember who she was now—Maatkare, the Son of Re. It would be terrible to forget that it was not necessary to live in fear and to fail to recognize that God lived inside her. Surely her Ka would not condemn her to being born in a place where Amun-Re remained hidden and Maat suffered even more than she had during the time the Setiu ruled in the north. If there were no High Priests of Amun to educate her and reveal her true nature to her she would be like a seed planted in the desert. Perhaps in her next incarnation she would look up and marvel at the Monuments of Heh erected by Maatkare. When she saw them, whoever she was then would recognize her timeless Ka as she read the words she had ordered inscribed on one of their shining bodies:

"Now my heart turns this way and that, as I think what the people will say. Those who shall see my monuments in years to come, and who shall speak of what I have done.⁹² I have made this with a loving heart for my Father, Amun, having entered into His initiation of the First Occasion and having experienced His impressive efficacy. I have not been forgetful of any project He has decreed. For My Incarnation knows He is Divine, and I have done it by His command. He is the one who guides me. I could not have imagined the work without His acting: He is the one who gives the directions. Nor have I slept because of His temple. I do not stray from what He has commanded. My heart is perceptive on behalf of my Father and I have access to His mind's knowledge. I have not turned my back on the town of the Lord to the Limit, but paid attention to it. For I know His temple is heaven on earth, the sacred elevation of the First Occasion, the Eye of the Lord to the Limit—His favorite place, which bears His perfection and gathers His followers.⁹³ I am His daughter in very truth, who works for Him and knows what He desires. My reward is life, stability, dominion upon the Horus Throne of all the Living, like Re, forever."⁹⁴

Menkheperre's gilded ship glided directly behind Maatkare's. The Keeper of the Seal of the King of Upper Kemet, the High Priest of Amun, followed both pharaohs on his own vessel. Thutmose was accompanied by his new bride, Meritre-Hatshepsut, to whom he had awarded the title King's Great Wife Whom He Loves. Satioh had yet to produce an heir and the bonds of friendship, even lifelong, could not compare to the force of sexual love. All of Meritre's best friends and pets had also been loaded onto barges and were accompanying her to Mennefer and from there to Perunefer. Her new husband's ardor did not permit him to even think of leaving her behind in White Wall. The girl who had once tried to kill the new queen had herself been poisoned six months later and died a painful death. And so justice was served and the unsavory event recorded by Seshat on her palette, where there would scarcely be room to list all the presents lavished on Meritre by both pharaohs.

The royal entourage did not dock in the Mansion of the Ka of Ptah until two months later for the Good Goddess and the Good God had made many stops along the way. In every port, Maatkare addressed their subjects while Menkheperre stood smiling beside her. Hatshepsut considered it a blessing, a gift from Amun-Re Himself in honor of her *heb-sed* that Anubis had finally come for the King's Mother. Isis was buried in Kemet's most ancient city of eternity, near the burial ground of all the sacred cows which had given birth to the sacred Apis bull and close to a pyramid ascending in great stone steps toward the sky.

During their stay in Mennefer, on more than one occasion she went hawking with Hapuseneb. Every time they did so, she recalled the afternoon he had said to her, "Together there is nothing we cannot do, you need only believe that for it to be true." He had been right, as usual. The last morning they enjoyed the sport together, they were not alone on the edge of an elevated plateau dominated by nine pyramids. Senmut was one of the officials she had asked to accompany them even though he had never really enjoyed hunting with birds. His falcon, however, was blissfully ignorant of the fact and served him well. Perhaps her unique friend's relaxed disposition won the royal bird's respect and loyalty more effectively than the tense and demanding attitude of other men, who seemed to think their virility was enhanced by the number of dead rabbits, hares and other assorted rodents their attendants collected and piled into baskets. Hungry people would eat almost anything; whatever prey the nobility rejected was distributed in the city's poorest district.

Hatshepsut kept smiling over at Senmut but he did not seem to notice and after annoying her began to worry her. He seemed oddly distracted by something. She wondered if perhaps he had left some important matter unattended and only just remembered it. She happened to be looking at him just as he sat down abruptly on a conveniently situated rock. One moment he was staring up at the sky attempting to follow the track of his falcon—which had flown so high it was barely visible—and the next he was sitting with his head resting in his hands. She lost sight of him as his attendants immediately surrounded him. A few moments later, she felt somewhat reassured when his head rose above them all as he regained his feet. Nevertheless, the incident disturbed her.

"What do you see, Maatkare?" Hapsuseneb said abruptly, his tone commanding her attention as she sensed what he was asking her had nothing to do with Senmut or the hunt.

"I behold heaven above us," she responded, "and below us the River receding and leaving behind the rich black land which will soon be sown with seeds. Beyond it I see the domain of Seth and Mansions of Millions of Years—the pyramids erected by great kings who all lived before the darkness brought by those who ruled without Re."

"Hundreds of years separate the nine pyramids and yet they are arranged in a carefully planned pattern. In the distant future, people will be able to look down upon earth like gods. Even though they will have forgotten much, they will one day be able to read the secret we have left for them written in the language of Number, which never changes or dies."

She completely forgot about Senmut as her gaze was torn between the pyramids and the High Priest's face. "What is the secret, Hapuseneb?"

He looked at her. "The equations through which the Hidden One reveals himself. I have taught you that Number is the doorway through which the Divine becomes incarnate."

"Yes…"

He turned his head and stared out across the desert plateau at the three great pyramids of Khufru, Kafre and Menkaure guarded by a colossal lion with the head of Pharaoh. "There is the key," he said.

* * * * *

Director of the Private Rooms in the Royal Palace, Trusted Councilor in the House of Amun, Keeper of The Royal Seal, Royal Scholar, First Speaker, One of the Ten Great of Lower Kemet, Superior Steward of the Lady of the Two Lands, Overseer of All Public Works of the King, Overseer of the Double Gold House, Unique Friend, the Great Steward of Amun, Senmut—his full list of titles took a scribe hours to write—lay dying.

Hatshepsut sat by his bedside from the time Khepri rose in the morning until late in the evening when Re, once vigorous and strong, transformed into the old and weary Atum as he unfurled the colorful sails of twilight and prepared for his journey through the night. There his youthful vitality would be restored and give birth to a new morning. First, however, twelve long dark hours had to pass—the One that became Two and created the stage of Three where the drama of corporeal life is played out. Whenever he was awake, she held Senmut's hand, attempting to communicate her faith to him with the strength of her grasp and with the love burning in her eyes. Every time tears escaped the dam of her self-control he reached up, gently wiped the salty drops from her cheeks and quickly brought his fingertips to his lips, as if her grief tasted sweeter to him than anything.

He murmured, "I like to imagine that the Primordial Waters to which I am returning will feel and taste like your tears, Hatshepsut."

"The Goddess loves you, Senmut!" She sounded angry because she was desperately not to cry. "She has proved it to you in every way she could!"

"She has." He turned his head away. "But even so, I have been lonely for her."

She thought of all the times she had sent him away after they worshipped Hathor together. It seemed so obvious now that her detachment had been a disguise assumed by fear and the tension it caused. Believing she could spare herself the inconsolable grief she would suffer if she lost him, she had pretended not to love and depend on him as much as she truly had. Maatkare, Powerful of Ka's, Foremost of Noble Women United with Amun, had behaved like a fool.

"Forgive me, Senmut," she whispered miserably. "Forgive me!"

He turned his head toward her again. "I fear I have broken beneath the weight of all the titles you have honored me with, Majesty." He tried to smile but the bark of his mouth was already drifting into the next world beyond his control.

"The Two Lands and their king will miss you more than Thoth himself could describe even if he spent millions of years writing!"

"Do not be sad for me, Hatshesput." He succeeded in gently squeezing her hand. "I will be seeing our daughter again soon. I dreamed with her last night. Nefi is waiting for me, rather impatiently, I think. She cannot understand why I insist on lingering in a body my Ka is no longer interested in sustaining."

She clung to his hand with both of hers wondering if he realized what he had said. "Thutmose engendered Neferure but in truth she *was* our daughter, Senmut, the child of our heart, and you know she was never very patient. However, on this occasion she will *have* to be, for even though I know it is selfish of me, I do not wish you to leave so soon!"

"It is not so soon. I am fifty-two. The Goddess has been more than generous with the time she allotted me, much more generous than she was with Nefi. You will see to it the monument above the tomb in which I will be buried is finished by the time my mummy is laid within it?"

He referred to another statue of him with Neferure's head emerging from the cloak flowing over his lap, like the lotus that rose from the Primordial Waters and bloomed the head of the child Khepri from a lotus flower—the solar disc illuminating the first moments of time and shining the petals of its rays across all of space. Abruptly, she recalled what Hapuseneb had said about the princess and Senmut, "To hear them speak was like listening to a single heart beat."

"You have not answered me, Hatshepsut."

She looked down into his eyes and was stunned by what she believed she saw there. For a moment she could not speak. Then she said quickly, somehow talking around her heart which had leapt into her throat from the shock, "Of course I will see to it, Senmut."

"My eternal home will never be finished. Only the first of the three chambers has been decorated."

"Do not speak like that." She reclaimed her hand and rose to leave, her heart beating hard and fast demanding she run from a suspicion impossible to tolerate. "Ibenre has told me you may live another month at least."

He said harshly, "I do not wish to!"

Her tears evaporated as she felt Seth taking possession of her emotions and herding them toward a hot arid desert of jealousy and wounded pride. Fortunately, her deeper feelings—allied to Osiris and the intelligence of her heart—promptly took control and mastered the selfish stampede. She sat down again, her back rigid and her hands gripping her knees.

In a completely different tone of voice he said, "Are you all right, Hatshepsut?"

She dared to look into his eyes again and the love she saw there shamed her. Whether Neferure was the Tefnut to Senmut's Shu, the Nut to his Geb, was irrelevant. Whatever form love took its force could not be denied, it could only be abused by those foolish enough to do so. More than ever, she felt it was true that love was the only real power in the universe.

She stood again but only so she could sit on the edge of his bed and kiss both his cheeks, even though it made her even more miserable how dry and thin, like old papyrus, his skin was.

"Sleep now," she whispered, kissing his lips very lightly for they were no longer a gateway to the desires of the flesh as they prepared to take their final breath— the gust of wind on which is Ba would fly free. "Sleep and dream with the Fields of Hotep, where we will all be together again soon! I envy you and Nefi for being wise enough to get there before me. I will see you again in the morning, Senmut, my unique and beloved friend."

As though he understood that she had given him her permission to leave, the Great Steward of Amun drifted off to sleep and never woke again on this side of the River. Ibenre told her his heart had simply stopped.

For three days, even while obeying an irresistible current of sadness, Hatshepsut experienced a profound relief that her unique friend was no longer suffering from the knowledge he was dying and leaving her behind. Instead, she could now mysteriously relax, confident Nefi had greeted him the instant his heart ceased to beat and, eagerly grabbing both his hands, led him into the beautiful Field of Reeds. When Senmut entered the golden hall of Osiris, the *neters* would all raise their hands to him in praise, recognizing the lord who commanded them all through the greatness of his heart. Son of the Honorable Ramose and of the Mistress of the House Hatnefer, Senmut, beloved of the Good Goddess Maatkare, would live forever.

Hatshepsut remained in Mennefer while her lover's body was in the *Wabet*. Understanding she needed to be alone, Hapuseneb returned to Waset and it comforted her to know he would be there waiting for her when she returned. The knowledge that her unique friend would never again greet her at the dock or join her in her garden was too bitter to swallow. For weeks, she savored this impossible truth with appalled reverence, as if it was a hard and bitter chunk of metal from heaven. Like a burned tongue, her emotions had gone numb. But eventually the wings of the Goddess that had been blessedly muffling her feelings slipped away. Like a fledgling fallen from the nest, she crashed against reality and fully realized that the very special person who had made her life worth living was gone forever. The profound strength of her faith, her duties and her responsibilities would all live on as Maatkare, but Hatshepsut was essentially gone. Her only comfort was knowing she would not have to remain too long on the side of the River which now felt so empty. It was astonishing, the ability a single man possessed to fill the world with wonder and vitality. All those years she had wanted to believe who she was, and all she had managed to become, existed apart from Senmut, thriving and growing in the mysteriously fertile plot of her individual mind. But such divisions were artificial, the scribbling of scribes. In truth, the roots of her perceptions and emotions had mingled with his to such an extent that, when his Ka plucked him away, she felt a vital part of her ripped from the earth with him. What she had always feared would happen had come to pass and left her bitterly regretting how foolishly she had attempted to deny the inevitable and, by so doing, made the person she loved suffer. She had honored him above all others, a commoner who had risen as high as any man could aspire, and yet what he had most desired—the simple nightly intimacy that made even the poorest fisherman and his wife wealthy— she had denied him. Not once in their life together had they experienced the sunrise lying in each others arms.

Senmut's Master of Life, and the stone container which would house it, were both in Waset but Maatkare ordered another temporary gilded wooden bed made for him and set on a dais in the center of his ship. To show the Two Lands in what honor Pharaoh had held her most beloved official, the royal barge sailed behind the vessel bearing his body back to the Town of Amun. Though he had been born in Iuny, it was at the foot of *Djser-Djseru* that his mummy would rest, the passages of his tomb magical roots reaching for her Mansion of Million of Years. It comforted her immeasurably to know she would be surrounded by the stone "kisses" he had placed there in secret intimate places, where they could not be seen but where her Akh would be able to feel his love eternally.

The voyage south felt longer than ever. If it had not been for the fact that Hapuseneb was waiting for her in Waset, the intense sorrow and regret she suffered would have drowned her heart, much as the River would have claimed her body if she had fallen overboard. Her thoughts were barely able to keep above a current of grief that threatened her desire to go on living. She had too much time to think during the journey home because there was no longer anyone she could talk to the way she had conversed with Senmut. Even more than she had appreciated the fact while he still lived, she understood after his death how he had always helped her alleviate the demanding pressure of her thoughts and feelings. They were building up inside her now so that her heart felt like a dam dangerously close to breaking and flooding the Two Lands with her unhappiness.

Senmut's most magnificent statue had been finished during his absence. It barely reached her knees but she had never seen anything more splendid. The face of Hathor was so exquisitely wrought, and her smile looked so alive, she felt herself reflecting it. On the goddess' head rested a sistrum, at the heart of which a cobra—crowned with horns and the solar disc—reared between two Ka arms rising above a *tiet* knot. Her beloved friend's unique way of writing *Maatkare* had never been more boldly and beautifully wrought as he knelt behind it holding the cryptogram in his arms. The long garment he wore was elaborately embroidered with hieroglyphs stating that the monument was made as an offering to both 'Amun-Re and Hathor, preeminent of Waset, who resides in Kha-Akhet on behalf of life, prosperity, health and favor every day for the Ka of the Steward Senmut, like Re'.[95]

She accompanied the statue when it was delivered to the temple, The Mansion of Kha-Akhet Amun, where it became the first offering to grace its newly completed court. The reverent sadness with which the High Priest, Senenu, welcomed her resonated soothingly through Hatshepsut's body. As they performed the libations together, pouring milk and water before the freshly painted statue of God—the brilliant colors of His erect plumes shimmering in the lamplight—she felt as though it was her heart the young priest held tenderly cupped in his hands. He stared boldly into her eyes and she knew he desired to offer her even more intimate comfort. She smiled at him then turned her head and concentrated on slowly empting the small round jar of its contents. Caught by a groove in the stone floor, the milk flowed away slowly. So too had Senmut's life. The baby who suckled happily at his mother's breast had become a handsome and strikingly intelligent man. He had lived a long life blessed by the Goddess, a life that passed much too fast and yet, her heart told her, ended exactly when it was meant to.

The way Senenu had dared to look at her—his eyes nakedly offering her all the comforts of his virile young body—planted the seed of an idea in her mind that, shocking as it was, swiftly took root in her heart.

In preparation for the funeral, the stone container intended for Senmut's Master of Life was hauled down from his offering chapel to the tomb where he would actually be buried. It had gotten as far as the entrance corridor when Maatkare abruptly commanded the work be abandoned and the tomb sealed. The Great Steward of Amun would not rest there. While he lived, they had never slept an entire night in each other's arms but inside her own Master of Life there was more than enough room for their mummies to rest side-by-side forever. It was necessary only to excavate a third supernatural portal off the burial chamber where her father already waited for her. Senmut would never be lonely for her again.

* * * * *

In the heart of Amun-Re's temple work began on The Palace of Maat. The intricate complex of rooms opened a new entrance to the section of God's house erected by Maatkare's predecessors and embodied her unique contribution to the sacred task of expanding His heart. The rows of intimate niches evoked the ribs of a skeleton supporting and protecting the organs of chapels and sanctuaries—the corporeal receptacles for Divine creative energy. A bark shrine made entirely of red stone and named *The Place of the Heart of Amun* would give life and peace to the Palace of Maat. The shrine erected by her mother's brother, Djserkare, would be replaced by one devised and emanating from her own incarnation.

While she still lived, and for millions of years into the future, whenever people read her inscriptions and beheld all her beautiful flourishing efficient monuments, they would know she had not been exaggerating her feelings but instead they would say, "How like her it is, to offer to her Father, Amun!"[96]

The *biat* transported from the Red Mountain in the north and the blocks of grey-black diorite from which the new bark shrine would be constructed were all painted yellow-gold so the inscriptions would stand out as vividly as possible. The bark shrine of Amun-Min would contain three doors and be open to the heavens. The forces contained in numbers became Hatshepsut's obsession. In her presence, all those who knew about it carefully behaved as if it happened every day that a king elected to share her Master of Life with an official who had been born a commoner. Nevertheless, after Senmut's secretly scandalous burial all the minor aches and discomforts she had been vigorously swimming away, or determinedly ignoring, rose to the surface and began plaguing her. For several weeks, she scarcely remembers she drank poppy juice to alleviate a stabbing pain in her gum from a tooth Ibenre finally insisted on pulling. The molar had been eroded almost down to the gum. The gap in the left side of her mouth was only visible when her lips parted in a joyful grin, which seldom happened anymore; it was not difficult to confine herself to smiling with her mouth closed. Most of her happiness had essentially evaporated. All that remained to her was the peace and contentment provided by her sacred work and Hapuseneb's company. Indeed, one could not be distinguished from the other. Swimming kept her strong but she tired more easily, and after a long morning sitting in audience both her feet itched as though they had been stung by a million mosquitoes. Ibenre, who seemed ageless, encouraged her to put her feet up as often as possible.

Djehuty suggested the new bark shrine be assembled and decorated in its intended location instead of stone by stone in the workshops. Hatshepsut was fascinated by the idea of raising the monument from the ground up in horizontal layers, as though it was literally blooming like a flower unfurling the petals of separate stone blocks, each one distinguished by a self-contained inscription even while forming part of a whole.

"It is a beautiful concept," she told Hapuseneb, more excited than she had been in more than a year. "Why has it never been done before?"

"Because you had not thought of it, Maatkare."

"The idea belongs to Djehuty."

"Yes, but it was you who inspired him to give birth to it. How freely and eloquently you express your feelings affects others as surely as the overflowing River enriches the earth and makes it possible for seeds to sprout and grow. The Place of the Heart of Amun will be as unique and special as you are, Hatshepsut."

It warmed her heart, as nothing else had the power to do anymore, when he used her birth name. It invariably took her back to the time when her family, and almost everyone else she had come to love, was still alive. Hapuseneb had warned her he was destined to cross the River before her but she had learned how foolish it was to worry and anticipate a sorrow that could not be avoided. When the time came she would endure his loss and survive it, just as she had lived through the deaths of her beloved daughter and her unique friend. Life was all that truly mattered because death was only a temporary illusion.

"This new system of construction," Hapuseneb went on, "also has the benefit of avoiding possible damage to the inscriptions as they are transported to the temple from the workshops. The artists can decorate each panel as it emerges."

The evening this conversation took place, they were dining alone together. Looking around her, she remembered the night Satis had become jealous of the fun her mistress was having and purring passionately attempted to rub herself into the sensual action. It shocked her to think Hapuseneb was fifty-seven, a very old man, for he still looked as handsome to her as he always had. Luxuriously tended, his golden-brown skin was only faintly traced with wrinkles. There was no denying his arms were not as strong and that his skin was beginning to tire of clinging to his bones—it sagged in places where it was once lean and firm—yet he looked better than most men only half his age.

"Do you mind being old?" she said bluntly.

"The young man does not desire to be a baby again and it would be equally foolish for the old man to want to be the youth he once was," he replied. "The different stages of life are the scales on the Serpent that swallows time with its tail. It is not merely your physical form I have loved and been attracted to from the instant we met, Hatshepsut. You will remember you were only a child and I was already a man who was obliged to wait for you to become a woman. It is a source of great joy to me that we have both lived long enough to watch each other grow old."

"You promised me I would not have to live very long after you left," she reminded him.

"And I will keep that promise, Hatshepsut." Pulling her to him, he repeated the words he had whispered to her so long ago in a moment which felt as if it had happened only yesterday, "Trust me!"

The Place of the Heart of Amun was Maatkare's testament to the love she bore Amun-Re and his High Priest, Hapuseneb, through whom the Hidden One had revealed Himself to her as through no one else.

The foundation blocks were decorated with a procession of kneeling women and men—the breasts and bellies of the latter sagging like those of Hapi, god of the River and prosperity—presenting offerings to Amun-Re. The standards over their heads identified the Nome from which they each came to give their hearts to the god who heard their prayers.

Above the offering register, Hatshepsut, wearing the ancient horned and plumed crown on her head, was shown entering the temple. She was met by the Oracle of Amun who confirmed her sovereignty over the Two Lands then led her to her throne, where she knelt and laid the foundation stone of the bark shrine in which the glorious events of her life would be inscribed.

The third layer of stones was consecrated to the festival of *Apet Aset* during which God's bark journeyed forth from the Divine realm into the watery womb of His consort Mut to be born in His bodily form in the Palace of Maat. Scenes from the Beautiful Festival of the Valley would also be rendered and show God crossing the River in His bark to spend the night in *Djser-Djseru* where He ruled as he did in Maatkare's heart, commanding all her deeds and actions.

In the fourth register, Maatkare offered life to the *neters* Amun-Min, Thoth and Horus—the Divine forces flowing through her incarnation become fully conscious of its transcendent nature, a spiritual achievement expressed by the crowns the three gods set upon her head.

The uppermost row of stones followed the return of God's bark to its new shrine in *Ipet Sut*, The Place of the Heart of Amun.

41

Beautiful Festival of the Valley

The High Priests of Re, Ptah and Amun feasted in private with the Female Falcon. More wine was consumed than food was eaten. The smiles on the faces of Kemet's spiritual leaders filled her with a profound satisfaction. She had succeeded in uniting the Two Lands even more strongly than they had once been bound before the first darkness descended in the form of the Setiu. It was Mentuhotep, born in Waset, who had restored Kemet to its former greatness with the help of Amun but it was Maatkare who had forged a perfect balance of power between the north and the south. Ptah was the body of God, Re was His celestial face and Amun was His supreme creative efficacy. In ancient times— when pharaohs first began calling themselves the Son of Re—Mennefer, the Mansion of the Ka of Ptah, and Iuno, the City of the Sun, had ruled as one. In those days Waset, now known as the Southern Iuno, had been as a seed—a small and seemingly insignificant town where Horus rose again in the form of Mentuhotep, the great king who had succeeded in banishing the Setiu and restoring the order of Maat. Although chaos descended a second time, the might of Re soon shone again in Ahmose-Nabpehtire, her mother's father. It could truly be said that never before had Kemet been so strong.

At the Head of the Year, on the day of the new moon, the greatest of the great participated in the Beautiful Festival of the Valley. The occasion was more splendid than ever for Maatkare's Mansion of Millions of Years, *Djser-Djseru*, was nearly finished. Their gilded doors sealed closed, the shrines of Amun, Mut, Khonsu and Hathor emerged from *Ipset-Sut*. They rode on the shoulders of priests who boarded *Userhat* and set the smaller barks of the deities on an elevated dais. Maatkare and Mekheperre stood at the prow of their own respective and resplendently gilded vessels, hers leading and his following the *neters* along the Canal of Amun Pure and Cool to the River. Eight barges rowed in their wake occupied by priests wafting incense over the crowds lining the banks. Behind the priests followed high-ranking officials—all of them bearing offerings carried by their attendants—musicians, dancers, chefs and acrobats. On earth men and women were joyfully reaping fields of wheat and barley while in the Dwat Osiris harvested the souls of the dead as they rose from the seeds of their mummies to live again. The people of Waset, both rich and poor, had dressed in their very best clothes and jewels to visit their deceased relatives in the west. To see and experience the Beautiful Festival of the Valley was to believe the living were going to their Ka for a day as small skiffs, larger boats and lavish pleasure barges crossed in droves from the east to the west bank of the River, all of them brimming with baskets and jars filled with offerings of food and flowers, wine and beer.

Excited voices and happy laughter traveled with almost supernatural clarity through that still, cool morning in the month of Pachons. Everyone was looking forward to spending merry hours with loved ones in the offering chapels of their tombs. For two days, justified souls would fly down from heaven to partake of the feasts prepared for them by their relatives. Even those Ba-birds whose tombs were only holes in the earth would perch on whatever shrine had been erected in their honor, no matter how small and humble. Paintings and inscriptions were desirable but not truly necessary. The hearts in which love burned were as clearly visible to the dead as fires lit after sunset were to the eyes of those who still lived on earth.

Hatshepsut's heart was so full it was difficult for her to take a deep breath. So many people she loved were waiting for her on the other side of the River in her Mansion of Million of Years—her father and her mother, her long dead baby sister Neferubity, her beloved daughter, Princess Neferure, and Senmut. On that special day her co-ruler's aura of impatience did not bother her. Thtumose had enjoyed his first military triumph in the north, capturing an important city of the Retenu riding in battle beside the new Army Commander, Djehuty, proving Pharaoh was the true head of Kemet's military. Meritre had written to her that ever since his victory Thutmose had been difficult to live with, preferring the flattering obeisance of foreign concubines to the discerning remarks of his Great Royal Wife, who never hesitated to let him know when his behavior annoyed her. Satioh was finally with child and the king paid more attention to her than to Meritre, who had, however accompanied him to Waset. She was there to attend the Beautiful Festival of the Valley as well as to receive the staff of God's Wife awarded to her by Maatkare and the High Priest of Amun. Her duties as God's Hand would oblige Meritre to divide her time equally between the north and the south. When Menkheperre looked at Meritre now his expression revealed only a guarded possessiveness.

Seshen, Hatshepsut sensed, was especially eager to see her mistress again, perhaps to apologize for surrendering to her fears and killing herself when she should have known better. She was now confident that her attendant had been mercifully received by Isis and Nepthys. The transcendently sweet sisters of Osiris would have washed Seshen clean of all her crippling doubts in the enchanted waters of their womb, through which she was born into a purer world whose beauty was limited only by that of her heart. Duauneheh and Dhout would also be there, along with Satepihu—the Headman of Tjeny who had so passionately supported her—it did not matter that his tomb was located farther north in Abedju. That morning when she woke, in the darkness behind her closed eyelids, she had seen Inet, no longer old and mindless but smiling happily at her, so proud of her statue, which the little girl she had nursed and who now ruled as Pharaoh had honored with a place in her Million Years Mansion. The mummy of Sitre—who had lovingly enfolded Maatkre in swaddling cloths against the chill of darkness when she was a helpless infant—

would lie comfortingly close to hers wrapped in linen bandages to ward off the cold of eternity, her personality held together by amulets and preserved by love's boundless magic. Akheperenre would also undoubtedly be pleased by the prominent place his sister had accorded him in *Djser-Djseru*, the monument he had begun and that she had transformed.

Also in her thoughts on that clear morning were Ineni and his physical opposite, Akheperseneb, free from the weighty duties of the viziership, his body now as light as the birds he had admired through the windows of the Seal Room. Senimen—the little head of Neferure blooming from his lap where they were both carved into the rock above the entrance to his tomb—always wore the same affectionate smile whenever she remembered him, an expression very different from Amenmose's, whose contagious grin she had never seen duplicated on another human face. She had devoted a chapel to her beloved brother in the sun court of her temple. Kanefer, who had carried her everywhere for years, Neferkhaut and Neshi, her efficient secretaries, Patehuti, the High Priest of Thoth who had taught her so much, and Meri, God's Wife who had told her it was a foolish heart that feared death—they all still lived inside her and were honored guests invited to the banquet she was hosting in *Djser-Djseru*. Ever since the day Seni taught her to write the hieroglyph that spelled *love* she had opened her feelings to so many people, all of whom had nourished her life with theirs and made it possible for her heart to grow so large it contained both the terrestrial and celestial words. On that glorious morning, the tireless pulse of duality that accompanies the endless feast of Divine forces becoming incarnate was echoed by drummers beating a rhythm for the temple dancers.

Userhat-Amun reached the canal on the west bank that flowed straight to the Mansion of Maatkare United with Life erected where the fertile land ended and the desert began. She disembarked and walked before the gods as Menkheperre strode behind them. The way was opened by the First and Second Prophets of Amun, who were closely followed by two rows of eight priests each carrying standards crowned by the deities of *Ipet Sut*—the forces commanded by the Hidden One whose face is the solar disc, His body formed by the head and feet of north and south and the arms and hands of east and west. The procession followed a straight path to the upper terrace of her valley temple, where the barks of the *neters* temporarily rested. The walls were brightly painted with *ankh* signs interspersed with cobras, their heads crowned by solar discs and *shen* rings of eternity growing from their chests. Alongside Wadjet, the vulture Nekhbet flew over another *shen* ring, her left wing stretching straight in the direction of the cosmic serpents while her right wing pointed down toward earth. Senmut was not physically present but Hatshepsut distinctly sensed him for she was surrounded by the special way he had devised to spell her throne name *Maatkare*. The Goddess dominated the temple resplendently decorated with the all the colors of The First Occasion. The water of life was offered to Amun-Re,

Mut, Khonsu and Hathor as plumes of incense ascended to heaven through an opening in the ceiling, uniting all those present with their true incorruptible natures as God entered their bodies through their noses, the physical seat of eternal life.

Headed by Maatkare dressed as Hathor in gilded mist-linen and the full vulture crown—her gold collar, bracelets and anklets set with turquoise reflecting the sun and sky—the procession flowed slowly out of the lovely temple and continued along a broad stone causeway lined with sandstone statues of the Female Falcon portrayed as a peacefully seated lion. Half way between the Mansion of Maatkare United with Life and *Djser-Djseru* another bark shrine offered rest and refreshment. Then at last, they arrived at the great gateway in the enclosure wall. The doors had already been opened and Hatshepsut's heart beat faster when she beheld the throngs of people lined up on the first and second terraces of her Million Years Mansion, all of them joyfully waiting to greet Amun-Re and his bodily sons. The avenue of lions crowned by her smiling face continued leading the way into a garden miraculously blooming in the desert. At the base of the first ramp, an abundant variety of trees planted in buried pots grew as if by magic from the lifeless sand around two T-shaped pools filled with floating lotus flowers. Directly west across the expansive courtyard, the theme of duality and the realm of the senses it engenders was repeated in the double row of columns supporting the ceiling of the lower portico. The outermost row was composed of pillars with square exteriors and circular interiors—the One that becomes the world and its four cardinal directions. The second row consisted of sixteen-sided columns. The bright colors of the falcon god Horus—wearing the double crown and perched on the hieroglyph for *palace*—stood out with striking clarity against the white limestone pillars, which were flanked on both the north and south ends by two colossal statues of Maatkare as Osiris, the embodiment of eternal Divine kingship.

Even though the procession immediately began ascending from the physical world toward the creative realm of the Ka, Hatshepsut's smile deepened as she mentally toured the shadowy space of the first portico. She often visited her Mansion of Millions of Years. She loved the way sunlight shone in spear-like rays between the columns, the ever moving illumination it provided stabilized by lamplight to reveal all the paintings decorating walls formed directly from the mountain. On the lower level of the southernmost wall, the Lord of the South, Dedwen, offered all its lands and towns to Pharaoh as she strode forward in the direction of victory to receive a rope attached to eggs from which hatched Kushite heads. On the back wall the birth and transport of Maatkare's first two Monuments of Heh was portrayed. The vessels carrying them traveled north along the portico to Waset, where the king received and offered them to Amun-Re. On the second side wall, the northern enemies of Kemet were trampled by a lion with Pharaoh's head. The east wall was devoted to pleasurable scenes of fishing and fowling and offering the first calves of the year to the *neters*. The paintings of the lower terrace culminated with the celebration of Maatkare's jubilee and her ritual run before Amun-Re in which she grasped the crook and flail of kingship and was urged on by Merit—the goddess of Number manifesting as music—who cried, "Come and bring! Come and bring!" order to chaos, courage to fear, wisdom to ignorance, fulfillment to hunger.

Hatshepsut blinked away tears made blinding by Khepri gradually transforming into Re as the procession—headed by two of the men dearest to her who still lived, Hapuseneb and Puyemre—climbed the steps carved into the center of the ramp. The sides of the balustrades were molded in the form of seated lions— the Guardians of the Gate of the Horizon that opened at the dawn of time and the birth of the world as *yesterday* and *tomorrow*. Before each lion, an *ankh* sign with human arms and hands held up a *shenu* ring containing her throne name *Maatkare*. At the head of the ramp, on top of the newel posts, sat two small but vividly painted lions crowned with her smiling face.

There to greet them when they reached the second terrace were eight colossal statues of the Female Falcon—two rows of four facing each other and kneeling with two small circular jars held in both her hands where they rested on her thighs. Her delicate features were framed by the *nemes* headdress, the royal beard thrust from her chin and it was not necessary to read the inscriptions on the bases to realize Pharaoh was offering Maat to Amun as he passed. The exercise of crouching—during which all her weight rested temporarily on her knees and toes—had been rendered permanent in stone. Eternity and the moments composing it had been perfectly balanced by sculptors who, by making her feet and legs larger and longer than they really were, had incorporated the vital element of growth into the visual equation.

Two rows of square pillars lined the westernmost end of the second terrace, twenty-two in total, eleven on each side. Only their upper portions were visible behind all the officials and their wives assembled there, including the Royal Ornament Amenhotep, who looked shockingly fat and old. The highly privileged spectators had undoubtedly spent the time they waited for the procession to arrive admiring the splendid inscriptions gracing the central portico. On nearly all four surfaces of the pillars supporting it, Maatkare was embraced by Amun. Only on every fourth column was Menkheperre shown before the god. Occupying the entire southern wall, her expedition to Punt was recorded in splendid detail. Just as her five ships had traveled to God's Land so did the vessel of her flesh and blood, captained by the five senses, journey from the supreme realm of the Ka for the sole purpose of experiencing the sensual pleasures made possible by God's Hand—Hathor, the Lady of Punt.

The northern walls of the covered central portico were the most meaningful to Hatshepsut because there her birth was depicted in a traditional ancient format known as *The Legend of the Divine Descent*. It all began with Amun assembling the gods and announcing His intention to engender a bodily son. God commanded Thoth to search the world for a woman worthy to be the mother of the

Supreme Being who would rule both heaven and earth. The ibis-headed deity needed to look no farther than the royal palace in Waset, to which he promptly led Amun-Re. Woken by his Divine scent, Queen Ahmose, the beautiful wife of Pharaoh Akheperkare, joyfully welcomed God and invited him to sit beside her. The bed on which they faced each other, their legs entwined, was drawn in the shape of the *sky* hieroglyph, studded with stars and supported by the potentiality of the Ka—the mysterious muscle of Divine creativity represented by two goddesses in whose hands the feet of the couple gently rested. The *hemusets* themselves perched on a lion-head couch representing the celestial womb of Mother Nut. Wearing the full vulture crown reflecting Amun-Min's double plumes, the queen inhaled Life from the *ankh* He raised to her face. A *tiet* knot hanging from a belt covered His sex as she cupped His elbow in her left hand and touched the fingers of her right hand to His in the time honored code for sexual intercourse.

Consummation of their union occurred when Amun-Re gave his heart to Queen Ahmose and flooded the palace with a uniquely Divine fragrance as Hatshepsut was conceived. The Hidden One commanded Khnum to fashion the child's Ka and body on his cosmic wheel. The two figures appeared standing side-by-side on a table while Heqet—the goddess of sensual abundance and Millions of Years—offered them both the *ankh* of life. The Lord of Time and Master of Measure, Thoth once again appeared to the queen and informed her that the baby was ready to enter the world. Khnum and Heqet led Ahmose to a room where she gave birth seated on a throne before a lion-head couch. Beneath the couch knelt a plethora of *neters* all performing the gesture of praise and rejoicing. The hawk-headed gods representing the North and the people of Pe, and those with jackal-heads standing in for the citizens of Nekheb in the South, expressed both the joy of the Two Lands and the union of heaven and earth when Hatshepsut-Maatkare was born. The Mistresses of the House, Isis and Nepthys, holding *ankh* signs in both hands, faced the queen in the next register where she sat with the child on her lap before a midwife and women bearing offerings. Beneath them knelt two *Heh* figures of eternity. Also present in the House of Purification were Sobek and Khnum, Bes and Tawaret, agents of transformation flanked by two *was* scepters of dominion and power between which stood the *sa* "protection" hieroglyph. Amun then entered the room to see and welcome his bodily son, who was offered to him by Hathor. He kissed and embraced His daughter who he loves and blessed her.

As the story unfolded, Hatshepsut's body and Ka were nursed to life, health and strength by God's Hand who took the form of two women with cow's heads crowned by bovine horns and discs representing the sun and the moon. The bed on which the goddesses sat—its ends carved with double lion heads—was supported by *tiet* knots, The Blood of Isis, standing on the *sky* hieroglyph, beneath which two celestial cows were depicted. The king's Ka was further nourished by three rows of male and female *neters*—the forces of manifestation employed by the Ka to fashion the physical body through which its abilities inscrutably grow. The child was presented by two gods to three mummified deities who, by the power of three times three, actually represented nine divinities and incorporated the numbers "one" through "eight" into the tale of manifestation. The development of her entity established, Thoth brought Hatshepsut and her Ka before Amun-Re, where she was given her name, invested with her Divine status and royal titles and crowned King of Upper and Lower Kemet, ruler of heaven and earth united in her. Four women—the number expressive of completion—held Maatkare and her Ka before Seshat and the wife of Thoth recorded how long her earthly life and reign would last.

The northernmost end of the central terrace was devoted to Anubis, Heir to the Throne of the godlike capacities nascent in every soul—the jackal-headed *neter* who leads the deceased by the hand through the frightening transformations of the Dwat. In Anubis' chapel, the powers of Osiris, and of the hawk-headed Sokar, a husband of the bloody Sekhmet, also played a vital part. A staircase ascended to an offering court supported by twelve columns. In the center of the western wall more steps led up into the innermost sanctuaries—three rooms, each narrower than the last, opening off at right angles so it was impossible to see from one into the other. In them were recorded the stages of transformation, beginning and ending in the smallest innermost shrine—the Divine seed—then moving on to the sensual realm and the spellbinding space of the Dwat. All the rooms were connected even while appearing separate. The outermost chamber was populated by the Ancestors, those beings who had perfected themselves and could now shed their flesh and slip it back on at will, a supreme faculty symbolized by the animal skin hanging from a golden pole before Anubis. In the second room the jackal-head *neter* was joined beneath the starry ceiling by Imentet—an aspect of the Goddess personifying the western Necropolis—and by Hathor, Osiris, Sokar and Ptah. In the innermost sanctuary, Hatehepsut-Maatkare stood alone making her own private offerings to Anubis, the Opener of the Way.

The southernmost end of the central portico was dominated by the Chapel of Hathor in which the female heads crowning the pillars faced both east and west to greet the sun as Khepri in the morning, and to bid him farewell in his from of Atum in the evening. More Hathor heads mounted on tall standards faced north and welcomed Amun-Re into her house as he was born through the gateway of incarnation enclosed in the golden womb of His shrine resting on a bark shaped like the crescent-moon. Crowning the north-facing heads of the Goddess were colossal stone sistrums carved with figures of Maatkare gripping the crook and flail and performing the ritual run of the *heb-sed* in the direction of Hathor's sanctuary. Inside the first offering room, directly to the right of the entrance, the celestial cow approached King Maatkare on her throne and licked her hand in an affectionate gesture unique to *Djser-Djseru*. The traditional order had been reversed—instead of Pharaoh proceeding deeper into the chapel, the *neter* who walked out toward her. Above the entrance to the small outer sanctuary were inscribed the words:

The doorway of Maatkare who is imbued with the vitality of Hathor, the supreme one of Waset.[97]

On both walls, Hathor in her bovine form stood on the *Per-Wer* coronation shrine and miniature figures of Hatshepsut knelt beneath them actively imbibing her Divine milk. Another image of Maatkare stood directly in front of Hathor, so that the large *menit* necklace hanging from the animal's neck embraced her human form. Both walls were lined with rows of cobras crowned by horns and held up by Ka arms—the unique hieroglyphs composed by Senmut spelling *Maat is the Ka of* Re, her throne name. In a panel to the left of the shrine was a monkey named *Flesh* with two baboons seated above him. This reference to sexuality and the forces of attraction was occupied by a seated lion facing east above which perched a falcon—symbols of time and space and the spiritual consciousness that transcends them. Kneeling out of sight behind the open door of the sanctuary was Senmut, smiling and offering praise. How much she missed him was intolerable and yet she somehow continued to exist, just another miracle to add to her ever-growing list. Inscribed alongside the entrance to the innermost sanctuary were the words:

The doorway of Maatkare, enduring of attraction in the temple of Hathor.[98]

Surrounded by offerings of life, Hathor's bark shrine was left resting in her chapel as the procession, flanked by onlookers, made its way back to the base of the second ramp. The balustrades leading up to the uppermost terrace were carved in the form of cobras, their flaring hoods facing east and their bodies and tails flowing all the way up into the celestial realm of the west. Perched on the heads of the serpents was the falcon god Horus clutching in his talons the hieroglyph for "eternity."

Only the *neters*, Pharaoh, priests and favored officials ascended the second and final ramp toward the awe-inspiring facade of twenty-four statues of King Maatkare rendered as Osiris. In addition to the traditional crook and flail she also held an *ankh* and a *was* scepter against her chest. Her skin was painted red like a man's and her smile transcended the characteristics of either sex as she guarded the entrance to heaven. Concealed behind a massive granite central gateway, three groups of sanctuaries spread out from the outermost courtyard into the mountain itself. As the procession approached, a trumpet sounded from within the summit of the temple and the gates of the uppermost terrace were opened to admit clouds of incense ritually uniting it with the second and first levels. For a few moments, Hatshepsut ceased to be aware of her mortal body as she was met by twelve invulnerably strong representations of her Ka, the mediator between heaven and earth. Kneeling and offering *nemset* vessels, her statues all wore the *khat* headdress proclaiming her commander of the Two Lands and General of Maat. On that day, it was easy to believe the moments after her death would feel even more sublime and effortless as she ascended the magical steps between dimensions.

The procession followed the east-west transit of the sun as it neared its destination in the heart of the mountain—the western end of the large open court surrounded by two rows of sixteen-sided columns decorated with falcons sitting on *serekhs* and wearing the double crown of Kemet. Two colossal striding statues of Pharaoh Maatkare flanked the portal leading into the central sanctuary. The entrance to Amun's chapel divided the west wall into two parts, the façades of both distinguished by five tall recesses housing statues of the King as Osiris. Between them were carved four smaller but deeper niches in which, accompanied by select *neters*, Maatkare was shown facing both north and south in the direction of God's sanctuary. The modest-sized statues of herself and of her family housed in the recesses, and the rituals depicted on the walls around them, were not visible for the double-winged doors were closed. And behind them all, she knew, knelt Senmut.

In the first and most spacious room of his rock-hewn chapel, God's bark was gently set to rest on a pedestal erected in its center beneath a dark-blue vaulted roof covered with golden stars. On both the eastern and western walls— beneath paintings watched over by winged solar discs in which the two kings made offerings to Amun-Re—a small square window was carved that twice a year admitted the rays of the sun and marked the beginning and end of the season of inundation. On a single day every twelve months a shaft of light penetrated all the way to the sanctuary's innermost chamber to illuminate the statues of Amun-Re and Hatshepsut-Maatkare seated beside each other forever.

With the temple's Divine heart safely residing in His chapel, the procession followed the royal north-south axis through the central court where the walls all bloomed with festival scenes. The painted figures became the reflections of the people walking alongside them, who magically transcended their mortal flesh as it was transformed into imperishable colors and imbued with the strength of the stone serving to preserve all their pleasures and joys. The inscriptions and images decorating the walls were an exquisitely deliberate effort to forge a vital creative connection between different states of being. At both the north and south ends of the westernmost wall, intimate sanctuaries dedicated to Amun-Re served as storage spaces for the cult items required to worship Him, and for all the splendid offerings He received.

The northern corner of the upper terrace—where Neferure stood beside her mother offering to the bark of Amun-Re—was dominated by the Sun Court, a sanctuary open to the sky and all the beauty and power of Re. The great altar, modeled after those in the temple of Iuno, was reached by a flight of steps. An opening in the northern wall led into a small chapel of Anubis dedicated to members of Hatshepsut's family.

Directly opposite the Sun Court, at the southernmost end of *Djser-Djseru*, the Ka's of two of Amun-Re's bodily sons were revered in the form of Hatshepsut-Maatkare and her father, Thutmose-Akheperkare, their separate sanctuaries accessed by a single vestibule supported by three columns. The ceiling of her offering chapel was brightly painted with golden stars and the twelve hours of the day and night assumed the forms of beautiful goddesses. On the east wall, to either side of the entrance, were scenes of cattle being butchered around piles of earthly treasures. The offerings were carried by rows of painted priests and noblemen walking deeper into the elegantly slender room straight toward the female figure enthroned before the false doors of red *biat* that dominated the western wall. On the walls around her smiling limestone statue, enthroned before the false door, Maatkare was shown sitting before a table piled high with loaves of bread as priests performed the rites that would sustain and nourish her Ka perpetually.

Present in the flesh that day, Hatshepsut laid a floral bouquet at the base of her stone feet. In the light cast by dozens of oil lamps, her incorruptible stone self shone with all the magic of her Ka. Smiling back at herself, she ignored the silent complaint of her knees as she regained her feet and turned away reluctantly. She could feel it in her body that she would soon be ready to remain there and become one with her Ka who had fashioned the beautiful face and figure so skillfully captured and immortalized in imperishable stone by servants of Ptah. Her Ka was powerful indeed, a master craftsman commanding all the forces of incarnation. There were those who Khnum had only recently fashioned on his wheel whose Ka's were as children still learning and growing, but Hatshepsut-Maatkare had fully grasped who she was—the bodily son and daughter of Amun-Re.

That evening she shared a table with the High Priest of Amun on the lower terrace of her Million Years Mansion. His ailing wife had returned to the spacious house they still shared on the other side of the River. They sat beside one of her pools beneath a sycamore tree. As the sun set behind *Djser-Djseru*, fires came to life around them and for as far as they could see all across the hills of the Necropolis. Families were spending two days and nights with their loved ones, feasting and drinking, playing music and singing, dancing and embracing each other beneath the cover of darkness. Newborn flames passionately savored the wooden sticks and cakes of dung sustaining the warmth and light emanating from the spirit of Fire, of which they were all a part and to which they would all return.

"Our mortal bodies are only a mysterious fuel," she mused out loud gazing in the direction of Senmut's second tomb and its empty burial chamber. The quarry was dark but beyond it, to the south, the prestigious cliff where he had excavated his offering chapel was illuminated by fires that were far enough away to resemble fireflies. She sighed. "It is as though heaven has fallen to earth tonight."

"It has." Hapuseneb held her eyes over the food resting between them. Lately she could feel her Ka beginning to abandon the mysterious roads of her digestion as it prepared to leave the physical house it had so much enjoyed living in.

Sitting on the opposite edge of the pool, Puyemre caught her eye and grinned at her. She could sense her childhood friend was far from finished with life even though she knew that beneath his wig his hair was entirely white.

"I would like to walk," she said. "Will you accompany me, Hapsueneb?"

He rose and offered her his hand. "Of course."

"All this music and dancing and laughing is making me sad because it celebrates the senses I will soon be slipping off like bracelets and anklets. The older and more wrinkled it gets, the more I am convinced my skin is merely a garment it will give me great pleasure to shed as I prepare to dive back into the magically refreshing depths of the Primordial Waters."

"That is a lovely image, especially because it involves you stripping."

She laughed.

Walking side by side, they leisurely began climbing the steps of the first ramp. Torches illuminated the crouching figures of lions crowned by her benevolent human face. No one followed them.

"However," he went on quietly, "your flesh is not *merely* a garment. Your Ka and your body are inextricably bound together through the supreme gesture of creation. Simply because you are preparing to leave physical life does not mean you should feel less serious and passionate about it than when you were younger."

As they ascended the final ramp, the sound of conversation, laughter and music wafted more gently up behind them. *This is what growing old is like* she thought contentedly. Soon only ghostly ripples of sound ascended like smoke from the fires below into the intense silence of a sky burning with more stars than she could ever count. Their endless abundance never failed to swell her heart with joy.

Torches and lamps burned everywhere in *Djser-Djseru* while God and His Hand were in residence there. Hatshepsut found her Osiride statues more inspiring by sunlight. Seeing their bases washed by darkness and their faces masked by shadows, she suffered an acute feeling of foreboding. Suddenly, she felt that her monuments were not as invulnerable as she believed. Uneasily she dismissed the thought. Nothing, she quickly managed to convince herself, would ever happen to her beautiful Mansion, on which she would sail through the Dwat like Re on her bark across the horizon of Millions of Years. During that time, her Ka would fashion and inhabit as many bodies as there were images of herself decorating its walls and lining its terraces, courtyards and chapels.

The silence at the summit of *Djser-Djseru* was mysteriously strummed and deepened by the forest of pillars, as if they were the strings of an instrument large enough for Mother Nut to play from heaven. They headed toward a small room opening off the southeast wall and dominated by a large window. Between her Osiris statues, the fires flickering below them on the bottom terrace felt strangely more distant than the stars. Seating themselves on gilded chairs, they stared out in the direction of *Ipset-Sut*, the House of Amun.

She whispered, "I feel as if we are still young and living on the other side of the River and that only here in the west have we grown old, Hapuseneb. I can almost believe that in the morning, when we return to Waset, all of life will still lay before us."

"All of life *does* still lie before us, Hatshepsut-Maatkare, and it always will."

She heard quiet footsteps behind them and Senenu's respectfully hushed voice said, "Is there anything you desire, Majesty?"

"I require no offerings as yet, Senenu," she replied, and then added with a smile, "Wait until I am dead."

When the new day was come, Maatkare and Menkheperre each ceremoniously extinguished a torch in a basin of milk. They stood in the Sun Court as the solar disc rose in the east between her two Monuments of Heh, their rays illuminating the town of the living and the cities of the dead across the River and filling the hearts of all those awaiting the day's rebirth with awe and hope.

On the second morning of the festival, the double doors at the western end of Maatkare's Mansion of Millions of Years were flung open and Amun-Re was carried forth from the Divine womb of His chapel to manifest again in the world.

42

True of Voice

Queen Satioh gave birth to a son she named Amenemhet.

Maatkare attended the celebrations in Mennefer. Upon her return to Waset, she commanded that the house of Amun-Re in the western desert—*Djser-set*, Holy of Place, where the body of Atum-Amun was believed to rest—be torn down and replaced with a much larger temple made entirely of stone. The earlier structure was too small and corruptible. When, every ten days, Amun-Re journeyed from *Ipet Sut* in the east to *Djser-set* in the west, he could see how his bodily son and daughter never stopped striving to beautify and improve the world He had created and sustained. Confined by her own aging flesh, it made Hatshepsut feel better to tear down old and inferior structures and to oversee the creative work of replacing them with imperishable buildings. The men and women she had loved during her long life would live forever in the paintings decorating her Mansions of Millions of Years. The gods and goddesses, offering bearers and priests carved on the walls were modeled after real people. She also began overseeing the production of *ushabtis*, made from *nebes* wood, for her tomb—small statues inscribed with her name all representing the countless Ba-birds and lifetimes commanded by her Ka currently integrated into Hatshepsut-Maatkare.[99]

Late one afternoon, Antef appeared in her Pleasure House where she was relaxing alone with Nafre. She had sent all her other attendants away for they were still too young to understand that, later in life, quiet introspection and conversation flowing on a gentle river of wine constituted life's greatest pleasure.

"My lady," Antef bowed formally, "the First Prophet of Amun desires to see you."

She was astonished Hapuseneb had asked to be formally announced into her presence. At once, she dismissed Nafre and told her herald to admit the High Priest. As always, she was exquisitely attired in mist-linen, but over her form-fitting tunics she now also wore long-sleeved robes tied closed in front by a red sash. Incorruptible gemstones set in gold enhanced the slenderness of her wrists and ankles and a fresh floral collar, worn beneath a shoulder-length wig, helped imbue her oiled and scented skin with a luminous aura of youth. However, whenever she looked, unsmiling, into a mirror she saw that her eyes revealed all the years she had lived. Her golden-brown irises were the same as always but all the grief she had suffered when, one after the other, loved ones and friends went to their Ka was visible in the dark half moons beneath her eyes, and in the fine lines at their edges which evoked the desert dunes beneath which they were all buried. And yet whenever she smiled—as she did watching Hapuseneb stride down the garden path toward her—she glimpsed again the lovely girl she had been and the beautiful woman she had become who, like a flower long past its bloom, was slowly drooping on the stem of her spine.

The High Priest walked lightly up the steps of the pavilion and sank to one knee before her. He grasped both her hands and kissed the back of each one two times.

"My lord," she said, "even though the sun is setting my garden appears more luminous and beautiful to me now that you are in it."

Without rising, and continuing to hold her cool hands in his much warmer ones, he gazed into her eyes and said gently, "I have come to say good bye."

"But you have only just returned to Waset," she protested in dismay.

"I am not bound for any city or town in the Two Lands," he explained.

"What do you mean?" She refused to acknowledge the meaning of the light shining in his dark eyes, which was akin to excitement yet somehow steadier and deeper.

"I will see you again very soon, Maatkare."

"But where are you going?" she insisted, absolutely refusing to understand him.

"I have said what I came to." Rising, he pulled her up out of the chair so she stood before him. He looked down at her face for a moment, then he pressed her body urgently against his and kissed her, thrusting his tongue between her lips and exploring her mouth as though he had never tasted it before. He released her just as abruptly and took three steps back. "I love you, Hatshepsut. *Never* forget that."

He turned, descended the steps and walked purposefully back the way he had come. Only after he had disappeared behind a sycamore tree, where the path turned toward the west, did she collapse back into her chair. She sat there unseeing until Nafre appeared a timeless while later carrying a lamp. Above the flame her features looked distortedly sinister. She said, "My lady? Is everything all right? It is getting cold out. You should come inside. Wadjrenput is dying to serve you the goose he prepared with a special new sauce."

"I am not hungry, Nafre. I fear the goose of my Ka has just laid the great egg of death and rebirth in the nest of my flesh and bones."

Her attendant did not ask what she meant but simply set the lamp down and knelt at her feet. "My lady, I have loved you more than any other person and have sworn to serve you always. When you rest from life, then will I also. Until then, however, I will drag my body behind me with both hands if I have to!"

She smiled sadly down at her attendant. "And I love you, my friend and sister. Stay with me tonight, please. I do not wish to sleep alone."

Early the next morning, a delegation of priests from *Ipet Sut*, headed by the Second Prophet of Amun and accompanied by Ibenre, requested an audience with Maatkare. They were immediately ushered into her presence by Antef, who she had told to expect them.

"Do not speak," she commanded, "for I know what you are going to say. The High Priest of Amun, Hapuseneb, has gone to his Ka."

Puyemre inclined his head as the other priests glanced at each other with varying degrees of surprise and respect.

"I will not ask you how it happened for I feel I know that as well. He opened the door to the Dwat himself and crossed the threshold between the worlds willingly and peacefully."

"As far as I can tell," Ibenre said, "that is exactly what happened, Majesty."

Hatshepsut felt as though Hapuseneb had failed, perhaps deliberately, to completely close the door between the worlds when he left and that her right foot was firmly wedged in the opening—her emotions went blessedly numb as she prepared to follow him. He had promised they would see each other again very soon and he had always kept his promises. She hoped there would not be enough time for her to visit the new Temple of Satis—where she had passed through the skin in the Chamber of the Other Word—which was currently being erected over the old one as her private tribute to the High Priest, whose beloved face was the first thing she had seen when he ripped open the linen bandages over her eyes on that morning she would never forget. She had somehow lived through his funeral by recalling countless times how he had laughed when she asked him if it was morning already, and then carried her back out into the light cradled in his arms. Following his Master of Life into the tomb, she had stood there remembering how he had thanked her for blessing it with her laughter. Menkheperre had been present and she did not doubt that his hawk-like gaze made critical note of the fact that in his eternal home the High Priest of Amun-Re, the Governor of the South, offered life and praise exclusively to Maatkare, Hatshepsut, United with Amun, even though he had also served three other kings.

She had believed Hapuseneb's burial would be impossible to endure but the days, weeks and months that followed it proved much worse for now she had nothing either to dread or to look forward to except her own death. She forced herself to travel north and visit the fledgling falcon, Amenemhet, a handsome but distressingly slow-witted little boy. She dearly hoped Meritre would give birth to a son more worthy of the double crown. While she was in Mennefer, the winds of Seth attacked the city more viciously than anyone could remember. She took a perverse pleasure in the discomfort, which could not compare to the hot sorrow pressing like a suffocating layer of sand against her heart and making it impossible for her to breathe the sweet air of joy and contentment ever again. Every sandstorm reminded her of that glorious afternoon when Hapusuneb pulled her into the shelter of Hathor's sanctuary. Reliving those intensely pleasurable moments was more painful than sand stinging her eyes and filling her mouth. She did not want to look back anymore. She wanted to look only forward to the instant when her Ba at last escaped the cage of her skeleton and flew straight to the High Priest's tomb in search of him. Even if she did not find him there she would not give up hope for it simply meant he was waiting for her in the shining nest of *Djser-Djseru.*

It was a relief to return to Waset, where almost everyone she loved was buried on the other side of the River she was so impatient to cross herself. Her new bark shrine, The Place of the Heart of Amun, was nearing completion and she visited it almost daily where it had taken root in the heart of *Ipet Sut* in front of the Palace of Maat. The glorious events of her life were all recorded there:

His Majesty Amun entered into the front of the palace of "I Shall not be Far from Him" in the Estate of Amun, having laid firm hands on His egg, Hatshepsut, having planned that she should take possession of the Two Lands, and having promoted her to the dais of the Unique Lord so she would be content as Ruler of Joy. He assigned her position on the great throne, He caused her to occupy the dais, she having been reared as a Horus, Lord of the Two Lands, in the presence of all.[100]

Nehesj, The Overseer of the Seal, rested from life and was replaced by his long time assistant. Maatkare appointed Ty even though, in most other affairs of state, she now deferred to Menkheperre's judgment. On temple reliefs, the young king now appeared striding forward ahead of the Female Falcon. When her Royal Butler, Amenhotep—who had seen serving as Steward of Amun since the death of Senmut—abruptly suffered a seizure he never recovered from, Hatshepsut mourned him like her own brother. A more considerate, respectful, gentle and pious soul she had never met and his distressingly violent demise upset her so much it made her ill. A fever that began as a strange feeling of lightheadedness intensified until she felt her insides were burning and returning to the Divine fire that forged them. The afternoon before she became sick— when she was swimming in her pool and surfaced from the weightless depths filled with writhing serpents of light—she had glimpsed Neferure's smiling face reflected in the mirror of the solar disc shimmering on the surface of the water. In that instant she had known the time would soon come for her to fly back up to the sky.

Lying on her bed, tended day and night by Nafre and Ibenre, it soon became impossible for her to distinguish the faces of people who were actually in the room from those populating her increasingly vivid dreams—dreams the bark of her awareness could not reasonably navigate as they rushed through her like the River's wildest waters.

"Nafre?" she whispered when sleep abruptly abandoned her on the painfully inhospitable shore of her waking consciousness. "It is so hot in here! Please open the screens and let in the cool north wind. I do not care if a cobra slips in through the window. I would welcome Wadjet and ask her to be as kind to me as she was to Nefi."

"The flies are terrible today, my lady," her attendant protested gently. "It is better to keep the screens in place."

She did not have the strength to protest. Already she was drifting off to sleep again feeling as though she was floating in mid air. She could not feel the bed beneath her and silently she thanked her physician. The poppy juice he had given her was helping her forget she still had a body even though its fleshly bark was the one on which she sailed along the mysterious canals of dreams all flowing straight into the dark river of the Dwat, which had no beginning or end. Then suddenly she found herself trapped in a gauntlet of priests all chanting "Horus-Anubis, Horus-Anubis, Horus-Anubis…"

She woke abruptly feeling as though she had never been ill at all. Her room was flooded with sunlight so intense it blurred the edges of its colorful furnishings.

"Nafre?" Her voice sounded young and healthy. "What day is it?"

"It is the tenth day of the sixth month," a man standing at the foot of her bed replied. "Twenty-one years and nine months since I placed the double crown on your head."

"Hapuseneb!" Her heart broke with joy and her Ba-bird flew out of her mouth.

Ignoring her body lying on the bed resting from life, Maatkare soared out a window and flew across the River to the garden planted on the earthly level of her Mansion of Millions of Years. The High Priest of Amun stood at the top of the final ramp. Also visible were Senmut and Neferure, their three figures heading a procession of people she loved all waiting to greet her.

Afterward

Approximately twenty years after her death, Hatshepsut's nephew, Thutmose III, set about systematically, but very selectively, erasing her name and images from her monuments. Her "representations as queen were never touched; the attacks were directed solely at her kingly representations."[101] In most instances, Thutmose replaced Maatkare's name with that of his father or grandfather, his direct male ancestors. However, the statues in her Mansion of Millions of Years, now called Deir el-Bahri, were completely destroyed and thrown into a pit that in the end mysteriously served to protect them. Centuries later they were discovered and lovingly reassembled. Perhaps these statues were simply too unique to be re-inscribed for someone else.

The original theory that Thutmose III hated his aunt has essentially been ruled out. I personally agree with the Egyptologists who believe "the obliteration of Hatshepsut's kingship may thus be linked with the determination to eradicate the possibility of another powerful female ever inserting herself, as the personification of Horus on earth, into the long line of Egyptian male kings."[102] After Thutmose III's death, the title of God's Wife of Amun, created for his wife by Hatshepsut's grandfather, fell into disuse, for it was "this powerful economic and political office that may initially have given her (Hatshepsut) special leverage to act in the name of Thutmose III during the years of his minority."[103] But it was Hatshepsut herself who took profound advantage of her position like no other queen before or after her.

Regarding Hatshepsut's so-called mummy, the Egyptian government has refused to disclose the full results of the DNA analysis done on the body identified as Hatshepsut in a 2007 television special. "So far, the science shown in the Discovery Channel's 'Secrets of Egypt's Lost Queen' has not been published in a reputable peer-reviewed scientific journal—the gold standard of scientific research worldwide."[104] Zahi Hawass, Egypt's Chief of Antiquities, "has never disclosed full results of the examinations, sometimes on grounds of national security. Though Zawass has never explained the reasons for this, apparently there is concern the tests could cast doubt on the Egyptian lineage of the mummies."[105]

Much of the evidence for Mr. Zawass' identification rests on a tooth and yet no independent confirmation based on forensic dentistry has ever been produced. It is also highly probable the box containing the tooth, along with a liver and intestines, was actually used by someone else. "It is remarkable that the package (with the visceral organs), that was found in the box is obviously too large for the box as it prevents the lid from closing properly. Therefore, it is possible that the package was originally accommodated in another container and does [not] belong to this box. Furthermore, it must be taken into account that the package indicates a re-use of the box in later times."[106] The box was not found in

Hatshepsut's tomb whereas a quartzite canopic chest *was* found at the foot of her sarcophagus. The stone chest was divided into four compartments designed to hold her heart, liver, lungs and intestines.

"The scientists have proved only that a tooth in a box belongs to a mummy. The identification is based on the assumption that the contents of the box are properly labeled and were once vital parts of the famous female pharaoh. And the box inscribed with Hatshepsut's cartouche is not the typical canopic vessel in which mummified organs are found. It's made of wood, not stone, and might have been used to hold jewelry or oils or small valuables. Some would say we have not found absolute proof and I would agree."[107] Personally, I do not believe Hatshepsut's so-called mummy really belonged to her. Based on all the other extensive material evidence the female Pharaoh left behind the identification does not make sense and to date it does not make for true science either. "The investigation's (perhaps inconclusive) results were never published, leaving the mummy's true identity in question."[108]

PRINCIPAL REFERENCES

An Ancient Egyptian Herbal, Lise Manniche, University of Texas Press 1989, published in cooperation with British Museum Publications, Copyright Lise Manniche, 1989.

Ancient Egyptian Book of the Dead, Translated by Raymond O. Faulkner, With an Introduction by James P. Allen, Barnes & Noble Publishing, Inc., Copyright 2005, Faulkner Translation Copyright 1972 The Limited Editions Club, New York.

Ancient Egyptian Literature—An Anthology, Translated by John L. Foster, University of Texas Press, fifth paperback printing 2007, Copyright 2001 by John L. Foster

Cultural Atlas of Ancient Egypt, Revised Edition, John Baines, Jaromir Malek, Published by Checkmark Books an imprint of Facts on File, Copyright 1980 by Andromeda Oxford Limited, Copyright 2000 by Andromeda Oxford Limited for Revised Edition

Daughters of Isis – Women of Ancient Egypt, Joyce Tyldesley, Penguin Books 1995, Copyright J.A. Tyldesley, 1994.

Egyptian Games and Sports, Joyce Tyldesley, Shire Publications Ltd 2007, Copyright Joyce Tyldesley 2007

Feasts of Light, Celebrations for the Seasons of Life based on the Egyptian Goddess Mysteries, Normandi Ellis, Quest Books, Theosophical Publishing House, Copyrwright 1999 by Normandi Ellis

Hatchepsut – The Female Pharaoh, Joyce Tyldesley, Penguin Books 1998, Copyright J.A. Tyldesley, 1996.

Hathor Rising—The Power of the Goddess in Ancient Egypt, Alison Roberts, Inner Traditions International 1997, Copyright 1995, 1997 by Alison Roberts

Hatshepsut – From Queen to Pharaoh, Published by The Metropolitan Museum of Art, Edited by Catharine H. Roehrig, with Renee Dreyfus & Cathleen A. Keller, Copyright 2005 by The Metropolitan Museum of Art, New York.

Her-Bak – Egyptian Initiate, Isha Schwaller de Lubicz, Illustrated by Lucie Lamy. First complete English edition including commentaries and illustrations published in 1978 by Inner Traditions International.

Jewels of the Pharaohs – Egyptian Jewelry of the Dynastic Period, Cyril Aldred, Photographs by Albert Shoucair, Ballantine Books, New York, Copyright 1971, 1978 by Thames and Hudson, Ltd. London.

Life of the Ancient Egyptians, Eugen Strouhal, with photographs by Werner Forman, University of Oklahoma Press, Norman, Publishing Division of the University, by special arrangement with OPUS Publishing Limited, London,

England, Copyright 1992 OPUS Publishing Limited, text Copyright 1989, 1992 Eugen Strouhal.

Love Songs of the New Kingdom, Translated from the ancient Egyptian by John L. Foster, University of Texas Press 1992, Copyright John L. Foster, 1974.

Maat Revealed, Philosophy of Justice in Ancient Egypt, Ph.D Anna Mancini, Copyright 2004 Anna Mancini, Revised version May 2006, Buenos Books America, Kindle Edition

Reading Egyptian Art – A Hieroglyphic Guide to Ancient Egyptian Painting and Sculpture, Richard H. Wilkinson, Copyright 1992 Thames and Hudsom Ltd., London.

Sacred Sexuality in Ancient Egypt – The Erotic Secrets of the Forbidden Papyrus, Ruth Schumann Antelme and Stephane Rossini, Originally published in French under the title *Les Secrets d'Hathor* by Editions du Rocher, Copyright 1999 by Editions du Rocher, English Translation Copyright 2001 by Inner Traditions International.

Symbol & Magic in Egyptian Art, Richard H. Wilkinson, Copyright 1994 Thames and Hudsom Ltd., London

Temples of Ancient Egypt, Dieter Arnold, Lanny Bell, Ragnhild Bjerre Finnestad, Gerhard Haeny, Byron Shafer, Edited by Byron E. Shafer, Cornell University Press, Copyright 1997 Cornell University

The Art of Medicine in Ancient Egypt, James P. Allen, The Metropolitan Museum of Art, New York Yale University Press, Copyright 2005 by the Metropolitan Museum of Art

The Complete Gods & Goddesses of Ancient Egypt, Richard H. Wilkinson, Text Copyright 2003 Richard H. Wilkinson, Layout Copyright 2003 Thames & Hudson Ltd., London

The Egyptian Miracle—An Introduction to the Wisdom of the Temple, R.A. Schwaller de Lubicz, first published in French under the title *Le Miracle Egyptien* by Flammarion, Paris 1963. Translated by André and Goldian VandenBroeck, English translation copyright 1985 Inner Traditions International

The Literature of the Ancient Egyptians – Poems, Narratives, and Manuals of Instruction, From the Third and Second Millenia B.C., Adolf Erman, Translated into English by Aylward M. Blackman, First published in 1927, Reissued 1971 by Benjamin Blom, Inc., New York, N.Y. 10025.

The Opening of the Way—A Practical Guide to the Wisdom Teachings of Ancient Egypt, Isha Schwaller de Lubicz, Inner Traditions International, First published in French by Editions Aryana, Paris, Copyright 1979 by Editions Aryana, Translation Copyright 1981 by Inner Traditions

The Temple in Ancient Egypt—New Discoveries and Recent Research, Edited by Stephen Quirke, Copyright 1997 The Trustees of the British Museum, First published in 1997 by British Museum Press

The Tomb of Hatshopsitu, Theodore M. Davis, First Published in 1906 by Archibald Constable & Co., Ltd., reprinted in 2004 by Gerald Duckworth & Co., Ltd. Foreward Copyright 2004 by Nicholas Reeves

Treasures of the Pharaohs, Delia Pemberton & Joann Fletcher, Consultant, Chronicle Books, LLC 2004, Copyright Duncan Baird Publishers 2004, Text Copyright Delia Pemberton 2004, Artwork Copyright Duncan Baird Publishers 2004.

Tutankhamen – Life and Death of a Pharaoh, Christine Desroches-Noblecourt, New York Graphic Society, Boston, Massachusetts 1976, Copyright 1963 by George Rainbird Limited.

Tutankhamun, text by T.G.H. James, photographs by A. De Luca, MetroBooks, An imprint of the Michael Friedman Publishing Group, Inc., Copyright 2000 White Star S.r.l., Vercelli, Italy

Tutankhamun's Cook Book—Ancient Egyptian Cooking, Jackie Ridely, Copyright 2007 Jackie Ridley

PRINCIPAL ONLINE RESOURCES:

Dr. Karl H. Leser's invaluable site, **Maat-ka-Ra Hatshepsut**, http://www.maat-ka-ra.de/english/start_e.htm.

Ancient Egyptian Kingship, Connor, D. & Silverman, D.P. (1994) Chapter Seven, *Beloved of Maat, The Horizon of Re: The Royal Palace in New Kingdom Egypt*, by David B. O'Connor, from The University of Edinburgh, School of History, Classics and Archaeology, *Crowns & Concubines: Court Society in the Ancient World* accessed on Oct 19, 2008 07:55:45 GMT at http://www.shc.ed.ac.uk/classics/undergraduate/ancient/ CCsourcebook.htm

Osirisnet.net, *The Red Chapel of Hatshepsut Reconstructed*

RECOMMENDED NOVELS: *Winged Pharaoh* and *Eyes of Horus* by Joan Grant

End Notes

[1] Some Egyptologists believe that when Ahmose (most likely a daughter of Ahmose I) married a non-royal man she forfeited the title "King's Daughter".

[2] The ancient Egyptians did not use the words "sister", "aunt", "uncle", "grandfather" or "grandmother." Hatshepsut's maternal grandfather, for example, she would have referred to as "my mother's father."

[3] Thebes, the modern Luxor

[4] What we know today as the Nile the ancient Egyptians simply called "the River."

[5] Based on Erman, A. (1971) *The Literature of the Ancient Egyptians*, 146-147

[6] *Ibid.*, 187

[7] Based on Foster, J.L. (2007) *Ancient Egyptian Literature—An Anthology*, 42

[8] Memphis, the modern Cairo

[9] What the Greeks called, and we now know as, a sarcophagus.

[10] Based on Antelme, R.S. & Rossini, S., *Sacred Sexuality in Ancient Egypt—The Erotic Secrets of the Forbidden Papyrus*, 78

[11] The ancient Egyptian month consisted of three ten day periods.

[12] Egyptologists spell the word *whdw*, I have inserted vowels to make it pronounceable.

[13] The Minoans from the island of Crete in the Aegean Sea.

[14] Foster, J.L. (1992) *Love Songs of the New Kingdom*, 17

[15] It's not clear when exactly the exteriors of New Kingdom palaces began to be decorated in this fashion. It's possible that in the time of Hatshepsut palace facades were not as elaborate.

[16] Foster, J.L. (2007) *Ancient Egyptian Literature—An Anthology*, 121

[17] Based on a prayer to Thoth.

[18] Wilkinson, R.H. (2003) *The Complete Gods & Goddesses of Ancient Egypt*, 146

[19] Based on an ancient Egyptian love poem.

[20] Based on a spell from the *Book of Coming Forth By Day and Opening the Tomb*

[21] *Ibid.*

[22] *Ibid.*

[23] Nepthys, the wife of Seth, secretly desired her sister's husband, Osiris, and one night, when he mistook her for his wife, Anubis was conceived.

[24] Based on an ancient hymn to the king of Egypt.

[25] Erman, A. (1971) *The Literature of the Ancient Egyptians*, 78

[26] Foster, J.L. (1992) *Love Songs of the New Kingdom*, 11

[27] Shafer, B.E. (1997) *Temples of Ancient Egypt*, 28

[28] Mancini, Anna, *Maat Revealed, Philosophy of Justice in Ancient Egypt* – Kindle Edition, Loc. 776-80

29 Erman, A. (1971) *The Literature of the Ancient Egyptians*, 82

30 *Ibid.*, 19

31 *Ibid.*, 58-59

32 *Ibid.*, 56

33 *Ibid.*, 57

34 Egyptologists seem to think Egyptians used the headrests found in tombs even while they still lived. I found this impossible to believe. It seems clear they were funerary objects designed for a mummy who would not suffer from any discomfort.

35 Tyldesley, J. (1996) *Hatchepsut—The Female Pharaoh*, 43

36 Ellis, N. (1999) *Feasts of Light—Celebrations for the Seasons of Life based on the Egyptian Goddess Mysteries*, 238

37 *Ibid.*

38 Wilkinson, R.H. (2003) *The Complete Gods & Goddesses of Ancient Egypt*, 205

39 A headless animal skin hanging on a lotus-bud pole by its tail, which circles it three times. The tip of the tail takes the form of an open papyrus flower.

40 Foster, J.L. (2007) *Ancient Egyptian Literature—An Anthology*, 62-63

41 My niece, Emily Pita.

42 Tyldesley, J. (1994) *Daughters of Isis—Women of Ancient Egypt*, 147

43 Quartzite

44 Leser, K.H., www.maat-ka-ra.de/english/start_e.htm

45 Tyldesley, J. (1996) *Hatchepsut—The Female Pharaoh*, 86

46 Roberts, A. (1997) *Hathor Rising—The Power of the Goddess in Ancient Egypt*, 84

47 Iron. In Hatshepsut's time, meteorites fallen to earth was Egypt's principal source of iron.

48 Faulkner, R.O. (2005) *Ancient Egyptian Book of the Dead*, 95

49 Keller, C.A. (2005) *The Statuary of Senenmut* in *Hatshepsut—From Queen to Pharaoh* (Roehrig *et. al*) 121

50 *Ibid.*

51 *Ibid.*, 117

52 Foster, J.L. (1992) *Love Songs of the New Kingdom*, 105

53 Smith, D.G. (2007) *Total Solar Eclipses in Ancient Egypt—a new interpretation of some New Kingdom texts*, 5, 21. Note: A total solar eclipse occurred over Thebes (Waset) on June 1 in the year 1478 B.C.E. The beginning of Hatshepsut's reign varies according to Egyptologists, but at least five of them cite the years 1478-1479. Hatshepsut could very well have witnessed the celestial event.

54 Leser, K.H., http://www.maat-ka-ra.de/english/start_e.htm

55 Breasted, J.H. (1906) *Ancient Records of Egypt*, 3:137-138

56 Translated as "the common people." Maatakare's "inscriptions seem to show a personal association with the *rekhyt* which at this stage is unrivaled." Kenneth Griffon, Swansea University in Wales, as quoted in *National Geographic*, April 2009 issue, in *Hatshepsut*, by Chip Brown.

[57] Evidence for such a window has only been found in Akhenaten's palace but there is no evidence to indicate it was the first one as very few palaces have survived to be excavated.

[58] Allen, James P (2005) *The Role of Amun* in *Hatshepsut—From Queen to Pharaoh* (Roehrig, *et. al*) 84

[59] *Ibid.*, 85

[60] In Hatsepsut's time earrings were worn mainly by women and associated with sexuality.

[61] Keller, CA. (2005) *The Statuary of Senenmut* in *Hatshepsut—From Queen to Pharaoh* (Roehrig *et. al*) 117

[62] Foster, J.L. (1992) *Love Songs of the New Kingdom*, 12

[63] Randall-MacIver, D. (archive.org) *Buhen*

[64] *Ibid.*

[65] *Ibid.*

[66] Roberts, A. (1997) *Hathor Rising—The Power of the Goddess in Ancient Egypt*, 46

[67] Selections from Foster, J.L. (2007) *Ancient Egyptian Literature—An Anthology*, 193-197

[68] Faulkner, R.O. (1955) *Journal of Egyptian Archaeology*

[69] Dorman, P.F. (2005) *The Career of Senenmut* in *Hatshepsut—From Queen to Pharaoh* (Roehrig, *et. al*) 111

[70] Based on Tyldesley, J. (1996) *Hatchepsut—The Female Pharaoh*, 81

[71] Based on Manuelian and Loeben (1993) *From Daughter to Father*, 5:40

[72] Lesser, K.H., www.maat-ka-ra.de/english/start_e.htm

[73] Based on Manuelian and Loeben (1993) *From Daughter to Father*, 5:53 and on the translation by Faulkner, R.O. (2005) *Ancient Egyptian Book of the Dead*, 86-87

[74] Wilson, J.A. (1956) *The Culture of Ancient Egypt*, 176

[75] Davis, T.M. (2004) *The Tomb of Hatshopsitu*, 37

[76] *Ibid.*

[77] Based on *Ibid.*, 39

[78] *Ibid.*, 40

[79] Keller, CA. (2005) *The Statuary of Senenmut* in *Hatshepsut—From Queen to Pharaoh* (Roehrig, *et. al*) 126

[80] Leser, K.H., www.maat-ka-ra.de/english/start_e.htm

[81] De Lubicz, R.A. (1986) *A Study of Numbers*, 17

[82] O'Connor, D., Cline, E.H. (2005) *Thutmose III*, 86

[83] Hayes, W.C. (Google Books) *Varia From the Time of Hatshepsut*, 84

[84] Based on Foster, J.L. (2007) *Ancient Egyptian Literature—An Anthology*, 137-138

[85] Mancini, Anna, *Maat Revealed, Philosophy of Justice in Ancient Egypt* – Kindle Edition, Loc. 602-5

[86] *Ibid.*, Loc. 940-52: "In the Egyptian world each human being is part of the cosmos. As 'living matter,' he has the ability to receive solar energy through the heart, to transform it, and to send it back out. One of the famous ways he emits solar energy is through speech... The ancient Egyptians... believed that a harmonious flow of solar energy, when transformed into words,

involved growth on many levels: inner growth, inner happiness, and outer growth through physical and material prosperity. They also believed that the obstruction of the flow of energy would mean a crisis: destruction, misery, and even death. The ancient Egyptians, like other ancient peoples, understood the importance of the proper flow of thought. They also understood how much physical as well as intangible exchanges bring wealth in the tangible as well as in the intangible world."

87 www.ancientneareast.net/texts/egyptian/speos_artemidos.html

88 O'Connor, D., Cline, E.H. (2005) *Thutmose III*, 91

89 Oakes, L. & Gahlin L. (2002) *Ancient Egypt—An Illustrated Reference to the Myths, Religions, Pyramids and Temples of the Land of the pharaohs*, 473

90 Based on Roberts, A. (1997) *Hathor Rising—The Power of the Goddess in Ancient Egypt*, 121

91 "Mars is also pictured in the Senmut map, but it is represented by an empty boat in the west. This seems to refer to the fact that Mars was retrograde so that in this backward movement (well known phenomenenon to the Egyptians) the Mars position was perhaps not considered to be "concreate". From *Senenmut: An ancient Egyptian Astronomer* by Bohan Novakovic. The decorations on the ceiling of Senmut's tomb are the earliest known star maps in Egypt.

92 Tyldesley, J. (1996) *Hatchepsut—The Female Pharaoh*, 210

93 Allen, James P (2005) *The Role of Amun* in *Hatshepsut—From Queen to Pharaoh* (Roehrig, *et. al*) 84

94 Tyldesley, J. (1996) *Hatchepsut—The Female Pharaoh*, 154

95 Keller, C.A. (2005) *The Statuary of Senenmut* in *Hatshepsut—From Queen to Pharaoh* (Roehrig, *et. al*) 126

96 Keller, C.A. (2005) *The Joint Reign of Hatshepsut and Thutmose III* in *Hatshepsut—From Queen to Pharaoh* (Roehrig, *et. al*) 97

97 Roberts, A. (1997) *Hathor Rising—The Power of the Goddess in Ancient Egypt*, 44

98 *Ibid.*, 46

99 Egyptologists believe that *shabtis* were images of the deceased used to get them out of any work they might be obliged to do in the next life. To me, this interpretation does not make sense. A king, for example, who never worked in the fields while he lived, would certainly not expect to have to do so in the golden Field of Reeds.

100 Based on Murnane, W. (1980) *Serapis—The American Journal of Egyptology* 6:95

101 From *The Proscription of Hatshepsut* by Peter F. Forman, in *Hatshepsut—From Queen to Pharaoh* (Roehrig, *et. al*) 267

102 *Ibid*, 269

103 *Ibid.*

104 FOXNews.com (2007) *DNA Tests Fail to Confirm Identity of Mummy Claimed to be Pharaoh Queen*

105 FOXNews.com (2008) *Egypt Planning DNA Test for 3,500-Year-Old Mummy*

106 Leser, K.H. www.maat-ka-ra.de/english/start_e.htm

107 Ashraf Selim, professor of radiology at Cairo University

108 Parchin, S. (2008) *Egyptian Museum Tests Mummy's DNA*, Suite101.com

Made in the USA
Lexington, KY
21 January 2011